The
CIRCLES
Trilogy

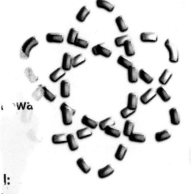

BOOK ONE

The Life in the Wood with
JONI-PIP

Artists

Short Allerton
James Boddy
Joni-Pip
David Durnford
Digger Durnford
Jane Durnford
Andrew Gibbons
Alex Hopkins
Eliza Hopkins
Sheena Hopkins

Bevan Kemp
Morgan Kemp
Carrie King
Paul Moon
Danielle Taute
Mark Taute
Beth Waites
Elle Sahara Waites
Rebekah-Paige Waites

(Carrie King especially appreciates the work done by the children of Milton Keynes, in providing some of the illustrations for this novel; the magnificent work done by James Boddy; the spectacular work by Paul Moon; the beautiful water colour Map by Danielle Taute; the painstaking cover photography by Fil Downs; the ingenious CIRCLES Logo by Phil & Sares; the superb cover Water Colour by Mark Taute and the great Cover Design by David Durnford)

Cover Design and Graphics by David Durnford
Cover Water Colour by Mark Taute

Published by Bothy Books

Printed in the United Kingdom

2 4 6 8 10 9 7 5 3 1

For Roger

Take a hold of your dream and realise it.
You know there's nothing left to stand in your way,
Except yourself and I know, though your heart's full of pain,
The Hope still remains, behind those eyes of 'green'.

Paul Carrack

Very special thanks to my Editor-in-Chief and his wife for everything they do for me.
Unending appreciation for Joni and all her tireless hard work.
My deepest thanks to all my family and special friends for their massive support in the making of this novel.
Grateful thanks to the late Derrick Davidson, who showed such enthusiasm for this work.
Special thanks to Roger and Ryan Ellory for their wonderful encouragement.

List of Illustrations   Page

Contents

Aerial Map of Edwinstowe and the surrounding areas

by Danielle Taute

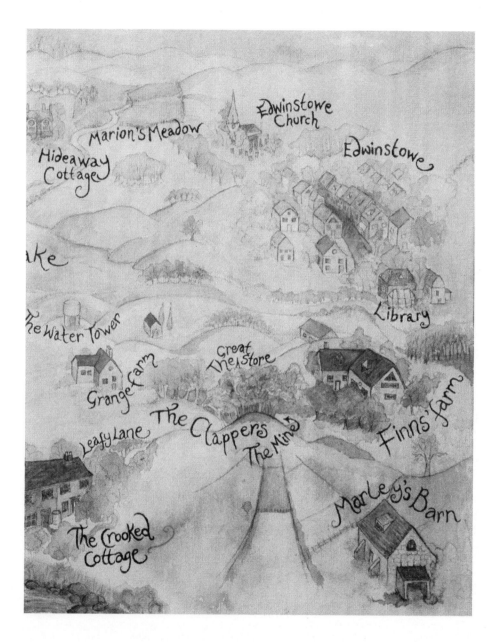

"To Joni-Pip's astonishment, there, in front of them, was a huge, spinning Orbit. Terrified, Ethelred-Ted went to run back but Joni-Pip dragged him by the arm and pulled him inside."

(Page 452)

Picture by David Durnford, based on an Illustration by James Boddy

Foreword

Within the heart of the Child,

Is the learning child.

Within the heart of the Man,

Is the yearning child.

So whether learning or yearning,

Or both,

This Tale is for all.

It is not a yarn of the underprivileged.

It is a yarn of the privileged.

This is not a story of making good.

This is a story of Good in the making.

In pocket or purse, most carry around small change.

If all that small change was collected together,

How great that Fortune would be!

Most have the power to carry out small changes for good.

If all those small changes were collected together,

How good that Good would be!

So let us all make some small changes for good.

Let us perhaps, make a BP (Bad Past)

Into a BF (Better Future)!

Read and enjoy!   **C.K. 10:01:10**

Chapter 1

Changes from the Skies

She tried skipping back to the tent but the little girl was wearing her brother's long outgrown dressing gown, which dragged on the ground. She kept hoisting up the bottom to stop it from tripping her up. Her mother had wanted to buy her a new one but she liked wearing this one because her big brother had given it to her, even though the sleeves had to be rolled over several times.

They had just been to the wash rooms on the Camp Site in Aberech Sands, North Wales and they could feel the crisp night air on their freshly washed faces. As they walked, they could hear the soothing sound of the waves crashing on the shore on the other side of the sand dunes. The five-year-old chatted excitedly; she could hardly wait to go to sleep in her family's large, white, bell tent.

It was just after they had returned from Portland, Oregon, where she had met her American Grand Parents for the first time. She loved being with them and hadn't wanted to leave the United States of America.

The little girl looked up into the clear, star-filled, night sky.

"Look, Mother, that star seemed to fall out of the sky!" she said. "I thought it was coming right down to the ground to see us!"

"That's beautiful, Darling! I wish I had seen it. We call that a shooting star or a falling star. Make a wish, quickly but if you want it to come true, you mustn't tell it to anyone."

The little girl closed her eyes and made her wish.

A few hundred miles away, a 31 year old man was watering his plants in his conservatory. He looked up and saw a shining, shooting star, arc across the dark blue velvet, night sky.

"I must make a wish!" he said out loud and he did.

* * * * * * * * * * * * * * * * * *

"Joni-Philipa, Joni-Philipa, wake up! Quickly!"

Suddenly Joni-Philipa felt strong arms encircle her and she was whisked out of bed. The twelve-year-old shivered from the cold air.

"Joni-Philipa, we have to go….now!" Father carried her over to the door.

A deafeningly loud and eerie wailing sound came from outside. Joni-Philipa hunched up her shoulders and put her hands over her ears. She was still half-asleep, so she wasn't quite sure if this was really happening. She wondered if it was just one of those awful dreams that she so wanted to wake up from. She shivered again.

As he passed the door, Father grabbed her brother's shabby old dressing gown she loved to wear and roughly wrapped it around her. When they got on to the landing, her mother was standing there holding a lighted oil lamp.

"Hurry!" she commanded.

Joni-Philipa blearily saw her brother, Alex, walk quickly across the landing and down the stairs carrying her little sister, Becky-Paige.

"Oh hurry!" Mother urged again.

The three of them swiftly crossed the polished floorboards on the landing and then practically ran down the stairs and along the hall. Mother walked through the opened door that led to the cellar and down the cold stone steps. She turned to guide them with the light from her lamp. Father carefully climbed down the uneven steps. Joni-Philipa huddled herself into him.

She was quite used to walking up and down these sixteen steps. The cellar was a place she often took her friends to explore. Neither Angela Stebbin nor Mona Royal, her two best friends had cellars under their houses, so when they came to visit this was the place that always interested them. However, now it was different.

When they reached the bottom of the steps, Joni-Philipa couldn't help but compare how things used to be when they came down into this cold, old room, with what she saw. In the light of Mother's lamp, she could see how the large, grim, uninviting and yet fascinating room under the house, which was usually empty, had completely changed.

She knew that the cellar had been undergoing a transformation for some time. The uneven flagstones had been covered with an old carpet. Old boxes, boots, tools, old magazines, toys, tea chests and sacks had been removed. The Household staff had then spent many months, sweeping, cleaning and painting. There had been a great deal of to-ing and fro-ing and getting things ready. Two armchairs and a long settee had been brought in from the Music Room and were now piled high with blankets and eider downs. Stacked on an old wooden table in the middle of the cellar was a Primus stove, tin mugs, plates, spoons, knives, forks and billycans. Usually the only times these were ever seen were when the Family went camping.

A couple of times recently when Angela and Mona had come round to play, the three girls had gone down into the cellar and started to 'have fun' by lighting a few lamps and eating a snack from the kitchen. Both times they had been scolded and shooed out, first by Reg and then by Cook. The cellar was out of bounds, it was no longer a place in which to have fun and play.

"Is it a raid, Father?" Joni-Philipa asked as the wailing outside continued, warning the people of Bath of the horrors this beautiful City was about to suffer.

"Yes," replied Father softly, "sit down and wrap yourselves up in these blankets."

He gently put her down on the settee next to her sister. As the two girls settled themselves comfortably, Father started to pump up the Primus stove on the table. Mother walked over to the side of the cellar. In the lamplight, Joni-Philipa saw the old kitchen sideboard, which was usually kept in the shed, outside in the garden. Now it was pushed up against the stone wall of this murky cellar. Mother put the lamp on the top of this battered old sideboard and Joni-Philipa could see that there were tins of food stacked on it: all manner of stuff....carrots, peas, potatoes, fish, corned beef, tomatoes, plums, pears and rice pudding, her favourite: things she hadn't seen the last time she and her school friends were down here. Mother bent down and opened one of the cupboard doors. She took out a large jug of milk, closed the door and then returned to the table where she poured some into the largest billycan and placed it carefully on the, now lit, Primus stove.

"Let's have a nice warm cup of cocoa," said Father, rubbing his hands together and then opening his palms, feeling the warmth from the roaring stove.

"Do you want any help?" asked Alex.

"Thanks, Alex," said Mother tentatively. "I think Father and I have everything under control....don't we?" she looked at her husband anxiously.

He smiled back at her reassuringly. Neither of them had any idea how that night was going to turn out. They just hoped that the cellar was going to prove to be a place of safety for all of them. Ever since the beginning of the War, they had prepared for this to happen but now that this **was** happening, they realised that nothing, absolutely nothing that they had done or could have done would have prepared them for **this**.

Becky-Paige snuggled herself up on the settee next to Joni-Philipa.

3

"I like….getting up….in the middle….of the night," said the four-year-old, stifling a yawn, "it's 'citin'!"

Joni-Philipa smiled at her, then turned to her father. She was desperate to ask what they should expect but she waited until they had all settled down and were drinking their warm cups of cocoa. The noise outside suddenly changed and they all became aware of a loud droning sound coming from the sky above the house.

Alex, Mother and Father all looked at each other.

"What's that Father?" Joni-Philipa started but before he had time to answer, a high-pitched screaming noise seemed to come right on top of the house. It was followed by the sound of an enormous explosion.

The house creaked, cracked, groaned and shook.

Everyone was powdered in dust and started to cough.

Becky-Paige began to cry and Mother immediately put down her drink, got up and sat next to her and then snuggled her little girl into her. She wiped away the dust that had settled on her tiny face and in her dark, curly hair. Nobody spoke as one loud thunderous crash and piercing whistling followed another.

Boom! Boom! Boom! Boom! Boom! Boom! Boom! It seemed endless!

Boom! Boom! Boom! Boom! Boom! Boom! Boom! It was terrifying!

The Bombardment of Bath had begun.

Large tears began to roll down Joni-Philipa's cheeks and she started to sob quietly. Father came to her; she closed her eyes and buried her head under his arm.

"Are you all right, Alex?" Father called across the cellar to his son.

"Yes, I'm as fine as I can be in this!" Alex laughed, steadying the shaking lamp on the table beside him. "I'm sure glad these houses are made of stone!"

Father looked relieved, turned and looked at the walls, smiled and nodded.

"It's funny really," Alex had to shout to make himself heard over the noise above them, "it's like a dream….like it's not really happening!"

"Sure! Believe me, though, it most certainly is happening….and some! Don't ask me why we're still living in this pesky Land!"

After what seemed ages, the sounds of the explosions from above seemed to end as suddenly as they began. Father asked everybody how they were.

"Oh, no," said Joni-Philipa. Everyone looked alarmed. "I've left Ethelred-Ted. Where did I leave him? I think he's in….oh, I don't know where he is!"

"Never mind, Darling, I'm sure Ethelred-Ted will be fine, wherever he is."

Joni-Philipa screwed up her face.

"Honey," Father said to her, "I'll go and look for him as soon as I can."

"Please don't be too long?" pleaded Joni-Philipa.

She took Ethelred-Ted everywhere. Father had bought him in Germany when she was just a baby. He was a very special kind of bear, called a Steiff. He was yellow with red arms and legs and had a little metal stud in one of his ears.

Mother made another mug of hot cocoa and they all sat silently sipping for a while but then the calm was broken by the haunting, unbroken cry outside. It was the air-raid siren, telling the people of Bath that the raid was over and all was now clear.

Becky-Paige started nodding off to sleep. Mother took her empty mug, wrapped an eider down snugly round her and kissed her.

"Night, night, Mother," she said sleepily.

"Night, night, Darling," Mother replied and then she returned to the cupboard, took out a cake tin and went back to the table.

"Would any one like a piece of fruit cake?" she asked, as if it was a warm, lazy, Summer afternoon in the garden.

"Not for me thanks, Honey," replied Father, then he added, "even though it's probably the best fruit cake in the world."

"Probably?" Mother questioned, laughing. She then turned to Joni-Philipa.

"Do you want a slice of cake, Darling?"

"I couldn't, thank you, Mother, especially with Ethelred-Ted all by himself."

"Of course."

Alex remained silent. He was trying to tune in the wireless in order to be able to hear any news of the raid. The speaker hissed and squeaked.

"Alex," Mother's voice could hardly be heard, "do you want some cake?"

Alex didn't reply, so Mother left the cake tin on the table, returned to the settee, plumped up the pillows behind Joni-Philipa and then started to settle herself down.

"Did anybody mention cake?"

Mother laughed and while Father lit another oil lamp on the small table beside his armchair, she opened the cake tin, took out 'probably the best fruit cake in the world' and cut him a slice.

It probably wasn't the 'best fruit cake in the world': these were hard times and dried fruit was not readily available but Cook had carefully preserved fruits for some years before the War. So, using these, Mother

5

had made a pretty good cake, anyway.

Alex continued trying to tune into the BBC Home Service but despite all the tables and columns that he had prepared, he had nothing to fill them in with. He was still hoping to pick up a report of the raid. The wireless continued to hiss and squeak. He just hoped things had gone well for the people of Bath.

"Alex, leave it," said Father. "You won't get anything at this hour."

Alex continued for a while and then gave up and switched off the wireless. He was sixteen and all he seemed interested in were trains, really. He was fascinated by facts and figures. Joni-Philipa thought that this was most extraordinary. He would get up very early some mornings, when it was still dark, just to take down the number of some dark green, black or dark red train that was passing through Bath.

Alex was studying hard at Prior Park and Father hoped that he might become a Banker, like him. With his son's love of numbers and tables, that seemed quite likely to happen. Although he didn't have much time to talk, when he did, Joni-Philipa always enjoyed it, he seemed so clever and grown up.

Joni-Philipa didn't really understand everything that was happening in the skies above them. She was born in 1929 and it was now 1942, a time we refer to as, 'during the War'; so she was twelve going on thirteen. She knew that over the last three years there had been this awful, terrible, World War going on but up until then, it was something that hadn't affected her very much, apart from the Fire Drills at School and the Gas Masks they carried.

She looked around the cellar. The painting of Father's parents' house in Portland, Oregon, USA, hung crookedly on one of the walls. He kept it in the cellar as it made him too homesick to see it all the time in the library. Father's name was Phillip. He was an American and had come to England to live, after meeting and marrying Mother, who was then a student nurse. Mother's name was Sarah and Joni-Philipa thought she was amazing. She was kind and gentle and baked the most tasty cakes. Father was fun, he took them out for walks, helped them fly kites and when he was at home, he always read them stories at bedtime. Joni-Philipa had been to Portland, after all she was half-American but only once, when she was five: so, although she remembered going, it was a bit vague to her. She did remember, however, how much she loved her Grandmother Garador and was so sad to leave her; she would have loved having a Grandmother living nearby.

Becky-Paige had never been to Portland.

Alex, on the other hand, was born there and felt that he was all

American. He had been back several times. He was determined, too, that one day he would settle permanently in the United States. Father had intended to take them to visit their grandparents again but he had become too busy with his work in England and then with this War, he never got round to it.

Joni-Philipa's life in Bath was perfect. She lived in a pale cream, Georgian Town House, which stood on the end of a large curve of houses, called a Mews. All the houses had black wrought iron railings and front doors, with shiny brass letterboxes and doorbells. The Garador Family had three people working for them, to help Mother run the Household. There was Reg the Butler, Cook (whose name was Ginny), and Mary the Maid.

Joni-Philipa could have really enjoyed being in the cellar if she hadn't been worrying about Ethelred-Ted. What an adventure! She waited a while then decided to go and find him. She made the excuse that she needed to brush her teeth. At first Father said, 'No' but after she pleaded, he allowed her to leave the cellar. She took a lamp and climbed the stone cellar steps, alone. It was quite creepy. She then slowly climbed the wooden stairs to her bedroom and after looking round and seeing that nothing was damaged, she remembered she had been playing in the shed when Cook had called her in for tea the afternoon before. She went back down the stairs, along the hall and straight through to the back door. She quietly unlocked it and went out into the cool night air. She shivered and pulled her dressing gown tightly round her.

There was an acrid smell of smoke and burning. It was really scary but Joni-Philipa so wanted, so needed to find Ethelred-Ted. She walked very quickly down the garden path towards the shed. When she was but a few metres away from the gnarled and knotty shed door, she was startled by a face that appeared looking through the dusty glass of the window. Joni-Philipa gasped and cried out. The person, whoever he or she was, quickly looked away and all Joni-Philipa saw was the side of a grey hood, the figure then disappeared from view.

"Who on earth is that? What is he doing in **our** shed?" she said out loud and very indignantly, shaking her head and frowning as all spoilt children seemed to constantly do, "I must get Father and Alex! I must get back, I must get back! How dare he be in our shed without permission!"

Suddenly above her, there appeared, as if from nowhere, two low flying aeroplanes. She looked up and to her horror, the first plane opened fire and Joni-Philipa saw dust flying in the air as the bullets peppered the ground in front of her. She froze, thinking she was going to be hit. The next plane was flying really low by now and as it banked slightly, she looked up again and this time she saw the face of the pilot. He turned and looked straight at her. She shook and shivered, fearing that he, too, would open fire but he didn't, he just smiled. Joni-Philipa shook her head. A strange feeling of recognition flooded over her. As quickly as it had appeared, the second plane then suddenly banked away and followed the Messerschmitt into the blazing red sky.

Chapter 2

The Move

It didn't take long for Father to decide to move his family to Knotty Knook, the newly thatched cottage he owned in Nottinghamshire. The cottage lay close to the woods. He was very concerned about the danger the family could be in. The raid had caused considerable damage to Widcombe, the area of Bath in which they lived and although it had not yet harmed them, he was not prepared to take any chances. This was a wise move, as it happened, as the beautiful City of Bath was bombarded very heavily again the next night.

His initial reaction was to transport all of them back to his parents' beautiful house and farm in Portland. After all, Alex was born in Oregon and longed to live there and Joni-Philipa yearned to see her grandmother. However, Mother felt it would be very difficult for the children to leave England permanently; as well as the fact that she didn't think that she could leave her father behind, the children's other beloved grandfather.

Grandfather lived away from Bath, in Nottinghamshire. He lived alone in an old stone, crooked, cottage with his cats. He helped in the forest as a sort of gamekeeper and had this extraordinary way with animals. He was probably Joni-Philipa's favourite person in the whole world.

The very next morning, Father told them to collect a few personal things together because they were leaving as quickly as possible. They didn't even have time to say a brief good bye to all their friends in Bath. Father arranged for the rest of their belongings to be removed in a large van later that day. As the servants lived with their families outside the City of Bath, Father asked them, when it was safe to do so, to keep an eye on the house. He was grateful and re-assured them that they would still be paid!

By twelve o'clock, midday, everyone was loaded up in the Bentley, the Family's beautiful old car. Soon they were purring through the English countryside, on their way to the pretty village of Berry Bush, just outside Edwinstowe in Nottinghamshire.

During the journey, Joni-Philipa was silent. She sat staring out of the window, clutching Ethelred-Ted very firmly on her lap. It was kind of strange seeing girls from the Land Army driving tractors and working in the fields. It wasn't something she had seen much before but as most of the young men were away fighting, that is how it was. She didn't want any of this. She was so happy, living in her beautiful and beloved city of Bath and was quite content to go to her exclusive private school for girls. She was ecstatic about being friends with Mona Royal and Angela Stebbin. They were just about the most 'Spiffing' friends ever, she was always boringly telling everybody. Not that anyone really listened to her.

Joni-Philipa sat back in the plush leather seat of the Bentley thinking that the life in the wood was 'all right in the holidays'. Well, after thinking about it some more, it was really good fun in the holidays, for a few weeks that was but to live in the wood permanently? She just couldn't imagine being separated from all she loved in Bath, all year round, forever even. Not much of a Drama Queen then?

She felt that her life had ended abruptly. It had; just her life in Bath though. Little did she know it but that day, 26th April 1942, was to mark a complete change in her life: a wonderful, exciting change. Never was she to return to that life in Bath again, not life as she had known it, anyway.

As the miles from Bath grew and the miles to Berry Bush lessened, many thoughts went through Joni-Philipa's mind. She couldn't exactly remember what had happened the night before when she had walked into the garden.

She knew the sky was red and she knew she had seen something strange. However, when Alex had suddenly grabbed her and pulled her back into the house and demanded,

"What the blazes do you think you are doing?"

She had no answer.

None what-so-ever!

Joni-Philipa continued staring out of Father's car window, pulling her Teddy Bear even closer as she relived the memory of being reunited with him that morning. All the time she had been worrying about him, he had been sitting on the windowsill in the Library. It had seemed a very long night, spending it in the cellar without him.

As they continued on their journey through the English countryside, the fields, in all their different colours, patched together by hedges and walls, reminded Joni-Philipa of the quilt on her bed in Bath. She wanted to be with her grandmother right now: she would understand. She had sent the quilt from Portland and had written that, as she had used pieces of material from Father's and his brothers' and sisters' clothes, which they had worn as children, to make the quilt, she was sending her a bit of America. Joni-Philipa loved her patchwork quilt! She hated this horrid war! She thought about Father's sad face at the breakfast table that morning. He had explained that, as they very well knew, the War had now reached them in Bath. Mother had poured the tea, while Father had told them that it was no longer safe to stay in Bath and that after breakfast they were to get ready to leave immediately for Sherwood Forest.

Joni-Philipa remembered suggesting that they stay down in the cellar for the rest of the war. She also remembered Alex laughing at that and calling her a name. She didn't like that much, she preferred his head in some silly book rather than him calling her a 'Twerp'. Mother had told Alex not to be so mean. Father had explained that, although it seemed a good idea, living in the cellar for the rest of the war, he thought living in the countryside in Berry Bush, Nottinghamshire was an even better one. Joni-Philipa was mortified. She could hardly bear the thought of leaving her house, her home, her school and her friends. She decided that morning that she was never, ever going to be happy again, not until she returned to Widcombe. When she protested that it wasn't fair, Father agreed with her but he had explained that there was nothing fair about war, anyway. He was adamant that they were leaving and he didn't want to hear another word about it! Joni-Philipa obviously had other plans and began to cry as she had never cried before, which made her face blotchy and red and puffy!

Mother tried to pacify her, Becky-Paige hugged her and Cook said how sad she was for them all and explained how she knew Father didn't want to leave but he couldn't risk the lives of all his family, by staying in Bath, any longer. Despite all this, Joni-Philipa would not stop her wailing. Only when Alex came to her and cuddled her, did her determination to stay obstinate, waiver slightly. She couldn't remember the last time that Alex had shown her any affection. In fact she couldn't remember him ever showing her any affection. Her brother's support for her really touched Joni-Philipa and for just a brief moment her crying stopped. Unfortunately it was just a very brief moment, so the household had to get on with the leaving preparations to the sound of Joni-Philipa's noisy weeping.

As the family continued on their sad journey, Joni-Philipa couldn't help but compare the difference between this and all the other trips that they had made to their country retreat in Berry Bush. Instead of the excited voices of the children, planning how they would spend the days of their holiday, either in the woods or up on the hills; there was silence. In fact the silence was so unusual that it was almost deafening. Joni-Philipa thought that this definitely was the most disagreeable day of her life. It didn't occur to her how fortunate she was to have another home to escape to and how selfish and ungrateful she was.

When they had driven through Widcombe, instead of the once proud and stately buildings, all they had seen was smouldering rubble, house bricks scattered in uneven piles, chairs and tables upturned and broken, mattresses ripped apart, children's toys laying scattered and abandoned. People, her neighbours, were walking around dazed. Some just stood motionless, staring; others were groaning and crying. Uniformed men were working hard, trying to clear up the devastation. In actual fact, over those two nights of the Raid, Bath suffered nearly 1,300 casualties and 20,000 buildings were damaged.

Joni-Philipa had no idea of the suffering that could have befallen her own family, had they remained in that fateful city. She had no understanding of the pain that the people of Widcombe were bearing. She thought only of the hurt that she was going through, having to leave behind everything she loved. She could only think of the ache that she had, not knowing how long it would be before she saw her beloved Bath again. She was unbelievably self-centred, not even the sorry sight of the plight of the people of Bath, moved her.

Three times on their journey they were stopped by the Home Guard and Father had to show his Identity card and those of his family and he had to give them their Berry Bush address: a raw reminder that they were living

 during a war.

When they had been travelling for a few hours, Father pulled the car off the main road and drove down a lane. He parked beside a stretch of grass that led down to a river. It was a very pretty place.

"Let's stop and have some tea," he said enthusiastically.

"What a good idea!" Mother agreed.

Father got out, walked round to the back of the car, lifted up the lid of the 'trunk' as he called the boot and took out a picnic hamper. Mother joined him and took out a couple of blankets. As their parents crossed the grass, Alex and Becky-Paige left the car and followed.

"Bring the Primus, Alex!" Father called. Alex turned round and returned for the stove. Joni-Philipa stubbornly remained in the car, clutching Ethelred-Ted and staring out of the window.

From behind the car, Alex called to his sister,

"Come on J.P., let's have a serious game of Skimmers!"

Normally that invitation would have made Joni-Philipa leap for joy. Skimmers! The light was good; the river gleamed like glass and was as calm as a millpond: perfect conditions for Skimmers. How she loved that game, especially as it was one thing that she really seemed good at....but not today. In fact just then, she thought that she would probably never have another game of Skimmers: ever. She didn't even reply to Alex's appeal.

Suddenly, a teenage girl rapped violently on the car window.

"Open the window, open the window!" she said, wildly turning her hand round and round, miming an unwinding action.

For a moment, Joni-Philipa just stared at the girl. She had a faint feeling of recognition but she couldn't think how or from where she knew her.

"Hurry, Joni-Pip, hurry!" the girl urged.

Joni-Philipa wound down the window, grimaced and didn't say a word.

"I need your help: desperately!" said the girl. "Please think carefully. This is so important for us. Can you remember where the Old Mine is?"

Joni-Philipa looked confused. She had no

idea what the girl was going on about. She knew she knew the girl somehow and obviously the girl knew her but where did she come from and why did she call her 'Joni-Pip'? Silly name! Joni-Philipa didn't reply. Then suddenly two older boys arrived; they walked round from the back of the car.

"Have you found out, Flip?" asked the younger of the boys.

"Not yet."

"Give her a chance, Craig!" the other boy said.

"But we must hurry!" Craig replied.

"Look," said the girl to Joni-Philipa, "I realise this is all very sudden and most confusing but it's a matter of great urgency! Life and Death even!"

"Joni-Pip, have you any idea how difficult it has being trying to work out where you would be?" laughed the older of the two boys.

"We've tried Marley's Barn a couple of times!" laughed the girl. "But I guess we were way, way, out with our timing!"

"So?" asked, Craig, looking at Joni-Philipa expectantly. "Where is it, then? The Old Mine? We really, really need to know....right now! "

Joni-Philipa just stared blankly.

"The Old Mine? Where exactly is it? I can't remember!" said the girl, shaking her head, then she added, "I don't actually think I have ever been there, myself....or you....you in actual fact...." she laughed, "but I thought you might just remember the location...." she suddenly stopped talking and looked right inside the car at Ethelred-Ted. She waited a second and then laughed out loud. "Oh, M. M. and M., we are way, way too soon, way too early, what a Nolly I am!"

As she did so, Joni-Philipa was sure that she saw some glittery stuff, sparkling in the girl's long hair. It was very odd.

"We had better go then?" asked Craig.

"Oh yes!" said the girl emphatically.

"Not very good at our calculations then, Flip!" laughed the older boy.

"I can but try!" laughed back the girl. "Let's go!"

The three of them started to walk away, then the girl turned round and called back to a very bemused Joni-Philipa.

"By the way, don't forget to ask Father....your father....where we are right now, where this place is exactly! Bye then!"

"Bye J.P., see you soon!" called back Craig.

"Cheerio, Yankee Girl!" waved the older boy.

With that the three figures disappeared behind a bush. Joni-Philipa frowned; she was sure she saw some tiny stars twinkling above the bush.

'Stars in the day? That's not possible!' she smiled to herself....'I must be dreaming!' She then slowly wound the window back up and just stared at the bush. When the window was fully closed she was amazed to see, instead of her reflection in the glass, the face of the Fighter Pilot, smiling at her. It didn't scare her or frighten her. It wasn't eerie, at all. His face then disappeared again and all she saw was her own reflection in the car window. She wasn't afraid, she merely thought to herself,

'I must be tired, I think I just dropped off to sleep. What a strange dream I've just had. What was it now? Oh....I wish I could remember!'

After Alex had carried the Primus stove, kettle and water carrier down to the riverbank, he helped Father to light the primus stove and make the tea. Mother busied herself preparing the picnic. Alex had sent Becky-Paige off to search for flat stones. He then returned to the car, hoping to persuade Joni-Philipa to join him in a game.

"Come and play Skimmers, J.P.?" he pleaded.

14

Joni-Philipa didn't reply; she was far too preoccupied, trying to remember her 'dream' to play and had no intentions of changing her mind. Alex walked back down to the river and bent down to examine the beautiful, smooth, flat stones that Becky-Paige had gathered in a little pile for him.

"Well done, B.P.! They are just perfect!"

Becky-Paige beamed and promptly set off in search of some more.

Joni-Philipa's resolve not to take part waned slightly as she watched Alex skilfully skim the flat stones across the smooth surface of the wide river. They bounced several times until they disappeared into the water.

"One, two, three, four-five-six er....seven!" Alex cried, as the stone bounced five times across the river. "A Sevener!"

"Seven! No, it wasn't!" Joni-Philipa shouted through the car window. "It was five, it bounced five times, it was a Fiver!"

Alex continued examining the next stone and just as skilfully as before, he leant over to one side, bent his arm behind him and then threw the stone forward as low as he could, across the still waters.

"One, two, three, four-five-six-seven-eight!" he shouted as the stone skimmed gracefully over the river, bouncing seven times. "An Octo!"

Joni-Philipa wound down the car window.

"Alex, you are cheating, it was a 'Sevener'!" she yelled.

Alex ignored her and picked up yet another perfect stone and skimmed it effortlessly over the water.

"One, two, three, four-five-six-seven-eight-nine-ten!" he declared and added loudly, "A Gladstone, aye?" A 'Gladstone' being the name that they gave to a stone that bounced ten times. "Now we are getting somewhere!"

This was all too much for Joni-Philipa; she put Ethelred-Ted on the seat beside her, flung open the car door, leapt out and stormed across the grass.

"Cheat! Cheat! Alex Garador, you are nothing but a cheat. I counted that go and it didn't bounce ten times, it was eight and it was most certainly not a Gladstone!" Alex turned, looked at her and laughed as she shouted at him.

"Don't you be such a Grump!" he yelled back. "Come and beat me?"

Joni-Philipa finally surrendered: so, as Mother busied herself with the picnic, she and Alex began a vigorous game of Skimmers.

The sun was quite low in the sky by now and there was a slight nip in the air. Mother told them to put on their jumpers. Becky-Paige obligingly obeyed but the other two were too pre-occupied to heed Mother's request, so she continued setting out the picnic: a freshly baked loaf, with butter and strawberry jam, a pot of Marmite (Joni-Philipa's favourite), cheese, homemade pickles, some apples and the remainder of 'probably the best fruit cake in the world'. Father made tea and then settled down on the rug.

"Why don't you come and eat before your game?" Mother asked the older two children but they were too busy competing, to listen.

To anyone watching this peaceful, family scene: the sound of the stones skimming quickly across the gently flowing water, the birds singing their late afternoon sonatas, the excited voices of Joni-Philipa and Alex as they achieved wonderful scores: father reclining on the blanket and sipping his freshly made tea, Mother spreading butter and strawberry jam on crusty homemade bread with Becky-Paige sitting beside her munching away at a rosy apple: it would have been hard to imagine that this family was going through such a traumatic upheaval in a land wrenched apart by war. What a difference from the night before! The Bombing of Bath and this game of Skimmers seemed in two different Timescapes. The only thing that disturbed the peace, was the loud sound of a convoy of Soldiers in their heavy trucks, as they rumbled by, on the main road.

After the game, The Two Competitors joined the others for tea. Joni-Philipa settled herself down on the blanket beside Becky-Paige, while Alex stood with his hands on his hips.

"That was a great game, J.P.," he started. "It's such an incredible science, Skimmers. I have used a numerical method to simulate a skimming stone and have derived an equation to describe a stone's motion. This confirms the ideal angle of 20 degrees. There are several parameters to describe the motion of a skimming stone," he explained. "While the incident angle between the stone's velocity and water surface affects bounce....the smaller the better, there are other variables to be considered.

"Of course I've focused only on a single impact of a skimming stone but a stone thrown against water generally bounces a few times. If you are interested in studying skimming stones properly," Alex suggested, "studying classical and fluid mechanics is probably the best idea."

Joni-Philipa sat staring at her brother with her mouth wide open.

"That's lovely, my Darling," said Mother, "would you like some cake?"

"Good for you!" said Father with, sort of, double glazed eyes. "Bravo!"

Becky-Paige chewed away on her marmite sandwich.

"Father?" asked Joni-Philipa. "Where exactly are we?"

16

Table of Scores for Skimmers
By Alex Garador

Number of Bounces	Name	Score
0	Plop	-1
1	Singleton	1
2	Duo	2
3	Triple	3
4	Quad	4
5	Fiver	5
6	Sixer	6
7	Sevener	7
8	Octo	8
9	Niner	9
10	Gladstone	20
11	Yellowstone	22
12	Firestone	24
13	Rhinestone	26
14	Brimstone	28
15	Stone Valley	30
16	Flagstone	48
17	Moonstone	51
18	Stonewall	54
19	Silverstone	57
20	Rocky-Road	60

Five throws per game

Three games per set

Three sets per match

Rules for Skimmers

*(**For those who might be slightly interested in playing.
If not skip to page 20!**)*

Alex being Alex and having a love of tables and figures and scientific data, devised a scoring system for Skimmers. He said that he was sure that one day Skimmers would become so popular that, after the War, it would become an event at the Olympic Games: World Championships at least.

Skimmers was an easy game to play; any amount of people could play it. The first requirement was to collect a fair sized pile of smooth, flat stones. Each player then took it in turns to skim the stones across the water, albeit a lake, pond, stream, river or the sea.

Great care must be taken at all times to make sure that everybody played safely and kept well away from deep water. At best, the game should be played under the supervision of an adult.

The scoring went thus: each bounce counted one point. If the stone just landed in the water without bouncing it was called a Plop and the player scored minus one. Each throw was given a name: a Singleton scored one point, a Duo two points, a Triple scoring three, four times a Quad, five times a Fiver, six times a Sixer, seven times a Sevener, eight times an Octo and nine times a Niner. From ten bounces onwards, double points were awarded and each skim was given a special name, denoting extra

18

achievement. A skimmer that bounced ten times was known as a Gladstone and merited twenty points. Eleven bounces scored twenty-two and was called a Yellowstone. Twelve was a Firestone, scoring twenty-four, thirteen was a Rhinestone with twenty-six points, fourteen scored twenty-eight and was known as Brimstone, fifteen bounces scored thirty and boasted the name Stone Valley. From then on if somebody was skilful enough the points tripled. That meant a sixteen-bouncer scored forty-eight and was called a Flagstone. Seventeen was named a Moonstone and won fifty-one points, eighteen scored fifty-four points and was known as a Stonewall, nineteen was called Silverstone, scoring fifty-seven and twenty scored sixty points and was given the name Rocky-Road.

The most Alex had ever scored was a Stone Valley but he reasoned that with training and practice, a true Athletic Skimmer might be able to bounce a flat stone more times than he could! ((Little did he know but in 2006 the World Record for Skimmers was 38 bounces! He would have been elated!))

Five throws made a Game, three games made up a Set and three sets made a Match.

How on earth, one might ask, could a score be recorded whilst walking along by a body of water?

The answer was simple: if no pencil or paper was available, a twig was found and the scores were scratched out in the sand or mud. The number was erased each time, the new score was added and then the new number was written down. To some it might seem that the figure work was too difficult for a smaller child but smaller children would only play this game under strict supervision of an adult and they were not likely to achieve as high scores as older children. One assumes that an older child should be able to do more difficult sums!

Chapter 3

Awakenings at Knotty Knook

The cosiness of the cottage hugged them, as it always did, when they walked in; only this time, the fragrance from the freshly thatched roof still lingered in Knotty Knook, making their arrival even more welcoming than usual. Father had telephoned through to the village Post Office, notifying Mr. Broft of their arrival and Mrs. Broft had gone in and aired the beds, lit some fires and left a cold supper for them in the kitchen.

They all felt very tired after eating, so Joni-Philipa and Becky-Paige went off to bed not much before Alex, Mother and Father.

The next morning Joni-Philipa was slightly bewildered when she woke up in her bedroom in Berry Bush. After a few minutes she realised where she was, leapt out of bed and ran to look out of the window. She pulled back the red check curtains and there they were....her very own Windy Woods. They hadn't changed, not one bit. She could see The Log and Chain Path that Father and Grandfather had laid many years before and she could see the trees standing to attention at the top of the hill. She so wanted to run up the hill and into her beloved woods. As she started to get dressed she looked up and saw her face in her dressing table mirror. Her eyes were still swollen and puffy from her crying....almost the entire day before....and she couldn't help but laugh at herself because she thought how much like a frog she looked.

The stubborn twelve-year-old heard the sound of aircraft above her. In the reflection of her mirror, she saw, through her window, four RAF aeroplanes flying in the skies. She stood still and watched them as they flew over the top of the woods and disappeared from view.

Joni-Pip shuddered, remembering the horror of the night in the cellar in Bath. As she continued looking into the mirror, she strained her neck forward because she couldn't believe what she was seeing. It wasn't her face looking back at her, in the reflection of the mirror, it was the face of the pilot she had seen in her garden. Surprisingly it didn't frighten her. The Pilot smiled at her and for some reason, she smiled back. The vision then slowly faded. As she stood staring in the mirror, another four aeroplanes flew over, they reminded her why she had come to Knotty Knook. Her mood immediately darkened.

"This silly War!" she said out loud. "This silly, stupid War!"

She promptly put her pyjamas back on and climbed into bed.

Mother brought up a breakfast tray but Joni-Philipa left it untouched.

Father came up later and tried to persuade her to get up. She remained adamant. She did not want to be in Berry Bush during Term-Time. She wanted to be back in Bath, with all its majestic buildings. She wanted to be with Mona and Angela. Joni-Philipa slightly waned when Alex came into her room and asked her to join the rest of the family for a walk in the woods before lunch. She remembered with affection how Alex had let her win at Skimmers yesterday afternoon. Although her brother's invitation to enjoy the walk was tempting, she declined. Alex then told her that Chardonnay; one of Grandfather's cats, now had three beautiful kittens. Joni-Philipa had to think about that one. Still, she obstinately refused to join them. She did, however, creep over to the window to watch them all, as they climbed The Log and Chain Path and disappeared over the top of the hill and into the trees. The sulking twelve-year-old opened her window and even though they were out of sight, she could still hear the muffled sound of their voices as they excitedly chatted to each other. It was very tempting to join them, very tempting indeed.

When Joni-Philipa could no longer hear the sounds of her family enjoying their walk, her thoughts were turned to her hunger. Her first thought was to run downstairs and raid the larder. Her second thought was to stay stubbornly in bed, which she did, eventually dropping back off to sleep.

"Wake up, Cherry-Plum," came a familiar voice an hour or so later, "as you didn't come and see me, I thought that I had better come and see you."

At first Joni-Philipa didn't realise where she was.

"Are you going to stay in bed all day, wasting precious eating time?"

Joni-Philipa threw back the covers and looking down at her was her most favourite person on the entire planet, apart from Ethelred-Ted, of course.

"Grandfather!" she exclaimed. She sat up and went to throw her arms around him.

"Steady as she goes, or you might have an accident!" cautioned Grandfather, protecting the laden tray he held in his arms. "Look, Cherry-Plum, I've brought you up some food. Mrs Broft has just handed it to me. I'll not call it breakfast because it is far too late and I'll not call it lunch because it is far too early. So we'll settle for food, shall we? I suppose we could compromise and call it Lunchfast; that seems satisfactory."

"Oh, Grandfather!" said Joni-Philipa, being very careful not to upset the tray. "Everything is so awful! Everything is so different! Everything is so horrible! I want to go back to Bath....right now!"

Grandfather removed the tray from the bed and put it on the floor: he then held out his big strong arms so that Joni-Philipa could collect her hug.

21

She leapt out of bed and sat on his lap and snuggled her face into his curly beard. Suddenly everything didn't seem half so bad.

"How can everything be so horrible, now that I'm here?" he asked.

Joni-Philipa pulled her head out from the comfort of his woolly beard and looked into his eyes; then she started to cry. Grandfather pulled her back close to him and stroked her uncombed hair, while she related to him all the things that had happened to her, since the night before last.

"It's all this silly war's fault," she lamented. "Why are people so stupid that they have to go to war in the first place, Grandfather? It just doesn't make any sense to me!"

"Indeed, Cherry-Plum, I couldn't agree with you more," said Grandfather kindly, "but at this moment in time there is nothing we can do about that. What we can do, though...." he paused and looked at her squarely in the eyes. "What we can do, is make the most of what we have and you, well, you, Joni-Philipa, you have the 'most' indeed and more than Most, come to that!"

"Me?" Joni-Philipa asked in genuine amazement. "What d'you mean, I 'have the most and more than Most come to that'? I have nothing, I have lost every-thing. I have had to leave my school, my friends, my house. My house, Grandfather, our house, our beautiful house: I have had to leave Bath."

"Look, Joni-Philipa Garador, I realise that you had a very frightening time down in the cellar when Bath was bombed and by the way, what did you think you were doing venturing outside? Alex told me you could have been killed." He then gestured around the room, "What do you call all this? You have so much and so much, much, more than most people to be grateful for!"

"I don't want to talk about all this stuff anymore, Grandfather," said Joni-Philipa, listening to her grumbling, mumbling, empty tummy. "I'm so hungry. What did you bring up for me?" Her eyes quickly ran over the tray. There were two slices of freshly made crusty bread, a few slices of cheese, a couple of pats of butter and a glass of milk. Then she laughed.

"Thank you Finn's Farm! Good old Mrs Broft! Thank you, Grandfather."

He lifted up the tray for her, determining that he would talk to her about how grateful she should be at another time. He wanted to discuss with her the very serious issues that faced everyone living in Europe at that time. He so needed her to understand how much more she had than most other children in England, in fact in all of Europe during those terrifying times. He would look for an opportunity to teach her how thankful and how appreciative she should be and especially how privileged she was.

His opportunity came quite quickly. That afternoon, Joni-Philipa, Mother and Becky-Paige set out to walk back home with him to The Crooked Cottage. Becky-Paige chatted excitedly about Grandfather's new kittens, while her older sister walked in silence. Mother joined in with Becky-Paige's enthusiasm. She, too, was looking forward to seeing the tiny, fluffy new members of Grandfather's, already large, cat family again. As she walked, Joni-Philipa clutched Ethelred-Ted closely into her side; she felt that he was the only one who fully understood her.

Half-way between Knotty Knook and The Crooked Cottage, stood the Ruins of an old Workhouse. The Ruins looked abandoned and forlorn: just like Joni-Philipa. It was here that she decided to rest for a while. She settled herself down, sitting, leaning up against one of the trees that stood guarding the once magnificent but sombre house. She held Ethelred-Ted very tightly on her lap: confirming that she was fully justified in being sullen because she had been wrenched unwillingly from her beloved City. Mother and Becky-Paige walked on. The four-year-old was far too eager to stop and rest. Grandfather's new kittens beckoned but Joni-Philipa was in such a bad mood that she showed no interest in them at all.

Grandfather walked slightly away from her and picked up a crumbling brick, which had once been part of this great house.

"D'you know what a Workhouse was Cherry-Plum?"

"No," Joni-Philipa replied slightly rudely.

"It was a place where poor people went when they had no place to live and no money to live on," said Grandfather. "It was sometimes called a Poor House."

"There's one in Bath," said Joni-Philipa, again rather rudely. "Not used, of course, well not used for all that, I mean," she added hastily.

"Of course not. Anyway, they were not very nice places. The Poor Unfortunates who happened to be in these awful houses lived wretched lives. They had to work from the moment they got up, very early in the morning until they went to bed at night. They had very little food to keep them going."

Joni-Philipa was not in the least bit interested in all of this. She just looked at her Grandfather and shrugged her shoulders.

"All in all," he continued, "people who lived in Downing House, the Workhouse, right here in Windy Woods, had very unhappy lives."

Joni-Philipa went to shrug again.

"But," Grandfather added very strongly, "despite all this misery, despite all this cruelty, one little girl found hope."

"Grandfather, I don't care about any silly little girl."

"When I was foraging around up here one day, I found an old envelope, hidden in the remains of the fireplace," he pointed to the stack of bricks propped up by two planks. "Inside was a piece of paper. Would you like to read it? It's a bit crumpled and brown with age but you can still see the words quite clearly. Have a look at it."

Joni-Philipa shrugged again.

He slowly took out of his pocket an old faded envelope. Inside the envelope was a piece of paper, folded in half. He carefully unfolded it and stretched out his hand towards his granddaughter.

"Go on, Cherry Plum, have a look at it."

"What on earth for? I'm not interested in an old piece of torn paper. How could anything like that have any interest to me? What's it got to do with me, anyway?"

"Come here, Joni-Philipa," requested Grandfather, ignoring her rudeness. "Please?" he added more as a command.

His granddaughter knew he meant business, by the fact that he had called her by her full name. She stood on her feet and propped up Ethelred-Ted, so that he was leaning against the tree. She slowly and very deliberately walked towards Grandfather's out-stretched arm and Joni-Philipa read the beautifully written words.

Despite her bad-mannered behaviour, her rudeness and her uncaring attitude, she was, in actual fact, extremely curious to know all about this old piece of writing. She ran her eyes quickly over it.

"What's it about, anyway, what's this silly old piece of paper got to do with me?" she asked grumpily.

"Everything, Joni-Pip!" came a girl's voice from behind her. Joni-Philipa spun round and there was the girl again, the one she had briefly encountered the day before, while she was sulking in the Bentley, down by the river.

The two boys walked out from the wood.

"Hello, again, J.P.," laughed Craig.

"We're trying to get it right once more!" said Steve.

Joni-Philipa smiled.

"Good to see....you....smiling at last!" laughed the girl.

"Y' know what we're after, Yankee Girl, don't you?" asked Steve.

"We just have to know the whereabouts of the Old Mine, remember?" the girl put her head on one side as she spoke.

Joni-Philipa half-smiled. What was it about this girl that was so familiar?

Where had she seen her before? Where did they all keep appearing from? Why did one boy call her Yankee Girl and the other J.P.?

"It's so important, have you any idea, yet, J.P.?" asked Craig.

Joni-Philipa shook her head gently.

The girl turned and looked at Ethelred-Ted and stared at him, then said, "Oh M, M & M! I've done it again, we're too soon, Steve, let's go!"

"You're priceless, Flip!" replied Steve, giving her a friendly nudge. "It's a good job your Ancestors didn't all have your memory, or they would have forgotten where they were going when they were crossing the Atlantic to sail to the New World! They probably would have ended up in Timbuktu....hmmmm!"

"I know, I know but we have to go!" laughed back the girl.

"Right back we JIT! 'Bye J.P., we'll see you soon!" he said waving and as he walked off, Joni-Philipa was sure she saw something glittering and shining in his hair, like little sparklers.

"Thanks for not getting upset, You Two!" said the girl, then she turned to Joni-Philipa. "Look I realise where you are right now, so all I have to say is this. Please try and be kind? Please try and 'think' kind? Everything is for you, you know: just for you! Listen to what Grandfather has to say, please? Please? It will make things so much easier for you, so much nicer. Believe me it will. You know what, I think it might be that you actually change yourself...." She then walked forward and to Joni-Philipa's surprise, she hugged her. Joni-Philipa didn't hug her back. Oh, no!

Joni-Philipa began to feel peculiar; very, very peculiar. There seemed to be a spark inside her and it felt as if it was slowly getting warmer and warmer, until it finally grew into a toastie glow. She pulled the girl back and really returned her hug and then all of the anger inside her, all of the frustrations of leaving Bath, all of the pain she was feeling, didn't seem important anymore. She felt incredible, in fact she felt so amazing that she just started to laugh.

"Well, I must be off, Joni-Pip. You have no idea what a privilege this is. One day you will understand. Don't forget....feel really, really, really sorry for Amelia Plate and those Poor Little Children! You must! You will thank me, well actually you will more like thank yourself one day. Your Future depends on it! Just think of others and be kind. Your Future will be so, so much better! I promise you! I must go back and then I will be back. 'Bye for now!" she then ran to join the two boys. Joni-Philipa looked totally perplexed.

When the girl caught them up Steve waved to Joni-Philipa and shouted, "See you again....no doubt very soon, Yankee Girl!"

The three of them quickly disappeared into the trees.

25

Joni-Philipa was mystified. She waved back and as she did so, she was sure she saw some glittery stars go up from the woods into the sky. She watched them and then the face of the Fighter Pilot, flying past her in the night sky, came into her mind. He turned and smiled; then disappeared.

"Are you listening to me?" asked Grandfather gently. He was still holding up the piece of paper with Amelia Plate's writing on it. "I just told you it had everything to do with you!"

"Er....what?"

"What d'you notice about it?" he asked.

"What?" replied his granddaughter slightly abruptly.

"Can't you see? Look at the beautiful writing!" he pointed to the piece of paper. "What kind of girl do you think Amelia was, do you think she was poor?"

"I don't know I'm sure, Grandfather," Joni-Pip muttered, still confused.

"Indeed she was not," said Grandfather earnestly, answering his own question. "Anyone who could write so perfectly had to be well educated and obviously came from a family, which was probably quite rich at one time. No doubt the unfortunate family had fallen on hard times and that's why little Amelia Plate was in the Workhouse."

Amelia Plate
May 4th
1892
Age 8 years
Yesterday I worked
all day
Today I worked
all day
But Tomorrow
Who knows?

"Grandfather, do I want to hear anything else about this girl, Emily Dish?" came a strained Joni-Philipa. "No, not at this moment, in Time."

"Amelia Plate," Grandfather corrected, smothering a smile. He then read a line out loud. "'Yesterday I worked all day'. Have you ever done that?"

"Well....I always work all day at school," Joni-Philipa spluttered.

"You do, do you? Amelia Plate probably worked ten hours a day; if not twelve hours, Cherry-Plum and when I say 'worked', I mean worked. It might have been scrubbing or mending clothes or polishing floors...."

"Did they? Did the children do that, how awful!" said Joni-Philipa softly.

"Er....yes....they had a really hard time...." Grandfather was quite taken aback by this sudden change in Joni-Philipa's voice.

"Yes, Cherry-Plum and worse, much, much worse."

Suddenly Joni-Philipa began to feel really sad and sorry for this little

26

eight-year-old Victorian girl, Amelia Plate and she started to cry and sob: only this time she was not thinking about herself, Bath, her friends or her school.

"Oh, Grandfather!" she wept. "How horrible it must have been for her, for them, all the little children. How horrible! It must have been so wretched for them, for Amelia; just so awful!"

"About time too," came an unfamiliar voice from behind her.

Joni-Philipa looked around to see who it was talking but nobody was there, only Ethelred-Ted, propped up against the tree. She was surprised that this strange voice didn't frighten her. She thought she must have imagined it.

"Oh, Grandfather, what a horrible time those poor people must have had, especially the children," she said, resuming her sobbing.

"As I said, it's about time too," the strange voice from nowhere came again. "You sound as if you are really sad you sound as if you mean it!"

Joni-Philipa swung round and once again nobody was there.

"Grandfather," she said very slowly, "did you hear a voice just then?"

"What were you saying about those poor unfortunate people?" replied Grandfather, totally ignoring her question.

"I am sure I just heard....." she shook her head and after checking that nobody was there, she shrugged, ".....never mind: what was I saying?"

"You were telling me how horrible it must have been for those in the Workhouse, especially the little children," answered her grandfather.

"Hmmm," Joni-Philipa sighed. "I didn't mean all those horrid things I said about the poor people in the Workhouse, Grandfather. I do care about them. I am so sorry. It must have been so scary for them. I do think it's terrible about their poor lives. I know that I have everything compared to them: Mother and Father and Alex and Becky-Paige and you."

"Aren't you forgetting somebody?" a strange voice came from behind.

Joni-Philipa spun round. Nobody was there except Ethelred-Ted. She looked at him, thought for a few seconds and then shook her head again.

She turned back to Grandfather.

"Grandfather, you must have heard that voice. It seemed to come from nowhere. It was a different voice, one I have never heard before."

"Well, Cherry-Plum, I am so pleased that you are sad and sorry for the poor people in the Workhouse. I am also really happy that you, at last, realise how much you have and what a privileged child you are. Let's catch the others up!" With that he gave her a hug and set off in the direction of his cottage.

Joni-Philipa was puzzled and said out loud,

"He hasn't listened to a word I've said about this voice I keep hearing."

27

"That's because he can't hear me at the moment, only you can. This is your Awakening. It is a very private time, a very special time, just for you. A time you will never, ever forget; no matter how long you live. Up until now, you have been the most incredibly self-centred, little girl. You have now begun to think about others, for a change, not just yourself. By the way, the person you 'missed out', was me. Do you know how long it has been that I have wanted to speak to you? I am fed up with you treating me like a stuffed toy!"

Joni-Philipa spun round yet again and to her absolute amazement, no longer propped up against the tree but standing up on his sturdy little red legs, was Ethelred-Ted. He walked towards her! He seemed so tall, so much taller than she ever imagined him to be. Was **he** the one talking?

"I must be dreaming!" she exclaimed, then she felt her forehead. "Perhaps I am running a high temperature!"

"Tosh! Munchy Mash 'n Mustard!" said Ethelred-Ted crossly. "It's me speaking and please, in future, would you mind how you hug me? Sometimes I can hardly breathe. Everybody loves to be hugged but there are limits. Some hugs are almost suffocating and I feel as if my stuffing might pop out. Yes, I like 'Huggerlies" that's what I call really nice satisfactory hugs. No more 'Sufferlies' for me, thank you. I do believe in hugs though. 'More hugs, Less Thugs', that's my motto!"

"I….I see," said Joni-Philipa cautiously, not believing she was actually engaging in a two-way conversation with her Teddy Bear. "Good one, very good indeed! 'More hugs, Less thugs'. Would you mind if….I sit down?"

"Be my guest," invited Ethelred-Ted. "Er….by the way, do you happen to have anything to eat on you? I could really do with a slight morsel right now."

Joni-Philipa looked at him in amazement, shook her head, walked over to the tree and sat down, leaning up against the sturdy trunk.

Nobody's Teddy Bear could speak?

Nobody's Teddy Bear could walk

Nobody's Teddy Bear could possibly be *hungry?*

This was all very ridiculous. She must be in a Dream.

"Right, now that you're sitting down, I just want to get a few things straight. First of all, are you sure you haven't anything to snack on?"

"What? D'you mean you need a Munch Break? I have nothing to eat."

"Munch Break? Yes, that's exactly it. My….er….Munch Break is well overdue? No? Oh well, what was I saying? Yes, next time we travel in the Bentley, please give me 'Huggerlies'. I'm not a particularly good traveller and all the time we were travelling here you were giving me 'Sufferlies'. I thought that my glass eyes might explode at one time and I felt decidedly queasy."

"I am so terribly sorry er –er -" said Joni-Philipa not knowing exactly what she should call him now. "I-I am sorry. I'll remember in future, er...."

"Ethelred-Ted. 'Ethelred-Ted', is still my name, you know and what a fine name it is, indeed! A fine, noble name....indeed a royal name!" said the Teddy Bear, waving his red arms in the air. "I am named after a King of England!"

"Please, Sir....er....Ethelred-Ted, how can you speak? Why do you speak? What's happened? What's going on?"

"Because, my dear Child, you started to consider others....at last! I am so pleased. What you must remember is that it isn't Me who has changed. I have always been able to speak. I have been speaking all around you for years but of course you haven't noticed: you couldn't, you hadn't had your Awakening. It is You: you are the one who has changed. People don't understand. All around them are toys and animals talking, walking and carrying on busily together but most people can't even see them. They are invisible and silent but and this is most important, there are people, really unselfish people....not just kind people....some kind people are still very selfish....there are some really unselfish people who consider others more than themselves and these are the ones who can see the beautiful and amazing world of TAW, all around them. TAW stands for Toy and Animal World. You have to be or become a truly special person to enter it and now, you have! When you speak to me and walk and laugh with me, nobody else, apart from other TAWPs, that's Toy and Animal World People, will see anything but a twelve-year-old girl carrying her teddy bear under her arm and any animals that might be with you, will be totally unseen to them, completely invisible. You are blessed indeed and so welcome! You are officially, from now, a TAWP!"

"I don't know what to say," said Joni-Philipa quietly, "except thank you very much, I am honoured indeed, thank you so much!" she bowed.

"Good, good," replied Ethelred-Ted, then he frowned earnestly. "Look Dear Chap, sorry to go on about it but I am rather peckish, might you have a spare apple in your pocket or failing that, a couple of slices of Mrs. Broft's apple **cake**? Very partial to that, indeed I am....no? Oh, my tummy is indeed rumbling; grumbling even. I just need my Munch Breaks that's all....anyway, Joni-Philipa, what shall I call you? You have rather a long name!"

"How about Joni-Pip, then?" asked Joni-Philipa, thinking to herself,
'Where on earth did that come from?'

"Yes....yes....yes....excellent....excellent. Joni-Pip! Good choice! Such a fine name: Joni-Pip. Pip, hmmm, Pip. 'Pip' was the name of the boy in

Great Expectations by Charles Dickens, wasn't it? I've always liked the name Pip, it has a nice ring to it. Joni-Pip, I read Great Expectations when you left me in the Library at home in Bath one day. I so enjoyed it! It was most entertaining!"

Ethelred-Ted seemed to talk non-stop and Joni-Pip dare not interrupt him, even though she wanted to ask him how long it took him to read Great Expectations. It had taken her a whole term at school. Could he possibly have read it in just one day: one single day? That was surely not possible. It was so long! She loved the name Joni-Pip, though; she recognised it from somewhere.

"By the way, I wondered if you could get hold of a copy of David Copperfield for me?" asked Ethelred-Ted. "I am ashamed to say that I haven't read it yet: Oliver Twist, yes but David Copperfield, no. I can't wait to do so."

Joni-Pip nodded. She felt very ashamed that she hadn't yet read David Copperfield, herself.

"I find some of these books quite hard, actually," she said bravely.

"What d'you mean 'quite hard'?" questioned Ethelred-Ted indignantly. "Books can't be hard. The Classics are a must for anyone who wants to be anyone and I want to be anyone."

Rather confused by that sentence, Joni-Pip thought that it would be safe to make a comment about the books she did like.

"My favourite book is The Wind in the Willows."

"The Wind in the Willows?" bellowed Ethelred-Ted. "The Wind in the Willows? How could anyone really enjoy a book about animals talking and behaving like humans? They don't believe it!"

Joni-Pip looked puzzled at her Teddy Bear and even more puzzled by what he said next.

"The same goes with Winnie the Pooh and Peter Rabbit; they don't make any sense to me: none whatsoever."

"Well, I think that they are all jolly good books," said Joni-Pip boldly, "and I love to read them over and over again. I love Mole and his friends, Winnie the Pooh and his friends and Peter Rabbit and his friends."

"Each to his own," said Ethelred-Ted. "Each to his own, suit yourself, if you like that sort of thing. Did you notice that all those books about animals talking have boy leading characters, it's about time we had a few more girl leading characters in books about animals talking, if that is your sort of thing, of course. "

"Well, it is," said Joni-Pip crossly, "and what about Alice in Wonderland, then?" she asked proudly.

"I didn't mean that there weren't **any** books with girl leading characters.

I didn't say there weren't **any**, did I? It's just the ones you mentioned only had boy leading characters," retorted Ethelred-Ted.

"There's bound to be some more," replied Joni-Pip. "Let me think."

"Very well, if you must but I think that you will be hard pushed to find many more," he said knowingly, adding, "perhaps I should write one?"

Both of them remained silent for a while. Joni-Pip was rather sad that her first, two-way conversation with her beloved Teddy Bear had ended, thus.

"I think that now is a good time for you to meet some of **my** friends," Ethelred-Ted said, breaking the silence and then he put one of his red paws to his mouth and whistled loudly. Joni-Pip put her hands over her ears.

"What **are** you doing?" she asked.

"You'll see, you'll see," came a superior reply.

Joni-Pip turned and saw a bird flying towards them; it landed on one of the few remaining stretches of the Workhouse wall.

"This is my Wood Pigeon friend, Poppy-Plump-Pij," said Ethelred-Ted.

"How do you do?" said Joni-Pip getting up and walking to the rounded bird. She stretched out her hand towards her. The Wood Pigeon extended one of her wings and they shook 'hands'.

"You must be Joni-Blipipa," Poppy-Plump-Pij said innocently.

"Joni-Philipa," corrected Ethelred-Ted. "Only she wants us to call her, Joni-Pip." He turned to Joni-Pip and explained, "Poppy knows all about you, even though she's sometimes a little forgetful."

"I see. Do you live around here, Poppy?" she didn't want to call her 'Plump-Pij' because she thought it sounded a little rude. She remembered Cook being most upset once because Reg had called her plump.

"I have a little home yonder," replied Poppy, pointing into the wood.

"It's spotless!" encouraged Ethelred-Ted. "You should see it. You could eat off her floor, it's so clean and swept and scrubbed!"

"Perhaps you would like to come to tea one day. I could make some Oat Scones, Boni-Blip?" Poppy-Plump-Pij beamed.

"I'd love to," said Joni-Pip enthusiastically. "I've never actually tried Oat Scones but I'm sure that they are delicious."

"Absolutely scrumptious," exclaimed Ethelred-Ted, "especially smothered with Poppy's bramble jam!"

"That sounds even more delicious," said Joni-Pip happily. She suddenly felt good inside. Perhaps the life in the wood during term time wasn't going to be quite so bad, after all?

"Here comes Hetty!" shouted Ethelred-Ted.

Joni-Pip turned round and at first, she couldn't see anybody.

"Hello, Ma Pets," came a soft voice.

"Hetty!" exclaimed Ethelred-Ted. "Come and meet Joni-Pip!"

Joni-Pip still couldn't see anyone until Poppy-Plump-Pij flew down on to the ground and put her wings out and hugged a spiky, brownie-grey hedgehog. Yes hugged: the prickles didn't seem to bother her!

'So much hugging!' Joni-Pip thought.

"Hello, Het, isn't it marvellous? Baloney-Jip has awoken at last!"

"Joni-Pip," corrected Ethelred-Ted.

The hedgehog walked towards Joni-Pip and stretched out her little paw.

"Good day, to y' Hen," she said. "I've heard so much about y' and we've bin waiting so long f' this moment. I am so delighted f' yer."

Joni-Pip beamed.

"Hetty is known as 'Hetty the Wee'. Her name is, of course, Hetty and she is Scottish and compared to some....not all of course, she is small and the Scottish word for small is 'wee' so she is 'Hetty the Small' in English but don't let that fool you, she may be small in size but she is huge, just huge in her knowledge and wisdom," explained Ethelred-Ted.

"P'raps we should call her Hetty the Huge then?" suggested Poppy.

Ethelred-Ted smiled lovingly at the Wood Pigeon and then continued.

"I expect you are wondering how a Scottish hedgehog could be living here in Nottinghamshire, Joni-Pip?" he asked. "Tell her, Hetty; tell her how you came to be living in Windy Wood, miles away from Scotland."

Hetty took a deep breath, ready to tell her the story.

"She lived in Edinburgh and she went to sleep one day and woke up in Sherwood Forest! She had fallen asleep in a box and the box was put in a van and driven down here, as the people were moving!" said the Bear seriously.

Hetty the Wee looked slightly annoyed and then she turned to Joni-Pip.

"Well, it's so nice to speak to y' face t' face, Joni-Pip, I hope y' liked me tellin' ye ma story!" then she laughed. "It's all right, Lassie, I'm quite used t' him. I call him ma Toyfriend: now that's not t' be confused with the word, Boyfriend, remember that, Ma Pet, remember that?"

Joni-Pip laughed.

Suddenly, a grey squirrel shot out from the trees.

"Out of my way, out of my way!" he said rudely, pushing his way through the three friends. "Can't stop; loads to do. I'll pick up your rubbish, so we don't leave the wood untidy."

"W'd y' like t' meet Joni-Pip, Nuttingham Squirrel?" asked Hetty.

Nuttingham Squirrel pulled himself up as tall as he could.

"Certainly not!" he snapped. "I'm far too busy!"

Joni-Pip looked rather bemused.

"Don't mind him," said Ethelred-Ted.

"That's Nuttingham Squirrel," said Hetty the Wee quickly, before Ethelred-Ted had time to tell her. The scurrilous squirrel scurried off.

"He's a bit of a....well, I don't know exactly what he is," said Poppy.

"He thinks he's some sort of Warden of the Forest," said Ethelred-Ted. "Bad case of delusions of grandeur, if you ask me. What's he ever done to think he deserves that title? All he does, is pick things up! What bunkum!"

"That's right, he's always in a hurry and always picking up rubbish," said Hetty the Wee. "He seems t' have some fascination fer it...."

"As well as his love of rubbish and litter, he's very bossy," said Poppy.

"He's a bit too big for his boots, if you ask me," said Ethelred-Ted. "Why he thinks that he can tell us what to do, I don't know."

"I know one thing, tho, ma Pet," Hetty said to Joni-Pip, "there aren't that many in the Wood that get on wi' him: we all try: we really dooo!"

Joni-Pip tutted and then told her friends that she must be on her way to Grandfather's Cottage. Now, she was looking forward to seeing Chardonnay's new kittens; in fact, she couldn't wait!

As she walked down the hill towards the Crooked Cottage, two men wearing long, black coats and Officer's hats, came walking towards her.

"Haff you zeen zrree people 'round here?" asked one of the men in a foreign accent. "Zrree Strangerzz?"

Joni-Pip didn't reply, she just went to walk past them. She wasn't scared.

"Didtt you nott 'ear me?" repeated the man. "Haff yu zeen zree young...."

"Er...no," Joni-Pip interrupted him. "I'm just catching up my grandfather, he lives in that cottage," she said, pointing to the Crooked Cottage.

"I didn'tt askk vare yu verr goingg," said the man abruptly.

"Vee haff llorstt zemm. Haff yu nott zeen **zwei** boyzz 'en vun **Mädchen** [1]?" said the second man, half-smiling nervously.

"Vee needd to torkk to vun girl en two boyzz," corrected the first man.

Joni-Pip shrugged.

"**Sie weiss nichts! Wir müssen gehen, wir müssen rechtzeitig springen,**" [2] said the nervous man and they both quickly walked off.

She let them go for a minute and then turned round to look but to her

---

[1]   two, girl

[2]   "She knows nothing! We must go, we must Jump In Time!"

33

surprise, they were nowhere in sight. She did see, however, stars rising above the trees, which gave her a very strange feeling. She didn't know quite what it was but it made her scratch her head. She then instantly forgot about them.

Later, she was so pleased to discover that Grandfather was a TAWP and she asked him how long he had been one. He said he didn't know but there were a lot of them around and they were always kind and thoughtful folk.

Joni-Pip and her three new friends went on walks, wrote and sang songs, drew pictures, played games and enjoyed picnics together. Ethelred-Ted's favourite games were Pirates or Cowboys. Hetty, Poppy and Joni-Pip weren't too keen on these rowdy games but they indulged him. Swash-buckling, to him was the height of excitement and adventure. They would use parts of the Ruin as a Galleon and sail The High Seas on it. Then they would jump on to another 'ship' and capture it, by noisily swashbuckling into the air with imaginary foes, clashing wooden sticks as swords, removing chests of treasure and thousands of Ducats. The Ruin also doubled up as The OK Corral but mostly they used the wide open spaces of the Nottinghamshire countryside as Prairies and Ranches. Many a time they were shooed off, as 'Wild Buffalo Eth' and his Posse tried to round up neighbours cats and dogs. Although the Girls joined in, they preferred to laze around and talk: a bit too normal for him!

Of course life was not normal. Soldiers and Servicemen were always around when they walked down Edwinstowe High Street. Quite often, a small regiment of the Home Guard would march past them, as they lay in the long grass beside the lanes; or a squadron of planes would thunder overhead, as they walked across the meadows.

Mother and Father always discussed War Matters in low tones, in a whisper as if they were trying to shield their children from the true horrors of the War. Alex would turn down the volume on the wireless when Joni-Pip entered a room; he seemed to want to protect her from anything that might distress her. Mother was so fearful when Joni-Pip wanted to go out for walks and always made her promise to be careful and she insisted she came home long before it was dark, long before the Blackout.

It was a constant strain, living in such an apprehensive atmosphere, never knowing what each day might bring, never knowing what the outcome of the War might be. Everyone always seemed a bit anxious; living under a continual cloud of vigilance, living in the shadow of uncertainty. There was a strange, inexplicable mood and a special camaraderie, which people today, not living in War Time, perhaps could never ever understand, imagine or comprehend.

Chapter 4

Poems and People

Bath seemed a long way away now and Joni-Pip only occasionally missed it. One thing that really pleased her, though, came through Reg. On his return from Bath one week, Father brought back a letter for Joni-Pip, from the bright and breezy Butler, with news and new addresses of her best friends. Both had left Bath, temporarily. Angela was living in Wales with her grandmother and Mona was now in Vancouver, Canada, living with an aunt. Joni-Pip quickly wrote to both of her friends telling them about her life in the wood. There were so many new things she was discovering, places to explore and wonderful things to experience. Joni-Pip had no idea how exciting her life was going to prove to be or of the amazing things that would happen to her and her new friends and she had no idea how exceedingly fortunate she was. She just knew she was happy again and all in all, Joni-Pip thought that the life in the Wood was wonderful!

It was a bright day with a few fluffy clouds in the blue sky and Joni-Pip, Ethelred-Ted, Poppy and Hetty decided to spend the whole day in the woods. As Grandfather was busy, they walked on past his cottage, down the hill, over the railway bridge and up onto the Clappers. 'The Clappers' was the name given to a small hill. It was a very pretty area smothered in trees. There was no stream or spring but they all loved looking down the hill and over at the view across the plain. They could see the water tower, Loxley Lake, the Grange, the railway and a few isolated farms. At one time the Clappers had been fenced off by Old Farmer Finn, who owned the land

PRIVATE LAND

TRESPASSERS WILL

BE PROSECUTED

KEEP OUT

and nobody was allowed to wander over them. He had put up a large white sign with a bold red warning written on it, declaring:- 'Private Land - Trespassers will be prosecuted – Keep out'. That threatening sign had been removed by the present Farmer Finn, so anyone who wanted to could now wander over the Clappers in freedom, enjoying the beautiful countryside.

"Did you see that?" asked Joni-Pip, pointing.

"What....did we see what?" asked Ethelred-Ted, straining to see.

"It looked like....stars....coming off the top of Marley's Barn."

"Stars? But you can't see stars in the daytime, can y'? Ye couldn't have seen them!"

"I did see them. I know I did!"

"Not there now!" laughed Poppy, straining her neck to try and see them.

"They were there. Definitely! I saw them!"

"And we believe you!" laughed Ethelred-Ted.

"No, you don't!"

"Where did y' say they were, Pet?"

"They were most definitely there, above Marley's Barn but they appear to have gone!" Joni-Pip was disappointed.

Her friends had one more look. They saw nothing, so they all shrugged, looked at her, looked at each other and laughed.

Joni-Pip looked and looked again but saw nothing. She said she must have imagined it; although she knew....she knew....

They all had a packed lunch and were looking forward to enjoying a picnic. As they walked, they sang 'Life in the Wood' quite a few times. It was a song that they had all composed together with Grandfather. He and Ethelred-Ted had painted a picture to go with it. They loved singing it!

"Munchy mash n' mu-u-stard!" he sang, changing the tune.

"That sounds like Camptown Races," said Joni-Pip.

"Does it?" he replied, singing it again, "Munchy Mash n' Mu-u-stard!"

"Doo dah! Doo dah!" sang Hetty, Joni-Pip and Poppy-Plump-Pij.

"Munchy Mash n' Mu-u-stard!" Ethelred-Ted sang again.

"Doo dah, doo dah day!" chorused his three friends again.

"That sounds good!" said Ethelred-Ted, pleased.

"I think it needs another line, though," said Poppy-Plump-Pij.

"Does it? I suppose it does....let's think....what sounds good with Munchy Mash 'n Mustard?" mused Ethelred-Ted.

"Mustard? That's a mite difficult word t' rhyme with, isn't it, Lambs?"

"Hmmmm! What on earth rhymes with mustard?" questioned Joni-Pip.

"Bustard....the bird, of course!" replied Poppy-Plump-Pij.

"Hmmm!" said Ethelred-Ted thoughtfully.

"What about 'dusted'?" asked Joni-Pip.

"Hmmm!" said Ethelred-Ted, thoughtfully again.

"Trusted," tried Hetty.

"I know!" said Ethelred-Ted triumphantly. "Let's sing it again!"

"All right, y' start and we will join y'."

"Munchy mash n' mu-u-stard!" sang Ethelred-Ted.

"Doo dah, Doo dah!" sang the other three.

"I like mine with cu-u-stard!" sang Ethelred-Ted.

Wherein there followed an uproarious blast of laughter.

"Wha-at?"

"Trust you to be thinking about your stomach!" laughed Joni-Pip.

"We-ell?"

"I think it sounds good," said Poppy-Plump-Pij sweetly.

"Thank you, Pops and so do I but it needs more."

"There's a middle bit. Let's compose some more," suggested Joni-Pip.

"Ethelred-Ted is Red!" sang Hetty the Wee loudly.

"Poppy-Pij is plump!" sang Poppy-Plump-Pij.

They all laughed.

"Joni-Pip and Hetty said...." sang Ethelred-Ted.

"Over the Wall we'll jump!" sang Joni-Pip.

They all stopped laughing and singing and just stared at Joni-Pip.

"Why did you sing that?" asked Ethelred-Ted.

"Which wall? How could we jump over a wall, Lambie?"

"We could fly....well, I could fly over a wall!"

"That's strange. Why did you sing that?" asked Ethelred-Ted again.

"I don't know. I don't know," she said quickly. "What does it matter?"

Even though she said these words Joni-Pip felt peculiar. They all did.

"I think I am going to write a song," declared Ethelred-Ted.

"A song?" his friends all questioned together.

"You mean another song?" groaned Joni-Pip.

"Yes," Ethelred-Ted replied grandly. "Possibly a sonnet but this time I want to do it entirely on my own."

"A sonnet?" his friends all questioned again.

"Oh, no," lamented Joni-Pip, "Angela once wrote a sonnet at school."

"Was it good, Ma Hen?"

"Frightful and she insisted on reading it out loud to us."

"What on earth did y' say t' her when she had finished it?"

"I just looked at her and said very politely, 'Hmmm, interesting'."

"Well, I am going to write a song about the River," said Ethelred-Ted pompously, "and I am sure; quite, quite sure, that it won't be 'frightful'. I think that possibly, too, I shall become the very first Teddy Bear to be published!"

Hetty the Wee and Joni-Pip sniggered at his arrogance.

"Well, I actually know of a Cat, who has been published," said Poppy.

"You have?" questioned Ethelred-Ted indignantly.

"Yes, most definitely," Poppy-Plump-Pij replied emphatically. "There

38

was this Cat once, his name was Digger. His Owner's called him Dig-Dig."

"Silly name!" sneered Ethelred-Ted. He was very put out.

Joni-Pip and Hetty the Wee sniggered some more.

"Anyway," Poppy continued, "this Writer was working in the house, where the Cat lived and Digger walked across her typewriter and spelt out the word 'juju' on the top of one of her pictures.[*] She thought the Cat was very clever. His Owner said he was telling them that his name Dig-Dig, was in fact 'juju', in Cattish! So the Writer kept it in her book! In truth, Digger Durnford was the very first Cat to be published and it was all his own work!"

Eth looked aghast that some Cat had got there before him! Joni-Pip and Het could no longer smother their smirks and erupted into unbridled giggles.

"How clever is that Cat? Digger Durnford, the first ever cat to be published!" said Hetty gleefully.

"What a triumph for the TAW!" teased Joni-Pip.

"TAW? Humph!" said Ethelred-Ted. "Digger Durnford? What a silly name! Uh, whatever! Anyway, I need space to compose my sonnet!"

"But d' y' know how, Laddie?" Hetty was still laughing.

"Indeed I do! Nothing to it! I feel that inside me, right deep down within me, buried deep in the depths of my stuffing, is a Poet, is a bard no less."

"Isabard?" echoed Joni-Pip. "Didn't he build bridges and things?"

How she loved to keep digging at this self-important Bear!

"Is a bard? Bridges and things? What are you talking about, Woman?" snapped Ethelred-Ted.

"Oh, nothing. My wit is wasted, obviously. Isabard Kingdom Brunel, he was a great Builder. He built bridges and viaducts and things," said Joni-Pip.

"You do mean Is-am-bard Kingdom Brunel, don't you, Joni-Philipa? There is an 'm' in his name, you know," corrected Ethelred-Ted with great majesty; then he added in quieter reverence, "I might not be 'The Bard'; that, of course, is the epithet reserved only for William Shakespeare, himself."

"What's an epithet then, Hen?" asked Hetty, trying to stop laughing at Joni-Pip, as she made a, 'Quite frankly, My Dear, I couldn't give a viaduct', face behind Ethelred-Ted's back.

"An epithet: 'a descriptive word substituted for a person's name'," quoted Ethelred-Ted authoritatively.

"Have y' swallowed a dictionary, Ma Lambie?"

---

[*] Look out for it!

40

"That would be terribly painful," said Poppy-Plump-Pij seriously.

Joni-Pip and Hetty the Wee laughed heartily again.

"No, I have not swallowed a dictionary! Ignore them, Pops," said Eth tetchily, "it's just we call Hetty, 'the Wee' because she's Scottish and small, so 'the Wee' is her epithet. King Ethelred, my namesake, was known as Ethelred the Unready because he was not ready for the Danes, when he ruled over England. 'The Unready' is his epithet. Shakespeare's renowned as the greatest Poet or Bard in the world, so he's known as 'The Bard'….that's his epithet."

"Danes? Were they naughty? So that must be where we get the word 'Dangerous' from!" declared Poppy, which made them all look at her and say nothing.

"How do you know all this about an….an epi-what's-it?" Joni-Pip asked.

"An epithet," finished Ethelred-Ted. "I read it on the back of a box of tea! Anyway, I….um, I um….yes, I need some words that rhyme with River."

"Joni-Pip thought for a bit then she smiled.

"I know," she said, "LIVER."

The hedgehog and the Wood Pigeon sniggered this time. Ethelred-Ted didn't. He just looked kindly; that's if you can look kindly about a word like 'liver' and smiled.

"Liver?" he repeated, half smiling.

"I've got a good one," said Poppy-Plump-Pij, excitedly. "SHIVER!"

"Now that is a good one, Ma Lamb!"

Poppy-Plump-Pij beamed.

"Liver is a silly word." Joni-Pip felt totally stupid.

"Not at all. I can easily fit it into my song of the River." Ethelred-Ted didn't know how but he knew he must give it a jolly good try. "Can anybody think of any other words that rhyme with 'River'? Any other 'good' words?"

"Quiver!" shouted Joni-Pip, triumphantly.

"Good one!" cried Ethelred-Ted. "Good one, indeed!"

Ethelred-Ted thought and then laughed, then he thought again and suddenly, as if a light had switched on in his brain, he shouted loudly,

"Munchy Mash 'n' Mustard! I've just thought of the perfect word that rhymes with 'River'!"

"What is it?" the others all asked.

"Wait and see! Wait and see. Now please, My Dear Friends, would it be all right for you to give me some time and space to compose my 'Masterpiece'?"

He marched over to a tree stump. He sat on it and seemed like he really

Life in the Wood
by
Poppy, Hetty, Ethelred-Ted
Joni-Pip and Grandfather

Life in the Wood	Trees grow so high	Life in the Wood
Is so good.	Up in the sky.	Is so good.
Life in the Wood	Trees grow so high	Life in the Wood
Is fun.	And green.	Is fun.
Life in the Wood	Birds fly so high	Life in the Wood
Is so good.	Up in the sky.	Is so good.
Come, come along,	Lean by the stream,	Come, come along,
Come everyone.	Lean, dream and dream.	Come everyone.

meant business, so they left him to it. He scribbled and frowned and screwed up loads of pieces of paper. This process went on repeatedly, for quite a long time. His friends thought that he just might be amazingly clever but it was a bit boring for them, so they wandered away from him. Hetty curled up in a ball and had a nap and Poppy flew off. She fancied a flight in the beautiful blue sky. Joni-Pip ambled over towards Marley's Barn, alone.

Suddenly a familiar girl and two boys appeared from behind the bushes.

"Found you! I hope I've got it right this time!" Flip laughed.

"Can you be trusted to do that, Flip? Hi, J.P.!" Craig lowered his brow.

Joni-Pip was surprised that the sudden appearance of this girl and the boys didn't startle her. Both times it happened before, she hadn't said a word.

"Who are you? Why does he call me J.P., like Alex?" asked Joni-Pip.

"Er....it doesn't matter who or why....let's just say we know you very well, we are close friends," answered Flip.

"Very close but it's too complicated to explain right now!" added the older boy, Steve. "All we need to know is the location of the Old Mine."

"Haven't you asked me that already?" replied Joni-Pip. "Didn't I tell you, before? I have no idea what you are talking about. The Old Mine? What Old Mine?" She felt very strange as she looked at the girl. What was it about her that was so, so familiar? "Who are you? I know I know you. I can't remember how or from where I know you but I do, don't I?"

"Yeah, yeah, you know us....very well," laughed Steve, "only you don't know it yet!"

Joni-Pip looked puzzled.

"Why do you want to know where the Old Mine is, anyway?"

"We need it and right now," started Flip, "for a very special purpose...."

"Leave it, Flip, it's too difficult to tell her," cautioned Craig.

"Difficult? Why?" echoed Joni-Pip.

"It has to be kept a secret," added Steve.

"Right," said Flip, nodding her head, slowly. She turned to Joni-Pip, "we just need to know, that's all. We have to know!"

"I'm sorry," said Joni-Pip, "I've been coming to Berry Bush for years but I didn't know there was an Old Mine around here. Are you sure you've got the right place?"

"Yes," said Flip, looking around her, "It's most definitely somewhere near the Clappers. I've just forgotten where. I don't actually think I ever went there. I've just come too soon, again."

Joni-Pip frowned, looked at her and said puzzled,

"What I find most peculiar is that my friends now call me Joni-Pip."

43

"Look, Folks, I don't mean to rush you or anything but this is a matter of Life and Death!" Steve urged.

"Then we must go and come back again!" said Craig. "Now!"

"'Bye then," said Flip, "we'll be back soon but you'll forget us 'til then!"

With that the three of them ran off and disappeared back behind the bushes. A sprinkle of sparkling stars, rose in the sky.

Joni-Pip frowned and thought to herself,

'I wonder if Ethelred-Ted has finished his work, yet?'

She walked back, along the woodland path, to join him.

When they met up, he looked at her and smiled and then he held his written 'Masterpiece' high up in the air and shouted, "Finished!"

He was so keen to read it to them all but he had to wait until Poppy returned from her flight and Hetty the Wee had woken up from her nap. He wasn't so good at being patient. While they were waiting, however, he noticed that Joni-Pip was very quiet: she seemed far away: so unlike her.

Finally, they were all together again. He gathered them all around him, climbed up on to the tree stump and recited his SONG OF THE RIVER.

Song of the River

by Ethelred-Ted

In the waters of the river,
Fish quiver in the river
By the reedz of the river
Ducks eat weedz in the river
There are loadz in the river
Of toadz in the river.
On the toP of the ri
Lilly pads.

We shiver in the river
When wE wash in the river
We splash in tHe river
When we fish in the river
When we gO on the river
WE kan row oN the river
We eat LIVeR by the river
With oUr Dadz

After he had finished, he gazed expectantly at his audience.

They remained silent. Not one of them flinched.

"Hmmm," said Joni-Pip politely. "Interesting!"

She then looked over at Marley's Barn and again, she was sure that she saw sprays of twinkling stars, coming out from the top. "There they are again," she pointed and cried out, "stars above Marley's Barn!"

Everybody looked towards the barn but they all saw nothing.

"Don't be so silly, Joni-Pip," laughed Ethelred-Ted, "What could stars possibly be doing over at Marley's Barn, anyway?"

"Who's that?" Joni-Pip pointed towards a clump of trees in the distance.

"Who's what?" asked Ethelred-Ted. "Where are we looking?"

"Can't you see there's someone walking into the woods?"

"No," replied Hetty, Poppy and Ethelred-Ted.

"It looks like they're wearing a hat: fancy wearing a hat on a sunny day. Oh, they've gone now. I wonder who it was, I've never seen them before."

Song of the River

by

Ethelred-Ted

In the waters of the river,

Fish quiver in the river.

By the reeds of the river,

Ducks eat weeds in the river.

There are loads, in the river,

Of toads in the river.

On the top of the river,

Lily pads.

We shiver in the river,

When we wash in the river.

We splash in the river,

When we fish in the river

When we go on the river,

We can row on the river.

We eat liver, by the river

With our Dads.

juju

Chapter 5

Marley's Barn

It had been steadily raining for a few days and Joni-Pip missed being out with her new friends. It was so difficult trying to spend time with Ethelred-Ted: that is real time, real talking time because Becky-Paige never seemed to leave her side. Her little sister just wanted to play with Joni-Pip, that's all and nobody else.

"Play dolls with me, Sissa?"

'Sissa' was the name she had called Joni-Pip, ever since she could speak. Mother had always said to her, 'Joni-Philipa is your big sister' and 'Sissa' was the best way she could pronounce 'sister'. So Sissa had stuck. Joni-Pip didn't mind, she really enjoyed having this special name.

As Joni-Pip was now far away from her beloved Bath and school, Father had decided that he should employ somebody to tutor her at Knotty Knook. Mother thought that was a wonderful idea and decided to do it herself. Alex was trusted to get on with his own studies and Becky-Paige was to join in with Mother and Joni-Pip as much as she could.

They all worked together to make the Play Room at the cottage into the School Room. It wasn't too difficult, both Alex and Joni-Pip had desks in the Play Room and Becky-Paige had a large blackboard with plenty of white and coloured chalks. This large, spacious room had always been well stocked with books; the bookcase taking up the whole of one wall. So, with a bit of shifting of furniture, bringing in a table and chair for Mother to use as her desk, pushing all the toys into one corner, including Alex's old rocking horse (Joni-Pip's was still in the Play Room in Bath), transferring Alex's train set up into his bedroom (which pleased him immensely, although it meant Joni-Pip saw even less of her beloved 'train-mad' brother) and generally re-organising everything: in one day, Knotty Knook's School Room was ready.

Mother and Father had agreed that after lessons in the mornings, Joni-Pip could spend time doing whatever she liked in the afternoons.

Unfortunately, while it was continually raining, Joni-Pip was not allowed to venture out much, so she devoted her time to playing with her little sister. They played Snakes and Ladders, Ludo, Tiddly-winks, Snap and endless hours of 'dolls'. Becky-Paige liked it best of all, when the two girls snuggled up in the window seat together and Joni-Pip read to her. It was especially cosy listening to the rain pitter-pattering down the window pane.

Like her big sister, 'The Wind in the Willows' was most definitely Becky-Paige's favourite. Joni-Pip insisted on Ethelred-Ted sitting in the window seat with them at these particular readings, snuggling, 'huggling' together!

Finally, a new day dawned and Joni-Pip awoke with the sun streaming in through her window. At last it had stopped raining. The wind had been howling most of the night but now it was still. She leapt out of bed and pulled back her curtains. How lovely it was to see clear blue sky, instead of grey, heavy, clouds, full of rain. She begged Mother to let her have the day off lessons, as she had done so much reading with Becky-Paige. She hadn't seen Grandfather in days and wanted to visit him that morning. Mother said that she couldn't at first, so Joni-Pip begged and pleaded until she finally agreed. However, she told Joni-Pip not to run, as the ground would be so slippery following the continuous rainfall and she didn't want her to have an accident by sliding about in the mud and falling.

As she set off on her walk, Joni-Pip thought about the last time she had been out walking with her friends. It seemed ages ago! She had enjoyed it so much but she still puzzled about the stars she had seen above the bush and Marley's Barn. She seemed to think about stars and look at them at night a lot, now. Nobody else had seen them. While Ethelred-Ted had been reciting his 'interesting' Song of the River, dark clouds had gathered and a strong wind had started up. Then the Heavens released the rain! Hetty the Wee had suggested that they quickly make their way to Marley's Barn to take shelter. They collected together the remnants of their picnic and Ethelred-Ted stuffed all the discarded pieces of screwed up paper into his

47

bag. On these pages were his first attempts at solo-poetry: he had thrown a fair few away. Indeed there were so many bits of paper that his bag looked very fat, bulging and lumpy.

"Why is it that all these pieces of paper fitted neatly into my bag before?"

"For that very reason, Ma Pet," Hetty had replied, carefully putting her half empty flask of water and an uneaten sandwich, back into her little wicker basket.

"What d'you mean, 'for that very reason'?"

"I mean, ma Friend, the first time you put them in y' bag, they were put in **neatly**."

Ethelred-Ted paused and thought for a second and then continued cramming into his bag, the last few, decidedly 'un-neat' pieces of paper. This, of course, meant there was absolutely no room for anything else, so Joni-Pip put his lemonade bottle into her bag. It goes without saying; he had no food left over. She was surprised at how good it felt to be helping her friend by carrying his heavy drink for him. She found this new, 'thoughtful' person, called Joni-Pip, very agreeable!

The rain had started to fall just as they had finished packing everything up, so they all ran as fast as they could to Marley's Barn. Apart from Poppy-Plump-Pij, of course, she just took off and flew there, waiting for them in a nearby tree. When they arrived at Marley's Barn, Ethelred-Ted pushed open the large wooden door and they all ran in, just as a storm wind brought the rain down in heavy torrents. It was so windy that they all had to help push the door shut.

Marley's Barn belonged to Finn's Farm, which was on the other side of the Clappers. The barn wasn't really used any more. At the outbreak of the War, the farm had been taken over by the War Office and now sheep didn't graze on the hills, as they used to. Any suitable field was ploughed up and every available space was used to grow vegetables and cereals, to help provide food to feed the country. Mostly, Girls from the Land Army worked on the fields, these days. Shepherds, who had tended their sheep here, had used Marley's Barn to keep the sheep warm and sheltered from the icy winds, driving rain, sleet and snow storms, which hammered across the hills during the cold Winter months.

Now, however, it was sheltering one twelve-year-old girl, one yellow and red, very talkative, Teddy Bear, one wood pigeon and a particularly prudent Scottish hedgehog.

It was quite dark in the barn, although some light did come in through the broken windows in the roof and the few scattered windows round two sides of the building. The barn was divided up into several sections. They

48

wandered around trying to decide where it was best to rest and wait for the storm to subside.

"How good it is that I didn't eat up all my lunch," Poppy-Plump-Pij had remarked and continued, "so if we have to stay here until this evening, I'll have enough left for supper!"

"Well, I have eaten all of mine," lamented Ethelred-Ted. "I hope we aren't kept here too long, I quite fancy a Munch Break right now, well actually, a substantial supper even; not too big mind, just substantial. Three or four slices of hot buttered toast, well, possibly five or six slices, thickly spread with Mrs Broft's homemade strawberry jam, followed by a bowl of vegetable soup with another couple of slices of thickly buttered toast...."

"Not much then?" came Joni-Pip.

"Well, on reflection, I suppose celery soup seems a special sort of super supper," said Ethelred-Ted.

All of his friends turned and just looked at him.

"What?"

"Did you just construct that?" asked Hetty the Wee seriously.

"Where shall we sit?" asked Poppy-Plump-Pij.

"There are plenty of places," replied Joni-Pip and promptly set off in the semi-darkness. "Come on, You Lot, if we've got to stay here until the storm is over, we might as well make ourselves comfortable."

They all followed her and continued their search for a suitable place to ride out the storm. The squarish sections each had bales of hay and straw, with empty troughs of water, ready for the sheep. Although the barn hadn't been used for some time, it didn't smell musty, in fact the smell of the hay and straw was very pleasant.

"This one looks good," said Joni-Pip enthusiastically, sitting on a bale of hay. "Shall we stay in here?"

"It must have been quite cosy in this barn, for all the sheep and their soft sheeplets," said Poppy sweetly, "and the bulls and their baby bullets."

The other three smiled and chuckled to themselves but said nothing.

"I'll just be happy to sit down," said Ethelred-Ted, "pushing that heavy door quite tired me out!"

"This is fine, Ma Pet," said Hetty the Wee, settling herself down on another bale of hay. "Very snug!"

"I think I'll just flap up and look around, first," Poppy said, taking off. "I'm looking for a new holiday home and this looks just right."

"I can't imagine living in a barn," mused Joni-Pip. "A Cellar, yes but a barn...."

"Ooh, I can, Ma Pet, dry, warm and cosy: perrrrfect, just perrrrfect!"

"That's because you are used to the comforts of life," Ethelred-Ted said to Joni-Pip, almost as if he was scolding her, "carpets, curtains, coal fires and comfy beds."

Joni-Pip felt very silly, her friends were so close to her that she really imagined them as humans, enjoying the things humans enjoy. Rather than dry, warm and cosy, to her, hay, straw and barns meant draughty, cold and prickly.

"Of course, Eth, how ridiculous am I!"

"It's lovely up here," came Poppy's voice, high above them. Joni-Pip was relieved, she felt rescued by her flying friend.

"Is it? I would love to be able to fly, Poppy, it must be amazing!"

"It is, it is so, so amazing," came Poppy's pleased reply, as she soared above them. There were not many things that Poppy could do better than her friends but flying, well, that was her thing.

"There's a kind of loft up here, above the beams, it's really roomy!"

"I'd love to come and see, Poppy! D'you think I could get up there?"

"Oh, no you could na' do that. Ye can stay right here, on the ground wi' us, where it's safe!"

"But I'm sure that I could get up there....easily....look there's a ladder," said Joni-Pip walking towards a wooden ladder, which was propped up against one of the horizontal beams.

"Come on, then," called Poppy, excitedly, "you'll see exactly what I mean. It's really homely up here!"

Hetty the Wee jumped off her bale of hay and ran as fast as her little legs could carry her, putting herself between Joni-Pip and the ladder.

"Oh, no ye don't, Young Lassie," she said sternly, very sternly for such a small creature. "That's a foolish thing fer yer t' do: yer can't see in this dim light where the ladder is leaning at the top. There might be holes in the loft. The ladder might slip. Anything could happen and how ever hard ye try y'd never, ever fly like Poppy! Y'd fall like a stone!"

"Oh, come on, Hetty, please let me go up? I'll be fine, nothing will happen," laughed Joni-Pip.

"Ethelred-Ted, reason with her, I could do wi' a bit of support here. She must na' go up, Ethelred-Ted, must she?" Hetty the Wee pleaded with her furry friend, not taking her eyes off Joni-Pip.

Unfortunately, Ethelred-Ted had not been taking much notice of this whole episode. He was exhausted from spending the day composing his **Song of the River** and then having to push open the heavy barn door on his own, so he was enjoying sitting on a bale of hay just thinking about what other tasty things he quite fancied for his supper.

'Hmmmmmm!' he thought to himself. 'I would really like a hot buttered crumpet. I haven't had one of those delicious yummies for ages. What a tasty Munch Break that would make! The last crumpet I had must have been before the beginning of the War….yes, I'm sure it must have been. Hmmm! At least three of four would be nice….perhaps?'

For once, he didn't have anything to say: much to the frustration of his friend Hetty. Cross with his lack of response, Hetty the Wee turned towards him, turning herself away from Joni-Pip.

"Did ye not hear what I said, Ethelred-Ted? Stop her from going up that ladder, it's far, far too dangerous, she'll hurt hersel'!"

As Hetty the Wee was no longer looking towards her, Joni-Pip seized the opportunity and walked round the hedgehog and started to climb up the ladder. Hetty turned round and ran towards the bottom of the ladder.

"Joni-Pip, Joni-Pip please don't do this! D'ya want t' get yersel' killed?"

Strangely, Joni-Pip thought and thought but she couldn't re-call anything else.....

BECAUSE THIS IS WHAT HAPPENED:-

A blinding flash of lightning lit up the whole barn: at least that's what they all thought it was. In silence, they waited for the thunder to follow, their figures silhouetted against the brightness of the light. However, instead of the expected thunder, they saw something unbelievable. Right in front of them, a structure slowly built up. Each brick emerged, like liquid, out of another; from the floor of the Barn, upwards and then set into perfect blocks. They formed a wall like no other!

The spectators froze in horror.

Aren't walls usually made up of bricks or stone? This one wasn't! It was an extraordinary, transparent wall. The structure continued to grow in front of their eyes. Instead of bricks made of baked clay; impossible as it seemed, all the bricks were made of fluid. Each brick quivered and glistened, like pools of water and yet they were solid and firm.

Nobody dare speak; well, nobody apart from Poppy, of course.

"What's happening?" she asked, still flying, not only above them but also above the wall of water. "What's going on....where did this Wall of White Jelly (Jello) come from? Oh, I can see new people up here, it's extraordinary...." suddenly her voice trailed away and she disappeared from their sight, flying over to the other side of the water wall.

Strange music and talking voices came from nowhere.

Joni-Pip, Hetty the Wee and Ethelred-Ted still stood as stone, in dread.

Suddenly, as if flying in mid-air, three unknown figures appeared above the top of the water-brick-wall. They landed right in front of the three motionless friends. In the light, although stunned by all that was going on, Hetty, Eth and Joni-Pip could make out a boy of about twelve or thirteen, a blue and yellow parrot and a somewhat vaguely familiar looking red and yellow Teddy Bear. The three intruders brushed themselves down and the red and yellow Teddy Bear started towards the ladder.

"Joni-Pip, Joni-Pip!" he grabbed her while she still stood on the ladder and hugged her so tightly that she felt that she could hardly breathe. "You're safe! You're safe! Joni-Pip, Joni-Pip, you're safe. It's been so long!" The Teddy Bear then turned to the boy and said, "Wasn't that the most amazing thing, Jack? I couldn't believe all those colours....just in time, too, thankfully!"

"Amazing?" replied the boy in an American accent. "I don't think there is a word big enough or fantastic enough to describe it!"

"Are you all right, Joni-Pip?" the visiting Bear asked, looking at her.

Joni-Pip was staggered. How on earth did he know her name? How on earth did they get there? How on earth was music coming from a small, flat box in the boy's hand? It sounded like an extremely large band.

Who were these strange visitors?

The boy stepped towards Joni-Pip and held out his hand. He was dressed in very peculiar clothes. He was wearing, kind of, farm trousers, with a baggy, jacket-like top, with NYC in big letters written across it. On his head he wore, what seemed like, a large school cap, only the peak was at the back and his shoes, looked terribly heavy and cumbersome; a bit of a cross between football boots and plimsolls, complete with unusual signs emblazoned on them.

"Hello, Auntie Joni?" he said and then shook her by the hand.

"Joni-Pip, Auntie Joni-Pip," laughed the vaguely familiar looking Teddy Bear, adding, "I think it's a bit rude listening to the music on your 'phone

when meeting new friends and relations, Jack."

"Sure! Sorry!" replied the boy and he pressed a button on his small, flat box and the music stopped. He put it in his pocket. "I was curious to see if it would work when we jumped, that's all!"

Unable to hold back any longer, Ethelred-Ted stood up, walked towards the Intruders and demanded some answers.

"Who are you? Where do you come from? How did you get here?"

"We are JITs but I will explain that soon," laughed the visiting Bear. "Don't you recognize me, you Silly Oaf and stop thinking about three or four buttered crumpets....you won't taste another one until after the War is over! Let's see now this Time is 1942....the War won't end until 1945, so you have at least three more years to wait!"

"Huh! What are you talking about? What makes you think that you know when this War will end then? That's a rather stupid thing to say….do I recognise you? Well, I suppose you seem **slightly** familiar….in a funny sort of way and what do you mean….you are 'JITs'? What a silly word," replied Ethelred-Ted uncomfortably, "and what's more, how on earth did you know what I was thinking about?"

"Look," said the Stranger, "why don't we all sit down? This setting up and jumping over the Wall, although truly spectacular, mind blowing, even….well, it takes a great deal out of me. It makes me a bit tired to say the least and as you can see, I'm not as young as I used to be. I must say I certainly was a fine figure of a bear, in my younger years, wasn't I?" he added, looking exceedingly closely at Ethelred-Ted, as if he was a Judge at a Cruft's Dog Show.

Ethelred-Ted felt most peculiar.

"The first thing I….you….must do, is to make Joni-Pip get down from that ladder," said the strange bear.

All this time, Joni-Pip had stood silently on the second rung of the ladder.

"Make her get down, er….Ethelred-Ted, make her get down now," he continued urgently, "or you will regret it for the next sixty five, long years!" He pulled Ethelred-Ted by his arms and led him towards Joni-Pip. "Believe me, you will so, so regret it, if you don't and sixty five years is a very long time, a very long time indeed!" Ethelred-Ted just stared at him still not quite believing what he was seeing and hearing. "Just get her down and I'll explain," the visiting bear urged. "Do it!" he commanded. "Now!"

Ethelred-Ted looked at the Stranger.

"Steady on, My Good Fellow," he said in a kind of whisper.

"Do it, Ethelred-Ted," came Hetty's little voice, behind him. "I think y' must. Don't ask me why but I am sure y' must. It might not sound like sense, it might not be important to ye but do it. I know y' just have t'."

"All right, all right!" replied Ethelred-Ted, crossly. "I'll do it!" He turned to Joni-Pip, "Joni-Pip, please get down from the ladder….NOW." He gently pulled her and she obligingly came down the two rungs on to the floor. As she descended the ladder, a strange feeling came over her and suddenly a vision flashed across her mind. She saw a pilot in a cockpit. He was wearing a balaclava and goggles. He smiled at her. She shook her head and the image went from her mind.

The Macaw, the bird that came with them, until this time had said nothing and done nothing but then he suddenly took off and flew up over the wall.

In a moment, he re-appeared.

"It's a workeda," he shouted excitedly. "It's a workeda!"

54

Chapter 6

Dark Days

The Log and Chain Path was, as Mother had warned her, very slippery underfoot, as Joni-Pip had started to climb up it. This wasn't surprising, considering the amount of rain that had been soaking the Nottinghamshire soil over the last few days. Nevertheless, she still whizzed up the path at quite an alarming rate. How pleased she was, to be released from the School Room, at last! Although, Joni-Pip enjoyed sitting in the window seat, reading **The Wind in the Willows,** to Becky-Paige, how spiffing it was to be free!

Her restraint had been but a few days; however, to her, it had seemed like a lifetime!

Actually, it was.

She was in such a hurry to get to see Grandfather, that she had left Ethelred-Ted behind in the School Room....much to his annoyance. He was so frustrated because while he was with other people he had to stay as a dumb, cuddly toy....something he never relished but had to tolerate, not out of choice, of course, just necessity. His only solace lay in the fact that he had a great deal to think about. A great deal indeed!

55

It was only when Joni-Pip arrived at Grandfather's cottage, that she realised that she had left behind her beloved Teddy Bear.

Grandfather was always pleased to see his granddaughter but this particular morning, for some unexplained reason, he had an overwhelming desire to hug her and tell her how much he loved her. So he did. Joni-Pip was quite taken aback, not because she didn't love him but it was the earnestness in which he did it. He kept looking at Joni-Pip and feeling he wanted to hold her again and again. However, he resisted and did the next best thing. He poured her out a glass of her favourite cold drink ....blackcurrant cordial....accompanied by two oatmeal biscuits. Yummy!

"What have you been doing, Cherry Plum?" he asked her, as she munched away at her delicious snack.

"Not much, Grandfather," she replied taking a hearty gulp of her drink and leaving a purple moustache around her mouth. Grandfather took out a crisp white handkerchief from his dungarees' pocket and wiped it away. "Not much at all."

How little Joni-Pip knew!

Perhaps it was as well that she didn't know what had happened to her, that day of the storm, in Marley's Barn. Of course she couldn't know really. Nobody could. That's not how it worked. It hadn't happened as you have read it, Dear Reader: no, not at all. Something catastrophic and horrific had happened that day and she had absolutely no recollection of any of it, none whatsoever. She had no idea how the events of that day had affected all of those she loved for a very long time: a lifetime even. She had no idea how that day had brought such sadness to the Garador family and more importantly, she had no idea how events would eventually turn out and what is more, how fortunate she had been!

Let's go back to Marley's Barn, during the storm and re-live the terrible events of that day....and see what really happened?

Let's pick up the conversation again, shall we?

"Did y' not hear what I said, Ethelred-Ted? Stop her from going up that ladder, it's far, far too dangerous, she'll hurt hersel'!" Hetty pleaded.

As Hetty the Wee was no longer looking towards her, Joni-Pip seized the opportunity and walked round the prickly little hedgehog and started to climb up the ladder. Hetty turned round, looked at her in horror and ran towards the bottom of the ladder.

"Joni-Pip, Joni-Pip please don't do this! D' y' want to get y'sel' killed?"

"Please stop fussing, Hetty, I'll be fine!" replied Joni-Pip, climbing higher and higher up the ladder.

Hetty the Wee was frantic and ran towards Ethelred-Ted.

"Stop her Ethelred-Ted!" she practically screamed. "She'll fall and die!"

Ethelred-Ted took no notice of his wise hedgehog friend and continued musing about delicious, hot, buttered crumpets.

Joni-Pip finally arrived at the top of the ladder and scrambled out, onto the loft floor.

"See, Hetty," she shouted down, "you're worrying over nothing. It's as safe as houses up here!"

Of course, this was war time and some of the things that most definitely were not safe, at this particular time, were houses. Joni-Pip had seen them on her sad journey through Widcombe: crumbled, torn and broken.

Poppy-Plump-Pij eagerly showed her around this new place she had discovered. At first Joni-Pip was quite cautious in the steps she took. However, as her confidence grew, her care lessened. She began to move quickly around the loft, paying very little heed to what she was walking into or on to.

"What a lovely place, Poppy," she said and as she did so, her foot suddenly slipped and disappeared down a hole in the loft floor. Dust, bits of wood and straw fell beneath her. She quickly pulled her foot up again. "Whoops!" she laughingly said. "I had better be careful where I tread!"

"What's going on up there?" came Hetty's worried voice from below. "Where's all this stuff coming from? Be very careful Joni-Pip, please?" The Hedgehog brushed off the dust and straw that had landed on her prickles.

"Oh, Hetty, I am fine, honestly."

"Well, please come down now: then I can stop worrying!"

Joni-Pip stayed up a little bit longer, exploring Poppy's new Holiday Home.

'This,' she thought, 'is more like it! I could live here. Yes, I could definitely enjoy living here! A bit different from the cellar but nevertheless it looks good. I think it would be real fun to live in a hay loft.....up a ladder even!'

"Joni-Pip, that's quite enough. Now come down: very carefully, mind!"

"All right, all right, Het! I'll come now and yes....I will be careful."

Reluctantly, the twelve-year-old then began her perilous journey back down the ladder. Unfortunately, the difficulty did not begin by descending the rungs of the ladder. Before that, she had to negotiate actually getting on to the ladder itself. This proved to be very tricky stuff. Somehow she would have to stretch her leg across the front of the top of the ladder, so that she could go down the right way round, facing the ladder. First of all, she tried backing up to the edge of the loft floor. This didn't work; she just couldn't do it that way round.

Hetty the Wee watched anxiously from below.

"Do be careful, Hen, this looks so dangerous to me!"

"Nothing to it, Het, I'll manage somehow. I think it ought to be as easy to get down as it is to get up....but it's not....that doesn't seem fair to me. Oh well, I'll be down in no time!"

The ladder was quite a bit taller than the floor of the loft, so Joni-Pip held on to one side of it with one hand. She then put her foot on the rung a bit below the loft floor and she swung herself across, turning her body as she did so and grabbed the other side of the ladder with her other hand. Her other foot landed firmly on the rung of the ladder. So she was facing the ladder at last. The ladder wobbled a bit and Joni-Pip began to descend.

Hetty the Wee sighed with relief.

When Joni-Pip was about halfway down the ladder, a flash of lightning suddenly lit up the old Barn, immediately followed by an almighty crash of thunder! Frightened out of her wits, Joni-Pip lurched backwards, letting go of her tight grip on the sides of the ladder, the ladder shuddered and swayed about and then, to the horror of all of them, went crashing to the ground.

Joni-Pip was thrown off and landed with a loud crack on the concrete floor below her.

For a moment everybody just stared without moving and then suddenly all three of them rushed to their friend lying on the floor.

Hetty the Wee was the first to reach her.

"Joni-Pip! Joni-Pip! Are y' all right?" she asked, knowing what a hopeless question that was.

Joni-Pip lay motionless, her little body crumpled, torn and broken.

Poppy-Plump-Pij flew down beside Joni-Pip, put her little head on one side and gasped.

"Joni-Pip, what have I done? You must be all right. You have to be all right. Please be all right?"

Ethelred-Ted stroked Joni-Pip's ashen face.

"Joni-Pip, Joni-Pip, open your eyes? Please?" he whispered but she didn't move: he knew then she was badly injured. A tear rolled down his furry face.

"What are we going t' do, Ethelred-Ted? We must do something to help her," sobbed Hetty the Wee.

"I'll go and get Grandfather!" shouted Poppy-Plump-Pij and immediately she flew off towards one of the broken windows.

"But the Storm, Poppy?" questioned Ethelred-Ted anxiously. "Will you be all right?"

"It's all my fault....wanting her to see up in the loft with me! Of course I'll be all right!" she shouted down to him and then disappeared through the skylight, into the angry weather outside.

She was hardly able to see from the tears streaming down her little feathered face but courageously she began her battle, despite being terrified of the storm, as it raged relentlessly around her. The Lightning flashed and cracked, practically blinding her. The thunder claps exploded and crashed, almost deafening her and the torrential rain hammered at her drenched, little flying body but on she fought! The wind was so strong. How she managed to get to Grandfather's, she'll never know but she did. It was the most terrifying but earnest flight of her life.

She banged on Grandfather's door and waited.

She banged and banged again.

Nobody came.

Poppy was desperate.

Where could he be?

Terrified, she mustered up all the strength she had and flew back up into the blackened, angry clouds, reasoning that she might get a better look high up. She could hardly see anything and the furious wind kept blowing her away from where she wanted to be!

She was frantic.

She decided to fly over the wood to Knotty Knook.

This meant another perilous journey!

How she wished she was safely tucked up in her little cosy bed at home, instead of flying against the whipping wind in all its fury and being driven by the unrelenting, ruthless rain.

The thunder and lightning continued to flash and crack, all around her but when she became faint hearted, she remembered a little twelve-year-old girl, lying broken and still on a hard, unyielding, concrete floor.

At last she reached Knotty Knook and yes, she could see Grandfather through the kitchen window!

She practically threw herself at the pane!

With all the noise of the wind and rain, lashing at the windows, at first nobody took any notice. So, the exhausted Poppy had to keep circling the house, trying to find a way in, or some way of letting them know she was there. She thought it was hopeless and finally had to rest and landed on the kitchen window sill, where, thankfully, for some reason, Grandfather turned and saw the pathetic, bedraggled creature, pressed up against the kitchen window.

He ran out. All of the family had been so worried about Joni-Pip's whereabouts during the raging storm and this was the sign they needed, to bring them some news.

Poppy-Plump-Pij was so exhausted she could hardly speak but eventually she mustered up the strength to whisper to Grandfather,

"Marley's Barn!"

In no time, Alex, Father and Grandfather set off in the Bentley, towards Finn's Farm. Mrs Broft had already made a thermos flask of hot, sweet tea and brought down warm blankets to put in the car. She was always ready for any emergency.

Poppy-Plump-Pij was made to stay behind with Mother, Mrs Broft and Becky-Paige. The poor wood pigeon was half-dead from exhaustion, so they lovingly dried her off with some warm towels, wrapped her up in a woolly blanket and then Mother gave her some hot whiskey and water with sugar to sip, in order to revive her aching body. Finally, Mother cradled her in her arms and sat cuddling her by the blazing log fire in the kitchen.

Although she was safe and warm, Poppy's thoughts were miles away.

The driving rain made the journey up to Finn's Farm really difficult and that was on the road. It was almost impossible to drive up the muddy track to the farm.

When they finally pulled in to the farmyard, Farmer Finn came running out to see what was going on. He was wearing a thick yellow rain coat and sou'wester.

"Joni-Philipa is in trouble up at Marley's Barn!" shouted Father, through the opened car window.

"What did you say?" shouted back Farmer Finn. "I can't hear you!"

"Joni-Philipa is in trouble! Marley's Barn!" Father shouted and mouthed.

"Joni-Philipa? Marley's Barn? In this? Let's use the Land Rover!" shouted back the farmer. "You'll never make the rest of the track in that!"

Father pulled the Bentley over to the side of the yard and the three of them practically tumbled out, getting drenched in the torrential rain. They slopped across the slippery yard and then all piled into the Four by Four. Alex got back out and ran back to the Bentley, picking up the thermos flask and blankets. He had hardly got back into the Land Rover, before Farmer Finn pulled away. They all lurched forward and then backwards, as he started to race up the rugged track.

It seemed to take ages and a couple of times the wheels of the vehicle spun as they hit a deep mud patch. It was so difficult trying to battle against the wind and rain but Farmer Finn was an expert in his four-wheeled drive and they finally arrived at Marley's Barn.

All four men jumped out, pushed open the huge, old door and ran inside. It was dark in the Barn but they all had torches. They searched frantically, calling Joni-Philipa by name.

It was Alex who finally found the little group. Hetty the Wee was snuggled by her arm and Ethelred-Ted sat close beside her with his paw lying gently across her.

"I've found her!" he shouted. "Over here!"

As he shone his torch down on her little face, he froze. She was so pale and still. He threw down his torch and knelt over her. He touched her face.

It was so cold!

In horror, he felt for her pulse on her neck.

He could find no sign of a beating heart.

"NO!" he screamed. "NO! NO!"

He lifted her little broken body and cradled her in his arms.

Father, Grandfather and Farmer Finn all ran to find Alex.

Father shone his torch like a spotlight on his two children.

"Alex! What is it? Alex, is she all right?" he shouted, his voice shaking.

Alex didn't reply.

"Alex, what is it?" yelled Father.

Alex didn't say a word. He just turned his face towards his father with tears streaming down his cheeks.

"NO! NO!" screamed Father.

Both Grandfather and Father fell on their knees and cradled Alex in their strong arms, while he held his little sister.

All three men sobbed and sobbed.

Farmer Finn looked on in sheer disbelief.

Joni-Pip's broken body was taken back to Bath, where she was buried next to her grandmother, who had died during the Spanish 'Flu Epidemic in 1919.

Chapter 7

The First Circle

After the funeral, Father moved his grieving family permanently back to Bath: shut up Knotty Knook and they never returned to Berry Bush again.

Mother didn't recover from the shock of losing her little girl and she became quite frail, until she died ten years later, in 1952.

Alex eventually became a Scientist, it was said he rarely laughed out loud again and he moved to the United States, where he married and had two sons and a daughter, whom he called Elizabeth. His three children all married in America and they produced seven grandchildren between them. One of his grandson's was called Jack.

Becky-Paige found life very difficult without her big Sissa and after Mother died, when she was fourteen, Father moved her back to his parents' farm in Portland. There, they all shared in making her life as full and as happy as possible despite the tragic loss of both her sister and her beloved Mother. Eventually she became a nurse, like Mother, married and had two sons, who then also married and gave her three granddaughters. One of whom they named Joni and another they named Philipa and the third she called Paige. This pleased Becky-Paige so much, to think that they did this in memory of her sister, who died so prematurely and of course herself!

Hetty moved in with Poppy-Plump-Pij into Poppy's cosy little home in Windy Woods and they stayed with each other, neither having families, for the rest of their little lives.

Grandfather moved in with Mother and Father and spent the rest of his days in Bath.

Marley's Barn was boarded up by Farmer Finn and nobody ever went in there again.

What about Ethelred-Ted?

Alex took him wherever he went and allowed nobody to touch him, so the red and yellow Teddy Bear ended up living in the United States of America. To Alex, Ethelred-Ted was his last link with his sister, Joni-Philipa: a treasured link indeed! Alex was always conscious of Joni-Philipa's love for her Teddy Bear: so keeping him close, gave her brother great comfort. He almost had a feeling of Joni-Pip's presence when he looked at him and many a time did his wife find him hugging Ethelred-Ted and still feeling sad over the loss of his little sister.

Although they say that 'Time heals': anybody who has ever suffered the horrors of an unexpected and avoidable tragic accident in their family, will always say that 'it never goes away, you just learn to live with it'.

Jack loved his Grandfather's tatty old Teddy Bear and constantly asked if he could have him. Only after a great deal of soul-searching did Alex actually allow his grandson, Jack, to 'play' with Ethelred-Ted and only after a great deal of pleading, was it agreed that he could even 'borrow' him, now and again, as long as he took extra special care of him.

Chapter 8

The Wall of Time

So, Dear Reader, how come, after all these tragic events, do we see Joni-Pip munching away at her oatmeal biscuits, in Grandfather's cottage and slurping down blackcurrant cordial? How is this happening only a few days after the tragic accident in Marley's Barn?

The answer lies in the visit of the Three Strangers that came to Marley's Barn on the day of the storm. Once again, through the magic of the printed page, we are going back on another journey. We are returning to the time when the wall of water unfurls in Marley's Barn and the three visitors jump over it. Poppy-Plump-Pij has disappeared over this amazing, wet water wall and the visitors all seem to know Joni-Pip, Ethelred-Ted and Hetty the Wee. The visiting Bear, who is most familiar to all of them, makes Ethelred-Ted get Joni-Pip down from the ladder and the colourful macaw flies back over the wall of water. In a second he returns.

Let's pick up the scene here, shall we?

"It's a workeda," he shouted excitedly, "It's a workeda!"

"Workeda?" questioned Ethelred-Ted. "What exactly does 'workeda' mean?"

The macaw began to sing the most beautiful operatic aria.

Joni-Pip, Hetty the Wee and Ethelred-Ted listened in amazement. The notes, coming from out of his beak were beautiful; his pitch was perfect and his diction faultless. The only thing they couldn't understand was what he was actually singing about. They didn't understand the language, at all!

Sensing their wonderment, the visiting Teddy Bear said to them,

"Don't mind Macca, he's always singing. His owner was an Italian Opera Singer and he's always doing his scales and singing his stuff: in Italian, of course but he usually speaks in English with a very strong Italian accent, mind you. He is a Macaw. So, what is 'workeda'? he is just telling us that 'it has worked, it has worked'."

With that Macca took off, flew over the thick bricks of water and disappeared.

By this time, Ethelred-Ted was getting pretty fed up with not knowing what was going on. It was all very puzzling and he didn't like it; he didn't like it at all.

"Look here, My Good Fellow," he said rather pompously, "what exactly is this all about? Who are you? Where do you come from? Why are you here? What exactly has workeda....I mean worked and what exactly is this, this stupendous 'thing'?"

The visiting Teddy Bear smiled.

"Atta Boy," he chuckled, "you haven't changed, even after sixty five years!"

"What do you mean 'even after sixty five years'?" Ethelred-Ted said crossly.

"Look, My Very Dear Self, don't you understand any of this? Can't you guess who I am? Where we have come from? No, of course you can't, how could you? Only H. G. Wells had written about it by 1942. Do you realise he wrote that incredible book in 1895?

"Come on, all of us, let's sit down and I will tell you all that has happened and it is one amazing story that you will find impossible to believe. I know....I did!"

The storm still ranted and raged outside the barn: the squally wind howled and the unrelenting rain lashed against the windows. The thunder and lightning continued to flash and crack but the group seemed oblivious to it all. They each settled themselves down, sitting on bales of hay and when they were ready, the Teddy Bear stranger began his most extraordinary story.

"I **am** Ethelred-Ted."

Ethelred-Ted jumped up and said rather crossly,

"Of course you are **another** Ethelred-Ted."

"Let me continue, please, with no interruptions!" said the stranger with great authority. Ethelred-Ted immediately sat back down. "I am Ethelred-Ted and I **was** here with you in Marley's Barn, sixty five years ago. How d'you think I know you all? Why d'you think I'm familiar to you? How d'you think I knew you were thinking about hot buttered crumpets, Ethelred-Ted? It's because I **remember** thinking about them. Why d'you think I keep calling you all 'My Dear Friends'? It's because you are. We live in the year 2007 but we have jumped back in Time...."

"Jumped?" Ethelred-Ted, Hetty the Wee and Joni-Pip gasped.

"Yes," replied Jack, "we jumped over the Wall of Time and wasn't it SOME jump, Red-Ted?"

"Oh, yes," replied Red-Ted, "incredibly wonderful....The Wall of Time!"

"The Wall of Time?" repeated Joni-Pip, Hetty the Wee and Ethelred-Ted.

Red-Ted pointed to the wall of water, which still stood in the middle of the barn; silent, rippling and glistening. He nodded.

"Yes, the incredible Wall of Time. We were in the United States, in the year 2007, just a few minutes ago and when we have finished our Mission here, we will jump back over the Wall of Time and land back, once more in the States, in 2007."

Ethelred-Ted, Hetty the Wee and Joni-Pip all gasped again.

"So, if this is true, why have you come, then?" asked Ethelred-Ted.

"A very good question, Old Chap….well, actually, you are still a young chap aren't you and what's more, a very fine young chap, indeed!" laughed Red-Ted. He turned to Joni-Pip. "We have jumped back sixty five years from our day, for a very special reason. It was for you, Joni-Pip, just for you, my very Dear Friend," he faltered. "Do you remember what you were doing when we arrived?"

"I will never forget it, yes," replied Joni-Pip, feeling very strange as she said the words, "I was just about to climb up the ladder, to explore the loft with Poppy."

Red-Ted walked over to Joni-Pip and took her hands in his paws: a tear rolled down his furry face.

"Yes, Joni-Philipa Garador, you did go up the ladder in 1942….er….I mean a few minutes ago....in your Circle, in your Time....now, even....I suppose it is….and sadly, as Hetty warned, you did have a terrible accident….in fact you were killed."

Ethelred-Ted, Hetty the Wee and Joni-Pip all drew in their breath, very loudly. Joni-Pip jumped up.

"What? What do you mean? Am I in another life? This is terrible. Am I dead?"

"Calm down, Joni-Pip, don't worry, please, just listen to me?" pleaded Red-Ted kindly. "It sounds impossible but it isn't, it's all true, very true indeed. You see, if we hadn't come back when we did, that's how it would have happened and continued to happen for you all. You would have died about now, Joni-Pip and it would have caused so much pain for all of your friends and family. Believe me it was awful, the worst thing I have ever experienced."

Red-Ted then told them what had happened to all of Joni-Pip's family after the tragic accident and finally he began to tell them about Jack and how he had asked to have Ethelred-Ted from his Grandfather, Alex.

"It all started with Jack, really. You should be grateful to him, Joni-Pip."

"What started?" asked Ethelred-Ted, Joni-Pip and Hetty together.

"I didn't actually know too much really, not at first, anyway. Sure, I knew that Grandpa once had a little sister who had died…." answered Jack.

"When Jack says 'Grandpa' he means Alex, your brother and you, Joni-Pip, are the 'little sister', he's talking about, who died," clarified Red-Ted.

Ethelred-Ted, Joni-Pip and Hetty the Wee all nodded seriously.

"Then I got with Red-Ted, sorry, to you he is 'Ethelred-Ted', isn't he? You know we Americans, we always manage to abbreviate words....you see my top....the Letters NYC....guess what they stand for?"

"No idea!" said Ethelred-Ted. "I thought at first they must be your initials but then er....Red-Ted called you 'Jack' and I couldn't see a 'J'!"

"They stand for New York City!" laughed Jack. "We have another City we like to know by its initials now and that is Los Angeles! L.A.."

"Well, I think Alex must have started all that! He almost always calls me J.P., instead of Joni-Philipa and he always calls Rebekah-Paige, my little sister, B.P.," she laughed. "What's she called now; my little sister?"

"I didn't know her name until just now. She's my Great Aunt, my Dad's, Dad's sister; my Grandpa's sister and we always call her 'Tauntie'!"

"Tauntie?" repeated Ethelred-Ted.

"Yes, because she's my Great-Auntie....that became T'Auntie....we just call her Tauntie....she loves it, she says it's a special name, just for her!"

"Little Becky-Paige, a Great Auntie?" Joni-Pip shook her head.

"Well, it's true. Anyway, you will be interested to know that the English have started to use abbreviations now, in the Twenty First Century. Great Britain is hardly ever called that now...." said Red-Ted.

"It's not?" asked Hetty, who had been listening silently for some time.

"What's it called then?" asked Ethelred-Ted.

"It's called the U.K." replied Red-Ted.

"'U.K.'? What on earth does that stand for?" asked a puzzled Joni-Pip.

"The United Kingdom!" replied Red-Ted and Jack together.

"United at last!" laughed Hetty. "The Scots and the English! Although I'm sure John Buchan used that term, didn't he? It's not so new!"

"And the Welsh and the Northern Irish!" laughed Red-Ted.

"There's a city in the U.K. too, that's growing very fast, my Father goes there a lot to do business and it's known by its initials," said Jack.

"Which city is that then?" asked Ethelred-Ted.

"Milton Keynes....only it's known as 'M.K.', " replied Jack.

"Milton Keynes?" repeated Joni-Pip and Ethelred-Ted together. "That's a tiny village in Buckinghamshire!"

"Oh no....not now, it's not!" laughed Jack.

"Milton Keynes is where Reg was born....he's our Butler in Bath!" laughed Joni-Pip. We have actually been there once!"

"Well, it's not a village now!" laughed Jack. "M.K....Milton Keynes....has become a huge new, sprawling city."

"Look You Guys," said Red-Ted.

"'You Guys'?" repeated Ethelred-Ted, Joni-Pip and Hetty the Wee.

"Oh dear!" laughed Red-Ted. "How American am I? As usual we have digressed: I'm supposed to be explaining how we came to be here."

"Well, y' never were short of a few words and it will be the same fer the next sixty five years, it seems, Lambie!" chuckled Hetty the Wee.

Red-Ted took a deep breath and tried again.

"It all started when Jack had a visitor; no actually he had some visitors."

"Three in fact," added Jack.

"We were just about to go swimming in the lake, near Jack's house, weren't we Jack?"

"Sure, Red-Ted. Dad was away on business in the U.K.; right here in England, in Milton Keynes....M.K., in fact and Mom was at some meeting."

"She's always busy on some committee, isn't she, Jack?" said Red-Ted.

"Yeah, she never seems to be at home. My older brother, Grant, was supposed to be keeping an eye on me but his friends came over and they were upstairs, practising their music. Grant plays drums and they have this band. They reckon they are going to be the next best thing on the Rock Scene," Jack said, sounding far from convinced.

"Rock Scene?" asked Ethelred-Ted. "Is he a Musical Geologist?"

Jack and Red-Ted burst out laughing.

"I suppose that's just what it sounds like ....'Rock' in the Twenty First

Century refers to Music; not just rocks we find on the Earth....it's the type of music some kids love....look it isn't important....let's just say Grant's band plays music like....like...." Jack sought for a word.

"Glen Miller!" laughed Red-Ted. "Only a bit different....and they call themselves Rock Salt....that's their band's name. One day you will be telling your children off for playing it too loud, Joni-Pip, I'm sure!"

Ethelred-Ted, Hetty the Wee and Joni-Pip looked confused.

"Anyway, on this particular day, Jack wanted to go swimming in the lake. I remember telling him I thought it was a bit cold but he didn't think that would be a problem," said Red-Ted.

"It was so strange, I was just going to dive in, when suddenly The Wall of Time grew up, right in front of us, by the edge of the lake....any closer and it would have been in the water itself!" Jack told them.

"This girl and a very, very old, very tatty Teddy Bear and a macaw appeared jumping over the wall!" said Red-Ted very seriously.

Ethelred-Ted, Joni-Pip and Hetty the Wee gasped.

"Yes, you guessed it! It was Me again, my Future Self....how long do Teddy Bears last? This time I was with **Jack's** Great Niece, Jemmy and of course Macca's grandson, Acker: named after a famous clarinettist from the Sixties, apparently. We had come from the year 2042. Anyway, they told Jack that he did swim in the lake and it was too cold and he got cramp and he got into difficulty. So, My Future self made **Me**....you won't guess what I was called....'Reddy'....that's a turn up....knowing my namesake, Ethelred the Unready! Anyway, they made me stop him from diving in," explained Red-Ted.

"So had you drowned then, Jack?" asked Joni-Pip and then added quietly, "Had you died....like me?"

Jack looked confused, frowned and then shook his head.

"No! I didn't drown or die! You don't understand. You've got it wrong!"

"He didn't die!" Red-Ted took over. "As Jack was struggling to keep himself above the water, he made a lot of noise in the lake. Grant, who had stopped drumming, heard all the splashing and looked out of the window."

"Thank Goodness fer that, Ma Pets!"

Red-Ted shook his head.

"Hmmm, not quite, Hetty....my Dear Friend, hold your hedgehogs! When Grant saw his little brother in difficulty, he ran out of the house and down the bank to the lake, where he dove in fully clothed."

"'Dove' what do you mean, he 'dove' in?" asked Ethelred-Ted indignantly. "What kind of English is that? You know the correct word is, 'he 'dived' in'!"

"You are quite right, Old Chap. I was always determined that I wouldn't allow 'Americanisms' to be included in my vocabulary but sometimes one or two do creep in. I stand corrected. Do you know, Americans also say 'I snuck into the room', instead of 'I sneaked' into the room'. I won't use that one, believe me. As well as all that, they've brought in adding a comma before and after the words 'and' and 'but'!"

"What?" yelled Eth. "What? A comma before and after 'AND' and 'BUT'? Don't they know the words 'AND' and 'BUT' are conjunctions and never need a comma, ever! Those two words 'AND' and 'BUT' act as a comma, do the same as a comma. Why would any one want to put two commas together? Who isn't clever enough to work that one out? What is the world coming to?"

"Er....You Two, I know correct English Grammar is terribly important and I'm sad that the Americans....and I am half-American, so I feel I can say this....have mutated the English language by 2007 but I am keen to hear how Grant saved Jack. It was so wonderful that he dived in to save him!" said Joni-Pip authoritatively. "Grant was so brave to jump in and save you, Jack!"

Jack half-smiled and said gravely,

"My brother was indeed brave, very brave. He swam out to me and grabbed hold of me. By this time I had gone under three times. He pulled me up out of the water and pushed me into shallow water, I struggled. It was terrible. I didn't know what I was doing. Finally I lay on the small beach of the lake, half dead from exhaustion...."

Ethelred-Ted, Hetty the Wee and Joni-Pip all sighed with relief.

"But Grant, my brave, brave, big brother was nowhere to be seen...."

"They found reeds and weeds caught up in his shoes....wrapped all around them....that's what they said pulled him under," said Red-Ted.

"So it was Grant who drowned?" asked Joni-Pip gravely.

"It was Grant that they had come back to save?" asked Ethelred-Ted.

"So, Grant was given another chance to live, like Joni-Pip?" asked Hetty.

"You've all got it!" answered Red-Ted.

"So, in the next life....the next Circle, Jack didn't go in the lake and Grant didn't have to dive in to save him. I understand." said Ethelred-Ted.

"That's exactly right, Old Chap....look, I would love to talk about this some more but we haven't got too much time left....you won't remember it anyway....just as we won't, once we get back to 2007...."

"That seems a bit pointless, then," said Joni-Pip rather disappointedly.

"Well, that's how it is, I am afraid," said Red-Ted kindly. "But we aren't left entirely without ANY memory because we are given a special gift."

"A special Gift?" asked Ethelred-Ted, Joni-Pip and Hetty together.

"Yes, a special Gift, a very special Gift!"

Chapter 9

The Gifts

Ethelred-Ted sat on the School Room windowsill in Knotty Knook. He didn't mind too much that Joni-Pip had left him behind. He watched her silently from the window as she went speeding off up the Log and Chain Path and disappeared into Windy Woods.

'No doubt she will be drinking black currant cordial and munching away at oatmeal biscuits in Grandfather's kitchen soon!' he thought to himself. 'Now that I do mind. I could really do with a Munch Break right now.'

As usual his tummy was rumbling. He had enjoyed a good supper the night before, however; some cold potatoes, which he was very partial to, a lump of cheese, some of Mrs Broft's pickled onions and a hunk of crusty bread. Delicious!

He decided, in order to deviate his thoughts from food, that he would carefully try and remember some of the events that had happened in Marley's Barn, on the day of the storm. He couldn't remember much at all, although as he sat there, things began to float through his mind. Soon bits and pieces came back to him. He knew, definitely that he held in his hand something very special. He also knew that he had to use it **for** something very special and very soon....but he hadn't a clue what that might be.

Although he couldn't remember everything that had happened in Marley's Barn, Dear Reader, **we** are able to recall all that happened and everything that was said.

Let's go back again....

Red-Ted was explaining how, although they would remember hardly anything that had happened, they would have a slight inexplicable memory, thanks to a special gift.

"Gift?" questioned Hetty the Wee, Joni-Pip and Ethelred-Ted together.

"Yes an amazing gift!" said Jack.

"It is amazing, indeed," agreed Red-Ted. "It's something that makes you think, 'I have done this before' or 'I have been here before'; although you can't remember when or how; in fact you have no other memories about it other than this feeling of familiarity. Usually you actually **say** out loud, 'I have done this before' or 'I have been here before' or 'I have seen this before' and yet you know there is no way you could have done. In fact you haven't, not in this 'Circle' anyway!"

"Hmmm….that does sounds a bit familiar to me," said Ethelred-Ted thoughtfully. "So what's this gift, this special gift called?"

"Déjà Vu!" replied Jack and Red-Ted together.

"Déjà Vu?" repeated Ethelred-Ted, Hetty and Joni-Pip.

Once again, Joni-Pip had a flash of memory. She saw the face of the pilot, she had seen in her garden the night of the Raid on Bath. Then it quickly disappeared.

"Yes, Déjà Vu," said Red-Ted. "That's the name of this special gift."

Ethelred-Ted smiled and nodded his head knowingly and thinking,

'Perhaps this is all a dream and I will wake up soon!'

Red-Ted turned to him.

"No it's not a dream, believe me!"

Ethelred-Ted looked confused, wondering how on earth Red-Ted knew what he was thinking.

"I remember the word now, 'Déjà Vu'," said Joni-Pip thoughtfully. "Father used it once. We were driving into a pretty village, which we had never been to before and he said that he knew the village, he knew where the village pond would be and that he remembered being there with us before and that he knew exactly what Mother was going to say and what Alex was going to reply, even though he had never been there before in his life: ever! I didn't understand it too much, just a bit strange, I thought but I definitely remember the words 'Déjà Vu'."

"Déjà Vu," said Red-Ted. "I'm going to explain what it means and how it works but sadly you won't remember what I tell you because that's how it works, as well."

Hetty the Wee, who looked very thoughtful, put her little paw up, as if in class. Red-Ted smiled at her lovingly. He hadn't seen her for so many years and how pleased he was to be with her again!

"Yes, my Dear Friend," he said gently, "my very Dear Friend?"

"This Déjà Vu thing….what's the point of it, if we don't or won't even ever remember it?"

"It's amazing!" answered Jack looking down at Hetty the Wee. He, too, was so pleased to meet Red-Ted's friends properly, at last. He had heard so much about them and it was so exciting to be talking to them and actually to be with them in the flesh. "The whole point of it….as we have explained what happened with Grant….is to go back to sad events in the Past and turn them round so that they never happen."

"Go back?" asked Joni-Pip in amazement. "How on earth do you 'go back' and 'turn them round'?"

"This is just too far fetched for me!" said Ethelred-Ted, pompously.

"If you let me finish, I will explain it all," replied Red-Ted. "Trust me."

Up until then nobody had noticed, that since flying over the Wall of Time, Poppy had not returned. Suddenly there was a whooshing noise and the pigeon came flying back flustered and excited. She settled down on the bale of hay beside Hetty.

"You will never believe what has just happened to me! It was so amazing, so unbelievable!" These were words that Poppy-Plump-Pij hardly ever used and her friends were dumbfounded at their rapturous feathered friend. Red-Ted smiled at Poppy, he was delighted to see her again after all these years. They had crossed paths when he had arrived, so he hadn't actually seen her properly. He stood up and went and stroked her.

"Poppy, my very Dear Friend, how wonderful to see you!"

"It's so wonderful for me to see you, too!"

"This is all very well," said Ethelred-Ted rather crossly, "but we are in the middle of a very interesting explanation and I want to hear the rest of it."

Poppy-Plump-Pij looked at Ethelred-Ted.

"Well, what has just happened to me and what I have just seen, was so fantastic, that I think you should all listen to what **I** have to say, for once!"

Ethelred-Ted was a little taken aback.

"All right, Poppy," he said humbly, "but would it be too much to ask you to tell us all about it….afterwards?"

"Actually, that would be a good idea, Poppy," said Red-Ted gently, "because that will really prove to you all, that what I am about to tell you, is indeed true."

This statement made Poppy-Plump-Pij feel very important, so she once again quietly settled herself, next to Hetty the Wee.

"I am explaining the meaning of the term 'Déjà Vu' and how it has affected all of you today," continued Red-Ted.

"'Dinner and Stew'?" asked Poppy, returning to her usual self. They all stifled a grin and politely, none of them laughed out loud, although Jack got up and stroked her. How pleased he was at last to meet this sweet character that he had heard so much about. Poppy-Plump-Pij beamed.

"Déjà Vu," corrected the visiting Bear, smiling lovingly at his old friend.

"We are all going to be very quiet and attentive, Poppy," said Joni-Pip. "You see, Poppy, this is Ethelred-Ted, only Jack….Jack is Alex's grandson ….well, Jack now calls him just 'Red-Ted' and he is visiting us from years in front of us: from the Future!"

"I know. I just didn't know it was called such a silly name."

Red-Ted smiled again.

"Oh, Poppy, how I have missed you! So much! Right, now where was I?

Yes….I know….it is actually French, 'Déjà Vu' and it means 'already seen' and that's exactly what it is all about….hmmmm!"

"Could we please, get on?" inquired Ethelred-Ted impatiently. He was most intrigued to find out what exactly was happening to them and for once, he wasn't thinking about his next Munch Break.

"Very well," replied his Future Self, "I will tell you all, the amazing secret of Déjà Vu. Remember, I told you it started with Jack; well that's

how it works. We always think of 'Life' as going forwards, don't we? Well, actually it does but it also goes backwards and sideways. It's like a Giant Kaleidoscope, you know what I mean, one of those things that is full of different coloured beads and as you turn it, the beads move and change into beautiful patterns. These keep on changing as it turns and the patterns are never the same."

"That's right, there are so many different, pretty patterns. I loved my Kaleidoscope," said Joni-Pip, "but sadly I dropped it in the stream one day and when Alex pulled it out, it was all soggy and the cardboard split and all the beads came out, I was so upset."

"I remember," said Red-Ted smiling.

"I don't understand, Ma Lamb."

"I suppose an easier way of explaining it, then," said Red-Ted, "is using a circle."

"Hmm," said Ethelred-Ted, "I noticed you've said 'Circle' a few times."

"Yes, yes I have, that's because Life is a Circle. Poppy, Hetty, Joni-Pip and you, Ethelred-Ted, my, this is so strange, talking, actually talking to you, talking to myself, I want you all to picture a circle in your minds. Hold on a minute, of course, Ethelred-Ted, could I please have a piece of paper from your bag....and a pencil?"

"How did you know I have paper and a pencil?"

"Because you have just composed your 'Song of the River', Silly, haven't you?"

Ethelred-Ted obediently went to his bag and opened it, a few pieces of screwed up paper fell out. He put his paw in the bag and searched around for some paper but there were too many balls of paper in the way, so he lifted up his bag, turned it upside down and shook it. The remaining discarded pieces of paper fell out; as well as lots of other stuff.

"That's better!" he said, putting his paw in the heap and taking out a handful of unused pages. He walked back over to the visiting bear and handed him the clean pieces of paper.

"Thank you....do you think I could use your pencil, too, please?"

Ethelred-Ted walked back over and dipped his paw deep into the heap.

"It's a good job I didn't stuff these pieces of paper back in, isn't it?" he said nodding towards the floor, littered with screwed up pieces of poetry.

Everybody laughed.

"Mind you do, though!" said Hetty the Wee chuckling.

Jack ran and picked up a few of the pieces of paper, sifting through them.

"Wow, am I really touching....do I really have in my hands some of the original work on 'Song of the River'? This sure is neat! What an honour!"

They all turned and looked at him puzzled.

"Not now, not now," said Red-Ted slightly embarrassed.

"Oh tell them!" replied Jack, to which Red-Ted gave him a scornful look, said nothing and then proceeded to draw a large circle on a plain piece of paper. It was quite dark in the barn, occasionally lit up by a flash of lightning from the raging storm outside and so it wasn't that easy to make out Red-Ted's Circle. Jack saw them straining to see, so he took out of his pocket what looked like another pencil.

"I think this will help," he said, switching on his pencil torch and lighting up, not just the piece of paper but the entire section of the barn. The wall of water glistened and quivered in the light. It looked stunning.

"What on earth is that?" asked Ethelred-Ted in wonderment.

"Just a little torch," replied Jack nonchalantly.

"Little?" gasped Eth. "Well, for a little torch it certainly gives out a big light!"

Red-Ted laughed.

"You will be amazed at what Man thinks up in the next sixty years or so....do you know we can take a laptop....it's like an opened flat box with a small screen, like a tiny cinema screen in the lid....we can take one outside and watch a film....a movie....like the Wizard of Oz....from beginning to end. It's in full colour with full sound and we can do all this while we are drinking sparkling lemonade with ice and eating cheese and pickle sandwiches, with just a touch of mayonnaise, in the garden!"

"What?" cried Joni-Pip. "That's not possible! That just can't be true!"

"And d'you know what this is?" asked Jack taking out his mobile 'phone from his other pocket.

"No idea," said Ethelred-Ted after examining it closely. "I saw and heard it when you first arrived. It looks exceedingly clever."

"This is my cell 'phone. Do you want to know how it works?"

"Don't tell him yet, Jack, do you mind?"

"Sure, Red-Ted," replied Jack and he put his cell 'phone, as he called it, back into his pocket.

"Now, thanks to Jack's pencil torch, we have good lighting as well as the good lightning from outside!" said Red-Ted, at which they all laughed. "Can everybody see what I have drawn?" he asked, holding up his drawing of a large circle; everyone looked and nodded.

"Now....can anyone tell me where a circle begins?" the bear inquired, then added, laughing, "Just ignore my overlapping lines....I am not too good at drawing a perfect circle....just imagine it is....so can anyone tell me where a circle begins then?"

Everybody thought for a second and then they all shook their heads.

"Can anybody tell me where the circle ends, then?"

Once again everybody thought and then shook their heads.

"So, if you follow the line of a circle you would just keep going round and round, wouldn't you? Constantly moving."

Everybody nodded this time.

"And that's like Life....it's always on the go....always in motion ....never stopping," said Red-Ted, then he drew some tiny circles in the

76

middle of the large circle and larger circles going around these tiny circles in the middle. "Does anybody know what this is? It's something to do with **all** life, in fact everything in the Universe; everything is made up of them, built from them, like building bricks."

"It's an **atom**," said Ethelred-Ted.

"Exactly! Trust Old Myself....I always loved science," Red-Ted said, then he added seriously, "Mind you, Man will make something so terrible....so dreadful....from his knowledge of the atom....but that will be felt in about three years time for you....yes, August 6th 1945....now that will change the History of Mankind....anyway, Ethelred-Ted is right. It is an atom....does anyone know what the smaller circles are?"

"Yes, I know, the tiny circles in the middle make up the nucleus," said Joni-Pip smiling and thinking to herself, 'We only did this last week with Mother in our science lesson'. "The nucleus is actually only a 10,000th of the atom."

"The other circles are the electrons, going round and round the nucleus," said Ethelred-Ted.

"Exactly!" said Red-Ted enthusiastically.

"You Two know all that? I didn't think you were taught about such things in the Forties....I learn something new every day!" laughed Jack.

"Jack, even before the War I loved to read and study 'Niels Bohr's research notes for his atomic theory' and he wrote them in 1913, twenty nine years ago!" said Ethelred-Ted crossly. "He was a Dane and I love anything to do with the Danes!"

"Jack, we haven't gone back to the Dark Ages, you know, we have only jumped back sixty five years!" laughed Red-Ted.

"Yes, I suppose so, Numpty Me!" replied Jack.

"Well, in actual fact, the Atomic Theory....the teaching that we and everything else, are all made up of tiny atoms....is much, much older than this century," said Ethelred-Ted authoritatively. "It's believed, it was first discovered by some very clever Greeks. Democritus is the name of one of them and he is best known for his Atomic Theory....and that was way back....he was born in 460 BCE....that's getting on for two and a half thousand years ago!"

"Wow!" gasped Jack. "So, Einstein and all that, is just 'old hat'!"

"Absolutely! In fact Democritus was not the first to propose an atomic theory," replied Red-Ted, "his teacher, Leucippus, had proposed an atomic system even before him, as had Anaxagoras of Clazomenae. Actually, traces of an atomic theory go back further than this, perhaps to Pythagoras."

"Well, we have all heard of him!" said Joni-Pip. "For a right angled triangle, 'the square on the hypotenuse is equal to the sum of the squares on the other two sides'."

Both Ethelred-Ted and Red-Ted smiled at her and nodded.

"Well, you know what? It's thought that the Babylonians knew all **this,** about a thousand years before and that Pythagoras and his followers just proved it!" laughed Red-Ted.

"This is all too difficult for me!" said Poppy sweetly. "I have absolutely no idea what you are all talking about, Puddings."

"Ah, Poppy, I forgot you call people that! It's so cute! Don't worry, about understanding, Pops, it's not important. You know what I....we .... Bears are like," said Red-Ted, stroking her back lovingly.

"Getting back to Democritus a minute," said Ethelred-Ted to Red-Ted, "do you remember how Democritus explained all changes in the world, as changes in motion of the atoms, or changes in the way that they were packed together?"

"I do! I may be over seventy now but I still have all my stuffing," he replied, tapping his head with one of his paws, which made them all smile.

"Hmm.....interesting," said Eth thoughtfully, "so taking that theory even

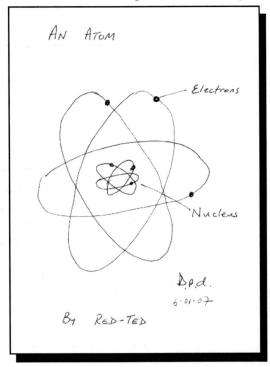

further, as in your case; you coming back from the Past to change things....just by coming, you have changed the motion of some atoms and no doubt, stopping the accident from happening, it's as if you have re-arranged the atoms, somehow and with what consequences I wonder?"

"Exactly!" said Red-Ted raising his eyebrows.

"What have these circles, these atoms got t' do wi' what's going on now?" asked Hetty who had been listening carefully to everything that was being said and watched very carefully everything that was being drawn.

"Sorry, I will get back to my picture...." said Red-Ted, holding up his drawing of the atom. "I'll try and say this as simply as I can. If any of you

78

don't understand then please tell me and I will try and explain it further until you do."

"Good." said Poppy and settled herself back down next to Hetty.

"Everything in the Universe....humans, bears, toys, animals, rocks, grass....just everything, is made out of tiny little things called atoms....this is my very bad drawing of one."

He pointed to the circle on the paper.

"Yes, well we all know about y' drawing, Laddie. Ye did, not a bad one of 'Life in the Wood' wi' Grandfather, remember?"

"Yes, I do and I will very shortly draw a picture of my 'Song of the River' with Grandfather, if I remember rightly!" laughed Red-Ted.

"That's a very famous poem now," said Jack, "Grandpa got it published, along with a few others you have written, he found them in Joni-Pip's desk and thought they were really funny, so they're recited in schools now!"

Ethelred-Ted stood up.

"Really? I will become a published poet one day?" he asked amazed.

"You sure will, Red-Ted....er....Ethelred-Ted," laughed Jack.

Joni-Pip, Hetty and Poppy clapped. Ethelred-Ted went very red, well as red as a red Ted can go red. He was delighted with the applause, although it made him feel extremely embarrassed. He nodded shyly and sat down.

"This is all very well, let's get on, we haven't much time," said Red-Ted equally embarrassed, he then picked out one of the little circles he had drawn inside the large circle, not the one in the middle, not the nucleus, "This electron is going round and round in circles around the nucleus and every time it completes a circle it is called...."

"An orbit!" interrupted Joni-Pip.

"That's right, Joni-Pip!" said Red-Ted relieved that the poetry thing had now gone away; he turned back to his drawing and he drew a line from the electron right round the nucleus and made another but much larger, circle. "So that's an orbit....and it keeps on moving round and round the nucleus. Here's another electron and this one, too, is going round and round the nucleus; orbiting it," he continued drawing another circle and another until all the electrons had a ring going through them.

"Everything is spinning around, inside an atom; it's similar to our solar system, isn't it?" Ethelred-Ted contributed to this very important science lesson. "It gives off power, it gives off energy."

"My thoughts exactly!" smiled Red-Ted.

"Polar wisdom?" asked Poppy, innocently. "Is that to do with clever bears that live in the snow?"

The two bears smiled and looked sweetly at their wood pigeon friend and then at each other.

"She still delights me!" chuckled Red-Ted. "Even after sixty five years!"
Ethelred-Ted gave a smile and nodded.

"No, Ma Pet, it is called our 'solar system'. That's our sun in the sky and all the things that go around it. The Earth, for instance, the planet we live on, it goes round and round the sun, spinning as it does it."

"And the moon, Poppy, the moon goes round the Earth and other planets orbit our sun, too," added Joni-Pip. "Some of those planets have moons that go round and round them, too...."

"....All the planets that orbit the sun; together, are known as our Solar System, Pops," said Jack.

"The Earth is spinning right now? Won't we fall off?" she said alarmed.

"Poppy, don't worry, we won't fall off because there is a very big power, a very big force that keeps us very, very firmly here!" smiled Red-Ted.

"Gravity!" chorused Jack, Joni-Pip and Hetty the Wee together.

"Grab a tea?" asked Poppy-Plump-Pij. "I'd love one! I need one!"

Everybody else burst out laughing. Poppy-Plump-Pij looked confused.

"Well, Poppy," said Jack, stroking her back, "it has been well worth all the effort of working out everything and finally going over the Wall of Time and JITTING back sixty five years, just to hear you!"

The pigeon beamed and smiled, shrugging her little shoulders.

"Look," said Red-Ted, "I'll just explain a bit more, just a little bit more."

"But y' said we won't remember it, so is there any point, Laddie?"

"You will, though, when you use your 'Gift', of course," replied Jack.

"There'll be a time, or even times, when you, yourselves use the Gift and you will remember all this information, even after you return for a while but then suddenly you will forget like a light switch suddenly turning off," said Red-Ted.

"M, M 'n M!" said Ethelred-Ted.

"Anyway, I will just quickly explain at least try to....without any interruptions!" laughed Red-Ted. He then once again held up his drawing of an atom and once again Jack shone his torch on the paper. "So, Life is like this, it goes round and round in circles and what we have done today, is change the direction of Joni-Pip's Circle, Joni-Pip's Orbit. Now, because you were in that Circle, that Orbit, then your lives will change with her, too and you will re-live the next sixty five years very differently. Everyone has their very own Orbit. It is called a POOL....Personal Orbit of Life."

"Oh, I see, now, Ma Lamb, that's marvellous!"

"This Gift, the Gift of Déjà Vu, includes the ability to go back in the Past and change horrible events that have happened to friends and family, making their lives, which were unhappy, into something better....happier," explained Jack.

80

"How do y' 'go back'?"

"Yes," said Joni-Pip, "I want to know, how it works," as she said this she was sure she heard footsteps behind her. She turned and in the dim light she saw the shadow of a tall figure, wearing a long cloak, disappearing into the darkness: scared but curious she pointed in the direction he had gone.

"Hello!" she called out, running into the gloom, "Who are you? Why do you keep coming near us? What do you want? Where are you from?"

"Joni-Pip, where are you going? Who are you talking to?" asked Eth.

"It's the man in the cloak again!" called back Joni-Pip from the darkness.

"Come back here, you'll fall, in the dark!" ordered Eth, "we aren't the only ones allowed to use Marley's Barn for shelter, you know, there is a wild storm still raging outside and I wouldn't want to be outside in it!"

Joni-Pip reluctantly returned to where she was sitting, frustrated that no-one seemed interested or would pay attention to this figure she kept seeing.

"Where were we?" resumed the visiting Bear. "How does it work? How do we go back? I don't really know. We just put our heads together and tried a few things until finally we managed to produce the Wall of Time!"

"Produced The Wall of Time?" exclaimed Hetty, Eth and Poppy.

"Yes, the amazing Wall of Time," replied Red-Ted.

"Is this normally done alone?" asked Poppy.

"It can't be done alone. It's always best to do things like this with others, isn't it? So you can help each other, in case, when jumping over the Wall of Time, something happened and you couldn't get back," said Jack.

"How awful it would be to be left stuck somewhere in the Past or Future, with nowhere to go and no way of getting back home?" said Red-Ted.

Poppy-Plump-Pij, Hetty the Wee and Joni-Pip nodded.

"Is that exactly what you make?" asked Ethelred-Ted, gesturing towards the wall of water, which still quivered and glistened in the dim afternoon light. "Is that how it always looks, the Wall of Time?"

"Exactly!" replied Red-Ted. "It all started, simply because Jack felt sorry for me. I was just left sitting on a window sill in Alex's Study, getting an occasional hug from him but mostly just sitting there. Jack came along and what a change in my life! Of course, as he was a caring person, straight away I was able to talk to him. I remember telling him about all of you three, Joni-Pip, Hetty and you, Poppy. He was so sad about your accident, Joni-Pip. I remember him saying, 'If only I had been there, I would have done something to stop Joni-Pip from climbing up that ladder!' That made me feel awful because I should have stopped you, Joni-Pip but I didn't and I've had to pay with that terrible feeling on my mind, for all these years. However, the whole point of this is that I think....and this is purely a thought....I think Déjà Vu only works if somebody really cares about other people's sadness. Anyway, quite a bit later, as we have already told you, we had the visit from Jemmy, Reddy and Acker from 2042 and the Gift was passed on to Jack. He knew he had something very special. It was this amazing material with strange numbers and figures on it. It was like a small handkerchief but it opened up into something incredible. He was puzzled because he had no idea where it came from and yet at the same time he kind of knew where it came from. Of course when he showed it to me, we both decided to take it to Joni-Pip's brother Alex, Jack's Grandpa."

"Actually, I held on to it for a few days....a few very thoughtful days," added Jack. "I kinda knew I had a mission and this was something so, so special....I knew I had been given a wonderful gift....I had no idea who from or where from, I just knew it was so important that I use it as soon as I could. I also knew it was connected to JITTING....but that's all."

"JITTING?" questioned Ethelred-Ted and Joni-Pip.

"Yes," replied Jack. "Jumping in Time, only we call it JITTING."

"We took it to Alex and he explained that it was a very special formula," continued Red-Ted. "He said that although he had worked with formulae for years, he couldn't remember seeing such a strange one. Then he thought about it and said that somewhere in the back of his mind he had this notion that he had actually seen this formula before: this very one! He couldn't understand why he felt this way because he couldn't recall when or where he had seen it; he just had a strange feeling about it. We asked him to explain it to us. Alex said that it was very complicated but that he would study it and then get back to us. Alex always loved figures, tables and numbers, so he was able to work it all out for us. He said that it was some amazing formula that made power from water. Don't ask me to explain it, ask him!" laughed the Old Bear.

"From Grandpa's working out of the Formula, we were able to make energy from water and we made the Wall of Time appear!" Jack went on. "We had to practice at first and we made a few mistakes. Once, we landed in Germany, where Red-Ted born, some battle was raging on and we think it was you there, Joni-Pip, with two boys. It was so strange and so dangerous. Whoops! We soon got out of there!"

"Me?" questioned Joni-Pip, "Why, that's impossible! What would I be doing n Germany? In the middle of a Battle....did you say?"

"You were older than you are now, so it's obviously going to happen in your Future. We didn't stop long enough to find out what was going on!"

"No, we didn't," laughed Red-Ted, "it was peculiar!"

Joni-Pip looked at Red-Ted and Jack and the faces of a young girl and two boys flashed around inside her head.

"D'you think these Circles, can join up, somehow? You know, overlap?"

"Sure, they must be able to," ventured Jack, "or perhaps come out of each other, as the water bricks on the Wall of Time do."

"Now, there's a thought," said Joni-Pip. "What I mean is do you think it is possible that these Circles can join together like links in a chain?"

"Hmmmm, not sure," added Red-Ted. "In the end it turned out to be really simple....the F.B.....much simpler than we thought. Our time is running out, I think we only have an hour when we JIT. I don't actually know! It just seems right and I don't want to find out and get stuck in Time; so we must be getting back real soon...."

"One last thing," said Jack, "the person who is given the Gift of Déjà Vu has to pass it on to somebody he or she meets in the Past. It's strange really, I pass it on to you but I keep it as well....it's a bit like love, isn't it? If you want to keep it in your life, you have to give it away!"

"That's so nice!" said Joni-Pip.

"Isn't it just? So, Ethelred-Ted, I am passing this on to you," said the young American, thrusting a neatly folded, sort of handkerchief into his paw. "You won't remember anything about this soon but you will have the Formula and you will realise what you will have to do with it....change an unhappy event in somebody's life. It's all so remarkable! It has been really, really neat meeting you!"

"When we jump back over the Wall of Time," said Red-Ted, "you'll begin your New Circle, your New Orbit and that will start a few minutes back in Time, from your Old Circle. You know I suppose they do link, Joni-Pip, as you said, like a chain an enormous chain....

"Right so you will go back to the time when you arrived at Marley's Barn and you will do everything exactly the same but one thing, Joni-Pip....I....er....he....er.... well....Ethelred-Ted, anyway....will stop you climbing the ladder. You, Joni-Pip, you will have the feeling of the Gift you have been given, the Gift of Déjà Vu because it will be something that will drastically change your life. It will be the Kaleidoscope of Life turning, or more accurately, it's referred to as, the Turning of the KOL."

"Whew!" she said.

"It's a bit sad that we won't remember this though!" said Hetty the Wee.

"Yes," said Poppy, at last able to tell them what had happened to her, when she had flown over the Wall of Time, "when I flew over, the Wall, I knew that I was in another Time, in the Future. There you were, Joni-Pip, an old lady but we both knew each other straight away. It was the most amazing feeling; it was out of this world!"

"Yes," said the Red-Ted, "that's exactly right; indeed, at the moment of Déjà Vu, everybody both from the Past and the Future has a glimpse of what is going on. Only a glimpse mind but for a few moments Past and

Future join and unite, it's called the **Pasture**."

"Pasture? That sounds so peaceful, so beautiful," said Joni-Pip.

"Doesn't it? I hope this explains why we sometimes get strong feelings about things that have happened way back in the Past and we haven't a clue why," said Jack.

"It's been amazing, thank you so much," said Ethelred-Ted.

"It has been our pleasure, believe me. I'm so glad that we have been able to do this, not just for you, Joni-Pip but for all of your friends and family. Not to mention, myself. I won't have to live with this terrible guilt that it's left me carrying for 65 years until 2007. How glad am I!" said Red-Ted.

"We had better get ready to leave, Red-Ted," said Jack.

Eth laughed again when he heard his new name and thought to himself, 'Oh well, I suppose if life can turn and change, then so can names!'

"There's one more thing I want Jack to do before we go, though," said Red-Ted, turning to Jack. "Now you can use your cell 'phone, Jack....why don't you dial your Grandpa's number?"

Jack looked puzzled.

"We are still in the Pasture, so it might work," smiled Red-Ted.

"O.K., I'll do it!" said Jack, taking his 'phone from his pocket. He tapped away at some numbers and then held the 'phone to his ear. "It's ringing!"

"Hello?" said Jack into the 'phone. "Is that Grandpa?"

"He is talking to Alex!" Red-Ted whispered. The others gasped.

"Yes," came the reply from the 'phone. "Is that you, Jack?"

"Yes, it is, Grandpa," Jack replied.

"I'm so glad you rang because there is someone here who has just arrived from England. She wants to speak to you. She says it seems like ages since she's seen you and spoken to you," said Jack's Grandpa. "I'll hand the 'phone to her, here she is."

"Hello," said Jack cautiously.

"Jack, Darling, where are you?" came a slightly familiar voice.

"Who is this?"

"Jack, how are you, Darling, don't you recognise my voice?"

"No. Grandpa said you were over from England...."

"Stop mucking about you Bad Boy, hurry on home I need a hug!"

"Oh it's you!" Suddenly Jack's face lit up.

"Where are you, Darling?"

"A wonderful place!" answered Jack. "You could never imagine! It's so amazing to hear your voice!"

"Are you feeling all right, Sweetheart, you sound a bit strange?"

"Do I? Not surprising really. You've no idea how neat this is!" said Jack.

"Jack, you really sound odd now, are you sure you are not unwell?"

"No, I am most definitely not unwell. In fact I am feeling spectacular!"

"Now you are making me laugh, Darling. Thank Goodness!"

"I've someone who would love to speak to you. I'll put her on," Jack walked to Joni-Pip and handed her the 'phone. "Say 'hello'," he laughed. "Say 'hello' to my great aunt." Then he whispered, "I don't know much about her yet but I'll learn all about her in the OOMU, on the way home!"

Everyone looked puzzled. Red-Ted shrugged. Joni-Pip was confused, she had no idea what Jack was going on about. She'd never seen a mobile 'phone before; she took it from Jack and spoke into it, as Jack had done.

"Hello."

"Hello," came the voice, the voice of an older lady.

"Who's that?" asked Joni-Pip.

"It's Jack's Aunt. I am his Great Auntie Joni-Philipa!"

As the two visitors prepared to JIT, Macca, who during all this time had busied himself exploring the lofts in Marley's Barn, returned. He didn't care much for Science. Music was his main interest in Life and a certain pretty little wood pigeon. He flew over and landed on the bale of hay, next to Poppy. He looked at her.

"I'll be meetinga you soona and when you firsta see me you'll thinka, 'haven't I meta him befora?' Anda you will hava but no mattera 'ow 'arda you racka your braina, you willa nevera be hable to recalla whena or howa because it is all parta of Déjà Vu. It willa slightly frustrata youa, however! Buta you willa flattera my feathers and I willa flattera your feathers too. You ara so Baby!"

Poppy blushed slightly but it pleased her greatly. All of the group hugged each other and said their 'goodbyes' and then in an instant, the three visitors jumped and disappeared over the Wall of Time.

When Joni-Pip entered Marley's' Barn, she had this incredibly strong feeling that she had been 'there before' and she remembered the conversation and she remembered that she had started to climb the ladder.

"You know what? I've been here before. It's all so familiar. I know exactly what you're going to say. I'm going to climb a ladder. Peculiar! Talk about Déjà Vu!"

As she said this, the face of the pilot came into her mind and he had the girl, called Flip, alongside Craig and Steve, standing behind him. They were all smiling at her. It was so weird.

After this, she saw the two men, wearing long black coats walking along in the woods. All of them then vanished.

Chapter 10

Strange Happenings at Hideaway Cottage

"What are you going to do, today?" asked Grandfather as Joni-Pip continued drinking down her blackcurrant cordial.

"Not sure yet, Grandfather," replied Joni-Pip, wiping the dark red droplets of her drink from off her chin with her hand. Grandfather took a clean tea towel from out of a drawer and went over and wiped both her damp face and her blackcurranty hand.

Of course, neither of them had any idea of what had really happened but that's why he had had these terrible urges to hug his granddaughter. When Déjà Vu affects anyone, although they have no recollection of the life they have lived through, when it changes, they still feel strange about certain things. In reality, he had lost his granddaughter many sad years previously, in the First Circle: something he never recovered from but now with the Turning of the KOL, he was doing it all again. This time, he had no tragedy to live through. As the Orbit had changed, though, it still left him with these unexplained feelings. He just took Joni-Pip's glass tumbler from her hands, put it on the table, gently pulled her up from her chair and gave her the gentlest but strongest hug he had ever given her in her life.

"I love you, Joni-Philipa."

"You O.K., Grandfather?" she wasn't used to him using her full name.

"Wonderful!" he replied.

((So, Dear Reader, if ever you have the urge to hug somebody close to you, then do it, don't hesitate or question why, just do it….you never know what you might have just lived through or indeed what that other person might have just experienced. I am promoting Hugdom here, as you will read!))

Feeling bad about leaving Ethelred-Ted behind, Joni-Pip decided to walk
back for him. On the way across the hill she bumped into Nuttingham Squirrel. Normally she was a bit scared of his brusque manner but this time, she was pleasantly surprised to find that he was very pleased to see her. He too, had been so sad when he had heard of her terrible accident, so he had this happy feeling this time he saw her.

"How are you feeling, today, Joni-Pip? Where are your friends? You are looking really well."

"I am feeling fine," she replied, wondering why everybody seemed so very odd today. "I am just on my way to pick up Ethelred-Ted now. We will probably go for a walk. Would you like to come with, us?"

"Thank you so much for asking me and most certainly, I'd have liked to but as it has been raining so much, I'm very behind with my work. Another day, I would be delighted to join you. Goodbye!"

With that, he dashed off.

For a moment, Joni-Pip just watched him disappear from her view, she couldn't believe how nice he had been, even though the conversation had ended somewhat abruptly. She smiled to herself and went on her way home.

How pleased Ethelred-Ted was when she finally picked him up from the Schoolroom windowsill. He had been thinking about things. Of course he couldn't remember everything but he did know that he had this amazing Formula and he knew that he could use it and he was hoping that soon he would find an opportunity to do so. The strangest thing about anything connected with Déjà Vu, is that you don't remember what has happened, it just leaves you knowing things and you don't know why or how even. Peculiar.

At first they had a game of Pirates in the garden of Knotty Knook. Ethelred-Ted just adored running in and out of the freshly washed white sheets, which were pegged on the line. It was indeed a game that smelt so good! The white wind-plumped cotton panes, provided perfect sails for his Armada, as they billowed in the breeze. That was until Mrs Broft caught sight of Joni-Pip hoisting the Main Sail and shooed her off. They were a bit put out, to say the least, especially as it was the one time that Joni-Pip had really entered into the spirit of the game and was enjoying it immensely. The two of them examined Joni-Pip's hands and both agreed that the term 'grubby' most definitely didn't apply; not entirely anyway.

They were crestfallen that the battle had not been won and the Treasure had not been seized; in order to give it to the Poor, of course. Captain Fry (Ethelred-Ted's tribute to Captain Cook), modelled himself on Robin Hood and rarely kept any Pieces of Eight for himself! So, the scuppered Pirates set off to find Poppy-Plump-Pij and Hetty the Wee. Both of them were delighted to see Joni-Pip and once again she was given two warm hugs from them.

'Oh, dear, what's the matter today? Everybody keeps hugging me!'

The four friends decided to walk to Edwinstowe Library. Everywhere seemed fresh that day; they thought it was purely the sunshine on the well watered grass and trees, a result of the days of endless rain. Of course, it was more than that for them: it was, in truth, a fresh day for them, a brand new start. They chatted excitedly as they walked across the woods; past Grandfather's Crooked Cottage and then took their way down Lily Lane, into Edwinstowe. A squadron of Spitfires flew across the blue skies, above them and a regiment of the Home Guard, marched past them: raw reminders of the War.

Edwinstowe was the place where Robin Hood had married Maid Marion. People were odd and called that a legend but if you go into Edwinstowe Church, you can read the record of their marriage, even today.

The village was very pretty with thatched cottages, a few little shops, the Butchers, the Bakers, a little Grocery Store and the Post Office. Edwinstowe also had a very old Blacksmith's Forge and the Old Stopping Cells. These had been used years before when transporting villains from the North of England, down to prisons in the South. They were stop over cells, used for the captors and their captives to rest and sleep on their journey (down to London usually). Then of course there was the Library. Poppy-Plump-Pij had never been there before, she was very excited.

As they walked along together they heard the sound of more big boots. They had to stand very close to the wall this time, as a large regiment of soldiers marched along beside them and past them, on their way to the Camp where they were stationed, a few miles outside of Edwinstowe.

Every time the Four Friends walked through the village, they always stopped when they came to a dilapidated, old, empty shop. It didn't seem to belong to anybody. It was all boarded up, so it wasn't possible to see much of what had gone on inside it. Nobody seemed to know anything about it; just that it had stood empty for years.

"I wonder who used t' own that wee shop?"

"I wonder what they used to sell?" asked Joni-Pip. She stepped up into the little porch in front of the shop and peered through a small hole between two of the crossed over planks that had been nailed together to stop any intruders. The other three joined her. Poppy-Plump-Pij flew up and perched on a wooden beam that held up the ceiling of the porch. She twisted her little body round so that it was almost upside down and tried to get a good view above the wooden planks.

"Not much to see….the glass is so dirty."

"Oh could you wipe it?" asked Joni-Pip. "I want to know what's inside."

"This shop is such a mystery," muttered Ethelred-Ted, straining to see through another crack between the planks.

"I have a hanky in my pocket," Joni-Pip said, taking out a crisp white handkerchief, which Mrs Broft had ironed that morning. "Couldn't you have a go at cleaning the window, please?"

Poppy flew down and took the handkerchief, then flew back up to the beam. She perched herself rather precariously upside down once more and gently wiped away at the dirty glass.

"Oh, dear, I seem to be making it worse, it's all smeary."

"Probably because it's dry, Hen. Can't we wet the hanky somehoo?"

"What a splendid idea!" exclaimed Ethelred-Ted. "With all the rain we've been having recently, the path is covered in puddles. Sling it down Pop," he continued affectionately, "and I will do it!"

The Wood Pigeon obeyed and the handkerchief floated gently down towards him. He caught it and walked off and dunked the, now black smeared, once white, cotton square in the deepest puddle he could find. He squeezed it out and returned to the porch where Poppy flew down, took it from him and returned to her vantage position above them. With the wet handkerchief in her little beak she rubbed away at the grime, until a little round, clear patch allowed her a glimpse into the dark shop, below her. Shafts of sunlight through the cracks in the planks, as well as the light from above, gave the sight below her, quite an eerie glow. The sunlight cast dusty beams, which cut through the gloom, like the search lights in the darkened war skies of 1942.

"What can you see, Poppy?" asked Joni-Pip excitedly.

"Yes, Ma Pet, what's therrr?"

"Can't see much," replied the pigeon, peering into the gloom.

"Is there a counter in the shop? Are there any sweet jars on the shelves?" asked Ethelred-Ted, pondering about his next possible Munch Break.

Poppy strained her little eyes to see what was below her. She scanned round the room.

"No, no sweet jars....plenty of shelves though....and yes, yes I can see a counter....lots of big tubs on the floor....and do you know what else?....There's a....is it?....No, it can't be...."

"What....it can't be, what?" asked Joni-Pip excitedly.

"What can you see, Poppy?" chorused Ethelred-Ted and Hetty.

"Yes, it is....I can see it clearly now...."

"What are you three up to then?" came a loud, booming voice behind them.

The three friends jumped in surprise and turned round to see Constable Cruckleton smiling at them with his big, red, round rosy face. He was tall and huge and could be as ferocious as a roaring lion, if need be but most of the time, as was now, he was as gentle as a flowing mountain stream.

Poppy, still trying to describe what she was seeing, paid no heed to him.

"It is....it is...." she said loudly. "I can see a very large gr...."

"Hello, hello, hello," interrupted Constable Cruckleton. "I didn't see you up there….all I saw were these three backs, looking through these cracks and I wondered what you were all at."

"We were just curious, that's all," said Joni-Pip.

"Yes, we weren't prrrying….just being inquisitive," added Hetty the Wee.

"Well, I wasn't," said Ethelred-Ted boldly, "I was simply being downright nosey!"

"Nosey, eh?" Constable Cruckleton chuckled.

"Not nosey," said Poppy flying down to be with them all, "just interested."

"What's the story behind all this, then, Constable Cruckleton?" asked Ethelred-Ted, gesturing towards the rundown, abandoned shop.

"Not much to tell really….a bit of a mystery….hmm….but if you want to find out anything, the best thing you can do is to take a walk across to Mr Spindlethrop's cottage, Archimedes Spindlethrop….he lives in Hideaway Cottage not a mile from here….go straight through to the other side of the village….you'll come to a stile on your right, climb over it and cross Marion's Meadow….there on the other side is Spindlethrop's strange little house."

"Who is he, this Mr Thimblestop?" asked Poppy-Plump-Pij.

Constable Cruckleton grinned.

"Mr Spindlethrop will tell you all you need to know….and more….er….if you do decide to go….be careful….he doesn't like people too well….I don't know how he is with little 'uns….let me know how you get on?"

With that he went on his way.

The four friends watched him walk up the High Street, away from them until he disappeared round the corner by the Stopping Cells.

They all felt slightly strange and didn't speak for a while.

Ethelred-Ted finally broke the silence.

"Well, he was obviously a TAWP, wasn't he? What do you think? Shall we pay Archimedes a visit or what?"

"A TAWP?" questioned Joni-Pip, looking at Hetty.

"One of those Toy and Animal World People, who hears us," said Hetty.

"Or what, what?" Poppy-Plump-Pij asked Ethelred-Ted.

"Or what else shall we do?" replied Ethelred-Ted kindly.

"I do have library books to pick up for Alex," said Joni-Pip.

"What aboot, if we go to see Mr Spindlethrop first and then come back t' the library?"

"Spiffing idea!" exclaimed Ethelred-Ted. "Now what exactly are we going to say to the old boy then?"

"Well, we can just ask him about the shop. We can ask what happened, so that it had to be boarded up?" suggested Joni-Pip.

"Yes, and we can ask what they sold in the shop, too," added Poppy-Plump-Pij. "Don't let's forget the library, though, I have never been in there."

"And we can ask him how long the shop has stood empty," said Hetty.

"Splendid!" exclaimed Ethelred-Ted. "Let's get going!"

The walk across Marion's Meadow was quite difficult. The constant rain had soaked the ground, making the going heavy and boggy. As they got nearer to the other side, they saw the four tall chimneys of Hideaway Cottage, above the hedge. None of them had ever been here before, in fact none of them had ever heard of Archimedes Spindlethrop, either, or Hideaway Cottage.

On the far side of the meadow, there was a large iron gate. They tried to open it but the lock had rusted so badly, it was impossible. They all clambered over....well, Hetty the Wee was helped by Joni–Pip and of course Poppy-Plump-Pij flew over. As they got closer to the cottage, all of them began to feel a trifle uneasy. It was an ugly cottage....nothing at all as any of them had imagined....Hideaway Cottage sounded so pretty....the windows were small and latticed and they were positioned on the building in such a way that the house seemed to have a very grumpy, cross face; it definitely was frowning!

Nobody spoke as they began to walk slowly up the path towards the front door. Half-way up the path, they were all startled by a black cat, which suddenly leapt out of the hedge. He stationed himself on guard, in front of them and started hissing, growling and spitting at them. Poppy-Plump-Pij immediately flew up into the air terrified. Hetty the Wee nearly jumped out of her little body and Ethelred-Ted ran and hid behind Joni-Pip!

"Well, thanks for all that!" she said. "Great support You Lot are...."

She then bent down in front of the raging cat and extended her arm bravely. The cat continued to hiss and spit but Joni-Pip persisted in her peace making and spoke to the cat gently.

"It's all right, Little One," she said and after a bit of coaxing, she finally managed to stroke the cat and eventually he started to purr.

"That's amazing, Joni-Pip!" said Ethelred-Ted in awe. "How do you do it?"

"Nothing to it, Grandfather always taught me that animals respond, usually in the way you treat them....so if you are ferocious with them, then they will be ferocious with you....and if you are gentle and kind to them, usually they will be gentle with you. See?"

91

The cat continued purring and then walked up and down by Joni-Pip as she stroked him and then backwards and forwards around her legs, rubbing his side against her with his tail pointing straight up in the air, like a flagpole.

"Don't you see how friendly he is now? All it takes is a bit of gentleness and a lot of fuss!" laughed Joni-Pip.

The four friends, along with the cat, made their way up to the front door. Ethelred-Ted, feeling rather ashamed that he had hid behind Joni-Pip, decided to absolve himself by knocking boldly on the front door.

Knock, knock, knock. They waited. Nobody came. He knocked again. Knock, knock, knock, knock. Nobody came.

There wasn't a scrap of noise coming from within the house but they could all hear a strange whirring sound, coming from outside the cottage: behind it somewhere.

No-one spoke. They walked towards the noise. At first they thought the noise was coming from the large workshop at the very back of the cottage but after investigation they realised it wasn't coming from there at all. They continued following the strange noise, which got louder and louder as they moved closer and closer to the far end of the cottage. The noise was like no other that they had ever heard. It was kind of like a very noisy tractor and a very noisy motor car and a very noisy motorbike all revving up at the same time. They had to cover their ears to save themselves from being deafened.

"What on earth is that?" shouted Joni-Pip into the air.

Nobody heard her, the noise was thunderous.

As they turned the last corner of the building, before they got back to where they had started their search, they saw the wooden shutters of the coal cellar. They were vibrating violently. This racket and clatter was most surely coming from beneath those brown wooden shutters.

They all ran back to the corner they had just turned and peered apprehensively from the safety of the grey stones of the cottage. They were so scared of this dreadful noise but so intrigued. None of them had the remotest idea of what was going on down in that cellar but they were dying to know. Suddenly, the shutters, covering the hatch of the coal chute, burst open and a huge cylinder shaped object came hurtling through them and was launched up into the air. For just a moment it was propelled forward….then the strange object nosedived back on to the grass and slid along a few feet, until it stopped abruptly. Clouds of black smoke came billowing out of the back of the cylinder. The four spectators could hardly make out a thing through the murk of the strange smelling smoke. After a while, the foggy gloom began to clear.

The contraption was something, the like of which, they had never seen before….it was literally like a giant cigar case, a metal cylinder, covered in nuts and bolts and covered in black soot!

Everybody looked in amazement, as a small door on the top of the strange missile, was flung open and an unusual Creature immerged. The Being was wearing a leather balaclava and goggles. It lifted itself up, out through the small trap door and looked around until it saw Ethelred-Ted, Joni-Pip, Hetty the Wee, Poppy-Plump-Pij and the cat, standing in utter disbelief watching this spectacle. The Life Form, which was of questionable nature, was covered from head to toe in black soot. It marched excitedly towards them and lifted up Its goggles, resembling a human panda….a black face with huge white patches round its eyes....where the goggles had been and where no soot had managed to force its way in. Suddenly the Creature smiled.

"What year is it?" It asked enthusiastically.

The four friends looked at It blankly.

"I said, 'What year is it'?" It repeated.

"1942," they all said together.

"Oh, Cough Drops!" exclaimed the Sooty Soul and promptly walked round the corner of the cottage and disappeared.

A second later It re-appeared and called to the cat,

"Come on, Eureka, time for your breakfast or lunch or supper or whatever, I don't suppose I have fed you for days."

The quiet, black cat lifted up his tail appreciatively and walked off; both of them disappearing round the corner of the cottage.

Chapter 11

Archimedes Spindlethrop

"What are you going to do this afternoon, J.P.?"

"I don't know yet, Alex."

"It's just you forgot to pick up my library books yesterday."

"Alex, I did. I forgot. I'm so sorry. I didn't get to the library in the end."

"What did you do then? Didn't you walk into Edwinstowe?"

"Yes, we did....I did," she corrected.

"So where did you end up then?"

"I walked across Marion's Meadow to Hideaway Cottage."

"Hideaway Cottage, isn't that Archimedes' place?"

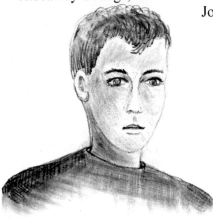 Joni-Pip crossed the dining room, to the table where her brother was tucking into his lunch of cheese on toast....well, it wasn't actually lunch, it was eleven o'clock in the morning....but Alex, like Ethelred-Ted, always seemed to be eating. She was surprised that her brother had heard of Archimedes Spindlethrop. He had never mentioned him to her before....however, she was more surprised that her sixteen year old brother was engaging in a conversation with her, at all.

Alex had been affected by the Turning of the KOL and had these protective feelings towards her. This morning, surprisingly, he appeared to make time for Joni-Pip and was decidedly filial towards her. He got up and gave her a little hug. Joni-Pip was flabbergasted.

"So what was my little sister doing round Archimedes' place then?"

"Nothing really," she replied nonchalantly. She didn't know quite how to explain about Hetty, Poppy and Ethelred-Ted and their interest in the old dilapidated shop in Edwinstowe and the amazing spectacle they had all witnessed at Hideaway Cottage; how they had walked back home, excitedly chatting about all that they had seen and heard; understanding very little but being totally intrigued by it all.

"Nothing really...." she repeated to her brother.

"Look, J.P.," said Alex, "I've finished all my work, what say you about us taking the bikes and cycling into Edwinstowe to get my library books?"

Joni-Pip was amazed. Her brother had never invited her to join him on a bike ride, ever! She kept wondering what exactly was going on in her life.

"So?"

"So? So what?"

"So, so are you going to come with me, you Twerp?" Alex laughed.

"Alex, what do you know about Archimedes?" she realised that actually she and her friends had discovered almost nothing about him, other than he had a cat called Eureka whom he fed now and again and also that he came whizzing out of the cellar at a very noisy and alarming rate, in some sooty, silver, sausage-shaped machine.

"He's a wonderful character, J.P. but let's get going and I will tell you all about him on the way. I'll go and clear it with Mother."

While Alex was talking to Mother, Joni-Pip slipped into the School Room and had a quick word with Eth. He had been feeling rather bored just sitting there while Joni-Pip had been having her lessons. Geometry was not one of his stronger points, he preferred English Literature himself or Cookery, which was an excellent lesson. Joni-Pip would prop him up in the kitchen on the work surface, where they would be preparing a delicious War Time dish. He would then just savour the tantalising aromas coming from the wood burning stove: maybe from a thick tasty vegetable casserole or a yummy strawberry jam roly-poly. Joni-Pip would always manage to save him some, which he would savour later on with such relish, pleasure and appreciation.

Joni-Pip told Eth she was going on a bike ride with Alex. He begged her to take him but she said that her moments with her brother were so rare that this time she wanted to be alone with him; he was a bit put out. She said that she was going to find out as much as she could about Archimedes, so Eth felt consoled. He was fascinated and needed to know more about Archimedes and his weird and wonderful contraption.

"Before you go, could you just get me a hunk of bread and jam, I'm dying for a Munch Break?" he asked as Joni-Pip was about to leave the School Room. She laughed and ran off to the kitchen to grab him his wish.

As they cycled Joni-Pip had this wonderful feeling of 'belonging'. It was something inexplicable: they chatted together as they never had before.

"Oh blow!" said Alex, stopping and getting off his bike, "I've got a flat!" He felt his tyre, "False alarm it's just a bit soft. Hold on a sec, it won't take a jiff!"

"That's an awfully long train," Joni-Pip said as Alex pumped up his tyre.

"Probably a Troop Train," Alex didn't look up, "how many engines?"

Joni-Pip stood straddling her bike and counted the engines as they steamed past.

"My Goodness, there's three at the front and one at the back!"

"It's a Troop Train without a doubt, probably heading for Hull. Fixed!"

Everything seemed just perfect as they cycled side by side, through the country lanes, shaded in places by lush, overhanging trees. They were reminded that everything wasn't perfect, though, as they passed the Prisoner of War Camp, a few miles outside of Edwinstowe, in Norton Cuckney. It was more of an agricultural camp, really, with military security. They sometimes saw the leather-clad military policemen roaring around on their big, black motorbikes. The Inmates, including East European soldiers and former Russian Tzarist Officers were sent out to do field labour: digging potatoes mainly.

"Tell me, Alex, what does Archimedes Spindlethrop do? What is he?"

"Didn't you know he's an Inventor, mad as a Hatter, everybody says but I'm not so sure. I find him totally absorbing; not crackers at all. He has some amazing ideas, incredible theories. Why don't we go and see him? I'll introduce you then we can go and pick up my library books on the way back we might even get a cuppa offered us."

Alex didn't wait for his sister to reply, he just headed off towards Hideaway Cottage and Joni-Pip followed. As they got off their bikes and leaned them up against the wall of the Workshop round the back of the cottage, Joni-Pip once again felt uneasy but her fears were dispelled when her brother marched confidently up to the back door and firmly rang the bell, which hung on a string, beside it.

"Claaaaang!" Nobody came.

Alex rang the bell again, "Claaaaang!" Nobody came.

"Let's try the door," suggested Alex.

"Are you sure?" Joni-Pip shrank back; she wasn't quite prepared for that.

"He won't mind….he knows me," he said, trying the door.

Joni-Pip was scared, to say the least. She wasn't brave like her brother.

"Don't you think he would be cross, Alex?" She offered.

Just then the sound of a loud explosion echoed over their heads and bounced back off the cottage wall. A high pitched whistling came towards them, getting louder and louder. Suddenly Alex dived on to Joni-Pip, pushing her to the ground and covering her with his body. Something rushed closely above them and crashed into the wall of the cottage. Pieces of brick and stone sprayed out all over them.

"What the….?" exclaimed Alex as Archimedes appeared from behind the Workshop and came running up towards them….and past them….and began to examine the hole in the wall, which the missile had just made.

"Astonishing! Astonishing!" he exclaimed. "Now where did it land?"

The Inventor hadn't seemed to notice the two bodies, looking up at him in utter disbelief, lying beside his back door. He was so oblivious to them that as he went on his way, searching for his errant missile, he just stepped over them and disappeared round the corner of the cottage. Alex got up and helped his sister to her feet. They both brushed themselves down and slowly walked in silence towards the Workshop.

The large, wooden, double doors, of the Workshop, were wide open and Alex just wandered in. Joni-Pip had never seen anything like it. The whole, huge space of the building was filled with strange contraptions. There were tables and desks, crammed with papers  of all shapes and sizes, with strange writings and formulae on them. There were wires stretched across the area above them, forming criss-crosses, loops and patterns in a higgledy-piggledy fashion. In one corner there was a mini laboratory with a large assortment of all different sized and shaped test tubes, glass jars and several bubbling beakers, by a Bunsen burner. The entire floor was littered with thousands of burnt out matches. There were, what seemed like, literally hundreds of glass bottles, filled with chemicals in beautiful, different shades of green, purple, red, yellow and blue. The whole place had a surreal feel about it and Joni-Pip wouldn't have been surprised if Albert Einstein, himself, had walked in!

Right in the middle of the Workshop, was the huge sausage-shaped cylinder that Joni-Pip and her friends had seen hurtling from the cellar. It was propped up on four huge ramps and the trap door, on the top, was open. Archimedes Spindlethrop was nowhere in sight. Joni-Pip felt that she had entered a new world, a world that she neither knew nor understood but one that she found totally fascinating and exciting.

"Archimedes!" shouted Alex. "Archimedes, where are you?"

"Perhaps he is in the cottage, Alex," Joni-Pip offered.

"I hardly think so, J.P., it was obvious he was in the middle of some experiment. He sometimes spends days out here, not even stopping to sleep until he has finished whatever project he is working on."

"My Goodness, Alex, doesn't he get tired? Doesn't he get hungry?"

"Archimedes Spindlethrop, hungry? No, I don't think eating is something he is much fussed about; not like me!"

'Not like Ethelred-Ted, either,' thought Joni-Pip.

"He never seems to get tired, either, he always seems like he is on some Mission: something drives him to keep going forwards and...."

"Upwards!" interrupted Joni-Pip laughing. "And downwards!"

Suddenly Archimedes entered the workshop carrying a small sausage-shaped object. Joni-Pip noticed it was the exact replica of the large Missile that she had seen him climbing out of, the day before. He was muttering.

"Splendorous, splendorous indeed!" he exclaimed, as he passed Joni-Pip. Then he turned and spoke to her as if he had known her all of his life and certainly not in the way he would speak to some stranger who had entered his laboratory, uninvited.

"If it can work on such a small scale, then it must work when everything is increased in size, multiplied by thirty one. What do you think?" he asked her, not stopping to hear her reply but walking straight on towards the large sausage-shaped vehicle in the middle of the workshop.

"Yes," Joni-Pip replied meekly.

Alex followed him, as he approached the large Missile.

"What is it, Archimedes?"

"What is it? What is what?" the Inventor replied rather irked.

"This great Invention of yours?" Alex pointed to the giant metal sausage.

Archimedes suddenly looked at both of his visitors and shook his head.

"Who are you? Are you from the Council?"

"No, Archimedes, it's me Alex Garador, from Knotty Knook, in Berry Bush, the one you talk to about steam trains," replied Alex.

Archimedes looked at him blankly through his spectacles then he lifted them up and peered closely at him.

"Why did you say you had come from the Council?"

"We haven't come from the Council, Mr Spindlethrop," ventured Joni-Pip, "but we are jolly interested in your wonderful Inventions."

"Humph! If you haven't come from the Council, then let me get on! I am far too busy to talk. Good Day to you!"

With that, he walked over to his 'laboratory' and with his back to them, he began to examine the small cylinder, on one of his benches.

Alex looked at Joni-Pip, shrugged and started to walk over to him.

"We have come to ask you about the old shop in Edwinstowe," said Joni-Pip bravely. Alex turned and looked at her puzzled. He didn't know about his sister's attempts to see what was inside the dilapidated old shop.

Archimedes slowly turned round and gave Joni-Pip a smile.

"How about a nice cup of tea?" he asked her. Alex was dumbfounded. Joni-Pip suddenly had a very warm feeling about this eccentric older man. The kitchen in Hideaway Cottage was large and cluttered but comfortable enough to enjoy a cup of tea. Archimedes led them to a cosy corner of the room and settled his two visitors into two easy chairs round a beautiful, small, octagonal, table. The Old Inventor filled the copper kettle and put it on the wood burning stove. He fed Eureka. Then he took out his best, blue rose patterned china, from a rather grand but terribly dusty, glass cabinet. He washed up the cups, saucers, plates, teapot, milk jug and sugar bowl and dried them with a surprisingly crisp, white tea towel.

"It's not often we have guests, is it, Eureka?" he asked his black cat. Alex was surprised that Eureka was so friendly towards them, as last time, the cat had been far from sociable, in fact he had been downright ferocious towards him. Alex was even more amazed to see that after Eureka had polished off his tin of sardines and licked his saucer of milk clean, he jumped up onto Joni-Pip's lap and started to wash himself.

Archimedes sat down in a large, leather arm chair and poured them all a cup of tea from the beautiful bone china teapot and handed them round.

"Forgive me," he said, "I don't think I have any biscuits to offer you....well I might have...." He put the teapot down and got up. He walked over to his magnificent, painted dresser and pushed off loads of papers, exposing a large, red tin. "There might be some in here," he said, opening the rusty old tin. He looked inside the tin, gave a very large sniff and then shook his head, "P'raps not!"

He settled himself back down, picked up his cup and saucer, took a large gulp and then turned to Joni-Pip.

"So you want to know all about the shop in town then?"

Joni-Pip nodded.

"Who do I have the pleasure of addressing, young lady?"

Alex leaned forward.

"This is Joni-Philipa, one of my sisters, Archimedes."

"So you are young Garador's sister, then, I know him well, lives over at Knotty Knook," he said, as if Joni-Pip had nothing to do with Alex.

"Yes," answered Joni-Pip, thinking, 'so do I but what does that matter to this old gentleman?'

"Your brother is quite a clever chap, did you know, Joni-Philipa?"

Joni-Pip smiled and nodded.

"Well, let me tell you all about the Pretty Posy," the old man said, rather wistfully. Alex, knowing nothing of the shop then said,

"The Pretty Posy, what's that?"

"The Pretty Posy?" asked Joni-Pip. "The Pretty Posy? How lovely!"

"It was my sister's, her husband was Edmund Plate, the Explorer."

Joni-Pip's heart began to race, she knew she had heard of the name PLATE but couldn't remember where. She began to rack her brain.

"He was always away on Expeditions, travelling the world, so Jemimah, my sister, ran the little flower and craft shop. It was such a beautiful shop. Jemimah kept a baby grand piano in there and she used to play wonderful music to her customers. People came from miles around to buy the pretty little baskets of flowers she sold: as well as all the amazing, unusual potted plants Edmund would bring back from his journeys. Jemimah could boast that some of the biggest and most famous Gardens in the country, had bought some of their exotic plants, from the Pretty Posy. She also sold little samplers, tea cosies and handmade lace....lots of things ....buttons and bows and all colour pretty ribbons!" the old man's face was really glowing, as he fondly recalled the memories of his sister's busy, little shop.

"What happened to change everything?" asked Joni-Pip.

"It all started to go wrong when Edmund was reported lost at Sea; Jemimah could not cope with the thought of losing her beloved husband. She wasn't a very strong kind of person, really ....that's why she played the piano to her customers, it was easier than actually having to talk to them. Anyway, when Edmund was reported as being lost at Sea, she just went to pieces. She took to her bed and never recovered properly....I just wish things had been different ....but I was so young, you see, only twenty six....I was only twenty six, a single young man full of ideas and plans....she just didn't fit into my schemes....that's why they put her there........," his voice trailed away.

"Put her where?" asked Alex, by now intrigued with the whole story.

"In the Workhouse. She shouldn't have gone there, she was so young; such a pretty little thing but what was I to do with her? A young, single man with so many other things on my mind. So many things I wanted to do. I have never forgiven myself, believe me, I haven't. There are so many things I regret," the Inventor sounded so sad. "So many, many things....if only I could go back in Time and put the clock back...now wouldn't that be grand....to put everything right and have no regrets. Oh, I wish!"

100

Chapter 12

The Workhouse

"Honey, what are you going to do today?" asked Father.

"I wanted to walk over to see Grandfather. Is that all right?" Joni-Pip replied. She really wanted to spend time with her friends, as she had found out so much about The Pretty Posy but she knew she would have to be alone with them to do so. She was quite torn. She rarely seemed to spend time with her wonderful father these days: he was so busy travelling from Bath to Berry Bush and back again. The War was still raging on and he wouldn't allow his family to return to live in the City, until it was all over. Petrol was rationed at this time but because Father was an important Banker, he was allowed so much more petrol than most people; a bit unfair really.

"I have some business to discuss with Farmer Finn and he asked if you would like to come up to the Farm with me. He has something he wanted you to see up there," said Father, putting on his overcoat: Joni-Pip crossed the kitchen to help him, she pulled down his collar, standing on tip toe.

"My, we are getting tall! You will soon be as high up as me!" he joked.

"Hardly, Father!" she replied and as she did so, he turned and gave her a really warm hug, which he was always doing but because of the Turning of the KOL, at this particular time, he had the most tremendous urge to do so.

"Are you coming then, Honey?"

Joni-Pip didn't know how to reply. She was curious enough to want to find out what it was that Farmer Finn wanted her to see but so desperate to talk to her friends about Archimedes Spindlethrop and his story.

"Father, I would love to," she ventured, "but I really must get to Edwinstowe Library. Alex and I forgot again yesterday and Seamus O'Hara, you know, the Librarian, has had some books waiting for him to be picked up for three days now!"

"O.K., Honey, but Farmer Finn wanted to see you so much; he will be disappointed that you aren't coming."

Farmer Finn had witnessed the sad scene, sixty five years before, in Marley's Barn, so now, he too had experienced the wonder of Déjà Vu.

"Would you like a lift to Grandfather's?" he asked, as he was about to leave.

"No, thank you, Father but please tell Farmer Finn that I will come next time."

As soon as Father had left, Joni-Pip ran to the School Room to fetch Ethelred-Ted. He had felt decidedly abandoned over the last couple of days. It goes without saying that he was extremely pleased to get out of the house and up on to the hill in Windy Woods, where, once again, he became himself. He was not cross with Joni-Pip: since that 'Day' in Marley's Barn he had become terribly protective towards her.

"I think it would be a good idea if we go to two places today, Eth," said Joni-Pip, "when Poppy and Hetty the Wee join us, of course!"

"And where might they be?" asked Ethelred-Ted curiously.

"Just wait and see," she said smiling. She had so much she wanted to share with them but wanted to wait until they were all together.

On the top of the hill, overlooking Knotty Knook, Joni-Pip settled herself on the ground and leaned up against a friendly rock. Poppy flew up to join them.

"Hello, You Two, how are you both?"

"I am very well, now," came Ethelred-Ted's reply. "It's so good to get out, after being stuck in the School Room for a day and a half!"

"Sorry, Eth, I didn't mean to leave you but it was so good to spend some time with Alex, he's quite amazing and such fun to be with!"

"And I am not?"

"Of course you are, Silly but how often do I get to be with my big brother?"

"Only teasing," laughed Ethelred-Ted.

"I wonder where Het is? I've been worried about her as it's been so windy. P'raps her little house had been swept away," said Poppy, looking very concerned.

"Well, it's not windy now," said Ethelred-Ted. "There's no wind at all."

"How do you know there's no wind at all?" laughed Joni-Pip.

"Easy, Silly You, this time, look at the smoke coming out of the chimneys at Knotty Knook!" he pointed towards the cottage. The smoke was going straight up.

"Can you see those stars?" asked Joni-Pip, sitting up and pointing, "they look as though they are coming from behind Knotty Knook!"

"Oh, yes, of course!" said Poppy-Plump-Pij.

"Yes, I can see them," said Ethelred-Ted, "So they are not imaginary?"

Joni-Pip turned and gave him a look.

"We see so many stars and glittery things, these days, don't we? Well, at least, I have, up until now. It's got to mean something, surely," she said.

"Who are **they**?" asked Poppy-Plump-Pij, as two men, in long, black coats and Officer's hats, started walking up the Log and Chain Path.

"Joni-Pip settled herself on the ground and leaned up against a friendly rock"

"They are looking for the three visitors I have had, I suspect," said Joni-Pip; suddenly remembering all the other encounters she had experienced.

"Who are they? Which three? Why didn't you tell us?" asked her Ted.

"I think I only remember all about it when they appear," she replied.

Joni-Pip remained sitting on the ground, as the two men approached.

"Ach, eet iss yu. Haff yu zzeen za gurl?" one of the men asked Joni-Pip.

"**Guten Morgen,**" said Ethelred-Ted, "**Kann ich Ihnen helfen**?" [3]

Joni-Pip and Poppy stared, open-mouthed, at their friend, in amazement.

"**Guten Morgen. Haben Sie irgendwelche Zeichen von drei jungen Menschen gesehen? Ein Mädchen und zwei Jungen?**" [4] replied the other man.

"He wants to know if we have seen two boys and a girl?"

"I see loads of young boys and girls," replied Joni-Pip, "all the time!"

"Ha, ha!" laughed Ethelred-Ted. He turned to the men, "**Nein, schade.**" [5]

"**Dann müssen wir zurück wieder springen. Ich bin sicher, dass wir den richtigen Platz haben.**" [6] said one of the men, to the other.

---

[3] "Good morning. Can I help you?"
[4] "Good morning. Have you seen any signs of three young people? A girl and two boys?"
[5] "No, sorry."
[6] "Then we must jump back again. I am sure we have the right place."

They then marched off, back down the Log and Chain Path and then disappeared round the back of Knotty Knook.

"Where did you learn to speak like that, then?" asked Poppy, impressed.

"Pops, my friend, I was made in Germany, remember? I am a Steiff!"

"There goes the stars again!" Joni-Pip pointed down the hill.

"Talking of stars, did you see the stuff on their hats? It was all shiny!" asked Ethelred-Ted. "I wonder what they're after? Not sure I like them."

"Me neither," said Joni-Pip thoughtfully, wondering why she didn't want these two men to find the girl and Steve and Craig, whoever they might be.

"There's no wind, today, is there?" asked Poppy and they all carried on as if the men hadn't come or gone. "The smoke just goes straight up in the air. If there was any wind the smoke would be blown in the direction of the wind. Birds use signs like these all the time, they help us with our flying. I remember flying once in this terrible storm...." her little voice trailed off.

"I see," said Joni-Pip. "That's very clever....when was that then?"

"I can't remember exactly when, I just know that I did....it still frightens me to think about it," said Poppy shaking her head.

"Funny, you've never mentioned it before, Pops," said Ethelred-Ted.

"Hmmmm," nodded Poppy-Plump-Pij, "that's quite strange really."

A small pile of leaves began to move in front of them and it spoke.

"I think I nearly got blown away last night, it's so good t' see y' all."

The three onlookers remained speechless. A self-moving pile of leaves was strange but a talking, moving, pile of leaves was something else!

"What are we going to do today?" inquired the speaking leaves.

Nobody replied.

"Are you all right Ma Pets?" the leaves said in a concerned voice.

"Hetty the Wee!" they all chorused together.

"Are you in there?" asked a curious pigeon.

They all pulled at the leaves, which had stuck on to Hetty's prickles.

"That's better, Het," said Joni-Pip, as she pulled at the last remaining leaf. "You are You again!"

They all had a chuckle together and Hetty told them how she had scarily nearly lost her little home in the strong winds of the night before.

"Hmmmm!" said Poppy very faintly remembering a tiny shadow of her ordeal on the night of the storm when they were up at Marley's Barn.

Joni-Pip felt this was a perfect time to tell what she had learned about the Home of many an unfortunate child, living in the century before them.

"Let's walk to the Ruin!" she suggested excitedly. "I've something very important to tell you about. Look!" she pointed. "Am I seeing things?"

They all turned and saw two men galloping across the fields in front of them, behind Knotty Knook....followed by a Regiment of mounted soldiers wearing scarlet jackets and white safari helmets.

"That's ridiculous!" said Ethelred-Ted, "They look like something out of your History Book, Joni-Pip."

"Rather!" she said, watching the riders tear across the land before them.

"Who are they? I'll go and investigate!" said Poppy taking off.

"The soldiers are chasing those men, aren't they, Ma Pets?"

"Looks like it! I wonder who they are?" Ethelred-Ted lifted himself up.

"They look like soldiers in the desert, with those hats on!" said Joni-Pip.

"That's it! They look like Royal Engineers in Africa!" Ethelred-Ted said.

They watched the two groups hurtle across the plain below them.

"Look!" cried Joni-Pip. "They are heading straight for those stars!"

They all looked. There were thousands of stars amassed together, making up a kind of structure: like a huge wall of stars. Suddenly the first two riders leapt into the stars and disappeared; followed by the Regiment of scarlet-coated, white-hatted, mounted soldiers.

The stars then rolled up like a scroll and disappeared.

"What were you going to tell us about?" asked Poppy, circling in front of the others; none of them remembered the spectacle they had just witnessed.

"Yes, tell us, Ma Lambie!"

They were eager to find out what it was, right then but Joni-Pip said they needed to be at the Ruin to hear her story. Intrigued, they walked off together, questioning her but she would give nothing away until they were finally settled at the Ruin. Ethelred-Ted sat leaning up against his favourite tree, The Major Oak, which still stands tall and proud to this day: Poppy perched on top of one of the broken down walls, Hetty snuggled up next to Ethelred-Ted and Joni-Pip stood in the middle of them on the sandy path.

"We all know what this big building used to be, don't we?"

"Indeed we do, Ma Lamb."

"A Work Shop!" answered Poppy-Plump-Pij.

"A Workhouse," corrected Ethelred-Ted.

"Right," said Joni-Pip, "do you know who used to live and work here?"

"Work people?" asked Poppy-Plump-Pij sweetly.

Ethelred-Ted stifled a laugh.

"Um," said Joni-Pip kindly, "sort of but they were a bit more than that."

"Yes, a lot of wee people worked here, didn't they?"

"That's right," answered Joni-Pip.

"Poor people, usually," added Ethelred-Ted.

"That's right, too," replied Joni-Pip, "but not always poor people: sometimes rich people lived here, ones whose family had fallen on hard times." She suddenly heard herself speaking in the very same words that Grandfather had used, when he first spoke to her about the Workhouse.

"However, the most important thing, has something to do with the very first time you spoke to me Ethelred-Ted."

"It has?"

"Do you remember why it was that you first started to talk to me?"

"Let me see now, was it to do with my need of a Munch Break?"

"It was when Grandfather first showed me the envelope and the piece of paper he found in the chimney of the Ruin," Joni-Pip replied, ignoring Ethelred-Ted's comment and pointing towards the pile of bricks that made up the last remains of one of the Workhouse chimney breasts. It was now propped up by two long planks leaning up against it at a precarious angle.

"I remember that piece of paper. I've never seen it but you told us it was about a little girl called Suzie Saucer or something?" enthused Poppy.

Amused, they all burst out laughing.

"Suzie Saucer?"

"You mean Amelia Plate," said Joni-Pip smiling, then she remembered that she too had referred to the little Victorian girl as 'Emily Dish'.

"She was a very pretty little girl," replied Joni-Pip.

"How could you possibly know that, Joni-Pip?" asked Ethelred-Ted.

"Ah....I found out so much about her....from her Uncle."

"Her Uncle?" the other three questioned together.

"Yes, her Uncle....Archimedes Spindlethrop!"

"Archimedes Spindlethrop?" Her three friends gasped.

"The very same! Can you believe it? Archimedes Spindlethrop is Amelia Plate's Uncle."

"The Mad Inventor?" asked Ethelred-Ted.

"Oh, Eth, despite what we saw when we all went to Hideaway Cottage, despite that amazing Machine that came out of the Cellar....." Joni-Pip began.

"I thought it was like a Flying Cucumber!" said Poppy innocently.

"A Flying Cucumber?" the other three laughed.

"Yes, I did....just like one."

"Well, it wasn't green!" exclaimed Ethelred-Ted.

"No, it wasn't but it was the same shape."

The other three decided to leave it at that.

"Anyway, Joni-Pip, what were you saying about old Archimedes?" asked Eth.

"Despite how it looked, when we first saw him....he is not a Mad Inventor!"

"Are yer quite sure now, Hen?" asked Hetty the Wee, really laughing. "An' ye know....seeing a large....seeing a large....Flying Cucumber.... erupting from the cellar, as we did....and then the Inventor emerging....as

106

he did....like a huge Panda....was quite somethin'.....somethin' bordering on madness!"

"He is a very determined and forthright man but he is not mad. In fact he was quite sweet when we had a cup of tea with him."

"Sweet?" repeated both Poppy-Plump-Pij and Ethelred-Ted, laughing.

"Yes, sweet. Anyway...." Joni-Pip sounded quite irritated by now, "the whole point of what I was going to tell you, was to prove to you what an amazing man he is....but I don't think that I will bother now."

She turned away from them and walked over to the propped-up chimney. She had been so eager to tell her friends about Archimedes Spindlethrop but now it all seemed spoilt by their amusement and lack of support.

She looked down towards The Crooked Cottage but something rustling in the bushes beside her made her turn sharply and she was just in time to see a strange, hooded figure disappear into the woods behind her friends.

"Who on earth is that?" she asked, pointing towards the trees.

The other three turned and followed the direction of her finger.

"Who?" they asked together, seeing nothing and no-one.

"I saw a person, somebody wearing a long, grey cloak with a hood and they went into the woods behind You Lot!"

The three others laughed and shook their heads.

"Are yer seeing things again, Ma Lamb?" asked Hetty kindly.

"No I am not! Why don't you ever believe me?" she shouted.

"But we didn't see anyone, Joni-Pip, honestly," replied Poppy gently.

"Why do I bother? You never believe anything I say," she shouted again. "I did see somebody and they were strange looking. Who wears a long grey cloak with a hood, for Goodness sake? What's he doing round here?"

Ethelred-Ted stood up, walked over to her and put his arm around her.

"Sorry, Joni-Pip, we didn't mean to upset you. We really didn't see anyone. Why don't you tell us all that you have learned about this amazing Inventor, Archimedes? Amelia Plate's Uncle eh? This is really intriguing."

"Yes, please do, Ma Pet; please? We all need to know, we all want to know what y' have to tell us," pleaded Hetty as she walked over to her.

Poppy-Plump-Pij flew across to the chimney.

"Was this, the very chimney where Grandfather found the paper, written on by Celia Slate?"

Joni-Pip burst out laughing.

"Oh, Pops, you are priceless....her name was Amelia Plate."

All four of them laughed together at Poppy's confusion. This laughter was a good thing. Joni-Pip quickly forgot about the mysterious hooded figure and returned to her enthusiasm about the story she had so wanted to tell them. They settled themselves down and she began.

Chapter 13

Finn's Farm

There was something about a farm that always fascinated Joni-Pip. Maybe, it was the constant noise of the chickens wandering freely around the farmyard? How busy they always seemed, pecking and scratching; scavenging tirelessly in the muddy straw, in between feeding times. They always seemed in a desperate search to find some 'left over' morsels from their last meal. Or perhaps it was the muddy ducks walking in short steps, swaying from side to side, stopping now and then to quench their thirst by taking a drink from a murky puddle; 'drurdling' across the water with their flat bills? Possibly it was the sound of the cows lowing from within the darkness of their milking sheds? Or was it, by chance, the ruddy faces of the farmhands, wind burned and raw from constantly working outdoors? It may have been none of those things; it may have just been purely the many different and unusual, farmyard smells!

Whatever it was, Joni-Pip loved visiting Finn's Farm.

Farmer Finn was delighted to see Joni-Pip. He hadn't seen her since that terrible night up at his Barn, Marley's Barn, where he witnessed the saddest scene of his life: the still body of a little girl, lying lifeless in the arms of her big brother.

All was changed now, of course!

"I have been waiting for you to pay me a visit, young Joni-Philipa," he said eagerly and for some unknown reason he gave her a friendly hug. This unexpected show of affection took her quite by surprise but Joni-Pip was pleased. She always enjoyed being in his company although sometimes she felt he carried something sad in his heart, something secret that caused him to sigh now and again. She had no idea what or why. He wasn't a typical farmer. He was tall and straight and very well spoken. Somehow, through the pages of the books she had read and the children's progrxammes she had heard on the wireless, farmers always seemed portrayed as chubby, jolly with very ruddy cheeks and broad country accents.

This farm, Finn's Farm, had been in the Finn Family for generations. Farmer Finn had been sent away by his parents to Eton and then to Oxford, to be highly educated, in true British style. That's where he had met Joni-Pip's father, at University. Farmer Finn's own father, Fred Finn, had wanted him to go on and do great things to change the world but all Farmer

Finn wanted to do, was to return to the farm of his Forefathers and keep it running as smoothly and efficiently as his own father had done and his father before him.

"It's all your fault, Father," he said, "you shouldn't have made life so good here for me and then perhaps I wouldn't have farming in my bones!"

So, with his PhD in Physics, safely tucked up under his muscular and very tanned arm, he ended up becoming a happy and successful farmer. His father learned the lesson that parents can only encourage their children to go in one direction but if that isn't the way in which their children want to go, then they will turn around and go in the direction they choose: following their own heart's desire, their own dreams.

"Father said that you had something you wanted to show me," said Joni-Pip. She loved this warm feeling she kept getting. Of course she had no idea why. She didn't realise how her Old Teddy Bear and her great nephew Jack had given her the opportunity to live the life she should have had, the one that had been so cruelly snatched away from her, sixty five years previously, in The First Circle.

Farmer Finn took her by the hand and walked her across the farmyard to one of the barns. As they crossed the muddy yard, the ducks and chickens clucked and quacked noisily. Joni-Pip loved it.

"The animals seem very pleased to see you today!" laughed Farmer Finn.

When they got to the barn, he called out to one of the farmhands inside.

"Have you seen Franco this morning, Bernie?"

"He's up at Marley's Barn, fixing some of the windows," came a reply from within the darkness of the barn. Joni-Pip poked her head inside and took a big sniff. It was wonderful, the smell of the stored hay and straw. Somehow that had changed within her since going through her 'Pasture'.

"Is he alone?" asked Farmer Finn.

"No," laughed Bernie, "he has his friend with him!"

"Good," replied the Farmer and then he turned to Joni-Pip. "Fancy a stroll up to Marley's Barn? Let's call your Dad, he's coming too!"

Father had driven Joni-Pip up to Finn's Farm but he had been lured away by the farmer's wife to enjoy a cup of freshly brewed tea and a slice of her Victoria sponge, filled with lashings of fresh cream and thickly spread, strawberry jam. Such were the advantages of living on a farm during the War: plenty of fruit to make jam and fresh cream from the cows!

Father reluctantly turned down Mrs. Finn's offer of a third cup of tea and soon the three of them were heading up the track, towards Marley's Barn.

The sun was shining and the hedgerows were full of pretty Spring flowers. The birds were singing and they all enjoyed a feeling of joy and freedom. Joni-Pip wondered if the soldiers in Europe were enjoying the

109

Spring, too. Farmer Finn and Father began to whistle a happy tune together. They had forged a great friendship since being Room Mates at Oxford years before. They were similar in personality and stature and they just seemed to get on well, in everything they did. Joni-Pip walked on slightly ahead of the two men; she so enjoyed hearing their whistling.

"In competition with the birds?" she laughed, looking back at them.

"Sure," said Father, "but I think we will win! Most definitely."

A few girls were working in the fields, either side of them. When they saw the Walkers, they turned and waved. So much of the farm work was done by women at this time as most of the men were away.

Walking on, Joni-Pip couldn't help but think what a fortunate girl she was, surrounded by so many very nice people. Just then, she was a little startled by the fluttering of feathers by her face.

"Jolly day for a flight!" came a familiar voice from within those flying feathers.

Joni-Pip turned and saw her pretty bird friend.

"Poppy!" she exclaimed. "How lovely to see you!"

The wood pigeon flew up and down the track beside her. Father and Farmer Finn were not aware of Joni-Pip's conversation with Poppy-Plump-Pij, they just continued enjoying their walk together, whistling and joking.

"Where are Ethelred-Ted and Hetty?" asked Poppy-Plump-Pij.

"I don't know where Het is but Ethelred-Ted is on the window sill, in the Schoolroom," said Joni-Pip. "He was feeling very tired today. He said that he had a lot to think about since I told him about Amelia Plate, yesterday."

"Yes," said Poppy-Plump-Pij, soaring past her friend, "that was a lot to take in, how sad....so sad....that poor little girl....those poor little children."

Poppy sounded very serious and very sensible; something that Joni-Pip was not familiar with. This was the very first time that she had spent time alone with her flying friend and how different she seemed! Joni-Pip couldn't help but be reminded of the serious and sad looks on the faces of her three special friends the day before. They had sat silently listening to her, surrounded by the crumbling bricks and walls of the Ruin, as she told them of the tragic events which had brought an end to the Workhouse.

"Archimedes Spindlethrop told us, Alex and me, how his little niece, Amelia Plate, had been sent to the Workhouse, after her father had disappeared at Sea and her Mother had become too ill to care for her."

For once Ethelred-Ted was quiet, as she told them this sombre story. Hetty the Wee and Poppy remained as still as statues. She continued relating the Tale.

"Archimedes felt so sad that he had been too young and too busy to take care of Amelia. The little Victorian girl had to live and work in the Workhouse, with no mother, father or uncle to look after her."

All of her three friends had sighed at the thought of that.

"After she had been in the Workhouse for one and a half years, Archimedes decided to make a place for her in his little house."

"How lovely, Hen!" Hetty the Wee had said enthusiastically but that enthusiasm was fleeting. Joni-Pip then started to speak slowly and very solemnly.

"He painted up a little room for her and decided to go and pick her up the following Monday."

"About time, too," declared Ethelred-Ted, "what was the Man thinking of, leaving her there so long?"

"This is the saddest part of all." Joni-Pip looked at each of her friends in turn. "On the Sunday, the day before he was to pick her up, something terrible happened. It was after he had finished painting her little room and hung pretty curtains up on the windows for Amelia and when he had bought her a brightly coloured patchwork quilt, to put on her little bed and he had filled the room with fresh flowers, yes on that Sunday...." she paused. Her friends all looked at her expectantly.

"On that Sunday....a fire broke out at the Workhouse!"

The Listeners all gasped.

"A fire?"

"It started in the cellar. Mr Paddy O'Hara was the name one of the men who ran the place; he kept a cellar full of bottles of wine and stuff and that night, he had too much of this drink and he fell over while he was smoking his pipe; a bottle smashed and the pipe lit the drink and whoosh, soon the fire spread to the rest of the house!"

"What happened to all the people who worked there?" asked Poppy.

"This is the sad part," said Joni-Pip seriously. "Although all of the Grown Ups escaped, none of the little children was saved, none of them got out of the fire alive!"

Her three listening friends all remained silent.

"Archimedes was so heartbroken, as you can well imagine, that from that day forth, he lived alone, never getting married, being sad all the time."

"I should think he was, what a terrible thing to have t' live wi'."

"Then, after the Great War, he read a book," said Joni-Pip.

"A book?" asked all of her three friends together.

"Yes, a book....called The Time Machine...." she started.

"By H. G. Wells," finished Ethelred-Ted.

"Yes, Eth, by H.G.Wells."

"It's all about Time Travel," continued Ethelred-Ted.

"Time Travel?" asked Hetty the Wee and Poppy-Plump-Pij together.

"Yes, H. G. Wells first called it that. It's about this man who invents a machine that takes him backwards and forwards in Time. It's a great book," answered Eth.

"What an amazing story," said Hetty. "How did he manage that?"

"I have no idea about all that," said Joni-Pip almost impatiently, "but what I do know, is that from the day Archimedes finished the book....he began his 'Quission'."

"Quission, eh? What's that then? It sounds exciting!" said Eth, grinning.

"Archimedes explained that was his special word....it means he began a Quest and he began his Mission...they are the two words mingled...."

"That makes it doubly important really, doesn't it?" Hetty interrupted.

"Rather!" came Ethelred-Ted's enthusiastic reply.

"So, from the day he began his Quission, he started work on making his very own Time Machine, only he called it his Time Tube," Joni-Pip went.

"So that's what it was, a Time Tube? It's jolly exciting!" declared Eth.

"It is so, Ma Pets!"

"I am not quite sure....what exactly you're all talking about," said a puzzled Poppy, "all this talk about Cushions and Tubes."

Her three friends chuckled.

"Do you remember, Pops? When we went round to Hideaway Cottage, what did we see?" asked Eth, trying to help; Poppy thought for a second.

"A cat?" she said sweetly.

"No, Poppy," said Hetty the Wee.

"But we did."

"We did, indeed," said Eth kindly. "Pops we did see a cat but can you think what else we saw, something that reminded you of a Vegetable?"

The pigeon thought for another second and then her little eyes lit up.

"I know, we saw the Silver Sausage!"

They all burst out laughing. This was just as well as the atmosphere had become terribly tense and sad about the Workhouse Fire.

Poppy looked a trifle hurt that they had laughed so heartily at her. Ethelred-Ted got up from sitting, leaning up against his favourite tree and walked over to her. He put one of his red arms around her and hugged her.

"Poppy, Dear Friend, how we love you so, don't ever change, please,?"

Joni-Pip smiled to herself as she remembered those words. How changed Poppy seemed to her, flying up and down, weaving her way in and out of the gaps in the hedge, which lined the track. She chatted to Joni-Pip in such an adult way. This was so different from the usually forgetful Poppy, whom Joni-Pip had come to love so dearly.

"How did you say Ethelred-Ted was today?" asked Poppy.

"Very thoughtful and very quiet."

"Same as usual then."

Joni-Pip said nothing. She put her hands on her hips, turned her head on one side and grinned at her pigeon friend.

The truth of the matter was that since hearing about Archimedes Spindlethrop's Quission to build a Time Tube, Ethelred-Ted had begun to think very carefully, very carefully indeed. In fact, he had so much to think about and he needed time to think everything through before he decided to tell his friends about his wonderful plan!

Before long, the two men, Joni-Pip and Poppy caught sight of Marley's Barn. In this new Orbit, the Barn was no longer boarded up, Farmer Finn had the windows and doors replaced, so that he could use it once more. As they approached Marley's Barn, they were amazed to be greeted by the sound of beautiful singing coming from within the hollow emptiness of the building. The good acoustics produced an enchanting echo, enhancing the wonderful performance of two magnificent male voices. Joni-Pip recognised the piece they were singing. It was the superb male duet from the Opera, The Pearl Fishers, by the French Composer, Bizet. Joni-Pip remembered it for two reasons. The first was that Father had a gramophone record of it, which he played frequently and the second reason was because she had heard a live performance of it at Alex's School, Prior Park, during one of the School's marvellous Concerts.

So incredible was the singing coming from Marley's Barn that all four of them stopped and just listened in awe. Poppy-Plump-Pij perched herself affectionately on Joni-Pip's shoulder. It was such an amazing experience for all of them. There they were, listening to splendid French Opera, while standing in the middle of beautiful English countryside. The sun was streaming on their smiling faces; the birds were singing their Spring Love Songs: everything seemed so peaceful and tranquil. Joni-Pip wondered if the fighting soldiers could still get to hear music. The War seemed so far away, as they drank in the sheer beauty and wonderment of the moment: one that they would constantly relate to their friends and family. It was a totally unique occasion, one that they would never, ever, forget.

((If that fabulous Duet doesn't move you, Dear Reader, then, I wonder if anything would!))

When the song was over, they all burst into appreciative applause and Farmer Finn grinned and beckoned to Father and Joni-Pip to follow him into the large old Barn. The heavy door was wide open and the sunshine cast deep beams of light into the darkness within. As they entered, Joni-Pip was rather startled to feel a strange, cold, feeling wash over her....

Straight in front of them, lit up by the shafts of sunlight, they saw the back of a man standing on a ladder, which leant up against one of the white walls of the barn.

"That was amazing, Franco!" exclaimed Farmer Finn. The singer turned round.

"Thanka you, Farma Finna," replied the man, smiling and from the top of his ladder he made a very small bow with his head.

"Come down and meet my friends, Franco."

The singer slowly and carefully started coming down the ladder. As he neared the bottom rung, a large, colourful, blue and gold mass, flew straight towards him, brushed past his face and then headed up into the darkness of the loft above. The ladder wobbled.

Joni-Pip ran towards the ladder to steady it and stop it from falling sideways. The man jumped off safely but Joni-Pip grabbed one side of the ladder with both hands. As she did, she felt a sharp burst of energy, running up through one of her arms, across her body and down the other arm. She quickly let out a scream and released her grip on the ladder. All three men ran to her.

"What ever is it, Honey?"

"Are you all right, Joni-Philipa?" asked a worried Farmer Finn.

"Whata 'appen?"

"I don't know....it just hurt me....like burning through me!" Joni-Pip looked round at each of the puzzled faces.

"Is it still hurting, Honey?" Father put his arm around his daughter and gently pulled her out of the shade and into the bright light of one of the sunbeams, streaming in through a broken window. He examined her closely. "No sign of damage, anyway!"

"What on earth must it have been?" Farmer Finn shook his head.

"Eeta is a stranga thinga."

"I'm all right now," she forced a smile.

The three men still stood around her, like sentries on guard.

"Honestly!" she laughed.

"It makes no sense to me," said Farmer Finn. "P'raps you've torn a muscle?"

"That's it," exclaimed Father somewhat relieved. "I've done that a few times playing golf. It really hurt!"

"Me too," added Farmer Finn. "The pain kept me awake for nights!"

"Well, whatever it is or was, it has gone now!"

The two tall men looked at each other, realising that she couldn't have pulled a muscle then, as pulled muscles hurt for days.

They both decided not to pursue that thought and started to talk to Franco.

"The singing was amazing, as usual, Franco," said Farmer Finn. "Please let me introduce you to Philip Garador, an American friend of mine, who has decided to make England his home....and his lovely young daughter, Joni-Philipa."

Franco extended his hand towards Father and the two men shook hands. The Italian was quite small compared to the tall American, so Father leaned forward slightly and Franco bowed his head respectfully.

"Pleased to meet you, Franco, I sure enjoyed your song."

"I am charmeda to meeta a frienda of Farma Finn's and I ama glad you likeda our singing," beamed the Singer.

It suddenly occurred to Joni-Pip that Franco had said 'our' singing and she distinctly remembered hearing the sound of a duet...two male voices. She looked around the barn to see where the other singer was.

Still searching for the missing singer, Joni-Pip appeared to rudely ignore him.

Father noticed.

"Joni-Philipa, this is Franco from Italy, he would like to shake hands with you."

The Italian brushed his right hand on his dungarees to clean it, wondering if that was why she had refused to shake his hand.

"Oh, sorry!" said the twelve-year-old, holding out her hand towards him. They shook hands. "I was just looking for the other man who sang with you."

"Man?" the Italian looked puzzled, thought for a minute and then he laughed. Farmer Finn started to laugh, too.

"That's why I brought you here, that's who, I wanted you to see, Joni-Philipa!"

"I am not quite sure I understand."

"I will showa you the 'mana' I singa with," laughed Franco. The Italian then turned away from her, looked up towards the loft and called out.

"Coma ona downa!" he shouted. "Coma an' meeta the friendsa ofa Farmer Finna, Macca. Coma Nowa!"

There was a rustling coming from the loft, which really interested Poppy. She took off from the bale of hay and flew up to investigate. In doing so, she nearly collided with a blue and gold mass of feathers that flew down and landed on Franco's shoulder. Very slightly ruffled, Poppy continued her flight and landed up in the loft, silently watching the proceedings below her with great interest.

The proud Italian smiled at the big, bright bird on his shoulder. He stroked him and then turned to Joni-Pip.

"Joni-Philipa, thisa isa my singinga partner, mya Macaw, Macca."

"That's incredible! A singing Macaw! How spiffing!" said Joni-Pip extending her hand to shake his wing and then she stroked the Macaw's lovely back.

Another very strange feeling, came over her.

"Haven't we met before?" she asked straining her brain wondering where.

"Hmmmm, I don'ta thinka so! I woulda remema such a beautifula younga lady, lika yoowa!" laughed Franco. Joni-Pip, of course, was speaking to Macca but she let Franco's reply stand. It would be just too complicated and sound rather strange to start explaining that she meant that his pet macaw, was the one that seemed familiar to her.

"It's sort of unbelievable, isn't it? An Opera-singing Macaw!" exclaimed Farmer Finn. "Franco was an opera singer in his home town of Pisa, before the War. Then he was shot down over England, somewhere and he became a Prisoner of War. He's staying at the Camp in Norton Cuckney and he has been sent to work on the Farm with me. I had no idea we had such a Celebrity among us, until he was first heard singing in the Barn. After lots of questions, we discovered that he had sung in all of the famous Opera Houses in Europe."

"Including Coventa Gardena!" added Franco, slightly bowing respectfully.

"So," asked Father, "how come he sings with his parrot?"

"So simpla!" replied Franco. "Macca, 'ee nota ha parrot, 'ee a macawa, 'ee was givena meyah when 'ee wasa just a littla mora thana a few feathersa, nota mucha mora than a hegg! Always 'ee heara me practicesa ma scalesa and singa ma songsa and 'ee ees a little one....so 'ee learna so quicka to singa ma songs and ma scalesa....showa them, Macca....singa

116

the scala ofa Gee...."

Macca was not too keen to obey, he was far more interested in the beautiful creature that had flown past him and up into the confines of the loft. He remained silent and kept peering up into the darkness above him.

"Macca, singa youra scalesa. Hara youa too shya for a my newa friendsa?"

Macca's curiosity finally got the better of him and with a loud fluttering of his wings, he took off and disappeared from their view.

Once away from the humans below, Macca soon located Poppy. She, too, had been very fascinated by this extremely talented Macaw and was so pleased that he had sought her out. How cosy it seemed to her, up in the semi-darkness of the loft. She was pleased they weren't in brilliant sunshine, as they had been outside, it afforded her the opportunity of blushing, without Macca noticing.

"You ara so Baby!" said the Macaw softly.

A pretty pigeon blushed once more.

Chapter 14

The Plan ?

The sun streamed in through the School Room window from outside, beckoning a thoughtful twelve-year-old. She so wanted to take a walk with her friends up to Marley's Barn. Joni-Pip didn't want to be sitting listening to Mother's voice right then; even though it was a beautiful voice. She was sure that it was very important to know it was in 1768 that Captain James Cook set sail from Whitby Harbour, England and travelled with his crew in his ship The Endeavour and discovered Australia. She knew it must be even more important to her, as her Grandmother, six times back, or was it five times back, she couldn't quite remember; well, anyway, her Grandmother was Captain Cook's sister, Margaret. This history was all very well but not today, she was not in the mood for lessons at all.

Mother sensed her distraction.

"Darling, are you all right? Is anything the matter?"

"I'm just not in the mood for History, at present, Mother. Sorry!"

Of all of Joni-Pip's friends and relations, Mother was affected most by Déjà Vu. She was not aware that because of the loss of her daughter, her heart had ached so in the Past; so much so that it had completely broken. Now, however, it had mended and how amazingly glad she felt to be with Joni-Pip. Since the Turning of the KOL, she was re-living her life: only this time without the pain. Mother was always gentle, caring and cuddling Joni-Pip and all she wanted to do, was to make her daughter happy.

Joni-Pip would never want to hurt Mother, so she reassured her that everything was all right. Which of course it wasn't.

Mother suggested that Joni-Pip might like sit and read silently, while she tried to teach Becky-Paige how to do long division.

Happy at this idea ((wouldn't you be?)), Joni-Pip got up and searched through the shelves of books. She searched and searched....so thorough was her search that she ended up getting the step ladder to read the titles of the books, high up, on the top shelf.

"What are you looking for, Darling?" asked Mother, who by this time was quite distracted herself by her daughter's fervent search.

"Oh, just a book, Ethelred-Ted was looking for...." she started, then realised that would sound quite ridiculous to Mother and Becky-Paige.

"Don't be so silly Sissa, he can't read!" laughed Becky-Paige. "He's like Puppalove!"

She was referring to her favourite toy: a soft, squashy, cream puppy, who constantly enjoyed, or endured, wearing bonnets and being pushed around in a doll's pram with squeaky wheels and lacy covers.

"No, I meant, I would like to read it with Ethelred-Ted....outside....if that's all right," she quickly covered herself, stumbling as she did.

"Hmmmmm. Joni-Philipa, I do not want you wandering off when you should be at your lessons, so I think it best you just sit and read, in here, for a while," replied Mother. "Which book did you say you were after?"

Joni-Pip didn't answer that question, she just continued to look through volume after volume, until, at last, she was rewarded for her persistence. Her eyes suddenly fell upon a particular book. She pulled the volume out carefully but there was a large tome next to it, which fell forward. To stop it from crashing to the ground, she grabbed at it but its sheer weight caused her to lose her balance, slightly. She swayed. Mother glanced up and saw her, she slid her chair away from herself quickly, stood up and ran to the step ladder, climbing a few steps, so that she could help her daughter down.

"Steady, Darling, please be careful. You gave me such a fright. I thought you were going to fall!" Mother exclaimed, having a slight reminder of the pain she had felt in Joni-Pip's First Circle, when her daughter had fallen from the ladder in Marley's Barn. Joni-Pip, too, had a strange feeling and when both of them stepped off the step ladder safely, Mother took the book from her and held her so tightly and spontaneously that both of them didn't know why but tears began to well up in their eyes.

"Please be careful, Joni-Philipa, I couldn't bear anything to happen to you again!" Mother said, to her surprise.

Joni-Pip just held her mother tightly for a while.

"Don't be silly Mother, I'm fine," but she puzzled over the word 'again' and then said, "Nothing is going to happen to me!"

Soon Joni-Pip was settled down in the window seat. Mother hadn't allowed her to bring Ethelred-Ted to lessons that morning, which caused him some dismay as his favourite lesson was History. However, he had asked Joni-Pip to get out this most interesting book for him, as some form of consolation.

She opened the book but her eyes were not running over the pages, her mind was far too distracted to take anything in. She just couldn't stop thinking about the things she had heard and learnt about, the day before.

It was the day after meeting Franco and Macca, his talking, opera-singing Macaw, up at Marley's Barn with Father and Farmer Finn. Ethelred-Ted had called a Meeting of the four friends, to be held by the Ruin. A special meeting he had said, a very special one indeed.

Joni-Pip just stared hazily at the book in front of her and recalled the events of the day before. This is how they went:-

"It's like this," Ethelred-Ted said authoritatively, "I think we could do it....well, we could have a jolly good go at it, anyway."

"A jolly good go at what, Eth?" asked Joni-Pip.

"Yes, Ma Pet, what are y' talkin' of?"

"I'm feeling very lifeful today," said Poppy, totally unaware of what the others were talking about. Her mind was still on the wonderful day before, the day she had met Macca in the loft of Marley's Barn. Her tiny heart skipped a little beat at the thought of the amazing Macaw. Not only was Macca a beautiful bird but he was a beautiful singer, too and Italian!

'What more could a girl ask for?' she mused to herself.

"Yes, I think we should have a really good crack at it," continued Ethelred-Ted, then he looked at Poppy. "Lifeful?"

"Yes," replied Poppy, not in the least bit embarrassed at her misuse of the English language. "I am indeed feeling very lifeful, everything is so wonderful, so perfect. Everything should be 'full', always and it will be so, from now on."

Her three friends looked at her and decided to ignore her.

The wood pigeon started to hum happily to herself.

That definitely changed things.

"Are you feeling all right Pops?" asked Joni-Pip, not really understanding why a happy, humming pigeon should warrant such an inquiry.

"I am feeling wonderful! Lifeful to the full!"

Joni-Pip looked puzzled and then turned her attention to the matters in hand....Ethelred-Ted's new business but as she did so, she was sure she saw something glittery rising above the Crooked Cottage.

"As I was saying," continued the red and yellow Teddy Bear, trying to establish some kind of order to this gathering.

"There they are again! The stars!" Joni-Pip pointed. The others looked and they all saw them and agreed they were peculiar and couldn't fathom them out. "It's odd, I keep thinking about stars! Why? What's going on?"

Joni-Pip sat perched on one of the walls of the Ruin. Hetty the Wee had found a convenient smooth rock on which to settle herself down and Ethelred-Ted stood in front of one of the remaining fire places of the Workhouse, the one that was propped up with two large planks.

As for Poppy-Plump-Pij?

Well, she wasn't settled down at all. She just kept wandering around sniffing the wild flowers and humming to herself.

120

"What are ye trying to say, Hen?"

"I want to tell you about my Plan, my Top Secret Plan!"

"Top Secret?" Joni-Pip and Hetty the Wee chorused together.

Ethelred-Ted smiled. At last he felt he had their attention.

"Top Secret indeed!" he replied enthusiastically.

"Tell us then, Ethelred-Ted?" encouraged Joni-Pip loudly.

"Yes, Ma Pet, tell us. I am all agog with anticipation!"

"Before I begin," Ethelred-Ted said, lowering his voice to almost a whisper, "I must have your absolute, total word that you will tell this to no-one, you will breathe this to no-one and you will speak of it only when we are together, all four of us?"

"Of course!" said Joni-Pip. "You have my word on it!"

"And, mine too, Ma Lamb, I promise!"

Ethelred-Ted turned to Poppy to receive her sworn oath on it as well, only to find her gazing up into the sky, singing a little song to herself. Usually he had all the time in the world for his little friend but the weight of his Daring Plan lay heavily on his heart right now, which unbalanced his true feelings for the wood pigeon.

"Poppy, whatever is the matter?" he growled. "You haven't listened to a word I've been saying, have you? Do you actually want to be here? Do you want to be a part of our Daring Plan? Are you ill or something?"

Hetty and Joni-Pip were quite taken aback. They had never ever heard him get even slightly cross with Poppy before. They looked at the little plump wood pigeon, expecting her to burst into tears but she didn't, she just carried on in her own little world, singing and smelling the flowers.

"Are ye keeping quite well, Lassie?"

Poppy-Plump-Pij just ignored her and continued singing a few bars of Green Sleeves: her very favourite song.

Her three friends just watched her for a moment, then Joni-Pip jumped off the wall and walked over to her. She put her arm around Poppy's small body and turned the little pigeon's head towards her, looking straight at her.

"Poppy, my Lovely Friend, are you in there?"

"Mmmmmm!" came the little bird's reply.

"Well, how are you feeling? Swell?"

"Swell?" questioned Ethelred-Ted.

"Yes, swell," she said firmly. It wasn't often she used such a term, Alex did it all the time, so why shouldn't she? She was half-American, after all.

"Swell?" questioned Poppy-Plump-Pij. "No, I don't swell. Well, I suppose I do, when I get too hot but not enough that you would notice."

Everybody laughed, even Ethelred-Ted, who wasn't usually a lover of the Americanisation of the beautiful English Language. However, in this instance it was a very good thing because firstly, it brought Poppy-Plump-Pij out of her mesmeric mood and back to her friends and secondly, it broke the rather tense mood Ethelred-Ted was in.

"Poppy, you're priceless!" Eth laughed. "No wonder we love you so!"

Poppy-Plump-Pij looked puzzled.

"What?"

"Nothing Poppy, you have just made us laugh," said Hetty the Wee. She knew that to try and explain to the wood pigeon that the word 'swell' in this American term meant 'good' or 'fine' and not a 'bloating of something', would have just confused her even more.

"Are you feeling all right, though, Poppy?" asked Joni-Pip. "You seem a little sidetracked today. It's important that you are not distracted right now, as Eth has something very important, something very secretive to tell us."

"Then why didn't he say so before?"

Her three friends all decided silently to let that explosive statement go. Joni-Pip got back up on the wall, Hetty settled herself back on the rock, Poppy-Plump-Pij flew up on to a branch of The Major Oak and Ethelred-Ted, himself, resumed his upright standing in front of the fireplace.

"It's like this, my Dear Friends, I don't know whether or not you have noticed but something has happened to us recently, something extraordinary. I am not entirely sure what it is but it is very exciting. Haven't you noticed?"

The three others thought to themselves, then they all shook their heads.

"No, I canna say that I've noticed anything, Ma Pet."

"Nor me!" said Joni-Pip.

"What exactly are you talking about?" asked Poppy-Plump-Pij, not daring to mention her feelings for her new feathered friend, Macca.

Ethelred-Ted shrugged his shoulders.

"All right then, perhaps it's just me but I know, just absolutely know that something truly outstanding, something truly spectacular, even, has happened to all of us and it's all connected with Marley's Barn."

Poppy-Plump-Pij blushed a little, hoping the others wouldn't notice.

'Do they realise what happened to my heart, in Marley's Barn the day before?' she thought to herself.

"What d' y' mean, Hen?"

"When are we talking about?" asked Joni-Pip. "When did this amazing thing happen to us then?"

"It was the day of the storm, remember, when we were up at Marley's Barn?" replied Ethelred-Ted.

Poppy-Plump-Pij sighed with relief, realising that it was only yesterday that she had met Macca. Yesterday, was most definitely not the day of the storm. Yesterday had been bright, sunny and very warm. The day of the storm, however, had been rainy, windy, very black and very cold. Very black and very cold indeed!

"Haven't you noticed anything, anything different about us at all?" Ethelred-Ted asked his friends, almost pleading with them to recall some tiny detail, which would make them realise that changes had occurred in their lives. He knew things had changed, he didn't know what exactly but they had; oh yes, indeed they had: his deep stuffing feeling told him they had!

"Joni-Pip, hasn't anything seemed at all different these last few days? Anything?" he asked in earnest.

Joni-Pip thought and thought.

"Yes, something is different. You're right, Eth, thinking about it, you're right; well, I think you are. I don't know quite when it all changed. I only know that recently everybody seems to have acted very strangely towards me."

"Strangely Ma Pet?"

"Yes, I suppose that's not such a good word really. It's just....well...."

"Yes?" asked Ethelred-Ted excitedly.

"You'll all think I'm being silly. It's nothing," she shrugged her shoulders.

"No, it's not 'nothing'," the Teddy Bear said comfortingly. "Tell us more!"

"It's....well....I don't know quite how to explain it," she hesitated.

"Please try? Take your time and tell us all how you think people have been 'strange' towards you recently," encouraged the earnest Ted.

"All right, I'll have a go, as long as you don't think I'm being stupid or thinking of myself as overly important." Joni-Pip kind of laughed.

"Of course we won't, Lovey. All we want t' hear, is what ye have t' say."

"Here goes then but don't forget I'm not trying to make myself out as something special or anything...."

She jumped off the wall and walked over to where Ethelred-Ted stood.

Respectfully, the Teddy Bear left his position by the fireplace and went and sat down on the ground, leaning up against The Major Oak.

Joni-Pip cleared her throat and started,

"I don't actually know when it began....or how it began, even."

"You must," said Ethelred-Ted most urgently.

Hetty the Wee cast him a look and he stopped talking.

"....All I know is that over the last few days, everybody and I mean

123

everybody, even Nuttingham Squirrel, would you believe....yes, everybody has treated me in a....a....surprising way," said Joni-Pip, still worrying that her friends might think that she was thinking too much of herself. How Cook used to scold Mary the Maid, back in Bath for doing such a thing....

"You think too much of yourself, young girl, by Scarry Crow you do!" Joni-Pip remembered hearing Cook say those words to Mary many times. "Nothing good isn't goin' to come from it, look you. Mark my words, young Mary, just you wait 'n see!" she always added, in her beautiful Welsh accent.

Joni-Pip had changed so much since her new Life in the Wood and she didn't want her friends to think badly of her, so she was very cautious.

"Surprising? How d'you mean?" asked Ethelred-Ted.

Once more Hetty the Wee shot him a look.

"I told you that I didn't want to sound as if I think that I'm important."

"No, we don't think that, at all," reassured Ethelred-Ted.

"Let her speak without being interrupted!" said Hetty very firmly.

Ethelred-Ted then tried really hard to keep quiet, despite his total absorption in this exciting affair. He was desperate to understand and make some sense of all that was going on and all that was going through his mind.

"Well, everybody I meet recently, hugs me....hugs me as if....I don't know....as if....I can't explain it....they seem....all of them....they seem so pleased to see me...." said Joni-Pip slowly and carefully.

"What d'you mean? Is it different from how they usually are with you, Joni-Pip?" asked Ethelred-Ted softly. This time, Hetty the Wee shot him no disapproving glance.

Joni-Pip thought for a minute, walked slowly away from her friends and then turned round.

"It's most definitely different but I can't really explain how it's different."

"Are ye sure, Lassie? I dinna want him t' put strange ideas inter yer pretty wee head."

"No....Het....absolutely not!" Joni-Pip, shook her head. "There has been a difference....a strange difference....why, as I said before, even Nuttingham Squirrel seemed genuinely pleased to see me the other day!"

"Nuttingham Squirrel?" laughed her three friends.

"So that pretty well proves something strange is going on," laughed Joni-Pip, "doesn't it?"

More laughter.

"This strange way they....everybody....greets you," Ethelred-Ted asked, "can you explain the feeling it gives you....what is it like exactly?"

"I have thought about this a lot over the last few days….it's not as if only a few people treat me strangely….no, not a few….it's everybody….and that started me thinking. "

"Thinking? Thinking about what?" asked Poppy, who, by this time, had completely put out of her head, all thoughts of the magnificent Macca.

"I knew I had almost had the feeling it gave me, before….almost but not quite…." she replied.

"What feeling? What's it like?" asked Ethelred-Ted excitedly.

"Give her time, give her time," Hetty the Wee said to him kindly.

"Well, the only other time I have had this feeling, is when I have been away for a long time and then I come back....yes that's it….everybody, yes everybody without exception….when they first meet me recently, has treated me as if they haven't seen me for ages….almost as if I have been away somewhere….oh, it's so silly….I have been nowhere….but they give me the feeling I get when I go back to School….the feeling I get when Mona Royal hugs me; when Angela Stebbin hugs me. It's after I have been away on my Summer Hols….up here for six weeks….oh, I don't know….am I just being silly?" she sighed.

"You most definitely are not!" exclaimed Ethelred-Ted. "Can you tell us, Joni-Pip, think carefully, can you tell us when it was that things began to change?"

Joni-Pip thought for a moment then she said quite definitely,

"That's the thing….the strangest thing….things didn't **begin** to change."

"What do you mean?" asked Poppy-Plump-Pij seriously.

"It wasn't a gradual thing….no not gradual….it suddenly happened ….suddenly everybody treated me in this way, always so terribly happy to see me. Mrs Broft surprised me, she always pretends that I am this naughty girl and treats me in a kind of joking way, as if she is telling me off but when I got back from Marley's Barn after the storm, she hugged me so tightly I thought I would stop breathing…." Joni-Pip chuckled.

"A true 'sufferly' then!" laughed Ethelred-Ted. "Now you know how I used to feel!"

"So, this suddenly began when, then?" asked an intrigued Hetty the Wee.

"Since it stopped raining….no before that….it was before then….it was….it was….when I got back home….yes it was just after that terrible thunder storm up at Marley's Barn....just as I said!"

"Munchy Mash and Mustard, I knew it! I knew it!" Ethelred-Ted jumped up and resumed his position by the fireplace. Joni-Pip remained standing beside him. "But you are wrong, Joni-Pip, it didn't start when you got back home."

Joni-Pip thought for a second and then said rather puzzled,

125

"Hmmmm, I was pretty sure it was!"

"No, it definitely started before then….it started right in the Barn….and I know it did!" the Teddy Bear said excitedly.

"How do you know that, Eth?" asked Poppy, totally absorbed in it all.

"Because I remember when we were going into the Barn….do you remember what you said, Joni-Pip?"

"Not really," she replied, then she thought a little. "Oh, yes, I do, I remember quite clearly….in fact, I said it to you all, didn't I?"

"I remember….yes you did!" Hetty jumped off the rock she was sitting on and scrambled over to be at Joni-Pip's side.

"Well, I can't remember," said Poppy-Plump-Pij, "or can I? Was it something to do with some sugar stew?"

They all laughed….including Poppy because the thought of sugar stew sounded so preposterous and unappetising, even to her.

"Almost," laughed Ethelred-Ted. "Actually, I remember the exact words ….and something else! Joni-Pip you said,

'I have been here before, this is all so familiar. I know exactly what you are all going to say. I am going to start to climb a ladder. Most peculiar! Talk about Déjà Vu!' "

Joni-Pip was slightly distracted at this point, as the face of a Fighter Pilot came into her head and then it disappeared, as quickly as it came.

"As you said it, I had this feeling for you, Joni-Pip, I was so pleased, no, that's not enough, I was very, very pleased to see you!" said Eth, excitedly.

With those words bringing back memories to her little heart, Poppy flew down and landed on Joni-Pip's shoulder so she was close to her.

"That's right….I remember you saying that and I felt this feeling….yes I felt it….it was this amazing relief as well….I couldn't understand it. I just knew how much you meant to me, my friend….my good friend, Joni-Pip!" Poppy-Plump-Pij then nuzzled her little head into her.

"Why y're all correct. Thinking about it now, I was so very happy to see yer Joni-Pip….even though we had all just scurried to the barn together ….most strange! I had this bonny feeling for y', Ma Pet!" Hetty smiled.

They all surrounded her in a little circle and made her feel very secure.

It didn't occur to the four of them that, although they now all realised that something had happened to them up at Marley's Barn, which made them all very happy….they still had no idea what it was exactly; what it was that they were so happy about!

Ethelred-Ted still wanted, however, to discuss a matter with them….a matter of such serious concern….and it was all connected with Déjà Vu. Consequently, after a short break from his serious talking, he began to hustle them once more into 'Meeting Mode'.

126

"Right," he said with great authority, "now we have established that something has happened, I want to tell you what I think it is connected with ....and it concerns all of us....and I want to tell you of my Plan."

"Yes! Your Plan!" said Hetty, Joni-Pip and Poppy together.

"Yes, my Plan....it's not my Quission, like Archimedes' but it is similar.... the difference being that through some amazing way....a way of which I have absolutely no knowledge....I have access to something that Our Old Inventor has sought, so sorely, for many years...." continued the Bear, suddenly sounding terribly intense.

"Something? What exactly is that 'something' that Archimedes Spindlethrop seeks, Laddie?"

Just then Flip, Steve and Craig appeared.

"Hello Folks!" said Flip happily.

"Hi Flip!" said Ethelred-Ted.

Joni-Pip looked at him, then looked at Flip.

"Do you know her then? How? Who is she?" she asked stone-faced.

"....Er....we've met a couple of times....when I was in the Bentley, I told her you hadn't had your Awakening....then we met here, at the Ruin, just moments before your Awakening."

"Oh!" said Joni-Pip, noticing they all had glittery bits in their hair.

"Er....what is exactly going on?" asked Ethelred-Ted. "I think you might have some people following you. We had Two, German-speaking, Men in Long, Black Coats, asking if we had seen a girl and two boys, recently."

"Huh, I wonder why?" asked Steve shrugging. "We just must find the whereabouts of the Old Mine, that's all....nothing more and nothing less!"

"Two Men in Long, Black Coats? I wonder who they are?" interrupted Craig. "They sound pretty interesting."

"Hmmm....are you sure they are after **us**?" asked Steve.

"Anyway, do you yet know where the Old Mine is located?" asked Flip.

They all shook their heads.

"We must be off then....I wonder who those men are who are looking for us? Did you tell them that you had seen us?" asked Flip.

"Absolutely not!" said Ethelred-Ted.

"We didn't think we should," said Joni-Pip.

"Right," replied Flip, "I don't see that it would matter though...."

"Anyway, we're going and we hope in a few minutes, when we catch up with you, it will be at the right time, if my cousin can finally get it right!"

As he said this, the silver in Steve's hair glinted in the bright sunlight.

"I think you mean **in** the right Time!" laughed Craig.

They disappeared into the wood and stars billowed above the trees.

"Vee haff verry important matterrz to discuss!" a voice boomed behind.

127

They all spun round and there were the Two Men in Long, Black Coats.

"Vee zink zatt you haff seen ze peoples vee haff to talk to!" said the other man abruptly.

"Who are you? Where do you come from?" asked Joni-Pip boldly.

"Warum suchen Sie nach diesen Leuten? Vom welchen Interesse sind sie zu Ihnen?" [7] asked Ethelred-Ted.

"Sie haben etwas von Uns, das wir sofort brauchen! " [8] one of them replied.

"Was? Sagen Sie, dass sie es stahlen? " [9] asked Ethelred-Ted.

"Wir sagen nichts. Es ist von der am meisten äußersten Dringlichkeit, dass wir wiedererlangen, was uns gehört!"[10] snapped the other man.

"Was ist es? Was haben sie, der gehört Ihnen? " [11] asked Ethelred-Ted.

"Es ist keines Ihres Geschäfts. Sie wissen nicht, worin Sie sich einmischen. Das ist von am meisten äußerster Wichtigkeit zur Staatssicherheit! " [12] snarled the first man.

"Hey, you guys," Steve appeared from the woods, "I forgot to ask you to actually **ask** the next grown up, you see about the......whoooooops!"

When he saw the Two Men in Long, Black Coats, he about-turned, very quickly and headed off, very swiftly, back into Windy Woods.

The two men turned and saw him and ran speedily after him.

"Oh no! Do you think they will catch him up?" asked a worried Joni-Pip.

"Dort ist er! Das muss einer von ihnen sein! "[13]One of the men said, pointing at Steve, as he continued to run towards him.

"Fangen Sie ihn! Lassen Sie ihn nicht loskommen! " [14] yelled the other man.

Very quickly, both of the men disappeared into the woods.

"What on earth was that all about? Do you think Steve should have stayed and talked to them?" asked Joni-Pip, as they all stood and watched two batches of stars twinkle up into the blue sky above the trees.

As if none of this had happened, Ethelred-Ted reached for his bag, which was on the ground in front of him and took out a small piece of folded

---

[7] Why are you looking for these people? Of what interest are they to you?
[8] They have something of ours that we need immediately!
[9] What? Are you saying they stole it?
[10] We are saying nothing. It is of the utmost urgency that we recover what   belongs to us!
[11] What is it? What do they have that belongs to you?
[12] It is none of your business. You do not know what you are meddling with. This is of utmost importance to National Security
[13] There he is! That must be one of them!
[14] Catch him! Don't let him get away!

cloth. He unwrapped it....it was not 'normal' material. It was a kind of shiny green cloth. It almost looked as if it was lit up....like a green traffic light on 'GO'. The others crowded round to get a good look and were amazed to see that as he unfolded it, all the creases left and it took on the form of a large, hard board. It was covered in figures and letters....it didn't seem to make any sense.

"That's amazing! What is it, Eth?" Joni-Pip gasped.

"Where did you get it from?" asked Hetty the Wee, still not quite believing what she had seen. "What does it all mean?"

"Is it a trickful or something?" asked Poppy-Plump-Pij.

"No, Pops, not a trick....not a trick at all....it is quite splendiferous, isn't it? It folds up into such a tiny piece of cloth and then, when I unfold it, it becomes this big, rigid board....and as to where I got it from? Well, I have no idea....I just know I came back from Marley's Barn with it, after the storm."

"This gets more and more intriguing as we go on, Laddie!"

"It's all such a puzzle," said Joni-Pip. "I really want to hear all about your Plan and what it has to do with Archimedes Spindlethrop."

"Me too!" said Poppy-Plump-Pij.

"I would like t' know what all those letters and figures mean....they have t' mean somethin', somethin' so special!"

"I suggest you all go back to where you are comfortable and I will begin to explain, as best I can," said Ethelred-Ted kindly: so they did.

"I know that you might have questions during my explanation....many of them I am sure....but I wondered if I might ask you to refrain from asking them until I have finished?" Eth requested, looking at them all in turn.

"That's rich," Hetty laughed, "coming from you!" The others sniggered.

"All right, all right, I know that's quite a tall order and I am, well, at least I try to be, aware of how good I am at interrupting!" said the bear sheepishly.

"Or how 'bad' ye are at interrupting!" said Hetty, still laughing.

"All right I take your point but please try and bear with me because what I have to say is going to sound so preposterous, so impossible that you'll think I'm talking about some Fairy Tale, some work of Fiction," said Eth seriously.

His three friends stopped laughing and listened attentively.

"What is it that Archimedes has sought after for so long?"

Everybody remained silent.

"Well?"

"I thought you didn't want us to speak!" ventured Poppy, bravely.

"I didn't mean you not to answer any questions I might ask," he said irritated.

Hetty smothered a smirk and said, as if she was reading the words,

"He has sought t' find the secret of Time Trekking.....or somethin'."

"Exactly! Exactly!" exclaimed the Bear, then he held up the large, solid, fluorescent, green board. "And this, my Dear Friends, this is, I think, the secret, the very Formula that Man, including Archimedes....that Men have sought....the secret.....the way we can....Jump in Time!"

His three companions were stunned and silent.

"Us? Jump in Time?" Joni-Pip shouted after a considerable pause. "Don't be so ridiculous, Ethelred-Ted, that's impossible!"

"Hey, there, Laddie, aren't y' gettin' a bit carried away....a bit far fetched with yer ideas?"

"D'you really think we could jump in Time, do you, Eth?" asked Poppy.

Of the three of his friends, she was the most convinced about Jumping in Time or as in Poppy's case, Flying in Time but then, although she had no clear recollection of it now, it had only been Poppy who had flown over the Wall of Time and seen Joni-Pip as an older lady in her seventies. As well as that, when she met Macca in the loft of Marley's Barn with Franco, she felt very definitely that it wasn't the first time that they had met.

Ethelred-Ted walked over to The Major Oak and looked up at Poppy-Plump-Pij, perched perfectly on the branch above him.

"Yes, Pops I surely do, in fact I shouldn't be surprised if some of us already have!" He looked straight into her eyes almost as if he knew, then he added, "All right then, Hetty....as you are so unbelieving....how do you explain this astounding board? It is a tiny piece of flimsy cloth that when unfolded, becomes this huge firm board? Not only that, it has its own built in light from nowhere....and....it contains strange letters and figures that obviously mean something!"

"I don't quite understand why you think this has any connection with Jumping in Time, though," stated Joni-Pip, very reasonably.

"That's a valid point, Joni-Pip," said Eth, "one I have had to think about a great deal. I knew what I had was incredible....you have seen it....I also knew that I was so glad to see you when you opened the Barn door with me....I, too, had this intense feeling for you, it was so strong....and then I remembered you saying....'talk about Déjà Vu'....I merely guessed.... that's all it is....sheer guess work....and a strong sense that I have been given something for a reason....after all, where on earth did this Formula come from....it just appeared suddenly in my hand? It had to come from somewhere, didn't it? I knew I would have to use it. Don't ask me how I knew....I just did. Added to all these feelings, was the fact that I felt that you had gone away somehow and now I was so glad, so very glad to see you again. As a consequence, I thought what must have happened is that you did go away....for a long time....only you were trekking about in Time, as Hetty said. You said, 'I know that I am going to climb a ladder'....which you did. I think you came back from your Jumping in Time, only you arrived slightly sooner than you left!"

"I don't remember any of that!" said Joni-Pip, screwing up her face.

Hetty, who had been thinking and listening very seriously, suddenly said,"All right, I'm not saying that I believe all this that y' are talkin' about but I have seen the remarkable Formula Board so I do accept something is extraordinary right now. I also remember feeling this relief, this joy when Joni-Pip said, 'talk about Déjà Vu': what exactly is that? I don't mean what is Déjà Vu, I know it's when we think, or know even, that we are doing something that we have already done before, exactly the same as before and that we are re-living it; we know what is going to happen next; I know all that but why does it happen? What makes it happen? What's exactly going on at those times?"

"This is all so confusingful," said Poppy-Plump-Pij.

"I think Déjà Vu has to do with Jumping in Time," said Eth decidedly, "and the only way we can find out, is to take the F.B., the Formula Board to an Expert; one who can be trusted, of course. To me, I don't know what you all think; to me the only person I know who fits that bill is...."

"Archimedes Spindlethrop!" his three friends exclaimed together.

"Exactly! How about we go to see him right now?"

Everybody agreed and so they set off on the walk to Edwinstowe. They couldn't stop talking. They were so excited. It was yet another beautiful, sunny, cloudless day. The English countryside smelt fresh and new as Spring was indeed, 'springing up'. All this new life that was emerging, made it so difficult to believe that almost the whole of the European countryside was, at that time, filled with the terrifying sound of marching boots, exploding gunfire, battering and bombs.

"So, say y' have the secret of Jumping in Time....the secret Archimedes has so dearly sought....what exactly do y' intend to do with it?" asked Hetty, as she trotted alongside Ethelred-Ted. "Not that I am totally sure of all this yet, I still keep thinking this has to be impossible, Ma Lambie."

"Even though you don't believe me, quite; I'll tell you what I would like to do with it....no, on second thoughts, you all tell me what you would do, if you could jump, either back or forward in Time."

All his friends thought for a moment.

"That's a bit of a difficult question to spring on us....we need time to think, I think," said Joni-Pip smiling.

"Take yer time," he quoted in a Scottish accent. "Take yer time!"

"Are y' being cheeky, Young Bear?"

The mood was one of joy and enthusiasm. Poppy-Plump-Pij had managed to put all thoughts of Macca out of her head. Her little heart still had a glimmer of 'almost recollection' that she had, at one time, experienced something amazing and yet something very, very frightening.

"If we could fly back in Time, I would want to change a few sad things in the Past....to make a better Future!" said the little pigeon.

"That's such a jolly good idea!" said Joni-Pip. "Much better than mine. I was thinking how much I would have liked to meet some of the people I have learned about in History lessons: like Good Queen Bess, Sir Frances Drake, Sir Walter Raleigh....even my Great, Great, Great, Great, Great, Great Grandmother's brother, Captain Cook....or a Fighter Pilot."

Her three friends just stared at her.

"What did I just say?" She shook her head.

All of her three friends just looked at her.

"I have thought of both of those," said Ethelred-Ted. "I have also thought of perhaps combining those two things, as well!"

"What d' ye mean? I kind of thought that I would like t' go back in Time t' meet my Great Grandfather, Angus McFarlan, he was a brave hedgehog, the bravest. When the Forest of Kinlardine caught fire, he saved them all. He ran back into the furious flames carrying out all the little ones and the older ones. Aye, he was a fearless One indeed!"

"That's interesting, Het, did he get hurt carrying out this brave deed?" asked Poppy-Plump-Pij.

"No, I think not, his prickles just got very badly singed."

Ethelred-Ted and Joni-Pip stifled a laugh. Hetty turned and glared at them both.

"Here, Ye Two, it's nay laughing matter to get yer prickles singed....it smells se bad."

Joni-Pip and Ethelred-Ted disintegrated into fits of laughter.

"What are Y' Two like? I repeat, it's nay laughing matter....prickles take forever to recover from a nasty singeing!" Hetty sounded very serious.

At this last expression, even Poppy-Plump-Pij could contain herself no longer and she too joined the Errant Twosome in their unbridled laughter. The three of them were laughing so much, they had to hold their sides. It was really hurting! Hetty the Wee tried to remain serious but the sound of the laughing and the sight of the effects of the amusement, finally embraced her, too and she began to laugh with them.

"I think that ye are so unkind to me....laughing....how would you like t' have yer prickles scorched? It's nay laughing matter, believe me!"

The four of them ended up laughing so much they had tears running down their faces. Each time they tried to stop, they just looked at each other and burst out laughing again. ((I remember doing that with my best friend in School Assembly once and got into great trouble but I just couldn't stop)).

"Scorched prickles!" Eth gasped and then re-creased up with laughter!

"Singed prickles!" laughed Joni-Pip breathlessly.

Finally after about ten minutes or so, Ethelred-Ted slightly composed himself enough to say,

"Actually, You Lot, I still haven't told you why I summoned the Meeting, up here by the Ruin."

"Oh, don't worry about that, Eth," said Joni-Pip. "You can tell us later....this is much too much fun to spoil!"

"Yes, yes, you are right, Joni-Pip" he replied and they all continued on their way to Hideaway Cottage.

Even though he had shelved telling them of his daring Plan, it still kept going round and round in his mind. It excited him so much he just hoped it would all work out but he knew there was so much to discover first, so much to explore, before the Plan could be put into action.

After knocking at the large door a few times and searching round the back of the house, it was obvious that Archimedes was not at home and out somewhere; so they all agreed to walk back and try him again the next day.

As they walked home, Ethelred-Ted asked Joni-Pip if she could get hold of a particular book for him. Of course, after the discussions of the day, she understood his fascination for such a subject and realised why he was so eager to read it.

The sun was still streaming in through the School Room window, warming her legs, as she sat, stretched out in the window seat. A pretty passing butterfly flew in through the opened window, disturbing Joni-Pip.

This ended her day-dreaming about the events of the previous day, so she decided to have a good look at the book she held on her lap.

Mother and Becky-Paige were still engrossed in their struggle with long division, so she read to herself the beautiful gold writing, embossed on the spine. Softly and gently, she slowly slid her fingers over the grey cloth, dipping them smoothly within the grooves of the gilded letters.

"THE TIME MACHINE, by H.G. Wells," she whispered to herself excitedly.

Chapter 15

The Formula

"This is splendorous! Where did you get it from?"

The old Inventor pored over the large green board that now took up most of the remaining space left on his kitchen table. The unavailable part of the table was strewn with papers, pens, cups, saucers, empty milk bottles and very, very old newspapers.

"I have no idea."

"Oh....did you?"

Ethelred-Ted realised that Archimedes was not listening **to** him but at least he was looking at the Formula Board **with** him. It had taken a Dickens of a job to get him to look at it at first. When the four friends had finally found him outside in his garden, he had said he was far too busy to entertain guests. Eth had hastily explained that they were not guests, well, not guests in the true sense of the word and they didn't need any-thing from him, quite the contrary: they had come to share some-thing with him.

He still wasn't remotely interested. It was only when Eth, in frustration, had thrust the Formula Board, in its minutest form, into the Inventor's hand that he had taken any notice, at all. Even then, he didn't seem to be listening to what the Bear was saying.

When wrapped up small, the F.B. (as it had begun to be called), felt like a tiny, soft, silk handkerchief; nothing, the like of which the Professor had felt before. It was similar to paper to touch but squashier and smoother, almost like liquid, water even. This intrigued the Inventor, as it did anyone who happened to be fortunate enough to hold it in their hands but not anywhere near as much as it did when he began to unwrap it. When the soft, liquid-like material turned into a solid, board-like, substance. The old man's ruddy face lit up like Ethelred-Ted's always did, when he knew he was on his way to having his next Munch Break. The bristles of his white moustache shook and quivered as his smile spread widely across his face, into a delighted grin.

"In all my years, in all my work, in all my life, nothing like this has ever been shown to me....or ever been put into my hands!" He was almost unable to contain his joy. "This truly is a day to remember!"

When the F.B. was completely unwrapped and had been transformed into the unbending, lit up, green board, the Inventor hurried off with it, disappearing round the side of his house. The others just stood silently, not knowing what to do. After a short while, the old man's face re-appeared looking round the wall of the house.

"Well," he said, almost impatiently, "aren't you coming in?"

That's how they all came to be standing on and around Archimedes' kitchen table, watching the old man as he ran his eyes over all the strange symbols and figures that made up this incredible Formula.

"Did you steal it?" asked the Inventor furtively. "I jolly well hope not!"

"Steal it?" repeated Joni-Pip incredulously.

"Most certainly not!" exclaimed Ethelred-Ted indignantly.

"Why, he would never do such a thing!" defended Hetty. "Ethelred-Ted is the most upright of Bears, such a thing would ne'er enter his head, would it?"

"Most certainly not!" repeated the red and yellow Teddy Bear strongly.

He felt so happy to hear these words from Hetty the Wee, especially as he had laughed so heartily the day before, at the thought of her grandfather's, however many times back, scorched and singed prickles!

"Because if you did steal it, we had better hide it and prepare for an attack!" said Archimedes fervently.

"No, Archimedes, I most definitely did not steal it....it was given to me."

He knew, once more, that the old man heard nothing.

"Not a good thing that, stealing, don't hold with it," the Inventor shook his head.

Poppy-Plump-Pij, who until now had said very little, decided enough was enough, of the Inventor's rude behaviour. She took to flight and landed on the old man's head. The Inventor at first took no notice, so she walked forward to the front of his head and stretched her neck and looked down over the top of his face until, upside down, her little eyes were looking directly into his.

"Now look here!" she said firmly. "Look here, Karkiweedies Twindlestop, I have just about had enough of....hearing the rudeful, extremely rudeful way you treat my friends!"

The old man stopped examining the F.B. and peered straight into her fearsome eyes. Her three friends watched in awe. This was an intrepid Poppy; one they had never seen before and quite frankly hoped they would never, ever, have to face themselves!

"What?" asked Archimedes puzzled. "What have I done?"

"Done?" repeated Poppy. "Done? You've done nothing but ignore everything that Ethelred-Ted has tried to tell you. You have rudefully suggested he might have stolen this wonderful and quite incredible F. B.. He didn't have to show it to you. You aren't the only Inventor in the world. The world is full, quite packed even, with Inventor's like you. Why, in some countries they have more Inventors than people," she said, much to the amusement of her three friends. "Just for once, in your extremely self-centred life, could you consider other people and other people's feelings? This is no way for a grown up man to behave. I don't care how cleverful you think you are. I don't care how importantful you think you are. All these things mean nothing if you can't treat others kindly and thoughtfully. So please listen to what others have to say? What a selfish person you are, only to listen to your own words, your own voice; only to be interested in your own thoughts! D'you not realise how easy it is to be selfishful? Anybody can be selfishful, that's no achievement, nothing to be proud of. You could have no brain at all, you could not be at all clever but if you're considerate of other people and other people's feelings and care about what others have to say and you listen to their words, then you could be the greatest person in the whole world. Who wants to be with rudefish folk?"

Archimedes went very red in the face, very red indeed, redder than he had ever been before: redder than the ripest red apple and redder than the brightest red poppy.

"So?" he bellowed.

Poppy was still perched on his matted mop of wiry, wayward, white hair. She looked as though she was nesting. Of course she wouldn't have dreamt of settling for such an untidy nest! Ethelred-Ted, Hetty and Joni-Pip so wanted to laugh at how comical they both looked but they didn't dare.

"So?" he bellowed again, making the unwashed, empty milk bottles on the table rattle furiously. "So, you think that I am rude, do you? You think that I am thoughtless do you? You think that I don't listen to anyone but myself, do you?" he thundered, looking at each of his visitors in turn, who just stood and shook in terror....terror that they might burst out laughing as it was very difficult to take a man with a nesting bird plonked on his head very seriously.

"So?" he yelled again. "Will anybody answer me for Goodness sake?"

The three friends stood motionless and silent.

"Yes," came Poppy-Plump-Pij's firm and loud reply, "and I think that I have made that quite clearful, haven't I?"

"You do, do you, you think I am boorish?" screamed the old man.

The atmosphere at Hideaway Cottage was so intense that his friends thought that there might very well be another explosion....but there wasn't! As if he had burst, like a big balloon, the old man suddenly became deflated: a soft, soggy old rubber shell.

The whiskered Inventor looked intensely at the plump little wood pigeon who was still staring into his bright red face and he slowly sat down in his comfy, old armchair by the fireplace.

"You are so right! You are indeed, 'rightful'! I am totally rudefish!" he laughed.

Poppy's three friends had quite expected the old man to tell them to leave his house but much to their relief, they saw that he had completely changed. He put his hand up above his head and gently lifted the wood pigeon into his hands, cradling her softly. He ran his hand over her, somewhat ruffled feathers.

"My, my, you are a little fire cracker!" he said kindly. "Who would have thought it of such a sweet little creature? I think that I have a bit of apologising to do, don't I, Pretty Poppy? Before I start, though....how about we put the kettle on and make a nice fresh pot of tea. Hmmmm?"

The Formula Board

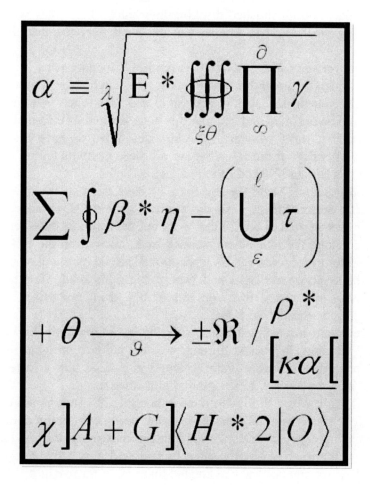

Chapter 16

One Man and His Cat

All five of them sat in Archimedes' kitchen, drinking cups of hot tea together. How brave Poppy had been and how she had surprised her three friends! They were so grateful to her. Suddenly, their relationship with Archimedes Spindlethrop had changed. Joni-Pip had witnessed this 'other' side of this unusual man when she visited him with Alex, on her bike. It occurred to her that he only became the rude, absentminded, Professor Spindlethrop when he was dealing with scientific matters: when he was talking about every day affairs, then he was very nice and kind.

After they had all finished drinking their cups of tea, they went back to examining the F.B.. Archimedes ran his hand over the incredible green board.

"I've never seen anything like it in my life. I wonder what it is made of? What a splendid invention! Just fancy, you could carry important doc-uments in your hand....so tiny and small and then when you needed them they could be unfurled and become this huge amount of information!"

"It is marvellously wonderful, Archimedes. What we have been puzzling over is: what does it mean? What are all these symbols telling us? Where will all this take us?" asked Ethelred-Ted.

"Good gracious!" said the old man. "I have been so occupied with the wonderful material this....what did you call it, this F.B. is made of....that I haven't even started to see if I can work out the formula! Now let me see!"

Immediately, the four others stepped back, away from the F.B., to allow the Inventor more room for his inspection. The old man looked and looked at all the symbols and signs and kept nodding his head. Then he took off his glasses and rested them on top of his head, muttering to himself, looking even closer at the F.B..

There was a meowing from outside the backdoor. Joni-Pip got up and opened the door. In walked Eureka, with his tail bolt upright. She went to the cupboard, took out a white saucer and poured him a little milk. He lapped it all up eagerly, so she poured him some more.

"Well, well, what? Well who'd have thought....?" Archimedes muttered.

His four visitors politely remained quiet, each determining not to distract this amazing character. Despite his thunderous temper, they had all grown to really like him; especially since he had said how sorry he was for his bad behaviour and how he had begged them all to forgive him.

It's so much easier to forgive people who are truly sorry, isn't it?

Archimedes continued to examine the F.B.. In fact it was after about an hour that Joni-Pip realised how late it was and whispered to Ethelred-Ted that she really must be getting home or Mother would be starting to worry about her safety. It was War Time when life wasn't normal and since that terrifying night in the Cellar in Bath, she knew everyone was always on the brink of panic, wondering what events might transpire for the People of this Beautiful Island.

Reluctant to leave the F.B. with the Old Inventor, Ethelred-Ted tried to talk to him but as usual, the old man was so engrossed in the work at hand that he didn't hear him. His Observers all whispered to each other and decided to leave the cottage quietly, letting him continue in his silent, solitary, wonderful world of working out.

Of course Archimedes didn't see them leave or even notice that they had gone. Not until midnight, that was. By this time, he had filled endless pages with his notes and calculations. His work was only brought to a halt by Eureka. His usually uncomplaining pet was tired and hungry, very hungry. He needed some food and he needed his bed. Eureka was a very tolerant and generally a very quiet cat. He allowed his Master to ignore him and neglect him. He even put up with having, what most people would think of as, a female-sounding name but....this tolerance only went so far. He would only allow Archimedes to neglect him and ignore him up to a point and then he no longer was a quiet cat: that point was now well and truly reached. So he began to meow and meow and meow and meow and meow and meow and meow.

As you can imagine, Dear Reader, this was not a very pleasant sound to the old Inventor's ears, it was most bothersome. So finally, he had to leave his precious notes and calculations and see to the cat. While he was feeding him, he realised that perhaps it was time that he, too, fed himself and went to bed. So he got himself a light supper of bread and jam, with a hot cup of tea and fell into bed, exhausted.

The next morning when Joni-Pip, Ethelred-Ted, Poppy and Hetty arrived, Archimedes came to the door with his clothes crumpled and his hair ruffled; not an unusual sight.

"Forgive my wayward appearance," he said smiling, "it's just I didn't have time to get ready for bed last night, I was too tired!"

His visitors were ushered into the kitchen, where Joni-Pip immediately put the kettle on and made a fresh pot of tea for all of them. Archimedes disappeared for a little while and returned with his hair combed....well, re-arranged....and smelling fresh and scrubbed.

"So, Archimedes, how did it go?" asked Ethelred-Ted, surveying the floor, where every available space was strewn with pieces of paper, emblazoned with numerous mathematical symbols and figures.

"Well, I am not too sure," replied the old gentleman, "something is missing....I don't know what it is....what exactly is this formula proving? What is its purpose?"

"I think it is something to do with Jumping in Time," said Ethelred-Ted cautiously. He didn't want to disappoint the old man, in case it was nothing to do with Time Trekking, although he was pretty sure it was.

The old Inventor's eyes lit up.

"I thought it might be....no, no, no I knew it had to be...." he said excitedly, "....I knew one day it would come to me, if I searched long enough, if I waited long enough....'everything comes to he who waits' and all that....I never dreamt it would actually be handed to me, though....that's the surprise....but I am not there yet....it's going to take some time...."

"Can we help?" asked Joni-Pip.

"Not unless you are amazing at mathematics....my weakest point, actually ....never was any good at the difficult parts....loved the chemistry, loved the physics but was rubbish at maths...."

Joni-Pip thought for a moment then her eyes lit up.

"I am no good, no good at all, at maths but I know somebody who is. Shall I ask if they would come?"

"Who are you thinking of?"

Chapter 17

The Inventor's Assistant

"Alex?"

No answer: typically, Alex had his head in some book about trains and didn't appear to hear his sister.

"Alex…..Alex, could you help me with my maths homework, please?"

For some reason, the word 'maths' took Alex away from his reading and he looked up, over the top of his book into Joni-Pip's eyes.

"Maths, J.P.? Something you're not clear on?"

"Something like that," Joni-Pip smiled and thought, 'Not clear at all!'

"It's not like Mother to leave you with something she hasn't fully explained."

He put his book down on the garden table and took the exercise book Joni-Pip was holding, out of her hands.

It was another beautiful, sunny, Spring afternoon. Alex had been ushered into the garden by Mrs Broft, so that she could give his bedroom a well needed 'wash and brush up'. At first Alex had complained, he loved the solitude of his room. In Bath, the family home was large and spacious and Alex could escape to a number of places to be alone. Here, at Knotty Knook, a much smaller country cottage, his bedroom was the only sanctuary where he could get away from the noise and bustle of family life: especially away from his little sisters and their noisy games. Sometimes Joni-Pip longed to just sit with Alex quietly in his room, reading but Alex was an insular person who enjoyed his own company and made that quite clear to everyone by displaying a large sign on his bedroom door which declared and warned,

'PRIVATE LAND TRESPASSERS WILL BE PROSECUTED KEEP OUT'.

Alex had seen the sign in Farmer Finn's barn one day. It appealed to him as a great deterrent for anyone who dared to invade his territory. He had asked where it had come from and what the farmer was going to do with it and was told that it was the actual sign **his** Father, Old Farmer Finn, had put up to keep people off his land.

This Farmer Finn, his son, James Finn, did not much care for it and didn't see the need to stop folks from enjoying the lovely views over the English countryside from up on the hills, so he had removed it from the copse by Marley's Barn.

"For some reason, my father didn't like people walking over the

Clappers, so he put the sign up by Marley's Barn, to stop people from wandering around up there."

PRIVATE LAND

TRESPASSERS WILL

BE PROSECUTED

KEEP OUT

Alex asked if he could have it. Farmer Finn chuckled and readily agreed.
"What on earth d'you want it for, Alex? Of what possible use is it?"
"It keeps people out of my room, it warns them off!" replied Alex.
Therein followed a roar of laughter.
"That might do the trick for some; not so sure about Mrs Broft though, she's truly a mighty foe. No amount of warnings will quash her determination to enter!"
"You are so right, what is it with that woman and cleaning? She's obsessed! She is indeed a force to be reckoned with though and I don't much like confronting her when she is wielding that very large broom, with that very long handle. I think if The British got wind of that Lethal Weapon, this War would soon be over, make no mistake!"
"If only," said Farmer Finn thoughtfully, looking up into the sky: then he turned and added, "I think it will need a lick of paint, though!"
The old sign was transported to Knotty Knook, where Alex painted it and then nailed it, very firmly, to his bedroom door. He made a few holes in the door in the process. Father wasn't too happy about that but Mother had pleaded his cause, saying that as the door was solid oak, it wouldn't really do much harm. So there it remained.

"What's the maths about then?" Alex, surveyed Joni-Pip's exercise book.
Joni-Pip gently took her book back out of Alex's hands.
"Er....how good are you at algebra, Alex?"
"Algebra? Nothing to it!" he laughed.
"Do you find it easy then, Alex?"
"Really simple."
"Try this then." She opened her book to the last page and Alex glanced over the page, expecting to see a simple, childish, algebraic formula.
"I'll soon sort this out for you...." he said positively then he jerked his head forward and had a second look at the Formula....and a third....and a

fourth...."What the....?" his voice trailed away.

Joni-Pip had carefully copied the Formula. It wasn't anywhere near as impressive as on the large fluorescent Formula Board....but impressive it still was.

$$\alpha \equiv_{\lambda} \sqrt{E * \oint \prod_{\xi\theta}^{\partial} \gamma \sum \int_{\infty} \beta * \eta - \left(\bigcup_{\varepsilon}^{\ell} \tau\right) + \theta \xrightarrow{g} \pm \Re \rho * [\kappa d\chi] A + G \langle H * 2 | O \rangle}$$

"Where on earth did Mother conger this up from?" Alex demanded to know. "It's amazing, truly spectacular!"

Joni-Pip cleared her throat nervously.

"Tell me what you can make of it and I'll tell you where it came from."

"I see," said Alex, sounding as absent-minded as Professor Spindlethrop. "I say, this is spiffing! What's it all about then?"

Joni-Pip wanted to say,

"Don't be such a Twerp, Alex, I wouldn't have shown it to you if I had known what it was all about, now would I?"

But of course she didn't: instead she said,

"We....I....wondered what you could make of it?"

Alex examined the Formula, very carefully for some time.

"Time....yes this will take time, J.P....a lot of time!....the only thing I know, is that it has something to do with water....well sort of water....it's to do with energy....some sort of force...."

"Oh, Alex," said his admiring twelve-year-old sister, "you're so clever!"

"Look J.P., this needs very careful investigation, calculation and careful observation. Mind if I take it away to examine it alone in my room?"

"Of course I don't, Alex." She was slightly sad that she was not invited to watch him work. Ever since she could remember, her brother always seemed to have his head in some 'silly' book, writing number upon number, doing calculation after calculation, much to her annoyance. It had always seemed such a waste of time. Now, however, when she would love to have been watching him, he wanted to do his work away from her, alone in his room!

Alex stood up and made his way towards the cottage door, clutching the exercise book firmly in his grasp. Joni-Pip suddenly remembered what she had been instructed to do. She called him back.

"Alex, hang on a minute! Eth....er....I have another copy of the Formula....it's in my room....it will be easier than this little one....easier to follow, I mean."

The instructions from Eth had been written thus: **If Alex isn't interested**

in the Formula, leave it with him just seeing the small version. If, however he is interested, show him the large Formula I have copied.

Joni-Pip ran to her room and pulled out the large copy Ethelred-Ted had beautifully made during the quiet of the night. In the morning, they hid the copy under Joni-Pip's bed, concerned that Mrs Broft might be curious when she discovered it during her sprucing up of Joni-Pip's room: so they covered it over with an old sheet.

"Er....Mrs Broft," Joni-Pip had said tentatively that morning, as she passed the House Keeper on the landing. Mrs Broft stopped and looked at Joni-Pip expectantly. She had a mop and bucket in her hands, with a feather duster under her arm and she stood looking at the twelve-year-old. Joni-Pip looked blank and said nothing.

"What is it, My Lovely?"

"I have something in my room," said Joni-Pip, thinking how silly she sounded.

"Do you now and what could that be?" asked the jolly woman. "A lot of dust 'n that? That's the usual, Miss Joni-Philipa, lots of dust and clothes 'hung up' on the floor and books, tidily flung under your bed...."

Joni-Pip suddenly panicked.

"Under my bed? Yes that's it....yes that's it, I have something under my bed!" she suddenly felt vulnerable: she hadn't wanted Mrs Broft to discover the copy of the F.B. but now she had directed her to exactly where it was!

"What have you got under your bed, then?" asked Mrs Broft, still patiently holding the mop and bucket. The water in the bucket was steaming. Mrs Broft had just got it from the copper boiler, down in the scullery and Joni-Pip looked at it in horror.

'What if Mrs Broft was to get the Copy of the F.B. wet....accidentally? ....What if she was to ruin it?' she thought to herself. 'Oh no that will never do, all that work Ethelred-Ted has done....it will be wasted. I must do something and very quickly!'

"Mother and I are doing an Art Project," she lied, thinking 'how on earth am I going to muddle my way through this one?'

"An Art Project? She didn't say," replied Mrs Broft, putting the bucket down and resting on the mop. "What exactly are you doing then: something exciting?"

"Exciting?" repeated Joni-Pip, suddenly seeing her escape. "Yes very exciting. In fact it is so exciting, that it is Top Secret, very Top Secret!"

Mrs Broft, dubious about this last comment decided to keep silent.

"So what do you want me to do with this exciting, Top Secret, very Top Secret, Art Project an' that, then?"

"Nothing, absolutely nothing....could you **not** mop my room today?"

"Miss Joni-Philipa, I most certainly could not, whatever next?"

"All right then, Mrs Broft but could you not mop **under** my bed? The art work is there and it shouldn't be moved....yet," said Joni-Pip weakly.

Suddenly her story seemed to be very transparent....and full of so many holes....in fact, so many, it possibly had more than Mrs Broft's cream, enamel, green edged and green handled colander. The one that hung up in the scullery, next to the many cream, green handled spoons and spatulas.

Mrs Broft smiled to herself. Although she guessed Joni-Philipa was hiding something, she was a good sport and reckoned that 'under the bed', could go without a mopping just this once....but just this once, mind! Actually, as she was doing Joni-Pip's room that morning, she almost forgot her promise and as she reached with the broom under the bed she hit up against the copy of the F.B.. She was very curious but being a woman of principle, she refrained from investigating the so called 'art work', even though she was tempted, extremely tempted indeed.

Joni-Pip lay on her floor and pulled the F.B. copy from under her bed.

"That's huge!" said Alex startling his sister. He had been intrigued by the Formula and had followed closely behind her.

Joni-Pip was so pleased to find that Alex had followed her. She thought it must be one of the few times in his life that he had taken an interest in something his younger sister had done.

Alex helped Joni-Pip carefully remove the old sheet. His eyes lit up when he saw it and they both stood staring at it. He decided it needed closer investigation. He kneeled on the floor and peered at it, running his eyes over and over the strange and yet somehow, familiar characters. Neither of them spoke. Alex just kept letting out sighs and gasps of wonder as he followed the signs and symbols, sometimes running his finger over them, as if he was invisibly drawing them.

"So, this is your Top Secret, very Top Secret, Art Project, then Miss Joni-Philipa?" a voice came from above them.

The brother and sister jumped with surprise and Alex turned round, trying to shield the Formula from their industrious House Keeper who had appeared from nowhere and now stood towering over them. He didn't know why he did this. His sister had not asked him to keep it a secret; he just knew it was not for all eyes, it was not to be shared with everybody and he felt that J.P. trusted him to keep it that way.

Alex's attempts at concealing Joni-Pip's 'Top Secret, very Top Secret Art Project', were in vain. They were totally unnecessary, anyway because the curious cleaner had stood watching over them for some time before she had deemed it appropriate to speak.

"What's it all about then, that there Art Project? Art Project, my eye? Now I'm not the sort that did a lot of art at school, much preferred cookery m'self but I do know one thing....that there stuff, those there figures and things," she said gesturing towards the Formula. "Those funny, squiggerly what-knots, that's nowt to do with art, now is it, my Lovelies? That's to do with science, that is. It's a bit of that there science and clever stuff like that, innit?"

Alex got up from his knees and started to explain.

"Yes, Mrs Broft, you are quite correct....it is indeed something to do with science....incredibly difficult science....and it is beyond me, right now but I am going to have a jolly good crack at it."

"So, what's it all about then, Master Alex?" asked Mrs Broft, with great interest. "What does it all mean?"

"Well....I know....this Formula....it has something to do with water....see these symbols at the end here....H_2O....the symbol for water but it has a symbol I don't recognise, after the 'H' for hydrogen....you see, this one." He pointed to the star-like symbol between the 'H' and the '$_2$'.

"Looks like a snow flake to me," said Joni-Pip, coming in to the conversation for the first time. She had felt like a spectator, up until now but was pleased to finally contribute something.

"Hunting Hockey Trees!" exclaimed Alex. "You're brilliant, J.P., you're right....it does look like a symbol for snow....why didn't I think of that? Yes, yes, yes....snow that's it....that makes sense....why didn't I see that?"

Joni-Pip was elated.

Once more, Alex got down on his knees and examined the Formula. This time he was joined by Mrs Broft, who had no idea why she was looking at it, she only knew it fascinated her and she was so taken by Alex's enthusiasm.

"What is it, Master Alex?" asked the Curious Cleaner. "What's it all about, that there formulation? What does it add up to, what does it mean?"

Alex turned and looked at her for a moment, scratching his head.

"Well, Mrs Broft, it's like this....it's a....um....it's...."

"Yes?" asked Mrs Broft and Joni-Pip together.

"It's...." Alex continued to scratch his head. "I've absolutely no idea!"

All three of them burst out laughing.

Joni-Pip couldn't quite believe that all this was happening. Here she was, cycling across the fields toward Hideaway Cottage, laughing and chatting with her big brother. The Formula had drawn them really close together. The one 'downer' on the occasion, was that Ethelred-Ted, who had worked so hard to reproduce the F.B., had to be left out. Alex had no idea that he was alive, a real character, a real talker! Eth had taken it much better than she had, after all it was 'the Formula that was the important issue here', he had explained but that didn't make Joni-Pip feel any better. She felt that he had earned the right to be there with all the excitement that was going on, especially after all the work he had done in copying out the strange signs and symbols. However, he was as magnanimous as he was industrious and he had bowed out with dignity. He made it clear that it was just until they had 'sussed out' what it all meant that he would remain a dumb, stuffed toy....only until then. Joni-Pip loved him.

When they arrived at the cottage, Archimedes, as usual, was nowhere to be seen. They leaned their bikes up against the wall at the front of the cottage and walked round to the rear. They knocked on the back door for a while. Nobody came, so they walked over to the Quission Hut, his laboratory. They called out first and after receiving no answer, they then cautiously opened the door. After quite a long search, they discovered he wasn't there either.

"Where on earth could he be?" Alex thought out loud.

"I have absolutely no idea!" Joni-Pip replied to the audible thought.

"Archimedes! Archimedes! Are you around?" yelled Alex.

As if using a mega-phone, Joni-Pip circled the outside of her mouth with her hands and shouted,

"Archimedes! Archimedes! It's us....Alex and Joni-Philipa, we have come to see you about a matter of great importance!"

Still the air was silent.

After a small discussion, Alex decided they should leave and come back the next day so they collected their bikes and wheeled them round from the side of the cottage to the front. They were both disappointed that their journey had proved fruitless. Reluctantly they mounted their bikes in silence and started slowly pedalling down the wide, overgrown path.

"Where do you think you are going?"

The Cyclists stopped their bikes, got off and leaned them up against the wall, then they walked over to get closer to the house but neither of them could see anybody.

"Why are you leaving me?"

Alex and Joni-Pip looked all around them.

"I thought you said that you had come to see me about a 'matter of great importance', I think you said, didn't you Joni-Philipa?"

"I did....we did...." Joni-Pip replied, "where are you? I can't see you."

Alex and Joni-Pip searched all over with their eyes but they saw no-one.

"Archimedes, where on earth are you?" asked Alex, almost laughing.

"Where am I? Well, that's a silly question. I am here....of course!"

His visitors looked up towards the cottage. They looked at the Quission Hut, beside the cottage. They looked at the cottage windows. They saw nothing, nothing at all.

"I am here!" shouted the old man. "Up here! I seem to remember this happening before!"

Both Joni-Pip and Alex looked up and there was Archimedes balancing, very precariously, on top of the roof between the four tall chimneys, which stood majestically guarding the cottage. What on earth he was doing there, neither of his callers could imagine but up on the roof he was. Archimedes was always surprising them when they came to Hideaway Cottage and this time proved to be no exception.

"That looks very dangerous to me, Archimedes, what are you doing up there?" shouted Joni-Pip. "Please take care?"

"Got some experiment going on, Archimedes?" Alex shouted.

"Experiment? Experiment? I wish!" laughed Archimedes.

The notion obviously tickled the old man and he began to laugh out loud.

"Experiment you say? That's rich!" he continued, his laughter getting louder and louder until it was almost uncontrollable.

"Steady, Archimedes! Steady!" shouted Alex, watching uneasily. The Old Inventor started to wobble and held his side laughing.

"Archimedes, please, please be careful, you will fall!" urged Joni-Pip.

Just then they heard a loud 'meow' and Eureka appeared on the top of the roof between two of the chimneys. He confidently walked along the ridge past his Master, down the angle of the tiled roof to the edge by the gutter. He strolled along the gutter until he was above the large, green, water butt. He then jumped down effortlessly, landing softly on the lid of the butt on all four paws. He took one brief glance around at Joni-Pip and Alex and then he leaped off the water butt and walked majestically with his tail straight up in the air, like a mast on a sailing boat. He greeted his twelve-year-old friend. Joni-Pip leant down and stroked him. Appreciatively the cat rubbed around her legs and began to purr loudly.

"Eureka!" shouted Archimedes, pointing towards the cat but still continuing to laugh. This was rather unfortunate for the white haired, white whiskered mountaineer. His arms began to wave wildly in the air, signalling towards Eureka.

This action was not sensibly thought out.

Anybody knows that, as a rule, standing on the top of a roof, laughing, hanging on to nothing, is not something one should do many times in one's life. The Inventor was no exception to this rule and started to wobble, sway and balance from one foot to the other.

Alex and Joni-Pip started to laugh, in fact they laughed even more, as they watched Archimedes, enveloped in unconstrained laughter, fall on to his bottom and slide down the tiles of the roof.

"Wheeeeeeeee!" he shouted. "This is fun....ha ha....! Wheeeeeeeeee!" he continued and when he had reached the edge of the roof, by the gutter, he put his hands down by his sides and pushed himself off. This mighty push propelled him, from the roof and down to the ground. He landed in the overgrown grass below.

Alex and Joni-Pip stopped laughing and ran quickly to his aid, followed by Eureka. Well, actually, they only stopped laughing for a second or two because coming from the depths of the long grass, came the most uproarious laughter they had heard that afternoon.

They waded through the overgrown garden to the Professor's Landing Pad. They were so relieved to see him still in one piece, still laughing.

"That....ha ha....that....my....ha ha....he he....my....friends....is....that....that is my experiment!" he laughed pointing.

They looked around.

"That...." laughed the Inventor pointing straight at Eureka, "that cat is my experiment! Haha....oh what fun it has been!"

Alex and Joni-Pip helped Archimedes to his feet, which was rather a difficult task as they were all still laughing so much. A couple of times he nearly got up but he fell back into the grass, laughing.

"The main thing is, are you all right, Archimedes?" laughed Joni-Pip.

"Any broken bones sustained?" grinned Alex.

"Broken bones?" repeated the Inventor, feeling his arms and legs. "Broken bones? Ha....ha ha....well we will have to see....ha ha....I don't exactly know yet!"

Happily, the chuckling, careless climber was not hurt. He had a few little grazes and a few large bruises but on the whole, considering what had happened, Archimedes had come out of the entire hilarious episode almost unscathed; well, practically, anyway.

Alex and Joni-Pip stood either side of the Inventor and helped him walk back to the cottage.

"I'm fine," he said, still laughing. "All I need is a nice cup of tea!"

"Of course. I'll make you one," said Joni-Pip. "By the way, what did you mean when you said that Eureka was your experiment?"

"I was up on the roof trying to rescue him. I thought he was stuck!"

More hysterical laughter ensued.

Joni-Pip was staggered at this whole episode. Archimedes gave the impression that his cat was surplus to requirements most of the time; why he only fed him when he remembered or Eureka reminded him! So it defied all reason to see the quirky old Inventor, up on the roof, risking life and limb, trying to rescue this neglected moggy, when everyone knows that cats delight in heights and invariably come on down when they are good and ready; steadily, safely and softly, landing on all fours!

All three of them made their way into the kitchen, Joni-Pip scolding Archimedes for his reckless behaviour and telling him that it was a wonder he didn't fall and have a nasty accident! A bit rich, coming from her but she didn't remember her own accident at this particular moment in Time!

While Joni-Pip made them a cup of tea and fed Eureka, Archimedes went off and changed into some fresher and cleaner, crumpled clothes.

On his return, they all settled down in the kitchen. Joni-Pip sat in one of the big armchairs, thinking how good it made her feel being with both Alex and Archimedes; especially now they had seen him laughing so much. She felt very close to him. He reminded her of someone but she couldn't think who.

"I suppose you should now tell me of this 'matter of great importance', you have come to see me about!" said Archimedes smiling.

"Oh yes!" exclaimed Joni-Pip. "I told you that Alex was brilliant at maths, didn't I? I think he's worked out the Formula, haven't you, Alex?"

"You have?" asked Archimedes enthusiastically, looking straight at Alex. "Wonderful!"

"Yes, he is wonderful, he's worked it all out!"

"Steady on, J.P., I'm most certainly not wonderful. I don't think I've exactly worked it out; I just get the gist of it and you, Archimedes?"

"Same here, Alex but what do you make of the 'H*2|0' at the end? That was the thing that stumped me," Archimedes said frowning.

"It's the strange symbol after the H for hydrogen, which puzzled me, too. I knew it was producing some sort of energy and making a kind of water," replied Alex.

"Same again. So what conclusions did you come up with, then, Alex?"

"I think and it is only a thought," Alex answered slowly, "that the water produced isn't water; not water exactly but how about.....a bit like snow?"

"Eureka! That's it! Snow, yes snow!" exclaimed the old man, standing up. "Why on earth didn't I think of that? It's perfect, so, so simple!"

"I only said a bit like it," laughed Alex.

"Indeed!" the white haired Inventor replied with a grin and then he said, "So? Tell me, how did you work that one out?"

"Well, in actual fact, it was J.P. who got me on to that," said Alex looking across at Joni-Pip and smiling at her.

Joni-Pip beamed back.

"J.P.?" the old man questioned.

"Joni-Philipa," answered Alex, "my very clever, younger sister."

The old Inventor nodded and smiled at Joni-Pip. She grinned back at him. She was so thrilled with it all. She thought that Alex might have forgotten that she had contributed to the solution.

"Hmmm?" said the old Inventor, raising his eye-brows and once more looking at the twelve-year-old. "So not only can your sister make tea and feed my cat, she can work out almost unfathomable formulae!"

"Rather!" replied Joni-Pip, laughing.

"Actually, I don't think you needed my Input, at all," laughed Alex generously. "My little sister seemed to manage perfectly capably, without me. If you ask me, she makes a proper little Inventor's Assistant!"

Chapter 18

The Clappers

"Why don't we all go up to Marley's' Barn?"

"What for, Poppy?" asked Ethelred-Ted.

"Er....I just thought it would be a nice place to go."

"What you mean, Pops, is that it would give you another opportunity to see the singing Macaw, wouldn't it?" He knew!

"It's such a lovely day, it seems a pity to waste it," ventured Poppy weakly.

"Ma Lamb, when do we ever waste a day?"

"I don't think it would be such a bad idea, though," said Joni-Pip.

Her comment was made, knowing that she had so much to discuss with them all. The meeting with Alex and Archimedes had been very productive. Marley's Barn was a fair walk from Knotty Knook, so it gave her plenty of time to tell them everything.

A train chuffed past them as they walked alongside the fence by the railway track. In true British style, they all stopped and waved at the passengers. The passengers all waved back.

"Have you noticed all the trains seem to be black, now?" asked Joni-Pip, still waving as the train chugged on towards Nottingham.

"It's the War. All of the passenger engines round here would have been LMS maroon before but now they have all been painted black, so they can't be identified from the air," replied Ethelred-Ted informatively.

"Thank you, Alex," said Joni-Pip, smiling cheekily.

They all laughed at this comment and then they continued their walk along the beautiful country pathways. These walkways had been forged over many centuries, by the thousands of footsteps made by travellers who wandered through the forest, woods and fields of Nottinghamshire. Robin Hood and his Merry Men, who enjoyed many an adventure here, were included in those ramblers.

Now, however, this particular little 'band of men' was about to embark on an adventure of its own. An adventure that was to be so amazing....one that they could never have imagined....not even in their wildest dreams!

"Look over there, above those trees, it's the stars again!"

Everybody looked and saw them.

"Prepare for some visitors, then," said Ethelred-Ted, only looking briefly; he was more eager to find out what had gone on with the Inventor and Alex.

"I got on really well with Alex and Archimedes, Eth."

"You did?" he tried not to sound too keen.

"Yes, especially after the funny start to the afternoon. When we arrived we couldn't find Archimedes anywhere."

"That's not unusual, Hen, he's never around when y' first arrive, is he?"

"He's usually shooting out of the ground in a silver sausage!" chirped Poppy, walking along beside Hetty. She wanted to fly on ahead and get to Marley's Barn really quickly but after Eth's remark about Macca, she decided to take her time. Her little heart was pounding at the thought of seeing the beautiful, talented Macaw again. However, she resolved to lay low and pretend nothing was going on.

They all laughed about Archimedes hurtling out of the cellar in the Time Tube.

"Anyway, to get back to yesterday, guess where he was this time?"

"I can't imagine, Ma Lambie."

"No idea!" came Ethelred-Ted.

"Up a treeful?" suggested Poppy-Plump-Pij.

"He was up on the roof, standing on the ridge, between the four chimneys!"

"What?" questioned Ethelred-Ted incredulously.

"And what business could he possibly be doin' up there, Lassie?"

"For me, that would be wonderful," said Poppy dreamily, "but not for a human."

"You're right, Poppy, it most certainly was not a sensible thing for any human to do....especially not when a human is laughing!"

"Laughing?" the three chorused together.

"Alex asked him if he was carrying out an experiment, up on the roof."

"That's a pretty normal question to ask Archimedes," said Ethelred-Ted.

"Because **he** knew why he was actually on the roof and how far it was from an experiment; it made him laugh; no shriek. In fact he laughed so much that he lost his balance and fell off the roof! Worried me when he said he'd 'been there before'!"

"That's nay laughing matter, Pet," said Hetty sternly. "Was that Déjà vu?"

"I'm surprised at you for laughing!" said a disapproving Poppy-Plump-Pij.

"I say, that must have been pretty spectacular!" exclaimed Ethelred-Ted. Then feeling slightly guilty, he added quietly, "Was he hurt?"

"Yes, Joni-Pip, was the Poor, Wee Lamb hurt?"

"A bit. He's got a few little cuts and bruises; well, a few very big bruises

153

on his back and legs. Interesting point about Déjà vu, Hetty, we will have to see."

"Poor thing, I hope you put some diniment on them," said Poppy.

"Diniment? Ah....liniment? No," said Joni-Pip, "we didn't think about anything like that! We were all laughing so much!"

"So?" quizzed Eth. "What did You talk about? What did you discover?"

"Yes, Ma Pet, tell us the outcome of all this merriment?" Hetty grinned.

"Did you solve the big problem?" asked Poppy-Plump-Pij.

"Yes, we did solve the 'big problem'."

"And?" Eth waited, trying desperately hard not to sound too impatient.

"The problem," started Joni-Pip, then she turned and looked at Poppy, "the big problem, was with the special symbol at the end of the Formula."

"Ah!" exclaimed Ethelred-Ted. "That confused me, too....you are talking about the star-like symbol aren't you: the one between the H and the little 2?"

"I know enough science t' know that H_2O is the symbol for water," piped up Hetty the Wee, "but what that little spiky symbol means, beats me!"

"What does that all mean, then?" came Poppy's little voice.

"I will tell you," replied Joni-Pip, "and it's so simple."

"It is?" asked Poppy-Plump-Pij surprised.

"I suggest I explain a little to you, first," said Eth. "Everything is made up of tiny little atoms. Hydrogen is a gas, have you heard of it, Pops?"

Poppy-Plump-Pij nodded.

"Er....Hyprogen? I think so, I think I have heard this before, somewhere."

Ethelred-Ted ignored her new word and continued.

"Well, two atoms of hydrogen, mixed with one atom of oxygen, makes...."

"Three atoms of oxyhypro?" ventured Poppy-Plump-Pij.

Hetty the Wee, Joni-Pip and Ethelred-Ted all stifled a laugh.

"Er....not quite, Pops....but nearly," said the Teddy Bear kindly.

"It makes something important; so important we couldn't live without it, Pet."

"Oat Scones?"

"No, I don't quite think so," said Joni-Pip, trying again not to laugh.

"Hmmm....now we're talking! I could just do with a Munch Break!"

"They are probably the most delicious Oat Scones in the world, Pop but I think we could just about manage Life on Earth without them," said Joni-Pip.

"Ethelred-Ted always says he can't live without them, my Oat Scones."

"They are truly wonderful, Poppy. A work of art!" exclaimed Ethelred-

154

Ted.

"But, Ma Pet, we don't quite need them to support Life on Earth, do we?"

"Well, we would starve if we didn't have them!" Poppy reasoned.

Her three friends decided to abandon the subject of the Oat Scones.

"Pop, two atoms of hydrogen and one atom of oxygen, make water," said Eth.

"Water? Water? Is that all?"

"What d' ye mean, Pet, 'is that all' ?" asked Hetty slightly prickly. "My, it's wonderful n' all....just think two gasses together n' they make water? Amazin'!"

"I had never thought of it before, Het but you're right," said Joni-Pip. "Isn't **everything** amazing? The stars....the moon, the sun, the Earth, the birds, the animals, Us? How we are made. Yes, the stars are truly amazing!"

"It's all so bonny, y're right, so right!"

"And so are my Oat Scones! One day you'll learn how crucialful they are!"

They all laughed with her, not realising how true her words would prove to be. Walking and chatting, they continued on until they got to the Clappers and were just about to sit down, when suddenly, Flip, Steve and Craig came running out of the trees.

"Hello, You Lot!" said Ethelred-Ted. "So, you got away safely then, Steve and no, we still don't know where the Old Mine is!"

"Just about!" laughed Steve. "That was a bit close. Are they the ones you told us who keep asking about two boys and a girl: the men who chased me?"

"They are! Where do you keep coming from and why always with glittery stuff in your hair?" asked Joni-Pip. "Is it to do with the stars we see before you arrive?"

"What stars?" asked Craig.

"Please, this is so terribly confusing, we were just going to sit down. Why don't you sit down with us and explain a few things?" asked Joni-Pip.

The three visitors all looked at each other.

"O.K. but not for long, we're in the middle of a Quission," said Steve, settling himself on the ground in front of Joni-Pip. Flip and Craig joined him.

Soon everyone was sitting down on the grass in a circle.

"Can't you just tell us something about yourselves? Who you are? Where have you come from? Why are you looking for the Old Mine?" asked Joni-Pip.

155

"Only a little because it's so pointless answering all those questions. When we have gone, you will forget everything," said Flip.

"I know we know each other but is it in a different world or something?" asked Joni-Pip. "A little while ago, when Bath was bombed, I was in my garden and I saw a pilot in a plane....he smiled at me....which was incredible....he seemed to know me and I seemed to know him. I know he has something to do with you because every time his face comes into my mind, it's either after you have appeared or the men in long black coats have spoken to me, or chased after you! Who is he?"

"We have no id...." started Steve but he was interrupted by the sound of heated voices coming from the woods behind. They all turned round to see a motley band of soldiers emerge from the trees and march purposefully towards them.

"Who on earth are these?" asked Craig. "Strange uniforms!"

The Officer in charge strode up to the little circle of friends and spoke to them. Joni-Pip just sat there, nonchalantly pulling up the little white flowers scattered around her and started making a chain. She didn't want this interruption.

"We are looking for two men in long black coats," said the soldier abruptly, "have you seen them? We need to inter....speak with them!"

Joni-Pip now pricked up her ears but still lazily continued threading the fresh green stalks of the pink-edged daisies, weaving them through each other, forming a pretty floral string.

"No, no, I haven't. Should I have?" Craig truthfully replied.

"Who are they?" Steve asked the Officer.

"It's a matter of National Security. If you see them you must report them to the Constabulary! Do not approach them. They are desperate men!"

"Where do you come from?" asked Flip.

The Officer shrugged.

"We must be going! Right, Men, quick march!"

The circle of onlookers watched them disappear back into the trees.

"Some questions for you," Joni-Pip began. "We had visitors from the Future."

"Yes, we...." interrupted Flip.

"Let her speak," said Steve.

"I had an accident and these ones from the Future changed everything for me, which was wonderful but things are different with you. Since you first arrived when I was in the Bentley, I have been seeing these stars all the time before you appear and after you leave," Joni-Pip sounded serious, "you also have glittery bits in your hair."

Flip, Steve and Craig all brushed their hands across their hair and

156

examined the glitter in their palms.

"Hmmm!" they all said and smiled cheekily.

"Why is it that when Red-Ted, Jack and Macca came there were no stars and no sparkly bits on them? What's the difference?" Joni-Pip asked.

Ethelred-Ted, Poppy and Hetty all looked bemused at this question, it wasn't something that they had ever considered.

"I have no idea," grinned Flip, "have you Lads got any thoughts on it?"

"No, I'm stumped, too. What d'you think, Craig?" Steve chuckled.

"Haven't a clue!" he said looking at the other two and they all laughed.

"I almost feel that the stars are a sign of something; it drives me mad wondering what it's all about," said a frustrated Joni-Pip. "Look there they are!" she pointed to stars rising above the wood. They turned and looked and were amazed to see, a long way away, countless stars, billowing into the air.

"Hey....eey, that's neat. Is that what happens before we arrive, then?"

"Not actually that many but yes, Craig. Now tell us, where are you from, the Past or the Future?" asked Joni-Pip. "We want to know, don't we, Eth?"

Ethelred-Ted didn't reply, his thoughts seemed miles away.

"Hey, hang on a minute, J.P., those Two Men in Long, Black Coats, aren't they the ones that chased me and aren't they the ones those weird soldiers were asking about? D'you think they're the same ones? Why didn't you tell the soldiers you had seen the men in long black coats?" asked Steve.

Joni-Pip screwed up her face.

"I have no idea. It's all so peculiar. I am convinced it has something to do with the stars we keep seeing. I sure hope I understand all this one day."

"You will," said Flip, leaning over to her and gently rubbing one of her shoulders. Joni-Pip smiled back at her.

"You all right, Ethelred-Ted? What's up?" asked Craig.

Ethelred-Ted remained silent.

"Thinking about our next Munch Break, are we?" asked Hetty: more silence.

"Is he ill or something?" Poppy walked over to him. He still stood, staring.

"I don't believe what I am seeing," he said slowly. They all turned and followed his gaze. "Is that a huge....fence, growing in front of me?"

"What?" they all said. "Where?"

"It is a fence, isn't it? Well, it jolly well looks like one!" Eth continued.

"What can it be, this huge fence?" asked Joni-Pip.

"The Fence of Time?" answered Poppy.

They all looked at her, paused and then looked back at the 'Fence'.

"Can't you see, all those pointed spikes up on the hill?"

"Yes, yes I can, what on earth...." Steve strained to get a better look.

"What's happening? They're getting higher. It's huge!" Craig gasped.

"Is it the Invasion?" asked Joni-Pip.

"Invaded by a Fence? I don't think so!" said Steve seriously.

"No worries, Joni-Pip," Flip leaned over and gently squeezed her shoulder again, "there was no Invasion of Britain, written in History, during World War Two."

As they watched the pointed stakes grow and grow, they realised how huge the structure was. It grew until it was just a bit taller than a man but so wide! It stretched all along the top of the hill opposite them.

"I think we had better take cover," suggested Craig, looking round.

"There are those rocks over there, let's go behind them!" said Joni-Pip, standing up, climbing the hill and making her way quickly over to the enormous stones. They all followed her until they were standing in the shelter and the shadow of these rocks.

Suddenly a very loud, eerie whooping sound filled the air. The fence began to quiver and move rhythmically and a deafeningly loud clapping sound was heard.

"I know what they are!" shouted Steve above the noise.

In disbelief, they watched the spectacle below from behind the rocks.

"So do I!" said Ethelred-Ted. "I think we are in grave danger!"

"What is it, Eth?" Joni-Pip was horrified.

"Zulus!" came Craig, Steve and Ethelred-Ted together.

"We must keep out of sight," Steve commanded. "The clapping sound is made by the Warriors hitting their shields with their spears. They are preparing to attack!"

"Edwinstowe?" asked Poppy; how preposterous this seemed: however, the thunderous sound of the clapping of spears on shields told them this was all too real!

"How did they get here? This is impossible!" said Joni-Pip.

Suddenly, at the bottom of the hill, a small regiment of mounted soldiers wearing scarlet jackets galloped in the direction of the Zulu Wall of Warriors!

"And where on earth did they come from? Who are they?" asked Poppy.

"Royal Engineers! They're done for! What can we do?" Craig sighed.

"Call them to come up here," suggested Eth, "but would they hear us?"

Everyone looked at him, hopelessly.

"Then we'd all be done for!" resigned Joni-Pip. "We've seen these before!"

"Yes, we have," agreed Ethelred-Ted, "and I presume we have seen those two men down there, as well," he pointed below them. "It was when we were up in Windy Woods and they galloped along the fields, behind Knotty Knook!"

All of them gazed unbelievingly, as lower down, on the other side of a hill, out of the view of the Zulus, two tall men suddenly appeared from behind some huge rocks. They ran in front of the mounted soldiers. The horses reared up and the soldiers halted. The Commanding Officer raised his arm in defence and shouted out something but the two men shouted back and pointed up towards the rocks, behind which the onlookers were hiding. The Commanding Officer helped one of the men to climb up on to the back of his magnificent stallion and another soldier helped the other man up on to his. The regiment then headed up the hill, directly towards the viewers.

"They are coming up here!" said Flip in panic.

"Stop worrying, they might not see us. Even if they do, why would they think we were a threat when they have Zulus to deal with!" said Steve.

The horses quickly ascended the small hill and stopped just beside the rocks that harboured the concealed spectators. They all held their breath in fear of discovery.

"I think you'll be safe here, Colonel Durnford," said the man on the back of the Commanding Officer's horse. Joni-Pip gasped at the sound of his voice.

"If you follow me carefully, I will guide you to a safe hiding place," said the other man on the back of the other soldier's mount.

"He sure will!" came the familiar voice again. Joni-Pip couldn't see his face, she so wanted to know who it was. "He knows this place like the back of his hand. He was born within a mile of here!"

"Yes, I was. What a noise those Zulus make! No wonder they intimidate their enemies. It's like ten thousand people applauding!"

"Do we know him?" Joni-Pip whispered to Ethelred-Ted.

"He sounds a bit familiar, doesn't he? In fact both of the men do who stopped the soldiers. I'll go and look, perhaps we know them."

Joni-Pip tried to drag him back but he walked round the side of the rock.

"Hello," he said, "do you know the whereabouts of the Old Mine, please?"

There was a pause.

"A red and yellow, talking Teddy Bear!" came the voice of one of the soldiers. "With manners, as well. Now, I've seen everything!"

"My name is Ethelred-Ted. I am a Steiff Bear. I was made in Germany."

"Germany? I'm going there for part of my Post Graduate Course. I'll buy

159

one. I like you you're so neat! Right now, though we have important business to attend to!"

The whooping suddenly stopped and everything went disturbingly silent.

"They are ready. They are coming!" said the Commanding Officer. "I must get my men away to safety. Lead the way, please Gentlemen! Thank you, so!"

"You won't be blamed for this little regiment being wiped out, now, Colonel Durnford. History will be re-written. Follow me," said the local man, "I'll take you to the Old Mine. You will all be safe there, until I can escort you safely back to Natal."

Flip, Steve and Craig drew in their breath.

"I cannot thank you enough. Her Majesty is so indebted to you both."

"I thought it was very unfair that you were blamed for losing most of your men. Now it has been put right," came the voice Joni-Pip recognised.

The tumultuous clapping noise of spear on shield began again.

"I think your Dad should call this hill 'The Clappers', don't you, Jim?" laughed the voice, Joni-Pip recognised. "Let's get to the Old Mine!"

With that the horses and their riders disappeared into the woods.

The man turned and looked at Ethelred-Ted.

"Bye then!" he said and waved and then Ethelred-Ted knew!

Joni-Pip and the others watched them disappear into the trees.

"The Old Mine? Why can't we follow them, Steve?" asked Flip.

"Because my dearest Flip, they are on horseback. How could we keep up? The Old Mine might be miles away from here. Anyway just look!"

Way below them, the whole area was flooded with whooping warriors, wailing their war cries, running down the hill.

They just watched the sight before them in amazement! It was incredible!

"How many are there do you think?" asked Craig.

"According to the History books, Colonel Anthony Durnford had his whole regiment wiped out, apart from two men who escaped to tell the tale, by over twenty thousand Zulus! It was in a place called Isandlwana."

"D'you think there are that many here? asked Flip.

"There are thousands," said Steve, looking at the Zulus swarming like locusts across the fields below them and up on past them and out into the pretty Nottinghamshire countryside: not a typical sight.

They watched them until they disappeared over the brow of another hill.

"I hope they are not heading for Edwinstowe. Seamus O'Hara won't want them making that noise in the Library!" said Joni-Pip, very seriously.

Just then two figures in long, black coats appeared on the hill, by Marley's Barn.

160

"Hello, hello, I think we have more trouble!" said Steve, pointing towards the Barn. "I know these blokes, don't I?"

"Who are they? Where do they come from?" asked Flip, frowning.

"They must be the ones the strange soldiers are looking for but I wouldn't wait around to find out!" said Joni-Pip. "They're always asking about two boys and a girl: kind of scary: most peculiar: a bit sinister. They speak very abruptly and don't have any manners but the silly part is why didn't I tell those odd soldiers about them?"

"Not like us, then!" Craig laughed. "I think we should go, don't you?"

"They're definitely the ones who chased me?" Steve strained to see them.

"Shall we wait and see what they want us for?" asked Flip.

"Er....no!" said Craig. "Let's get out of here! Fast!"

"O.K., I expect we had better go, considering we've been here so long, already. 'Bye then, You Lot!" Steve shouted as he ran into the woods.

"See you later!" said Flip. "I hope I manage to get it right next time!"

"Sorry we still haven't explained!" said Craig and he and Flip ran into the trees after Steve; they turned and waved.

The Two Men in Long, Black Coats came running up.

"Sahen wir gerade die drei Menschen, nach denen wir suchen?" [15] one of them said to Ethelred-Ted.

"Nach welchem drei Menschen suchen Sie? Wie ist ihre Namen?" [16] Ethelred-Ted replied.

"Wir wissen ihre Namen nicht," [17] said the other man abruptly.

"Dann weiß ich nicht, nach wem Sie suchen!" [18] Ethelred-Ted stated.

The men looked perturbed by this curt reply. Joni-Pip couldn't help but turn and look at the stars that were rising above the trees. One of the men watched her suspiciously and then turned and looked and saw the stars, too.

"Sie sind da drüben! Wir müssen eilen!" [19] he said and headed off in the direction of the stars. The other man followed. They ran really fast and soon some more stars drifted up into the Spring sky.

"Well, good bye then! Nice speaking to you again!" laughed Ethelred-Ted.

"Why aren't we worried?" asked Joni-Pip anxiously.

"I don't know, anyway, the others are long gone I should imagine."

"What's this all about?" asked Joni-Pip. "What's going on? Where do

---

[15] Did we just see the three people we are searching for?
[16] Which three people are you looking for? What are their names?
[17] We do not know their names.
[18] Then I do not know who you are looking for.
[19] They are over there! We must hurry!

they come from? Where are they going? Why do they all have glittery bits on their heads and how the Dickens did all those Zulus get here? The answer has to be in the stars!"

"Aye, it just has t' d' wi' the stars in the sky. It must." Hetty stood staring at the stars, glowing like fireworks. "How can we see them in the daytime?"

Joni-Pip then saw the image of the fighter pilot in her head.

"Uh-oh," said Ethelred-Ted, pointing towards the horizon.

They all looked and to their horror they saw the army of Zulus returning.

"They've obviously been thrown out of Edwinstowe Library!" said Hetty.

All four of them ran back to the safety of the rocks and watched and waited. The sound of thousands of bare feet, thundered down in front of them.

Ethelred-Ted wanted to get a better look, so he poked his head round the side of the rock, just as one of the warriors looked sideways! Their eyes met and the Zulu started immediately to run up the hill towards them.

He got so close, they could hear his deep breathing.

"This is it," whispered Joni-Pip, "now we are done for!"

The Zulu started to go round the side of the big rock that was shielding them when a stern voice from lower down shouted out in a strange tongue. The Zulu replied in a very loud staccato voice and then continued to search around the back of the rock. Joni-Pip crouched down low on the floor, grabbing Ethelred-Ted as she did so. Poppy flew up into a nearby tree and Hetty curled up into a neat ball. The Zulu then came round the back of the rock. He made a short loud noise. Joni-Pip froze. She heard the whooshing sound of the spear being raised. She felt the warrior's breath on her face. She lifted her head up and looked him straight in the eyes. He moved his arm quickly and brought his spear down....gently touching her on the head with it. He tapped her head lightly several times, as softly as if with a feather. Then he grunted and ran back round to the front of the rock and down the hill to join his warring comrades.

"Whew!" said Joni-Pip and Ethelred-Ted, laughing. "That was close!"

"Actually, I am still shaking!" Joni-Pip hugged her Teddy Bear.

"Don't they run fast!" said Poppy from the branch of a tree.

"Where are they, Ma Pet? Can y' fly up and see where they are going?"

"Odd," called Poppy, flying above them. "All I can see is a mass of stars!"

"And so can we!" said Hetty, Joni-Pip and Ethelred-Ted, watching thousands of tiny sparkling stars rise in the sky over towards Berry Bush.

As Joni-Pip was gazing at the stars, in the corner of her eye, she saw movement in the trees beside them, she turned and saw the tail end of a figure wearing a long grey hooded cloak, disappearing behind a tree. She ran towards the woods. Ethelred-Ted ran after her.

"Where d'you think you're going?" he laughed, as he caught her up.

"It's him again! The man in the hood. Who is he? Where's he going?"

"Steady on Joni-Pip and what makes you think it is a 'he' it might be a 'she'? It's really strange that we never see him or her!" Eth laughed again.

"This is another time that I have seen him and you haven't," Joni-Pip sighed. "It must mean something. I'm confused. Who do you think he is?"

"Don't worry about him, he's probably some tramp looking for food and shelter round here, Joni-Pip, "he's got nothing to do with us, I'm sure."

The four of them then continued on their way up to Marley's Barn, chatting away as if none of these startling events had happened at all.

Nuttingham Squirrel came rushing round the corner of the woodland path that led back to Berry Bush. He had come from the Clappers.

"Lovely day!" called out Ethelred-Ted, waving.

Nuttingham Squirrel appeared not to see him and moved hastily on.

"Hey to ye, Nuttingham Squirrel, 'n how 're ye t'day?" Hetty greeted him.

The Squirrel continued walking very quickly and paid no heed to her.

"Where are you off to, today, Nuttingham Squirrel?" Joni-Pip attempted.

The squirrel seemed oblivious.

"Oh, Nuts to him!" said Ethelred-Ted. "Why should we bother any more?"

This comment made Hetty the Wee and Joni-Pip laugh. However, Poppy took off and flew directly into his path, flapping gently in front of him.

"Out of my way, you Potty Pigeon!" he shrieked, madly waving his arms. He was irked and annoyed by Poppy's invasion of his space. He flayed his arms faster and faster, round and round, like a windmill, as Poppy got closer and closer to his face. The flapping of her wings became wilder and wilder.

"You will not ignore my friends!" Poppy whacked Nuttingham Squirrel on his face with her wide-spread wings The squirrel began to cough and splutter, as little feathers got in his mouth and up his nose.

"Don't ever do that again! Do you hear me? When anyone says 'hello' to you, then you stop and listen and reply! Do you hear me? Are you heeding?"

"Get off me, you dangerously unbalanced Bird! Yes I'll speak to you and your friends!"

With that he ran off and disappeared into the woods.

"Youa ara quita magnifisso. I ama so impresseda witha youa strength."

164

Poppy spun round in horror and saw Macca perched directly above her.

"Er....how long have you been there?"

"Longa enougha," he said gently; then he turned to Ethelred-Ted.

"Ees she allaways like-a thissa?"

"Er....Poppy....er....no," came his straight reply, "she's much worse!"

Everybody roared with laughter, even Poppy-Plump-Pij managed a smile.

"She's actually the sweetest, kindest creature you could ever imagine," explained Joni-Pip, worrying that Poppy might be sad if nobody told the truth.

"Area youa sure-a about thessa, I notta see thessa witha the squirrel!"

Poppy made a thoughtful face. Macca turned and looked at her.

"Woulda youa likea to coma upa fora flighta? Eet is a beautiful daya."

"I would like that very much," she replied softly and blushed.

At that, the two love birds flew off into the clear blue sky.

"You ara so Baby!" he said gently to her as they started their ascent.

Poppy didn't understand what he meant but it sounded so romantic!

"So, please, tell us, what was the outcome of the meeting between Alex, you and Archimedes?" Ethelred-Ted asked Joni-Pip, as they walked to Marley's Barn, oblivious of the Pageant that had just unfurled before them.

"Well, you know we were discussing the little star-like symbol between the H and the 2?" Joni-Pip stopped and looked at her friends.

"Yes," they both replied.

"Well, we....they think it's the symbol for....snow," she said slowly.

"Snow?" questioned both Hetty the Wee and Ethelred-Ted together.

"Yes, snow!"

"Snow? M,M 'n M! Snow? Unbelievable! So simple!" enthused Ethelred-Ted.

"They decided that water turning into snow, was the secret behind the Formula!"

"Hmmmm....sno-ow, that really is fascinating!" said Ethelred-Ted.

"What fer, Ma Pets? Why would they want t' make water into snow?"

"Something to do with JITTING?" Eth said slowly. "I never got round to telling you of my Plan. What I would use the Formula for, if I only knew how to use it!"

"No, you didn't, we're always being distracted!" laughed Joni-Pip.

"Right then, we had better get to and do it!" Ethelred-Ted stood up.

"Do what?" Hetty the Wee and Joni-Pip asked together.

"Get on with some trials. We must consult Alex and Archimedes and find out what we need. Look, You Two, all I know is we have been given a gift, an amazing gift. I don't know why, I just know I had it when we came out of Marley's Barn, the night of the Storm. Something happened in there that night and we have to do something about it....we just can't waste it, now, can we?"

"Of course not!" came Hetty the Wee and Joni-Pip.

"We have been given it for a reason, it must be so that we can do something good with it. I know what I want to do with it but I am not telling you what that is until we successfully come up with something positive." Ethelred-Ted sounded so earnest.

"I will pick Alex's brain, Eth and then we can go and see Archimedes," said Joni-Pip.

The next few days were very exciting. Alex and Archimedes worked on the Formula and kept trying it out in the Laboratory. All they did was produce water and flooded the place, many, many times. Eth silently kept storing up the information he had gleaned, determining that one day, he, too, would have a go.

He questioned the old Inventor and asked him how long he had been a TAWP. Archimedes replied that he had no idea. He hazily remembered that it was something to do with the Past but he couldn't remember how. Joni-Pip, Eth, Hetty and Poppy just presumed he must be a really kind and caring but very misunderstood, TAWP.

After a few days of relentless experimenting and coming up with nothing.....except gallons of very wet water, reluctantly Alex and Archimedes decided to leave things for a while and 'go back to the drawing board'; well, the Formula Board, at least!

Chapter 19

Success

It was a rainy day and Mother, Joni-Pip and Becky-Paige had just finished having morning lessons in the School Room at Knotty Knook.

"Is anything the matter, Darling?" Mother asked.

"Hmmm....nothing really," Joni-Pip replied dreamily.

"You don't seem quite here with us sometimes. This morning you were always looking out of the window. You're sure there is nothing you want to talk about?".

"You all right, Sissa?" Becky-Paige copied Mother's concerned face.

"I am fine, You Two, stop fussing!" laughed Joni-Pip.

Mother looked relieved. Becky-Paige looked relieved.

"You make me laugh, Becky-Paige, that's such a funny face you are pulling!" chuckled Joni-Pip. Her sister looked hurt so Joni-Pip hugged her.

"Becky-Paige, I love you so much, please don't ever change, will you?"

Mother walked over to her two daughters and put her arms around them.

"Joni-Philipa, so everything is fine? You seem so far away these days."

"Mother, I think I'm just becoming more and more like Alex, that's all. Probably I'm spending too much time with him!" laughed Joni-Pip, then she once again looked out of the window. "Do you think I could go and see Grandfather, please? It seems ages since I saw him last and forever since I was at the Crooked Cottage!"

"But it's raining, Joni-Philipa, you will get soaked," replied Mother.

Joni-Pip slopped about in the mud as she tried to run up the Log and Chain Path leading into Windy Woods. It hadn't taken much persuasion for Mother to allow her to go and see Grandfather; she had spoken to him the day before, asking him to try and find out what was troubling her twelve-year-old. So, togged up in her Macintosh, rain hat and Wellingtons, Joni-Pip was venturing forth, despite the pouring rain.

"Come in and get those wet clothes off, Cherry-Plum!" said Grandfather, ushering Joni-Pip into the kitchen and helping her off with her Macintosh. Joni-Pip pulled off her dripping rain hat and shook it, sprinkling the kittens that were peacefully sleeping in the basket. They all stirred gently, yawned and promptly went back to sleep. She sat on a wooden chair and Grandfather knelt down and pulled off her muddy Wellington boots.

"I'll put these in the sink, I think that's best. I'll rinse them off and they

167

can dry out while we have a nice cup of tea," said Grandfather, getting up from off his knees.

Joni-Pip ran her fingers through her tousled hair and then crouched down to stroke the kittens.

"It's a bit rough out there, today, Grandfather but I enjoyed the journey across the wood. I haven't seen Hetty the Wee or Poppy-Plump-Pij, yet."

She tunnelled her fingers in the soft, kitten fur.

"I should think they are being sensible and staying in the warm somewhere. Where's Ethelred-Ted? Didn't you bring him?"

Joni-Pip looked a bit sheepish.

"I suppose I should have brought him. He hates being dependant on me for his freedom but it was raining so hard. Mother would have stopped me anyway," she replied, consoling herself, "and of course he hates getting wet: soggy fur and all that!"

"What's he doing then, anything exciting?" Grandfather asked casually.

"Well...." started Joni-Pip: she hated having secrets from the grown-up she adored the most in the whole world but after thinking about it, she knew she couldn't tell him anything; it was so Top Secret. "He's probably got his head in some book, some Dickens' Novel. Grandfather, where is the place you took us to once, you know the place that came straight out of Dickens' Time?" She cleverly steered the subject.

"Dickens' Time?" Her grandfather frowned.

"Yes, don't you remember it? Father drove us in the Bentley and you showed us this wondrous place. The beautiful little cottages went right down on to the beach and there was a weir and a Blacksmith's....you said it was just like Jo Gargery's in Great Expectations; not that I've read it. There was this old breakwater made up of dried out stakes of wood. You said you could just imagine a witch going past on a boat."

"A witch? Now you have lost me!" puzzled Grandfather. Then he thought and chuckled. "Ah....you mean 'Magwich'....he was a character in the book! I know where you mean, it's a place in Somerset, near Minehead, it's called Porlock, Porlock Weir."

"That's it, Porlock Weir, Grandfather. I remember it was this extraordinary place. It was kind of odd but very fascinating."

Joni-Pip was relieved. Her desire to tell her grandfather about all the wonderful things that were going on in her life had subsided. She felt happy that these incredible secrets about the Formula were still safely tucked up in her heart and mind.

"Where's that cup of tea you promised?" she grinned at her grandfather.

"Let's go into the parlour. The kettle is boiling on the fire," said Grandfather, gently rubbing the top of his granddaughter's head.

The two of them walked arm in arm down the hall and into the parlour. Halfway down, Joni-Pip stopped and looked at the painting on the wall. It was a Landscape.

"I love this picture, Grandfather. Who painted it?"

"I did, Cherry-Plum, when I was at College. It's very old now, like me! Come on the kettle will be boiling its little bottom off!"

"That's silly, Grandfather."

"What's silly, Cherry-Plum?"

"You said, 'the kettle's boiling', it's not the kettle that's boiling, is it?"

"Yes?" came a puzzled reply.

"It's not, Grandfather, it's not the kettle that's boiling," laughed Joni-Pip.

"And what exactly is it that's on my fire in the Parlour and is boiling then?" smiled Grandfather.

"People always say that....Mrs Broft....she says, 'That there kettle, that's a boilin' '....Mother says, 'the kettle is boiling, Alex, please would you make us a nice cup of tea?'....Father says to Mother, 'Honey, the kettle is boiling, how about a coffee?'....and you of course....you just said it to me, 'The kettle will be boiling its little bottom off'. Well it's not, is it?"

"Cherry-Plum, if it's not the kettle that's boiling, what on earth is?"

"The water, that's what's boiling, the water **in** the kettle is boiling!"

"Of course! You're right! I've just never thought of it before. We always say, 'the kettle's boiling'. You're a One, Joni-Philipa," he chuckled.

"If the kettle was boiling, then the metal would melt....the only way I think you could actually boil a kettle is, quite frankly, in a furnace!"

Grandfather pulled his granddaughter into him and gave her a hug.

"You are a special child, what would we do without you?"

Of course at this moment in Time, Grandfather had actually once lived the rest of his days without her but thanks to the Turning of the KOL and the Gift of Déjà Vu, he now was re-living these years in another Circle. This time, however, it was not with the sadness of being without her but it was with the joy of being with her.

Like Knotty Knook, the Parlour was one of those rooms that hugged you, the moment you walked in. The logs on the fire hissed, crackled and spat, producing beautiful red and yellow flames. Joni-Pip nestled herself in the big armchair at the side of the hearth and cuddled her hot cup of tea. Three of the cats were curled up, latticed together on the rug in front of the fire. The Grandfather clock ticked away in harmony with the rain, which was still beating on the windows outside. It was so cosy. Grandfather went back to the kitchen and returned carrying his large biscuit tin. He levered off the lid and held it out for his granddaughter. Joni-Pip peered in.

"Rock cakes, Grandfather, how delicious!" Her face lit up and she took one out and bit into it. Grandfather took one for himself, put the tin on the low table in front of them and settled down in his very favourite, fireside chair.

"Everything all right?" he asked.

Joni-Pip nodded, she was far too busy enjoying her rock cake to talk.

"You're happy?"

Joni-Pip nodded again.

"Nothing is bothering you, right now?" He tried not to sound too serious.

Joni-Pip shook her head.

"So....everything's all right?"

"Grandfather, I'm fine. The tea is yummy and the rock cake is scrummy."

"No, Cherry-Plum, I wasn't asking you about the tea and the cake, I meant are you fine? Is your life happy at the moment?"

"Grandfather....my life is very happy right now. I hardly ever think about Bath. Please don't think I've forgotten my beautiful city, of course I haven't, or Angela or Mona. It's just that I'm settled here now and I have so many exciting things going on at present that I don't really have time to worry about missing my school, my friends and my house," said Joni-Pip, taking another crumbly bite of her delicious cake.

"Good, Cherry-Plum. Can you remember how sad you were when you first left Bath? You said you felt you would never be happy with the Life in the Wood, do you remember? Tell about these exciting things that are going on in your life right now?"

Joni-Pip screwed up her face.

"Grandfather, I can't tell you," she replied slowly. "I'd love to but I can't."

"Why not?" Grandfather looked concerned.

"Because they are very secret, very Top Secret, even," replied Joni-Pip in a whisper, as if people were listening to their confidential talk.

"Has it got anything to do with this terrible War?" He looked very serious.

"The War? The War, Grandfather?" repeated Joni-Pip. "No."

Grandfather looked a bit surprised but very relieved.

"So what's it to do with, this very Top Secret stuff that seems to be occupying your time and energy, leaving you no room for anything else?"

"Hmmm," said Joni-Pip politely. "Interesting!" then she laughed.

"What do you mean 'Hmmm. Interesting'?" asked Grandfather.

"I can't tell you what it's all about, it's Top Secret. Just so that you don't worry, though, I will say that Alex and Archimedes Spindlethrop are both connected with it."

170

"Archimedes? Archimedes Spindlethrop? What has he got to do with it?" Grandfather roared. Joni-Pip was a bit taken aback. All her life she had known her grandfather and she had never ever heard even a glimmer of anger from him.

She felt quite strange. It was not nice.

"Are you all right, Grandfather?" she asked quietly.

"I just don't want you having anything to do with that....that awful man."

"Awful? Grandfather, Archimedes...." Joni-Pip started.

"And I won't have his name mentioned in my house, if you don't mind, either!" He snapped and shook his head violently.

Large tears began to fill Joni-Pip's eyes and she let out a little sob. Immediately Grandfather felt cross with himself. He got up from his chair and went over to his granddaughter and put his strong arm around her shoulders. The broken tears began to roll down her cheeks. He took out his handkerchief and wiped them away.

"Cherry-Plum, I am so sorry, so, so sorry. Please forgive me? I didn't mean to growl at you like that. I don't know what came over me. That was a very bad thing to do and I regret it so much. I hope you will still love me?" he pleaded.

Joni-Pip smiled.

"Of course I love you, Grandfather. I didn't mean to make you cross."

"No, no you didn't, my Little Cherry-Plum and I'm not cross with you, at all. I'm simply cross with myself. Let's forget it ever happened shall we?"

For some reason Joni-Pip felt sad: not just because her grandfather had momentarily been cross with her but because she was puzzled at how Archimedes could have had that effect on him. As she sat sipping her tea, she couldn't help but be intrigued by what it could possibly be that had caused this bad feeling between them. She wondered if it was Archimedes' usual rudeness but then she thought that Grandfather was much too nice a person to allow such a trivial thing to upset him. He was such a kind man, always ready to forgive and understand. No, she decided, it had to be something much more serious than that. She couldn't think what it might be but she was determined that some day she would find out.

"I wonder what happened between them, then?"

"I don't know, Eth but it was something pretty important to make Grandfather so cross about him," replied Joni-Pip.

Surprisingly, her Teddy Bear hadn't been too upset that he had been left in the School Room the day before. He had been so busy trying to sort out the Formula recently that he hadn't had the time to start reading, **The Time**

171

Machine, the book Joni-Pip had got down from the book case for him, some days earlier. He spent the whole day reading it. It was quite cosy sitting in the window seat with the rain pitter-pattering down the panes. In fact he was quite glad he hadn't had to go outside with Joni-Pip. One thing that was for certain, was that Teddy Bears really hated getting wet and another thing that was for certain, was that rain was always wet! Wet fur didn't only feel horrid but wet fur smelt unpleasant as well and it was such a bother to dry! So for him to stay warm and dry in the School Room reading, was far preferable to getting wet and soggy in the pouring rain. Anyway, he was hoping that H.G. Wells, who wrote the book The Time Machine, might give him some clues as to how to get Time Travel, or in their case, JITTING, in motion. It was published in 1895; it was only just over 100 pages long but acclaimed as a very progressive story. He wondered if H.G. Wells had experienced Déjà Vu, himself, as he wrote about such an incredible subject as Time Travel. Did the great Nineteenth Century Writer give the Inquisitive Bear any signs?

Well, unfortunately he didn't: none at all: not even a wisp of a trace.

Despite this lack of help, Ethelred-Ted really enjoyed reading The Time Machine, although he did feel it was a little far fetched.

After the rain of the day before, the wood felt fresh and clean. Poppy said it was a natural cleansing when it rained: she was always in favour of a good downpour. The persistent rain, however cleansing it might have been, left the ground too soggy to sit on the grass so the four friends decided to sit on the crumbling walls of the Ruin.

Hetty, Poppy and Ethelred-Ted had all been intrigued about Grandfather. They were so surprised when Joni-Pip related to them what had happened in his Parlour, the day before. Joni-Pip said that she couldn't stop thinking about it and kept wondering and trying to guess what could have happened between the two old men.

"I'm sure we'll find out one day, Ma Pets, we just have to be patient in these matters."

"I don't want to be patientful," said Poppy-Plump-Pij firmly, "so when I see him next, I am going to ask Archimedes what went on."

"That seems a very sensible idea, Pops!" laughed Eth. "Straight to the point!"

"I worry that might not be too sensible," Joni-Pip said cautiously. "Perhaps there is a big problem between the two of them, Poppy...."

"Yes, thinking about it, we need Archimedes in a good mood while he is working on the Formula, we really don't want to upset him, do we?" interrupted Ethelred-Ted, "We don't want to set Poppy on him, again, do we?"

"No!" Hetty, Poppy and Joni-Pip chorused together.

Everybody then burst out laughing.

"What I would like to do," said Ethelred-Ted, still smiling, "is get into Archimedes' Quission Hut and have a go at the Formula myself....now that would be worth a try!"

"What, break in?" questioned Joni-Pip excitedly.

"No, not exactly," replied the Teddy Bear, looking a bit naughty.

"What d' y' mean 'not exactly'?" laughed Hetty the Wee.

"Well, not exactly 'break in'...." he replied, "more like....sneak in!"

This last comment caused more bursting forth with laughter. In fact Poppy made a very high pitched, giggling sort of noise. Her friends all looked at her.

"What was that?" asked Joni-Pip, still laughing. "It sounded most peculiar; a cross between a squeak and a giggle!"

"A squiggle!" squiggled Poppy.

More squiggles then emerged from them all!

"So, Ma Wee Lamb, how do y' propose t' do this....this sneaking in without breaking in?" asked Hetty, still laughing,

"I don't know, I haven't decided yet!"

This remark brought about even more laughter from all of them, so much so, that they all ended up holding their sides with the pain of their aching.

"It strikes me we laugh a lot these days!" said Ethelred-Ted.

They all carried on laughing while thinking about his comment.

"I love us being laughful!" exclaimed Poppy-Plump-Pij. "Isn't it lovely and do you know, it's been since the storm up at Marley's Barn?"

"Ye are so right, Hen!"

For some reason they all stopped laughing and became very quiet.

"Something wonderful happened up there, that day. Something that has affected us all. I don't know what it is. I have my theories mind, as you know," said Eth seriously and then added, "whatever it was, it was a good thing!"

"Especially so, if it makes us laugh a lot!" said Joni-Pip happily.

"Well let's go over to Hideaway Cottage and see if we can 'sneak' in?" suggested Poppy. "That will really be a good thing....and a good laugh!"

They looked at each other; started laughing again and then they set off.

Eureka came walking up towards them, as they arrived at Hideaway Cottage. As usual, his tail was bolt upright and he was purring very loudly. All of them felt so welcomed. How different this was from the first time! They called out to Archimedes and as usual, silence was their loud reply!

"Let's go round to the Quission Hut!" laughed Ethelred-Ted.

"Vision Hut?"

"I think that's a pretty good description, Pops." He thought for a second, "Well, sometimes!"

They all laughed again and made their way round to the side of the cottage and on to Archimedes' Laboratory. They rattled on the door. Nobody stirred. They knocked on the door. Nobody came. They called out. Nobody answered. Ethelred-Ted tried the door and it was unlocked, so he pushed it open and poked his face round the edge, straining to see if anyone was there. The place was deserted, so he beckoned his friends to follow him in. They were very surprised to see that things had changed in the Quission Hut.

In the middle of the room, Archimedes had put a large metal tank. Proceeding from the sides of the tank, were two pipes, which then led on to a second tank. Under the first tank was a kind of log fire. It was just a metal basket really, holding three or four logs.

"Hmmmm!" said Ethelred-Ted, examining the equipment in front of him. "I see what's going on here, don't you?" He ran his paws over the pipes, following their course from one tank to the other.

"I haven't the faintest idea!" answered Joni-Pip, in awe of her Ted.

"They are distilling....heating up some gas in this tank," he said pointing to the first tank, "and then cooling it down in this tank," he gestured towards the second tank.

"And, Ma Pet?"

"I think he....they....are trying to make snow....well sort of....it's latent heat transfer, isn't it?" he continued, sounding exceptionally clever.

"Latent heat transfer?" Joni-Pip screwed up her face.

"Late and heat tans fur?" asked Poppy-Plump-Pij sweetly.

Ethelred-Ted smiled.

"Nearly, Poppy," he said kindly, "but I think we call it 'latent heat transfer'....let me explain."

"Aye, please do!" said Hetty the Wee eagerly.

"Right," Eth instructed, "what I want you all to do is lick.... Joni-Pip, your wrist ....Poppy, your leg....and Hetty, your paw....immediately afterwards, I want you to blow on it and then tell me what it feels like." [20]

All three of his friends obeyed.

"Why it starts off warm and then it feels so cold!" exclaimed Joni-Pip.

"Aye, it does!" said Hetty the Wee excitedly, which was very rare.

"Even I can do it!" cried Poppy, thrilled. "It's hot then cold!"

"That's it....you have all done it....you have made heat, by licking your wrist, leg and paw and then you have transferred that latent heat you made, by blowing on it and you made it transfer into cold," he said proudly.

"I'm beginning to understand....do you think then that Alex and Archimedes are trying to make...." started Joni-Pip.

"Snow?" questioned Hetty the Wee.

"Yes, I do and very clever they are as well!" replied the Bear and then he added, "I wonder if they succeeded? They are such very clever Boys."

Hetty the Wee, Poppy-Plump-Pij and Joni-Pip all looked at Ethelred-Ted admiringly and Hetty spoke for them all, when she said,

"And so are ye, Ma Pet!"

Ethelred-Ted smiled modestly and whispered,

"I don't think so," sounding very pleased, all the same.

Joni-Pip couldn't help but notice how different this was from the bossy, arrogant bear she had first come to know at her Awakening. She wondered,

'Could this be something else to do with the storm at Marley's Barn?'

Just then, she heard the noise of someone closing the door of the Quission Hut, she turned sharply to see the handle being turned from the outside of the door.

"Who is that? Who is there?" she called running up to the door.

"What are you doing, Joni-Pip?" asked Ethelred-Ted.

"Somebody has just closed the door, I'm going to find out who it is!" she replied opening the door and looking out. She saw no-one.

Ethelred-Ted, Hetty and Poppy all joined her and looked out of the opened door.

"There's nobody around, Joni-Pip!" said Poppy surveying the empty garden in front of them.

"But someone closed the door, I saw the handle move!"

---

[20] Grateful thanks to the Refrigeration Expert I met in the Lobby of the Coppid Beech Hotel, Bracknell, during the Summer of 2005!   Carrie King

"Seeing things again, are we?" asked Ethelred-Ted gently.

"No I am not seeing things!" shouted Joni-Pip.

"What are you seeing then?" asked Poppy.

"Things," replied Joni-Pip, which was followed by a pause and then heaps of laughter.

"Look!" said Joni-Pip pointing up the hill. "There he is again, the man in the cloak with the hood!"

They all looked but saw nothing. Joni-Pip just caught the back of his cloak as he disappeared into a clump of thick bushes.

"Oh, he's gone again. One day you will believe me!" said Joni-Pip sadly.

"I am sure we will. Look, You Lot, there's a whole heap of logs stacked over there, we can replace the ones we use: why don't we go and light the fire and try the experiment? Let's make some snow!" Eth suggested enthusiastically, trying to raise Joni-Pip's spirits.

Everybody looked shocked.

"You....don't really mean that, do you?" laughed Joni-Pip nervously.

"Y' are joking aren't y'?" half-laughed Hetty.

"Let's do it!" said Poppy; always ready to try something new.

Just then the door burst open and in ran Flip, Steve and Craig.

"Hello Folks, it's us again!" said Flip. They all exchanged greetings.

"I still have no idea where the Old Mine is," laughed Joni-Pip. "Why is it I don't remember you, when you have gone?"

"I think you could work that one out for yourself, if you think about it long enough!" replied Flip, nodding her head.

"No, I don't think I could," said Joni-Pip thoughtfully.

"It will come!" laughed Craig. "What we've learnt, is that we can JIT as many times as we like, as long as it is to do with the same Orbit."

"Really?" asked Ethelred-Ted. "I wonder if I will remember that?"

"You won't. Sorry!" replied Steve.

"So tell me, who are you? Why do you want to know where the Old Mine is? How come you keep turning up? You seem to know exactly where we are, all the time. Are you following us? How come I know you?" asked Joni-Pip.

"All these questions!" laughed Flip. "Inquisitive Little Person wasn't .... aren't you? There's no point in us telling you because you will forget everything when we leave."

"Why do you need to know the whereabouts of the Old Mine, though?" asked Ethelred-Ted. "You can at least tell us that!"

"Er....no I don't think we can," said Craig. "It is for your protection. We have no idea who these men are, these ones who are following us but they could be...."

"Dangerous and we don't want to put you at any risk!" finished Steve.

"Vee 'aff you at last!" came a loud voice from the door.

They all spun round and in horror, they saw the Two Men in Long, Black Coats, standing in the doorway. Joni-Pip was nervous, this time.

"Vy are you zo difficult?" asked the other man.

"**Wofür wollen Sie diese?**" [21] asked Ethelred-Ted.

"**Es ist nicht für Sie, um zu wissen. Es ist eine Sache der Staatssicherheit.**" [22] replied the first man.

"What are we going to do?" asked Steve. "What do they want?"

"Wait until they come in and then run round the back of the tanks and out of the door," ordered Ethelred-Ted without looking at them. He then said,

"**Eingegangen und lassen uns darüber vernünftig sprechen.**" [23]

The two men walked towards them, away from the door.

"Now!" said Ethelred-Ted quietly. Steve, Flip and Craig ran round to the back of the tanks. The two men gave chase. Ethelred-Ted immediately ran to the door. Steve, Craig and Flip came round the other side, from the back of the tanks and ran straight out of the door.

"When you speak to Archimedes, Alex or Mother, don't forget to ask them where the Old Mine is. The location!" shouted Flip, as Ethelred-Ted quickly closed the door and bolted it behind them.

"**Sie dummer deutscher sprechender Bär!**"[24] shouted one of the men. When they got to the door they both tried to unbolt it and a struggle ensued.

"**Verlassen Sie es! Lassen Sie mich es tun!**"[25] shot one of the men, pushing the other one out of the way.

"**Wirklich bin ich nicht nur ein deutscher sprechender Bär, ich bin ein deutscher Bär!**" [26] said Eth, as they finally opened the door and ran off.

"I hope they got away all right!" said Joni-Pip. "Did you learn anything?"

"I'm sure they did. I think these men are spies!" he replied.

"Spies?" echoed Hetty and Poppy.

The face of the Fighter Pilot then went flying through Joni-Pip's mind.

Everything returned to normal, they remembered nothing.

Excitedly, they lit the logs under the tank. That was very easy to do, as

---

[21] What do you want these for?
[22] It is not for you to know. It is a matter of National Security.
[23] Come in and let us talk about this sensibly.
[24] You stupid German speaking Bear!
[25] Leave it! Let me do it!
[26] Actually, I am not just a German speaking Bear, I am a German Bear!

Archimedes and Alex had obviously set it all up to start again. The logs burned very quickly and soon the tank was getting warm.

"Are we boiling the tank like a kettle?" asked Poppy-Plump-Pij.

"No we are not!" replied Joni-Pip.

"But we are, Joni-Pip, that's exactly what we are doing, boiling the tank...." explained Ethelred-Ted.

"Not you as well," said Joni-Pip and she sighed.

"What d'ye mean, 'not him as well'?"

"I had this conversation with Grandfather, yesterday." said Joni-Pip.

"But Joni-Pip that's what we are doing; there's no getting away from it....we are boiling the tank...." tried the Bear once more.

"No, Eth, we're boiling whatever it is IN the tank!" she said crossly.

Ethelred-Ted thought for a minute and then laughed.

"Munchy Mash n' Mustard!" he exclaimed. "You're right....so right!"

"Right? I know I am!" laughed Joni-Pip, shaking her head.

Suddenly a noise was heard coming from the door. They all froze.

"We are discovered!" whispered Hetty the Wee.

"Let's hide!" Poppy-Plump-Pij suggested and promptly flew up on to a large rafter above and disappeared from view.

"It's all right for some." said Eth quietly. "Teddy Bears weren't given wings....!"

Hetty the Wee and Joni-Pip started to laugh.

"Shhhhhh!" reprimanded the wingless bear. "We had better find somewhere where we can't be seen. I have seen some barrels around: maybe we can hide behind them?"

"Where are they then?" asked Joni-Pip softly. "I haven't seen any."

Although it was daylight outside, the light in the Quission Hut was not very good. Possibly this was due to the fact that there weren't many windows in the building and those that were, hardly allowed any light to filter through, anyway. It was a point of debate as to whether any of the windows had ever been cleaned, since the place had been built. Even if they had, Archimedes used up every available space on the window sills to stack up various items and articles necessary to carry out his experiments, so it just wasn't possible to see either in or out of the murky, green, mildew-covered glass!

"It's a bit dark to see anything!" said Hetty the Wee, as quietly as she could. "Where did you say the barrels were, Eth?"

"Not quite sure but if you follow me I think I will find them," whispered back Ethelred-Ted, beckoning with his paw for them to follow.

The door creaked and slowly opened. The three friends suddenly panicked and all scuttled off in different directions. Joni-Pip managed to

178

find a pretty good hiding place, crouching down and lodging herself under Archimedes desk. Hetty found a little empty box and crept inside it.

Ethelred-Ted was not nearly so fortunate. In his haste to find the barrels to hide behind, he bumped straight into one and fell forwards, giving it a mighty knock. The barrel immediately began to roll, so he desperately tried to stop it. [[I don't know if any of you Readers have ever tried this....well, don't!]] This resulted in his body being pulled over with the barrel and he ended up being thrown upside down against the tank that had the fire burning under it. Unbeknown to him, there was a lever on the side of the tank and in his quest to stop himself from falling further, the Bear grabbed hold of this metal bar, to steady himself. The lever moved. There was a dial behind the lever and on the dial there were different settings, set out like this :-

MINIMUM/ COOL/WARM/HOT / MAXIMUM/ **DANGER**

When Ethelred-Ted took hold of the lever it was pointing to:-

WARM

When he let go of the lever it was pointing to:-

MAXIMUM.

....but of course he didn't notice.

The noisy barrel continued on its ramble through the Quission Hut, running over and cracking or squashing anything that came in its path: pots, pens, pencils, pieces of paper or pipes. Eventually, it came to rest up against Archimedes' desk. Joni-Pip, who was still bent up, crouched underneath it, let out a little cry, as the barrel thudded into the wood, shaking her folded body and trapping her up against the wall, with no way out. Fortunately, she could see through the tiny crack that was left between the top of the barrel and the bottom of the desktop. She listened, as the door continued to creak open. The usually intrepid Ethelred-Ted, held his breath and ducked down, behind one of the experimental tanks. Joni-Pip's eyes looked anxiously through her tiny peephole.

As for Hetty? She just closed her eyes and did what most hedgehogs would do under the circumstances....she rolled up into a tight ball.

Poppy-Plump-Pij, who was surveying all these shenanigans from her vantage point behind a large beam, poked her head gently round to have a good look and see who was coming into the Quission Hut.

The door finally hit hard up against a wooden bench and everybody feared what discovery might bring.

"Meow!" came a familiar voice. "Meow, meow!"

"Eureka!" chorused all four of them.

The black cat strolled into the Quission Hut, totally unaware of the panic that his arrival had caused.

179

"Get me out of here!" laughed Joni-Pip, from her crunched up position.

"Where are you then?" asked Eth, immerging from behind the tank.

"I'm over here!"

"Where? I can't see you!" he called out.

Hetty the Wee, by this time had unfurled her prickly little body and walked in the direction of the voice.

"She's under the work desk, up against the wall!" called out Poppy.

Ethelred-Ted walked over to the barrel and tried to shift it away from the desk but it wouldn't move. Joni-Pip looked through the gap and laughed,

"Hmmmmm. Perhaps this wasn't such a good idea after all, was it? Whose idea was it to sneak in, anyway?"

Poppy-Plump-Pij flew down to help and Hetty the Wee used her little body against the might of the barrel.

"Come on Eureka, help us!" invited Ethelred-Ted. "After all, it was your entrance that caused all this! Anyway, why don't you talk? Aren't you a TAWC, a Toy and Animal World Cat? It doesn't make sense."

"I must admit I have wondered that myself, Hen. He does appear to understand us, doesn't he but he never utters a word!"

"There has a to be a good reason why he's not talkful: maybe we'll find out one day," added Poppy, looking at the bemused cat.

"It's all very intriguing but I really need you to get me out!" said Joni-Pip.

The four of them, Hetty the Wee, Poppy-Plump-Pij, Ethelred-Ted and Eureka all pushed and shoved at the barrel but it seemed unmovable.

"Isn't there anything you can do to help, Joni-Pip?" asked Poppy.

"It's a bit cramped in here, to say the least but if I twist myself a bit, I might be able to give the barrel a nudge with my feet."

With great difficulty but incredible force, she managed to swivel her body round and sit on the floor. Both feet were now resting on the side of the barrel.

"Right, I think this will take some Team effort!" she encouraged. "When I say, 'push', then all push on the side of the barrel, away from the desk: right?"

Everyone nodded, which of course she didn't see, positioned themselves up against the barrel and braced themselves for an almighty thrust.

"Ready?" questioned Joni-Pip.

"Yes!" her three friends replied, audibly this time.

"Meow!" came from Eureka, who actually wasn't much help, his attention had been slightly diverted, by a mischievous field mouse, who had strayed into the Quission Hut and was now running across the length of one of the beams, above him. Although it was quite out of reach, it was much too tantalising to stop Eureka from observing the scurrying creature.

"Here we go then! Push!" shouted Joni-Pip. They pushed and pushed.

The barrel didn't move.

"Again!" came Joni-Pip's command. They used all their strength and might to try and budge the barrel but to no avail.

"I think you had better settle down and we'll go and get help," said Eth.

"But who will you get? You can only talk to Archimedes."

"And Grandfather!" said Poppy-Plump-Pij proudly.

"Er....bit of a problem here, I think," said Joni-Pip, "remember they are not friendly and all that!"

"Goodness gracious, yes, Ma Pet."

"There has to be a way. We can't leave you here....it might be all night. We don't know where Archimedes is now, do we?" asked Ethelred-Ted.

"We have to think of something!" said Poppy. "Shall I go and get Macca?"

"No!" chorused her three friends.

"Oh!" she said disappointedly.

"I don't actually know that he would make any difference, Pops," said Ethelred-Ted kindly and then added, "but it was a good suggestion!"

Poppy-Plump-Pij blushed and felt much better!

As they busily discussed Joni-Pip's imprisonment, they were all unaware of what was happening, a small distance away from them.

"What's that noise?" asked Hetty the Wee.

"What noise?" asked Ethelred-Ted.

"It's a kind of whirring, a kind of bubbling," replied Hetty. "Listen!"

They all remained silent and distinctly heard a whirring, bubbling sound.

"I can hear it now!" called out Poppy-Plump-Pij.

Suddenly Ethelred-Ted looked towards the tanks. He looked at the fire blazing underneath one of them. Next, much to his horror, he noticed the dial on the side of the largest tank. The pointer quite clearly was on the **MAXIMUM** setting. He worried it might move into the **DANGER** zone.

"Take cover! Everyone!" he yelled. The bubbling grew into a gurgling and the gurgling grew into a groaning and the groaning grew into a rumbling and the rumbling grew into a moaning, in every different sharp and flat. It finally gave way to an almighty explosion.

The Quission Hut shook. Everybody shook. The whole building became filled with smoke! Dust filled the air and everybody began to choke.

The barrel gently rolled on by, away from the desk. Joni-Pip was free.

Amid all the chaos and confusion, Eth told everyone to be quiet.

"Shhh! Listen! What's that? Shhh! Shhh! Listen! What's that?"

Out from the gloomy, smoky mudge, came a strange noise.

"Chink, chink. Chink. Chink, chink, chink. Chink, chink, chink!" it went.

"What on earth is that all about?" said the Bear, trying to work out where the noise was coming from.

"Chink, chink. Chink. Chink, chink, chink. Chink, chink, chink, chink!"

He groped his way around in the fog, until he came to the large tank. He saw nothing and realised the chinking was not coming from there.

"Chink, chink. Chink. Chink, chink, chink. Chink, chink, chink, chink!"

He then made his way through the murk, following the chinking, as best he could. The smoke made him choke but he didn't care. He knew he was on the brink of discovering something wonderful. Finally, he reached the pipe that came from the second tank and there it was!

"Eureka!" he shouted. "Eureka!"

The cat followed him.

"No, I don't mean you, sorry!" he said to the cat apologetically stroking him. "I mean Eureka! The Greek word for, 'I have found it'. It's worked! It's worked and we are all wrong! Come and see!"

Everyone stumbled through the devastation the explosion had left behind and made their way through the smoke, to get to the triumphant Eth.

"See!" he said, pointing to a bucket.

"Chink. Chink. Chink. Chink, chink, chink!" continued the noise.

"Look at it! It's wonderful!" said the Bear.

They all watched in amazement as they saw, coming out of the pipe and dropping into the bucket....lots of little, glassy, cubes.

"Don't you see, You Lot, why didn't I think of it? The little star symbol, you know, the one in the Formula Board....Alex and Archimedes....and you Joni-Pip....you were all **nearly** right....but it wasn't **snow** that it was making....that it formulated....look at what it is!" he was ecstatic.

"What?" they all asked.

"Look!" said Eth excitedly shrugging his shoulders and pointing once more into the bucket.

They all looked. "Can't you see what it is?" he asked again.

His friends all examined the contents of the bucket: they looked at each other and then looked back into the bucket. This time they looked back up and smiled at each other.

"Ice!" they all shouted. "Ice!"

Chapter 20

The Wall of Time - Again

"Alex, what's the date today?"

"May the 14th 1942," replied her brother without looking up from his book.

"Would you like me to bring you your pot of tea in the garden, You Two?" asked Mrs Broft.

"That would be nice thank you, Mrs Broft," replied Joni-Pip, answering for both of them. She was quite sure Alex didn't mind where he drank his tea but she, well she always enjoyed the fresh air and drinking outside made her feel really happy. Nothing could compare, in her mind, with the joy of drinking her tea while having the sun on her face and a slight breeze gently kissing her, somewhat spiky, hair. That, she thought to herself, you could never get in any dining room, no matter how beautiful and comfortable it might be.

"Alex, what do you know about the Workhouse?"

Alex didn't stir from his book.

"Alex, what date was the Workhouse burnt down?"

"May the 5th 1892," came her brother's automatic reply. Joni-Pip had come to realise that figures and facts fascinated her big brother and no matter how absorbed he might be in some 'silly' book, when asked a question that involved such things, his brain seemed to register and he would always find time to reply. Actually, since she had lived the life in the wood, Joni-Pip had gained a much greater understanding of her brother. Although in her heart she always thought of Alex as having his head in some 'silly' book, she realised that these books that took all of her brother's time and attention, were indeed, far from 'silly'.

"Hmmmm!" said Joni-Pip. "So, that's fifty years ago."

"Yeah!" replied Alex once more without looking up from his book.

Mrs Broft came into the garden carrying a tray stacked with a fresh pot of tea, a milk jug, a sugar bowl and tongs, two plates, two cups and saucers and four currant buns.

"Currant buns!" said Joni-Pip excitedly. "Why, we haven't had those for some time, have we, Mrs Broft?"

"This 'ere War, makes it difficult sometimes but I did find an old jar, full o' currants, at the back of that there pantry. I think they must have been there some years, mind but the lid was sealed. So you have a treat today!"

"Yippee! That's so good! Thanks so much, Mrs Broft," smiled Joni-Pip.

The jocular Mrs Broft couldn't help but notice how much nicer Joni-Pip had become recently. She smiled back approvingly and replied,

"That's my pleasure Miss Joni-Philipa. You know what, You Two? There may be this there War on but what with your grandfather's fruit and vegetables and all the things that Mr Broft grows for your father, in Knotty Knook's garden and all that there stuff he gets given by his friend, Farmer Finn and we mustn't be forgettin' all your Mother's preserves and dried fruits and jams 'n that, You Lot don't do too bad, at all, not too bad, at all, when it comes to eatin' and that; not like some."

Joni-Pip smiled and nodded politely. She couldn't really appreciate the hardships most people had to face during the War she was living through. The only changes in her life had been having to leave her beloved Bath and spending one fearful night in the cellar. What Mrs Broft said was so true. Although most families had strict rations during this terrible time, the Garadors still did indeed have plenty of supplies in preserves and jams and such things. Cook, in Bath had always had plenty of stocks before the War and Mrs Broft, here in Berry Bush, had always kept the Country Pantry at Knotty Knook filled with bottled fruits and jams. They were running lower than before the War, of course but still there was a supply to be used and always something, somewhere, to be found.

Had there been an observer, other than you Dear Reader, it would have, once more, been very difficult to appreciate the horrors that were going on in the world at that time. Everything was so calm and peaceful in this little cosy part of the Nottinghamshire countryside. Nothing looked as if it could disturb their tranquillity as the brother and sister sipped their tea and nibbled on their currant buns, well, actually Joni-Pip nibbled, Alex gnawed.

Joni-Pip's thoughts were far from tranquil and Alex obviously didn't want to engage in any form of conversation, so Joni-Pip leaned back in her white, wicker, garden chair, allowing the warm May sun to shine on her face. She then closed her eyes and re-lived the exiting events of the day before in the Old Inventor, Archimedes Spindlethrop's Quission Hut.

184

After the dust had settled, following the explosion, the five in the Quission Hut gathered together. Well, actually four of them did. Eureka was still taken up with watching the mouse on his journey across the beams.

"I thought the Quission Hut was filled with smoke," said Ethelred-Ted, "but it's not is it?"

"Isn't it?" asked Hetty the Wee.

"No, it's steam....I think we rather overheated the tank!" he replied.

"Did we?" laughed Joni-Pip.

"I have had a good look round and there doesn't appear to be much damage. To be quite honest, I don't think Archimedes will even notice that we have been here," the Teddy Bear said quite confidently.

"Are you sure?" Hetty, Poppy and Joni-Pip said together, then roared.

"The important thing here, is to realise what a great discovery this is!" said Ethelred-Ted seriously.

The others stopped laughing.

"I brought the Formula Board with me and I think this calls for another detailed look at it, don't you?"

His audience all nodded.

"Where shall we examine it, Ethelred-Ted?" asked Joni-Pip. "There's not an awful lot of space in here, is there?"

"There's enough room right in the middle of the Quission Hut, by the tanks; that's if we clear a few things out of the way. Let's do that, we don't know when Archimedes is likely to come back but we can always say we wanted him to re-look at the F.B. can't we?"

With Ethelred-Ted in charge, everybody felt confident and all nodded.

In no time at all, the various pencils, pots, pieces of paper, pens and odds and ends, which were strewn about on the floor, were pushed out of the way and Eth opened his paw and put the tiny F.B. down. He gently unfolded it and as usual, they all gasped. No matter how many times they had seen it done, it was still so overwhelming to see the tiny silk handkerchief-like material, grow into a stiff, green, lit up, very large and hard F.B.! They all looked once again at the strange symbols and figures on the floor in front of them. Eth gestured towards the four star-like symbols and said,

"These, then, we have discovered today...."

"Accidentally....Ma Lamb."

"These then, these symbols we have **accidentally**," he emphasised, "discovered today, mean ice and not snow, right?"

Everybody nodded.

"The problem is this," he said authoritatively. "The problem is this...." he repeated and they all looked at him expectantly.

"The problem is this...." he paused for a considerable time. "I haven't the faintest idea what to do with the stupid ice!"

They all burst out laughing.

That was all except Eureka. The naughty, fearless little mouse had seen the cat spying on him and the intrepid creature had decided to run down one of the upright beams, which supported the roof of the Quission Hut, in a bid to escape and leave the building.

That was Eureka's cue! He leapt forward in the direction of the courageous mouse and in the skirmish that followed, sent the bucket of ice cubes hurtling into the air.

Everybody turned and looked at that which was going on and although Ethelred-Ted put out his paw to try and stop the bucket from emptying on to the F.B., it was in vain!

The bucket landed on the floor with an almighty claaaaaaang! The racket was so loud it nearly deafened them, resounding mercilessly through their ears. Most of the ice cubes landed on the floor beside the F.B. but a few rolled right on to the Board, itself. Nothing had ever been allowed to touch the F.B. before. Nobody knew why, it was just an understanding that something so amazing and wonderful had to be protected. Besides that, nobody knew the effect that anything might have on the truly incredible substance from which the F.B. was made. Not until now, that was. They all looked in horror as three of the ice cubes continued on their way, rolling across the board. One of them rocked from side to side as it finally finished its journey, landing right on top of one of the Ice symbols. Amazingly the other ice cube did the same, stopping on one of the other Ice symbols.

For some reason Ethelred-Ted worried that these three ice cubes would make the F.B. soggy, so he stretched out his paw to try and remove them. As he did so he was amazed to see that his paw became transparent! He could see right through it! Everybody gasped as they, too, saw this happen. He very quickly withdrew his paw and once more it became red. The third cube landed on another of the Ice symbols.

"What's going on?" he said breathlessly.

"I have no idea," said Joni-Pip seriously, "but something is just about to go on and I think we should just stand back and watch!"

"Aye, Hen, that's a mite good suggestion," said Hetty the Wee.

"I'm going to look from up there," said Poppy-Plump-Pij and promptly took off and flew back up to her perch on the beam.

"Coward!" laughed Joni-Pip.

"That's me! Cowardful to the full!" Poppy-Plump-Pij laughed back.

Suddenly, there was a kind of rushing noise coming from the F.B.. Hetty the Wee, Ethelred-Ted, and Joni-Pip stood back a bit, well actually as far back as they could but the Quission Hut was pretty cramped for space, what with all of Archimedes' bits and bobs that littered the place. They stood on tip toe and pulled themselves in, as small as they could, by breathing in deeply and holding their breath.

The area where the three ice cubes stood on the star symbols began to shake. The vibrations got stronger and stronger and the rushing noise got louder and louder. Then....everything stopped and silently, in front of their very eyes, they saw the ice cubes open up and another ice cube came out of each one, then another and another and another and they watched in awe, as silently the ice cubes began to expand and grow into brick sized ice blocks. They weren't solid any more, they were like water but appeared solid. Gradually an amazing wall began to form: a solid wall made up of watery ice blocks. The spectators gasped in wonderment.

"The Wall of Time!" Ethelred-Ted said very quietly.

"Aye, I remember it now," said Hetty the Wee, "in Marley's Barn!"

"The Wall of Time!" whispered Joni-Pip. "Yes, we've seen it before!"

"It's amazing up here!" Poppy-Plump-Pij called down softly. "I can see right over to the other side....I have done this before....I remember it on the night of the storm. I'm going over!"

She took off and flew out of sight.

"What do we do now, Ethelred-Ted?" asked Joni-Pip excitedly.

The Teddy Bear shook his head and said, "I'm not quite sure."

"We'll know soon enough, Ma Pets. Just be patient."

"We have to jump!" said Joni-Pip. "We have to jump, are you ready?"

"How do you know, Joni-Pip?" asked Ethelred-Ted.

"I just do. Come on....get as close as you can and jump....don't worry how high, Hetty, we will be 'taken'!"

Joni-Pip stood in front of the Wall of Time and jumped in the air. She felt this unseen force lift her up and over the top of the Wall she went!

Eth did exactly the same and up and over the Wall he went, too.

At first Hetty hesitated. She was a hedgehog, after all and well, have you ever seen a hedgehog jump? Hmmmm! She then remembered Joni-Pip's urgings. She mustered up her courage, took a tiny leap of confidence and found herself, too, lifted up into the air and over the Wall of Time.

While all this was going on, Eureka had been desperately trying to catch the mouse but when the three friends disappeared, he stopped and stared in front of the Wall of Time....

A little mouse scurried away under the door, totally unaware of the wonderful things his tiny presence had brought about.

Chapter 21

Wonderment

Joni-Pip continued to nibble on her currant bun. Alex, on the other hand, wolfed down both of his in a very short time. Joni-Pip's thoughts were far too intense to allow something as mundane as food to cloud her beautiful thinking, however delicious currant buns might be. Alex was different, he always allowed food to come between himself and his thoughts; his reading, anyway. In many ways he was so like Ethelred-Ted.

"J.P., will you be wanting another one of Mrs Broft's yummy currant buns?"

Joni-Pip was sad to have her thrilling thoughts arrested. She wanted to go back to re-living those feelings she had on her fantastic journey. She was revelling in those marvellous memories of jumping over the Wall of Time. She knew they wouldn't last. She just had to make every moment count. Unfortunately, her brother did not share her spectacular experiences, so she had to deal with his gastronomic demands before she could be left in peace to indulge herself in more JITTING joys.

"Oh, Alex, how many have you eaten already?" Joni-Pip laughed. She sat up from her lolling position on the white wicker garden chair and examined the blue willow patterned plate. Only one solitary currant bun looked back up at her. Well, it looked like it did. Two of the currants stuck out of the top of the shiny bun and they looked decidedly like large eyes. Yes, it most definitely was looking back up at her but it wasn't sad. No, it seemed to say to her,

"Eat me! That's my sole purpose, my sole mission in life to be eaten and thoroughly enjoyed!"

"I'm afraid not," she laughed, speaking to the beckoning bun.

"Spiffing!" exclaimed Alex. The white, wicker garden chair squeaked as he lifted himself up from his laid-back position and grabbed the final bun from off the plate. "So you won't mind if I have it, then?" he said, taking a very large bite of the bun. Joni-Pip laughed as his teeth sunk deeply into the soft shiny bap because it made an eye of the bun look decidedly as if it winked at her!

Joni-Pip laughed at herself and thought,

'That will teach me to speak my thoughts out loud! Oh well, I hope the bun is happy because I know Alex certainly is!'

Joni-Pip settled herself back into her chair to reminisce about yesterday's incredible events. She closed her eyes and felt the welcoming sun on her face, as she was transported back to the wonderful sensations of the day before.

Joni-Pip had always envied Poppy's ability to fly and as she was taken up, over the Wall of Time, she imagined this was what flying must feel like. It was glorious. She felt weightless and free. She kept thinking to herself,

'I must remember everything. I must remember everything. I must remember every feeling, every thought, every movement!'

As she went up, the roof of the Quission Hut changed into beautiful shapes and colours and she had the magnificent sensation of motion without effort. The colours were so vibrant, forming vivid, beautiful patterns, which swirled and moved constantly around her. Everything kept changing. She couldn't believe how beautiful it all was. This carried on for some time. She was enjoying it so much, she didn't want it to end....ever!

All of a sudden, thoughts came into her head....amazing thoughts....some good and some not so good....she remembered what had happened up at Marley's Barn, on the night of the storm. She remembered the visitors from the Future. She remembered Red-Ted, telling her that she had had an accident and sadly died. She remembered how he explained that he, Jack and Macca had come back from the Future, from 2007, jumping over the Wall of Time, to save her. They had JITTED to stop her from climbing the ladder that had led to her falling to her death. She remembered him explaining to her the secret of Déjà Vu. It all made so much more sense. Now, she understood why everybody had kept hugging her because she had entered another Orbit of Life and she was re-living her life with all of her friends and family. She understood, too, that she would now have to use her knowledge to help somebody to re-live their life.

It was so clear!

It was so wonderful!

The beautiful coloured shapes of red, blue, yellow, violet, purple, orange, green, pink, turquoise, burgundy and mauve continued to twist and turn in front of her. It was the most sensationally, spectacular sight that she had ever seen and was ever likely to.

Suddenly she knew where she was.

It was all so simple.

She was there....right inside it....a giant tube, actually watching its amazing patterns changing continually with every unique twist and turn.

'So this is it!' she thought. 'The Kaleidoscope of Life!'

Joni-Pip felt out of this world. Not quite out of, more like, along side it.

The feelings were nothing she had ever felt before. They were a mixture of joy, wonderment, understanding, happiness and just sheer bliss, multiplied by thirty one! Everything she loved in life seemed to be all joined together in one single beautiful feeling.

A snowball fight with friends.

Being with special people.

Building sandcastles.

Collecting shells in a bucket.

Eating delicious food.

Eating in the garden on a sunny day.

Eating warm bread.

Enjoying a favourite drink.

Footsteps, squeaking while walking through fresh snow.

Having a cool drink by the river on a Summer's evening.

Having a warm drink in front of the fire in Winter.

Hearing the wind rustling through the leaves of the trees.

Hearing the rain lashing against the windows.

Hearing the wind howling outside, while warm and snug indoors.

Laying in the long grass, looking up at a cloudless, blue, sky.

Listening to favourite music.

Looking down on the river from a bridge watching the fish.

Looking up at the stars on a clear night.

Picnics with friends.

Playing Wee Sticks.

Pretty snowflakes falling, especially watching them through the light of street lamps.

Reading a very good book.

Scoring a goal in a match.

Singing.

Sitting on the river bank, dabbling toes in the clear waters.

Soaking in a warm bath.

Soft, fluffy towels.

Stroking the soft fur of kittens.

The beach.

The cosiness of being snuggled under the bed clothes.

The early morning sun.

The mist across the fields.

The moon's reflection, shining across the sea.

The smell of freshly baked bread.

The smell of freshly baked cakes.

The smell of puppies.

The sound of the rain on the conservatory roof.

Waiting in anticipation for the sea to flood the moat, after building a sand castle.

Walking in the woods on a Summer's day.

Warm hugs and cuddles.

Watching a log fire crackle and sizzle on a cold night.

Watching kittens play.

Watching the sun set.

White fluffy clouds moving gently across the sky.

Writing in the sand.

She didn't want it to end.

As suddenly and as quickly as she had been taken up over the Wall of Time, she was back in the Quission Hut. Ethelred-Ted and Hetty the Wee stood next to her. The Wall of Time had gone. The F. B. was closed again and sat in the middle of the floor looking very small.

"Whew!" exclaimed Ethelred-Ted.

"Whew, indeed!" said Joni-Pip. "That was some incredible jump!"

"Thank you for making me jump, too, Ma Pet, I have had the most wonderful time. No hedgehog in the world could ever have imagined such a thing!"

"Something is not quite right though," said Ethelred-Ted seriously.

"What do you mean, 'not quite right'?" asked Joni-Pip.

"Well, for a start we didn't actually go anywhere did we?"

His two friends nodded.

"And what's more I remember everything. I remember the life I lived after you, you died....Joni-Pip....I have such memories....that's not right is it? We're supposed to forget everything, after we've jumped over the Wall of Time and returned."

"Perhaps we didn't do it right, Ma Pets. I remember when y' came back from the Future, Ethelred-Ted, y' know, when y' become Red-Ted; he told us that the first time he, Jack and Macca jumped over the Wall of Time, they landed in the middle of some Battle during this War," said Hetty seriously, "and y' saw Joni-Pip in the Future."

"That's it, Het, you're a Genius," said Eth, "why didn't I think of it? I think we were all so taken aback by what happened that we didn't think straight."

"What's a Genius?" Hetty chuckled to herself. "Only someone who discovers something that's always been there, just waiting to be found!"

"What are you on about, Eth, what did we do wrong?" asked Joni-Pip.

"We didn't set the date, did we? We just jumped. That's why we didn't go anywhere. We just came straight back!"

"Set the date; how do we do that then?" asked Joni-Pip.

"What's the procedure, Hen?"

"Er....well it has to be simple....we can't get this far and not be able to set the date....can we?" asked the Bear of his friends.

"So?" asked Hetty the Wee and Joni-Pip together.

"Well....er," Ethelred-Ted fumbled.

"What do we have to do to get it right, Clever Crumpet?" asked Joni-Pip.

Ethelred-Ted looked up at the roof and then looked down.

"Er...." he stumbled some more.

"Well?" asked his friends again, looking at him expectantly.

"I haven't the faintest idea!" he said weakly.

Hetty the Wee and Joni-Pip burst out laughing.

"I love it!" chuckled Joni-Pip. "That doesn't make me feel half so silly!"

Ethelred-Ted smiled.

"But you are never silly, Joni-Pip, in fact I think you are very clever!"

Joni-Pip beamed; she had never dreamt this was what he thought of her.

"Where's Poppy I wonder, Ma Pets?"

"Oh, no! I hope she isn't lost!" said Joni-Pip.

"When she flew over the Wall of Time, before she had a great experience. There must be something different from jumping over it, to flying over it. I remember she saw you as an old lady, Joni-Pip. That must have been amazing for her," said Eth.

Joni-Pip nodded and smiled, remembering the incredible feeling she had, when she actually heard her own voice on the other end of Jack's strange telephone from the Future. It was quite incredible talking to herself, only when she was seventy seven! It was so emotional for her, especially as the voice on the other end of the 'phone seemed really happy to talk to her. Joni-Pip wondered if the older, Great Auntie Joni-Pip might have had some idea whom she really was?

"Poppy will be fine, she's probably having a good time with Macca," said Hetty.

"I heard that and I most certainly was not having a good time with Macca. I only wish I was," said Poppy sadly, from up in the rafters. "Something very weird was going on. I flew down and landed in a tree. There were four young men, three were about Alex's age and one was quite a bit older. Anyway, they were talking together in a very familiar wood. They were getting a bit cross, well one of them was very cross."

"I wonder who they were then?" asked Ethelred-Ted.

"The silly part was that I knew two of them....I knew exactly who they were and yet I have never known them at that age," Poppy continued, "and one of them I don't know too well but he looked a bit familiar."

"Who were they then, Poppy? The ones you know," asked Joni-Pip.

"Yes, tell us who they were, Pops!" urged Ethelred-Ted.

Poppy-Plump-Pij flew down and landed on the runaway barrel.

"You won't believe it....well I suppose you will....one of the two young men I knew, was Grandfather. The one I kind of recognised but didn't know was, well I think it might have been....it could have been Old Farmer Finn....not young Farmer Finn....not the one at Finn's Farm now but his Father...."

"I know who you mean, Old Farmer Finn, who now lives in one of the Farm Cottages. He doesn't seem to like anybody much!" said Joni-Pip.

"That's right....but guess who the other young man was?" Poppy asked eagerly.

Her three friends thought.

"No idea....have you, Joni-Pip?" asked Ethelred-Ted.

"I can't think, Ma Pet," Hetty the Wee shook her head.

"I can!" said Joni-Pip.

"Who then, who do you think the other young man was?" asked Poppy.

"Archimedes Spindlethrop!" said Joni-Pip triumphantly.

"You clever thing! How did you know?" laughed Poppy-Plump-Pij.

"Only because of the conversation I had with Grandfather, a few days ago."

"I wonder who the fourth one was?" questioned Ethelred-Ted.

"That, I guess, must be the key to the trouble between them," replied Joni-Pip.

"Something must have happened....I wonder how you managed to end up there, Poppy?" asked Ethelred-Ted thoughtfully.

"Aye, most strange, Ma Lambs!"

"Something was most definitely differentful from when I flew over the wall of Time before," the pretty pigeon sounded very experienced.

"Differentful? What d'you mean different?" asked Ethelred-Ted intrigued.

"The Wall of Time, it wasn't the same. It's really amazing that I now remember everything that happened in Marley's Barn, though."

"So how was the Wall of Time different?" asked Ethelred-Ted.

"It just was and these young men were arguing, really angrily until I flew down and they stopped and looked at me and two of them turned to me and said, 'Hello Poppy!' They seemed really pleased to see me but I just said, 'I don't know you!'"

"Which ones: which two of the boys knew you Poppy?" asked Joni-Pip.

"I know the answer t' that question, Silly, it must have been Grandfather and Archimedes who recognised y', Ma Pet!"

"But that's the silly part, Het. It wasn't, it was the young man, who I think is now Old Farmer Finn and the older man I didn't recognise who called out to me. I don't know Old Farmer Finn, well, I only know what he looks like, as I said but Grandfather and Archimedes didn't seem to know me, at all!" said Poppy-Plump-Pij, shaking her little head. "The ones I knew didn't know me but the ones I didn't know, knew me and spoke to me, as if they were old friends of mine!"

"That **is** so odd, Poppy," said Joni-Pip.

"Aye, most peculiar, Hen!"

"This is bizarre and there's bound to be a reason for it, You Lot but before we can fathom it all out, the next thing we must work out, is how to set the date for when we want to end up and we must set up the place where we want to arrive but now we must turn our attention to more pressing things!" said Ethelred-Ted enthusiastically.

"What's that then?"

"When's my next Munch Break?"

Chapter 22

Questions for Alex

Joni-Pip chuckled to herself as she recalled all the startling happenings of the day before. The most wonderful part was that for the time being, she was able to remember everything. She knew it wouldn't last. She knew that once they had got it right, the memories would be erased, just as Red-Ted had said. Until then, however, she felt so privileged. How many people had been inside the Kaleidoscope of Life, the KOL and remembered it? How many people had seen the beauty and the wonderment of the Colours of Life turning? How many children had experienced jumping over the Wall of Time? How many people understood what Déjà Vu was all about?

"You all right, J.P.?" asked Alex, closing his book and putting it down on the garden table in front of him. "I say, do you think Mrs Broft can come up with any more of those currant buns? Do ask her? They were very nice, weren't they? What were you laughing at then....just now?"

"Alex, why don't **you** ask Mrs Broft for more currant buns, yourself? You really remind me of somebody I know very well and actually, I was laughing about lots of things, including that very friend," said Joni-Pip. She then asked him seriously, "Alex, did you know that Grandfather and Archimedes Spindlethrop don't speak to each other?"

"Yes," replied Alex matter-of-factly.

"You've never mentioned it before. Why not?"

"Dunno. I never tell Grandfather when I go to see Archimedes and I am certain that Archimedes has no idea that I am Grandfather's grandson," said Alex laughing.

"Have they always been enemies then, Alex?"

"No, they used to be friends, very good friends. They spent all of their childhood together. Mother told me all about them....there was a group ....four of them."

"Four?" asked Joni-Pip nonchalantly.

"Yeah, they went around in this group, you know....knocked around together."

Just then a squadron of War planes thundered in the blue skies above, both of them looked up and watched them go over.

"There was Grandfather and Archimedes, which makes two of them

195

....who were the other two?" Joni-Pip brought the conversation back, trying not to sound too keen.

"There was Old Farmer Finn and a beautiful young lady called Mimi...."

"Mimi? It couldn't be...." said Joni-Pip authoritatively.

"And why not, J.P.?" laughed Alex.

"There were four young men; there wasn't a young woman....Poppy saw them!"

"What are you going on about, J.P.? Poppy saw what? When? Who is Poppy? I don't remember you mentioning her. Is she one of your school friends from Bath?"

"No, Alex, Poppy is one of my friends but she is not from Bath, she is from here, right here in the wood," laughed Joni-Pip.

"She is? Where in the wood? Why haven't you told me about her before? I don't remember her," he shook his head, lowered it and laughed. "Is she good at Skimmers?"

"No, Alex, you don't understand. I've never told you about her before because, well, she isn't quite like any of my other friends....you know ....like the ones in Bath."

"She's not? Why? What's wrong with her?" asked Alex intrigued.

Joni-Pip now faced a dilemma: was she going to fob Alex off with a silly made-up story or was she going to risk it and tell him the truth? Was she going to tell him all about her special friends she had made and the wonderful things that they were experiencing right now?

"Er, well you might find this a bit difficult to believe...." she started.

"Oooh, a mystery! I love those!"

"It's not a mystery, Alex, just a trifle odd; a bit unusual," Joni-Pip ventured.

"Look J.P., I'm really interested in this Poppy friend now, so do tell all?"

"Well, Poppy's full name is Poppy-Plump-Pij," started Joni-Pip.

"And how plump is this Poppy then?" said Alex and burst out laughing.

"Not very: I don't think she is plump but I suppose, compared to a normal pigeon, she's slightly plumper than that," said Joni-Pip as if she was talking to herself.

"**Normal pigeon**? What are you talking about J.P.? Am I getting this right? Is this Poppy-Plump-**Pij**," he really emphasised this last word, "is she a real live pigeon?"

"Yes, Poppy is a bird. My friend is the sweetest little, slightly rounder than most pigeons, Wood Pigeon," replied Joni-Pip smiling.

"This Pigeon friend, she speaks to you?" Alex tried hard not to sound sarcastic.

"Yes," said Joni-Pip firmly.

"O.K.," said Alex, "and did I hear you correctly earlier, did you say she, this Poppy, she saw Grandfather and his friends when they were young men?"

"Yes."

"I see, so how old is this Pigeon, for Goodness sake?"

"I have no idea, Alex, I have never asked her," she said, slightly crossly.

"She must be pretty old to have seen Grandfather as a lad!" he laughed.

"Don't laugh, Alex," Joni-Pip sounded as if she was telling her brother off. "She isn't old but Poppy did see Grandfather and Archimedes and Old Farmer Finn, only when they were still young men and she said she saw another man and they were all arguing together in the wood."

"So when was all this then?" Alex tried desperately to understand her.

"Yesterday."

Again he tried to take her seriously and smothered his urge to start laughing.

"O.K., J.P., let's start again. Am I hearing you correctly? You have a friend, a sweet friend, a plumpish friend, who is a Wood Pigeon and her name is Poppy?"

"Yes."

"And this, not very old pigeon, speaks to you and she told you that yesterday, she saw Grandfather, Archimedes, Farmer Finn...."

"Old Farmer Finn," interrupted Joni-Pip.

"Old Farmer Finn and another man, hanging around together in the wood; only they weren't older men, as they are now but they were young men?"

"Yes," said Joni-Pip, "three of them were your age-ish and the other was older."

Alex slowly nodded his head and said calmly, "Right!"

"Well, it's not quite right, Alex," Joni-Pip said slowly.

"Now you're going to tell me this is all a pack of lies you have been telling me?"

"Of course it's not lies Alex, it's all true. I knew you wouldn't understand. How could you? We only went over the Wall of Time yesterday and we didn't do it right and Poppy, well she flew over and managed to land but we didn't, we just came straight back, we didn't actually go anywhere. Ethelred-Ted said we forgot to set the date, that's all," Joni-Pip hardly stopped for breath.

"Ah, Ethelred-Ted!" said Alex thoughtfully. "Now I understand; this is all part of your Game, your imaginary Game. Why didn't you say so at the beginning J.P.? It's Winnie the Pooh and all that all over again: Christopher Robin and all his imaginary friends. Why didn't you explain?

Then I would have understood perfectly!"

Joni-Pip realised that it wasn't any good trying to involve Alex. He now thought she had concocted all of this as a Fairy Tale. She determined that although he thought it was all make believe, she was going to find out all she could about beautiful Mimi and the other young man with Grandfather, Archimedes and Old Farmer Finn.

Alex was still puzzled. Some of the things his sister was talking about seemed quite plausible. For instance, she had said about seeing Grandfather and his three friends. How did she know about them? Perhaps Mother had told her, or Mrs Broft? Mrs Broft? Alex thoughts quickly returned to the question of the extra currant buns.

"Go on J.P., be a jolly good sport and go and ask Mrs Broft for some more delectable currant buns?" he urged his sister.

"I will and then you must tell me all you know about Grandfather's friendship with the beautiful Mimi and Archimedes and you must tell me why they don't talk to each other now, even after all these years. Yes?" bargained his younger sister.

"O.K., J.P. but first....to the Buns!" ordered her brother.

She stood up and walked into the cottage, through the conservatory door.

A few minutes later she returned, carrying a plate of soft and sticky currant buns. Alex was leaning back in his garden chair, with his feet up on the white wicker table. His head was, once more, buried deeply into his book. Joni-Pip put the plate on the table and instinctively Alex leaned forward, in order to sample a requested currant bun. As he did so, Joni-Pip whisked the plate up into the air and out of his reach.

"Not so fast, Alex! First of all, get your feet off the table! Whatever next? What would Mrs Broft say if she saw them? 'That there boy ain't fit for no good'," said Joni-Pip laughing. In actual fact she mimicked their Housekeeper very proficiently: so proficiently that Alex immediately removed his feet from off the garden table.

"Sorry," he said meekly.

"And put this away!" said his sister lifting his book out of his hands, snapping it shut and putting it down on the table.

"I say, steady on, Old Chap!" he was shocked by his sister's sudden boldness.

"And before you eat any more of these...." said Joni-Pip once more waving the plate of buns over his head, out of reach, "you have a few questions to answer."

"You win J.P., so let's be quick! I'm starving!"

"Alex, you may want more currant buns because they are soft, fresh and delicious but not because you are starving. You've polished off three, including one of mine," she said authoritatively. "Now, tell all about this Mimi, this beautiful Mimi?"

Alex sat very upright and began his story.

"Mimi, Grandfather and Archimedes were all born in the same road. Farmer Finn was born on Finn's Farm and they all went to school in the village, together."

"Edwinstowe?"

"Yes, Edwinstowe."

"I thought so," said Joni-Pip thoughtfully.

"They were inseparable. Mimi was like one of the boys. They were all chums. They went fishing, walking and riding together. Old Farmer Finn's father used to keep horses and the four of them used to ride all over the hills and through the woods."

"That sounds wonderful, I would love to do that!" said Joni-Pip eagerly.

"Hold your horses! Let me finish!"

"Of course, Alex."

"Old Farmer Finn's father used to breed horses, even the Queen used to buy his beautiful stallions, for her Horse Guards."

"Which Queen are we on about here, Alex?" asked Joni-Pip.

"Victoria, of course. We're talking about the year 1882, when they were all sixteen!" laughed Alex, then he turned serious again. "At this particular time, in the stables there was a very beautiful stallion, he was magnificent but very, very difficult to handle; he was a Palomino. His name was Bullet: he was very seriously feisty. Only a couple of the older Trainers could ride him. One day, Mimi, who was indeed a very accomplished rider, decided to ride him. Of course she was told she couldn't, Bullet was much too strong for most riders to handle, let alone a young woman, no matter how good she was. Archimedes, who prided himself on his horsing skills, took Bullet out without permission and let Mimi mount him," he hardly paused at all.

"What on earth happened?" Joni-Pip asked earnestly.

"Grandfather saw them racing across Finn's Field and up on to the Clappers. He was furious with Archimedes. There was nothing he could do but hope she'd be o.k.!"

"And was she?"

"What do you think, J.P.?"

"I think she was thrown by Bullet and hurt herself really badly!" replied Joni-Pip. "And that's why Grandfather won't speak to Archimedes anymore."

"As they were galloping over the Clappers; it's hardly a place to be galloping, is it? There are trees everywhere, low branches and rocks and of course, the Old Mine."

"The Old Mine?" questioned Joni-Pip and as she did so, the face of the Fighter Pilot came floating across her mind and then disappeared. "What do you mean the Old Mine? I didn't know there was an Old Mine, up on the Clappers? Alex, we have been coming to Berry Bush ever since I can remember and I had no idea there was an Old Mine around here. Tell me more! Where exactly is it?"

"Now, Mother will be cross with me! When she told me this story she told me that I mustn't ever tell anyone. Oh, what have I done?" said Alex; cross with himself. Then he added, "Joni-Philipa Garador, you must promise me faithfully that you will never, ever, let Mother know that I told you anything about the Accident and the Old Mine Shaft. She might tell you herself one day....when she thinks you are old enough and you must pretend that it is the first time that you have ever heard the story. Promise?"

"I promise, Alex, but what do you mean 'the Accident'?" asked Joni-Pip, totally intrigued by now and really glad that her brother hadn't made her promise not to tell **anyone**, just Mother.

"J.P., I've said enough, in fact I have said more than enough. Let's leave it at that, shall we?" Alex said finally.

Her sixteen-year-old brother then promptly got up and walked through the conservatory door and into the cottage.

The fresh batch of currant buns, which sat expectantly on one of Mother's best, blue, willow pattern plates was totally and utterly ignored. ((What a waste!))

200

Chapter 23

Questions for Archimedes

"I am definitely going to ask him!"

"That's a bit risky, Poppy," said Hetty the Wee cautiously.

"Yes, Pops, this has to be handled delicately," added Joni-Pip.

"Why?"

"Because my Dear Poppy, we don't know exactly what happened yet and we might be opening up some very difficult memories, which our Inventor friend might just like to forget," Ethelred-Ted said, nodding knowingly.

All four sat in a row, perched on the wall of the bridge, which overlooked the stream in Windy Woods. They had been in the middle of a game, when Joni-Pip had told them all about the conversation with Alex that morning. It brought a rather hasty end to the game, which kind of upset Hetty, as for once she was winning. However, talk of all this intrigue and revelation overtook any annoyance she might have had.

All of Joni-Pip's friends shared with her in her curiosity about these things: especially as most of the details had come as somewhat of a surprise to them.

"And....he will probably know all about the Old Mine," said Poppy, trying to get her friends approval to interrogate Archimedes about everything.

"Hmmm....now that does intrigue me," said Ethelred-Ted. "I can't understand how we've never discovered it before. Where up on the Clappers is it, I wonder?"

"Anyway," said Poppy-Plump-Pij sweetly, "why don't we go back over the Wall of Time and change it all? You jump and I'll fly."

Her three friends all stared at her.

"What?" she said indignantly.

They all burst out laughing.

"Poppy, there is nobody like you," said Ethelred-Ted, stroking her feathery back, "everything is so black and white with you. Everything seems so easily solved."

"What?" she said innocently.

Once more, all her friends just stared at her and burst out laughing.

"For some reason....actually, we know why....I'll start again....because we made a 'worm's web' of our first attempt at going over the Wall of Time...." she began.

"Worm's web?" echoed all of her friends.

"Yes, a worm's web....have any of you ever seen a worm spin a web?" she answered looking at them with her eyebrows raised.

Ethelred-Ted, Hetty and Joni-Pip thought for a moment and then they all shook their heads.

"No? Exactly!" Poppy said nodding and once again raising her eyebrows. "Our first attempt at going over the Wall of Time was no better than a worm's web; fortunateful, though, we still remember everything and that includes knowing that it's possible for us to go back in Time and change a bad Past into a better Future."

Her friends all stared at her again.

"What?" she asked, somewhat puzzled by their gaze.

"Poppy, you're amazing, truly amazing!" said Joni-Pip.

"What? What have I done now?"

"Y've done nothin', Hen, we just love y' so, that's all!"

"Poppy, you look at life so simply and so perfectly. You're right, we do have the means to change things for the better and how wonderful that is! I don't think we have quite mastered the art of jumping over the wall of Time yet. We are not proficient in the art of JITTING but with practice, we will be able to do it successfully. There seems a number of pressing events we might be able to change; that's if we ever find out exactly what some of them were and I don't know if there is a limit as to how many we can change. Whatever, I know we'll give it our very best try!" said Eth.

Joni-Pip and Hetty the Wee clapped.

"Let's have one more game and then head off for Hideaway Cottage, not forgetting to stop at Grandfather's for a yum Munch Break!" said Ethelred-Ted enthusiastically.

They all picked up pieces of wood and got ready to throw them

"I think we are using sticks that are much too big twigs," said Eth.

"Me, too," said Joni-Pip, snapping her twig in half to make it smaller.

"We need wee sticks to manage this game, Pets."

"What shall we call this Game, then?" asked Poppy.

They all thought for a moment then each of them shrugged and lobbed their Wee Sticks over one side of the bridge and ran to the other side, to await the floating twigs. Hetty's emerged first.

"I know it seems a silly question, now that we are halfway through the game," asked Poppy-Plump-Pij, "but how do I win?"

Therein ensued a silent interlude; closely followed by uproarious laughter.

Walking along, they kept suggesting places where the Old Mine might be. They had no idea where it was on the Clappers. There were several working mines in the Edwinstowe area but they had never heard of an old, disused one.

At Grandfather's they grabbed a Munch Break and then set off for Archimedes' cottage. Eth thoroughly enjoyed the very deeply filled, egg and cress sandwiches, with Grandfather's special mayonnaise; washed down with blackcurrant cordial.

They really wanted to question Grandfather about the Old Mine, as well as the beautiful Mimi and her accident. However, as Alex had made Joni-Pip promise not to mention anything about all these things to Mother, they decided it was best, for now, to leave well alone, just in case Grandfather mentioned anything to his daughter.

As they neared Edwinstowe, clouds gathered, crowding out the beautiful blue sky. A squadron of Spitfires roared overhead. At first the wind began to blow quite gently but by the time they reached Edwinstowe High Street, it had become very blustery. When they approached the old boarded-up Pretty Posy, they couldn't help but take a look through the nailed-up, gnarled planks and into the darkened showroom.

"It's such a shame that nobody has ever done anything about this place," said Ethelred-Ted, shielding his eyes with one of his red paws in order see into the gloomy space.

"It is," said Joni-Pip, peering through one of the gaps between the planks, "it all seems such a waste." Suddenly she gasped, for there inside, caught in the dismal light, she could see a man, a soldier, sitting on a chair. He was smiling, looking over at a figure bathed in shadows, sitting at a piano. She heard the most beautiful melodic piano music and felt mesmerised by the mood. A wonderful feeling came over her and then disappeared. Joni-Pip strained her head forward and just saw the empty shop.

"Did anyone hear that?" she asked still desperately trying to re-capture the scene, which she had just witnessed in the misty light.

"What? Hear what?" asked Ethelred-Ted.

"The piano music....it was enchanting!"

"Music? No. You must be hearing things," said Ethelred-Ted shaking his head and looking at her peculiarly. Joni-Pip shrugged and pondered.

"What I don't understand, Lambs, is why didn't Archimedes d' anything aboot the shop himsel'? He must have inherited it, if Jemimah died? After all Edmund Plate was lost at sea and Amelia Plate died in the Workhouse Fire, so surely it would have come to him?" asked Hetty thoughtfully.

"Good point, Het," said Ethelred-Ted, still looking into the shop through the darkness.

"Well, I think you might all be running up a gun tree," said Poppy-

Plump-Pij, flying up on to one of the higher planks. She twisted her little head so far round that Hetty the Wee, who was looking up at her from below, wondered if it might screw itself right off!

"'Gun tree'?" came three puzzled voices.

Poppy-Plump-Pij ignored them and continued,

"Until we ask Archimedes some questions, we don't know what happened to Jemimah Plate and we only know that Edmund Plate was **thought** to be lost at sea," she said quite authoritatively.

"That's very true Pops," said Eth. "I hope Mr. Archimedes Spindlethrop is in because we really could do with some answers, right now."

The wind suddenly blew with such a force that one of the planks came loose on one end. Another flurry of wind followed and the plank was pulled clean away from the wood it was fixed to, exposing the pointed end of a long, thick, rusty nail. The plank hit Ethelred-Ted very squarely on his head. Instinctively, he put his paw in front of his face to protect himself. The wind once more blew a hefty gust and the long rusty nail ripped into Ethelred-Ted's arm, leaving a big, jagged tear in his fur.

"Munchy Mash n' Mustard! That hurt!" he shouted.

His friends all heard the sound of the tearing fur and looked at him.

"Are you all right, Eth?" asked Joni-Pip anxiously. She walked over to him and took his arm, cradling it in both of her hands. Very carefully she pushed the flap of his fur back over so that it fitted together. "Mrs Broft will have some sewing to do. Actually, I think I could do it....I do needle work at school. It will be a chance for me to show off what I can do."

Ethelred-Red withdrew his arm and rubbed a red paw over his wound.

"Thank you Joni-Pip, that's very kind but I think I can manage."

"What's the matter, Ma Pet? Are y' worried she'll have y' arm beautifully repaired in pink chain stitch?"

Everybody, including Ethelred-Ted, laughed.

"Something like that!" he replied, grinning.

"Are you in much pain, Ethelred-Ted?" asked a concerned Poppy. "Maybe we can put something on it at Hideaway Cottage? Some dinnerment perhaps?"

"Dinnerment!" laughed Joni-Pip. "That's so apt for Our Friend who is constantly thinking about his food!" The thoughts of the Piano Player and the Soldier had been dispelled from her mind.

The wind continued to blow and then a few drops of rain began to fall.

"It's sprinkling!" said Poppy-Plump-Pij, who by this time had flown down to be on the ground by Ethelred-Ted, "so I think we had better get going, before it really starts to pour."

"Sprinkling, Pops? That's beautiful!" said Ethelred-Ted. "No wonder we enjoy being with you, you look at everything in such an uncomplicated way, so simply but so wonderfully. You've made me forget my poor old torn arm already: all of you, actually. Thank you, for being my friends!"

"That's nice," said Joni-Pip, "but I think we must do as Poppy suggests and get a move on, those big, black clouds are definitely coming over in this direction. Shall we run?"

The four of them set off, going as fast as Hetty's poor little legs could take her. By the time they reached the stile at Marian's Meadow, the rain was coming down quite steadily.

"Look, shall we shelter under the trees or make a dash for it to Hideaway Cottage?" asked Eth, surveying the skies and watching the rapid approach of some exceedingly black, menacing clouds. Even he had found the going difficult because as he didn't want any rain to get into the stuffing in his arm, he had travelled holding the torn flap together. "I hope those planes, we saw earlier don't run into too much bad weather. I think we might."

"Yes," agreed Joni-Pip. "Shall we shelter, Het?"

She hoped Hetty would say, 'No', as she loved walking in the rain: in fact Joni-Pip seemed to love everything, these days.

"Well, I suggest Poppy flies off and we get there as quickly as we can. Ma prickles protect me from the rain, I just don't care f' the wind too well, it tends to blow me about a bit!"

"Then I think we should make you a little trolley we could put you on and push you on, at times like these," said Joni-Pip lovingly.

"Goodness no, oh Prickledy Dee, that would never do, Ma Pet! I'm not old and I love t' use ma legs, however short and spindly they may seem to be to y' but thank y' all the same. I may take a bit longer than y' but I always get there in the end!"

"Of course, Hetty, how silly of me!" said Joni-Pip, slightly embarrassed.

"If that's the case, Het, let's make a run for it!" said Ethelred-Ted.

It got decidedly darker as they ran across Marian's Meadow. How pleased they were when the four, tall chimneys of Hideaway Cottage came in to view, above the hedge that surrounded Archimedes Spindlethrop's home. They all clambered over the Iron Gate, which was much quicker than taking the path around the back of the hedge and up the drive.

Poppy didn't think that it was cheating to fly from the gate, so she took off, arrived first and pulled down the old black bell on a string, in front of the house. She loved the clanging noise it made and rang it several times. Archimedes, true to form, was, of course, not in, so after enjoying her campanology for a little while, she flew round to the back of the house and through the opened door of the Quission Hut.

The Laboratory was completely empty.

"That's strange," she thought, "I wonder where our Inventor Friend is?"

Just then three soaked figures appeared at the door. They were drenched from the rain, which by now was thundering down like Niagara Falls. They came in and slopped across the littered floor.

"He's not here, it's emptyful," Pops smiled at her bedraggled companions.

"Tried to get him up at the house, then?" Eth laughed at her oxymoron.

"Yes, I rang the bell but he most definitely was not in at the cottage."

"I wonder where he is then?" mused Hetty, shaking her prickles and showering Poppy. The pigeon laughed and flapped her wings gently, to dry the raindrops off.

The rain hammered down on the corrugated roof of the Quission Hut, like a hundred mallets knocking in tent pegs.

"Oooh, isn't it cosy?" said Joni-Pip. "Shall we stay in here?"

"I think that would be a pretty good idea, right now," said Ethelred-Ted, examining the wound on his arm. "I just wish there was somewhere in here where we could sit down and **be** cosy!"

He was very tired and in a lot of pain.

"Aye, me, too," laughed Hetty the Wee.

Suddenly, there began a loud vibrating noise, like the sound of a motorbike revving up, only thirty one times louder....like thirty one motor bikes, in fact. The Quission Hut began to shake. The four friends looked round to see where the noise was coming from and together they ran into the squally rain outside. They headed for the cottage door and as they ran past the brown, wooden shutters of the coal chute, the volume of the vibrating, the 'motorbike like' revving noise, got louder and louder. The shutters jumped about as if they were on a trampoline.

"Head for the wall!" shouted Ethelred-Ted. He was soggy and soaked from the pouring torrents but of course nobody heard him above the racket of the revving and the racket of the rain. As it happened, all of his three friends took to the cover of the side wall and just peeked round the corner of the cottage, intrigued by what was about to happen next. Had anyone else witnessed this scene, other than You, Dear Reader, they would have thought how comical it looked. Joni-Pip's head was the highest, looking round the wall, Ethelred-Ted's head was next in line lower down and Poppy stretched her little head, so that it was just above Hetty. For all intents and purposes they looked like a row of vegetables on a kebab stick. They all knew, kind of, what to expect, after all this was not new to them.

As the shutters continued to vibrate violently, the four spectators shrunk lower and lower to the ground until each head rested on the other, like a four light traffic signal.

Suddenly the shutter doors flew open and out shot the silver, sausage-shaped vehicle....the Time Tube....only this time it whizzed up into the air at least as high as the tall chimneys. The four onlookers all stood up and stretched their heads, straining to see through the driving rain and up into the black, angry clouds above.

For a moment, the Time Tube seemed to be suspended in mid-air but then it spun round very fast a few times. As they watched, it slowed down in its circular motion until it gradually lowered itself gently on the ground.

Everyone watching sighed with relief but also felt sad that the Time Tube hadn't gone very far. Most of all they were happy that its Inventor had not blown himself up!

After about a minute, the Time Tube stopped making the dreadful noise, the hatch door flew open and out clambered the Tube Traveller.

His four friends ran across to see him and surrounded him.

He looked at them.

"Sir, we're all extremely sorry that it didn't work out again for you but we're so glad that you appear to have come back to us safe and sound; despite the failure of yet another experiment," shouted Eth consolingly.

The old Professor looked at him and shook his head.

"Failure?" he bellowed through the rain. "What do you mean 'Failure'?"

"Well, the Time Tube didn't go back in Time again," replied Joni-Pip.

"I see," said the White-Whiskered-would-be-Time-Tube-Traveller sadly.

Everybody put their arms around him lovingly and supportively. There was a moment of silence and then the Old Inventor leaped in the air.

"Failure? What do you mean Failure? It was wonderful! It is the very first experiment that has worked. The first one that has ever worked. Do you hear me? Don't you see, it worked? It worked!" he shouted loudly.

"What worked?" asked all his friends frowning.

"Silly," grinned the eccentric old man, "I have at last perfected it!"

His four friends looked decidedly puzzled and said,

"Perfected it?"

"Exactly!"

"Perfected what?" came back four voices.

"The art of Landing!" triumphed the White-Whiskered-Wonder.

With that he grabbed hold of one of Ethelred-Ted's paws and one of Joni-Pip's hands and started to dance around in the rain. Joni-Pip grabbed Hetty's paw and Ethelred-Ted grabbed Poppy's wing and then Poppy and Hetty the Wee joined up and they danced around and around and leaped about in a circle, splashing and sploshing in the thunderous rain!

"I've landed, I've landed!" sang one soaked bloke but very happy chap.

The four visitors stood on the rough, red, quarry tiles, laid unevenly on the floor of Archimedes' kitchen. They all dripped steadily, from the rain they had managed to absorb over the last twenty or so minutes. They shook and shivered from the cold. Pools of water began to grow on the floor beneath each one of them. Archimedes seemed oblivious to their plight. He was wearing his special Time Tube, waterproof flying suit, with big hefty boots, a leather balaclava and goggles. The only part of him the rain managed to find was his large, white, whiskery moustache.

He walked over to his large dresser, opened a drawer and took out a beautifully folded, white fluffy towel.

"I knew these would come in handy one day. Edmund brought these back for me from Turkey, years ago: years and years ago," he said, rubbing his face and moustache dry. The towel was still obviously brand new, unused and unwashed, as it left tiny bobbles of white cotton, speckling his coarse, white, whiskers. "I have never seen the like of them in England....quite honestly, I have never looked....but I am quite sure you couldn't buy them here....well, I expect you can in London."

"Archimedes, do you think we could all use one of your beautiful Turkish towels to dry ourselves please? Or any old one come to that," asked Joni-Pip.

Archimedes Spindlethrop didn't reply, he just continued to dry himself and then removed his balaclava and goggles.

"Do you think we could dry ourselves with something?" asked Ethelred-Ted slightly loudly.

The old man turned and looked at him, stared for a moment and frowned.

"Did you say something?"

"We are all a bit in need of a towel, Hen," Hetty the Wee replied.

"Yes, Mr Bindledrop, Hetty and I aren't as wet as Joni-Pip and Ethelred-Ted but we could all do with a rub down with a towel, please? We are all very coldful, as well," added Poppy-Plump-Pij.

"What did you say?" he said looking back at her.

Poppy decided enough was enough, so she gently flapped her wings. This time she sprayed her hedgehog friend, then she took off and landed on the dresser beside the Old Inventor.

"We actually have been walking, running and dancing in this dreadful rain for some time this afternoon, which means we are all a bit wet, to say the least, Joni-Pip and Eth particularly. It's all right for you. Look what you are wearing! We are just drenched and need to be dry, can't you see?" she then flew over and landed beside one of the pools of water on his kitchen floor. His eyes followed her. At first what she had said didn't seem to register in his very complicated brain, so Poppy-Plump-Pij decided to demonstrate by jumping up and down in the water and splashing about.

"My Goodness me, what am I thinking?" exclaimed the eccentric old man. "I will get you all towels, immediately!"

With that he walked over to the door at the other end of the room, lifted up the latch and disappeared, walking up his wide, wooden stairs.

Joni-Pip, Eth, Hetty and Poppy remained silent for a couple of minutes. At first they could hear the Inventor walking up the stairs and then across the floor above them in his heavy boots. The footsteps stopped, the floor boards creaked and then no sound at all came from upstairs, just silence.

All Four Wet Ones looked at each other and shrugged their shoulders. They waited for another few minutes and then Joni-Pip said,

"Oh blow this, I'm going over to warm myself by the fire! Coming?"

"Yes, indeed!" said Ethelred-Ted and Hetty the Wee together.

"And I will join you!" said Poppy taking off and flying over to the huge range at the other end of the kitchen. The others all followed, squelching and squeaking as they walked across the cold, stone, kitchen floor. They didn't think it was taking advantage of Archimedes' kindness because they knew he was just absent-minded. As she walked past the dresser, Joni-Pip opened the same deep drawer as Archimedes had done and took out some more fluffy white, Turkish towels. None of them thought he would mind, so they all dried themselves and warmed themselves up, by the open range.

When they were all much more comfortable, Ethelred-Ted decided that he should make up the fire because it was pretty much dying. He picked up the coal scuttle with some difficulty because of his wound and shook some coal on. He made a little bit of a mess and choked Hetty and Poppy with the coal dust but eventually the fire began to liven up again. Meanwhile, Joni-Pip busied herself making them all a nice hot drink. It was no problem for her; she had done it before and knew where everything was.

Soon, they were all sitting round the range, draped in thick, white, fluffy Turkish towels, snuggled in Archimedes' comfy chairs, cosily sipping at the best thing in England ((well, some people think it is, anyway! I am enjoying one at this very minute)), a freshly brewed cup of tea!

The wind still howled outside and the rain still lashed at the window panes. Cosily, they discussed the events of the afternoon.

About three quarters of an hour later they heard the floor boards squeak again, followed by footsteps coming from above them. The footsteps walked across the floor and down the stairs. The stair door latch was lifted and the door opened. Archimedes appeared, holding a large book. He didn't seem to notice them as he walked across the kitchen floor and opened up the back door. A squally gust of wind blew into the kitchen, the rain started to pour in and something else was literally blown in.

"Eureka!" called Joni-Pip, as one very wet and very bedraggled, soggy moggy ran into the sanctuary of the cottage. He shook himself violently on the door mat and then ran across the room and jumped up on to Joni-Pip's lap. She put her cup and saucer down on the floor and immediately wrapped the towel she had used for herself, around him and began to mop up his sopping fur. Soon he was purring contentedly, as he washed himself.

This was something Joni-Pip could never understand. Why on earth would a cat want to add more moisture to his fur, by washing, when he was already inundated with the stuff from being soaked in the rain? This was a question that was beyond her comprehension. Nevertheless, he continued to do it, however peculiar this process might seem.

Archimedes closed the door and pushed out the unwelcome wind and rain. He walked over to Eth and opened the book he was carrying. He didn't seem to appreciate that he had left them for nearly an hour. Why should he? He didn't notice that they were drinking his tea, in his cups. He was totally oblivious to the fact that they were all wrapped up in his very expensive, white, fluffy, Turkish towels that he didn't think you could buy in England, not out of London, anyway. In fact, he didn't seem to think it was strange at all to see four visitors snuggling in his comfy chairs, cosily huddled around his fire, even though he hadn't invited them to do so.

He just took it as normal.

"What do you make of this then?" he asked Ethelred-Ted.

Ethelred-Ted peered at the title of the hefty tome he was being shown and there he read the words '**Time Travel Attempts Through the Ages, by Matthias Ulwalker Gastion.**'

Archimedes very slowly turned the pages and Ethelred-Ted saw many drawings and pictures of strange and wonderful contraptions and machines that Man had invented and tried, unsuccessfully, over the centuries.

"Trekking around in Time is something that will always interest Man, Archimedes and this book does appear very interesting but I think you need search no further," said the Bear holding his torn arm. "I've pored over **The Time Machine by H.G. Wells** and that didn't help. How-ever, we have here, something that is far more amazing, far more astonishing!"

"But isn't this book marvellous? It has given me some brilliant ideas to really work on," replied Archimedes, paying no attention to what his visitor had said.

Ethelred-Ted continued to fiddle with his arm. He always tried to be brave: nonetheless, the torrential rain had drenched him and consequently some of his stuffing had got very soggy, making his arm very swollen and extremely painful.

"Are you all right, Ma Lamb?" Hetty could see that Ethelred-Ted was not himself, so she climbed up on to the arm of his chair and started to try and do something for him, with his tear.

"Thank you, Hetty. I am feeling a trifle under the weather....especially this weather," he laughed.

Archimedes continued turning the pages of his book and paid no attention to the ailing bear, which infuriated Poppy-Plump-Pij. She promptly flew up and landed on the opened book.

"Do you want to see?" asked the Professor gently.

"Thank you but no," she replied politely, "but I would like you to shut this book right now and pay attention to Eth. Can't you see he is hurt?"

"Shut the book, did you say? Whatever for?" questioned the puzzled Inventor.

Poppy-Plump-Pij opened her wings gently, so that they completely covered the two pages Archimedes was looking at.

The old man tried to look around and under her wings but with some nifty movements, she made it impossible.

"Marchimedes Shindleshop, please do not let me get crossful with you again?" begged Poppy. "I want you to look at my face and watch my beak and listen to and really concentrate on, what I am saying to you. Understand?"

"What?"

"Just pay attention because I do not want to have to tell you off again."

"What?"

Poppy-Plump-Pij used her wings and gently held the old man's face with them, looking straight into his eyes,

"Now, I hope I have your full attention. Please listen very carefully. Are you listening?"

"Well, it seems I don't have any choice, with you holding my face, do I?" laughed the old man.

"Ethelred-Ted is hurt and he is in pain and he needs you to help him sort himself out," she said, still looking straight into the Inventor's eyes.

"Who is hurt? Let's go and find him!" said Archimedes urgently.

The other three spectators stifled a laugh at this typical response coming from their eccentric but eager friend.

Poppy-Plump-Pij kept a tight hold of his white whiskered face. She knew this was going to be tough but she also knew that she would get there, if she was patient enough.

"Ethelred-Ted, who is sitting right in front of you, has a torn arm. He caught it on a rusty nail. Some of his stuffing is very wet, on account of the buckets full of rain that we have been soaked with. This all happened while we were coming to visit you, at your place. He is in a great deal of pain because his arm is swollen and very heavy, as well as the fact that his fur has been torn. Now please will you help him?"

The old man wrenched his face away from Poppy's tight grip and turned to Ethelred-Ted.

"You have torn your arm on a rusty nail? Where was it; in my kitchen? I will find it and remove it, at once!"

Ethelred-Ted rubbed his aching arm with his red paw.

"I'm afraid so but no, I didn't do it here. It was outside the Pretty Posy....the wind caught a plank...."

"You are in pain?" interrupted the Professor.

"Yes, that too," replied Ethelred-Ted.

The old man made a grimace and said crossly,

"Then why the Dickens didn't you say?"

Everybody burst out laughing.

Immediately the Old Inventor took action. Out came his medical box and liniment and a poultice were administered to the painful limb. When that was all beautifully carried out, the ailing arm was carefully wrapped up in

212

a fresh, soft, clean, crepe bandage.

Archimedes might have been one of the most eccentric and absent minded men on this Planet but he was also one of the kindest and he was very, very efficient, when it came to first aid.

"I think we best leave the stuffing to heal and then we can get you stitched up in a couple of days, when the stuffing has dried out thoroughly and the swelling has gone down." He then gently put Eth's arm in a sling and told him to rest awhile. "If we stitch it now, you might end up with a very lumpy and uneven arm and we don't want that now, do we?"

Ethelred-Ted was extremely grateful.

"That's a bonny sling, Ma Pet!"

"Thank you, Archimedes. Yes, it is 'bonny' indeed, Het," Ethelred-Ted said appreciatively. "It feels so much better now."

"I remember doing something similar to this, a long time ago."

"When was that, then, Archimedes?" asked Ethelred-Ted.

"Oh a long, long, time ago," replied the old man sadly.

"Had somebody torn themselves on an old rusty nail, too?" asked Joni-Pip, desperately hoping that this was the opening they so keenly sought.

"No, no, nothing like that." The Inventor shook his head.

"What was it then?" asked Hetty the Wee.

"It was my friend," he started.

"Did she have an accident?" asked Poppy-Plump-Pij, hopefully.

"No."

"Oh," said Joni-Pip, trying not to sound too disappointed. All of Archimedes' visitors were eager to find out as much as they could about the beautiful Mimi and why Grandfather wouldn't speak to Archimedes. Of course, they wanted to know all about the Old Mine Shaft, as well but they were afraid to make him angry or sad, so they just trod very gently.

"Well, I suppose he did, Silly Me!" said the Old Inventor.

"He?" questioned all of his visitors together.

"Yes, he hurt himself very badly. I patched him up as best I could but I hardly had anything with me. It was so dark down there and I could barely see."

Poppy, Hetty, Ethelred-Ted and Joni-Pip all looked at each other.

"Where? Where was it dark, Archimedes?" asked Ethelred-Ted gently.

"It was all so stupid," answered the Inventor and then continued as if he was in a dream, "in the Old Mine, up on the Clappers."

The face of the smiling pilot then came into Joni-Pip's mind.

Joni-Pip thought to herself,

'Why do I need to know where the Old Mine is? I know I do. I wish I could remember! What's going on? Am I supposed to ask him where it is?'

Chapter 24

Family Affairs

Sarah Garador gently mopped the rain from her twelve-year-old's hair and face with a soft towel.

"Joni-Philipa, when will you learn that when you see the weather changing, you must come home."

"Mother, I'm fine. What harm does a bit of rain do? Why, the trees, the grass and the flowers have to put up with it all the time," replied her daughter, "and you don't hear them complaining!"

Mother laughed. Her middle child never ceased to amaze her recently. What a different child she had become in the last few weeks. How grown up! How less brattish and spoiled she behaved! How much happier and kind she was! How funny she had become, how much nicer she was to have around!

"I worry that you will catch a cold and then you won't be able to wander over the woods, enjoying all the trees, grass and flowers you love, will you?" chuckled Mother again.

"We are pretty waterproof, Mother, aren't we? Our skin doesn't let the rain in does it? We might get wet but we don't actually drown in the rain or go down in the drain, do we? What's more....when have you ever heard a tree or bush cough and sneeze?"

Mother burst out laughing.

"Just promise me you will try....at least try....not to keep getting drenched in the rain, Darling? How many times has it been recently?"

Soon, both Mother and daughter were snuggled up in easy chairs, nestled by the roaring fire in the kitchen at Knotty Knook. Every now and then they took a sip of the delicious, warm, smooth, milky hot mug of cocoa they cupped in their hands and took tiny bites of the French Toast, which Mrs Broft had prepared for them; that was before the House Keeper had bundled Becky-Paige upstairs to bath and bed.

Ethelred-Ted had been persuaded to spend the night at Hideaway Cottage with Archimedes Spindlethrop. It hadn't been without thought that he had decided to stay. There were several things that he wanted to find out from the Inventor. There were several things that he wanted Archimedes to know, as well. There was a break in the storm, so Joni-Pip, Hetty and Poppy had left at about four o'clock, leaving The Two Intellectuals to talk into the night. The other three nearly made it without getting wet but as

214

they reached the Ruin the Heavens opened and once again, down came the rain.

"So where have you been this afternoon, Darling?"

Joni-Pip decided to be courageous.

"First of all, we popped into Grandfather's for a Munch Break: that was delicious. Then we walked into Edwinstowe and ended up at Archimedes' place."

"Oh, that's interesting, what did you do there?" Mother didn't flinch.

"I made tea and Archimedes bandaged up Eth because he caught his arm and tore it on a nail outside the Pretty Posy," said Joni-Pip matter-of-factly.

"That was kind, Darling, by the way I didn't see you come in with Ethelred-Ted. Where have you left him?"

"He's spending the night with Archimedes at Hideaway Cottage. His torn arm got all soggy in the rain and Archimedes is going to stitch him up when his stuffing has dried out."

"That's so thoughtful of him, Darling. I'm surprised though that you could leave him for a night. Do you remember how worrying it was for you down in the cellar, all night in Bath without him?"

"I will never forget that night. You're right, Mother but I thought it was for the best," said Joni-Pip and then she took a deep breath.

"Mother, why doesn't Grandfather like Archimedes?"

Once more Mother didn't flinch. She just smiled and replied gently,

"So Grandfather has been talking to you, then, Joni-Philipa?"

"Yes, he told me not to have anything to do with him. I find that just too difficult. Archimedes Spindlethrop is one of the most fascinating, as well as irritating, people, I have ever met. I love being in his company. He makes me laugh so much!"

"Does he, Darling? Does he remind you of anybody?"

Joni-Pip thought for a moment and then shook her head.

"Nobody comes to mind at the moment. Should he then?"

"I just wondered."

Joni-Pip took another sip of her delicious drink and a nibble at the tasty toast. Mrs Broft had dunked the bread in freshly beaten eggs and fried it gently in butter for them. It was such an advantage having Farmer Finn as a friend of Father's, during War Time.

"So, tell me, Mother, why doesn't Grandfather like Archimedes Spindlethrop?"

Mother tasted some more of her hot, chocolatety drink and then leaned back in her comfy armchair. Joni-Pip felt very warm inside and a little bit special. She had the feeling that Mother now thought it was time to unlock a secret of the Past.

"Grandfather and Archimedes used to be great friends," started Mother. Joni-Pip was about to say 'I know' but then thought better of it and decided to simply listen as Mother spoke. "They were born here in Edwinstowe and they spent all their time together as boys. They had other friends; Fred Finn was one of them. Fred, is Old Farmer Finn: not Father's friend but **his** father, do you know who I mean?"

Joni-Pip nodded.

"So that's his name," she said and then added, "what's the current Farmer Finn's name, then? I know Father calls him Taff but that's not his real name, is it?"

"No, that's just his nickname. His name is James, James Finn. Anyway they were all friends together," Mother continued.

"Tell me what happened, Mother?" Joni-Pip ventured.

"Patience, Darling, I'll get there," Mother said softly.

Joni-Pip settled back in her chair. She felt very grown up indeed having this important conversation with her mother and she was desperate not to spoil things.

"All right, Mother, I'll try really hard not to interrupt....but you know me?"

"In the village there was a very beautiful young girl who was the same age as Grandfather, Fred and Archimedes," said Mother seriously.

Joni-Pip wanted to say, 'this must be the beautiful Mimi' but she had promised to be quiet and not interrupt. She sipped her warm, comforting cocoa and just nodded.

"Anyway, Mimi....that's the name of the beautiful young girl....loved to spend time with the boys, all three of them: Fred Finn, Archimedes and Grandfather, even though she was a girl. We are going back a few years of course....over fifty....yes, well over fifty years....it must be....more like sixty years, actually....and there weren't as many living in the village as now, of course. Mimi and the boys were really the only children around here, at the time; who were of a similar age, that is. There were younger ones, like Colin Finn, Fred Finn's brother and a few other little girls....I'm wandering off, aren't I? I must get back to the story!" laughed Mother.

Joni-Pip laughed, thinking how much she, too, was always going off on tangents when she was trying to relate important events to her friends.

"The four of them did everything together....including riding the horses up at Finn's Farm. At this particular time there was a very big, difficult horse there," said Mother. "He was a magnificent Palomino."

'Called Bullet!' thought Joni-Pip but amazingly she remained silent.

"Mimi wanted to ride Bullet, that was his name but of course she wasn't allowed. The stallion was much too big for her; he was far too dangerous for her to ride. She was a very headstrong girl...." Mother stopped and looked at Joni-Pip.

"Is everything all right, Mother?" asked Joni-Pip, breaking her silence.

"Yes, Darling, sorry. One day, your Grandfather was walking up on the Clappers, when to his horror, he saw Archimedes and Mimi galloping over the hills. They were going really fast. Mimi was in front and she was riding Bullet! He was furious and ran after them but it was impossible to catch them as they were on horseback. He couldn't believe that Archimedes would be so stupid as to let a young woman ride the feisty animal, no matter how much she might have pleaded. Mimi was only sixteen. They galloped through the trees and up on to the Clappers, you know how dangerous that must have been. There are so many low hanging branches and rocks. It was treacherous and most certainly **not** the place to be riding at such great speed. Suddenly, they came to a clearing in the woods and on one of the pathways, Fred Finn and his younger brother came into view. They were just walking their dogs. They must have been about ten feet apart from each other. Archimedes shouted out to them to get out of the way. Fred tried desperately to run and grab hold of

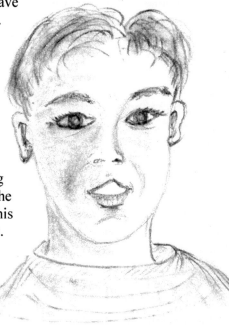

Colin's hand to pull him out of the way of the thundering horses but it was impossible. In his desperation to get out of the horses way, the terrified lad started running. Fred chased after him to try and save him but suddenly he disappeared. Fred had fallen down one of the Old Mine Shafts. Nobody had used it for years. The entrance had become overgrown and hidden, so Fred had no idea it was there. The horse and rider tried to avoid Colin and reared up, knocking the young boy on to the rocky ground. Mimi fell off the horse of course and Bullet, in panic, fell badly, breaking one of his legs."

Mother was silent for a while. Joni-Pip started to cry.

"Oh, Mother, that's terrible, so, so terrible....I had no idea all that happened...."

Mother stood up and went to Joni-Pip and hugged her.

"Darling, perhaps I shouldn't have told you, I didn't mean to make you cry. It's just that both Alex and Grandfather have told me that you have spoken to them recently. Alex said you were asking questions and he felt you should be told about the accident. I thought now was the time. Perhaps I should have waited?"

"No, Mother, I have so wanted to know. Archimedes told us something this afternoon but he got all upset and so we left it. Thank you for telling me. I would have cried, anybody would have, about such a terrible story, no matter how old I was."

"Thank you, Darling. I just wanted you to understand why your Grandfather is still cross with Archimedes; even after all these years."

"So what happened to poor Fred Finn....he's still alive, I know that.... what about Colin....and Mimi and Bullet?"

Mother walked back to her chair and settled herself down again.

"It was terrible. Grandfather soon arrived on the scene. Mimi was lying on the ground, pale and unconscious. Archimedes was in shock and so bewildered as he ran from one to the other, not knowing who to help first. Colin was unconscious, too, lying on the ground with a terrible, bleeding gash on his head. Bullet was making a terrible noise as he was in such pain. Grandfather had no idea that these weren't all the casualties. He didn't know that Fred Finn was lying at the bottom of the Mine Shaft, moaning in agony from his injuries."

"Poor Grandfather! It must have been so horrible for him!"

"It was. He quickly realised that Colin needed something to stop the bleeding, before he could run for help, so he took off his shirt and tore it into long pieces and wrapped it around the poor boy's head. He had a clean handkerchief in his pocket which he used as a kind of pressure pad and he put it straight across the huge gash under the make-shift bandage. He then checked that Mimi wasn't bleeding and ran off to Finn's Farm for help. He left Archimedes to stay with the two casualties. In the meantime Archimedes searched for the place where he thought he had seen Fred disappear. He finally found the gaping hole, between two large rocks and he called down into the dark chasm beneath him. He listened and heard Fred's groaning. He called down to him and told him that he would get there as soon as he could. He knew he couldn't climb down: it was too steep and too deep but he reasoned that there must be a better entrance somewhere. He called down to Fred and asked him if there was any light coming from any other direction. Fred's voice came back and said there was and he reckoned it was further on towards the farm. Archimedes realised from the weak sound of Fred's voice, that his friend was in a lot of pain, so he rushed around trying desperately to find the proper entrance to the Old Mine."

"Did he find it?" asked Joni-Pip. "Where is the Old Mine, Mother? Do you know exactly where it is?"

Mother shook her head.

"No, Darling, he didn't find it and I have no idea where it is, other than it is somewhere up on the Clappers. When all the men came up from the Farm to help, however, one of them knew where to look."

Joni-Pip felt very disappointed.

"Does anybody know where it is?"

"I don't know, Darling, it is a very dangerous place, very deep and full of water I should think, by now. Why do you want to know? I think they filled in the Entrance, if I remember rightly, so that it was safe and nobody would fall down in it again. I'm not sure though. Why did you say you wanted to know where it is?"

"I just need to know, I really do!" replied Joni-Pip, thinking to herself, 'Why?'

"Surely not, Darling, why would you need to know that?"

For a moment, both of them sat in silence, looking into the fiery flames of the blazing kitchen fire.

"So, what happened to everybody and Bullet of course?" Joni-Pip asked.

"It was terrible," replied Mother gravely, "Colin had brain injuries and they were so serious that he never recovered properly. He was sent to a special Sanatorium in Bristol. It broke his parents' hearts. Fred was rescued by Archimedes and a Farm Worker. Amazingly he had slid down the shaft, more than fallen, so he had only broken one of his arms and both his legs. Mimi suffered from concussion and shock and as for poor Bullet? He had to be shot as there was nothing they could do for him."

"M, M 'n M! Mother, that's all so terrible! What a tragedy!" said Joni-Pip, in almost a whisper.

"Archimedes insisted that he did everything to stop Mimi from riding off on Bullet. Apparently, he had hold of a lead rein but some visitors, some Inspectors from the Palace, who had come to see about the Queen buying Bullet, suddenly appeared on the scene unannounced and scared the animal to death. The horse just bolted," said Mother very seriously.

"Oh poor Bullet," said Joni-Pip sadly. "I expect those Inspectors felt that, as they came from the Queen, herself, they could just turn up when they liked. What a cheek! I'm so cross. Didn't they realise what terrible sufferings they had caused?"

"I don't know about that, Darling. They probably thought that to turn up unexpectedly was a good thing, as they would see the Stable and Bullet as they really were: without all the Staff and everyone putting on a show," continued Mother; then she said, "Well, that's not all, I'm afraid, Joni-Philipa."

Joni-Pip looked alarmed.

"Mimi felt so terrible about what she had caused through her headstrong personality that she just couldn't eat. She became very poorly, very weak and very frail. She blamed herself for Colin's brain injuries and she was never quite the same again. She lost her vibrant personality and became like a little mouse. Mimi quickly grew from a beautiful young girl, into a beautiful young woman and she married the first young man who courted her. She was only seventeen when she got married. Unfortunately, Grandfather didn't approve of this, either," said Mother seriously.

"Was it anything to do with him, then?" asked Joni-Pip innocently.

"Hmmm, I suppose it wasn't but Grandfather was a very close friend of Mimi's and he wanted what was best for her, at least, what he thought was best for her!"

"Did Grandfather love her then, Mother?" asked Joni-Pip.

Mother smiled.

"My Darling, you never stop amazing me, recently. Yes, Grandfather loved her. He didn't realise how much though, until he was told that she was to marry somebody else. The problem was, the man who was to marry her was much older than her and he spent a lot of his time away, out of England. Grandfather felt that if a man took on the responsibility of a wife, then he should at least be there to take care of her: especially his special friend Mimi. Archimedes told me that there was once the most terrific argument, just before the wedding. All four of them were there, up on the Clappers, right by the site of the accident...." started Mother.

"I know about this...." said Joni-Pip excitedly, "There was Old Farmer Finn....Fred....Fred Finn and there was Grandfather and Archimedes and obviously the man the beautiful Mimi married!"

"How d'you know?" asked a puzzled Mother and then she smiled. "Of course, Archimedes must have told you!"

Joni-Pip smiled and thought to herself,

'Actually, no....it was my friend Poppy-Plump-Pij, when she returned from flying over the Wall of Time!'

"Mother, who did the beautiful Mimi marry? Who was he? What was his name?" Joni-Pip questioned.

"He was an Explorer," Mother replied. "His name was Edmund Plate."

220

Chapter 25

A Voice from the Past

"So, the beautiful Mimi and Jemimah Plate are one and the same?" said Hetty.

"And....they are both Archimedes' sisters!" said Poppy-Plump-Pij.

"Well, I never!" said Ethelred-Ted.

"Actually, Poppy, there are not two of them....Mimi is just the shortened form of the name Jemimah!" said Joni-Pip.

"Just like we sometimes call you Pops or Poppy, when actually your full name is Poppy-Plump-Pij, Poppy," explained Ethelred-Ted.

Poppy-Plump-Pij looked confused.

"Lassie, there are not two or three of ye, are there? Even though y' have more than one name."

"So, Jemimah Plate is Archimedes' sister and her friends used to call her Mimi for short," said Joni-Pip. "My name is Joni-Philipa but you all call me Joni-Pip. They are both me; actually my brother calls me J.P. all three names are me! Rebekah-Paige is my little sister's name but I've never called her it. We always call her Becky-Paige. Even Mother and Father do. She calls me Sissa. I have four names but they are all me!"

Poppy-Plump-Pij smiled and said no more.

"Jemimah Plate and Mimi, the beautiful Mimi, are one and the same person. It's so simple!" Ethelred-Ted said, then he added, "Why didn't we guess that?"

They all shrugged their shoulders.

"Poppy when you flew over the Wall of Time and landed, you were watching the argument between Grandfather and Edmund Plate. Fred Finn and Archimedes were mostly just looking on. Grandfather was telling Edmund that he shouldn't marry Jemimah because he was an Explorer and he would always be away leaving her alone. Edmund didn't listen, though because they got married and had Amelia Plate."

"I see. I understand it all at last!" Poppy smiled and nodded her head.

It was a beautiful warm, sunny day and the four of them were on their way over to visit Grandfather for lunch. They all felt good. The rain had left the ground a bit soggy and muddy, underfoot, so they tried to walk on the grass as much as possible.

"What I would like to do today," said Eth, "after I have filled you in with all that I learned from Archimedes, is write down, collate even, all the facts we have and decide what it is we want to achieve. When we finally make it over the Wall of Time."

"What a sensible thing t' do, Ma Pet, that's supposing we do eventually get it right! It kind of gives us a Plan. Isn't it marvellous that we made a mistake the first time and we can remember all that has happened? The visit of Red-Ted and Jack...."

"The pilot in my garden, not to mention the man in the hooded cloak," said Joni-Pip. All her friends looked at her, shook their heads and shrugged their shoulders in puzzlement.

"Well, none of us have seen the cloaked stranger, except you and why do you keep going on about some pilot?" asked Ethelred-Ted. "Who is he? When did you see him in your garden?"

"I....I think I saw him in Bath, the night of the raid. I'm not sure. By the way, I meant to tell you, I found out where the Old Mine is!"

All her friends stopped walking and said together,

"Where?"

"I don't know," she said in a high pitched voice.

"But you just said you found out!" said Ethelred-Ted.

"What I mean is I know whereabouts it is but not exactly whereabouts it is."

"Hmmmm, very clear," said Ethelred-Ted, blankly.

"Explain, Hen?" laughed Hetty the Wee.

"Mother told me the Old Mine Shaft, the one which Fred fell down, was up on the Clappers but she doesn't know and nobody else seems to know, exactly where it is....it's just....'somewhere up on the Clappers'."

"Fred fell down?" asked Poppy-Plump-Pij.

"Let's go to Grandfather's and I'll tell you all Mother told me on the way."

As they walked she related to them the entire conversation with Mother. Everybody was very sad, especially for Colin Finn and Bullet. After Joni-Pip had finished Ethelred-Ted continued telling them about his conversation with Archimedes.

"I told Archimedes that we had discovered the Formula made ice and the Formula Board works with ice," said Ethelred-Ted.

"What did he say?" asked Joni-Pip.

"Did y' tell him it was by accident that we discovered it, Hen?"

"Did he notice the mess in the Quission Hut, after we had left?" asked Poppy.

Ethelred-Ted put his free arm up. The other one was still in a sling.

"Steady on, You Lot, one at a time!" he laughed.

222

"He was thrilled we had discovered it was ice; his face really lit up when I told him," started the Bear. "I told him it was an accident but he wasn't really paying much attention, he was re-working out the Formula, trying to make it make ice and no, Pops, he didn't notice the mess we had made!"

"That was a silly question, really," said Poppy, "but I did wonder."

"I asked him how he thought we might set the date and the place we would like to go back to, when we jumped over the Wall of Time," said Ethelred-Ted sighing, "but he was far away in his mind, up in the clouds with the Formula. It was hopeless!"

Poppy frowned and said,

"That silly Man! He misses so much because he doesn't listen!"

"Let that be a lesson t' all of us, then!" said Hetty the Wee, chuckling.

"So, doesn't he know we have already had a little JIT?" asked Joni-Pip.

"No he doesn't! Believe me, though, it wasn't for lack of me trying to tell him."

"I wonder if the Gift of Déjà Vu is only f' us and only f' us t' know about?"

"You know, Het, that very thought has gone through my mind again and again," said Ethelred-Ted seriously.

"If that is the case....then we're on our own," said Joni-Pip. "I think we should just get on with it and make our own plans to save Amelia Plate and the other children from the Workhouse Fire, as soon as possible!"

Ethelred-Ted turned and looked at her in amazement.

"So you're thinking the same as I've been thinking....these last few days, Miss Garador? Well, I never!"

"Y're not the only Two. That same thought has gone over and over in ma brain, since the day we jumped and remembered!" Hetty raised her eyes.

"And me!" said Poppy, taking off and flying gently around them, just above the ground. "All I think of, is saving A Mealy Plate and her friends in the Workhouse!"

Everybody stopped walking and just stood still, in silence, with big grins on their faces. That is, everybody except Poppy, who, silently, swayed and turned effortlessly in the air. They then all burst out laughing.

"A Mealy Plate, indeed! Pops, it's Amelia Plate and now we know she is the daughter of the beautiful Mimi....as you say....we **must** save her!" said Joni-Pip.

"And to think I thought I was the only one with a Plan!" laughed Ethelred-Ted.

"I did too," said Joni-Pip, smiling. "I haven't been able to sleep properly. I keep on wondering how on earth we will get **all** the children out in an hour?"

"Ma thoughts exactly, Ma Pet, we're all a silly set of sizzling sausages!"

"Hmmm!" grinned Ethelred-Ted. "I wonder what Grandfather's got for lunch?"

With that they all dissolved into fits of uncontrollable laughter! After they had gained a considerable but not total amount of control, Eth began on a serious note.

"I don't think it's a coincidence that we have just found out about Grandfather's grudge against Archimedes. Something tells me that these two things: Amelia's note and Jemimah's accident: perhaps they both could be put right at the same time?"

"My thoughts, too!" said Joni-Pip. "I have searched for a solution but up until now, I have not had an idea, not a single sardine!"

"Hmmmm!" said Ethelred-Ted. "Now we're talking....on toast I hope!"

Once more the group melted into a heap of laughter.

"I hope you don't start thinking about food when we are trying to rescue those poor children!" said Hetty. "We won't want any distractions!"

"Of course he will, Het, don't be silly," said Poppy-Plump-Pij seriously.

"No, I won't, Pops, I will be very serious and I will be exemplary. Why, when I came back from 2007, as Red-Ted, I didn't think about food did I?"

"Come on!" said Joni-Pip impatiently, "let go to Grandfather's."

"All right, Eth! Let's get to Grandfather's," encouraged Joni-Pip.

"I think we should sit down and work out some sort of plan though, don't

224

You Lot?" asked Ethelred-Ted.

"How do we set the date?" asked Poppy, landing gently beside them.

"I'll pick Grandfather's brains and we'll just have to wait and see," replied Eth.

"Come on!" said Joni-Pip impatiently. "Let's go to Grandfather's!"

"All right, we're coming, Ma Wee Lamb, don't fret!" Hetty laughed.

They walked in silence for a while. All of their minds were crammed with their own thoughts. They all knew that a huge adventure lay ahead of them. They didn't know if it would work or not. They still had a few minor things to sort out first: like working out how to get to the right place, in the right year, at the right time: minor things.

Also, they all wondered how changing the Past might affect their Future; that was something very sobering. Would they come back to a different Life in the Wood? Would they still be friends? Would Ethelred-Ted just be a stuffed toy on an armchair? Would they even like each other?

It was all quite scary. The one thing that united them in their thoughts though, was this strong desire to save the children and that was all they were concerned about. That thought was, of course, the secret of why they had been blessed with this task and given the Gift of Déjà Vu in the first place. It was this compelling urge to put this dreadful tragedy right, which made them all such excellent candidates to enter into the Secrets of the KOL and qualified them all to JIT.

As they neared the Ruin, they saw Nuttingham Squirrel hurrying along.

"I wonder if he would like to join us at Grandfather's?" Joni-Pip said.

"You can but ask," suggested Ethelred-Ted.

They met up at the Ruin. He was in a very bad mood and went to walk by them.

"I wondered if you wanted to come and have lunch with us at Grandfather's?"

"It would be very nice if y' could join us," added Hetty the Wee kindly.

Nuttingham Squirrel pulled himself up as tall as he could.

"Certainly not!" he snapped. "I am far too busy! I have my work to do!"

"What's that you've got in your hand, Nut?" asked Ethelred-Ted.

Nuttingham Squirrel quickly put his hand behind his back.

"C'mon, show us! We only want t' see it, we dinna want t' take it."

"It's none of your business!" the rude rodent responded.

Poppy flew up and circled round him so she could see what he was holding.

"Nuttingham Squirrel, you've got Jack's little telephone!" she shouted.

"What?" chorused Ethelred-Ted, Joni-Pip and Hetty in absolute astonishment.

"How on earth did you get that?" asked Poppy-Plump-Pij.

"None of your business!" snapped Nuttingham Squirrel again.

"Unfortunately for you, My Friend, it **is** very much our business right now!" said Ethelred-Ted assertively. "Hand it over this minute....if you please?"

The grumpy Squirrel began to walk off but the three of them very quickly stopped every way he tried to go and Poppy dive-bombed him from above.

"You don't even know what it is, Nut Old Boy, do you?" quizzed Eth. "So you definitely don't know how it works or what it's for, do you? We, on the other hand, have been looking for this everywhere as we need it to fix something very urgently, this actual minute," he went on, slightly over-exaggerating and bending the truth!

"What might that be then? This urgent 'something', you need to fix?"

"It's not for y' to know but we will tell y' this, Laddie....y' found it in Marley's Barn, didn't y'?" said Hetty the Wee, very cleverly.

"How did you know that?" the squirrel asked.

"Because I was the last to use it and the last time I saw it, was in Marley's Barn," said Joni-Pip truthfully.

"It doesn't belong to you, Nottingham, so give it to us now!" shouted Poppy.

The Squirrel had bad memories of his last encounter with this 'dangerously unbalanced' wood pigeon. He most certainly didn't fancy any repeat performances. He immediately thrust Jack's 'phone into Joni-Pip's hands and went scurrying off!

Nottingham Squirrel pulled himself up as tall as he could, "Certainly not!" he snapped, "I am far too busy

"That was easyful!" laughed Poppy-Plump-Pij.

"We must put the Fear of Poppy in him more often!" laughed Ethelred-Ted.

They then examined Jack's mobile 'phone for a few minutes, pressing several, if not all the keys, one at a time but absolutely nothing happened. They tried again and again using all manner of combinations. Still the mobile 'phone lay dormant.

"What's that you've got there?" came a gruff voice behind Joni-Pip. She spun round to see the small band of strange soldiers they had met previously, when they had been all sitting in a circle with Steve, Craig and Flip.

"Nothing, just one of my brother's things he uses for his Calculus," Joni-Pip replied, surprising herself by her quick response.

"I see," said the man in uniform, "where are you going?" he asked sternly.

"To my Grandfather's Crooked Cottage," she pointed down the hill.

"Have you seen any strange men around, wearing long, black, coats?"

"No," she knew she was lying but she didn't know how or why.

227

"Well, if you see anything suspicious then you must report it to the Constabulary!" said the Officer and the soldiers marched off, back in the direction from which they came. As they did she turned and watched. Her friends turned their attention back to the telephone. Of course, none of them had any idea how it worked.

"Let's be logical about this, we must get this back to Jack, yes?"

"Yes!" they all chorused.

"Yes, we must....mustn't we?" he asked again.

"I suppose so, I expect he needs it," offered Joni-Pip.

"Yes," the rest of them said quietly, all nodding their heads.

"Why?" asked Poppy-Plump-Pij.

They all smiled and shook their heads.

"Poppy, I have no idea but I should think Jack will miss it," said Ethelred-Ted.

"So how do we get it to him, then?" came Poppy's next question.

"I have no idea!" laughed Ethelred-Ted. "We don't know anything do we?"

"But we do know a bit....a little bit," said Joni-Pip.

"Yes, yes, Joni-Pip that's good, that's good. So, let's start by thinking about all the things we do know about it. Yes?" he suggested.

Everybody nodded.

"The first thing we know is...." Ethelred-Ted hesitated.

"It's Jack's!" exclaimed Poppy-Plump-Pij firmly.

"Yes," said Eth, "it most certainly is! So that's the first thing we know about it."

"Aye, it's....er ...." stammered Hetty the Wee, "it's a wee telephone!"

"Good, Hetty, that's two things we know about it," said the Teddy Bear happily.

"I know...." said Joni-Pip, "it's from the Future!"

"Yes," said Ethelred-Ted sounding very teacher-like. "We're definitely getting somewhere, now!"

The Four of them desperately searched their minds for some scrap of information, about the 'phone, they might have stored from their hour with Jack, Red-Ted and Macca. Unfortunately, the cupboard was bare. Not a crumb was to be found.

"This calls for some drastic measures!" declared Ethelred-Ted.

His friends all looked at him hopefully, like soldiers with their heads stretched forward, awaiting his command.

"Yes, definitely....drastic measures!" repeated the Bear.

"Yes, Ma Lamb?"

"Well....of course we could....er...." Ethelred-Ted hesitated.

228

"Could what?" asked Joni-Pip expectantly.

"Well, we could....um....we could....um....yes....that might work...." this was one, totally perplexed red and yellow Teddy Bear.

"What might work?" questioned Poppy. "Ethey, what is the plan?" the Wood Pigeon loved saying that word 'plan'. She thought it sounded terribly important.

Hetty, Poppy and Joni-Pip all looked at Ethelred-Ted in anticipation of his instructions.

"I haven't the faintest idea!" declared the Bear.

His three friends looked horrified.

"Look, You Lot, what d'you expect? I'm only a Stuffed Toy!" said Ethelred-Ted crossly and then added, holding up his sling, "With a torn arm that needs stitching!"

His three friends looked aghast at this statement: they all looked at each other for a moment and then burst into laughter!

"I think we should pick Grandfather's brains!" laughed Joni-Pip.

They started walking down the hill towards Grandfather's Crooked Cottage, still laughing at Ethelred-Ted's statement. Joni-Pip carried Jack's mobile 'phone carefully in both of her hands. She wasn't quite sure how she was supposed to hold it.

Suddenly, the small screen on the 'phone lit up and the 'phone started to vibrate and ring. Joni-Pip was so startled that she panicked and the 'phone slipped out of her fingers. She quickly tried to grab it back but the 'phone once again bounced out of her hands and up into the air. The twelve-year-old desperately struggled to try and catch it and once again, the 'phone, still merrily ringing, seemed to leap in the air. A Juggler in a Circus, practicing her act....only very badly....comes to mind! All her friends looked on in horror, wondering if she was going to let it drop and smash on to the ground but she didn't! She finally caught the jumping, Jack's 'phone and held it very firmly in both of her hands and sighed with rapturous relief.

Her friends spontaneously applauded this wonderful performance and then looked at each other hopelessly. They had no idea what on earth to do with this strange Future 'phone. It continued crying out to be answered.

"What do I do? What do I do?" Joni-Pip said in panic.

"Answer it....answer it!" said Hetty the Wee in equal panic.

"Yeah right and how do I do that?" said Joni-Pip sarcastically. "Somebody make a suggestion!"

"Press a few buttons, can't you?" said Ethelred-Ted quickly.

Then, as suddenly as the 'phone started to ring, it stopped.

Everybody just stared at it in silence: willing it to start ringing again.

They were all so bitterly disappointed and gathered round to look at it.

"Hey, look what it says on the tiny little square, at the top of the telephone!" exclaimed Hetty the Wee.

"What does it say?" asked Poppy-Plump-Pij, straining her little head to try and read the words.

"I MISSED CALL" read Ethelred-Ted out loud.

"How cleverful!" said Poppy, with a gasp and then added incredulously, "How does it know?"

To these four friends in 1942, that didn't seem too much of a silly question, so Ethelred-Ted answered seriously,

"It must be someway of communicating....telling the person who is using it....I know....I've got it....the little telephone is telling us that 'I have just missed a call'. It has missed a call."

"Ye are so clever, Ma Pet."

Ethelred-Ted beamed.

"I wonder why it says 'I missed call' instead of 'I have missed a call' ?" questioned Joni-Pip.

"That's easy," said Poppy-Plump-Pij.

"It is?" all her friends asked.

"It's American! They always shorten things now....then....whatever Time it is....Jack told us!" said Poppy-Plump-Pij, shrugging her shoulders and slightly opening her wings, a bit like Fagin, in Oliver Twist.

"That's it!" said Hetty the Wee. "Y' are so clever, too, Poppy!"

The Wood Pigeon also beamed happily.

But the ray quickly faded as Joni-Pip put a small, loose screw in the machine....well dropped one, actually.

"We are so, so clever," she said sarcastically. "The 'phone has just informed us that it has just missed a call: which of course we **didn't** know! O.K. then, what do we do now?"

Everybody's mood darkened.

"Let's have a look at Jack's 'phone again," said Hetty the Wee, trying to raise some enthusiasm, "we might be able t' learn something."

"Good idea, Het!" said Ethelred-Ted; still smarting from Joni-Pip's harsh but truthful comment about them all.

He took his poorly arm out of the sling and very gently took the 'phone from Joni-Pip's hands.

"Do you mind if I have a look at it....a good look at it?" he asked, not waiting for a reply.

He ran his eyes over the key pad, scrutinising every part of it.

"Look!" he said excitedly. "There is a little red picture of a 'phone on this tiny button, here on this side....and a little green picture of a 'phone on this tiny button on the other side....that must mean something...."

"You're right!" said Joni-Pip. "I didn't notice it before. That's swell, Eth!"

Her Teddy Bear frowned at her Yankee phrase and then beamed again.

"P'raps it's to tell us if it's stopping or going," said Poppy-Plump-Pij sweetly. "Like the traffic lights in Nottingham."

"That's brilliant, Pops, that's marvellous! I'm sure you're right!" said Ethelred-Ted appreciatively. He stopped and thought for a bit then he said, "When have you **ever** seen traffic lights in Nottingham?"

"I am a bird. I fly. I travel. Do you know how far and how quick it is to fly over to Nottingham from Edwinstowe?" asked Poppy authoritatively.

"It must be quite close....as the crow flies...." answered Eth cheekily.

"Well, as this Wood Pigeon flies, it's only a few miles and I have done it several times; quite recently, actually, with a very nice friend, as well!" said Poppy saucily.

"Who's a pretty, proud pigeon then?" laughed Hetty the Wee, lifting her little paw and touching Poppy-Plump-Pij's wing affectionately.

"Traffic light or no traffic light," said Joni-Pip, "perhaps if it rings again, we should press the green button and then it knows it can go?"

"Let's just hope it rings again and we can try it, then," said Poppy.

They all nodded and just watched the 'phone for a few minutes.

Sadly, nothing happened.

The 'phone remained silent and still.

"I suggest we make our way to Grandfather's for lunch and we all keep our ears well and truly open, ready to press the little green picture of a telephone, if necessary," said Ethelred-Ted.

"Good idea!" his friends all chorused.

As they walked down the sloping hill towards The Crooked Cottage, Joni-Pip heard a twig crack. She spun round to see who or what had made the noise, just in time to see the back of the, now familiar, grey cloak, disappearing behind a tree.

"There he is again! Look!" she cried, running back to try and speak to whoever it was that wore the hooded cloak.

"Joni-Pip, where are you going?" Ethelred-Ted shouted after her.

"It's the man in the cloak!" Joni-Pip shouted back. "Hey you!" she called towards the empty space in front of her, "Who are you? Please speak to us, what do you want?"

"Ethelred-Ted ran back to be with her.

"There's no-one there, Joni-Pip, see!" he said putting his arm around her.

"Well, there was. I heard him and saw him.....well, the back of him!"

"Oh, him again, the man in the hood, was it?" asked Eth gently.

231

Joni-Pip nodded.

"Something tells me we will find out what this all means one day. Let's go to Grandfather's, I need a Munch Break of Mammoth proportions!"

When they arrived at Grandfather's cottage, he was up on the hill chopping wood. The cats walked in line to greet them, while Poppy-Plump-Pij stopped for a drink in the stream.

"Go into the kitchen!" called out Grandfather. "I've left you all a snack to be getting on with. I won't be long!"

After stroking all the cats and kittens, the group of friends walked down the slope and into Grandfather's cosy kitchen. Chardonnay and her three kittens, Oliver, Barnaby and Cleo followed them into the kitchen. Sebastian (Grandfather's fluffy, cream, Persian cat), Romeo and Millie stayed outside. They playfully chased the wood chippings that floated and twirled, while Grandfather chopped the logs.

In no time at all, all four of them had settled themselves to munching away at the delicious home-made biscuits and tasting the yummy black- currant cordial, Grandfather always made for them. Jack's 'phone, which Joni-Pip had rested on the kitchen table, suddenly came alive again. The little screen

lit up and the 'phone began to vibrate and ring loudly. All of them scrambled to get it. Poppy flew to it first and tried to pick it up with her beak. Of course, she dropped it. Fortunately, it fell down towards Hetty the Wee, who put out her little paws, ready to catch it but she grabbed it so tightly, it slipped out of her grip and up into the air. Joni-Pip lurched forward and tried to grab it. It landed on one of her hands and she tried to put the other hand over it, to secure it but as it was vibrating so fiercely, it literally jumped off her hand and back into the air: at which point Ethelred-Ted put both of his paws up in the air and the flighty 'phone came hurtling back down again, finally being captured in his resolute clutch!

"Quick! Quick! Let it go!" yelled Poppy from the air. "E.T. go phone!"

Ethelred-Ted turned and looked at her strangely.

The very last thing he was likely to do, was to let it go; it had taken such a palaver to finally constrain it! What was the Bird thinking?

"Press the little green telephone, quickly....quickly!" urged Hetty.

"Yes, quickly!" shouted Poppy-Plump-Pij. "Then it will know it can go!"

Joni-Pip suddenly understood what Poppy meant. She took the 'phone from him and put the shaking 'phone on the palm of one of her hands and fumblingly attempted to press the little green 'phone key. At first nothing happened. The 'phone continued to ring away. She tried again.

The ringing stopped.

Joni-Pip looked at the small screen on the 'phone.

She read the words GRANDPA HOME.

A cold shiver went right through her little heart.

"Hello," came a quiet voice from the small 'phone in her hand.

Joni-Pip lifted the 'phone to her ear.

"Hello," came the voice again, only it was much louder this time.

Joni-Pip shook and said in a whisper,

"Hello."

"Jack, is that you?" asked the voice in the 'phone again.

"Er....no....it's not...." Joni-Pip replied.

"Who is it? Don't I know you?" questioned the voice again.

'Don't I know **you**?' repeated Joni-Pip to herself but then replied,

"Er....I think we have met a few times...."

"Is Jack with you, then?" asked the voice.

"Er no....not right now....we have been together....er....I mean he has been here...." she stumbled.

"So where is he now?" came the voice; such a beautiful voice that had hardly changed: just a bit more of an American accent, that's all.

"Er....I have no idea....but please could you ask Jack to ring his telephone....as he left it here....with me....er....last time I saw him," requested Joni-Pip, cleverly.

"Sure!" said the voice. "Who shall I tell him to 'phone?"

Joni-Pip looked startled and stammered,

"Er....er....er....tell him....tell him....it's....it's....Joni-Pip!" she blurted.

The voice on the other end of the 'phone went silent.

"I beg your pardon....J.P. is that you?....But you sound so young....no it can't be....you sound like...." the voice trailed away.

"Look....please, just tell him to ring his 'phone and it will be answered this time....he will understand....thank you," said Joni-Pip bravely.

The voice on the other end faltered.

"O.K.....it was really nice speaking to you....really, really nice," came the old man's voice. "Goodbye!"

"Good bye!" said Joni-Pip sadly.

She put the 'phone back on the table.

"Who was that?" asked her three friends together.

Joni-Pip didn't reply. She walked over to the kitchen window and looked out at her very own Grandfather.

She shook her head.

"I have just spoken to another grandfather," she said almost not believing what she had actually done.

"What your other one....the one in Portland?" asked Hetty the Wee.

Joni-Pip turned towards her friends.

"No, Silly I have just been speaking to Jack's Grandpa....my brother...."

"Alex!" her friends all gasped.

"For just a moment I heard the excitement in his voice because I know he recognised my voice from the Past," she said wistfully.

"Well, it's a jolly good job that you have already received the Gift of Déjà Vu, Joni-Pip. It's a good job that....er....Red-Ted, Jack and Macca have already jumped over the Wall of Time and visited us at Marley's Barn. It's also a jolly good job that the KOL has turned....because if it hadn't....now....that would have been a terrible shock, for Alex....to hear your voice, after you had been dead for over sixty five years," said Ethelred-Ted soberly.

The 'Phone on the table began to crackle. They all looked at it.

"Oh, my and my again," said Poppy-Plump-Pij. "You forgot to tell it to stop....with the little red telephone presser!"

Eth was closest to Jack's 'phone, so he picked up the 'phone and pressed the little red 'phone key. The 'phone made a funny beeping noise.

"I expect that's the 'phone telling itself t' stop," said Hetty the Wee; then she sighed. "All this drama, I wonder my little heart can take it all!"

"You'll manage, Het," said Ethelred-Ted lovingly, "now where are some more of those scrumptious oatmeal biscuits?"

Everybody laughed. The little 'phone on the table beeped again but nobody heard it above the noisy laughter.

"Beep!" it went again. "Beeeep."

Chapter 26

A Voice from the Future

After having a delicious lunch at the Crooked Cottage with Grandfather, Joni-Pip and her friends went and played in the garden. Grandfather had a swing and a seesaw. The seesaw was just a barrel and a smooth plank but it served them well. Ethelred-Ted was in a happy mood. The lunch was one of his many favourites; hot fried egg sandwiches, followed by hot apple pie and fresh cream. He managed to devour several helpings of apple pie, not to mention that he polished off both Hetty's and Poppy's leftovers!

"Waste not, want not and all that," he said cramming the last delicious morsel, skilfully into his mouth. It left behind a beautiful white, creamy moustache on his furry, yellow face. Joni-Pip couldn't help but compare his face with Becky-Paige's at bedtimes. Eth's was after an Eating Marathon and Becky-Paige's was after a Toothpowder Spitting Marathon.

During this time, a careful watch was kept on Jack's 'phone. For some reason, Grandfather didn't seem to notice it, even though it often made a little beeping noise. They all presumed from this that it was because he wasn't part of their Gift of Déjà Vu and wasn't involved in this Pasture.

It was while they were taking it in turns on the seesaw: first of all Poppy and Hetty would have a go and then Joni-Pip and Eth would have a go: that Hetty noticed the little screen had some strange words written on it.

"Look!" she said, showing the 'phone to the others. "It says 'LOW BATT', what d' y' think it says that for?"

The other three crowded round her, offering suggestions as to what 'LOW BATT' might mean.

"D'you think it might be something to do with cricket?" asked Poppy.

"Good thought, good thought, Pops," said Ethelred-Ted.

"D'you think there are lots of Bats in America in 2007?" asked Joni-Pip.

"What, Hen, the flying sort? D'ye think it's some kind of warnin'....**Low Flying Bats**?" Hetty asked, glancing anxiously into the sky.

Joni-Pip nodded.

"A good thought....maybe....but how d'you spell that kind of bat?" Ethelred-Ted, shook his head and kind of smiled.

"You're right, Ethelred-Ted, I think there is only one 't' in that type of bat," said Joni-Pip nodding her head again.

"It has t' be somethin' 'low' whatever the 'batt' is, Ma Pets."

Everyone nodded.

As they were all huddled together, the small screen suddenly lit up and the 'phone began to vibrate and ring. This time, although startled, there was no panic.

Joni-Pip pressed the little green telephone key and put the 'phone to her ear.

"Hello," she said, sounding confident and loud.

"Hello," came the voice from sixty five years in her Future. "Hello, is that Great Auntie Joni-Pip?"

"Yes, it's me."

"That's swell! Wow, am I relieved that I have got hold of you, at last! I have been ringing for days and I worried I might have flattened the battery," came Jack's unmistakeable American accent.

"Battery?" asked Joni-Pip.

"Battery!" said Eth. "Of course!"

"Yes, my cell 'phone has a brilliant seventeen day battery but I wondered how long it would last, especially as it had JITTED!" laughed Jack.

"Oh, right," said Joni-Pip, "you had best talk to Ethelred-Ted about that, I don't know anything about batteries!"

"When Grandpa was puzzled, that a 'Joni-Pip' had answered my cell 'phone, Red-Ted and I guessed you still remembered our visit. There's so much I'd like to say but I must be quick. The first thing is this: as I left my cell 'phone in the Past, the Pasture hasn't ended yet. The Circle started to close up but it hasn't been completed, it's still open. Red-Ted reckons you must be still enjoying it, too, which you obviously are, as you know who I am! Isn't it brilliant? By now, our memories should have been long gone. As it is, we don't think the Pasture will end, or can end, until I have my cell 'phone back. Then the Circle will be joined up and perfect again, with no loose ends from another Time. We must end it as soon as we can, as we are holding up any Wall jumps, any JITTING you might want to attempt and each Pasture should only last one hour....we are breaking all the Rules!" Jack sounded as if he knew everything that Joni-Pip was thinking.

"Oh yes right....we are actually planning to jump over the Wall of Time very soon!" said Joni-Pip, hardly believing what she was saying.

"Hmmmmm! How well Red-Ted remembers himself!" laughed Jack. "That's exactly what he told me you would be planning....he mentioned something about the Workhouse Fire."

"Right! He's still so clever, then!" laughed back Joni-Pip. "Jack, how on earth am I....are we....going to get your telephone back to you in the Future? Er.....we nearly didn't have the 'phone, at all....it ....er...I ....er....it was left up at Marley's Barn. Fortunately, Nuttingham Squirrel found it."

"Did he? How is the Old Rodent? I meant to say, Red-Ted said not to be too hard on him, he can be very useful; no, he will be very useful to you..."

"Nuttingham Squirrel useful? I think not! Anyway, to get back to our pressing predicament....surely without jumping over the Wall of Time, it's impossible to get your phone back to you, in the Future and we can't jump over the Wall of Time, until this Pasture is over. Aren't we rather stuck in a loop somehow? Talk about going round and round in circles!"

"Sure, we thought, to our horror that was the case but your friend and mine, the Great Red-Ted, has come up with the most brilliant idea!"

Jack's 'phone beeped.

"Shucks! That was my 'phone....the battery must be low," panicked Jack. "What will happen, then?"

"The 'phone will die."

"The phone will die?" repeated Joni-Pip. "What happens then?"

"We bury it?" asked Poppy gravely.

"We won't be able to communicate! You must find a way of re-charging the battery! Remember this, Auntie Joni-Pip, whatever you do, or you'll be stuck in this Pasture forever. It has never happened to us before, so we're not quite sure what the consequences would be! Anyway, we haven't time to talk, just remember it's a **3.7** volt battery, that's all. Don't go using Grandfather's old car battery, that's 12 volts. Red-Ted said that will melt it....slightly!!!! So don't short circuit it. Listen very, very carefully. This might be a lot to take in....no wonder we couldn't stay in this Pasture....it would be too much ....knowing all the Future .... before it happened."

Jack's cell 'phone beeped again and the little screen continuously flashed up the words....'LOW BATT'.

"I heard that....listen carefully. Please take my cell 'phone, wrap it up in something and put it in a box and write on it 'Not to be opened until 2007' and then you must put it, remember this is so important, it's somewhere that is exactly the same in 2007 as it is, with you, in 1942...."

"Where?" asked Joni-Pip.

"It's...." the voice from the Future suddenly stopped. The little 'phone in Joni-Pip's hand was silent.

"Jack....Jack....are you still there?" Joni-Pip spoke into the 'phone. "Where have I got to put your little telephone? Where, Jack, where?"

There was no answer.

In sheer horror, Joni-Pip kept pressing as many keys as she could, trying

237

desperately to get the 'phone to light up again.

It was to no avail.

Jack's cell 'phone was lifeless.

The battery was dead.

Large tears began to roll from Joni-Pip's eyes.

"It's all my fault!" she sobbed.

Ethelred-Ted put his good arm around her and gave her a gentle hug.

"Joni-Pip, whatever is the matter? What has happened?"

"Everything is lost: everything can't be put right and it's all my fault," she continued weeping.

Hetty the Wee put a supportive paw on her leg.

"Don't y' be worryin' yerself, Lassie. I'm sure we can do something about....whatever it is that y' have done."

"But we can't, can we?" said Joni-Pip faltering.

Pops flew up and gently landed on Joni-Pip's shoulder. Stretching her little head to one side, she looked lovingly into Joni-Pip's tear-filled eyes.

"My Sweet Friend," she said, sounding very much like a certain red and yellow Ted, "there has to be something, we always find something."

Ethelred-Ted pulled Joni-Pip very gently over to the swing and sat her down on it and said encouragingly,

"Tell us what this is all about....we only heard your part of the conversation, so you need to fill us all in, then we can think about....what you think is 'your fault'....which, I am quite sure, it's not."

The swing remained still, as Joni-Pip began.

"Red-Ted said that as the telephone is still in the Past, this Pasture can't end. He said that probably we still remember everything because of that."

"Hmmmm!" said Ethelred-Ted thoughtfully and rather than making a comment, he let Joni-Pip continue.

"Jack said that when his Grandpa, Alex, told him, strangely, that a 'Joni-Pip' had answered his 'phone, then both he and Red-Ted knew that, we too, were still in their Pasture."

"Hmmmm!" said Ethelred-Ted once more but again he kept quiet.

"Anyway, Red-Ted has devised a clever plan," Joni-Pip paused. "Oh, sorry, I forgot to say that Red-Ted said to Jack, that he thinks we won't be able to attempt any jumps over the Wall of Time, until this Pasture is over. He also said they didn't know what might happen, as they had never left anything behind before...."

"How can they possibly know any of that, Ma Pets?"

"And the 'Clever Plan'?" asked Poppy; she just loved using that word.

"Yes, the Clever Plan, Red-Ted said I was to wrap up Jack's little telephone, put it in a box and mark it, 'Not to be opened until 2007' and put it somewhere that hasn't changed since now, in 1942," Joni-Pip said.

"What do you mean?" asked Poppy-Plump-Pij.

"We have to put it in a place that is still the same in 2007, as it is today ....now....in 1942," replied Joni-Pip.

"That Red-Ted is staggering!" said Eth, shaking his head and beaming.

The others all looked at him for a moment and then burst out laughing.

This was very good for Joni-Pip.

"Self praise indeed, Ma Pet!"

"What?"

They all continued to laugh as Joni-Pip started to move the swing gently.

"This is all very well and good: truly a 'clever plan' of your future brilliance, Ethelred-Ted....but there is one slight problem....one winsy, pinsy, tinsy, tiny detail that I forgot to mention....which of course is also the reason for my tears...."

Perturbed, her Friends all looked at her and raised their eyebrows.

"The little telephone has no life left...."

"And?" the other three said together.

"Jack didn't have time to tell me **where** we are to put the wrapped up telephone, in the box marked 'Not to be opened until 2007'!"

She jumped off the swing and walked away from them.

"The battery is dead!" she said sombrely, then she turned to face them.

For a while all of her friends remained silent, trying to take in the enormity of the hopeless situation they all now found themselves in.

"So....tell me, Hen....why d' y' think this is all yer fault?" asked Hetty, trying so hard to relieve the tension.

Joni-Pip walked back and got on to the swing. She didn't reply, she just began working the swing up high. Higher and higher she went.

"Of course it's my fault!" she shouted down, flying high above them. "I remember now, when we were in Marley's Barn, I was so deeply moved when I spoke to Myself as an Old Lady....Jack's Aunt....Great Auntie Joni-Pip or Philipa, whatever he called me. It was Me! Can you imagine how extraordinary that was for me, talking to myself, as I will be in sixty five years time? Not only that, can't you see how difficult it was? I'd just learnt that I'd been killed as a twelve-year-old! No wonder the Pastures can't last more than an hour, normally. It's awful thinking about it; my accident, my funeral, my grave. A headstone with my name on it. The flowers. My family crying. Alex crying and Mother, Darling Sweet Mother, eventually becoming so ill after losing me and dying young. It was just too much!"

Like a bursting dam, all the pain and emotion of the last few days, which she had kept closely locked up in her heart, guarded even from herself, came flooding out. She sobbed and sobbed and floods of tears fell down her face.

"I shouldn't have gone up the ladder! I should have listened to Hetty! Why did I do it? I was warned!" she shouted out the words.

The swing continued to rise higher and higher.

"Take heed, Lassie!"

"Slow down, Joni-Pip." Poppy flew up and landed on the horizontal bar on the top of the swing.

The swing began to shake violently and Poppy had to hold on with her little claws, as tightly as she could, to stop herself from being thrown off.

Eth could see what was about to happen and he called out loudly,

"Joni-Pip, can you stop swinging now? I have a plan!"

Of course he didn't but he could foresee the repeat of her accident. He worried that Joni-Pip, coming back to live a Second Circle of her Life, was not to be. He panicked she wasn't going to be able to cheat Death, after all.

"So you see....it's all my fault!" she shouted through her weeping.

The swing went so high they thought it would go over the top of the bar.

"Don't you see? I was so upset; in so much pain, **I forgot to give the telephone back to Jack**. I remember now, I walked off in a corner with it; I still had it in my hand. I remember it all so clearly. It was kind of like a link, that little telephone. It was so tiny but it was so huge to me. It was really special. I remember rubbing my hands over it, realising that I had just spoken to myself through it....I didn't want to let it go....then, Red-Ted said they needed to jump back over the Wall of Time...."

"Joni-Pip, please let the swing slow down now?" asked Eth, with large, tears in his eyes. "We understand how dreadful it must have been for you!"

"Anyone goin' through what y' were, Pet, could have forgotten to give it back....easily....we, no doubt, would've done the same, exactly the same!"

The swing began to shake, so much that the very bars in the ground, which stabilized it, began to come loose.

"I have forgotten so many things, Joni-Pip!" said Poppy, finally giving up her struggle to stay on the bar and perilously flying, fluttering in front of the uncontrollable swing, trying to stay as close to Joni-Pip as she could.

Soon all four poles had come loose, as the swinging, sobbing, Joni-Pip blurted out her final, confessional words.

"Don't you all understand? I just lied to you all a minute ago. I didn't forget to give back the telephone!" she wailed. "I didn't forget! I didn't forget! **I kept it on purpose....I wanted to keep it....I stole it!**"

The poles of the swing finally submitted to the forces above it and they all lifted up out of the ground. The entire swing fell forward. It thudded on the ground and Joni-Pip was catapulted high into the air.

240

Chapter 27

Light from the Torch

"Is she dead, Grandfather?"

"Dead? What do you mean 'dead'? Of course not, Hetty, just give her some space," laughed Grandfather.

Bear in mind he hadn't been privy to Joni-Pip's outburst. He didn't realise how awful her friends were feeling. The first he knew about this accident, was when Poppy-Plump-Pij came flying into the kitchen, all flustered, pleading with him to,

'Come quickly! We think Joni-Pip has killed herself!'

He immediately ran into the garden and after checking that she was breathing and that she hadn't broken any bones, he carried her carefully, very carefully, into the parlour and laid her on the huge, comfy sofa, in front of the fire and covered her with a soft, warm, tartan blanket.

He then wrote a note for Doctor Evans and tied it round Poppy-Plump-Pij's neck and sent her off to fetch him.

As Poppy flew into the village, she was reminded of the terrible night of the storm. That night, she had flown the flight of her life. Her perilous journey had taken her from Marley's Barn across to the Crooked Cottage and then over Windy Woods to Knotty Knook. This time there was no wind and rain to battle against, no thunder and lightning to terrify her: just clear blue, beautiful sky to fly in. There was no wind, at all, just beaming, golden sunshine and what's more, Grandfather had reassured her as she took off that Joni-Pip was going to be all right. She chuckled as she saw the obnoxious Nuttingham Squirrel below her, scurrying along in his usual officious manner. She didn't care for him much, so she felt a little bit smug and considered she had an advantage over him, as she flew way above him.

Back in The Crooked Cottage, Eth had immediately put the kettle on for the water to boil, so that in true English fashion, this German, Steiff Teddy Bear, could make a pot of tea. Hetty was anxiously watching over Joni-Pip as she lay motionless and pale on the sofa in front of the fire. Grandfather continued to re-assure her that Joni-Pip was still very much alive.

Despite his calmness, Grandfather was indeed worried. The last time he'd seen something similar to this was when young Colin Finn had had his accident and the poor boy had never recovered from his head injuries.

It wasn't too long before the sound of a big, old motorbike came throttling up towards The Crooked Cottage. Grandfather walked through, into the kitchen, pulled on his boots, crunched across the pebbly drive and waited for the rider and his passenger to get off the big, black bike. Soon, Doctor Evans walked into the cottage kitchen with Poppy-Plump-Pij.

"I've just had a ride on a motorbike!" she beamed.

"Well, I never: a bit different from flying!" said Grandfather, appreciatively stroking the pigeon's smooth back. "You were quick! Well done, Poppy Pigeon!"

"She was amazing!" said the kindly Welsh Doctor, taking off his leather balaclava, huge gauntlets and goggles and putting them on the kitchen table. "I have had to administer to casualties in many a terrible Mine accident in South Wales. You see, speed is the essence at these times. So, no sooner had I got your message from this pretty little pigeon, than I was on my way to see young Joni-Philipa. I left in the middle of looking at Mrs Botterton's bunions....but she understood, of course, so I got on my motorbike and rode here as quickly as I could....Now let me see my patient please? In the Parlour, isn't it?"

With that he disappeared.

After twenty anxious minutes for Eth, Poppy, Hetty and Grandfather, Doctor Evans reappeared in the kitchen. He went over to the large, white, porcelain sink and washed and scrubbed his hands thoroughly. He used the cream slab of Sunlight soap, on the draining board and Grandfather's wooden-backed, scrubbing brush. He turned his head, looked over his shoulder and spoke to them; his back was still towards them.

"She's going to be fine. She is slightly, very slightly concussed, that's

242

all. No bones broken. No cuts or bruises even: just a little bump on her head." He rinsed his hands under the gushing, running water. "I suggested to her that she just rested for a couple of hours and then I think she could be taken home."

"You spoke to her?" asked Grandfather, so relieved.

"Actually, yes," replied the doctor, "as I was looking at the back of her eyes with my special little torch, she asked me what batteries it took. I told her two little 1.5 volt batteries. She kept going on about these batteries. Batteries? I ask you. She kept saying she needed 3.7 volts. Look you, I said, I don't have 3.7 volt batteries: never heard of them, even. She was so going on about these batteries that thought I would pacify her, keep her quiet like, so, I took the two little 1.5 volt batteries out of my torch and gave them to her. I have more in the surgery see, down in the village: spares you know: plenty of spares. That seemed to still her a bit. She seemed almost demented about these batteries but now she's all right. She lit up like a little torch, herself, when I put them in her hands. Amazing what batteries can do!" he laughed.

While Grandfather was seeing the Doctor off, Ethelred-Ted, Hetty the Wee and Poppy-Plump-Pij hurried into the Parlour to see Joni-Pip.

"May I brew you a nice hot cup of tea?" asked Ethelred-Ted. "I'm sure there might be a bit of apple pie left over from lunch, as well."

Joni-Pip was sitting up on the sofa, with the blanket snuggled around her legs.

"No, I don't think there is any. Some bear ate the last of it; polished off the lot!" laughed Joni-Pip, then she winced and put her hand on her head. "Ooh, that hurt!"

"Be careful, Joni-Pip, y' had a nasty fall and the doctor, Doctor Evans, said y' must rest," cautioned Hetty the Wee.

"Only for a couple of hours, Het!" smiled Joni-Pip. "Thank you for caring, though. I would love a cup of tea, please, Eth? That would be so nice! English Breakfast?" ((My favourite, too, unquestionably!))

Soon, they were all sitting together in the Parlour, sipping hot tea. The two men had obviously struck up an interesting conversation piece, as through the window, they all could see them both, nattering by the sheds.

"Right!" said Joni-Pip firmly. "This is what we have to do. Jack said we must charge the battery of his telephone, if we need to talk to him again, which of course we do because we don't know where to leave the little telephone for them to collect in 2007. So we need to do that, as soon as we can. You probably guessed, the words 'low batt' stand for 'low battery'. The 'phone was telling us the battery, the one that made the little telephone work, was low in power and needed charging. That's why it finally

243

stopped working, when I was talking to Jack. So we have to find a way to charge it."

She seemed to be totally unaware of her emotional outburst about the mobile 'phone, earlier and so, kindly, all of her friends made no comment about it. None at all: in fact it was never, ever mentioned again. It was as if it had never happened.

"Charge the battery? Does it have to pay us?" asked Poppy, shrugging.

"Shouldn't be too difficult," said Ethelred-Ted thoughtfully.

"I haven't a clue how or what or even **if** we can do it. I just thought of the idea, while Doctor Evans was examining me. As he was looking into my eyes with his little torch, he complained that he had only just put new batteries in and they weren't working properly. He then hit the torch on the end and the torch lit up again. Anyway, he has given me two little 1.5 volt batteries. Do you think we can devise a way to use them, to charge up the battery in Jack's little telephone, Ethelred-Ted?"

Eth stood up and walked over to the window. He looked out across the fields for a moment, across the beautiful, English countryside. Then his eyes were turned to the skies, as a couple of new, huge Lancaster Bombers thundered over the cottage.

"Sometimes I forget we are living during a war. How selfish are we? How selfish am I? Generally, all I seem worried about is that I might be late for breakfast."

He sighed and then turned around to face his friends.

"To get back to Selfish Us, then; I don't think we are actually still part of Jack's, Red-Ted's and Macca's Pasture. The reason I say this, is this: after we left Marley's Barn, we had no recollection of what had just happened. All we know is that Joni-Pip said 'I know what is going to happen. I've been here before, talk about Déjà Vu?"

Joni-Pip screwed up her face, as the vision of the Fighter Pilot, once more came into her mind. Then Flip, Craig and Steve's faces shot across her mind, too. She shook her head, they disappeared and she forgot about them.

His three friends all nodded.

"I think through some fluke, well, actually because we made a 'worm's web'..." he looked at Poppy, smiled and gave her a little bow, "....of our first attempt to jump over the Wall of Time, we entered our own Pasture; we opened our own new Circle but it wasn't quite right. I'm wondering if each time we are affected in any way, we remember everything. You know what I mean; every time we go into the KOL or get the Gift of Déjà Vu, or jump over the Wall of Time, then we remember every other time we've done it. I think that must be the case. It might not, of course, my

244

thoughts might be purely boorish bunkum. That seems logical. Either way, we are very fortunate that this has happened at the same time; otherwise, when Jack's 'phone rang and Joni-Pip answered it, she wouldn't have had any idea whom she was talking to."

"I don't think I quite understand," said Poppy-Plump-Pij sweetly.

"It's very simple, Ma Pet," said Hetty the Wee, turning to her feathered friend, "because Jack left...." she looked at Joni-Pip and then smiled and continued talking to Poppy-Plump-Pij, "because we still have part of 2007 with us, through Jack's telephone, then the Circle of Life....you know the one Red-Ted drew for us in Marley's Barn....the Circle of Life is still not joined up for Red-Ted and Jack. At the same time we opened up a new Circle when we tried to jump over the Wall of Time ourselves. We now remember everything, so we know that the Circle has not been completed. Ethelred-Ted thinks there are two different Circles still open and that's why we can communicate with Jack."

"Er....right....right," said Poppy-Plump-Pij faintly.

"The question now, is," said Joni-Pip, "how do we charge the battery of Jack's little telephone? He gave me strict instructions that we mustn't overload the battery. He said the battery is 3.7 volts and it mustn't go over that, or it will melt. Doctor Evans has given me 3 volts with his two 1.5 batteries from his torch. That's not enough, is it Ethelred-Ted?"

Eth, who was still standing, looked at his friends and shook his head.

"So it has to be 3.7 volts, does it? That seems such a strange amount. I'm wondering how we are going to do that....now, let me think for a minute."

"Impossibleful, isn't it?" asked Poppy. "How can you have 3.7 revolts?"

The others all laughed. The pigeon turned up her little face and shrugged.

"Let's see what we've got and let's see what we need." Ethelred-Ted sounded very much like Archimedes Spindlethrop.

Joni-Pip handed him the two 1.5 volt batteries, which Doctor Evans had given her and Hetty the Wee gave him the lifeless telephone, which she had been guarding, ever since Joni-Pip had fallen off the swing.

"We have one dead telephone and....two 1.5 volt batteries. We need 3.7 volts and it must be that, or very, very close, or we will overload the telephone and 'melt it'!" said Ethelred-Ted.

All of the others remained very quiet. They knew he was a clever bear and they knew he had to work in silence, if he was to work at his best. He held the two batteries together and put them up against the telephone. He winced a bit.

"Are y' all right, Ma Lamb? Does y' arm still give y' some pain?"

"I must get it stitched up," replied Ethelred-Ted.

"Look why don't I do it now, while you try to fathom out the batteries?"

suggested Joni-Pip. She then turned to Hetty the Wee. "Hetty, Grandfather still keeps Grandmother's old sewing box in the corner. Could you get me some red silk, a largish needle and a thimble, please?"

"How long has Grandmother been dead and he still keeps her sewing box? That's amazing!" said Poppy-Plump-Pij.

"You don't talk about her much, Joni-Pip. What was she like?" asked Ethelred-Ted, hoping that he would divert her enough, so that she would forget about the 'painful needle work' to come!

"I know very little about her, other than she was poorly and died of Spanish 'flu in 1919. There's a picture of her in the dining room. Grandfather and Mother never seem to talk about her. It was 23 years ago that she died, Mother wasn't even married to Father then. I think it's too painful for them, so they just can't speak about it," said Joni-Pip very sadly.

"It's a pity we can't jump over the Wall of Time and save her!" said Poppy-Plump-Pij matter-of-factly.

"Hmmmm!....I can't see how that could work....catching some disease is very different from dying from an accident....we can stop accidents from happening, when we go back in the Past: just as Red-Ted and Jack made me stop Joni-Pip from going up the ladder....all accidents are avoidable....that's the horrible thing....the tragic part about being killed, as opposed to dying of some awful disease: which is terrible enough," said Ethelred-Ted thoughtfully, "but I can't see how we can stop somebody from contracting a fatal disease, can you?"

Everybody shook their heads. Hetty the Wee then walked over to Grandmother's sewing box, lifted up the lid, sorted through the beautiful coloured silks, took out the bright, ruby red one, chose a largish needle and picked out a thimble. She then closed the lid and walked back across the Parlour and handed them to Joni-Pip.

"Thank you, Het, you are a Love. Now, come and sit down beside me, Eth and I will get that poorly arm fixed for you, at last!" she said firmly.

Ethelred-Ted hesitated.

"Now!" Joni-Pip commanded.

Ethelred-Ted thought for a moment and then obediently did as he was told. He felt it wasn't worth protesting. The job needed to be done and now was as good a time as any. Joni-Pip threaded the needle, knotted the beautiful, shiny, ruby red, silk strand and commenced the operation. She prided herself that she could sew and so she very carefully began to use tiny stitches, to join the flap back to his arm again. Surprisingly, Ethelred-Ted reassured her that it didn't hurt and sat very still and made best use of this time by pondering over the problem of the batteries.

When the stitching was completed, Joni-Pip ended off her work by knotting the silk and biting off the end of the strand with her teeth.

Everybody examined her work.

"So prettyful and neatful!" said Poppy. "You can sew up my arm anytime!"

They all looked at Poppy's wings, shrugged and looked back at Joni-Pip.

"Aye, Lassie, that's a prime job!"

Ethelred-Ted walked over to the large mirror, hanging on the wall and surveyed Joni-Pip's handy work.

"M, M 'n M!" he said appreciatively. "You are a Master Sewer, Joni-Pip. I'd never have guessed you could have made such a good job of my arm!"

"You know there will always be a scar, don't you? The stitches won't fade, I'm afraid," said Joni-Pip sadly.

"They hardly show. You have made them so smallful," said Poppy-Plump-Pij, flying over to admire them again.

"I thank you **so** much, for **sewing** so much!" laughed Ethelred-Ted.

The others all laughed.

"Aye, I think now Joni-Pip must have her rest, or the Doctor will be cross w' us!" said Hetty. "I suggest she has a nap and we go and busy ourselves elsewhere."

"Good idea, Hetty," agreed Ethelred-Ted. "Why don't You Two come with me to Grandfather's shed? I'm sure we will be able to find something, somewhere, to sort out this battery business."

"Spiffing stuff, Eth. 'Bye for now, Joni-Pip, sleep wellful," said Poppy.

"Bye-bye, Pet, have a good rest. I'm glad y' feelin' so much better now." Hetty followed Poppy-Plump-Pij out of the cosy room.

"Thank you so much again for sewing up my arm, Joni-Pip. Now make sure you get some sleep, we have so much to do later!" Ethelred-Ted said, disappearing out of the door.

Reluctantly, Joni-Pip settled herself down and tried to fall asleep. She was far too excited to close her eyes and much, much too awake to fall asleep. However, once her friends had gone and the room was silent, apart from the flickering of the flames, from the log fire and the ticking of the clock on the dresser, she began to feel a bit weary. A few minutes later she slid herself down the sofa, until she was lying down. The door was pushed open gently and Sebastian effortlessly walked in and jumped up to be with her. He settled himself down beside her, as only cats can do and started purring. Joni-Pip stroked him gently for a little while, which made her feel remarkably comforted. Soon her eyes became heavy, very heavy, until they finally closed and she joined Sebastian in a peaceful, afternoon nap.

Chapter 28

The Abacus

The neat rows of tools hanging on the walls of Grandfather's shed, stood in stark contrast to the higgledy-piggledy chaos in Archimedes' Quission Hut. There was a line of varying sized screw drivers, then underneath was a row of pliers, wire cutters and spanners. Next came the wrenches and files and beneath them was Grandfather's collection of hammers and chisels.

The floor was swept clean and his workbench was clear, apart from a large vice, which was attached to one corner. Pushed neatly under the workbench, were two wooden laboratory stools. There were tidy piles of cables, wires and ropes, standing in one corner of the shed. A soldering iron, accompanied by rolls of solder, lay neatly on an old, mahogany, chest of drawers. The wide, wooden shelves were uniformly stacked with various sized tins: each dated and beautifully labelled, in Grandfather's immaculate Italic writing. There were nails, screws, tacks, pins, clamps, small washers, medium washers, large washers, rubber bungs and plugs. Grandfather kept so many things that one might wonder if there was something for every task or emergency, conceivable.

As it was, Ethelred-Ted did have an emergency and he wondered if Grandfather did have something for this particular task.

The Bear pulled out both of the wooden stools and sat on one. He laid out the two batteries and Jack's mobile telephone. Hetty the Wee tried to climb up on to the work bench, by using the cross bars on the stools. Poppy-Plump-Pij flew up and landed gently, beside Ethelred-Ted. There were so many advantages of being able to fly.

"I think Hetty needs a hand to get up," she said to Ethelred-Ted.

Ethelred-Ted was rather engrossed in his thoughts and ignored her, so she tried again.

"Ethelred-Ted, there is a little hedgehog here, who could do with a bit of help."

The Bear mumbled something to himself and picked up the telephone.

"The first thing we have to do is find out where the battery is," he said, examining Jack's cell 'phone.

Poppy-Plump-Pij walked determinedly across the workbench, thumping each footstep as she went.

"Is it just the Male of every species that seems to have this total lack of ability to communicate when trying to solve a problem?" she said to Hetty the Wee, who was valiantly trying to get herself higher and higher, threading herself in and out of the maze of wooden bars.

Hetty the Wee nodded.

"Some might think that might be a correct assumption of a lot of males," she laughed and then added, "but not all!"

Poppy jumped up on to Ethelred-Ted's head: something she had never done before.

"Hey, You, Archimedes' Apprentice, there is a small friend of yours that could do with a bit of help."

She bent her head down, right into his face.

"Pops, can't you see I'm busy?"

"I'm fed up with having to do this," said the little pigeon crossly. Then she spoke, very deliberately, mouthing her words, very definitely.

"Can you please give Hetty a hand to get up on to the bench?"

"Of course," said the Bear, getting off his stool and moving it back so that Hetty could use the seat as a platform to climb up on to the workbench, "you only had to ask!"

Hetty the Wee and Poppy-Plump-Pij looked at each other and made an 'O.K. so he **is** Archimedes' face and then chuckled.

"What?"

Poppy-Plump-Pij gently jumped off Ethelred-Ted's head and helped Hetty the Wee to complete the final part of her ascent, up on to Grandfather's work bench.

The little hedgehog paused for a minute, to catch her breath and then she surveyed the batteries and the 'phone.

"What exactly are y' trying t' d'?" she asked with great interest.

"Well, it's like this, Hetty...." Ethelred-Ted began.

Hetty the Wee waited for him to continue but of course he didn't: he was far too busy searching his brain for a solution to the, what seemed like, almost insurmountable problem.

"So, Ma Lamb, what are y' goin' t' attempt?"

"Hmmmm....Jack told Joni-Pip that the charge must be no more than 3.7 volts and no less than 3.7 volts...." He wasn't replying to Hetty the Wee; he was just talking to himself: something exceedingly clever people seem to do all the time, don't they?

"Hmmmm....I remember talking about this, in the Parlour," said the hedgehog thoughtfully. "Is that a big problem, then?"

"Hmmm...." mumbled the Teddy Bear to himself. "There has to be a way we can do it."

Hetty looked at the batteries and then picked one up in her little paw.

"So what is this volt?"

"'Volt'?" questioned Ethelred-Ted. "Ah you mean voltage....these batteries are one and a half volts each....so we have 3 volts, so far....that means we need 0.7 volts from somewhere and then we can try and fix it up to Jack's telephone battery....wherever that is...."

"Jasper Perry sells bolts in his store," said Poppy-Plump-Pij sweetly.

Ethelred-Ted looked at his little pigeon pal and smiled.

"Yes, Pops, he does in Edwinstowe but it's not bolts; we need volts. I have thought of getting hold of another **battery** to make more **volts**....but that makes 4.5 volts and that's too much. Somehow we need to reduce the voltage; we mustn't put too many volts into the little 'phone or we will make it too hot and it won't work any more. Jack said that will make it melt."

"You mean too much of those things....those yokes....will cook Jack's telephone. Um....I don't think that would taste very nice....I think you can cook the yokes, though, can't you? You like yoke sandwiches?"

"Poppy Pigeon, you are so lovely," chuckled Eth, turning and stroking Poppy's back. "Whenever we have a difficult situation you always manage to say something sweet to make us laugh. We should hire you out as a T.C., a 'Tension Calmer'; we would make a fortune!"

Poppy-Plump-Pij looked puzzled and Hetty the Wee laughed.

The sound of a motor bike, revving up, outside, echoed through the shed.

"Doctor Evans must be setting off, at last. I hope Mrs Botterton's bunions haven't been too upset, having t' wait so long for the Doctor's return," laughed Hetty the Wee.

Ethelred-Ted looked at her and laughed too.

"What I don't understand," said Poppy-Plump-Pij seriously, "is why he would be looking at her onions anyway."

Ethelred-Ted and Hetty the Wee collapsed into hysterical fits of giggles.

"What's going on in here, then?" came Grandfather's voice, from behind them. He stood in the doorway, with a smile on his face. "Can I share the joke?"

"Well, I don't know why These Two are laughing," replied Poppy-Plump-Pij, "all I said was, I didn't understand why Doctor Evan's had to look at Mrs Botterton's onions. Can't they grow on their own?"

Grandfather started to chuckle, too. He walked over to Poppy-Plump-Pij and stroked her.

"What are You Good Folks doing in here anyway? Is Joni-Philipa asleep?"

"We left her t' rest, so we hope so," replied Hetty the Wee.

Grandfather looked at the two batteries and Jack's mobile 'phone on his

250

bench.

"What have we got here, then? May I have a look?"

Ethelred-Ted gave a half-smile.

"Er....well...."

Grandfather picked up the 'phone and examined it closely.

"What on earth is this? Where did you get it from? I've never seen anything like it!"

"Er...." panicked Ethelred-Ted.

"What does it do? What's it for?" Grandfather pressed the numerous buttons on the mobile 'phone.

"It's a toy," said Poppy-Plump-Pij.

"Oh!" said Grandfather. "I see....of course."

"Yes, yes it's a toy....only we can't get it t' work properly."

"It's a toy? A toy what?"

"It's a toy....it's a toy....abacus!" said Ethelred-Ted, taking it out of Grandfather's hands.

"Abacus? This little thing is a toy abacus....not a real abacus?"

Ethelred-Ted stumbled on blindly. He knew he had to. He didn't know where he was going with the conversation but he knew he was at the point of no return. Grandfather couldn't possibly understand.

He **wanted** to say:-

"Actually, Grandfather, this is a little portable telephone that has been left here by visitors from the Future; sixty five years in the future: in fact, from the next century. The visitors are related to you, Grandfather. You know your grandson, Alex? Well, this little telephone belongs to his grandson, Jack. Not only that, Grandfather, there is something even more amazing: Jack, your Great, Great, Grandson, has actually telephoned us from the Future and Joni-Pip has spoken to him using this little 'phone."

But of course he **couldn't.**

Would Grandfather believe that story?

Would anybody believe that story?

Would you believe that story, Dear Reader?

Nah!

So, the Teddy Bear had to continue down the path Poppy-Plump-Pij had started and he made out that this was indeed an abacus, something, with which, to add up and subtract. To be honest, Ethelred-Ted was pretty pleased with himself that he had come up with the idea. The telephone had numbers on it. He thought it could easily pass for something like that.

"What does it do?" asked Poppy.

"It helps with arithmetic and all that," replied Ethelred-Ted, intensely frowning at her.

"How does it work then?" asked Grandfather, pressing the numbers down firmly.

"Well, that's what we have come into the shed for," replied Ethelred-Ted, "it has a re-chargeable battery that has gone flat."

"Now, I see," said Grandfather. "Is that why Joni-Philipa wanted Doctor Evans' batteries from his Eye Torch?"

"Exactly!" said Hetty the Wee. "Although I worry they won't work. Joni-Pip said he had t' hit the torch on the end t' get the light t' go on."

"That's a thought," said Ethelred-Ted casually. "The problem is, we haven't got enough volts to charge it up, to get it going again."

"How many does it need?"

"3.7."

"We mustn't have more and we mustn't have less," said Poppy-Plump-Pij sounding very clever. "If we have too many faults, we will cook it. It's a bit like 'too many faults, will boil the Math'....I think."

Grandfather looked at the pigeon and smiled.

"What had you thought of doing?" he turned and looked at Ethelred-Ted. "Are you sure it will only take 3.7 volts?"

"Absolutely," replied Ethelred-Ted. "If we use another battery....which I am thinking is the only way to go....that will make 4.5 volts....that's too many."

Grandfather stood silently for a few minutes. He picked up the batteries, one by one and then put them down.

"Where did you say these came from?"

"Doctor Evans' torch," replied all three of them, together.

Grandfather picked up Jack's telephone and examined it again. Once more he stood in silence. Nobody spoke.

He then walked over to the mahogany chest of drawers and pulled open the top drawer. He took something out.

"This," he said, "could be the answer to your problem."

"A torch?" questioned Ethelred-Ted, Poppy-Plump-Pij and Hetty together. They all looked at the large, metal torch, which Grandfather held in his hand.

"Yes....let me just check...." said Grandfather, unscrewing the cap, at the bottom of the torch. He put the cap on the work bench and let the batteries inside, gently slide out. He put the torch down and laid the three large batteries, side by side.

"These are 1.5 volts each, too," he started, "so that makes 4.5 volts. What did you say you needed?"

"3.7," they all replied.

"Well, My Friends, with this little bulb in the end, here," he said, lifting

252

up the torch and unscrewing the top, "I think we can do it."

He took out the torch bulb and examined it. He held it up to the light so that he could read the details on the metal stem of the bulb.

"Yes, this little bulb will help reduce the voltage sufficiently, to bring it down to 3.7 volts....now where are we?"

He again rummaged in the drawer and took out another torch bulb.

"Here we are! I like to keep a spare bulb or two."

Grandfather began to draw a diagram on a piece of paper. Ethelred-Ted stood beside him and watched carefully as he worked. Poppy-Plump-Pij softly walked over to the paper and strained her little neck to see. Hetty the Wee just watched his face.

"If we connect up five batteries like this, we will get 7.5 volts....what we need is 3.7 [27] volts, which is about half of that," explained Grandfather, "and if we connect these two bulbs up together, the voltage will be shared, or divided between the two of them, like this...." he added to his drawing. "We can connect the abacus to....one half and it will be 3.75 volts....will that do?"

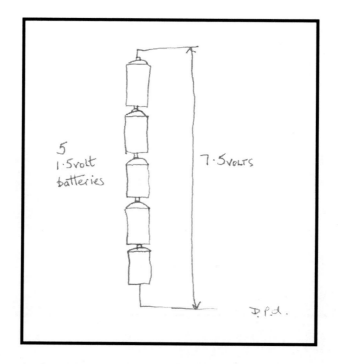

---

[27] For all you Anoraks out there: yeah, yeah, I know battery chargers for mobiles have to be a couple of volts heavier than the 'phone. I still think what David came up with is amazing, don't you? I 'phoned him from France wondering how on earth they would charge a battery in 1942: he astounded me with his ingenuity but then he is my very brainy brother!   C.K.

Grandfather turned and looked at them all in turn.

"That's so clever, Grandfather," nodded Ethelred-Ted, "and so simple....
the five batteries add up to 7.5 volts, the bulbs take the same voltage each,
so that leaves us with 3.75 each....I am sure that will do....at least it's not
too much....so it won't melt the tele....abacus."

"This is all very clever but how are y' going t' do it then, Ma Pets?"

"Just watch!" laughed Grandfather and then he turned to Ethelred-Ted,
"What exactly are you trying to do to the abacus?"

"We want to charge it up, so that it works again," Ethelred-Ted replied,
not having a clue as to how they were going to do that.

"Oh!" said Grandfather in amazement. "That is **so** clever. My, my, it has
a built in re-chargeable battery? What will they think up next? They didn't
have any thing like that when I was a boy!"

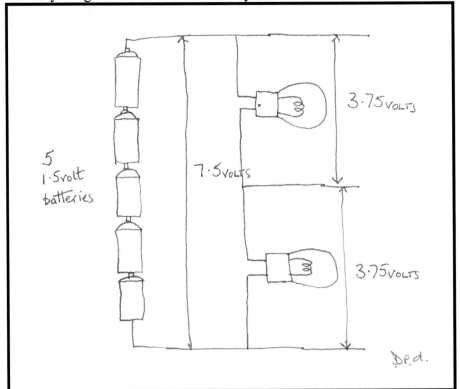

'No,' thought Ethelred-Ted, 'nor now!'

"Leave this to me!" laughed Grandfather.

The three spectators watched him work.

First of all, he went to the corner of the shed and pulled out a roll of
cable. He carried it over to the chest of drawers and laid it down, beside the
batteries. He took his wire cutters, from off a hook on the wall, pulled out a

length of the cable and cut it off. He then cut the cable into short lengths and stripped off a small piece of the rubber insulation, each end, exposing the copper wire inside. Next, he plugged in his soldering iron and unrolled some solder, from one of the rolls. Very carefully, he soldered one end of a piece of the wire, to the top of one battery and the bottom of another, until he had connected up all five. He then connected the first battery, to the first bulb and then he connected the other bulb, to the last battery. He rummaged through one of the drawers in the chest and took out a small switch. He connected the small switch, between the two bulbs. Finally, he connected two longer pieces of wire, to each side of one of the bulbs. He switched off the soldering iron and put it out of the way, to cool down. He picked up Jack's mobile 'phone and examined it again.

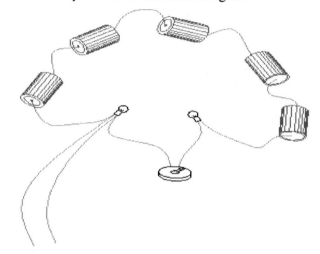

"Now where do I connect it and what do I connect it to?" he asked himself.

The others remained silent.

Grandfather looked very carefully at the telephone and turned it over a few times.

"There must be some way of getting into it," he muttered to himself.

"I think the back must come off, somehow," said Ethelred-Ted.

The determined man continued gently pulling and pushing at the back.

"Ah! Housey, Housey!" he said. "Look there's an arrow....it has to be pulled this way."

He pulled at the back of the 'phone. Nothing happened.

"Oh....obviously not," he said to himself. He then slid the back of the 'phone.

"At last!" he said, as the back came off. "Here it is! This is the little battery. Look! How amazing! How wonderfully made!"

The others all crowded round and took a look.

"Is that it?" asked Poppy-Plump-Pij disappointedly.

"Now where is the connection?" Grandfather asked himself. He removed the small flat battery. "Here are the connections....see?" He pointed to the little gold strips. "Now, I need to keep the torch batteries in contact with these tiny connections....while we charge it up....how shall we do that?"

Nobody answered.

"Yes, yes," said the old man delighted. "If I put the battery back...." he performed this little task. "I can simply push the two ends of the wire between this small gap here...." he did so and the wires stayed in place, "and they will all connect up together! Right," said Grandfather, "let's see if this works!"

He turned the switch on and the two bulbs glowed.

They all looked at the telephone and then back at the bulbs. They expected some kind of reaction....some kind of noise....some kind of sign....to let them know it was working.

They saw nothing because they were only looking at the back of the telephone, with the two wires sticking up out of it.

"Oh...." said Grandfather, "and I thought I had worked it all out!"

Just then, they heard the sound of a motorbike revving, as it climbed up the drive.

"It sounds as though I have a visitor," said Grandfather, walking over to the shed door. "It's Doctor Evans again; I wonder what he's forgotten?"

With that, he walked out.

"This just has to work!" said Ethelred-Ted, examining Grandfather's handy work.

"It **must**: otherwise we are in big trouble," said Hetty the Wee, seriously.

"He's probably forgotten to do something," laughed Poppy. "Just as I did once. I called in Lily, my toad friend who lives near me, one day because I couldn't get my little iron to work. I needed it to iron my freshly washed curtains. I plugged the iron lead up into my light socket but it just wouldn't work. Lily came round and looked at it and then said, 'Poppy things only work if you turn them on!' I had forgotten to switch my light on!"

"Grandfather is not that silly," said Ethelred-Ted slightly harshly. "Of course he would have turned it on."

"Aye, of course he would!" agreed Hetty the Wee.

"It was only a thought," said Poppy-Plump-Pij, a bit ruffled. She flew; well it was more like a long hop, from the work bench, over to the mahogany chest of drawers and landed next to the batteries and the telephone.

"I was glad Lily helped me, it kind of put things right. I had gone round to have lunch with her and she served up Egg Pie. I was rather hurt, to say the least. I asked her how she would have felt if I had offered her a slice of Tadpole Tart," said Poppy, more or less to herself.

The others sniggered. Poppy just ignored them.

"I wonder what we could call this thing that Grandfather has made. A tele-torch sounds nice!" said Ethelred-Ted, diplomatically steering the subject.

Poppy had a good look at it, following the wires with one of her sharp little eyes.

"Hmmmm...." she said, sounding very much like Archimedes Spindlethrop. "Hmmmm...." she continued, as she examined the contraption carefully with her other little eye and nodded every now and then.

"It strikes me, Young Miss Plump-Pij, that y've been spending far too much time in the company of a particular inventor friend and a wee red and yellow Teddy Bear!"

"Now let me see," said the persistent pigeon, scrutinising every inch of the telephone with her busy beak.

"Pops, my Dear Friend, I know you mean well," said Ethelred-Ted kindly, "but do you seriously think you could get it to work, when Grandfather couldn't?"

"Hmmmm....now what do we have here?" She pecked at the little red telephone button firmly with her bill. Nothing happened. She then poked and prodded other buttons on the little telephone. Nothing happened. She then turned the little telephone over to one side, very gently: there were two small buttons. She pressed one. Nothing happened. She pressed the other. The light bulbs flickered. They all jumped in surprise. All three of them watched the telephone. Nothing happened. All three of them continued to watch the telephone.

"Beep!" went the 'phone.

Three heads stretched forward and stared at the telephone. On the little screen they all read the words that came up: 'BATTERY CHARGING'

Little lines began to, systematically, go up the side of the telephone screen, from the bottom to the top. Again and again and again and again. They didn't stop.

For a moment nobody spoke.

Then they all clapped and cheered and hugged each other.

"Poppy, you are a Genius, I'm sorry that I doubted you!" laughed Ethelred-Ted.

"Me too, Ma Hen, you are indeed a wonder!" said Hetty the Wee, dancing up and down.

Chapter 29

New Life, New Ways

The Parlour door creaked as Ethelred-Ted gently pushed it open and popped his head round it. Joni-Pip stirred, stretched and smiled over at him. He joined her on the sofa, closely followed by Hetty and Poppy and handed her Jack's cell 'phone. They all gathered round her and excitedly told her how Grandfather had devised an amazing 'Battery Charger' and all that had happened while she had been busily sleeping. She was so delighted. They told her that through pushing lots of buttons on the little telephone and following the instructions at the bottom of the screen, they had finally brought the telephone back into use. It was alive again!

As if on cue, the telephone rang loudly. Everyone looked at each other, breathed in deeply then they looked expectantly at Joni-Pip. She stood up, glanced around at her friends and shrugged. The 'phone continued to ring; she shrugged again and then expertly pushed the little green telephone button and put the 'phone to her ear.

"Hello?"

"Hello!" came back Jack's cheery voice. "Am I glad to hear you, Great Auntie Joni-Pip! I have been trying my cell 'phone every half-hour, hoping that somehow you'll have worked out how to charge the battery and you have! How did you do it?"

"Eth said Grandfather used three batteries from his large metal torch and two batteries from Doctor Evan's little torch. He connected them together and took down the voltage by using a little switch and two little torch bulbs!" she said excitedly.

"Wow, that sure is neat," exclaimed Jack, "yet so simple! I hadn't a clue what you could do but I knew you would find a way....somehow....and HOW!"

"What do you want us to do now?" asked Joni-Pip.

"Just wait until you get a call....it should be in a few minutes. O.K.?" he said. "Be prepared for a shocker....things have really changed since the Turning of the KOL! Your POOL is full of surprises, Auntie Joni-Pip!" he laughed gently.

"What d'you mean?" asked Joni-Pip anxiously and as she did so she remembered the pilot in the plane, smiling at her and then she forgot him again.

"Your POOLS remember, your Personal Orbits of Life? Red-Ted said

258

we all have our own. Some have more than one! That's it then as , sadly, this is probably the last time that I will speak with you until we meet, when I am born in your new Circle. It's kinda depressing I won't remember all this. Let me say 'good bye' to everybody?"

Joni-Pip passed the 'phone to Hetty. They all said their 'Good Byes' to Jack, while Joni-Pip pondered on what on earth her surprise might be.

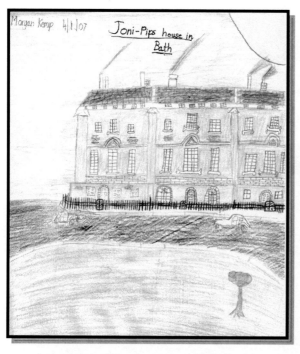
Morgan Kemp 4/1/07 — Joni-Pips house in Bath

After Ethelred-Ted had finished speaking, he pressed the little red telephone button.

"I didn't say 'good bye' to him!" cried Joni-Pip in panic.

Ethelred-Ted put his arm, his beautifully stitched up arm, around her and consoled her, by saying,

"Perhaps that's how he wanted it, Joni-Pip, perhaps it was too hard for him to say 'good bye' to you. Anyway, you will see him again and talk to him lots and lots, one day."

Joni-Pip smiled sadly. It was a strange sort of smile. They all sat still, in silence.

The telephone rang again. Joni-Pip answered it.

"Hello?" she said, nervously.

"Hello," came an unfamiliar voice. "Hello is that Joni-Pip?"

"Yes," she said cautiously, "who is that?"

"Jack has just 'phoned from the States and he said I was to tell you that I am Joni-Philipa's daughter, Amanda."

Joni-Pip drew in her breath loudly.

"Are you all right?" asked Amanda.

"Er....yes....yes....Amanda....I'm so delighted to speak to you....where do you live?" Joni-Pip's voice was shaking.

"I live in a very beautiful, old cottage, here in Nottinghamshire. It's called Knotty Knook. Jack says I am to tell you that my mother, who shares the same name as you; that's so unusual; anyway, she now lives here, at times but usually, she stays in her posh apartment, in Bath. It's overlooking the river, near that beautiful bridge, with all those little shops, on it. Do you know Bath? It's my favourite City. Mum gave us the cottage a few years ago. We love it! Uncle Alex has the house in Bath. One of my daughter's drew a picture of it, it's on my bedroom wall, it's a shame you can't see it, it's a beautiful, really old house."

"Mmmmmm," was all Joni-Pip could manage to say softly.

"My mother says she remembers being down in the cellar, when it was bombed in the War. That must have been pretty scary," said Amanda calmly: she had no idea how this conversation was astounding a listening twelve-year-old. "Uncle Alex also has a house in the States and Auntie Becky-Paige still lives in the Crooked Cottage: that's only a little way away from us. Just across the woods, Windy Woods. There are two people, here, who Jack says are to say 'hello' to you, too! Mellie, come and say 'hello to Jack's friend."

'Jack was right,' thought Joni-Pip, 'this is a real 'shocker'!'

"Hello!" came a bright voice. "This is Mellie, well, my full name is Amelia but everyone calls me Mellie for short. How are you?"

"Hello, Mellie," said Joni-Pip slowly, "I'm all right....I have been a bit poorly. I fell off a swing while it was going very high, today but I'm fine

260

now."

"Good show! You sound like me!" laughed Mellie. "Humph! Mum says I'm to pass you on to Jem, so 'bye 'bye for now!"

"Good bye, Mellie, so nice to speak to you!" said Joni-Pip wistfully.

"Hello, how are you, then?" came a voice, identical to Mellie's.

"Hello, who are you?" asked Joni-Pip.

"Me? I'm Jem....Jemimah, Mellie's twin sister!" laughed Jem. "You  can't tell who is who and that's so much fun, at times, especially if I'm naughty and Mellie gets blamed! That's so cool! Anyway, Jack says this is what we have to do................"

"Whew, that's so clever!" said Joni-Pip, listening intently to the instructions.

"Is it?" asked Jem, puzzled.

"Let me speak again, Jem, I like talking to Joni-Pip," came Mellie's voice.

"O.K., Mel....but so do I!"

"Hi, it's me again: Mellie. So where d'you live then?"

"Not too far from you, actually," said Joni-Pip. "Do you like living in Knotty Knook?"

"Yes, I love it. I much prefer living here, than in the town. Do you live in the town or in the country?"

"Er....both....." replied Joni-Pip.

"Both?....Cool....which do you prefer?" asked Mellie.

"Er....Cool? No, it's been quite warm recently," answered Joni-Pip.

"You are so funny!" laughed Mellie.

"Which do I prefer?" Joni-Pip thought for a second. "The Countryside, without a doubt, yes definitely, it's absolutely spiffing, especially in the Wood."

"Spiffing? You sound like you're in an Old Black and White Film!" Mellie laughed again.

"Do I? I suppose I do....er....could I speak to your mother again, please....to Ama....Amanda?" Joni-Pip shook.

"Of course you can. Here she is. Mum, Joni-Pip wants to talk to you again."

"It's me, Amanda again," came the voice from the Future. "Is everything O.K.?"

"Yes....I....think....so...." Joni-Pip faltered. "I just wondered how....you were? Are you all right? Do you like living in Knotty Knook? How is your....your mother?"

"Yes," said Amanda politely, "I love it here and Mum's fine, she's great!"

"M, M 'n M, is she?" gasped Joni-Pip. "Your mum, she's fine then, that's amazing!"

"What's amazing? Oh about Jack's 'phone, d'you mean? I suppose it is!" laughed Amanda. "I'm surprised he's done without it for so long. He hasn't been back to England for at least three months. Perhaps he has another one! Anyway, he made us laugh when he said that what we have to do is vital....for all of us!"

"Hmmm. Yes, yes, er....it's so nice to speak to you all," said Joni-Pip sadly.

"I look forward to meeting you; Jack insists we will one day. He was adamant about that, as well!" chuckled Amanda. "Good bye then."

"Good bye, Amanda, I really can't wait to meet you," said Joni-Pip wistfully, "say 'good bye' to the twins for me!"

Slowly she pressed the little red button and put the telephone down beside her.

"Well?" questioned her three friends together.

Joni-Pip just stared and said nothing, it was all too much to take in.

"Well?" asked Eth again, shrugging his shoulders and waiting for an answer.

Joni-Pip kept silent. She was totally in a daze.

"What was that all about, Ma Pet?"

Joni-Pip turned and looked at her friends.

"I....I....I don't believe this....I....I....have just spoken to my....my....my.... daughter." Large tears began to roll down her face.

"M, M 'n M! That **is** unbelievable!" exclaimed Ethelred-Ted.

"....And my twin grand daughters!"

For a while, nobody said anything. Ethelred-Ted then put his arm around Joni-Pip and patted her gently on the shoulders, soothing her as she sobbed.

Softly, he asked her,

"Are you all right? This must be so overwhelming for you."

Joni-Pip remained silent. She walked over to the window and looked out across the fields, towards the Clappers.

"Is this really happening?" she asked. "There are the stars again!"

The others joined her at the window.

"They are, too. I wonder what that means this time, Ma Lambies?"

"Await visitors," started Eth, "d'you think they're connected with this Pasture?"

"Hasn't most of what has happened with us been to do with **my** Orbits?"

"That's true, none of this seems to make any sense," said Ethelred-Ted.

"I think I am going to have a little flightful and investigate," said Poppy.

Ethelred-Ted opened the window for her.

"Flap off!" he laughed.

She turned and looked at him, grinned and then took off from the windowsill. They all watched her, as effortlessly she rose into the blue sky.

"How lovely t' be able t' d' that! At least I got to fly over the Wall of Time."

"Hello, I see we have The Two Men in Long, Black Coats, striding up the drive. I wonder if Grandfather will see them?" said Ethelred-Ted.

"Oh no! They've just walked past him and Doctor Evans and they didn't seem to notice them and they are hardly the normal type of men we see around here!"

"You're right, Joni-Pip. They're heading in this direction!" Eth replied.

"Close the window! Close the window!" shouted Joni-Pip. "Quick hide!"

Ethelred-Ted swiftly pulled the window shut and fastened it securely.

"They can get in the back door! Quick, quick, we must lock it!"

Joni-Pip ran out of the Parlour and along the Hall to the kitchen. Her heart was pounding; she was terrified. That Grandfather and Doctor Evans hadn't seen The Two Men in Long, Black Coats, made her feel so endangered. She had to lock them out! As she ran across the kitchen, her heart nearly stopped. She could hear the sound of big boots crunching through the pebbles, approaching the back door. She crouched down so she couldn't be seen through the glass in the door. Her fingers fumbled with the key above her. She couldn't turn it. She struggled, trying to rotate the large, iron key but it wouldn't budge. She couldn't let the men see her but that made this feat even more difficult. She could hardly breathe. She heard the men's abrupt voices and the key finally clunked the lock fast, at the moment the door handle was turned. Joni-Pip slowly slid down the lower part of the door and slumped on to the floor. She breathed out a very long, deep sigh as the door handle rattled violently but she was no longer afraid. This was England. She was held within a stone cottage that had withstood the ravages of Time. This sturdy little cottage had sheltered supporters of King Charles l, during the time of Oliver Cromwell, three hundred years previously. This rock-solid structure had hidden refugees fleeing from the

Reformation in the time of Henry VIII, a hundred years before that! This old cottage might be a tad crooked but with its solid oak kitchen door and strong iron lock, it had held off many an Intruder, Invader and Escaped Convict (who, previously, had been staying at His Majesty's pleasure in the Stopping Cells in Edwinstowe), so now Joni-Pip feared not!

Ethelred-Ted crawled across the kitchen floor to Joni-Pip.

"Well done, You!" he whispered and smiled.

"Where's Het?"

"I don't know, I presume she's still in the Parlour."

"What d'you think they want?"

"I've no idea but it must be pretty important as they keep coming back!"

"You Two, there's somebody knocking on the front door!" Hetty's little voice called across from the kitchen door that led into the Hall.

"What?" asked Joni-Pip.

"It must be The Two Men in Long, Black Coats!" said Ethelred-Ted.

"But they're still standing outside the back door, I can see them, Pets!"

"Oh, who can it be?" asked Joni-Pip. "Eth, I'm going to crawl round the edge of the kitchen and go and see who it is. I don't think they'll see me."

Immediately, she set off and Ethelred-Ted followed her. As she got to the door leading into the Hall, she looked round and up and saw the two men, peering through the glass. Their voices were raised. They sounded angry and frustrated.

"I hope they can't see me. Here goes!" she said, taking the last leg of the journey around the edge of the kitchen door on all fours like a little mouse, then once she had got into the Hall, she stood up.

'Rat-a-tat-tat!' went the knocker on the front door.

"Is anyone in?" came a low voice from outside.

Joni-Pip approached the solid, wooden door, cautiously.

"J.P., are you there?" came another whispered voice.

"You must be in!" said a voice she recognised.

Quickly she unbolted the door, unlocked the key and opened the door. Three figures almost fell into the Hall in front of her.

"At last! We thought you would never hear us!" said Steve, as he quickly shut the door and locked and bolted it behind them.

"Hi, You Lot!" laughed Craig. "Whew, this is some exciting stuff!"

"What exactly is going on?" asked Ethelred-Ted.

The Hall was quite unusual. All the walls, doors and the ceiling, were made of oak panelling and now that all the doors of the rooms, going off it, were closed, it made a pretty impressive, private, square room. The only furniture that stood grandly in it, was a very old, huge and heavy Hallstand, which included shelves for shoes, hangers for outdoor clothes, a large, deep cylinder for umbrellas and a square mirror for adjusting One's appearance; as well as beautiful, birch brushes, hanging on hooks, for brushing boots, clothes and hair, accordingly.

Suddenly, there was a very loud hammering on the front door.

"It's them!" whispered Craig.

"Can they get in here?" asked Steve.

"I suppose, if they chop the door down: other than that, no! What shall we do?" asked Joni-Pip, very, very quietly.

"I think I'll do this," said Flip, walking silently over to the Hallstand and looking in the mirror. She adjusted her long hair and went to take one of the brushes off its hook.

Everyone looked horrified.

"This is hardly the time to be preening oneself, Flip!" said Craig.

Flip just turned and laughed. She didn't take the brush off its hook, she simply lifted it slightly. As she did, there was a 'clicking' sound and one of the oak panels slid sideways. She turned and smiled at Joni-Pip.

"New ways, all days!" she laughed as everyone else gasped.

Straight in front of them was a solid, brick wall.

"Useful!" said Steve, walking over and tapping the rock-hard wall.

The banging on the front door got louder and louder. Flip deftly ran her fingers between two bricks on the right hand side of her. Almost invisible to them, there was a little wire. She gently pulled it and to everyone's amazement, the solid brick wall began to smoothly and silently rise! Everybody gasped again.

"Super, isn't it?" whispered Flip, turning round and looking at the astonished spectators. "We have no time to waste but I will tell you everything when we are in a place of safety. Come on, Lads and Lasses, time to go!" she encouraged as she walked through the hole in the wall. The boys followed.

"What on earth, where on earth?" asked Joni-Pip, staring open-mouthed.

"Let's investigate!" said Ethelred-Ted.

"Of course you must!" Flip called back quietly.

Joni-Pip walked through the opening and into the darkness.

"Hold back a minute!" said Flip.

All six of them stood still and silent, in a huddle just inside the hollow while she unhooked an oil lamp, which was hanging up on the wall. She ran her fingers along a shelf and took down a box of matches and lit the lantern. Soon they were basked in lamplight.

"Don't forget to shut the door behind you. You must always remember that. You know what? I really get cross when I go to the Cinema and watch films where people never close and lock doors behind them....especially when they are being pursued. It peeves me! Still, I suppose that's not in 'real life'!"

They all laughed.

"Shhhhh!" said Flip. "See here, Joni-Pip, there's a handle on the inside of the panel, pull it until the door clicks shut."

Joni-Pip pulled the panel and it clicked closed.

"Good. Now see these two bricks? There's a little wire here, look! When you pull it, it triggers off this amazing pulley system that lifts this piece of real wall up and down, in the cavity between the Hall and the Parlour walls."

"I can't find it," said Joni-Pip, running her fingers between the bricks.

Flip held up the lamp.

"Look here! It's really small but you can feel it."

Joni-Pip's fingers finally rested on the tiny piece of wire.

"What do I do?"

"Just pull it, really gently."

At first nothing happened. Joni-Pip screwed up her face.

"Try again," said Flip.

Joni-Pip gently pulled the wire and silently the brick wall lowered itself perfectly in place, in front of the panelled door.

"That's amazing!" they all said together.

"Right, Het, Eth, Joni-Pip, when you come back; if you decide to come back this way, remember to put the oil lamp back on the hook, see here, ready for the next person....you know how to raise the wall....and just pull down the handle on the panelling and the door will open. That's it!"

"How did you know it was here?" asked Joni-Pip incredulously.

"Well, actually, as you just saw....I showed you....!" Flip laughed.

Joni-Pip and her friends all looked puzzled.

"Lead the way, Flip!" cracked Craig. "Stop confusing these kind folks!"

After a few paces, Flip lead them down some cold, stone, uneven steps.

The light from the lantern, cast enormous, eerie and jagged shadows, along the rough walls, of the channel they trod. It was very scary!

"We're under the Crooked Cottage. These underground paths have been used for years: long before the Cottage was built, going back to Robin Hood's Day. He and his Men used to hide from the Sheriff of Nottingham and his soldiers, down here."

In silence, she led them through an extremely long and narrow passage that sloped downhill, it smelt very damp and musty and they could hear water dripping from the walls. Occasionally they would splash in a puddle.

"It's easy coming from the Cottage but it's a bit of a climb coming back up!" Flip laughed, stopped and gathered them around her. "From now on, I

266

want you all to keep close together. We're entering a very low and narrow tunnel that runs all the way from here to the Clappers. There are so many branches off. I think Grandfather told me there were ten miles in all, so it's pretty easy to get lost. I've done that a few times with Alex but he was only teasing me. He knew where he was, he just liked to worry me! If you do get separated, just remember the tunnel you need is marked by arrows, with a number 6 beside it. See!" she held the lantern up. "Just feel for them and they'll guide you back to an exit. Each particular route is numbered. These arrows and numbers were gouged out by the Cavaliers while hiding from the Roundheads!"

"Not The Two Men in Long, Black Coats then!" laughed Steve.

"Whew!" said Hetty the Wee, Ethelred-Ted and Joni-Pip.

"Are you all right, Het?" asked Flip, looking down at her.

"I'm fine Hen, just intrigued!" she laughed back. "We Hedgehogs don't mind the dark, at all. It's the wind that plays havoc with our equilibrium! Hey! That's nay laughin' matter!" she said as they all laughed.

"Actually, You Lot, if my memory serves me correctly, I don't think you'll come down here again for a couple of years but you will remember all this then."

Flip then led them along the dark, low, damp, tunnel. It reminded Joni-Pip of the time Mother and Father had taken them to Dover Castle. That was a strikingly symmetrical castle, improved by the Normans. The contours of the Towers, Courtyards and The Keep were so beautifully formed and the walls were so straight and the lines were so perfect that Joni-Pip had called them, 'Big Boxes'. It was a place once used by the Romans, under the Command of Julius Caesar, in 55 B.C., when they took, the then, Anglo-Saxon Fortress.

Under the castle, however, had been another matter. They had been guided through a series of long passages and tunnels; some first dug during the Napoleonic Wars, where the British Army had lain, preparing to be attacked by Napoleon's Hordes. Joni-Pip had been terrified by the darkness under Dover Castle, the uneven ground beneath her feet, the dripping, dank walls and the damp atmosphere. She had held on tightly to Father's hand.

Suddenly, through the shadows, they heard a groaning. They all stopped.

"What was that?" asked Joni-Pip, very nervously; she shuddered.

Ethelred-Ted caught her up and lifted her hand and put it in his.

The groaning continued, it was deep and pathetic. Flip fearlessly strode on, through the shadowy tunnels; expertly guiding them; following the pitiful moaning. Occasionally, they had to crouch on their hands and knees and crawl through tight openings into huge hollow chambers. Eventually, they scrambled through another cavity and clambered up into to an enormous cavern. The cavern was well lit by lanterns, hanging on the walls. Over in one corner was a stretcher. A man, covered in bandages was lying on it. He kept groaning. A girl was crouched over him and she was wiping his forehead with a cloth. All of them walked quietly and anxiously into the corner. The girl turned, smiled, stood up and walked towards them. She was tall and pretty and looked about sixteen. As they met up, the girl smiled broadly.

"Hello, I didn't realise we would meet you here!" the girl said, hugging a puzzled Joni-Pip warmly. "Col has just gone through the Seam to try and get help."

She pointed to a vertical, glistening sheet of water behind her.

"Hello!" came a voice from the gloom. "Amazing timing! Friend or Foe?"

They all turned round and looked into the face of a swarthy, good looking youth, who was about the same age as the girl. Their clothing was unfamiliar.

"What's going on? We don't know you, " said Ethelred-Ted.

"Ethelred-Ted, Joni-Pip, Little Hetty, how are you all? How wonderful to see you again! I never did get a chance to thank you. I felt so bad when you had left, we owe you so much. I didn't mean to be so rude," said the girl.

"Who are these people, how do you know them, Jem?" asked the youth.

"These are the ones, the ones I was telling you about," Jem replied.

"Who exactly are You Two?" asked Steve.

The tall girl walked forward and shook Flip's, Steve's and Craig's hands.

"I don't think we've met, I'm Jem and this is Freddie. Are you all JITS?"

"Yes!" replied Flip, Steve and Craig.

"Well, you are, too!" Jem looked at Joni-Pip, Ethelred-Ted and Hetty.

"Not yet!" the three of them replied.

"Ah!" said Jem. "That's why you don't know us yet, then but you will!"

"I do need to know something," said Ethelred-Ted, talking to Freddie.

"I don't think we have much time," said Jem, "could you help us, please? We need to get this poor man some Twentieth Century medical aid."

"Serious stuff to do, first, I'm afraid," said Craig. "Before that, even, this Lot have to go back through Tunnel 6. They locked all the doors from the inside, at The Crooked Cottage. If not, Grandfather will have to break in!"

"Of course we can help, we'll do anything we can," said Steve, "but we'll have to JIT first and then come back ten minutes ago. All right? 'Bye for now."

Joni-Pip, Ethelred-Ted and Hetty the Wee looked decidedly confused.

"Righto, thanks; apparently, we'll meet you all soon. Cheerio," said Freddie.

"We must go," said Flip looking around, then leaving through a tunnel.

"How on earth do you know where to go?" asked a confused Joni-Pip.

"Done this so many times, as you will find out! One day, these tunnels will be as familiar to you, as they are to me, Joni-Pip," Flip laughed.

Very soon they came out into brilliant sunshine, behind some bushes in Lily Lane. They hadn't got anywhere near the Clappers but they were well away from the Crooked Cottage. They watched in the distance as two men in long, black coats were seen running into the trees on Windy Woods and then disappearing in a cloud of stars.

"I think everyone's safe, now!" said Ethelred-Ted.

"I'm sorry about all this. We must have left you so many unanswered questions," said Flip, "but they will all be answered; just be patient, uh?"

"Yes, they will but we must get back. Even though we know the locations of the Secret Passages and the Secret Tunnels, we still can't find the entrance to the Old Mine! It doesn't make any sense! Now we've got something else to do, for Jem and Freddie. Oh, joy, more work!!" laughed Craig.

"Sorry we're always rushing; one day we'll get chance to talk!" said Steve.

"Hmmm, I know eventually, all this will be explained," said Joni-Pip.

"Until again, then!" grinned Craig. "Truly, soon, all will be revealed!"

"I brought you out here, so you know where Tunnel 6 leads to. You remember what to do?" said Flip, handing Joni-Pip the lamp. "Don't forget to follow the arrows with the number 6 and when you get back to the Cottage, don't forget to put the lamp back! There's Poppy! See you in a little while!"

"It's been such fun!" said Joni-Pip. "I only wish we could remember it!"

"Did you get the abacus to work?" Grandfather poked his head through the kitchen door.

"Yes, it's all mended now." Ethelred-Ted was filling up the kettle at the sink. "Thank you so much, Grandfather, you're a Genius!"

"My pleasure, it was quite fun to do it. Sorry I missed the exciting bit, it's just that I had forgotten that I had told Doctor Evans to come and get some wood for his fire. I think he must have turned round even before he was re-acquainted with Mrs Botterton's bunions, he was back so quickly!"

Grandfather took his Wellington boots off and left them outside the back door. He stood and waited in his big, thick, woolly socks until Ethelred-Ted had finished at the sink. Ethelred-Ted walked over to the kitchen range and put the kettle on. Grandfather went to the sink and turned on one of the tall, narrow taps that he had made from copper pipes. He washed his hands

" Jan-Pip write the message to Mother while Grandfather carried in some logs for the fire "

271

thoroughly and then dried them on the towel that hung on the rail, behind the green check curtain under the draining board.

"I seem to have been chopping wood most of the day! This must all be so boring for you, sorry! How's my granddaughter? Have you been in to see her?" he asked, pulling out his slippers from the low shelf behind the door.

"She's fine. I'm just making her a cup of tea. The others are with her. Would you like one?" Eth wouldn't have asked so casually, had he remembered the exciting things that had happened to three of them earlier.

"Would I like a cup of tea? Is the sun hot? I'd love a cup of tea, thank you," chuckled Grandfather. "What have you been up to then?"

Soon they were all together, sitting round the hearth, in the Parlour. Eth had already put fresh logs on the fire and now they were crackling, sizzling and glowing invitingly. Joni-Pip and her friends had no recollection of all the astonishing things that had taken place in the dark and damp Tunnel 6, under the Crooked Cottage. ((So, boring? I'll answer. No!))

"How about, you all stay for tea?" asked Grandfather. "Cherry-Plum, you can write a message for your mother and Poppy Pigeon, if you feel up to it, you can fly it over to her?"

Poppy was feeling very good at that moment: in fact she was positively 'shiningful'. She felt that, thanks to her, the telephone was now 'lifeful'!

"I would love to!" she beamed.

After he had finished his cup of tea, Grandfather walked into the kitchen. The others all followed him. He took out of his second green drawer, by the sink: two pieces of paper, two envelopes and a pen.

"Here, Cherry-Plum, write a message to Mother on one of the pieces of paper." He handed her the pen, a piece of paper and an envelope. Then he folded the other piece of paper, put it in the second envelope and handed it to her. "Keep this other one in the envelope, in your pocket and the pen; you never know when you might need it!"

"Always prepared, aren't you, Grandfather? Thank you, I will keep it for a stormy day!" his granddaughter laughed.

So, Joni-Pip wrote a message to Mother, while Grandfather brought in logs for the fire.

After Poppy had returned from her journey, carrying the message back from Mother, which said that it would be fine for Joni-Pip to stay for tea with Grandfather, the Wood pigeon was duly commanded to rest.

Everyone else prepared the late afternoon meal.

How Ethelred-Ted enjoyed Tea Time! Even during the War, in 1942, English Tea Time was not just the time one enjoyed a freshly brewed pot of tea. It was an early evening, eating time, accompanied by the drinking of several cups of steaming hot tea! Grandfather had made a beautiful, red, wobbly jelly (jello), using the ripe, plump strawberries that had been picked and bottled from his garden, the year before. Ethelred-Ted had great pleasure carrying it into the dining room. Grandfather had baked an enormous Victoria Sponge; sandwiched together by lashings of thick whipped cream, from Finn's Farm and some of Mrs Broft's delicious, damson jam. There were apples and pears, which Grandfather had carefully stored all Winter, in his small cellar, under the Cottage. He also insisted that his visitors eat salad: some freshly grated raw cabbage and carrot, as well as tomatoes and cucumber. Ethelred- Ted was not too keen on that sort of stuff but he obediently munched through it, knowing it was 'doing him good', as Hetty the Wee urged. However, he did like, the hard boiled, fresh eggs and of course the freshly baked loaf of bread with freshly churned butter.

Grandfather, Ethelred-Ted, Hetty and Joni-Pip walked in and out of the dining room getting Tea ready. Although they didn't remember anything about Tunnel 6, occasionally they had fleeting wisps of memory (WOMS). Every time Hetty, Eth and Joni-Pip walked past the oak panel that led into the labyrinth below, they stopped and stared at it: having brief feelings of Déjà Vu. As Poppy hadn't shared with them in this wonder and had been ordered to rest, she stood and studied Grandfather's map on the wall. It was entitled, 'The Voyages of Christopher Columbus'. Poppy was always fascinated by journeys and passages. She was a bird after all and most of her life was spent in the air, travelling. How she looked forward to doing some more, she told them when Grandfather had left the dining room to make a fresh pot of tea. She also wondered if they could draw a map of their journeys as they JITTED! They chuckled at that idea! ((Try it, hm?))

As she was flying to Knotty Knook, Poppy-Plump-Pij had seen some full, weighty, black clouds, coming over from Edwinstowe and now they were finally throwing out their load in a heavy downfall of rain.

While they continued to prepare Tea, a little face pushed itself hard up against the window pane of the dining room. Eth felt so sorry for Nuttingham Squirrel, seeing his forlorn, wet face, peering into the cosy, fire-lit dining room. He asked Grandfather if the squirrel could join them for Tea. Poppy wasn't too keen on this but after a lively discussion, they decided to invite him in out of the wind and rain. Ethelred-Ted was immensely pleased to usher the dripping squirrel into the warmth of Grandfather's kitchen. Joni-Pip gave him a soft towel to dry off some of the soaking rain. Nuttingham Squirrel, although happy to be invited, seemed decidedly subdued, still cautiously keeping a close eye on Poppy-Plump-Pij, lest she might break out into one of her strange, hostile fits. As it happened, she behaved herself because the squirrel was being polite and agreeable. She felt she had no need to meter out any form of avian attack. She even went as far as to show him a photo of herself with her parents, when she was very small. After the wonderful Tea, they all sat round the fire in the Parlour, drinking warm cups of cocoa and enjoying a last slice of cake. Everyone thought that Poppy looked very cute as a fluffy chick!

Chapter 30

Operation Teleport

"What an amazing day it has been!" thought Joni-Pip.

She was standing in the bathroom at Knotty Knook, cleaning her teeth, wearing Alex's old dressing gown. Her little sister, Becky-Paige, stood next to her, spitting white foamy bubbles into the porcelain sink. The four-year-old was so small she had to stand on the tips of her tiny toes and then she could barely see over the edge of the large, Victorian basin. Joni-Pip wondered if Becky-Paige did actually ever manage to clean her teeth as all she seemed to delight in, was seeing how far she could get her 'tooth powder' spit to reach.

"That was a good one, Sissa, did you see that?" asked Becky-Paige, after managing a prize effort, which was lobbed over the full width of the basin and splattered beautifully on the brass taps on the other side.

"Becky-Paige, I really think you should concentrate on actually giving your teeth a good brush rather than decorating the taps with your slobber!" said Joni-Pip, trying to sound a bit authoritative.

"But it's such good fun, Sissa, why don't you have a go?" laughed her naughty little sister.

"You remind me so much of Alex, Becks. No doubt, you'll soon be making up a set of 'Rules for Tooth Powder Spitting' and you'll think it should be an event at the Olympic Games; after this silly war is over!" laughed Joni-Pip.

She could never really, ever, get cross with Becky-Paige.

"That sounds good. I like games!" laughed the four-year-old as she pushed her dark, curly topped head as far back as she could and then thrust it forward, spitting as strongly and as far as she could! The white foaming spray rose into the air, shot across the porcelain basin and then landed; sploshing satisfactorily on to the white, shiny tiles behind the brass taps.

"Amazing!" Becky-Paige gave Joni-Pip a white, sudsy, toothy grin.

Joni-Pip finished cleaning her teeth and then hung her toothbrush in the rack at the side of the basin, alongside Father's, Mother's and Alex's.

"Don't forget to hang up your toothbrush," she said to Becky-Paige, pointing towards the empty space left on the rack for her little sister's toothbrush. "You know how Father doesn't like you leaving your toothbrush on the side of the basin!"

"I'll try not to forget!" laughed Becky-Paige, launching another foray of foam across the basin.

"Marvellous!" said the tiny rascal.

Joni-Pip couldn't help but smile. She kissed her little sister and left the bathroom. As she walked across the polished, wooden floorboards, she glanced back over her shoulder and down the landing.

'Now, that,' she thought, 'is truly what I call marvellous!'

She ran her hands over Alex's old dressing gown before she hung it on her door. It was, indeed, getting tatty but she didn't care. Alex had rarely given her anything, so when he passed this on to her she was thrilled!

She walked over to her window and pulled back the pretty red, gingham curtains. The moonlight shone into her bedroom. She looked up at the beautiful, twinkling stars and sighed, 'What are you telling me? What's this all about? Is it all really going to happen?' she thought to herself, then she clambered on to her bed.

"Joni-Philipa Garador, you should be asleep!" came a voice from Joni-Pip's doorway. She lifted her head up and saw Father's silhouette. He was standing on the landing outside her bedroom door. She had been lying there on the top of her bed for sometime, engaging in what she loved: reliving the events of her most extraordinary day. Her beloved father walked into her room. The moonlight shone directly through her little window, clothing everything in her bedroom with a shimmering, silvery glow. He walked over to the window, pulled down the black blind and closed the curtains.

"Sweetheart, how many times do we have to explain to you that we are living during a War? We must keep the curtains closed at night. Blackout, remember? You're so much like your grandfather. He never seems to remember to close his curtains. He says the woods shelter us from giving off any light but we sure must be good and do as we are told." He sat on her bed and stroked her hair. "Anyway, Honey, you should be asleep. Your grandfather has just been telling us about your accident on the swing. You really must be careful. We all love you so much and we don't want anything to happen to you....ever!" he said, helping her to climb under the covers and into bed.

"Father, it won't, believe me, I know. I'll grow up to become an old lady and I'll have a daughter called Amanda and she'll have twins called Amelia and Jemimah and we'll call them Mellie and Jem," said Joni-Pip.

"Will you, Honey? That sure sounds nice! So you have it all mapped out then?" laughed her father, whilst kissing her forehead and tucking her in.

"Oh yes, Father, you just wait and see!" she said quite emphatically.

That prediction was something her father would never forget for the rest of his life. How puzzling and unfathomable it was when it all came true!

After Father had said 'goodnight' to her and left her room, Joni-Pip settled down....not to sleep, of course.....but to wait. She had to wait until everyone had gone to bed and the house was silent. How glad she was that she had had an afternoon nap because that meant she still wasn't tired.

It wasn't too long before Mother, Father and Alex had said their 'good-nights', on the landing and then they had all gone to bed. Joni-Pip looked at the big face of the alarm clock, which she had hidden under her bed covers. She had set it to go off at one o'clock in the morning. That was her emergency back-up plan, just in case she had fallen asleep.

Soon the house was silent, so Joni-Pip quietly pulled back her bed clothes and slowly climbed out of bed. She slipped into her brother's old woolly, well worn, dressing gown and put on her slippers. She walked over to the window, opened the curtains slightly and said in a whisper,

"Everyone's asleep. Let's go!"

There was no reply.

"Are you awake?" she asked again in a whisper.

There was no reply.

"Ethelred-Ted!"

There was only silence.

Joni-Pip waited for a few seconds and then she gently prodded her Teddy Bear on his tummy.

"Er....what....er....yes....who is it?" he asked drowsily.

"It's me, Joni-Pip. Wake up! It's 'Operation Teleport' Time," she whispered urgently.

Bleary Bear eyes suddenly opened and he sat bolt upright.

"How dare you wake me up when I'm not even asleep?" he snapped. "Er, what was that? 'Operation Teleport' Time....? Munchy Mash n' Mustard! Have I missed it?" He said, leaping off the window sill.

"Of course not, Silly," laughed Joni-Pip softly.

Ethelred-Ted headed straight for the door.

"Wait....wait....just remember I can't speak once we're on the landing. Mother, Father and Alex might not be able to hear you talking but they most certainly can hear me!" she said, pulling him back lightly by his arm.

"Ouch! That's my bad arm!" he said.

"Sorry! Does that mean you won't be able to help me, then?"

"Of course I can....I do have two arms!" he laughed.

The two of them tiptoed across the shiny, wooden floor.

"Be careful....the last but one squeaks, remember?" cautioned Joni-Pip.

"Squeeeeeak!" went the last floorboard.

"Shhhh!" said Joni-Pip turning and glaring at him.

"Squeeeeeak!" went the door.

"Shhhh!" said Ethelred-Ted turning and glaring at her.

They both smiled at each other and stifled a laugh.

Very, very slowly, they walked down the full length of the landing in the dark. Joni-Pip drew back the landing window curtains so that the moonlight shone in, giving them a beautiful, free, silvery glow to work in. There wasn't any light coming **from** the cottage, so she felt she wouldn't be breaking the Blackout ruling.

Finally, they arrived at their destination: the large, wooden, Captain's Chest, which sat under the window. Excitedly, they grinned at each other!

Joni-Pip very, very slowly removed the dark red velvet cushions that always lay on the top. Sometimes the girls would sit on these, while Joni-Pip read a story. The landing was wide and spacious and the window afforded a beautiful view up and over the side of Windy Woods and further on across the fields and slopes of the rolling Nottinghamshire countryside.

Ethelred-Ted gave her a hand and they both very, very slowly started to lift the wide, wooden lid of this enormous, metal-hinged, storage chest. "Squeeeeeak!" They stopped, holding the lid half open. No sound came from the sleeping family so they looked at each other and nodded. They began to raise the lid higher. "Squeeeeeak!" They stopped again. There was still no sound coming from the slumbering cottage, so they continued squeaking and stopping and squeaking and stopping until it was finally, fully opened. They cautiously began to let go of the lid, worrying that it might slam shut. As the last finger and paw were removed, to their horror the lid started to close. Instinctively, they both lurched forward to stop it from shutting and in the process; they bumped their heads, very firmly and very painfully together! Both kept their lips very tightly closed and they grimaced as they rubbed their sore, struck heads but not so much as a whimper came. Ethelred-Ted then motioned Joni-Pip to lift up the lid again very slowly. Squeak-stop, squeak-stop, squeak-stop.

When it was finally fully opened again, he kept one paw on the lid, reached down and picked up one of the dark red, velvet cushions and wedged it under it, so that it couldn't and wouldn't close.

Joni-Pip smiled at him and raised her eyebrows in appreciation of his ingenuity. They then started very, very slowly, to empty everything out of the Captain's Chest. There was a thick, brown rug in front of the wooden chest. Mother always kept it there for the girls' feet so that they could be cosy in this little nook of the cottage as they read together. Mother's thoughtfulness meant that Ethelred-Ted and Joni-Pip could put all the things down on the rug, without making too much noise. There were old books and papers, old toys, old hats, an old tin soldier, Alex's first shoes, Joni-Pip's first dress, Becky-Paige's first bonnet, an old rag doll, an old train engine, an old scarf, an old box of greeting cards....it seemed to go on and on forever!

At last, Joni-Pip felt a cold, smooth, wooden surface under her hand. They had reached the bottom of the chest! She quickly removed the last few bits and pieces: an old lace curtain, a wedge of old handkerchiefs and a pile of old letters, tied together with ruby red ribbon.

As she touched this little parcel of letters, a strange feeling came over her and the smiling face of the Fighter Pilot, once more, came into her head.

Even though she really didn't have time, this little package intrigued her. She put it down and then promptly picked it up again. With nimble fingers, she quickly undid the shiny, satin bow and opened one of the beige envelopes.

"Do you think this is a very sensible time to do this?" whispered Ethelred-Ted. "Reading Love Letters in the middle of the night?"

Joni-Pip ignored him and unfolded the paper inside the envelope. Written in beautiful even letters, was a poem. It was penned, by a Timothy Scott Gore.

"This is magic....a real sonnet How many lines is it supposed to have?" she whispered after she had read it. "Very different from some people's efforts at writing!" she looked at Ethelred-Ted and then she stared at the name on the front of the envelope. She gasped. She showed it to him. He read the words and gasped, too.

'To Jemimah from Tim'.

"How did it get here? Are they all for her?" he asked, shaking his head.

Joni-Pip leafed through the little pile of letters and every envelope was addressed to Miss Jemimah Spindlethrop. She smiled affectionately and then wondered why on earth she did that.

"Very intriguing, I wonder who Timothy Scott Gore is? Hmmm....I suppose we had better hurry and get on, though?" she said, raising her eyebrows. Ethelred-Ted nodded. Reluctantly, she re-tied the red, satin, ribbon, into a perfect bow and put the little parcel of letters carefully down on the floor. The Captain's Chest was finally empty!

The two of them then ran hands and paws over the wood, trying to find

A Thought For You
by

Timothy Scott Gore

Moments appear and pass in such an incessant stream,
That to look for waves or ripples,
Would be a task of enormous effort.
The vast majority arrive unannounced
And quietly fade, without so much as a whisper.

So much of our lives run without fanfare,
Or trumpets, or melodies,
That to break away from the banalities,
Almost seems a hope spawned
From too much imagination.

And yet suddenly, this uneventful series of moments
Has been agitated by your presence.
Thoughts for you hang on each moment and jump to the next
In such a whirlwind of emotions, that life has now become
A succession of upward steps, reaching new heights constantly.

And so it is, that I now look down and see
The sea of humanity, quiet and placid,
As the distance makes it appear as no more
Than a melange of blues and greys,
People moving along in the same dismal course, as always.

And yet I'm happy, because my life has become
An ascending ride of contentment.
No more shall life pass under me and drift away into the forgotten.
Each piece of time is precious and worth remembrance,
For you are there!

Alas, this moment is fleeting, yes, it is gone;
And yet another one is knocking
And I will gladly let it in and go with it,
For now each moment is better than the previous one.
A thought for you and then I shall be lifted away to the next plateau.

how to remove the false bottom. They searched and searched and found nothing at first. The bottom of the chest seemed well and truly fixed but after lots of effort, they pushed it down very hard and it sprung up. The two of them then carefully lifted it out and laid it down silently in the remaining space on the rug. They had removed it, at last! They looked at each other and silently and smugly, smiled and nodded. Ethelred-Ted nodded again and pushed his head to one side as if he was heading a football. Joni-Pip looked at him very puzzled. He did it again. Joni- Pip shrugged again and looked at him, blankly.

"Put the telephone in," he whispered.

"What?"

"The telephone....Jack's telephone....put it in the chest!"

"What?" she questioned again. "Ah....it's in my bedroom...!" she said seriously and then grinned.

She set off walking back down the landing, trying to be as silent as she could. Ethelred-Ted couldn't help but chuckle at how comical she looked. She kept her arms stretched straight out each side of her and walked with

one foot immediately in front of the other. All she needed was a tightrope and a pole to balance her and then she would make the perfect Funambulist! [28]

The door and floor of her bedroom creaked and squeaked as she entered and crossed it. She then pulled out the top drawer of her bedside cabinet and reached right to the back of it. There was the little telephone from the future! Earlier they had beautifully wrapped it up in brown paper and then put it in one of Alex's old, empty pen and pencil cases. It seemed perfect for the job and they were sure he wouldn't miss it! The box was then wrapped again in brown paper and tied up neatly with rough, cream-coloured, whiskery string. They had written on it, 'NOT TO BE OPENED UNTIL 2007' in very exact and bold letters.

---

[28] Tightrope Walker

Joni-Pip took out the little package, closed the drawer and re-trod her footsteps across her bedroom. She walked out of the door and down the landing. She had past caring now about the squeaky, creaky, groany polished wooden floorboards: she had a very important quission and nothing would stop her from completing it! They put the neatly-packaged, little, mobile telephone under the false bottom of the Captain's Chest.

"'Bye Little Telephone!" she said softly. "Thanks for giving me so much!"

"I only hope the Twins find it," Ethelred-Ted said, "or we're in trouble!"

They very carefully pushed the false bottom back in until it clicked and then they reloaded all the stuff from the rug into the chest. Once more as she ran her fingers over the little ruby-red, ribbon wrapped letters, a warm feeling washed over her. It quickly changed to a very heavy heart. She knew that very soon she would forget all about speaking to her daughter, Amanda and her grand daughters, Mellie and Jem. She knew that she would forget about Alex's grandson, Jack and Red-Ted. Right now, she didn't want to. Sadly, she knew it had to be that way. They were the Rules! She realised that it was only by this fluke, or her holding on to Jack's little 'phone more like, that she had had this extra special joy.

Just as they were about to close the lid, Joni-Pip noticed that the old, green train engine was still standing on the rug. She grabbed it quickly and in doing so, it slipped through her fingers. The engine went into the air as if it was being tossed like a pancake! Both Eth and she held out their arms to try to catch it. Once again, in doing so, they painfully collided. The metal train engine fell heavily and noisily on to the hard, unyielding, wooden floorboards, "Claaaaaang!"

Joni-Pip froze in horror as she saw the light come on in Alex's bedroom. Quickly, she grabbed Eth and pushed him into the Captain's Chest and noisily closed the lid. She then lifted up her arms straight out in front of her, half closed her eyes and walked along the landing. Alex came out of his bedroom first and then Mother and Father came out of their room.

"What's going on?" asked Father.

"What's all that noise?" asked Mother.

"Shhhhh!" said Alex. "It's J.P., I think she's sleep walking. She must have bumped into the Captain's Chest on her travels."

"What? My Poor Child! What has made her do that?" whispered Mother.

"Maybe it was the bump on her head. Doctor Evans said she was slightly concussed," replied Father.

"Well, let's just watch her and see what she does!" suggested Alex.

Joni-Pip continued on her journey down the landing and through her bedroom door. She took off Alex's old dressing gown, hung it on the peg on the door and got into bed, pulling her covers very firmly over her.

Three figures stood in her doorway and watched in amazement.

"She seems to be all right now, Honey!" laughed Father.

"Well, I never!" said Mother. "I wonder when she will let me buy her a new dressing gown. She is so attached to that tatty old thing you gave her, Alex."

Alex smiled.

"A new one?" laughed Father. "She won't hear of it!"

Alex smiled again.

"She won't remember any of this in the morning!" he chuckled.

Then they all went back to bed.

'Oh, yes I will!' thought a little twelve-year–old, smiling to herself from under the bedclothes. 'I don't need a new dressing gown! Blooming cheek!'

Ethelred-Ted was not too happy. He didn't relish the idea of being cramped up all night in a hard, cold, wooden chest.

"What on earth did she do that for?" he said out loud.

"I sorry if I 'quash you, Monsieur!" came a little, sweet voice from the darkness.

"What?" he said. "Je....je...m'appelle...my name is Celeste, ze..... rag doll, je ....I am... ....Française......."

came the husky voice, "I once belong to Amelia. Now I stay 'ere all day and all night. I 'ave no life now," the very attractive French accent went on sadly. "I 'ave no friends. I... so....lonely! Eet is nobody who luff me!"

"Oh, don't be like tha-at!" said the suddenly chivalrous bear, gently.

"Pourquoi? Alors, you will be my friend now, Monsieur?"

"Of course," Ethelred-Ted said, thinking,

'Hmmm! Maybe it won't be so bad, after all, being left here all night long with a beautiful, French, Rag Doll! That accent! Whew! That accent!'

Chapter 31

Father's Folly

"Why on earth, is Cecelia Slate's rag doll kept in the Captain's Chest?"

"Exactly ma thought as well, Hen."

"And what is a pile of Love Letters for Jemimah Spindlethrop doing in there?" asked Joni-Pip seriously. "And who on earth is Timothy Scott Gore?"

"It strikes me there are a lot of unanswered questions right now. I can only tell you what Celeste told me!" said Ethelred-Ted wistfully.

The four of them were walking through the woods, on their way over to Edwinstowe Library. Today, was the last day they had left to make their final preparations. They had decided that, tomorrow, they were going to attempt to jump over the Wall of Time. Their mission was to save Amelia Plate from the Workhouse Fire. Thanks to Eth having a quick word with Freddie (although he couldn't remember how and when he received the instructions), almost everything was ready. They were on their way to the Library, to verify the time that the Workhouse Fire broke out.

"Now let's go over what we have to do," said Ethelred-Ted.

Poppy-Plump-Pij flew on ahead of them. A colourful sight flash past her.

"Won't be a minuteful!" she said, as she came back and soared, silently, above them. "I'll just do everything you tell me, tomorrow, don't worry! I'll get to the Library, one day!" she added and then disappeared above the trees.

"Wouldn't you just love to fly?" said Joni-Pip wistfully. "I remember thinking that I must be flying, when we were in the KOL."

"It was indeed!" sighed Ethelred-Ted. "What a feeling! I wonder if Poppy goes through the KOL when she flies over the Wall of Time?"

"I don't think she does, Ma Pets. I think it must be a bonus for us folks, who can't fly!"

"That makes me feel slightly better, then," laughed Joni-Pip. "It would seem so unfair if they flew in the Kaleidoscope of Life, as well as flying in the Circle of Life!"

"I wonder what would happen if she just jumped with us, then?"

"Hmmmmm!" said both Hetty the Wee and Joni-Pip together.

The three friends came to a clearing in the wood and two birds were seen flying high in the beautiful, blue, cloudless sky, above them. They could just make out that one of them was very colourful and the other one was

284

mainly pinky-grey.

"That's got be them!" said Joni-Pip. "Flying must be so exhilarating there's such a lot of sky! If all goes according to plan....we will have a little flight tomorrow!"

"Yes, so I'd like to go over a few things with you both, now: all right?"

"Of course!" the two girls replied.

"I think the reason we need ice, is because the Wall of Time is made up of water ....pure and simply H_2O but the amazing part is that it has the molecular make up of ice, so rather than the water spilling out everywhere, it stands up, as ice would."

"That's so incredible, Ma Lambs!"

"Isn't it just?" agreed Joni-Pip.

"So when we saw the bricks forming to make up the Wall of Time, they were being made, by reproducing the ice cubes: only they were made up of water. Did you notice it wasn't freezing or anything? That's because it was just like water....solid water! Although it is water, I don't think we could walk through it....as we could a water fall or a shower because it's still like ice."

"And we can't walk through that, believe me....I seem t' be pretty good at sliding on it, though!" laughed Hetty the Wee.

"The thought of you sliding....or were you skating, Hetty? giggled Joni-Pip.

"The problem is this; we can't go over the Wall of Time at Archimedes' because it's a tad too far to walk in the dark and that would take some explaining to Mother and Father but we need some ice. I noticed that Mrs Broft had some ice in a jug of lemonade last week, so I did a bit of investigating and in the kitchen at Knotty Knook, there's that large American refrigerator and it has an ice box inside it," said Eth.

"I could have told you that, Ethelred-Ted. That's one advantage of having an American Father. We've always had an ice box, ever since I can remember."

"Then why the Dickens didn't you say, You Silly Nolly? I've been worrying myself senseless; struggling, stressing and straining my brain, wondering how on earth we could get some ice for the F.B., without breaking into the Quission Hut again and making it! You are a pain!" Ethelred-Ted said crossly.

"I am really so sorry, Eth," Joni-Pip said humbly. She paused for a moment. "Hey, why am I being so stupid? I'd have thought you, of all people, would be well acquainted with the whereabouts and the wherewithal of our large refrigerator!"

Everybody laughed, including Ethelred-Ted.

"What? Me? Not so much of your cheek, Young Lady!"

"I don't suppose she realised it would be such a problem, Hen," Hetty laughed, "especially not with you and your stomach!"

"I am sorry, though, Eth, I didn't mean to be such a Twerp," laughed Joni-Pip, "I just didn't think!"

"I suppose there's no harm done...." smiled Ethelred-Ted. He didn't want there to be any bad feeling between them, right now. He knew how crucial 'Team Spirit' would be as they embarked on their amazing adventure.

Determined not to let her small omission spoil the moment, either, Joni-Pip linked her arm in his, then she pulled away and looked at his arm.

Ethelred-Ted looked at her strangely.

"I am just making sure this is not your poorly but very nicely sewn up arm!" she said affectionately. As it wasn't, she nestled back in, closely, to him and whispered, "So tell all about this pretty little French Rag Doll?"

Ethelred-Ted smiled.

"She's so sweet. She speaks with this beautiful French accent. I feel so sad for her. She's been sitting in the Captain's Chest for years and years. Can you imagine that? It must be terrible just sitting there all day and night ....waiting. All she wants, is to be loved again. I wonder why Mother has got her? I wonder why she doesn't let Becky-Paige have her, to play with?"

"That's such a mystery, isn't it, Lovies, I wonder if we'll ever know why she's in there? Why would Mother keep her? What did Mother have t' d' with Amelia Plate? What did she have t' d' wi' Jemimah Plate?"

"Such a lot of unanswered questions! I don't know how You Two feel but after talking all night to Celeste...." Ethelred-Ted smiled.

"Are we a literl bit in lurve?" interrupted Joni-Pip. Ethelred-Ted blushed and once again, he went really red, well as red as a red Ted can go red.

"I think he is! I don't know; it must be because it's Spring: what with Macca and Poppy and now you and Celeste!" Hetty teased.

"It's not like that....it's not like that, at all....I just feel so sorry for the pretty little thing," protested Ethelred-Ted and then he sighed.

"Methinks the Teddy doth protest too much!"

"Ay, Laddie, she's taken y' hearrrrt and that's f' surrrre!"

"What?"

Hetty the Wee and Joni-Pip looked at each other and exchanged winks: then burst out laughing.

"Look, we have some serious questions to try and answer and as I tried to say a minute ago, I wondered if we might do something else, before we go to the Workhouse tomorrow night? I understand if you say 'no way' but I thought I would put it to you, anyway," he said seriously.

"What's that, then?" asked Joni-Pip, pulling up a piece of long grass and doing what she loved to do, chewing on the juicy root.

Ethelred-Ted stopped walking and looked up into the sky as a squadron of RAF planes droned overhead. Joni-Pip shuddered: just hearing that sound, reminded her of the horrors of the night in the cellar, during the bombing of Bath. She put her hands over her ears; drowning the droning.

"I'd like to jump over the Wall of Time and stop Jemimah from getting on Bullet!" said Eth very rapidly, sounding almost afraid to say the words.

"I have already thought we should do that, Hen, that terrible accident seemed t' affect so many people we know," said Het very slowly and very sadly.

"Have you, Het? Have you really thought about doing that?" asked Ethelred-Ted eagerly.

"Me, too! So you needn't have worried about asking us!"

Ethelred-Ted hugged both of his friends.

"I love You Two, so much!"

"And we love you, oh so much more!" laughed Joni-Pip.

"So when do we go then, Ma Pets?"

"This afternoon."

Both Joni-Pip and Hetty the Wee took a sharp intake of breath.

"Whew!" they both said.

"D'you know the date and time it happened then?" asked Joni-Pip.

"Yes. Do you remember the time I stayed over with Archimedes, when I first had my poorly arm? We talked a little bit about the accident, I told you before. He told me it was on the night of May 4th 1882," said Ethelred-Ted.

"So what are we going t' do? What's yer plan, Laddie Boy?"'

"The reason I've left it and left it, is because I worried we might only get **one** chance to JIT. I knew how you all wanted to save Amelia Plate and I didn't want to spoil any chances of us doing that."

"I see, Ma Lamb."

"D'you still think that?"

"I don't know but I think it has got to be one of those things we will never know, until we try it!" he replied seriously.

"I agree! I think we just have t' try....and hope!"

"The fact that all of us have feelings about this, is a good indication. It's something that we all want to do and something we all must do! After all, what Hetty said is right; the accident with Bullet affected so many people we know. So it's agreed then?" asked Ethelred-Ted.

The other two nodded.

"All right....I suggest we get the information from the Library about the fire and then go!"

"This is so exciting!" said Joni-Pip. "I never dreamt we would be going into the KOL, today. I can't wait! It's the most amazing thing!"

They quickly hurried on, towards Edwinstowe. They were three young things with a mission and Poppy-Plump-Pij was nowhere to be seen!

When they arrived at the Library they were greeted by the jocular, if not puzzled Librarian, Seamus O' Hara. He was always happy; he had the most beautiful, velvety, Irish accent, which made him sound as if he was singing, when he spoke.

"Top of the morning to yers," he said to Joni-Pip. "What can we be doin' for yer t'day, Young Miss Garador?" then he turned to Ethelred-Ted. "So yer back again, this mornin'? Didn't you find it then?"

Ethelred-Ted looked at Seamus and shrugged his bear shoulders. He had never met Seamus before and he hadn't the slightest idea what the Librarian was going on about. He thought it must have been Irish humour. He grinned.

"I like your hat, Seamus, where did you get it from?" Ethelred-Ted gestured towards the knitted, multi-coloured hat, the Irishman was wearing. "I especially like the red bobble on the top!"

Embarrassed, Seamus quickly removed his woolly hat.

"So y' like it do yer? My Granny sent it over from Ballymahon. I hate t' thing, it's all itchy but I promised her it would be worn. Y' don't want it do ya?" he asked eagerly.

"I would love it, just love it. Thank you!" replied Ethelred-Ted, taking it from him and plonking it on his furry head. "Are you sure?"

"Y'd be doin' me a favour and it truthfully would be worn!"

Ethelred-Ted walked over to one of the glass cases that held the specialist books and examined his reflection. He re-arranged the hat rather saucily on one side and returned to the others. He was delighted. He had always wanted a hat! A Pirate's hat would be the ultimate but nevertheless....

"Seamus, we would like to look at the old newspaper articles about the day the Workhouse Fire broke out, please?" asked Joni-Pip politely.

"Ah would y' now? And why would y' be doin' that, again, then?"

"Er...." Joni-Pip was puzzled, "well, actually, Seamus it's to prove a point to my brother. I asked him when the Workhouse Fire was and he said May 4th but I'm sure I was told that it was on May 5th. I just want to check it."

"I see," said Seamus. "Follow me! Tell that brother of yours, t'at I have got in some more great train books. I think he might be interested in one especially. It is about the Old Wild West Railways of North America.

288

There are some wonderful photographs in them. I know how much he loves his trains, particularly the American ones!"

Seamus walked them across the beautiful, shiny, wooden floorboards of the Library, to the Reference Section. Their footsteps echoed through the spacious building. He then searched the large files, which stood side by side in row upon row. Each file was marked by the year. He started at the front row of the huge book shelf and then walked round to the back of it. He ran his hands up the spines of the files as he read the years.

"Ah! Where was it now?" he said. "We're gettin' warmer....this is the 1880's....88....89....90....91....here it is, 1892, isn't it?"

He pulled out the file, walked over to a large stand and propped up the file, so that they could turn the pages of the stored newspapers and find the one they were interested in.

"I'll leave you to it, then," he smiled and walked away from them. He turned round and said to Ethelred-Ted, "I hope you find what you are looking for this time. Didn't you find it earlier? T' hat looks great, by the way, much better on you!"

Ethelred-Ted looked extremely pleased, touched his hat gently and then, puzzled, he said,

"Thank you, Seamus but what on earth are you going on about?"

"I am going on about the fact that you came in here not more than an hour ago with a young lad, didn't ya and ya asked for exactly the same file." He walked to his desk and sat down. "How d'ya t'ink I remembered the year?"

The three friends looked at each other and frowned.

"What on earth was that all about?" shrugged Ethelred-Ted.

"P'raps Seamus is getting a bit forgetful in his young age!" came Joni-Pip.

"It strikes me as most peculiar, all the same, Ma Lambs."

Soon the three of them were reading all about the terrible tragedy of 1892. There was even a photograph of the Workhouse, before it was destroyed, by fire. Then there was one of the people of Edwinstowe, still trying to put out the fire, early the next morning.

"It says here," said Joni-Pip, running her fingers over the words of the newspaper, "'Fire broke out in the early morning of May 5th' but it doesn't say exactly what time. That's going to be a bit of a problem for us, isn't it? Hang on a minute....look who's in the picture....he's standing right at the front....it can't be! How silly of me, he must just 'look' like him!"

She pointed to a tall figure, who did look familiar to all of them. Hetty the Wee and Ethelred-Ted leaned over the picture and scrutinised it.

"It's Farmer Finn!" they both shouted out loud.

"Shhhhh! Silence please?" Seamus' voice echoed through the Library.

"But it can't be! He was....how old in 1892?" whispered Hetty the Wee.

"I don't think he was born! He can't be much older than....what....38 or 39 now! So he wasn't born until around 1903. It can't be him!" Ethelred-Ted said, looking extremely puzzled.

"Shhhhhh!" came Seamus' voice across the Library. "Silence please!"

"But it is him!" whispered Joni-Pip, ignoring Seamus. "I would know that face anywhere. It's James Finn....Taff....oh no! Look! I can't believe it! Just look!" She pointed to another figure, just behind him in the photograph.

Ethelred-Ted and Hetty the Wee both leaned forward again, looked at the photograph in the newspaper and gasped.

"It's Father....Joni-Pip....it's....Father!" they said together.

Joni-Pip went white.

"I know! I can see....I can't believe it! What is my Father doing in a photograph, years before he was born? It's not possible. He's wearing the new sweater that Grandmother Garador knitted him and sent over from Portland. He's only had it about a month. How can that be? Look at the date of the Newspaper....May 5th 1892. Father is 40 now, he was born in 1902. This picture was taken 10 years before he was born!" she was almost hysterical.

Seamus came marching over to the Reference Library.

"I'm sorry but I can't have ya makin' any more noise in the Library. Y' are disturbing all the other Readers," he said slightly ruffled.

Ethelred-Ted, Hetty and Joni-Pip looked around the empty Library.

Seamus looked around the empty Library.

"Oh well," he chuckled, "there might have been some!"

All his 'Readers' shrieked.

"All right then....y' can talk....but the moment anybody walks in, y' must be quiet....as quiet as mice....agreed?" he said, grinning.

"Agreed!"

"I can't be fairer than t'at now, can I?" Seamus said and walked off.

"In the light of what we have seen in this newspaper, we really have got some knots to untie. I think that it's imperative that we get back to Knotty Knook as soon as we can and ask Father some questions!" said Joni-Pip and then she added in an Irish accent, "Agreed?"

"Agreed!" came two more Irish accents.

Father wasn't in when they arrived back at the cottage, so the question was....were they going to JIT and stop Jemimah mounting Bullet, or not?

"I don't know what to think," said Ethelred-Ted, removing his hat and scratching his head. "Everything seemed straight forward this morning, until we saw that picture in the paper from 1892....I know....why don't we take a walk over to Finn's Farm and see if we can speak to Farmer Finn....James Finn or Taff or whatever it is that Father calls him?"

"Good idea!" said Joni-Pip. "We've got plenty of time. Oh, I wish Father was at home....have I got questions for him! Is your new hat itchy? It really suits you. You look a bit like Rob Roy....I think."

"No, my head is though! Rob Roy eh? I don't want to take it off now!"

As they walked towards Finn's Farm, Joni-Pip pointed to a clump of trees ahead of them.

"There are the stars, again! You do see them, You Two, don't you?"

"Yes, I jolly well do! I remember what happened last time, in Tunnel 6, as well? Crumbs that was amazing, fancy all those passages!" replied Eth.

True to form, a few minutes later, Flip, Steve and Craig arrived.

"Greetings!" said Ethelred-Ted. "Did you help Freddie and Jem?"

The face of the Fighter Pilot came into Joni-Pip's mind again and stayed.

"Hello, You Lot!" laughed Craig. "Yeah, thanks to Steve's quick thinking!"

"You got back through Tunnel 6, O.K., then, I take it?" laughed Flip.

"Eth, have you got any paper on you?" Joni-Pip asked. "I must do something. Quickly before it goes and I forget it!" Ethelred-Ted looked puzzled.

"I have!" said Craig reaching in his pocket. "A pencil, too. Mr Efficiency!"

"Thanks!" said Joni-Pip. She turned her back and started drawing.

"What are you doing?" asked everyone, trying to see over her shoulder.

"Something I just have to do! Not very well but there we are! Leave me!"

"By the way, Eth, I meant to say before, that was such a shock, hearing you speaking in German. How long have I known you and I had no idea? You sounded fluent!" asked Flip.

"I have no idea how long you have known me but I have spoken German since I was made!" laughed Ethelred-Ted. "I had to learn English when I was adopted by the Garadors."

"Of course, you're a Steiff! That makes sense!" laughed Steve.

"So, have you any news on the whereabouts of the Old Mine?" asked Craig.

"Yes!" said Joni-Pip, still with her back to them. "It's somewhere up on the Clappers."

"Er....actually....we did know that because of the time with the Zulus. Where on the Clappers? Where exactly?" came Flip.

"The Zulus yeah, M, M 'n M! The mine is somewhere," replied Ethelred-Ted.

"Is there any other where?" asked Craig.

They all laughed.

"The Zulus, that was so scary, up on the Clappers," replied Joni-Pip.

"Isn't there anyone who knows?" asked Steve. "Anyone at all?"

"Let me think now," said Flip, "I guess we'll have to come back later and Nuttingham Squirrel might shed some light!"

"Nuttingham Squirrel?" shouted Joni-Pip, Hetty and Ethelred-Ted.

"Sounds impossible but there it is!" Flip said laughing.

"Do you know this man?" asked Joni-Pip, handing them the paper.

The three visitors put their heads down, looking at her drawing. She noticed glittery bits in their hair.

"Is he supposed to be a Fighter Pilot?" laughed Steve.

"How and when have you seen him?" asked Ethelred-Ted.

"In the garden, the night of the Raid on Bath!" said Joni-Pip.

Everyone looked at Joni-Pip and then at each other. Joni-Pip frowned.

Just then, the Two Men in Long, Black Coats came towards them.

"At lastte we haff you!" shouted one of them.

"You haff corst uss meny trerbbles!" called out the other man.

"M, M & M, should we run?" asked Flip.

"I should jolly well think so and fast!" ordered Craig. With that, they sped off, in the direction, from whence they came.

"Be back later!" shouted Steve, turning and waving.

The two men chased after them. They both disappeared into the trees.

The small regiment of strange soldiers they had seen before, suddenly marched along the pathway. The Commanding Officer gave the order to halt.

"Have you seen two men in long, black coats?" he demanded to know.

"You have asked us that before," Joni-Pip replied.

"The moment you do, you must report it to the Constabulary," he shot.

"You have told us that before," she replied, once more noticing that all this little band of Militia wore very peculiar uniforms.

"Just make sure you do! This is of the utmost importance: a matter of National Security!" he snapped and then ordered his men to march off.

'Now where have I heard that before?' thought Joni-Pip, then she said,

"I wonder why I said that? I hope they'll be all right. It's so confusing!"

"Are they all connected? Why don't we remember any of this once they

292

have gone? Did you notice their odd uniforms?" questioned Ethelred-Ted.

Poppy-Plump-Pij flew down to be with them again. She landed on the pathway in front of them and said breathlessly,

"Well, that was such a strangeful time. I have so much to tell you!"

"Poppy, we love you dearly and we would love to hear all about you and Macca but not right now. We've much more pressing things to talk about. You won't believe what we have seen and discovered," said Ethelred-Ted seriously.

"But I have so much to tell you. You must listen!" Poppy pleaded.

"Not now, Poppy....later, Hen!" said Hetty the Wee, walking on.

"Please listen to me?" Poppy urged but none of them paid any attention.

"Poppy Pigeon, we know you've had a wonderful time with Macca, flying high up into the sky. We saw you earlier and we will hear all about it but not just yet. All right?" said Joni-Pip kindly.

Her three friends walked passed her and on towards Finn's Farm.

All right," she said crossly, "so I won't tell you that I've just flown over the Wall of Time, then!"

Ethelred-Ted, Joni-Pip and Hetty the Wee all stopped in their tracks.

"What?" they all turned and stared at her.

"Well, it was a little while ago, actually."

"When?"

"Nearly two hours ago."

"Who with?"

"Macca of course!"

"Macca?" came three voices again.

"And Father and Farmer Finn!" she said triumphantly!

"Poppy, you must tell us....how? You must explain!" said Ethelred-Ted.

"I don't see why I should, none of you wanted to listen to me a minute ago. I tried to tell you but you didn't want to hear it!" She then flew off.

"What have we done now?" asked Hetty the Wee, shaking her little head.

"We never learn, do we?" said Ethelred-Ted, mournfully.

"Poor Poppy, we didn't give her a chance. I don't blame her, at all, for leaving us, do you?" asked Joni-Pip.

"No," replied Ethelred-Ted and Hetty the Wee.

"Well, we kind of know why Father and James Finn are in the photograph at the Workhouse after the fire, don't we?" stated Ethelred-Ted.

"Do we?" shrugged Joni-Pip and Hetty the Wee.

"I think that if we had arrived at the Library any earlier, we wouldn't have seen them both in the photograph in the newspaper," replied the Bear.

"How come?" asked Joni-Pip.

"I think that they had only just JITTED. I think they'd tried to change something....obviously they hadn't prevented the fire from happening, as they were helping, when the Workhouse was still smouldering, according to the picture. Also, they **must** have been there, when the picture was taken, as they look exactly as they do today....I wonder what it was they wanted to change?"

"I don't understand, Ma Pet."

"If they had stopped the fire, Het, then there wouldn't be a picture of the Workhouse burnt down, in the paper would there?" explained Joni-Pip.

"I see."

"Perhaps they jumped over the Wall of Time for another reason," said Joni-Pip. "I wonder what that could have been?"

"I think you should go and ask Father, he should be home by now!" came a voice from above them. They all looked up.

"Poppy!"

"Yes, I have come back but not because I wanted to but because Macca told me I must," she said begrudgingly.

"Thank you, Poppy, please forgive us?" begged Joni-Pip.

"Well, I'm not going to tell you all that has happened: that would have made it easyful for you. As it is, you will have to go and confront Father, yourselves," she replied and flew off again.

"Oh dear, I really think we have upset her now," said Hetty the Wee.

"Let's go back and talk to Father, I'm sure Poppy will forgive us in time," said Ethelred-Ted. "I don't like it that Poppy is upset with us, I don't like it at all but it has certainly taught me a lesson....a lesson in listening!"

"And me!" agreed Joni-Pip.

"Me too!" echoed Hetty the Wee.

With that, they turned round and set off, back towards Knotty Knook.

Father was sitting, alone, in the garden, drinking tea, when they arrived.

"D' y' think y' should do this, all by yerself, Joni-Pip?"

"I don't know. What d'you think Eth?"

"I'll come, we both will come. If he doesn't speak to me, then I know he won't be able to see me....as alive and talking, that is....the same goes for Het....at least we will be there to support you, in any case."

"All right, thanks....here goes!"

Father looked up and his eyes lit up when he saw Joni-Pip. He got up and almost ran towards her, as she approached the white, wicker, garden table. He then looked down, as if he had been caught scrumping apples, in the vicar's garden.

"Honey, you are here! I'm so sorry: so, so, sorry, we both are. We were too late. Please don't go?" At first he looked at her and then he looked down. He reminded Joni-Pip of the Engineer, who came to fix some machinery, at Finn's Farm, one day. While he was speaking to Farmer Finn, he only ever seemed to be talking to his shoes. She remembered laughing when James Finn had said,

"You can tell when an engineer is friendly and outgoing, if he doesn't look at his shoes, when he is speaking....he looks at yours!"

Joni-Pip didn't reply to Father....she just sat herself down on the white, wicker chair, opposite him and listened. Poppy's words had really scored.

"It was wrong of us....of me....I just hope you will forgive me....us....but you must promise me, you won't go?"

Joni-Pip had absolutely no idea what her father was talking about; what he had done and why he was being so apologetic. He obviously felt it was very bad; so bad, that he had to beg for her forgiveness. She didn't recognise this 'morose', sad Father; the One who was pleading with her not to go somewhere.

"This is yours, I presume?" He looked up and put something on the table.

At first Joni-Pip didn't see what it was but then the small, folded-up handkerchief made a noise, almost as if it was lost.

"The F.B.!" gasped Ethelred-Ted, Hetty the Wee and Joni-Pip together.

"Father where did you get it from?" asked Joni-Pip, seriously.

"Er....let me explain...." he stumbled.

There was a kind of wailing coming from the F.B.. It was a very strange, pathetic sound, not like anything, any of them had ever heard before.

"Actually, Father, no, it isn't mine."

Father looked at her puzzled.

Ethelred-Ted walked forward and picked up the F.B., cradling it in his paws. The wailing noise stopped. The F.B. then began to, sort of....purr!

"It was given to me. It's mine!"

"I thought you might be the one."

Father wasn't surprised, at all, to be talking to Ethelred-Ted.

"Please explain how you managed to get hold of it and....why you used it this morning?" as Joni-Pip asked this, she couldn't believe how she now seemed to be the parent and Father seemed to be the child.

It was a very strange experience.

"It all started with Alex," started Father, again talking to his shoes.

As he put his head down, she noticed something sparkling in his hair.

"Alex?" repeated Ethelred-Ted, Hetty the Wee and Joni-Pip.

"Yes, Alex. He told me that you had shown him and Archimedes Spindlethrop, the most amazing formula. Immediately, that stirred something inside me for days. Then I saw the Formula, under your bed,

295

Joni-Philipa...."

"Mrs Broft!" the three of them said together.

"Mrs Broft?" questioned Father. "What has she got to do with all this?"

Joni-Pip shook her head.

"Nothing," she replied, feeling sad that she had doubted their, very confidential, House Keeper. Joni-Pip took another look at Father's hair and there it was again, something was most definitely gleaming. It looked like he had little gold and silver stars in his hair! They reminded her of something.

"No, I discovered it one day. I had gone into your bedroom, simply to borrow a pen and as I walked past your bed, I saw something sticking out. I simply pushed it back under at first and then I went over and picked up a pen, from off your dressing table. It was on the way back that I noticed the thing I'd pushed back under your bed, was very large. A piece of the sheet that covered one corner, had slipped off and I saw the amazing symbols underneath. I pulled it out, removed the sheet and there it was!"

"So what did you do?" asked Ethelred-Ted.

"That's when it happened."

"What happened?" questioned his Three Inquisitors.

"Everything came flooding back into my mind: The Wall of Time: The Gift of Déjà Vu: The KOL: POOLS: CIRCLES," he said this, looking up at them.

"What?" came three shocked voices.

"You've JITTED? Father, have you got little stars in your hair?" asked Joni-Pip rather inappropriately. "How did they get there?"

"What?" asked Father putting his hand on his head and rubbing his hair. "Oh those? You'll soon find out where they come from!"

"So you have JITTED, too?" repeated Hetty the Wee.

"Yes....yes of course. You do, surely, realise that you are not the only ones who have experienced these incredible things, don't you? For me, it all started when I was at University, with Taff. We shared a room together, at Oxford. I was the fresh American Student and he was assigned to show me around. One day, I came back from a Lecture and I said I was mad that a Colonel Anthony Durnford ((my fifth cousin, Dear Reader)), had been blamed for the defeat of a little Regiment of Royal Engineers in the Zulu Wars, in Africa, at a place called Isandlwana. So, I looked it all up in the College Library and I read that it wasn't his fault, at all. It was, in fact, his Commanding Officer, Lord Chelmsford, who had boned off, thinking he knew where the Zulus were. He took most of the soldiers with him, to go and find them and while he was gone, the Zulus attacked the little regiment that was left and practically wiped it out. Colonel Durnford did his best but the odds were too great. A couple of soldiers ran away and they took the British flag with them. They found Lord Chelmsford and fought again, in the afternoon at Rourke's Drift, against the Zulus. The two men, who ran with the flag, were decorated with the Victoria Cross but Colonel Durnford, who fought so bravely, was disgraced. I read that his daughter had tried and tried to clear his name but she hadn't succeeded. So I just happened to say to Taff,

'I wish I could go back in Time and help her to clear her father's name. This sure isn't good for her, or the rest of Col. Durnford's Family. It's not fair!'

"'Well, Taff said, 'That would be great, if only we could do that....go back in Time and change things and all that!' In reply, his friend Sanjay, who was having a drink with us in our room, at the time, just astounded us by saying,

'All right, I will take you both over The Wall of Time!'

"We both laughed and mocked him, of course!" continued Father. "Sanjay was such a nice guy, always friendly and helpful. He ended up owning a hotel by the harbour in Folkestone, he ran it with his friend, Dana: great place!"

"So?" asked his three very intrigued listeners.

"Right, I digress. We went with Sanjay, up to his room and he showed us the Formula Board. He explained that he had been given it, before he came to Oxford, when he was still at school, in India and although he had it, he didn't know quite what he was supposed to do with it; until I said I wanted to go back in Time! Then it all came to him....yes, we went over the Wall of Time and it was wonderful to stand looking out of the Keep of Good Memories, in the KOL! We then helped Colonel Durnford to clear his name....and if you look up the history of the Zulu Wars, you will see that's true. There's a plaque on the wall of Rochester Cathedral, commemorating Colonel Durnford's death and honouring him. Of course, I forgot everything about it....my memory of it was erased....until I saw the Formula....I knew this was just a copy, so I searched for the real thing, the Formula Board and sure enough, I found it in the School Room, in the top drawer of your desk, Joni-Philipa. It was one day when you were out with Ethelred-Ted," said Father, extremely sheepishly.

"So, tell us, Father, how did you help Colonel Durnford?"

Amazing memories started to flood her brain.

"Hmmm, that was quite something when we JITTED to South Africa. We tried to get hold of Colonel Durnford to warn him about the Zulu attack. Unfortunately, he wasn't with his regiment, at the time, he had gone off with one of his Scouts, to try and locate where the Zulus were encamped. James and I had a quick discussion and felt the best thing we could do, was to trick the little regiment of Royal Engineers into jumping over the Wall of Time....and coming back here, out of the way."

"So, when was this, Father?" asked Ethelred-Ted.

"In 1922, I was twenty, myself. James was nineteen."

"How did you trick them, Hen?"

"We waited 'til they were altogether and mounted on their horses and then we pretended to steal two of their horses and we rode off, they gave chase, we jumped over the Wall of Time and they did, too. We didn't bank on twenty thousand Zulu's following them back to James' Dad's farm!"

The other three shrieked with laughter.

"So....it was you and James Finn....I knew I recognised your voice, only you sounded much, much more Yankee! That makes sense, now," said Joni-Pip, remembering what had happened to them, up on the Clappers, "you hadn't been long in England but how come you were in 1942, anyway?"

"What are you talking about, Honey?"

"We were there, Father, don't you remember meeting me? We were all hiding behind those rocks you stood next to," grinned Ethelred-Ted.

"Good Garador!" said Father, scratching his head and leaning back in his chair. "Yes, I do! How come it was you? D'you know I had a devil of a job trying to buy a pesky teddy bear like you, in Germany? They said they had never heard of a red and yellow Steiff. In the end I left it and then, when Mother was having you, Joni-Philipa, I had to go to Frankfurt on business. I drove to a Steiff Factory and got one....You....made specially for the new baby!"

They all shook their heads, trying to work that all out!

"I thought your friend was called Jim and you still haven't explained how you managed to be in 1942? I was behind that rock, too, Father. I watched it all. I heard you talking to Colonel Durnford. It was only recently, we saw you and all the Zulus running in front of us, below the Clappers. Before then, we saw you and Taff galloping along, behind Knotty Knook, being chased by Colonel Durnford and his Regiment. At least we presume it must have been You Lot. It was most definitely in 1942. How come?" Joni-Pip asked seriously.

"Well, I never! That explains something. We wondered why everything looked so different! All the new houses. We must have set the F.B. to the wrong year! Oh well, I can't believe you saw it and were there, too, Honey."

"We saw you in two places. Did you JIT twice then?" Joni-Pip asked.

"Yes, on our first attempt, we got Colonel Durnford and his men to JIT

298

and arrive, here. We planned to stop them and explain but something startled the horses and they bolted. They ran round in a circle and jumped back again, over the Wall of Time, back to the Battle of Isandlwana, during the Zulu Wars, on the 22nd January, 1879! We thought we would never manage to save the Regiment. We JITTED back here and then set the F.B., to an earlier time. We did it all again and this time, the Regiment chased after us and strangely the horses weren't frightened and we hid behind some rocks...."

"That's when we saw you. You thought you were in 1922!" said Joni-Pip.

"1942 instead of 1922....easy mistake!" laughed Ethelred-Ted.

"Why, 'Jim', Father? I thought Farmer Finn was called James?"

"Oh, Hen, that's s' simple, every Scotsman, I know, called James, is known as Jim or Jimmy!"

"That's right, Little One. At College, Taff was always known as 'Jim'."

They all remained silent for a minute, trying to make sense of it.

"I still don't understand why you stole the F.B. from me, Father?"

"Stole it? Stole it?" repeated Father indignantly. "NO! Just borrowed it!"

"And that, you feel is acceptable behaviour?" Eth raised his eyebrows.

"No, of course not: I just wanted to help a friend, that's all," Father said meekly. "It was to help somebody else....not me.... I wasn't being selfish."

"And why did your friend need help, then, Hen?" asked Hetty the Wee kindly. She could see that Father was upset with himself and she didn't think that it was necessary to make him feel even worse.

"A long time ago, Taff's father, the Old Farmer Finn...." Father started.

"Fred Finn," they all said together and Father looked surprised.

"Yes, Fred Finn: well, he was out walking through the woods, up on the Clappers, one day, with his younger brother...."

"Colin," they all said together and Father looked even more surprised.

"Colin was in an accident with a runaway horse....called...."

"Bullet."

"So you all know this story, then?"

"Yes!"

"Well, perhaps you don't know this....Fred Finn never forgave a certain young woman...."

"Jemimah."

"D'you know why I wanted to use your Formula Board, then? Am I wasting my breath? Is it something you already know?"

"We know about the Accident, that's all," said Joni-Pip.

"Well, Taff heard somebody say that they thought that his Father, Fred Finn, determined that one day, he would get his revenge on Jemimah, for

299

ruining Colin's young life. I expect you already know that Colin Finn never regained consciousness, from the accident. He has been and still is, in a coma. That's sixty years: a living death really! He suffered severe brain injuries. Well, Jemimah married...."

"Edmund Plate!" finished the three onlookers.

"Do You Three know everything?"

"No."

"Well, Edmund and Jemimah had a daughter...."

"Amelia Plate."

"I expect you know she was put in the...."

"Workhouse."

"As it was almost ten years, exactly to the day, from when Colin had his accident, rumour had it that it was Fred Finn who had started the Workhouse Fire, in the first place!" said Father, sadly.

"What?" Ethelred-Ted, Joni-Pip and Hetty the Wee gasped.

"Ah, so you didn't know that? So you don't know everything, then?" he half-smiled. "A couple of eye witnesses said that they saw Fred Finn, running from the Workhouse, when it was on fire. Nothing was proved. So, my best friend, T....James, has had to live with this rumour, this terrible slur on his family, all his life. His Father, Fred Finn, denied it, emphatically but these rumours hurt him so much that he cut himself off from almost everyone, at first, after the Workhouse Fire. He kept people from wandering over his land, the Clappers, by putting up a sign. When he took over the Farm, Taff took it down....well, of course, you know that, Alex has the sign...."

"On his bedroom door!" chorused his listeners, making Father laugh.

"Why am I actually saying all this? I probably just needed to say that Taff kept saying to me, 'if only' he could have put the clock back, then he could have gone back in Time, to see who it was that started the fire. He said that he would give anything, to, actually, stop the fire. So when I saw the Formula, I decided to have a go for him." Father shook his head.

"So what happened?" asked Joni-Pip.

"To start with, the Formula Board didn't sound happy, it gave out a, kind of, moaning sound....it was most pathetic....I felt quite sad for it."

"What d'you expect....it was given to me....it belongs to me and you had taken it....you had kidnapped it! You had no right!" said Ethelred-Ted.

"This can't be true, surely, Ma Pets?" Hetty the Wee laughed.

"How would it know?" asked Joni-Pip.

"Well, whatever, it sure didn't sound too happy that we were using it."

"How did it work? The Circle we are in hasn't closed yet? We haven't even managed to JIT properly, either? How have you done it? What exactly happened when you JITTED with **my F.B.**?" asked Eth crossly.

"What? Your Circle? I never considered. You haven't JITTED yet? You must have! I don't understand. What happened to us? We arrived, Poppy and Macca came, too, as you probably know but it was too late. The fire was in full blaze. I was so disappointed: not just for Taff but in myself. I did know, I had no **right** to use the Formula Board and it served me **right,** that I didn't succeed. I almost felt that it was cross with me, for taking it and it didn't work on purpose. Then it happened," said Father looking down at his feet again.

"What happened?" asked Ethelred-Ted, Joni-Pip and Hetty the Wee.

"It was awful. Something that I never want to experience, ever, again!" said Father, as if he was about to cry.

"What Father? What happened? What has happened that has upset you so much?" asked Joni-Pip gently. She stood up and walked over to hug him but Father pushed her off.

"No, Joni-Philipa, please, don't do that? I have to feel like this. I won't remember these awful feelings when the Pasture is over. This is how it is when you try to cheat the Formula Board," he said, not looking up.

"Please, Father, tell us what has happened to you? I don't like seeing you like this. It frightens me," said Joni-Pip, walking back round and sitting down.

"Honey, I don't want to....it was too horrible!"

"But Father, you can help **us,** by telling what happened to **you.** It's a wise man, indeed, who learns from other people's mistakes," said Eth.

"No....no....no....I can't."

"Can't or won't, Ma Pet?"

Father looked at Hetty the Wee and smiled.

"You sure are a wise One, Little Hedgehog. You must be the Hetty my daughter is always talking about and we all thought you were an imaginary friend! When Poppy spoke to us this morning, I did begin to wonder if you were real, too, though. Then sadly, I found out you were real, very real!"

"Sadly?" whispered Hetty the Wee, anxiously.

"So, Father, what is it, you can't or won't tell us?" asked Joni-Pip firmly.

Father returned to his despair.

"Honey, don't ask me to do this?" he said; again, addressing his shoes.

"You must! You took the F.B., without permission. You hadn't been given the Gift of Déjà Vu. You jumped over the Wall of Time, uninvited.

301

You even went into the KOL, illegally...." said Ethelred-Ted, sounding very annoyed and then he added, softly, "Father, is this something we need to know about? Is this something that we should be warned about? Tell us, please?"

"O.K. you win...." said Father, sighing deeply, very, very deeply.

Ethelred-Ted, Hetty the Wee and Joni-Pip all held their breath.

"All the Children perished in the fire....they were overcome by the smoke....they all died of smoke fumes. We helped carry out the little bodies, it was so bad....so, so sad....and then I was handed this person...."

"And.....who was it?" asked Ethelred-Ted, Joni-Pip and Hetty, together.

They waited for an answer. Father looked at Joni-Pip and said slowly,

"It was You, Honey, You; Joni-Philipa Garador, my very own, little girl. Your body was carried....I carried you out of the fire, along with your little hedgehog friend!"

Joni-Pip, Hetty the Wee and Ethelred-Ted all gasped!

"Then, on the way back, after we had jumped back, over the Wall of Time, we....I....anyway....I....I entered into...." Father began, then paused.

"Entered....entered into what?" asked Ethelred-Ted.

"The Keep of Bad Memories!" He hung his head in his hands. "It was awful, so awful. Horrible! Terrifying! Living through my worst Nightmares! I knew if I ran from them that I would never get out. I knew if I screamed to get out, I'd be stuck in there, forever. That's the price I'd have had to pay. I just had to face them. Uh! That's enough! I can't talk anymore! Just remember, I'm really sorry. I'm really, really sorry. Please, please, forgive me....all of you?"

"Of course, we do!" they all said together.

"Don't forget, please don't JIT, to the Workhouse Fire?" begged Father.

All three of them frowned and looked at each other.

There was a silence.

Suddenly, Father looked up.

"Hello, Honey," he said brightly "what have you been up to, today?"

Joni-Pip look startled but then she realised that Father's stolen Pasture, was over. How pleased she was that he was back! How sad she was about what he had told her! How disappointed she was in him.

"How about a cup of tea, Honey? I'll call Mrs. Broft to make a fresh pot. Let's have one, together!" Father said cheerfully, not waiting for her reply.

'Well, at least, you are now back, safely, Father,' thought Joni-Pip. She so wanted to give him a hug but she didn't think he deserved one, for taking the F.B., so she didn't but she did, they all did, wonder in horror, what on earth he meant, when he had said,

'I entered into the Keep of Bad Memories!'

Chapter 32

Saving Bullet

"We have to make sure we do everything right, Eth, that's all!"

"I seriously don't think you should come, now, when we brave the Workhouse Fire; or You Hetty?" said Ethelred-Ted, firmly.

"Look, Hen, I understand your concerns but don't y' think this might have had t' happen, t' warn us?"

"Now we know things went wrong, then we must be very careful. Fore-warned is forearmed, right? I agree with Het, perhaps Father was meant to borrow the F.B., so as to warn us. Let's get on, please?" pleaded Joni-Pip.

"All right but I'm none too happy about all of this," relented Eth.

"The thing is, Ethelred-Ted, it really doesn't bother me. I'm so calm about it. For some reason, I feel my POOL is going to be fine and stay safe, for me. I have spoken to my daughter and my twin granddaughters and I am twelve years old. How many people have ever experienced that?"

Ethelred-Ted sighed: he knew, no matter what, she wouldn't give in.

"All right, but you have to promise me, any sign of anything going wrong and we are out of there like arrows from a bow! Yes?"

"Yes!" said Hetty the Wee and Joni-Pip, together.

"Right, we have ice. We have the F.B. We have....Us!" said Ethelred-Ted, trying to sound enthusiastic again. "Are you sure we're all set?"

"No, we haven't set the 3 'D's'!" said Joni-Pip. "We don't want a repeat of our last attempt, now, do we?"

"What, another worm's web?" asked Poppy-Plump-Pij, laughing.

Thanks to Macca spending a little bit of time with her and reasoning with her, she had forgiven her friends, for ignoring her and now she was excitedly awaiting another flight, over the Wall of Time. When she was told all that Father had said and all that Father had warned about Joni-Pip and Hetty the Wee, she wasn't bothered. In her little mind she felt that everything could be put right with another flight over The Wall of Time. It never occurred to her that there just might be a limited number of jumps! .

"Why are y' wearing a rope around yer body, Laddie?"

"Well, I wondered if we might have to lasso Bullet, to stop him, so I thought I would come prepared!"

"D'you honestly think that would stop him?" asked Joni-Pip. "Hey, is that my skipping rope?"

"It might be but right now it is my lasso! Anyway, I quite fancy myself as a cowboy. Do I look the part?"

"No!" shouted all his friends.

"Especially not wearing Seamus' hat!" laughed Joni-Pip.

"Oh," he said, disappointedly, "it has always been my dream to be a cow-boy....or a pirate! I have a close friend called Ricky and he thinks I am like one. We have played Pirates and Cowboys together many times...."

"Ricky who is he? I've nay heard o' him. Pirates? Cowboys? Ye look no more like a pirate or a cowboy, come t' that, than I look like a trapeze artist!"

Poppy-Plump-Pij and Joni-Pip burst out laughing and then Poppy said,

"I can't quite see you as a trapeze artist, Het. Do hedgehogs do that?"

"I expect that would be a sight, Hetty....you in a pair of pink tights and a little net skirt!" laughed Joni-Pip. "Is Ricky, Mona's brother in Bath, Eth?"

"Hey, Lassie, enough of y' cheek: I do have ma best kilt, y' ken. I like t' wear it on special occasions, with ma wee sporran and even tho' I say so masel', I think I look a mite bonny!" said the hedgehog seriously serious.

"Of course!" replied Joni-Pip. "I imagine you look very smart, Hetty."

"Yes, it's that Ricky. Anyway, I think we should be getting on and even if I don't look like a cowboy or a horse boy, come to that, I think I look like a Rob Roy, as you once said, Joni-Pip and I still think it's wise to bring this rope."

"So Ricky's a TAWP? He always was kind. I'm not surprised. Will we know, I wonder? Do TAWP's recognise each other? Wow! Ricky, eh?"

"How much does a Pirate's earring cost?" asked Ethelred-Ted.

"No idea, d'y ken, then, Hen?" replied Hetty, laughing.

"Poet! Yes, Ricky told me. A Buck-an-ear!"

They all groaned.

"That's so old, Eth. So, next time I skip with my friends in Bath, I won't remember that this is a very special rope, a JIT....shame!" said Joni-Pip.

"It's not a tight rope then, it's a Time Rope!" laughed Poppy-Plump-Pij.

They all chuckled.

"So," said Joni-Pip to Ethelred-Ted, "shall we set The '3 D's', then?"

"'3 D's'?" questioned her three friends, together.

"Yes, The '3 D's'....Destination, Day and Date!"

"Oh, we are so cleverful!" said Poppy-Plump-Pij.

"Aye we are! What about the time then, Ma Pet, haven't y' forgotten that?"

"Shucks," laughed Joni-Pip, "you're right, we mustn't forget the time."

"Right....so let's do it!" said Ethelred-Ted, enthusiastically.

He started to unfold the F.B. and they all watched, in awe, as miraculously, the flimsy, silk, green handkerchief grew and grew, until it formed the firm, fantastic, Formula Board.

"How ever many times I am likely to see that, I am quite sure it will never cease to amaze me!" said Joni-Pip. "It is nothing short of fabulous!"

"What amazes me, Ma Pets, is that the setting of the time and date....where we want to go....was there all the time," chuckled Hetty.

"And it's all so simpleful!" added Poppy-Plump-Pij.

"Well, let's do it, then," said Ethelred-Ted. "Give me a hand, You Lot!"

They all took hold of a corner of the F.B.....and turned it over!

"Isn't it amazing how we have never looked on the back of it before?" said Poppy-Plump-Pij, shaking her little head.

"And there was us, wondering how on earth we had to set it and it was all simply there for us....right here!" laughed Joni-Pip. "Makes me wonder what else might be here for us and we don't know it!"

"Exactly!" said Ethelred-Ted. "At least we know now. How do we know?"

The others all frowned and shook their heads.

The four of them were up on the hills, near Finn's Farm. For some reason, they thought that would make it easier, to arrive at the right place, when they jumped over the Wall of Time. It didn't occur to them that Macca, Jack and Red-Ted had come from the United States of America, all the way across the Atlantic Ocean and had landed in Marley's Barn, in Nottinghamshire, in the heart of England! So it really didn't matter, from where they jumped.

On the back of the F.B., they were amazed to see, a large, kind of, frame, with specific sections in it. Underneath this, there were loads of letters and numbers. They were stuck on with a Velcro-like substance.

"I was told that we have to pull these off the Board and fill in the details," explained Ethelred-Ted to the others. "This sticky stuff is so clever!"

"Who told you?" asked three voices.

"I don't know," said a puzzled Ethelred-Ted, "I just know I was told."

"That's odd," said Joni-Pip.

"A wee bit weird," said Hetty.

"Peculiarful," said Poppy.

Ethelred-Ted stopped and scratched his head, under his hat.

"All of the above!" he laughed. "Oh, well, we seem to have got it right, no matter where we got it from."

Everyone nodded and said nothing but they all wondered and pondered.

"Right, so the first section says: Destination. See! There are a few special lines for that," Joni-Pip pointed, breaking the silence.

"Yes, it says underneath: Address. Shall we start?" asked Hetty the Wee.

"Yes....we need: **Destination**:- The Stable Courtyard: **Address**:- Finn's Farm, Edwinstowe, Nottinghamshire, England," said Eth and then continued, "so we pull off the letters, spell out the words and press them back, on the lines of the **Destination** and **Address** section. Here we go."

As he pulled off the first letter, sprinkles of a gold and silver, glittery light, seemed to come off with it and a strange, whirring sound, came from the Formula Board. He stopped immediately. The whirring continued. The glittery sparklers kept coming and coming off the F.B.. Everybody gasped.

"That's s' bonny!" said Hetty the Wee.

"Spectacleful!" said Poppy-Plump-Pij, in wonderment.

"It's beautiful!" said Joni-Pip, trying to catch some in her hands.

"I wonder what that strange noise is?"

"I think that might be its engine starting up, Eth," said Poppy.

"Pops, I think you're right....let's carry on!" he replied, nodding.

As they began to press the letters back on to the F.B., they changed into strange looking letters and numbers, which none of them recognised.

"This is so amazing!" said Joni-Pip.

"Well, it all looks Greek to me!" said Ethelred-Ted.

Soon, amidst all the beautiful gold and silver, glitter stars, they completed the Address and then they had to fill in the **Year**, which was, of course, 1882. Then the **Day**: it was the 4th and then the **Month,** which was May. The last section was the **Time**. They had a bit of difficulty with this and then Ethelred-Ted realised that it used the 24 hour clock: so they put 14:30. By now, the F.B. was making quite a noise, as if it was raring to go.

At last everything was set. They all helped Eth to turn the F.B. back over and then he took out the four ice cubes. He had desperately tried to keep them frozen, by wrapping them up in a lot of cloths and a lot of newspaper.

"I think I know why the Wall of Time wasn't quite right before. It is just a thought, mind. I think we need **four** ice cubes, one for each ice symbol. We only had three before, so the other side of the Wall of Time couldn't form properly. We need one for each corner of the Wall of Time," he said, as he unrolled the newspapers and cloths, "two for this side of the Wall of Time, in 1942 and two for the Wall of Time, in 1882....right?"

The other three all nodded. They were very nervous but so, so excited!

Ethelred-Ted placed an ice cube on each of the four ice symbols and stood back.

The F.B. started to shake. The noise got louder and louder. The vibrations got stronger and stronger, until suddenly, each ice cube began to move from side to side. Then The Wall of Time began to grow. Each ice cube opened and out came some clear liquid: that fluid then made a newly formed ice cube that then opened and out came more water, which set like an ice block and the process continued. These bricks then stretched out and enlarged until they resembled great, solid, symmetrical lumps of iced water. Finally, the Wall of Time was fully constructed.

"It's so beautiful!" said Joni-Pip. "A wonderful, Wall of Water!"

"Yet, it doesn't fall. It's beyond doubt a marvellous, marvel, Hens!"

"It's prettyful!" said Poppy-Plump-Pij. "When can we go?"

"I wish I could remember this fantastic sight, forever," said Ethelred-Ted, wistfully. "How sad that we can't....all right everybody? Let's jump!"

Poppy immediately took off and flew up over the Wall of Time and out of sight.

Ethelred-Ted, Joni-Pip and Hetty all jumped together. Up they went into the air.

'I am flying! I am flying!' thought Joni-Pip. 'How spectacular is this?'

Δεστινατιον	Τηε Σταβλε Χουρτψαρδ
Αδδρεσσ	Φιννσ Φαρμ
	Εδωινστουε
	Νοττινγηαμσηιρε
	Ενγλανδ
Ψεαρ	ΙΛω϶ᔡ϶ᔡℤ
Τιμε	ΙΛωᔡℤᔡℤ϶ℤ϶₴
Δαψ	ᔡᔡτη
Μοντη	Μαψ

Suddenly she was in the KOL again: only this time it was different. Before she had just been surrounded by beautiful swirling patterns and felt all the amazing feelings of doing her favourite things. This time, after spending a few moments flying through the incredible coloured patterns, which surrounded her, she gently tumbled into a huge room. It was like a conservatory. The room was circular and its walls, from floor to ceiling, were all made up of little, glass windows. From each of these shone brilliant coloured light. She had landed right in the centre of the round room. She walked over to the outside wall and looked out through one of the windows.

Joni-Pip couldn't believe it: there, she saw herself with Mother, Father, Alex and Becky-Paige. They were having a picnic, sitting on blankets, by the river. She could hear their laughter and she could hear the sounds of the river. As she watched herself eating a marmite sandwich she could actually taste it! She was filled with indescribable feelings of joy and delight.

Joni-Pip looked through another window and there she was, with Grandfather and Alex, having a snowball fight in the woods. She could feel the snow squeak and creak beneath her feet, as she made fresh footprints in the clean, untouched, beautiful, white, crisp carpet. The joyful laughter rang through her ears. Her nose was glowing from the cold but she felt warm and snug inside. Not just because she was wrapped up in a woolly hat, scarf and gloves but because she was with people she dearly loved.

Joni-Pip looked into another, lower window. She had to get down on her knees to see through this one and there she was with Mother. She was seven-years-old. Mother sat on a large armchair, by the roaring fire, cradling a new baby wrapped in a large, soft, white, shawl. Joni-Pip remembered this time so well. She was so frightened of this tiny baby: her new, little sister, Becky-Paige.

The baby made a little noise, a tiny gurgling noise.

Joni-Pip was slightly startled but Mother spoke to the baby and said,

"This is your big sister, Joni-Philipa!"

Joni-Pip could feel all the apprehension and joy of being a 'big sister' again. She watched herself lean forward and kiss the baby on her smooth little cheek. She smelt so beautiful! She remembered feeling so excited about this small, soft, scrap of humanity and such love; a love that never, ever faded.

Joni-Pip stood up and walked right across to the other side of this vast observatory. She stood on tiptoe and saw herself in Portland with Grandmother and Grandfather Garador. It was wonderful! She hadn't been to Portland, Oregon, since she was five and yet, here she was, watching herself through the window. She could hear her grandparents' American accents. She watched herself laughing with them, holding both of their hands as they walked through a shady grove, on their beautiful farmland. How cute she looked in her dungarees, how high her little voice sounded.

"Grandmother, I wish you lived in England, then I would see you every day!"

Joni-Pip smiled to herself as she heard herself saying these words and remembering how she felt about it. She paused for a while, just watching and listening.

She decided to move on. She knelt back down on her knees to look through the window below and there she was, in class, at school, in Bath. It was an English lesson, her favourite! There was Angela Stebbin and Mona Royal: her two best friends. She could hear their laughter, as they were reading out loud about Mr Collins, in Pride and Prejudice. What a comical man he was! She could smell the polish on the wooden floorboards of the classroom and she could smell all the schoolroom stationery smells; the books, paper and pencils. She wanted to call out to Angela and Mona and tell them that she missed them but that the Life in the Wood was wonderful!

Joni-Pip looked through another window and there she was with Father, learning to ride her bicycle. She watched herself as she wobbled from side to side, not quite getting the balance right. She could hear Father's breath, as he ran along side her, holding on to the saddle to keep her upright. How excited she was when Father finally let go and she rode on her own for the first time! She felt such exhilaration, with the wind in her hair as she cycled, alone, in the Park in Bath. Joni-Pip felt incredible. She could hear Father's voice as he was saying,

"Atta Girl! Honey, you've done it! You've done it!"

She then crossed the large circular room again, to one tiny window. It was exactly at her eye level. Joni-Pip looked through the glass and down on to the scene. There she was with Mother: she remembered it so clearly. She watched herself as she tried skipping back to the tent but she was wearing Alex's long, outgrown dressing gown that he had given her, which dragged on the ground. She kept hoisting up the bottom to stop it from tripping her up. Mother had wanted to buy her a new one but she liked wearing this one, even though the sleeves had to be rolled over several times. They had just been to the wash rooms, on the Camp Site, in Aberech Sands, North Wales and they could feel the crisp, night air on their freshly washed faces. As they walked, they could hear the soothing sound of the waves, crashing on the shore on the other side of the sand dunes. The five-year-old chatted excitedly; she could hardly wait to go to sleep in her family's large, white, bell tent.

"I think I was five, here," she said to herself. "Yes, it was just after we had been to Portland to meet Grandmother and Grandfather Garador."

Looking down through the window, Joni-Pip saw herself, as a little five-year-old girl, looking up into the clear night sky.

For just a few seconds, their eyes met, there was a flash of light and a star fell out of the sky!

A sharp burning feeling ran through her body. Joni-Pip froze for a moment, leaving her feeling really tingly. She shook, then stepped back from the window.

"Look Mother, I have just seen a star that seemed to fall out of the sky!" said the little girl.

"That's beautiful, Darling!" her mother replied. "I wish I had seen it. It's called a shooting star. You know, they say you should make a wish and if you want it to come true, you mustn't tell anyone what you have wished for."

For some unexplained reason, Joni-Pip felt very serious for a moment.

She remembered so clearly and exactly what it

309

was that she had wished for!

When she stood up, she turned and looked behind her: she didn't know which window to look through next.

In the middle of the conservatory floor there was a trap door. She walked over to it. It had a large bolt on it. It was obvious to her that it was locked for a reason, so she left it. It didn't interest her. She was having the time of her life, re-living some of her many, beautiful memories. As she turned to walk back over to a window, she noticed an archway. She so wanted to look through some more windows but the archway intrigued her and she walked through it. In front of her was a staircase of stone steps; she walked up them and as she did so, she heard this strange, high-pitched, humming, spinning sound. When she got to the top of the steps, there was nothing there, just a pool below her. The pool was made up of so many different, incredible colours.

Without thinking, she jumped into it and travelled through a mass of beautiful, swirling colours and then, suddenly, she was flying over The Wall of Time again and landed in front of a beautiful light brown horse with a flowing, cream-coloured mane and tail! The horse reared up and the rider shouted out.

"Calm, Bullet! Calm, Bullet! Calm! Calm!"

"You Idiots!" came a voice, from the other side of the horse. "What the blazes d'you think you're doing?"

"Calm, Bullet! Calm, Bullet!" the rider shouted again.

"Get out of the way, you've terrified him!" the other voice shouted.

Joni-Pip looked and immediately recognised a young Archimedes Spindlethrop. He had a lead attached to Bullet's bridle and was having great difficulty in trying to steady him. His sister, the beautiful, sixteen-year-old, Mimi was on the horse and she, too, was trying to control the startled stallion. Ethelred-Ted and Hetty had come over the Wall of Time at the same time as Joni-Pip and they were trying to get out of the frightened horse's way.

Archimedes pulled on the lead, as hard as he could but Bullet just bucked and reared. Mimi shouted out to Archimedes,

"Archie, don't make it worse! Leave him to me!"

"Don't be so ridiculous, Mimi, you can't possibly take control of him! You Silly Girl! Why did you get on him in the first place? It's a good job he still had his leader rein on him: I expect one of the stable boys was about to muck out his stable, was he? Was he taking him into another stable? You Silly, Silly Girl! You know you mustn't mount him. How many times have you been told? Let me help!"

"No!" shouted Mimi. "I want to ride him and I will! Who are these people that startled him, anyway? It's their fault! He was fine before they turned up, with their....whatever it is!" She nodded towards the Wall of Time.

Archimedes turned to Ethelred-Ted, Hetty and Joni-Pip and shouted,

"Get out of the way! You Idiots! Who gave you permission just to bowl up here, unannounced, with....that....that, that....amazing....contraption? What the blazes is it? Can't you see you've startled Bullet! Go, go, go! Leave now!"

The Three Visitors stepped back out of the way.

Bullet struggled once more and reared up, nearly throwing Mimi to the ground but she held on tightly. He turned and bolted out of the courtyard.

Archimedes quickly ran into one of the stables, led out an un-saddled horse, jumped on his bare back and like a Native American, galloped off in pursuit of Mimi.

"Nice welcome, for our first JIT, Pets!" nodded Hetty.

Ethelred-Ted and Joni-Pip looked on helplessly.

"Well, we've done a lot of good here!" said Ethelred-Ted, sarcastically. "It appears it was us, who caused Bullet to bolt in the first place!"

"This is awful!" said Joni-Pip. "What can we do?"

"Fail!" replied Hetty the Wee, sadly. "We don't seem to have done anything right yet, do we, Hens? We've done nothing, except fail!"

"Fail?" came a familiar voice, from above them. They all looked up and perched, high on the wall of the Stable Courtyard, sat Poppy, who had been surveying all these comings and goings with great interest and amusement.

"Poppy!" they all said.

"This is my moment, obviously. Leave it to me!" she said, effortlessly taking to the air and disappearing over the other side of the red, brick wall.

Ethelred-Ted, Hetty and Joni-Pip ran through a tall archway and out of the Courtyard. They hoped that they might be able to see something.

They did: they saw Bullet and his rider disappearing over the hill and up towards the Clappers, followed by Archimedes riding bare back, holding on only by the horse's mane.

"He's some rider!" said Ethelred-Ted, scratching his head.

"I'm amazed!" said Joni-Pip, "You'd never believe it was our Inventor friend!"

"Y' right there, Lamb. Look there goes Poppy! I wonder what on earth she can d', t' stop the accident? I fear there's na much a wee bird can dee!"

They watched together until all of them had gone out of sight.

Poppy-Plump-Pij soared high above and over the first rider. Then she swooped down to the second rider and landed on Bullet's bridle. She found it pretty hard to hang on. The horse was going at such speed but she had had some jolly good practice.

'I knew there was a reason why I had to stay on Grandfather's swing, despite the turbulence,' she thought to herself, 'and this is it!'

The plucky little pigeon thought that her tiny head would be shaken off as she shook up and down so violently. The uncontrolled horse tore across the hills and up into the trees, which sat like a crown on the top of the Clappers.

"I must act quickly or it will be too late!" said Poppy out loud.

Valiantly she started to work her way up the bridle until she was as close to Bullet's ear, as she could get. That really took some strength. At times she had to hold on by one foot so that she could move closer. All the time her little body was being shaken and rattled. Up and down it went and then from side to side; like a tiny tug boat, on a raging sea. When she finally got really close to Bullet's ear, she saw in the distance a young man around Alex's age and a younger boy walking in the woods!

"Bullet!" she screamed. "You have got to stop! Stop! Woaw! Stop! Woaw!"

The horse continued heading straight towards the two walkers.

"Bullet!" Poppy screamed again. "You just have to stop. If you don't stop, you will die: you will break your leg and have to be shot! You stupid horse!"

Of course the horse continued on his course, ignoring Poppy's pleas.

The young man saw what was about to happen and he ran to try and save the smaller boy. The horse was nearly on top of him!

"Bullet, if you stop, I will give you some of my delicious Oat Scones!" shouted Poppy-Plump-Pij straight into his ear.

Bullet turned his head.

"Oat Scones? Why didn't you say so before? I love Oat Scones. I haven't had any since I was just a foal," he said eagerly. He veered away from the boy and the young man and slowed down.

Jemimah finally brought Bullet to a halt. She jumped off him and ran back to see both of her friends.

"Fred, Colin are you all right? That had me worried for a while!" she said shouting, "Some silly pigeon landed on my bridle, that didn't help!"

The young man was more worried about Mimi.

"What were you doing riding Bullet, you Ninny?" he laughed. "I can hardly get on him; let alone ride him. Did Father know you were on him? I bet not, you Naughty Girl! What pigeon? I can't see one!"

Just then Archimedes arrived. He saw that Bullet was munching at the grass under a tree or at least trying to; with his bit in his mouth, that wasn't easy. Colin was stroking him, that was impossible! Bullet was far too feisty to let anyone touch him!

And Jemimah? His foolish sister, whom he had risked his life to save, was chatting and laughing with one of their best friends, Fred Finn. They were both sitting on a tree stump. He dismounted his horse. The horse then promptly walked over to join Bullet in his snacking. Archimedes marched over to Jemimah.

"Jemimah Silly Spindlethrop, You Idiot, do you want to get yourself killed? You nearly killed me!" her brother scolded and then laughed. "That was amazing!"

Jemimah and Fred laughed.

"I have already told her off, Archie, don't worry. 'Mimi Minx' I call her! It's only because she wants to be one of the lads! I don't know what Father would say, if he knew? Bullet is being prepared to go to the Royal Stables.....if he's tamed in time."

Fred turned and saw Colin stroking the beautiful stallion and patting him on his head as the horse tugged on the long, juicy grass.

"It looks like he's ready now! That's strange, what's happened to your wild stallion then? How the Dickens did that happen?" Archie laughed.

Just then, Grandfather, then known as Sam Regan and who was also just sixteen, came running on to the scene.

"Is everyone all right?" he gasped, looking around at all of them.

"Yes," said Fred, "everyone is fine: despite Miss Spindlethrop trying to scare us all and kill herself!"

"Sorry! I thought I could handle him. Archie was so cross with me and he tried to stop me! Bullet's fine. I had the ride of my life but I don't want to try that again!"

"I should think not!" laughed Sam. "You gave me such a fright. I didn't know what was going on. Good show, Archie! Were you trying to stop her?"

"Yes, of course! The Little Twerp! I keep telling her she's not a boy! She won't do that again, I'm sure! I had better be getting back! Lots to do!"

With that, he whistled to his horse and the horse obediently came to him. He held him gently by the mane and walked off back towards Finn's Farm.

After he had gone a few yards he turned round and called to Colin.

"Would you like a ride back on Flame, Colin?"

"Rather!" replied Colin and he ran towards Archimedes, who grabbed him and scooped him awkwardly up in the air and wonkily plonked him on the back of the horse. They both laughed and the three of them then walked slowly back towards the stables. Fred watched them for a minute and smiled.

"Listen to Colin chatting away! He loves Archie, so much!"

"Who wouldn't? My brother is the kindest person I know!"

"I'll second that!" laughed Sam. "I must be off and get on. I have loads of homework to finish. Be of good cheer, then, one and all!" With that, he walked off in the opposite direction towards the Crooked Cottage.

"D'you need a hand to walk Bullet back, Mimi?"

"No, Fred, I'm fine, thanks," she replied, smiling.

"Are you sure? You didn't look too good, earlier, I must say."

"Didn't I? I must admit I was a bit shaken up before but I didn't think you noticed. I'm perfectly all right now!" she said, walking over to Bullet and leading him away. After walking on a few steps, Jemimah stopped and turned round. "I think the Inspectors from the Palace have arrived. It was their sudden arrival that got Bullet to panic in the first place. I hope I haven't stopped the Queen from buying him!"

"Don't worry. I would kind of like Bullet to stay here, especially as Colin seems to have tamed him. See you, later on, Mimi Minx!" Fred laughed and waved his arm.

He watched her for a while, smiling to himself. He turned round and whistled. His two dogs came running up to him, tails wagging and tongues hanging out!

"All right, Boys, you can have another ten minutes to sniff around the rabbit holes but then we must go home!" he laughed as he patted each one on its head, he then settled himself down laying on the ground, looking up into the cloudless sky, drinking in the beauty of the trees and enjoying the peaceful serenity of the silence. How nice it was after the noisy commotion Jemimah and Bullet had caused. How he loved the peace of the life in the wood!

As he lay there, he thought he heard a strange, little noise. He lifted up his head but the noise had stopped. The noise came again. He looked again. The noise stopped. Then he heard it again. He didn't know where it was coming from. He looked around but he couldn't see a thing. The little sound came again. It was a kind of moan. He knew something must be hurt somewhere: instinct told him that some small creature was in trouble. He stood up and looked around. There, a little way away from him, half hidden in the undergrowth he saw a Wood Pigeon lying on the ground, gasping.

He slowly approached it. He didn't want to scare it. He was surprised that it didn't struggle to get away from his grip. He picked it up very gently with both hands and whispered,

"You must be the pigeon Mimi was going on about."

The dogs came running up and started to sniff at the injured bird.

"Go away, You Two!" he shouted.

The dogs got really excited. They wanted to investigate some lunch, perhaps? Fred Finn put the gasping bird into one of his hands, picked up a large stick and lobbed it with all his might.

"Go get, You Two!" he yelled.

The dogs ran off, after it.

He gently sat down on a tree stump and cradled the ailing pigeon in both of his hands. Gently, very gently he examined it to see why it was gasping.

"Is it all right?" came a strange voice from behind him.

Fred jumped slightly and turned round to see a tall Stranger, looking down at him.

"I don't know yet....there, there, Little Bird....." he said, gently stroking the pigeon's back, "....I am not going to hurt you."

The pigeon closed its eyes.

"Is it dying?" asked the Stranger. He took his large canvas bag off his shoulder, put it on the ground and bent down on one knee, beside Fred.

"I don't know but he's in a bad way. His breathing is so difficult."

"Do you want any help?" the Stranger said, softly. "He's a fine looking little thing. What happened?"

"I don't know. I've just, this minute, found him."

"If you lay him in my hands, then you can examine him and see where he is injured. Right?" said the Stranger, opening out his large hands.

"Right," said Fred.

Very, very tenderly, he transferred the gasping pigeon, into the Stranger's outstretched palms and then slowly lifted up one of its wings. He spread it out and looked at it closely. He shook his head.

"Nothing wrong there!" he said, gently folding the wing back in, like a redundant concertina. He carried out the same procedure with the other wing and found no damage.

"Is he all right then?" asked the Stranger.

"I have no idea," replied Fred. "He must be gasping for a reason."

Both of the tall men leaned right over, studying the little pigeon closely.

The breathless bird opened its eyes.

"Yes, actually, I am gasping for a reason," said the pigeon sarcastically,

"I am blooming exhausted and so would you be, if you had just done what I have! I am shattered and for your information, I am not a 'he', I am a 'she'!"

The two men nearly jumped out of their skins.

"Oh, hello You Two!" said the pigeon, recognising them both, from the first time, she had flown over the Wall of Time.

"We don't know you!" replied the two men, shaking their heads and wondering why they were talking to a pigeon. They looked at each other.

The Wood Pigeon laughed.

'Pigeons don't talk,' they both thought.

"Yes, I talk!" said the pigeon, as if it was reading their thoughts. "Some of my friends say that I am too talkful but there you go!"

"I don't understand!" said Fred. "Where do you work....in a Circus?"

"No. I did always want to run away to the Circus but unfortunateful, I live alone. That meant I had no-one to run away from and it kind of spoilt the image....slightly!" the pigeon replied seriously, making both the men laugh. "Anyway, my name is Poppy-Plump-Pij, only my friends call me, Poppy. The reason I am exhausted is this. You are not going to believe any of this, I know but there we are....I have come, with my friends, over the Wall of Time, from the year 1942....we are living in the Second World War...." she started.

"Second?" both of the men questioned together.

"Yes, I'm afraid there has already been one. The First World War lasted from 1914 to 1918. Don't humans ever learn? When did you ever hear of a Pigeon War? Anyway, the Second World War began in 1939 and I am told, will end by 1945. Yes, we too, had visitors from the Future, who told us that!"

"Whew!" said both the men.

"I came back from the Future with my friends to help save a young lad called, Colin Finn and a horse called, Bullet," she explained, "to make a bad bit of Past into a good Future!"

"My little brother and my Father's prize stallion?" Fred Finn gasped.

"Yes, I know. Actually, Bullet was on his way to have the same accident: so I flew down on to his bridle and promised him some Oat Scones, if he stopped," said Poppy-Plump-Pij, matter-of-factly.

"Oat Scones?" the two men said, in disbelief.

"Yes, Oat Scones: my speciality. So when he slowed down and the accident was averted, I had to quickly fly back to the Wall of Time....which, incidentally, is still on your Stable Courtyard....Farmer Finn....I really must get back soon....anyway, I flew back over it, the Wall of Time, that is and back to 1942. I flew to my little house and picked up a

316

tin, my special Coronation Tin, my Mother gave me, in which was stored, a fresh batch of Oat Scones. I had only baked them today. Early in the afternoon, in actual fact: it was because I was upset with my friends; that is, a teddy bear, a girl and a hedgehog, you see: so I went home and did some baking. I love doing that, it always calms me," Poppy rambled on but the two men didn't mind, they were so fascinated by this talkative pigeon.

"I then had to fly back, over the Wall of Time, from 1942, the Time I live in and head straight back up here: carrying my Coronation Tinful of Oat Scones. I quickly gave them to Bullet. That's what he was eating for his lunch, only it was very difficult for him, with his bit in his mouth. So, in future, Farmer Finn, if you want to control him and make him happyful...."

"Give him Oat Scones!" finished the two men, for her.

"By the way," said Fred Finn, "why do you keep calling me, Farmer Finn? I'm not. My Father is. I'm still at school in Nottingham. I'm only sixteen!"

"Of course! Sorry!" laughed Poppy. "You are 'Old Farmer Finn', in my Day. Your son, James, is Farmer Finn now! You **will** be Farmer Finn! Don't forget, I have come from sixty years in your Future. That's why you can hear me speak. I must get ready to go back now, or the Wall of Time will be gone and I will be stuck here and the Pasture won't end and the Circle of Life won't close. That was so much trouble for us before!"

The two men shook their heads.

"My word, you are a spunky little bird, aren't you?" laughed the Stranger. "So do You Two know the beautiful girl, who was walking the big horse then?"

"Jemimah!" said Poppy-Plump-Pij and Fred together.

"She is so lovely!" said the Stranger.

"Well, I can tell you, now, she will marry a man, an Explorer called...."

"Edmund Plate?" questioned the Stranger, smiling broadly.

"Yes!" said Poppy-Plump-Pij. "How did you know?"

Fred looked at the Stranger, strangely.

"I just did!" laughed the Stranger.

"Are you from the Future, too?" asked Fred Finn.

"No, just an Explorer."

"So **you** are Edmund Plate?" smiled Poppy-Plump-Pij, laughing. "Now everything makes sense! That's how you knew me!"

"What are you talking about, now?" asked Fred.

"Well, it's so simple," explained Poppy, "it's like this, a little while ago, I flew over the Wall of Time and landed, probably, sometime next year...."

The two young men looked exceedingly puzzled.

317

"As I said, it's so simple....let me explain. When I flew over the Wall of Time before and saw you both, you were having an argument with Archimedes Spindlethrop, the lovely Jemimah Spindlethrop's brother and Grandfather....I don't know his name, sorry! It was here, in the wood, only it was sometime next year, as I said. I didn't know, either of you but you both recognised me, obviously because of now....and you both said to me, 'Hello Poppy' and you both seemed really pleased to see me again. I said to you, 'I don't know you!'

"I was puzzled before but as you are speaking to me in this Pasture, that means any other time we do meet, in a Pasture, you will remember me. So next year, Edmund, just before you marry Jemimah: yes, Edmund, you will marry Jemimah. It will be when she is only seventeen....anyway, a little while before your wedding day, you will be in this wood and three of Jemimah's friends will try and stop you from marrying her. They will tell you that you are not being fair to her, as you are always away on Expeditions. Well, one of them will be her brother, Archimedes, as I said before; the other two are her friends: you, Farmer Finn....or rather 'Farmer Finn to be'....and Grandfather. So, when we meet again, you will remember what I said and you will recognize me. Only sadly I won't recognize you because I won't have met you before. Sorry!" finished the exhausted, little pigeon.

"Well, that's easy then!" laughed Fred.

"Well, I am happy!" laughed Edmund. "It appears that I am to marry the lovely Jemimah! Are you going to introduce us then?"

"I'm not too sure about that. Are you going to leave her on her own, while you explore the world? Hmmm....perhaps, I shouldn't," said Fred, frowning.

"I must be off, anyway, You Boys," said Poppy-Plump-Pij. "Thank you for caring for me! See you next year!" She jumped off Edmund's hands and flew up on to the branch of a tree. She turned to Fred.

"Oh, Farmer Finn, I am so glad you didn't set fire to the Workhouse, in ten years time!" she said and took off.

"Huh?" said Fred Finn and then laughed.

"Wasn't that an amazing thing?" laughed Edmund Plate.

"**The** most amazing thing!" laughed back Fred. "And who the Dickens is 'Grandfather'?"

Poppy-Plump-Pij flew high and fast, up, above the trees on the Clappers and then down the hill and over the fields, until, finally, she swooped smoothly down, into the Stable Courtyard, landing perfectly, right in front of the Wall of Time.

"Just in Time, Pops and well done!" said Ethelred-Ted.

318

"We have just had a word with Archimedes and Jemimah. They told us that everything is all right. We don't know how y' did it but y' did, Ma Pet. Clever Girl!" congratulated Hetty the Wee.

"So, Poppy, you are the Heroine of the day! You did it, single handed! We are all so proud of you!" said Joni-Pip.

"We are a bit concerned about Archimedes Spindlethrop, though. We explained everything to him about Déjà Vu and how we were Jumpers in Time and his eyes lit up. I worry we have started something in his mind," said Ethelred-Ted, seriously.

"Oh well, it seems that we set Bullet off and now we have set Archimedes off!" Joni-Pip laughed. "Is there no end to our talents?"

"Right!" said Ethelred-Ted. "Are we all ready, then?"

"Er....one thing....before we go back, have you passed on the Gift, Eth?" she asked, then she had a strange feeling wash over her and the face of the smiling Pilot came into her mind. Next, Flip's smile, followed by Steve's and Craig's appeared. She desperately tried to hang on to these visions in her head but all too soon, they vanished.

"So have you passed on the Gift, Hen?" repeated Hetty.

"Of course!" Ethelred-Ted laughed. "I told all those, I got to speak to, that they would go back in Time a few minutes before Bullet bolted, only, of course, we wouldn't arrive to scare him!"

"That makes me feel a tad bad, Lad," said Hetty, then she laughed.

"You're a Poet, once again, Het! Anyhow, it's all going to be fine, don't worry. Jemimah will have the feeling of Déjà Vu, as Joni-Pip did."

"This doesn't seem quite the same as it was with my accident, Eth."

"Of course not, Silly, every incident is unique, there are no set patterns."

"You sound like Red-Ted, now!" laughed Poppy-Plump-Pij. "Let's go home ....I'm tiredful, so very, very tiredful!"

319

Chapter 33

Strangers and the Night

"So when are we leaving, then?" asked Joni-Pip.

"How tired are we? Do you want to go back to Knotty Knook for a rest and then we go later this evening?" questioned Ethelred-Ted.

"I could do with a little Power Perch. I'm pretty exhausted," chipped in Poppy.

"Power Perch?" repeated Joni-Pip and Ethelred-Ted.

"Yes, fliers have to have Power Perches. You don't think our 'engines' run on nothing, do you? We don't use petrol for power, we use the power of sleep. That's why birds nap a few times in the day," the pigeon explained.

Her three friends looked at her in amazement.

"Would y' rather not come, Ma Lamb?" asked Hetty thoughtfully. "We did nothing for Bullet, except make him bolt! Y' did all the work, Lassie."

"No. I don't want to miss the Workhouse Fire but thank you for being so kind, Het," replied Poppy. "A good Power Perch and I'll be all set again."

The four of them were sitting on the grass just above the Crooked Cottage, looking out over at the Clappers. The sun was getting low in the sky and a sharp breeze had whipped itself up making them all feel a tad chilly. They had decided to get going as soon as they had heard all of Poppy's amazing story. However, that story had been closely followed by an interesting discussion. At first they talked about Joni-Pip's wonderful time in the KOL and then about Father's revelation that Joni-Pip and Hetty had been lost in the fire with all the other children. They wondered what horrors Father must have experienced when he had entered the Keep of Bad Memories, the KOBM, as he was so disturbed. They came to the conclusion that Joni-Pip must have entered the Keep of Good Memories.

That had to be the most amazing thing she had ever experienced.

They had also decided that the trap door in the Keep of Good Memories, the KOGM, possibly led down to the KOBM. Perhaps one day they would find out: although none of them particularly relished the idea and felt it would be best to just keep out.

A spot of rain landed on Joni-Pip's face.

"It's started to sprinkle," she said, "I think that means I must run. So then, at what time are we meeting and where, Eth?"

Ethelred-Ted got up and brushed his fur down.

"I must run, too! I can't get wet again! Shall we say six o'clock tonight, up at the Ruin?"

"See you there, then?" said Hetty the Wee, scurrying off to miss the rain.

"Can't wait!" said Poppy, taking off and flying up into the dark clouds. She swooped back down again. "What will we do if it's raining? Can the F.B. get wet?"

"I have no idea, we will have to see. 'Bye Pops," answered Eth, waving to her as she flew back in the air and disappeared over the tops of the trees.

As Joni-Pip brushed the bits of twigs and grass from her jumper, she turned and looked down at the Crooked Cottage.

"Who on earth is that?" she said pointing down the hill.

Ethelred-Ted turned and looked.

"I have no idea but she certainly seems to know us. Isn't she waving?" he replied. "She probably thought I was waving to her when I was waving 'Good Bye' to Poppy."

"Yes. She must be visiting Grandfather. I will probably find out later. Perhaps it's Mrs Botterton with her 'onions'!" laughed Joni-Pip.

"Don't be mean!" Ethelred-Ted chuckled.

"I was only joking. Poppy has worked so hard today. If she comes with us when we JIT back to the Workhouse Fire tonight; she will have flown over the Wall of Time three times today! That's amazing! I wonder if it's a record? Who is that woman? Is she calling us? She is calling, isn't she? I think she must think we are somebody else! Oh, let's get back to Knotty Knook!"

"Yes please! I need a Munch Break before tea, I'm starving!"

With that they both ran off up and over the hill and into Windy Woods, trying to dodge the rain.

Just as soon as they had entered the porch at Knotty Knook, the Heavens opened and down and down came the rain!

Mother called out to Joni-Pip, so Eth slipped into the School Room.

"Don't forget my tum needs a Munch Break!" he whispered to Joni-Pip.

"Ethelred-Ted, your stomach and I are great friends. Of course I won't forget. See you as soon as I can. Don't forget to wake me up before you go, go!"

"Where have you been Darling? Did you forget about tomorrow? You said you would get the Painting finished," said Mother bending down and

321

helping her daughter off with her shoes and handing her, her slippers.

It was only when Joni-Pip was sitting on the bench in the porch that she actually looked at Mother.

"Mother, what have you done?" Joni-Pip asked alarmed.

"Darling, what do you mean, 'what have I done'? Nothing."

Joni-Pip stroked her mother's hair. Instead of the usual curls, Mother's hair was glossy and straight! How could that be?

"What have you done with your hair, Mother?" Joni-Pip said gruffly.

"Nothing Darling, it's just the same as it always is! Mousey and straight!" replied Mother laughing. "Unfortunately, a Rita Hayworth, with lavish curls, I am not!"

Mother leaned forward and hugged her twelve-year-old.

'That most definitely was a 'Mother type hug'!' thought Joni-Pip to herself. 'So this is most definitely Mother but something is wrong, most definitely wrong!'

Joni-Pip was disconcerted. She watched Mother as she followed her into the kitchen. She walked in the same way, she spoke in the same way.

As they entered the kitchen, Joni-Pip froze. This was not Knotty Knook's kitchen! This was most definitely not her kitchen! Where had it gone? The walls in the kitchen used to be painted light green. These walls were painted white. There was a picture on the wall, which Joni-Pip had never seen before in her life! Where had it come from?

"Mother, when did you have the kitchen painted?" Joni-Pip asked, almost too scared to hear her reply.

"Darling, what is the matter? You heard Father and I discussing having it re-decorated this morning. It hasn't been done for over a year!" Mother felt Joni-Pip's forehead. "Are you sickening for something? I hope not!"

Just then, Becky-Paige came running in.

"Phiapa! Phiapa! I have been waiting for you to come home. We were supposed to be finishing the Painting for tomorrow, this afternoon!" she said. "Can we do it now?"

Joni-Pip bent down to give her little sister a kiss on the cheek, when she saw, to her horror, that Becky-Paige had a little scar on her chin. She had never seen it before. Joni-Pip felt sick, really sick.

'This isn't my World!' she thought. 'I have come back to somewhere else. I am in a nightmare world! I am not here! I am not where I want to be! I want to go home!'

"Becky-Paige, why did you call me Phiapa? You always call me Sissa?" asked Joni-Pip harshly.

Mother turned round from washing her hands at the sink. She frowned.

"Joni-Philipa, Rebekah-Paige always calls you Phiapa, she never calls you Sissa....what's that supposed to be anyway? Darling, are you all right you have gone quite pale?" Mother looked alarmed.

"Mother you must answer me these questions. It is very important to me that I am told the truth, the whole truth and nothing but the truth," said Joni-Pip anxiously.

Mother looked decidedly worried.

"Darling, do you want me to call Doctor Evans? What ever is wrong?"

"Where did that picture come from? How did Becky-Paige get the scar on her chin? What Painting are we supposed to be doing? What is going on tomorrow and why the Dickens does my sister, who has called me Sissa, for at least two and half years, suddenly call me Phiapa?

"This is not my home! You can't be my real family! What's happened? Where are they? I want to go back to my World. I want to go home!" Joni-Pip started to cry.

Mother put down the towel she was using to dry her hands and walked over to Joni-Pip and hugged her.

"Darling, Darling, there, there, it's all right. I think you are just feeling a bit poorly. Right let's answer your questions. The picture? We bought it when we all went up to York with Grandfather and Grandmother. Rebekah -Paige's scar? She fell off Grandfather's swing, remember? You were both staying over at the Crooked Cottage, don't you remember? It was two years ago, when I went into hospital to have Elle-Sahara? Who, by the way has been asking for you all afternoon."

Joni-Pip continued to feel sick, very sick indeed. The room began to swim and spin and then everything went black.

"Joni-Philipa! Joni-Philipa!" Father's whispered voice echoed through Joni-Pip's head. She slowly opened her eyes and found herself in her cosy little bed in Knotty Knook. Father was leaning over her gently. "Honey, are you O.K.? You frightened us all! Doctor Evans has been over to see you and he says you are suffering from exhaustion. You have to stay in bed and rest for a few days. That's an order!" laughed Father: her beautiful Father.

Joni-Pip pulled herself up, so that she was sitting in her bed. She quickly examined his face and smiled, hugging Father as tightly as she could.

"Oh Father it's all right! You haven't changed! You are the same!"

"Honey, of course I am the same. We are all the same! Whatever is the matter?" consoled Father. "Have you been having a nasty dream?"

"Oh, yes, Father, I must have! How glad I am that everything is all back to normal again!"

"Well, you must try and get some sleep, Honey, so lay back down and close your eyes. We will see you in the morning, all right?" Father kissed her and tucked her covers back in.

"I'm all right now, thank you. I feel so much better! Good night!"

Joni-Pip settled back down and quickly ran her eyes around her pretty room. Her bedroom furniture was exactly in its place. The red, check curtains were up at the window and Alex's old dressing gown hung on her door. Everything was perfectly all right so she closed her eyes. She was tired, extremely tired. In no time at all she fell into a peaceful, deep sleep.

"Joni-Pip! Joni-Pip!" came a whispered voice from the darkness. "Joni-Pip, Joni-Pip do come on!"

Joni-Pip felt someone tug at her bedclothes. She was tired and didn't want to wake up. She turned over and pulled her blankets high over her head.

"Joni-Pip, do you want to miss the Workhouse Fire?" came the voice, only this time it was really urgent. "I have already had to sneak out and meet Hetty and Poppy at six and tell them that you were in bed sleeping," came Ethelred-Ted's voice.

Joni-Pip stirred again and mumbled sleepily,

"What?"

"We are meeting them at midnight, up at the Ruin, so come on!"

Joni-Pip sat bolt upright in bed.

"Why have you let me sleep? Oh no!" she said, leaping out of bed.

"Shhhhh! We must be as quiet as mice!"

Joni-Pip quickly pulled her trousers on over her pyjamas.

"That will keep me warmer!" she laughed.

"Don't lie!" laughed back Ethelred-Ted. "You're just lazy!"

Pulling her sweater on over her pyjama top, she drew breath to speak.

"I know, you don't have to tell me, that's to keep you warmer too!" chuckled Ethelred-Ted.

"Hole in one!" she laughed, then she added. "I'll have to clean my teeth, I don't want to breathe this sleepy breath all over You Lot, now, do I?"

"Yuk, no. Just be very quiet! You don't want to wake up the house as we did last time," started Eth. "On second thoughts, a night with Celeste...."

Joni-Pip grinned at him and pulled her shoes from under her bed, grabbed a pair of clean socks from her sock bag hanging on the wall and tiptoed across her floor silently.

'That's funny,' she thought, 'Father must have mended the squeaky floorboards!'

Then a horrible thought struck her.

'Perhaps he hasn't? Perhaps I **am** in another world?'

"Squeak!" went the floorboard beneath her. "Squeeeeeeak!"

She laughed at herself for thinking such silly thoughts!

The two of them tiptoed across the landing and Joni-Pip went into the bathroom, while Ethelred-Ted continued on and headed for the Captain's Chest, which sat still and silent under the landing window.

'I still can't believe how Jack got his 'phone back!' he thought out loud. 'That was incredible: pure Mastermindery! Golly, I sound like Poppy!'

When Joni-Pip got into the bathroom, she closed the door as quietly as she could and turned on the brass, cold tap. She reached for her toothbrush hanging in the rack at the side of the basin, she opened a round tin of tooth powder and squidged the bristles until they were thoroughly caked in powder particles and began to clean her teeth ((more like scouring, if you ask me, Dear Reader: grateful thanks to the Inventor of toothpaste)), as quietly as she could. She was conscious of every movement.

((Have you ever tried to brush your teeth silently, Dear Reader? Well, try it! It is pretty difficult!))

Joni-Pip laughed when she thought about Becky-Paige and her tooth powder spitting! How she loved her little sister!

After she had finished giving her teeth a jolly good scouring, er....of course I mean brushing....she remembered that she had gone to bed without doing so, which made her feel pretty yukky....she felt so much better! She looked in the mirror as she put her toothbrush back in the rack that was fixed to the wall, at the side of the basin. Her hair just stuck up in the air! She laughed at herself, ran the tap very gently and dampened her hair down, using both hands. As she was watching herself make her hair look slightly more controlled: she stopped dead in her tracks, her hands on her head. An icy cold shiver ran down and all through her body. She started to shake and just managed to stop herself from crying out.

'It can't be true!' she thought to herself. 'It can't be. I am in a nightmare! Something is horribly wrong!'

The basin in the bathroom was in one corner, so she could see it as plain as day. There it was, in the reflection of the mirror. In her entire Life, nothing had struck more terror in her heart. Nothing bad that she had experienced in all of her twelve years, came anywhere near the pain that was running through her right now.

'I am in another world. I am trapped here and I can't get out! That couldn't have been Father last night! It must have been somebody like Father, somebody pretending to be him! I want to go home!' she thought and started to cry.

Joni-Pip quickly dried her hands on the towel and opened the door to leave. She pulled the light switch as quietly as she could, leaving the bathroom in darkness. She started to walk away but she turned round once more and looked back. The light from the moon that shone across the landing, cast an eerie glow on it. How could anything be so dreadful? Her eyes were transfixed on it.

Ethelred-Ted was poking around in the Captain's Chest on the landing. Joni-Pip could scarcely breathe when she got to him.

"You will never guess what I've just seen. We must get out of here quickly!" she whispered, in fear of waking up the people, the Strangers who lived in this cottage.

Ethelred-Ted closed the lid of the chest and looked at her.

"What ever is wrong with you? You look like you've seen a ghost!"

"Oh....much....much....worse!" she stammered, quivering and shaking: she sounded so desperate, then pulled him by the arm along the landing.

"Let's get out of here. Now?" she begged.

Ethelred-Ted was puzzled as to why she was upset but he obediently walked along the landing. They tip-toed past Mother and Father's bedroom and crept past Alex's room. Joni-Pip suddenly froze. She slowly turned her head round and looked back. Her face went whiter still!

The bright moonlight made their journey up the Log and Chain Path not quite as difficult as they thought it might be. Eth had brought a large torch but he said that because of the Blackout, they shouldn't use it until they were well out of sight of the cottage and under the cover of the trees. Joni-Pip was still in shock over her discovery. She followed him in silence.

When they got to the bridge over the stream, she burst into tears. Ethelred-Ted put his arm round her and hugged her. He didn't speak, he just let her cry.

"We had better get on, or we will be late again," said Joni-Pip through her tears.

Slowly they walked along the woodland path together. He had one arm around her and with the other, he shone the torch, lighting up their way.

It was a beautiful, still, cloudless night. The stars sparkled and twinkled in the velvety, dark blue, arched firmament above them and the moon shone like a shiny, silver sixpence. The only sounds they heard were the cracking and the snapping of the tiny twigs under their feet as they walked; the babbling of the brook, as it made its way gently past them and the occasional call of a night owl.

"Aren't the stars, so beautiful?" Joni-Pip stopped and looked up at them.

"They certainly are, especially tonight."

"What exactly are stars, Eth? Can we go to them? Are there secrets up there? What are stars there for? What's it like up there? Do stars serve any purpose? What exactly do they do? They must be there for a reason."

"Steady on, Woman," laughed Ethelred-Ted, "all these questions and I have very few answers! You seem so fascinated with stars these days."

"There has to be some answers, some secrets in the stars, I know there are, I just know it!" Joni-Pip said, searching the skies as if it would reveal the mysteries it held within. "I know the stars can help us get home, too," she sighed, then she grinned and added, "Oh well, perhaps not right now!"

Ethelred-Ted chuckled at this comment and sent her a sweet smile.

"I wonder where this obsession with the stars has come from?" he asked.

Joni-Pip didn't reply she just sighed again. They then continued on their way and had just turned the last corner, before they made their final descent down to the Ruin, when something came flying around their heads.

"Hello, You Two. Isn't it fun? I haven't done too much night flying, so it's a good job there's a big moon tonight!" laughed Poppy, as she flew straight into the branch of a tree, bashing her head and falling to the ground.

"Are you all right, Pops?" asked Joni-Pip anxiously then she helped Ethelred-Ted to get the pigeon back on to her legs.

"I obviously need a bit of Night Flying practice!" laughed Poppy. "I'm fine, just a bit shaken! More importantly, are you all right, Joni-Pip?"

Joni-Pip, remembering what she had seen at Knotty Knook, broke out into some noisy weeping. Poppy looked at her friend worriedly.

"Joni-Pip......what is it? Are you all right?"

"Leave her until we get to the Ruin, Pops, if you don't mind: then she can tell us all about it," Ethelred-Ted sounded very fatherly.

"Of course. I'll get back to Hetty. See you in a minute!" with that, she looked all around her, took off cautiously and flew off, back down the hill.

In no time, they arrived at the Ruin. Poppy and Hetty stood waiting for them in silence. Eth had carried a blanket over his shoulder in case they needed it later. He took it off his shoulder, spread it on the ground and sat Joni-Pip down on it. Once she was settled, the others joined her.

"I say, this is exciting!" said Hetty, trying to lift Joni-Pip's spirits.

"Yes, Het, it is and as soon as we get Joni-Pip sorted out, then over we all go!" said Eth confidently. "Joni-Pip, are you ready to tell us what's wrong?"

Joni-Pip nodded and then looked at her friends in turn.

"Eth, Poppy, Hetty, I don't know where we are but we most definitely are not here!" she blurted out.

Her friends all looked at her puzzled and pushed their heads towards her in surprise.

"What do you mean?" asked Poppy-Plump-Pij seriously. "Where are we then, if we are somewhere else?"

327

"I wish I knew!" replied Joni-Pip.

"Why d' y' say such a thing, Hen?" asked a worried Hetty the Wee.

"There are so many reasons why I know that we are in another World. We are not in our World, at all and I only hope we can get out and go back home soon," said Joni-Pip mournfully.

"Joni-Pip, please explain?" asked Ethelred-Ted.

"Well, yesterday when we got back from saving Bullet, I noticed so many things had changed at Knotty Knook," she began.

"Changed? How, Lambie?"

"Well, for a start Mother. What sort of hair has Mother got?"

"Straight and shiny," said Ethelred-Ted.

"What? Where am I? You can't be real, either! You can't be You! I must go!" cried Joni-Pip, starting to get up.

"Wait! Wait!" said Ethelred-Ted, pulling her back down. "How do I know what Mother's hair is like? I can't remember actually ever looking at it. I am a Bear with fur, remember? That's just in case you had forgotten!"

"I remember Mother's hair. I looked up at her for ages while she cuddled me in front of the fire; the night of the storm. The night of your accident, when you...." Poppy-Plump-Pij started.

"Oh Pops, what was it like?" asked Joni-Pip anxiously. "What is it like?"

"It was light brown and curly," said Poppy-Plump-Pij firmly.

"Poppy, how I love you so!" exclaimed Joni-Pip, leaning over and stroking her back. "Yes, of course it's curly but now, the Mother in Knotty Knook has changed. Her hair is very straight, not a curl in sight and that isn't all. The girl called Becky-Paige has a scar on her chin, which she hasn't got in my real world and she doesn't call me Sissa any more but she calls me Phiapa and there's a picture in the kitchen that I've never seen before, although Mother says it's been there since a trip we all went on: a trip I have absolutely no memory of and the kitchen, which hasn't been painted for a year, is a different colour from my real kitchen. Worst of all, I have a little sister in this world....her name is Elle-Sahara and she is two!"

The other three gasped. Joni-Pip went on.

"Last night, Father cuddled me and I thought I must have been dreaming about all these other things. He seemed just right, so I felt happy again and fell asleep. Sorry I missed you all at six, by the way. Just before we came out a little while ago, I cleaned my teeth in the bathroom and hung my tooth brush back in the rack. Then I damped my scruffy hair down because it was sticking up everywhere. I did it with some cold water at the basin. As I looked in the mirror, I saw the most horrible thing I had ever seen!"

"What?" asked all her friends in panic, dreading what was coming.

Joni-Pip took a deep breath, held it and then hesitated.

328

"What was so horrible, Hen?" asked Hetty gently.

"I don't know whether I can say, it's too ghastly to even think about," Joni-Pip muttered.

"Tell us in your own time...." Urged Ethelred-Ted kindly.

"O.K., O.K., here it comes....I saw...."

"Yes?" asked all her friends, fearing the terrible revelation to come.

"**A little pink toothbrush!**" Joni-Pip finally blurted out.

"What?" asked all of her friends, much more than a tad disappointed.

"A little pink toothbrush that I had never seen before. I quickly counted the tooth brushes in the rack and there were six! I counted them once again, still looking in the mirror with my hands up on my hair, just to make sure I wasn't mistaken. No, I wasn't, there were six all right. Six used toothbrushes, hanging from the rack!"

"I think that's a song isn't it?" asked Poppy-Plump-Pij.

Ethelred-Ted and Hetty the Wee sniggered.

"Father's black one, Mother's red one, Alex's yellow one, my green one, Becky-Paige's little blue one (as that's her favourite colour) and a little pink one! There should only be five. There are only five of us in our family! But there were six! I just couldn't stop looking at the little pink tooth brush! Where had it come from? Who did it belong to? I was terrified!" Joni-Pip hung her head in her hands.

"Why would a little pink toothbrush upset you so, Joni-Pip? I don't understand," said Poppy, looking up at her friend, "I don't think they're scary!"

"Don't you see, Poppy?" explained Hetty the Wee.

"The little pink toothbrush must belong to Joni-Pip's little sister, Elle-Sahara," finished Ethelred-Ted.

"But she doesn't have a little sister called The Sahara," said Poppy.

Hetty, Ethelred-Ted and Joni-Pip all laughed: this was a good thing!

"There she goes again, our very own little T.C.!" said Ethelred-Ted.

"What's happened? Where must we be? I know we're somewhere else but where? What have we done? What does it all mean? How can we get home? Can we put it all back? How can we undo everything and put it back together again?" asked Joni-Pip, looking from one friend to the other.

"I know something is very wrong," said Ethelred-Ted, shaking his head. "The mere fact that we remember everything....Poppy you mentioned Joni-Pip's accident....earlier, I remembered making a noise when we put Jack's telephone in the Captain's Chest....so we are still in an unfinished Orbit, an incomplete Circle of Life....I know what Joni-Pip means about things changing, too. While she was cleaning her teeth, I thought that I would just pop by and say 'Hello' to Celeste...."

"Oh yeah?" his friends all said together.

Ethelred-Ted ignored them and continued,

"So I lifted up the Captain's Chest, expecting to see her pretty little face and all I saw were some old paintings and books and things. I was so shocked! I certainly don't remember any paintings when Joni-Pip and I emptied the Captain's Chest last night and who would have taken Celeste out since then?"

They all nodded and agreed that something most definitely was wrong.

"There was something else, so telling, so awful, which absolutely proves we are not here. Not where 'here' is anyway," said Joni-Pip.

"What on earth was that?" asked Hetty and Poppy gravely.

"It was when we past Alex's bedroom. It wasn't there. There was no sign of it. Ethelred-Ted and I both examined it thoroughly and it looked as though it had never, ever been there!"

"His bedroom?" asked Poppy and Hetty together again.

Joni-Pip and Ethelred-Ted burst out laughing.

"What?" asked Hetty and Poppy together. "What?" They looked confused.

Joni-Pip and Ethelred-Ted held their sides with laughing. Hetty and Poppy looked very puzzled but couldn't get a word out of the amused pair.

"That's what you said, Joni-Pip. You said, 'when we past Alex's bedroom it wasn't there, there was no sign of it'. I heard you!" said Poppy half-frowning.

"Not his bedroom!" spluttered Eth. "That's not what she meant!"

"Oh?" came two puzzled voices.

"This was supposed to be horrendous, not hilarious!" laughed Joni-Pip.

"The sign!" chortled Ethelred-Ted.

"Yes, she said there was no sign of it, I heard her distinctly, Ma Lamb!"

"No....no....no!" roared Joni-Pip. "It was the sign, the sign Alex has nailed up on his door. 'Private Land Trespassers will be prosecuted Keep Out', remember? It wasn't there! Eth and I examined his door really carefully."

"There were no signs it had ever been nailed to his door," explained Ethelred-Ted. "No holes where it was fixed. It most definitely had never been there! That's why she knew she was not...."

"In my world. Not here at all! That's another reason I was so distressed but thanks to You Two, I am feeling much better. At least I have all You Lot! Circle Hug?" she invited.

They all joined together in a circle and hugged each other.

"D'yer think we could 'a changed things by savin' Bullet?" asked Hetty.

"I think we must have, Het," replied Ethelred-Ted nodding his head.

"You know what? That thought never crossed my mind!" said Joni-Pip.

"I think we keep making the mistake of saying that we saved Bullet," started Poppy-Plump-Pij.

"Sorry, Poppy, we do realise it was only you," Ethelred-Ted apologised.

"No, Silly I didn't mean that!"

"Well, let's face it Pops," said Joni-Pip, "what part did we actually play in saving Bullet? First of all, it was Us who startled him and then we just stood around in the Stable Courtyard talking to everybody who walked in and out."

"What I mean is: was it only Bullet whose life we saved?"

"Oh! I see!" said Ethelred-Ted and Joni-Pip together.

"Good point, Ma Lamb!"

"We know that the accident caused so much pain and trouble," said Poppy-Plump-Pij earnestly, "young Colin Finn, for instance."

"You're right; saving Bullet changed so many things, Poppy," said Eth. "Now let's see, what changes were there? First of all Bullet didn't have to be shot. Right? Secondly, Colin Finn didn't have to spend the rest of his life in a hospital, did he?"

"I spoke to Jemimah when she was walking Bullet back into his stable," said Joni-Pip thoughtfully. "It was strange really, she said to me, 'Do I know you? You look familiar?' Of course I felt that I knew her because of knowing so much about her but I replied to her that I didn't think so. The silly thing is that when she spoke, I did feel that I knew her, she sounded so familiar. Of course we did change her life, she didn't spend the rest of her days worrying about what she had done to Colin Finn. She didn't become frail and ill."

"That is such a good point, Ma Pet," said Hetty the Wee nodding.

"We stopped people thinking Fred Finn wanted to get his revenge on the Spindlethrop family....on Jemimah especially," said Ethelred-Ted.

"Yes, that was good and do you remember how happy we all were when Archimedes came walking into the Stable Courtyard with Colin on Flame's back?" asked Joni-Pip.

"That was brilliant!" said Ethelred-Ted. "That was when we really knew that Poppy had made it!"

"We also changed things so that Grandfather and Archimedes were still friends. I heard Grandfather congratulating Archimedes for trying to stop Mimi from riding off on Bullet," said Poppy.

"So really then, Poppy is right, it's inaccurate of us to say 'when we saved Bullet'," said Joni-Pip, "we saved so much and so many!"

"This is all true," said Ethelred-Ted, "but this still doesn't answer two big questions....why has the Circle of Life not closed on this Jump....and why has everything changed for Joni-Pip? It obviously has something to do with, what did Red-Ted call it....her POOL?"

All of them nodded.

"It just goes to show that when you change the Past, y' have to be prepared for the consequences in the Future, Ma Pets."

"Hmmmm!" they all said.

"Well, I'm being selfish, very selfish," said Joni-Pip standing up. "We have children to save in a fire and right now, as it happens. Let's hope that after tonight, everything will return back to normal!"

"Yes!" they all said together again.

"We do know, Ma Pets, that the Workhouse still burnt down, though."

"How do we know that, then?" asked Poppy-Plump-Pij, taking off and landing on one of the remaining walls of the Ruin.

All of her friends looked at her.

"What?" she asked. "That was a very sensible question!"

All of her friends looked at her again.

"What?"

"Where are you standing, Pops?" asked Ethelred-Ted.

"On a wall," she replied, looking around her and shaking her head, as if to say, 'Where do you think I am standing, Stupid?'.

"And where are we?" asked Ethelred-Ted.

"At the Ruin."

"Ring any bells?" asked Joni-Pip.

"No."

"The Ruin of what?" asked Hetty the Wee.

"The Workhouse, Silly!" said Poppy-Plump-Pij.

Her friends all waited.

"Ah," said Poppy; then she laughed, "I was just testing. Making sure you are still awakeful at this time of the morning! Actually, it was probably the bump on the head I got, when I crashed into that branch a few minutes ago!"

"Aye! Are y' bonny now, Hen?" asked Het anxiously; Poppy nodded.

"Now we must re-set the F.B.," said Ethelred-Ted, unfolding it and turning it over, "Right, glitter coming up....First of all....Destination?"

"The Workhouse!" said Joni-Pip and Poppy-Plump-Pij.

"No!" said Hetty the Wee. "We need t' be in the Children's Dormitory first....don't y' remember they were trapped?"

"You are so wise, Hetty, of course!" said Ethelred-Ted.

He pulled off the letters and they all became sprinkled with clusters of beautiful, sparkling little stars. The F.B. began to make its usual whirring noise and then began to shake.

"The engine is starting!" cried Poppy-Plump-Pij.

"Don't the glittery sparklets look pretty in the darkness?" said Joni-Pip. "Even nicer than in the daylight. They twinkle like stars!" she said looking up into the sky.

"Sparklets? Is that a new word, Hen?"

"Of course!" laughed Joni-Pip.

Everybody felt relieved that Joni-Pip seemed back to her normal self. Ethelred-Ted finished fixing on the letters for, 'The Children's Dormitory, The Workhouse' and the more he pulled off, the more the sparklers covered all four of them and it made them all feel so good!

"Address?" asked Ethelred-Ted.

"Er....Windy Woods, er, shouldn't it say 'Downing House' somewhere?" asked Joni-Pip.

"Munchy Mash 'n Mustard! Joni-Pip you're right. We have put on the wrong Destination: can we take it off?" asked Ethelred-Ted, trying to remove the letters but they wouldn't budge.

"What do we do now?" he looked round at all of his friends in turn.

"Can't we just add, 'Downing House' underneath The Workhouse, Hens?"

"Good idea, Het. I bet that's how Red-Ted and Jack ended up in the wrong place....in the middle of a battle, if I remember correctly; they probably couldn't get the letters off. Right let's add 'Downing House'." He quickly added it and then said, "Right now, Address?"

"Windy Woods, Berry Bush, Nottinghamshire, England," said Joni-Pip.

The Bear added these letters amid a shower of tiny, gold and silver stars.

"Year?" asked Ethelred-Ted.

"1892," they all answered.

"Time?" he asked, after fixing the numbers for 1892.

"Ah....the paper just said 'early hours' or something like that, Ma Lamb."

"All right. Let's put 01:00....one o'clock in the morning seems about right....let's hope we are in time!" said Ethelred-Ted.

"That's so true....we most certainly will be 'in Time' only not in 'our Time'!" laughed Joni-Pip.

"Only have Day and Month left...." said Poppy staring in wonderment at the F.B., as all the letters and numbers changed into something she couldn't read, when they were pressed and stuck back on to the board. "Isn't it so clever?"

"Right, the day is the 5th; the month is May!" said Eth. "It's all done!"

They silently stood in front of it for a while, just looking.

"Doesn't it look beautiful?"

"Yes, Poppy, it surely does!" said Joni-Pip.

"Joni-Pip and Het, before we JIT, I just need to remind you again about what I said before. Father didn't want you to go tonight. He warned you and begged you not to do this. So, any signs of things not working out and we are jumping back over The Wall of Time?

Δεστιναατιον	Τηε Χηιλδρενσ Δορμιτορψ
Αδδρεσσ	Τηε Ωορκηουσε
	Δοωνινγ Ηουσε
	Ωινδψ Ωοοδσ
	Βερρψβυση
	Νοττινγηαμσηιρε
	Ενγλανδ
Ψεαρ	
Τιμε	
Δαψ	
Μοντη	Μαψ

Back here! Understood?" said Eth very seriously.

"Yes, remember that, You Two?" added Poppy.

"Yes, of course!" replied Joni-Pip and Hetty the Wee.

"Are we ready, then?" asked Ethelred-Ted.

Joni-Pip and Hetty the Wee nodded.

"Right! Jump!"

Hetty, Joni-Pip and Eth took a tiny leap and landed back down again.

They all looked at each other and shrugged their shoulders.

"Er....aren't we forgetting something?" asked Poppy-Plump-Pij.

"What's that then, Pops?" asked Ethelred-Ted, puzzled at their failure.

"Just a minorful detail: a little thing. Something called The Wall of Time?" said Poppy, pleased that she had got them all back, over her forgetfulness about the Ruin.

"The Wall of Time!" they all said together. "A minor detail, indeed!"

They quickly turned over the continuously-whirring-F.B., it sounded as if it was almost complaining. Ethelred-Ted then took out the ice cubes, well now they were more like ice wedges that he had carefully removed from the ice box just before they had left Knotty Knook. He worried slightly that they might have melted a tad too much to work. His fears were needless, however. It was a crisp night and they were still frozen, tightly wrapped up with vinegar and brown paper ((sorry, I mean)), brown paper and thick tea towels.

He placed them on the four ice symbols and they all watched in wonderment as the icy wedges waxed and wended their way upwards and outwards, until the watery wall was fully formed.

"That will never cease to amaze me! Right are we all ready, now? Jump!" Eth said and up they went, wafting over The Wall of Time.

334

Chapter 34

The Workhouse Fire

"Won't the Wall of Time melt, in this heat, Eth?"

They had landed, right in the middle, of one of the two aisles that ran down, the whole length, of the Children's Dormitory.

"I hope not, or we're done for!"

Although, it was hot in the room, the flames of the fire had not yet, reached the Dormitory. In fact, it was still quite clear, with just a small amount of smoke, drifting in, from under the door. All of the children still lay, sleeping, in their beds. There were three rows of black, wrought iron beds, which stretched the whole length of the room. One row ran down each wall of the huge, sparse room and the third row ran straight down the middle.

"What do we do now, Pets? Wake up the children?"

"I'm not sure, yet," said Ethelred-Ted, "let me go and see where we'll be able get them out."

The room was in darkness, apart from the light coming under the door, caused by the flickering flames, outside. Ethelred-Ted turned on his torch and walked over to the large door and tried it.

It was locked! He searched but he couldn't find a key.

"Well, that's clever of us! We never thought about the children being locked in. No wonder they perished!"

335

He walked back over to Hetty the Wee and Joni-Pip, who stood in between two rows of beds.

"I want to try something, Joni-Pip....where's Poppy, by the way?"

"I have no idea! Shouldn't we try the windows?"

"Good idea! You try them. Hetty, come with me!"

Joni-Pip walked over to the windows but as soon as she got there, she knew it was hopeless. Each wide window had a barred grille on it, from the top of the frame to the bottom and every single one was locked with a hefty padlock. With a heavy heart, she looked through the window and gazed into the starry, night sky. Something about the light they gave off: the twinkling; the sparkling; made her feel warm and safe inside. It was most peculiar.

"This is a prison," she whispered across to Ethelred-Ted and Hetty. "These poor, little children. They really made sure they couldn't escape!"

While Joni-Pip was checking out the windows, Ethelred-Ted put down his torch, letting it shine up into the room like a search light. He pulled off the tartan blanket, which he had added to his costume, along with the 'cowboy' rope that he had worn to travel in. He felt he looked a bit like Rob Roy, what with Seamus' hat and the tartan blanket draped across one of his shoulders and wrapped round his body, diagonally. He asked Hetty to hold one end of the blanket, with her little paws. He then twisted the blanket, with his paws, until it was like a long, coily sausage.

"I don't know if this will work, Het but we must try. Now, don't let go!"

He walked further down the aisle of the room, to The Wall of Time. It stood glistening and quivering in the light, coming from, both the torch beam and the orangey fire glow, under the door. The sound of the fire, taking hold outside, got louder and louder, as parts of the House began to crack and sizzle, in the force of the flames. Ethelred-Ted worried that his idea might not just mean the end of these poor, little children but also the end of Hetty, Joni-Pip and himself, too!

He was so conscious of Father's words of warning!

He lifted up his end of the tightly, coiled blanket and walked, directly, into the Wall of Time!

Hetty let out a little cry. She was in fear of his life and was so scared that Eth would surely die! As she watched, he just seemed to disappear.

"Where's Ethelred-Ted gone?" asked Joni-Pip, walking back over to Hetty.

"In the Wall of Time!"

"What?"

"It was his idea, not mine!" said Hetty, still holding on to the blanket, very tightly. It was so eerie. The blanket was visible from Hetty's little

336

paws, right up until it went into the Wall of Time. Then it was simply no more! The strange part, was that it still stood up in the air. It didn't fall down. Hetty had a wise mind in her little head and so the fact that the blanket didn't break off and fall to the floor, at the point where it had entered the Wall of Time, made her realise that it was still attached to Ethelred-Ted....wherever he was....

Thick, curly, smoke began to filter into the room, from under the large, wooden door.

"Am I supposed to break the windows to let the smoke out....or will that make the fire worse?" Joni-Pip called out softly to Hetty the Wee. "I could use the torch: that sure would smash the glass, pretty easily!"

"I think we should wait until Ethelred-Ted comes back."

Just then Ethelred-Ted came walking back out of The Wall of Time.

"Am I glad to see yooo, Hen? Are y' all right?"

"I am quite well, thank you, Hetty," replied Ethelred-Ted, as if he was exchanging pleasantries with a passing acquaintance, whilst walking in the Park on a sunny, Sunday afternoon. "What I have discovered is....the Wall of Time is made up of water....wet water!"

"I heard that! It sounded so funny, Eth. I have never yet come across dry water!" Joni-Pip laughed, from the other side of the Dormitory.

"What I mean is, the water that makes up The Wall of Time....well, it's not got the consistency of ice....which I thought it might have because of the Formula....it's still wet....liquid....consequently....not wanting to put a damper on the proceedings or anything but I am pleased to say that we now have one very wet blanket with us!"

He was jubilant and held up his dripping part of the tartan blanket.

"Come with me Hetty," he said walking towards the door.

They carried the half-wet blanket and laid it on the floor along the edge of the hot door, it made a frizzling noise and steam rapidly rose from it.

"That will give us a bit of time! Now, Girls, I want you to wake up all the children gently and get them to wrap themselves in the blankets on their beds, which look pretty threadbare to me. Poor Little Scraps, they can hardly keep them warm at night. I want you to get them to stand as far away from the door as they can. I'm jumping back over the Wall of Time, to go and get something!"

He then stood in front of the Wall of Time, jumped and disappeared.

He landed back over The Wall of Time at the Ruin, in 1942 and was welcomed with a far from friendly face. It was none other than his obnoxious friend, Nuttingham Squirrel.

"Not you again? What exactly do you think you're doing? Did I see some more fireworks up here again, a minute ago? Didn't I tell you earlier, there's a war on?" shot the squirrel.

"Again? Earlier? When? I don't remember. What I'm doing is none of your business. You might have seen some fireworks....I don't know....and why did you say 'more' and 'again'? I have only just arrived and yes, I am very well aware there is a war on....although I can't exactly remember needing you to tell me that. Any more questions?"

The squirrel was furious!

"You might think that you are a very clever, Teddy Bear, what with your fancy words and your worldly friends. Who was that noisy boy, anyway? I've got the measure of you and you are nothing more than a Stuffed Toy!" sneered Nuttingham Squirrel.

"My Dear Friend, your opinion of me is none of my business: right now I am on a Quission and you are just the fellow I need to help me accomplish it and why the Dickens can't we be friends....you had tea with us for Goodness sake....what more d'you want? What noisy boy?" replied a cheerful and slightly puzzled Ethelred-Ted.

"A Quission? What the nutkins is that? Do you honestly think that I would help you out, after the way you and your friends just treated me ....you were in such a rush! No time for me! I, too, began to think we could be friends after having tea with you and a very nice tea it was, too, I must admit but now, help you? Not a nut!"

"Quite simply, My Dear Fellow, a Quission is a Quest and a Mission put together and I can't actually ever remember me treating you badly, Old Chap: when was that then? Tell me and I will apologise profusely!" Ethelred-Ted was amicable but still extremely puzzled.

"Hmmmm....let me see now....apart from tonight....it was one day....yes, I know....your Potty-Plump-Pij friend....she attacked me!"

"I'm very sorry if she did that to you, especially if it was unprovoked....but I can hardly be responsible for a Wood Pigeon's actions, now, can I?"

"There was another time, I'm quite sure...." he said, scratching his head.

"I'll tell you of another encounter we had with you and if you think back to it, Old Chap, I treated you with the utmost courtesy," said Ethelred-Ted in a very gentlemanly manner, "and....it was me who wanted you to have tea with us at the Crooked Cottage with Grandfather."

"When was that then? When was it that you treated me with the 'utmost courtesy'?" asked the squirrel, rather taken aback by Eth's congeniality.

"It was when you found our friends cell 'phone."

"Cell 'Phone? What the nutkins is that? Oh, that thing in Marley's Barn, you mean? Quite honesty I think you were all very rude at that time!"

"Indeed I was not! I am every bit an English Gentleman for a German Teddy Bear!"

"What?" quizzed Nuttingham Squirrel, screwing up even more, his already very screwed up face.

"Now, my Good Fellow, we are wasting time, very precious time. We must get down to business. I need your help in a very urgent matter. Do you, perchance, in your wanderings and collections....as Warden of Windy Woods, of course," said Ethelred-Ted diplomatically, "ever remember coming across a set, a very old set of very large and very many keys?"

"Keys?"

"Yes, keys and believe me if you have the ones, the very ones we need, Your Very Good Self could be entirely responsible for saving the lives of many a poor child."

"Keys? Are you mad?"

"Yes, keys....you know, things that are used to lock and unlock doors."

"I know. I am not stupid. I just can't understand you. You have already asked me about the keys and I have already told you I couldn't help you."

"No, I haven't, Old Chap. I think you must be getting a bit forgetful," replied Ethelred-Ted. He didn't want to cause any bad feeling again, so he added, "or it could be me that had forgotten, of course but please rethink.... after all, it is to save the children?"

"Children?" bellowed Nuttingham Squirrel. "Children? I hate the things! They do nothing but cause me trouble. They climb and break branches off my beautiful trees. They are smelly, dirty and very noisy. What on earth made you think that I would want to do that....save them? Why should I help save them, just for them to come back and taunt me? Anyway, I have already told you that I can't help them and I can't help you!"

With that he scurried off without so much as a 'goodbye'.

Ethelred-Ted, although puzzled, was not one to be put off easily, so he tracked the squirrel as silently as he could. He followed him closely and deftly, dodging behind trees and hiding under bushes. He was really surprised when the squirrel walked down past Grandfather's Crooked Cottage and along Leafy Lane, towards Edwinstowe. Then he cut across the fields and climbed up the hill towards the Clappers.

'Munchy Mash and Mustard!' thought the stalking Bear. 'I had no idea he lived this far away from the woods!'

When they got on top of the Clappers, the Moon, which had been partially hidden by a few passing clouds until then, came out in all its silvery glory. It cast beautiful, shimmering light through the trees.

Nuttingham Squirrel stopped in a little clearing by a tree, close to the edge of one of the steep banks of the Clappers. He looked all around him, just to make sure that he wasn't being watched and then he pulled at something cleverly concealed in the grass. The squirrel used this to lift up a square trap door that was thatched in a roof of grass. He pulled out an attached piece of wood and propped up the door. Ethelred-Ted was amazed to see Nuttingham Squirrel disappear under the ground: shutting the door behind him.

The fascinated Bear left it for a few minutes and then came out from hiding behind a tree. He then walked over to where he thought the trap door was but he couldn't find it! It was so well hidden. After scratching around in the long grass for a little while, his paw finally hit something hard. It was the thick, metal ring, used to open the door.

Very, very slowly Ethelred-Ted lifted up the trap door. He pulled down the piece of wood as Nuttingham Squirrel had, which wedged the door open and looked in. There, in front of him were steep, stone, steps. He couldn't see where they led to as after about ten steps, there was a bend. Shafts of light lit his way so he decided to descend and investigate. He closed the trap door behind him and walked as silently as he could for fear of discovery. When he arrived at the bottom step, he came to a short landing. Lighted oil lamps were hung all along one wall. He couldn't help but notice how swept clean everywhere was! He walked along this landing and down another steep set of stone steps. When he got to the bottom, there was a long, low passage, lit this time, on both sides, by a number of oil lamps. He walked quickly along it only to find another set of steps at the end. As he descended this next set of stone steps the air became decidedly damp and musty. He met another, longer, even lower corridor and then two more sets of steps: he just seemed to be going down, down and down, further and further underground. He wondered when the descent would stop.

'Am I on my way to Australia?' he thought to himself and laughed.

At last he came to an opening and he looked in and gasped! There, in front of him, was a huge cavern! It must have been hundreds of feet high! It was lit by so many lanterns and looked quite beautiful and very definitely worth the walk!

"The way back might not be quite so pleasing. I wonder how many steps back up? Too many Munch Breaks, too much tum!" He tapped his tummy.

Down one side of the cavern he noticed an old railway line. There were a few old, open trucks still standing on the tracks.

"Munchy Mash n' Mustard!" he said under his breath. "I know where I must be now....I am in the Old Mine!"

"I thought you might follow me!" came a serious voice from behind him.

Ethelred-Ted spun round, nearly jumping out of his fur and was dazzled by a very bright lamp light. He couldn't see who was holding up the lamp but of course he could hear the unmistakeable voice of Nuttingham Squirrel; only something in his voice sounded different. It had more feeling, it was warmer, somehow.

Ethelred-Ted was amazed to see Nuttingham Squirrel disappear under the ground ...

"Come over to my drawing room for a cup of tea," he said kindly.

"Thank you, Old Chap, I would love one!" replied Ethelred-Ted happily: thinking to himself, 'Maybe a Munch Break might be forthcoming, too?'

The challenge of the steps had long fled his mind: as always, his tummy was decidedly in need of some kind of sustenance. Joni-Pip had gone off to bed and left him in the School Room for hours earlier that evening. He had only managed to grab a hunk of bread and a lump of cheese from Mrs Broft's pantry, before he went out to meet the others at the Ruin for six o' clock. So he was very hungry again when he went to get the ice from the ice box in the Garador's large, American Refrigerator. This was at about a quarter past eleven that night.

His eyes had lit up like a couple of head lights when they had spied what was packed in that huge refrigerator. Temptation? Of course!

The Teddy Bear's eyes grew as big as balloons!

"Hmmmmm! Don't mind if I do," he said out loud. "I think I might sample a few of the delicacies in here just to show my appreciation for Mrs Broft's amazing cooking! Anyhow, I don't see why all this food should sit in here, just resting!"

The Refrigerator was a harvest of delights; simply stacked with all sorts of splendid things. He went back and got a very large spoon from the cutlery drawer. He thought that nobody would notice if he sampled a 'small' spoonful of the 'red, wibbly, wobbly, strawbelly, jelly', as Becky-

341

Paige called it: or, perhaps a couple of spoonfuls.

"Hmmm, very tasty!"

He then decided that a spoonful of the creamy, pink blancmange would also go down a treat. Three large tablespoonfuls went down, equally well. Right at the back of one of the many shelves in the refrigerator, he spied an American Lemon Cream Pie! His absolute favourite!

"Surely nobody would miss a slight slither of that?" he reasoned.

So off he went to get a knife and a plate. He brought a dinner plate: after all he didn't want any crumbs or cream to fall on to the beautifully swept and mopped kitchen floor, did he? That would have been rather unkind of him, especially to Mrs Broft. He carefully took out the American Lemon Cream Pie and put it on the kitchen table next to the plate and knife.

"Am I being a bit mean using a clean plate and knife?" he asked himself. "Mrs Broft will have to wash them up."

He decided that would, most definitely, be making unnecessary work; so he sliced a tiny piece of the pie straight from the dish into his mouth with his well licked, 'strawbelly'-jellied and pink-blancmanged tablespoon.

It was delicious! Very, very delicious! So delicious, in fact, that he decided to indulge in a proper-sized portion....and another....and another.

This, of course, posed a problem for him. Was it worth leaving the tiny piece he had left in the dish? Hmmm, puzzling.....but no, not really.

So in usual Ethelred-Ted style he polished the whole lot off!

'I think somebody might be having a party tomorrow,' he thought to himself. 'I hope they jolly well ask me. Greedy Lot!'

Nuttingham Squirrel led the way, holding the lantern, high above him. They walked across the great cavern and through an archway. Then they came to a small passage, which brought them to a stairway. They climbed about six steps and walked on to a kind of veranda: that's if you can have a veranda underground. They entered a door that led into a hallway, which had about six doors off it. He hung the lantern, up on a hook, outside one of the doors, which he opened and walked through.

"Make yourself comfortable," said the squirrel, gesturing towards three armchairs, "won't be a minute, the kettle's on already," with that he left through another door.

Ethelred-Ted was amazed by the fantastic place he was in and also by the totally unexpected change in this, usually, most unpleasant person.

He chose an armchair by the fire and settled down. He looked around the room. It was beautifully decorated and tastefully furnished. The walls were plain and painted in a lovely, rich, creamy colour. The armchairs were deep and comfortable, made of soft brown fabric with cream scatter

342

cushions. There was a small, natural pine chest of drawers in one corner and a little matching coffee table beside each of the armchairs. A lantern hung on every wall, each one along side a beautiful landscape painting. What amazed the Bear most, was the fire place. A welcoming log fire sizzled and spat in the hearth.

'Where, on earth, does the smoke go?' he thought.

Nuttingham Squirrel returned carrying a full tea tray. There was a cream tea pot with matching sugar bowl, milk jug, two cups and saucers, two little plates and a cake stand crammed with buns and biscuits. Eth was delighted! Nuttingham Squirrel poured the tea into the beautiful tea cups.

"Milk and sugar?"

"Just milk, please."

"I don't know how much milk you like," he said, "I like quite a lot. My sister says I spoil the taste of the tea with so much milk and I make it look more like mushroom soup but I only think I have probably slightly more than most, that's all!" he laughed.

Ethelred-Ted suddenly felt warm towards his host. He had never ever considered that the squirrel might have any family.

"Well, I never! I like a lot of milk and come to think of it, my tea always looks a bit like mushroom soup, too!" smiled Ethelred-Ted.

The two of them chatted away over their tea and buns as if they were old friends. When Ethelred-Ted had devoured most of the buns and biscuits, washed down with at least three cups of tea, Nuttingham Squirrel told him he wanted to show him something he thought Eth might be interested in. They both got up from their armchairs and left the drawing room, entering the hall. The squirrel took a lantern from a hook in the hallway and walked down to the door right at the other end of the passage. A large key was in the lock, Nuttingham turned it, opened the door and walked through.

"Come on! I want you to know that you are the first person to see this, the first one who is not a squirrel, that is."

"I am honoured, Old Chap."

They walked down a long slope, at the bottom of which was another large door. Nuttingham Squirrel opened it but didn't go in.

"After you," he said politely.

Ethelred-Ted walked through the door.

He was totally taken by surprise by what he saw.

"Whew!" he gasped. "Whew! Amazing! This is unbelievable!"

It was two o'clock in the morning, by the time Ethelred-Ted left Nuttingham Squirrel's place. He ran all the way back in the direction of the Ruin. As he got closer, he noticed some sparkly fireworks coming from above the Major Oak.

"We thought we might catch you here!" came Flip's voice, as she emerged from behind the massive tree.

"Hi Eth!" said Steve. "What a beautiful night!"

"So where is the entrance to the Old Mine? Flip says you'll know, by now," laughed Craig.

"Well, I have certainly seen part of it tonight. It's so huge!"

"I knew it! I knew it! I knew soon enough we'd get it right, if I only kept on trying! My memory is such rubbish!" laughed Flip.

Just then the Two Men in Long, Black Coats arrived.

"Oh Dear!" said Craig exasperated. He turned to the men, "Why are you following us? Leave us alone!"

"Ve haff to talke viff you. Vere is he? Vot haff you done viv heem?" asked one of the men.

"Done with him? Who, on earth, are you talking about? I'm not hanging around here. Let's go, You Two!" said Steve, running off.

"Nine, you must not leaff. Ve haff to know vere he iss!" said the other man, trying to grab Craig's arm.

"We haven't the faintest idea, who you are talking about. Leave me alone! We don't have anyone. Who is this person, this man you want? We certainly haven't got him!" yelled Craig, as he struggled and fought not to be caught.

Flip ran off and then turned and saw that both the men now had Craig, wedged between them.

"**Verlassen Sie ihn allein! Sie können das nicht machen!**"[29] said Ethelred-Ted, trying to help Craig get free.

Steve and Flip ran back and joined in the tussle. Flip pulled at one of the men's coats and Steve pulled at the other man's arm.

"Leave my brother, alone! Let him go!" he yelled.

"Here they are!" a loud voice came from behind them.

The small regiment of soldiers in strange uniforms, appeared.

"Arrest these men!" the Commanding Officer ordered.

The soldiers joined in the disturbance and soon arms, legs and hats became embroiled in a brawl.

The way-out-numbered men in long, black coats put up a hardy resistance to the soldiers but the odds were too great. Finally, the Two Men in Long, Black Coats became the regiment's captives. Craig, Steve and Flip shook themselves like dogs after a paddle in a pond and brushed themselves straight.

"At last!" said Steve. "Perhaps we will be able to accomplish what we

---

[29] "Leave him alone! You cannot do that!"

are trying to do without having to run off all the time!"

"I'll second that!" laughed Craig, rubbing his arm, which had been pinched a tad too tight in the tussle. "What are these men; crazy?"

"Donnern und blitzen! Sie dumme Leute! Macht Sie sehen nicht, dass wir versuchen, ihm zu helfen!"[30] said one of the restrained men, to Ethelred-Ted.

"Wir sind hier, ihn zu schützen! Was haben Sie gemacht?"[31] said the other man.

Ethelred-Ted looked confused.

"Right! Mission accomplished! Back we go! Quick march!" the commanding officer ordered.

The regiment tramped off, escorting the Two Men in Long, Black Coats, roughly.

"Herr Geronnenblut! Sein Leben ist jetzt in Ihren Händen!" [32] shouted one of the prisoners as he was being marched off.

"Sie sind alle so unkluge!" [33] yelled the other.

"Come on, come on. Enough!" said the officer, disappearing into the darkness.

"What was that all about?" asked Steve.

"Yeah, what were the men shouting at you?" asked Craig, still nursing his bruises.

"Hmmmm!" replied Ethelred-Ted.

"Hmmmm? Hmmmm, what?" asked Flip.

"I....er....I wonder if you have done the right thing? Helping the soldiers, I mean," he replied, screwing up his mouth and shaking his head.

"What?" Steve, Craig and Flip gasped....

After watching the shiny stars climb into the black night sky, Ethelred-Ted ran on towards the Wall of Time.

"M, M n' M!" said the red and yellow bear. "I hope I am not too late!"

He could hear something going on at the foot of the door in front of him. The sound of sizzling steam came from under his side of the door as the wet blanket was put down.

"Het is that you? It's me, er....Ethelred-Ted?" he called through the door.

The noise of the flames swallowed up his voice. Nobody replied. His back began to feel very warm indeed. He daren't turn round, he knew he

---

[30] "Thunder and Lightning! You stupid people! Don't you see we are trying to help him!"
[31] "We are here to protect him! What have you done?"
[32] "Herr Geronnenblut! His Life is now in your hands!"
[33] "You are all so foolish!"

didn't have much time. Quickly he picked the biggest key from the large ring of keys he held. He tried it. It didn't fit. He tried another. It didn't fit either. He tried another and another. None of them fitted.

He then began to smell what he had dreaded most of all: singed fur! He could hear the flames behind him and he could feel the intense heat on his back. He tried so hard not to panic. He tried another key and another. The flames began to curl round him. He felt burning on his side and to his horror he saw that he was on fire. He quickly thumped his side vigorously, with both paws, until he had put out the flames.

He tried one more key. It didn't fit. He tried another.

'Click' it went; he turned the door handle and pushed on the door. The blanket blocked it, so he called through the small gap he had made.

"Joni-Pip! Hetty! Help me! Hurry!" he pushed the door as hard as he could. Two hands and two little paws appeared down the side of the door. A large crack was heard. Eth turned round and looked up. To his horror, he saw a large, burning rafter, falling towards him. The door suddenly opened, he burst in and shut it behind him just as the flaming rafter came crashing down on the other side of the door.

Ethelred-Ted couldn't help but laugh as he saw the Wall of Time in the middle of the room and watched a red and yellow bear jump over it and disappear!

"Hmmmmm!" he said. "Not so bad timing, after all!"

"I'm confused," said Joni-Pip, "You are just going, right now....so how did you get on the other side of the door?"

"It's a long story and we have children to save!" he replied. "Now, go and do just as I asked....what was it now? Yes, I know....wake up the children and take them over to the end of the room. I'm going to try and unlock the window grilles. I expect one will be all we need; we'll see. Hetty, you go and help Joni-Pip."

The Wall of Time rolled up and disappeared. Eth chuckled to himself.

Joni-Pip and Hetty the Wee gently woke the children and lined them up down the far end of the Dormitory. Hetty encouraged them to wrap their blankets around them. The poor little mites were scared to death and still half-asleep, so they obediently and blearily did as they were told.

Ethelred-Ted pulled one of the little wrought iron beds, which was about half-way down the row and pushed it hard up against the window. He tried a key in the large padlock, which was keeping the grille on the window well and truly secured. The key didn't fit, of course. He could hear the sound of the flames eating up the house on the other side of the door and he knew it was just a matter of time before the door would catch fire. He tried another key. He wanted to try another window but he thought that

346

would be counter-productive, so he carried on trying key after key after key. Finally the padlock clunked open. Ethelred-Ted hastily pulled off the padlock, undid the grille and tried to open the window. It was a sash window, which he thought probably hadn't been opened in ages, years in fact! The word 'fresh air' probably had no meaning here.

'M, M 'n M!' he thought. 'So near and yet so far!'

"Joni-Pip, come and give me a hand!" he shouted across the room. "I've got the grille unlocked but I can't open the window!"

In a tic, Joni-Pip had joined him and stood on the little black and grey, striped, horse-hair mattress, which lay on the black, wrought iron bedstead.

"Do you know they have no sheets?" she said indignantly. "Just this lumpy mattress and one thread bare blanket. Not even a pillow!"

"Yes, well let's try and open this window, right now, shall we?" laughed Ethelred-Ted. "You can do your social work later!"

The two of them bent slightly and pushed hands and paws up from under the bottom section of the window. They both went red with the exertion.

They tried again. It wouldn't budge. They tried again.

"Hang on a minute! I think it works better if you do this!"

Joni-Pip pulled back the metal catch on the top of the bottom window.

"Try again!" she said: they pushed and sure enough, the window opened!

Eth looked through the window and put his head out into the night air.

"Great!" he said. "We have risked life and limb to save these children. We have travelled a long way: many years, in fact. I have sustained a nasty burn on my side. I have even managed to get the keys successfully, with tremendous difficulty mind. We have woken up the children....well, you and Hetty have and they are all ready to save. We have finally opened the window; even though I forgot to release the catch; only to discover that we are two floors up and the children will probably not survive the jump!"

"What?" exclaimed Joni-Pip, poking her head out of the window and looking down. "I can't believe it! This room is going to be on fire in a few minutes. I can already hear the door blistering from the heat. What next?"

Totally dejected, they looked back into the room, got off the bed and walked hopelessly over to the children.

"Can't we tie the sheets together and make a long rope, Ma Lambs?"

"What sheets, Het?"

"What about the blankets?

"Het, they are so threadbare they will just rip to pieces; they couldn't take the strain." Ethelred-Ted was so miserable. All of their planning, all of their good intentions, all of their hopes were to no avail.

He sat down on one of the beds and put his head in his paws.

"Never fear! Helpful is here!" came a familiar voice from the window.

347

"Poppy!" shouted Hetty the Wee, Joni-Pip and Ethelred-Ted, together.

A clanging noise was heard on the window sill.

"That's it! That's fine!" said Poppy-Plump-Pij, sitting on the window sill, looking outside and addressing somebody they couldn't see. "I'll tie it to something!"

She lifted up a rope in her beak and quickly flew into the room with it. She then tied it to one of the metal bedsteads.

"We have already tied the other end of the rope to the top of the ladder," she explained to Ethelred-Ted. "Now get these children out of here!"

The ladder shook and footsteps were heard coming up. Suddenly a face appeared looking in the window. Followed by another! Two men climbed into the room both of them were carrying lanterns. One of the men leaned out of the window and tied a lantern to the back of the top rung, so that it hung down behind it, lighting up the ladder.

"Quickly! Bring the children over. I will walk down first and they can follow me. Archie, you stay here and help the children onto the ladder!" ordered one of the men.

"All right, Fred!" replied Archie.

"Is everything going all right, up there?" called a voice from outside, down on the ground. "Can we do anything?"

"Just hold the ladder still and when we get the children down, take them away from the house to safety. I'm sure the whole place will go up soon!" Fred shouted down to the men below.

Joni-Pip shook.

'I know that voice!' she thought. 'These men: don't I know them both?'

"Bring the children over quickly!" ordered Fred, climbing back out of the window and standing a little way down the ladder. Eth, Hetty and Joni-Pip led the file of children. They walked along the side of the room to the opened window. Smoke began to fill the room. Archie picked up the first child and put her on the ladder so she could walk down, facing the rungs.

"Don't be scared, it will soon be over and you will be safe," he said.

The little girl let her blanket go, as she held on to the ladder; it floated down to the ground. She shivered and shook with cold and fright.

"Don't fear, as soon as you get on to the ground, we'll get you wrapped up again," said Fred, helping the little girl down every rung of the ladder.

Three men stood at the bottom of the ladder, holding lanterns. When Fred arrived with the first little girl, one of the men put his lantern on the ground, wrapped her back up in her blanket and carried her over to the old barn, which stood about a hundred yards away from the huge house. The door was already open and a lantern was hanging up, lighting their way. He put her on the deep straw that covered the floor.

348

"I'll stay with the children, James. You bring them over as they come down and let Sam hold the ladder steady!" he shouted to the other two men who stood at the bottom of the ladder.

"Righto, Phil!" shouted the two men.

Soon everything was working well. Archie lifted the children on to the ladder at the top. Fred helped them down the ladder. Sam steadied the ladder at the bottom. James carried the children across to the safety of the barn. Phil stayed with the children in the barn.

And Hetty the Wee, Joni-Pip, Ethelred-Ted and Poppy-Plump-Pij?

They were getting hotter and hotter and beginning to choke in the smoke coming into the Children's Dormitory. True: they were but they were holding the children's hands as they waited in line to go down the ladder and....that made them feel very happy and very, very useful!

When about half of the children had left the room, Archie lifted up a little girl and started to tell her not to worry: she looked up at him and said,

"Uncle Archie, thank you for coming for me. I knew you would."

Archie looked at the little girl and gasped,

"Amelia!"

"Hurry Archie," said Fred, from out of the window, "we haven't much time left. The flames are already licking around the door. Look!"

Archie turned and saw red flames, curling their way all round the edge of the door. He lifted Amelia up and quickly put her on to the ladder.

"I will see you in a minute, Sweetheart," he said, "then I am taking you home to Hideaway Cottage!"

"I knew 'tomorrow' would be special!" said Amelia, beaming at him.

The Dormitory door was now on fire. There were only three little boys left. The flames quickly wrapped themselves round the door frame and the walls started to crack with the intense heat. The little boys were choking quite badly in the thick smoke, so Eth told them to crouch on the floor.

"We haven't time to wait!" called out Archie. "I will put the children on the ladder one by one and they will have to go down on their own. We can't wait for Fred to come back and get them one at a time!"

"All right!" said Ethelred-Ted.

Soon two of the boys were on the ladder. Fred came back up towards them and lifted them off the last few remaining rungs of the ladder. With a bit of difficulty, the last little boy finally made it! They were all safe!

Archie, in the meantime, had started to help Joni-Pip to get on the ladder but she couldn't. She just froze.

"Cough Drops, I can't do this!" she hunched her shoulders and shook.

"Cough Drops?" laughed Archie. "I like that, I think I'll pinch it! Of course, you can do it, I'm here to help you! Come on, Little Princess!"

"What's going on?" asked Ethelred-Ted, anxiously turning and looking straight into the wall of flames behind them.

"I don't think Joni-Pip dare get on the ladder," said Hetty the Wee.

Poppy flew and landed on Joni-Pip's shoulder and whispered in her ear,

"Joni-Pip, you can do this. I'm here with you. I'm not going to let you fall this time. It was my faultful the first time so this time I'm going to help you. Let's pretend we're in Windy Woods, shall we? We have just climbed The Major Oak by the Ruin and we have looked down at Grandfather's Crooked Cottage. Now he wants us to come down for tea. So that's what we are going to do. We are going to climb down the tree. All right?"

Joni-Pip nodded and let Archie guide her onto the ladder. Fred, by this time was back at the top of the ladder and he slowly helped Joni-Pip climb on to each rung. All the way down Poppy was talking to Joni-Pip about the wonderful things they were going to do once they got to Grandfather's.

"How are we going to get Hetty down?" Ethelred-Ted asked Archie.

Archie thought for a minute.

"I know," he said, coughing in the smoke. "Step into your carriage, at once, Milady!" He took off his jacket and laid it on the floor, "Hurry!"

Hetty rushed on to the jacket in front of her.

"Thank y' kind Sir," she replied as Archie wrapped her up in it quickly but gently with just her little head poking out.

"After you!" he said to Ethelred-Ted.

Ethelred-Ted climbed on to the ladder, quickly followed by Archie and Hetty. The room, by this time, was completely ablaze. When they got half-way down the ladder, there was a huge explosion. The intense heat had forced all the windows to blow out. Glass flew everywhere. Everybody put up their arms to protect themselves from the shower of shards and shattered splinters. The ladder swayed and Joni-Pip screamed. Poppy continued reassuring her friend.

"My knots held out!" laughed Poppy, poking the ladder with her beak!

When there were only about four more rungs to go, suddenly Joni-Pip felt some strong arms encircle her and she was whisked off the ladder.

"You are safe now, Joni-Philipa," came a familiar voice.

She strained her eyes to see in the darkness, who it was that was carrying her. She was too exhausted to speak.

It was only when they walked through the small crowd that had gathered and a man held up a lamp to light their way that she was able to see his face.

"Father!" she whispered.

"Honey, I was so scared I wouldn't make it," he said gently pulling his daughter closer, "and what would I have told Mother?"

Chapter 35

Circles in a Pool

After Joni-Pip, Ethelred-Ted, Hetty and Poppy were all settled in the barn with the children; Father, James, Fred, Archie and Sam, went back to the house to see if they could help put out the fire. By this time, the village folk had come to see if they could help. The Villagers made a human chain from the stream on the top of Windy Woods to The Work-house; passing buckets of water to be thrown on to the fire. Soon a horse-drawn fire wagon arrived from Edwinstowe and the firemen took over. Two firemen worked very hard, pumping two levers up and down on a large, mobile water tank. They looked like two men, travelling along a railway line, in a hand truck or Gandy Dancer, as the Americans call them; only they were pumping water through huge hoses to be used on the ferocious flames. Their main concern, now that everybody was out, was that the wind would blow the flames and all of Windy Woods would be destroyed in the blaze.

The local Newspaper Reporter, Gavin Fielding, arrived with a Photographer, Steve Pedder and all the Rescuers were photographed. They stood together in front of the smouldering house. The next day, the children were taken in by different homes in Edwinstowe and the surrounding villages, where they stayed until they were old enough or wanted to leave home.

Edwinstowe became famous for this self-sacrificing act of kindness.

Once the Firemen had taken control, all the men who had helped with the rescue went back into the barn. The Workhouse Children were already wrapped in blankets and were fast asleep on the straw. Consequently, a strange little band of people sat in a barn on bales of hay drinking hot cocoa and talking. The cocoa had been made down the hill at the Crooked Cottage. Women from Berry Bush who were keen to help, carried the hot drinks in flasks up the hill. It was most welcome and most appreciated.

How different this was from the First Circle, which was full of weeping.

Joni-Pip, black faced and exhausted, looked around the barn. She thought that it was so peculiar seeing all of these men together.

Even though Ethelred-Ted was charred and worn out, he still busied himself, going round and talking to everyone. They were sitting discussing the events on the tightly packed bundles of straw, which were arranged in a perfect Circle. Despite all that had happened on that moonlit night there was still something very cosy about them all sitting together in this lantern-lit barn, cupping their black hands around big mugs of milky, hot cocoa.

After he had spoken to everybody, Ethelred-Ted stood up in the middle of them and like a Master of Ceremonies, he addressed them,

"This, My Dear Friends, has been an amazing night for all of us but especially for me. Once more, through the Gift of Déjà Vu, I have been able to redeem myself."

Joni-Pip, Hetty the Wee and Poppy-Plump-Pij all looked at each other.

"What's he talking of? He was magnificent tonight!" whispered Hetty.

"Indeed, he was!" agreed Joni-Pip, shrugging her shoulders.

"How he likes to talk!" laughed Poppy. "Let him enjoy his moment!"

"I will go round everybody so that we all know who is who and how you all had a part in changing the life of one Little Girl," continued the bear.

"Amelia Plate," whispered Hetty, Joni-Pip and Poppy together, smiling: how good it felt that they had helped re-unite Archimedes and Amelia.

"As you all know, this is the year 1892 but not all of us come from this Time. We all come from different Times and for different reasons but tonight, all of our Circles have met. It is as if they have all linked together in a chain, within a Circle: kind of wheels within wheels. So right now, you can all remember your experiences from the Past and Future in this very special Pasture. It is so special that is called a Premium Pasture and it lasts two hours, well, I think it does but I may be wrong....!

"Let's get down to business, shall we? The first person I would like to introduce to you is somebody who has flown over the Wall of Time, no less than three times, today. She comes from the Year 1942. I don't like to think what might have happened, if it hadn't have been for her quick thinking and quick action, tonight.

"Ladies and Gentlemen would you please be upstanding for Miss Poppy-Plump-Pij!" He started to clap: everyone in the barn stood up and heartily clapped, too. The pretty pigeon was very embarrassed and looked down.

"Dear Friend Poppy, please come over here in the middle. We want you to explain all that has happened to you recently," invited Eth, walking to a space on one of the bales of hay and totally exhausted, slumping down.

Reluctantly, Poppy walked to the middle of the Circle. At first she didn't know what to say but then suddenly the words just seemed to flow from her as if she wasn't speaking at all but somebody was speaking for her.

"The first experience I had of the Wall of Time, The Gift of Déjà Vu, The Circles of Life and Pastures and Pools, was when I encouraged Joni-Pip to come up the ladder to see the Loft in Marley's Barn. Joni-Pip came up the ladder and on the way down, a flash of lightning and a crash of thunder made the ladder shake and the little Pudding fell and died. I always felt it was my faultful," said Poppy sadly.

Joni-Pip looked at Poppy-Plump-Pij stunned.

"I flew through a dreadful storm to get to Grandfather. Then Alex, Grandfather, Farmer Finn and Father went back up to Marley's Barn and brought her little body back. It was awful. I lived a good life with Hetty the Wee, my little hedgehog friend, in Windy Woods but we always missed Joni-Pip. Anyway, thanks to the Gift of Déjà Vu, we had visitors from the Year 2007; Jack, Red-Ted and...." Poppy blushed slightly, "Macca. They had jumped back, over The Wall of Time. They arrived in Marley's Barn just in timeful to save Joni-Pip from having her accident. Red-Ted explained to us that life was always moving, going round and round in circles like a....a pattern....like a telescope....and like an atom....in different loops. By the way, because I fly over The Wall of Time, I don't get to go in the Kaleidoscope of Life, the KOL....did I say telescope? Silly Me....I meant kaleidoscope, didn't I? I don't get to go in there but I do get to flyful in the skyful, all the time, which is the most wonderful experience in Life. So don't feel sad or sorry for us birds, ever, will you?"

Everybody laughed and shook their heads.

"So, by our visitors coming back and arriving, just in time to stop the accident, they put Joni-Pip into another Circle of Life....a new....a new....'More bit' of Life...."

Nobody laughed.

"I didn't realise this had all happened because as soon as Jack, Macca and Red-Ted had gone, we went back to the time before we had entered Marley's Barn and Joni-Pip said that she had these feelings of Déjà Vu.

"I didn't remember anything about the First Circle with Joni-Pip. I just enjoyed the beautyful of Life and I remember having these wonderful warm feelings for her. Then Ethelred-Ted showed us the F.B....that was amazing....and after lots of thinking and experimentfuls....well, that was with Alex and Auntiedes Spindledrop...."

Archie looked up and smiled broadly at her wonderful malapropism.

"By some fluke, we made the Wall of Time appear. I flew over it and landed on the Clappers and saw four young men....well, three and an older man. I recognised two of them they were Barky CD's Twindlestop and Grandfather. The two others I didn't know but I was shocked that the ones I knew, didn't know me but the ones I didn't know, knew me and said, 'Hello Poppy' and seemed really pleased to see me. That was in 1883. We really made a worm's web of that." Poppy shook her head.

Everybody laughed again.

"It wasn't our fault, we were new at this JITTING thingy but we suddenly remembered everything again so we knew we had to keep going to close up the Circle. I was flying out with Macca one day; it was yesterday morning, it seems ages ago. I ought to say it seems ages 'to come', I suppose it is, as we are now in 1892!

"We were flying really high and then down below us, we saw two figures walking up to Windy Woods. I love to swoop down, which I did, it's such a wonderful feeling and there, by the Ruin, were Father and Farmer Finn, James Finn. I wondered what they were doing so I flew back to Macca and suggested we went and took a look. We landed in The Major Oak, by the Ruin and I was astonished to see Father had the F.B. opened. Of course that meant I could talk to him, so I flew on to the ground in front of him and asked him where he had got the F.B. from. He confessed that he had borrowed it without permission. I guessed it had to be Eth's.

"He and James know Macca because Macca's owner is an Italian Prisoner of War who lives a lovely lifeful here, at the Camp in Boughtsome Chutney, working on the land, up at Finn's Farm. Macca told me that Franco loves it and wants to settle in England after the War. He says that he couldn't work for a nicer man than James."

"Aaaahhhhhh!" went everybody, making James blush.

"Macca said it was Eth's F.B.. I said that I was going immediately to tell Eth but then the Wall of Time appeared and I knew I would be too late, so I suggested that Macca and I go with them. I don't suppose Father had much choice because I had already been over the Wall of Time, so we just took off and flew over. We arrived here too lateful, the Workhouse Fire was blazing. I saw Fred Finn and he recognised me and I told him the children were trapped, so he ran down to the Crooked Cottage to get Grandfather and a ladder. Of course it was far too late. None of the children were saved, although James and Father helped carry out the little bodies. Father was very quiet but I knew my friends had planned to come back and save the children, so I wasn't worried too much. Then we went home. I don't quite know what we achieved.

"Eth, Hetty, Joni-Pip and I JITTED, well, I flew properly the next time because we wanted to save Nimi Spindleprop from causing Colin Finn to have a very bad accident, which made big trouble between Archimedes and Grandfather. The accident had happened while she was riding a runaway horse called Bullet. We stopped it this time, with my promise to give Bullet some of my freshly baked Oat Scones. I think I'm the only one I know who has stopped a Bullet with her Oat Scones!"

Everybody laughed.

"I met everybody from 1882," Poppy continued. "That was funny. I met the two young men who had spoken to me a year later but this time I knew them and they didn't know me! When we got back to 1942 we remembered everything: so we knew something was still wrong. I had left

354

my Coronation Tin there: which meant and still means that this Circle is still open. So when we flew over The Wall of Time, yet again and landed in this Time, 1892, instead of staying with Ethelred-Ted and the others, I flew straight to Fred Finn's but he wasn't there, he was already here with Archimedes, trying to help with the fire. I told him everything again and asked him to go and get a ladder. He ran and brought one back and then they all helped rescue the children!"

She walked over to Hetty and sat down. Everyone stood up and clapped and like a Ring Master in a circus, Eth walked into the centre of the Circle.

"Thank you, Pops. Isn't that all just amazing? Er....Pops, it's actually at Norton Cuckney, the Prisoner of War Camp, although Boughtsome Chutney sounds delicious to me, especially with cheese!" Everybody laughed. "Now I would like to introduce you to James Finn. James?" He beckoned him over.

James got up from where he was sitting next to Fred Finn, his father: everybody started clapping again. He walked into the middle of the Circle and began to speak.

"Hello, my name is James Finn and I run Finn's Farm at the moment in 1942, that is. The farm is below the Clappers, just outside Berry Bush.... soppy me....you all know that, don't you? After taking over from my Father, Fred Finn," he said gesturing towards Fred. "It's most peculiar seeing my Father younger than me. I have jumped over the Wall of Time a few times now and I'm 39 years old. My Father is only 26, here in 1892. That means I was 13 when my Father was born...." he paused and looked around. "Just a little 'Circle' joke, there! Anyhow, he is a wonderful man and has given me a great education and a marvellous family life. He'd hoped I'd become a doctor but I love to run the Farm. All I have ever wanted to be is a farmer.

"There has been a deep sadness in our family. My Uncle Colin, my Father's brother, was badly injured in an accident, caused by Jemimah Spindlethrop riding one of my Grandfather's stallions, Bullet without his permission. Colin has spent all of his life, since he was twelve, in a Sanatorium. Some people were very unkind and said that my Father started the Workhouse Fire on purpose, to get his revenge on Jemimah. Her little girl, Amelia Plate, was in the Workhouse. So really Phil....Poppy calls him Father, as he is Joni-Philipa's father....so, Phil and I jumped over the Wall of Time, for two reasons: to prove my father, Fred Finn, was innocent and to help save the children who had all perished in the fire of 1892. We JITTED and were too late to save the children but we knew that Fred Finn, my father, had run from the fire to get a ladder, so in that sense I was happy, at least. We went back to 1942, disappointed that the children had still perished but of course we forgot everything that had happened. Then last night....well, early this morning, my friend Phil, drove up to the farm in a panic. His daughter, Joni-Philipa," he gestured towards Joni-Pip, "had been poorly earlier on, last evening and so in the middle of the night he couldn't sleep and he checked up on her to see if she was all right. When he got to her bedroom she had disappeared! He searched everywhere. He didn't wake up the Household as he had an idea where she might be. The two of us then set off for the Ruin. When we arrived, we couldn't believe it. There was Ethelred-Ted coming out from behind one of the trees near the Ruin. He was flustered and said he was looking for some keys....a very large bunch of keys. This silly squirrel came along, kicking up such a fuss about the light from the Formula Board. He reminded us there was a War on and asked us, 'hadn't we heard of the word 'Blackout'?' Poor Ethelred-Ted asked him to help us save the children in the Workhouse Fire by giving us the keys. The dopey squirrel said he knew nothing about the Workhouse keys, they had never been found or something and he didn't like children, anyway. Then he went off moaning about us. Ethelred-Ted looked a bit dirty and tired but fine. The Wall of Time was already glistening in the moonlight, so Ethelred-Ted asked if we wanted to go back with him, over the Wall of Time, to help save the children. Of course we wanted to and just before we did, we saw something amazing....but I'll let Phil tell you all about that!"

Everybody in the barn looked disappointed.

"When we arrived," James went on, "the fire had really taken hold. Then we remembered that we had been here before, only all the children had died. This time, however, all the children were saved. Ethelred-Ted set the time slightly earlier; we still thought we only had one hour though, so we had to work fast. Poppy told my Father, Fred, to run back to the Crooked Cottage and get a long ladder, which he carried with Sam. Poppy knew the children were locked in an upstairs room, so happily all the children were carried out safely. I feel really good because my Father's name has been cleared now and of course, more importantly, all the children are safe."

With that he sat down. Everybody clapped.

"James forgot to mention that he carried all the children across the grass to the safety of this barn," said Eth, clapping as he walked back into the middle of the Circle.

"Now, I would like to introduce you to Archimedes Spindlethrop."

Archimedes, a twenty-six-year old man, stood up. As Joni-Pip looked at him, he turned and smiled at her. There was something about that smile that gave her a strange feeling. He looked so familiar to her but she couldn't quite think how that could be. She remembered the pilot again.

"Not much to say really," he started, "it's very, very weird, learning things about yourself, which are going to happen in years to come. I know that it has always saddened me that one of my closest friends has blamed me, over the past ten years for my sister's frail health but now, thanks to the gift of Déjà Vu and the Accident being averted, at least one thing has been put right. I'm told that Amelia Plate, my niece," he gestured towards

Inside The Quission Hut

Drawn by Ethelred-Ted

Amelia, who sat on a bale of hay next to Joni-Pip, "lost her little eight-year-old life in the Fire, in her first Circle but I haven't lived any time past this night, yet, as this is my Time, my Present. I'm so grateful that tonight I was able to be here to help save her. I was also told that I regretted not taking her home with me, sooner. Well, tomorrow, I am taking my sister Jemimah Plate, home with me and her daughter Amelia is coming back tonight. That's all. I think that puts both things right," he paused, looking at them all, in turn, "doesn't it?"

Archimedes sat back down. Everybody clapped.

"I think everybody should be reminded that Archimedes....Archie, risked his life tonight, to save all the children, including Joni-Pip, Hetty the Wee and myself. He was the last to leave the building!" said Ethelred-Ted.

Everybody stood up and clapped him, really loudly.

"Also, Archie, that sounds so strange; I only know you as an old, eccentric, white whiskered Inventor and I call you Archimedes. Did you know, you have the most amazing Laboratory, in 1942? We call it the Quission Hut: actually, I have drawn a picture of it, here!" said Ethelred-Ted, holding out a drawing. Archie took it and examined it, with great interest, shaking his head.

"Cough Drops, this is amazing, everything I have ever dreamed of!" he said, seriously....then he laughed, "well, almost!"

They all laughed. Joni-Pip laughed, too, especially at hearing her phrase.

"It is? Really?" asked Eth. "You know, Archie, it's really strange, somehow I never imagined you were ever young and good-looking!"

357

Everybody laughed.

"Archie? Good-looking?" Grandfather grinned. "It strikes me that this Ted, of yellow and red, needs specs on his head!"

"What do you mean? I am dashingly handsome and frightfully debonair!"

He bowed, waving his hand in front of him as if asking a lady to dance.

"What was that, Old Chap?" asked Fred Finn. "You're such a fright and you'll soon have mad hair!"

Everybody laughed again.

Ethelred-Ted tried to re-establish some sort of order but everyone was so amused at Fred Finn's last 'hair' comment that he had to shout out loud before they would all be quiet. Finally, everyone calmed down and once more, Ethelred-Ted resumed his role as Ring Master.

"Anyway, Old Chap, you haven't told us all about the Accident. So come right back! You were such a daring rider; we watched you galloping over the fields and up on to the Clappers, trying to catch Jemimah. It was breathtaking and....Everybody," said the Bear turning and looking at all those in the Barn, "he was riding bare-backed, no less! It was amazing to watch! Just like a Native Indian. So, Archimedes, get yourself back here!"

Everybody clapped again, as Archimedes, the Reluctant Hero, stood up once more and returned to the centre of the Circle.

"It was nothing. It all started one day, when my silly twin sister...."

Hetty, Joni-Pip, Poppy and Eth all looked at each other and gasped.

"....Mimi and I were up at Finn's Stud Farm, helping to muck out the horses. We were sixteen. We liked to do that because we'd get to ride the horses. On this particular day, I presumed one of the Stable Boys had been moving Bullet; the most difficult and feisty stallion on the Farm, as he still had a lead rein on. Sorry, I've jumped the gun. So here I am, laying down clean straw in one of the stables and I see my sister walk past on Bullet, this incredibly wild horse very few could control. I was furious. I remember throwing down my fork and running out. I grabbed hold of the lead rein and told Mimi to get off; I think I called her a Silly Twerp! Then these Inspectors arrived, oh no they weren't, I've just realised, it was You Lot! It was your fault Bullet was startled! The Wall of Time must have scared him!" said Archie, shaking his head and looking at the culprits.

"Sorree!" Eth, Hetty and Joni-Pip shrugged their shoulders sheepishly.

Archimedes let out a long sigh and shrugged **his** shoulders.

"Bullet reared up and Mimi and he went tearing off. I ran into a stable and pulled out Flame, my favourite horse; we kind of had this understanding. I literally jumped up on to his bare back and headed off after her. I was desperate and feared for her life. I tried so hard to catch her. Sadly, I didn't and there was this terrible accident. Fred fell down the Old Mine Shaft; Mimi was thrown and really never recovered, both physically and mentally. Colin sustained dreadful brain injuries: Bullet broke a leg and had to be destroyed and Sam, one of my best friends, never spoke to me again. That, happily however, was in the First Orbit. The second time it happened, the Inspectors didn't arrive so Bullet wasn't startled; I forced Mimi to get off him and there was no accident and Sam, Fred and I are still the best of friends. Colin is now a strapping young man of twenty two. I do remember the argument up on the Clappers, when Edmund was about to marry my sister, Mimi. Sam got really cross: he didn't want them to marry. A pigeon flew down near us and Edmund and Fred spoke to her as if they knew her. Now, of course I understand, it was Poppy. It's funny how when Jemimah was trying to control Bullet the second time, she said to me,

'I have been here before.'

"Of course, she had, it was the Gift of Déjà Vu! Well, I never did! I have said enough!" He laughed and sat down.

Everybody clapped him, once more. Ethelred-Ted, the Circle Master, stood up and whilst still clapping Archimedes, he said,

"Thank you, thank you, Archie, sorry about our....our....oh....well.... please forgive our untimely entrance into the Stable Courtyard? Now, I would like you to hear from Fred Finn."

"Like Archie, I don't have much to say really, either," started Fred as he was being applauded, whilst walking into the centre of the Circle, "it's all been covered pretty much. I wasn't actually mad at Jemimah or Archie, come to that. I've no idea where people got that from. I most certainly would never have taken out any revenge on little Amelia. Anybody who really knew me would know that. As I lay at the bottom of that Mine Shaft, in a lot of pain, believe me, I just kept thinking, 'If only I had done what Father had asked me, then I wouldn't be here!' My father had asked me to specially groom Bullet that morning. He knew that the Royal Inspectors were due to come, as the Queen had heard what a magnificent stallion Bullet was and she wanted to buy a horse, as a gift for her son. However, instead of getting up early and doing what my father had asked me to do at the Stables, I stayed in bed and hung around the farmhouse, reading some medical journals. I so wanted to become a doctor but Father wanted me to take over the Stud Farm. Although I enjoy riding and love horses, I have absolutely no inclination towards Farming of any kind. I just wanted to go to Medical School and study to become a surgeon. My father had other ideas, alas! So Friends, New Ones and Old, I felt that if I hadn't been walking the dogs with my younger brother, Colin, then he wouldn't have been so terribly injured. If I had been working at the Stables doing what I was supposed to have been doing, then Mimi wouldn't have mounted Bullet because I would have had him and he wouldn't have had to be destroyed. I've just felt, for the last ten years, that everything was my fault. The only person I've ever been mad at, was myself. I felt responsible for Mimi's health, too. How happy I was at the thought of being able to help save the children; especially Amelia. It was, kind of, paying her back for all the pain I'd caused! So many things have changed. I'm so happy and so grateful to Poppy. She is so special. The first time I experienced the Workhouse Fire....how many times has it been? Is it three? Anyway, the first time, she asked me to go and get a ladder from The Crooked Cottage. I left the Workhouse and ran down the hill to fetch Sam. We both carried the ladder back up the hill but we were too late. How fantastic it was to be able to re-live that, through the Gift of Déjà Vu. I remember thinking, when we were carrying the ladder the second time, 'I've done this before', which we had. That ladder was so vital in saving the children. Thank goodness I was given the Gift, as well, to be able to forget the last, painful ten years and they have been exchanged for ten happy years. One thing I forgot to say, was that our beautiful horse, Bullet, changed from a feisty, ferocious animal, into a really Soppy Softie, with a penchant for Oat Scones! So much so that my father kept him and gave him to Colin!"

Fred sat down. At first there was no applause. Everybody seemed quite stunned by his revelations, especially James, his son.

Eth stood up and applauded him loudly; then the others joined in.

"Thank you, Fred, thank you, indeed! Now it is the turn of Grandfather: Sam to some of you! Come on Grandfather, tell us your story!" said Ethelred-Ted clapping

loudly and then sitting back down. As Grandfather got up and walked into the middle of the Circle, everybody clapped.

"How strange is that? I am twenty-six, unmarried and a talkative Teddy Bear calls me 'Grandfather'. I am sitting in a barn with my forty-year-old son-in-law and my twelve-year-old granddaughter, however, thanks to the amazing events that are happening to all of us, nothing here seems unbelievable but all very, very sensible, not unusual at all! So odd!

"My name is Samuel Regan. After I had got my degree at Cambridge, I went back to live at home with my parents, in the Crooked Cottage. I am writing my first book. I think I must now write about all the things I have seen and heard tonight! It's true, I was very mad with Archie for letting beautiful Mimi, Jemimah, ride off on the wild Bullet. Mistakenly I thought that they were racing over the hills and up on to the Clappers. I only learnt that he was trying to stop her, after Déjà Vu and we lived in another Circle. I remember the Accident and how sad and how cross I was that Jemimah changed so much because she felt Colin's tragic injuries were her fault; as well as Fred's injuries and Bullet's death: which they were of course. It's funny how I never blamed her. So many things happened that day and I'm cross with myself that I didn't listen to any of that, which my friend, Archie, had to say! I also remember being very angry with Edmund for marrying Jemimah. She was so young, only seventeen. He was an Explorer

and left her alone so much. I loved listening to her, while she played the piano in her little shop, the Pretty Posy. Somehow though, she always seemed so sad. I remember thinking that if she hadn't had the Accident, then she wouldn't have married Edmund. How wrong I was! In the next Orbit, there was no accident and I didn't fall out with

361

Archie, we stayed the best of friends but Mimi still fell in love and married Edmund. I tried again to stop Edmund from marrying her but how could I stop the course of true love? The Accident didn't happen but still Jemimah suffered when Edmund was lost at sea: so much so that Amelia went into the Workhouse, anyway.

"The first time I was involved with the fire, my friend Fred had come banging on the door to tell us that the Workhouse was on fire and they needed Father's long ladder. The children were trapped in an upstairs dormitory. I remember I was in bed asleep. I quickly got dressed and ran with him and got the ladder from behind the shed and we ran as fast as we could up the hill. It was pretty hard going and we were so mortified that we were too late. All the children died, even Amelia Plate, Mimi's little girl."

Grandfather paused at this point. Everybody thought that he might burst into tears. He didn't but his voice became much softer as he continued,

"Can you imagine how cross I was....that I had bothered to stop and get dressed? Minutes count when it comes to fires. I thought that it was my fault that little Amelia had died. If I had just come straight out of the cottage with my pyjamas on, what would that have mattered? I could have thrown my coat on, if need be but I didn't. I stopped and got dressed....how stupid was that? I even cleaned my teeth!

"I'm so happy that I have had another chance to do things better.... properly. Thanks to the Gift of Déjà Vu, I was able to come straight out of the cottage with Fred, tonight and we ran up the hill and all the children were saved! I thought when I opened the cottage door to Fred that 'I had been here before' and I had! Look!" said Grandfather, opening his overcoat. "Pyjamas!" he sat down; everyone laughed and applauded.

"Well, I never!" said Ethelred-Ted, as he walked back into the middle of the Circle, again, clapping loudly. He then turned to Father.

"Our last story comes from Father. Get here now, then!" he laughed.

Father stood up and walked into the middle of the Circle.

"Hi, my name is Philip Garador. I am an American living in England during the Second World War in 1942. I'm married to Sarah Regan, Sam's daughter and Joni-Philipa is my daughter," he gestured towards Joni-Pip, who was now cuddling a sleepy Amelia, as she leant on her shoulder.

"I had two very good reasons, for wanting to come here tonight. James has already explained one. Mine was to save my daughter, Joni-Philipa. It's funny how being in any Pasture you remember all the other things that have happened to you in past Orbits. We had already jumped over The Wall of Time, illegally, as Poppy told you. We don't know how we managed to do that with Ethelred-Ted's Formula Board, as they were already in an opened Circle with it but nevertheless, we did. We had come

362

to try and save the children, though. For me, the horror of it was that I carried out my own little girl's body! I couldn't believe it. It was then that I realised that was why they had been given the Formula Board: they had come to save someone. Only I knew that something had gone horribly wrong. The awful thing for me was that knowing everything, being in a Pasture, I remembered that Joni-Philipa had had an accident in Marley's Barn and had fallen and died in 1942: in a previous Circle, of course.

"I'm told that my wife, Sarah, never recovered from that tragedy. So at the Turning of the KOL for Joni-Philipa, she had another chance and she didn't die. It was wonderful! Carrying Joni-Philipa's lifeless body from the Work-house Fire, however, all I could think of was, 'Does this mean that it is impossible to cheat Death? Will Joni-Philipa have to die at age twelve, no matter what we try to do to save her?' I jumped back over The Wall of Time to Knotty Knook and tried to warn Joni-Philipa and her friends. When she went missing, well, James explained all of that, so I won't go over it again....I just want to say, 'Thank you so much' all of you. Every one has had a part in tonight's drama. I suppose the person I should thank most, is Ethelred-Ted. I can't believe that we've been given her back again but I think that he should tell us his amazing story, Friends, don't you?"

Everybody clapped Father as he sat down.

"Just a minute, Phil," said Fred Finn, from across the Barn, "James....my son....said you saw something amazing just before you jumped over the Wall of Time with Ethelred-Ted, the second time. What was that?"

Father stood up again and shook his head and shrugged as he told them.

"Yes, it sure was something! Another Wall of Time appeared at the Ruin and another Ethelred-Ted jumped over and landed, just as we made our jump and disappeared over our Wall of Time!"

"Cripes, that sounds a lot to understand!" said Fred Finn.

Everybody looked puzzled. Ethelred-Ted said nothing. Father sat back down and everybody clapped. Ethelred-Ted stood up and said seriously,

"What I have found out and I hope it will be a warning to all of you, is that if you 'borrow' the F.B. and use it illegally, you can JIT, as James and Father did, even though you might be crossing over another Orbit in an opened Circle but you have to pay for this illegal action by going into the Keep of Bad Memories: which Father will tell you, is a pretty awful experience! The most horrible part, is that when you go in there, no matter what you see, hear or feel, you have to stay. If you curl up in a ball, cry out in fear or try to run away, then you are stuck in there with no way out!"

"It was dreadful," Father shuddered, "so unspeakable I can't even talk about it. It was the worst experience of my life. I felt I was living through some terrible nightmare, which got worse and worse and more and more ghastly. The images in my head got more and more grisly; with no escape!

"Well be warned, don't use the F.B., without permission! If you do, you will so regret it, even if your intentions are to help somebody. At least I am glad, I have learned my lesson and I will never do it again and soon, when this Pasture is over, I will forget all those horrible, hideous visions!"

A hush wrapped itself over them as they watched Father slowly sit down.

"Come on, Ethelred-Ted!" urged Archimedes, relieving the tension in the Barn. "Come in the Circle and tell us your story now?"

Ethelred-Ted seemed rather subdued as he entered the Ring for the last time. He just stood silently for a moment and looked down.

"Father is brave to confess his wrongdoing. I'm not so sure that I want to confess my actions, though," he paused. "To feel responsible for a friend's death once, is pretty awful but to feel it twice well, it's almost unbearable."

Everyone looked puzzled.

"Poppy said that she blamed herself for Joni-Pip's accident but I did and I carried that guilt for sixty five years in Joni-Pip's First Circle."

Joni-Pip looked up at him, surprised.

"So, when it happened again, I had to do something! After jumping over The Wall of Time, we landed in the Children's Dormitory. The fire was raging and to our horror we realised that we were locked in with the children, with no obvious way of getting out. I suddenly thought that I knew a way of escaping! I left Hetty and Joni-Pip in the Children's Dormitory and jumped back over the Wall of Time. I couldn't believe my good fortune when the very person I thought that I would have to hunt down came tearing out of the bushes. I asked him if he could help save the children and he said that he had already told me that he couldn't. He hated children! I didn't remember him saying that but he marched off, so I followed him and was amazed to discover that he lived in a lovely apartment under the ground in the Old Mine up on the Clappers. We had tea, buns and biscuits and then he showed me a Wonder! He took me into a massive cavern and showed me something so astounding, I couldn't believe my eyes. I was sworn to secrecy but You Lot will forget when this Premium Pasture is over. I'll tell you what it is, if you haven't guessed!"

Everybody looked puzzled and shook their heads, so Eth continued.

"Nuttingham Squirrel explained to me that it all began when an unfortunate incident occurred, in the time of Robin Hood and His Merry Men; right here, in Sherwood Forest. This was during the time when his Band of Jovial Outlaws were the ones who walked through the woodland pathways of Nottingham Forest, the pathways that all of us here, so love. One day, when they had three special visitors staying with them, they were having shooting practice and one of their guests wanted to have a go. Unhappily, the visitor was a very bad marksman and the arrow shot straight up into a tree. Immediately, a squirrel dropped down like a stone in a pond and landed at Robin's feet with an arrow sticking in him!"

All of them burst out laughing. Eth ignored them and pressed on,

"The unfortunate squirrel was half-dead. The Merry Band of Outlaws helped nurse him back to good health, including Robin Hood himself. The injured squirrel's family were so grateful to Robin Hood and his Merry Men for looking after the Patient they declared that from that day forth, they would take it upon themselves to look after the forest. They became the Official Guardians of the Forest: known as OGOFS; which they have been for hundreds of years, long before this area was mined. In their search for a fitting Head Quarters, the OGOFS discovered and took over, a huge natural cavern. So since the Days of Yore, the OGOFS have cleared up everything that people have dropped or left in the forest. No matter how small or insignificant it might be, they catalogue it, recording the time, day and date it was found and detailing what it is. Nuttingham Squirrel showed me into this Aladdin's Cave: only of course it was A Squirrel's Cave! The OGOFS Cavern is called The Great Store! The news of this soon spread over the length and breadth of this Island. It wasn't long before squirrels from all over the land decided to join the OGOFS in their mission, as Guardians of the Forests. It was then decided that every year, on OGOF

Day, contingents of squirrels from every forest would trek hazardous journeys, sometimes many hundreds of miles, from the four corners of Great Britain, carrying everything that they had found to be added to the Great Store!" this last statement made everybody raise their eyebrows.

"I have never seen anything like it....ever," Ethelred-Ted continued, "it looked like a Museum with lots of different sections and rooms with stands and display cases. It was stupendous!" He said, re-living the wonder of it.

Poppy-Plump-Pij leaned over to Joni-Pip and whispered,

"I feel so horrible I was meanful to Nuttingham Squirrel and flapped my wings in his face. We've never understood what he was up to when he collected things, have we? I feel so sad at the way we treated this noble squirrel. We didn't really give him a chance, did we? I feel awfulful!"

"I feel so bad as well, especially about Jack's telephone!" Joni-Pip grimaced. "What makes me feel worse, is that he's never, ever, breathed a word of this truly astonishing work he does. P'raps he is abrupt because he carries this amazing secret heavily on his heart, not being able to tell anyone the importance of what he does, not being able to share the wonder of his commission." Both Poppy and Joni-Pip half-smiled at each other.

"Squirrels from all the other forests would bring treasures, to be safely stored in the OGOFS Cavern," continued Ethelred-Ted. "There were long benches covered in all manner of things: shells, beads, pen-knives, toffee papers, mint wrappers, bags, purses, combs: so many combs: why do people use combs in a forest, I ask you? Everything was put in sections and beautifully labelled. There was an amazing collection of fountain pens; all different colours, shapes and sizes. There were crayons and pencils and collar studs and cuff links and necklaces and bracelets and watches: so many beautiful watches, some were gold....yes...and the gold rings! So many of them: plain rings, carved rings, engraved rings, diamond rings, ruby rings, sapphire rings, emerald rings. Then there were the coins! So many coins! There were pennies and half-pennies and Roman coins and crowns and half-crowns and shillings and three-penny-bits and sixpences and guineas.....the Great Store is indeed a Cavern of Treasure! Truly, a place to be guarded! My eyes could hardly take it all in! On the walls of the cavern were loads of hooks and on the loads of hooks, hung all kinds, of all sorts. There were rows and rows of different tools....yes tools, can you believe....as well as screws and nails and nuts and of course keys: big keys, little keys, rusty keys, shiny keys and bunches of keys. This, of course, was what I had come for....the keys....to....”

Joni-Pip suddenly jumped up, startling little Amelia.

“Sorry, Amelia,” she said, settling her back down again, by pushing her gently, so that she leant on her Uncle Archie. Eth stopped talking and everybody stared at Joni-Pip, as she marched purposefully towards him.

“You’re not Ethelred-Ted! You’re a fraud!” everybody gasped. “I knew something was wrong when you said about living sixty five years with the guilt of my accident. Caught you! Who are you? You most definitely are not Ethelred-Ted and I can prove it. Ethelred-Ted hasn’t lived through those sixty five years yet....he comes from 1942....and....” she said lifting up his arm, “where are your stitches on your poorly arm? See, there is nothing! You have a perfect arm, absolutely stitch-free. I know I am pretty good at sewing but I haven’t yet mastered the art of **invisible stitches**! You tore your arm outside the Pretty Posy in Edwinstowe and I sewed you up, only a little while ago! So what have you got to say for yourself?”

Everybody looked expectantly at the ‘guilty-looking-found-out-Bear’.

“Sorry Joni-Pip. Sorry everybody. I thought that I might, just might get away with it, if only to save my name, Ethelred-Ted’s name. I was confessing after all. I did say that I was responsible for Joni-Pip’s death, twice, don’t you remember?” he asked.

“Yes!” said almost everybody; the rest just nodded their heads.

Everyone then turned and looked as a strange figure ran into the barn.

Chapter 36

The Keep of Good Memories Re-visited

"I just hope it wasn't as hopeless as it looked, Father."

"Listen, Sweetheart, there was nothing we could have done. It might, just might not have been as bad as it seemed. Let's concentrate on this now, shall we? It has to be done."

Joni-Pip and Father stood in the middle of the large circular room, beams of different coloured light shone through the many tiny windows, which embroidered the walls. The shafts, in blues, yellows, reds, greens and

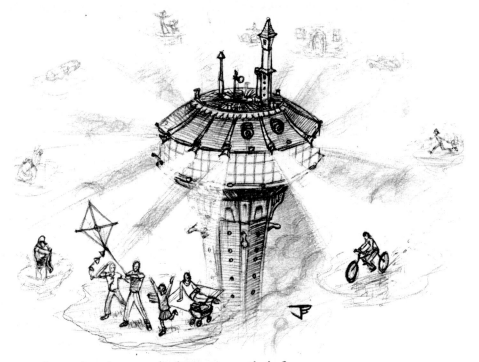

purples, painted pretty shadows across their faces.

"I don't understand, Father, I thought we only go into the KOL alone."

"That's true, Honey but as this is still a special part of your Premium Pasture, you're allowed one person to come with you in the Keep of Good Memories, the KOGM, that's why I'm here. It's called your After Pasture or AP. Don't ask me how I know because that I don't know: I just know!"

" 'After Pasture of my Premium Pasture'? That sounds spiffing. I'm happy that you're with me but I did enjoy it, being here on my own before. I wasn't afraid or anything. Is there a reason why you're with me? Is that what you mean by 'special'?" Joni-Pip asked, walking over to one of the little windows in the large, round room.

"Yes, Honey, there is a reason why and it is special, very special."

"Oh, look, Father; we're all flying kites on Dunstable Downs! Do you remember that? Look! There's Alex and me and you and Becky-Paige!" Joni-Pip cried excitedly. "Where's Mother? I'm sure she was with us. Oh, how I loved it there! We haven't been since this silly War began. We would watch the gliders taking off and landing down the hill. Look at the kites! I think everybody used to come and fly their kites here, don't you? Where's Mother, I can't see her?"

Father walked over to join her by the little window and said earnestly,

"Honey, I want you to listen to me. I need you to listen to me. Please?"

"It was so lovely feeling the breeze on my face, up on those Downs and hearing the kites flapping in the wind, I was only eight last time we did it but it seems like only yesterday, I'll never forget that feeling!"

Father took his daughter gently by the hand and steered her away from the windows, into the middle of the Keep.

"Joni-Philipa, you must listen to me!"

Joni-Pip look startled. She didn't want to be serious. She loved it up here in the Keep of Good Memories.

"Don't spoil it, please?" she begged. "This must be my favourite place in all the world. After all, Father, it is the Keep of **Good** Memories, isn't it? So there can't be anything **bad** up here, can there?"

Father put his arm around her, hugged her and said gently,

"No, Honey, there are no bad memories while we stay in here: none at all but I'm here for a reason. Let me explain what that reason is. O.K.?"

"You are scaring me now, Father. Am I not going to like this?" Joni-Pip asked tentatively.

"Of course you will like it....you will love it....now listen. When anybody jumps over the Wall of Time, something is always changed. There are what are called 'knock on effects' they are known as KOES. What is the purpose of the Gift of Déjà Vu? Do you remember?" he asked, putting his head on one side.

"Yes, Poppy explains it beautifully, she says....we jump back in Time to make a Bad Past into a Better Future! Or in her words....we JIT to make a BP into a BF," said Joni-Pip smiling.

"Sure! In the process though, things change. For example, Archimedes and Grandfather remained good friends after Poppy saved Bullet and the others, whereas in the Circle before, they didn't speak for years, did they?

369

So that was a change. Yes?" Father asked, raising his eyebrows.

"Yes. What are you saying? Have lots of things changed in my life, now that I have been given the Gift of Déjà Vu?" she asked casually.

"Yes."

"What? What has changed, Father?" she asked anxiously.

"That's why we come here, into the Keep. This is another, very special part of the KOL. There are things that have happened to you that you don't remember and there are other little windows here, so you can experience them for the first time. Let me explain. When you JITTED and saved Bullet, you changed many things. Jemimah Plate for example, she wasn't quite so frail. Then you saved Amelia Plate, didn't you? So, she would have grown up into a woman. There might have been things that you did with Amelia Plate, say for example when you were eight, she would have been in her fifties then. Let's see, she might have taken over the shop, The Pretty Posy from her mother Jemimah, so you might have gone in and bought something and she might have played a tune for you on her piano, as her mother did and that may have made a beautiful memory for you."

Suddenly, Joni-Pip felt herself looking into the Pretty Posy and she saw a beautiful woman playing the piano and a soldier was sitting listening.

"Yes, yes, Father, I have seen that before....no, no, I haven't.....or have I? I can see it right now in my head....I definitely can see a lovely lady at the piano but she isn't playing for me, it is for a soldier....who on earth are they? Do you know Father? The music is so enchanting! I really have experienced this before!"

"Honey, I have no idea. When did you see them before? When did you hear the music?"

"I was looking through the planks into the Pretty Posy, in Edwinstowe one day and there they were, it was misty but unmistakeable....a beautiful woman and an admiring soldier. They are still there in my head, can't you hear the music?"

"No, Honey, that's so strange but anything can happen in here."

The pianist and the soldier then disappeared.

"They've gone. That sure is weird: very odd, Father. What on earth was that all about?"

"I haven't a clue. You've stumped me, Honey. All I know is, one day all will be revealed to you: these things always are eventually understood. I am sure there is some logical explanation for it...." Father paused thoughtfully and then said cheerfully, "Let's get back to you, though. Just supposing Amelia did play the piano in the Pretty Posy for you, when you were eight; well, you are twelve now, so that memory has to be put in your head and your heart, as you haven't actually experienced it yet, have you,

370

even though it happened!"

"Hmmm, I think I understand what you're saying: you have to fill in my heart and mind the memories I have never actually gone through, although when I get back home they will be there, as the Past has been changed."

"Sure, so I want to go through a few new memories with you, Honey. Are you ready? Is that clear? Do you understand?"

"I think so."

"Don't worry, Sweetheart, everything is going to be fine!" reassured Father, holding her tightly. "It's going to be so neat!"

He took his daughter by the hand and walked over to the Archway Joni-Pip had gone through before. They walked up the steps and instead of jumping into the Pool of Colours, Father turned to the other side and there was a door, Joni-Pip hadn't seen it before. He opened it and they walked through together and up a flight of stairs. Then they heard a soft, rushing, humming sound, similar to a Spinning Top. Joni-Pip felt wonderful.

"This is another Observatory, in the Keep of Good Memories. We've now entered the Observatory of Memories Unknown, the OOMU. These windows point to unknown memories. Things that you have experienced in your next Circle but you don't remember yet. I'll go through some of them with you. The rest you'll encounter yourself," Father said as they entered into another huge, circular room with loads of little star-shaped windows.

Joni-Pip walked over to one and peered through it. There she was, with Becky-Paige, Father and Alex, flying kites on Dunstable Downs.

"Father here we are again! I've just seen this and I remember it so well!"

As she said this, she heard a baby cry. She turned and looked further through the window and on the grass behind them, was Mother sitting on a blanket with a tiny baby in her arms.

"Do you know who that is, Joni-Philipa?" Father asked very quietly.

Joni-Pip suddenly had these wonderful thoughts running through her head. She remembered Mother telling them that she was going to have another little baby and she remembered Mother getting a big tummy and she remembered helping to get the nursery ready for the new baby.

"Elle-Sahara, Father! My Baby sister is called....Elle-Sahara! Isn't she just the cutest baby? Just look at her, Father!" Joni-Pip couldn't stop telling her Father all about the new baby, as if he didn't know her!

For a few minutes Joni-Pip began to have her mind filled with wonderful memories; memories that she hadn't experienced but now she was being given them because of the Turning of the KOL. How exciting it was in the OOMU!

"I'm going to tell you something else. You weren't born when it happened, so I can't show you. Your Grandmother, Grandfather's wife, was a very frail person and as you know, she died in the Spanish 'Flu Epidemic of 1918/19. Well, your Grandfather's friend, Fred Finn, decided to go to Medical School instead of carrying on being a Farmer. He started studying later in life but eventually he qualified and became a great doctor. Colin Finn grew up and became the new Farmer Finn and guess who he married?" asked Father.

"Jem....no....she would be too old I think....it must have been Amelia?"

"That's right, Honey! Well done! Anyway, when your Grandmother died in the first Circle; Mother was only sixteen. She took it very badly. One of the effects of her grief was that it made her hair go coarse and curly. She had always had shiny, straight hair. Well, when everything was changed, after the Workhouse Fire and Fred became a doctor: he nursed Grandmother night and day and she recovered from the Spanish 'Flu. I want you to look through this window," said Father, pointing to a bigger window, straight in front of them.

Joni-Pip looked in eagerly and there she was, holding the hand of a woman. They were looking at paintings in an old Curiosity Shop. She could hear the woman speaking to her.

"My Darling, Joni-Philipa, which one shall we have? You choose!"

"Oh, Grandmother, I love this one!" she heard herself say and suddenly she remembered being there. It was in York; in the area known as the Shambles, where there were lots of lovely shops. How she loved her grandmother! She had all these thoughts running through and round and round in her mind. Beautiful thoughts about her grandmother! Unknown memories were becoming known to her: instantly!

Father held her as she watched and experienced sounds, senses and sights that just thrilled her! There were so many wonderful days she spent with Grandmother and Grandfather at the Crooked Cottage, up in the Woods, in Bath, at the Seaside, by the River: they just went on and on.

"It made life so much easier and so much nicer for Mother having Grandmother, her own mother, around when you children were born. That's why we wanted another baby. Grand-mother loved babies, too and she helped Mother so much," said Father gently.

Joni-Pip put her arms around her father, hugged him and whispered,

"This sure has been marvellous, Father! Thank you so, for coming with me! I can't wait to get home now!"

"Are you ready then, Honey?"

"Yes please!"

They walked out through another door and left the OOMU. There was the stairway they had climbed up together, they walked back down it, held hands and jumped into the Pool of Colours.

Chapter 37

New, New Life

"What time is it, Father?" asked Joni-Pip, walking up the garden path. Father held up his wrist, then looked at his watch.

"Six after three," he replied. "No noise, remember Honey?"

"I remember!" mouthed Joni-Pip. Father laughed and pretended to give her a clip round the ear. "It's as though I've been away for a life time," she whispered.

"I know what you mean," agreed Father, opening the porch door and walking in.

They sat on the bench, took off their shoes and leaned up against the wall, Joni-Pip noticed how different she felt this time she entered Knotty Knook. Father opened the door, took off his jacket, hung it on the hall stand and walked into the kitchen. Joni-Pip followed. He switched on the light and went and filled the kettle at the sink.

"Fancy a cup of tea, Honey?" he asked, putting the kettle on the kitchen range.

"Yes, please, Father," replied Joni-Pip in a whisper. She walked over to the painting on the wall and felt excited. "Isn't Grandmother good for letting me choose this? I love the sea and the beach. I love this painting. I find it hard to believe I didn't recognise it before but of course, that was impossible. I hadn't been in the OOMU!"

Joni-Pip studied the painting, which had once sent shivers of fear up her spine.

"Haven't we been here, Father?" she asked him, pointing to the painting.

"Sure, it looks exactly like the beach near Auntie Sylvia's and Uncle Richard's house, remember?" replied Father, taking out the teapot and tea caddy and spooning in the tea leaves. "That's why you said you wanted it so much."

"Who on earth are Auntie Sylvia and Uncle Richard?" asked Joni-Pip puzzled.

"We obviously didn't stay in the OOMU long enough! When you meet them, you'll remember them. Sylvia is Mother's younger sister and she has two sons. Don't tell me you don't remember them? They have two cats, Cinders and Candy."

"Nope!" she replied frowning; then she thought, 'Boy cousins? I don't think so!'

"You'll soon know them. You're spending most of your Summer Holidays by the sea!" said Father, pouring both of them a cup of tea through a tea strainer. When he had finished, he settled himself down in the armchair by the range and sipped his fresh cup of tea. "I am so English, don't you know?" he laughed.

"Can't wait to spend time there: is it so different from the life in the wood?"

"The life by the sea? Of course it's different but it'll be wonderful! There's plenty to do there. Come and sit down and drink your tea before it gets cold."

"Thanks," she said sipping her tea, "there is nothing as good as this!"

After enjoying their tea, the two of them walked up the stairs arm in arm.

"I must just do something, Father," Joni-Pip whispered and walked, across the landing to Becky-Paige's bedroom. The door was slightly ajar, she tip-toed in and there, lying fast asleep, cuddling her toy puppy, Puppalove, was her little sister. The light from the landing shone across the masses of dark curls that lay stretched across her white pillow case. Joni-Pip leant over her and kissed her gently on the cheek.

"Sleep well, My Becky-Paige," she whispered, "see you in the morning!"

Becky-Paige stirred and turned over. Joni-Pip smiled and just looked at her for a while. She turned to leave the room and drew in her breath. Sleeping in a bed next to Becky-Paige's, was a small, sweet soul. Her heart became filled with love. She was a pretty little girl with no dark curls, just straight, brown, shiny hair. Joni-Pip couldn't help but let out a little cry as she was cosily cuddling a certain familiar Rag Doll.

'Celeste!' she thought. 'What the? How? When? It can't be! Is it? Yes it is! How come? I'm sure she's happy now, being loved by a beautiful little girl and I'm glad but I wonder what on earth is my new baby sister doing with Amelia Plate's doll?

The small sleeper stirred as Joni-Pip pulled her covers up and leaned over and planted a kiss on her little cheek, which was rosy from sleep. Two little, soft, plump arms came out from under the covers and wrapped themselves around Joni-Pip's neck.

"Ni-night, Doni," whispered a little voice, "I miss you tonight," she kissed Joni-Pip softly on the cheek and went back to sleep, Joni-Pip didn't want to let her go.

"Honey, you must get to bed. There's a party for all the family tomorrow. You'll be too tired to enjoy it. Your cousins are coming. You girls painted a special picture for it but it's not quite finished. You'll can do it in the morning," whispered Father.

374

Reluctantly, Joni-Pip pulled her little sister's arms away from around her neck and tucked them back under the covers; a large tear rolled down her face.

"Ni-night, My Darling, Elle-Sahara, 'Doni' will meet you in the morning!"

"Come on, Sweetheart, you must get to bed!" urged Father from the door.

"All right, Father," Joni-Pip replied, "but do you mind if I just go and get a glass of water from the kitchen?"

He smiled and went into his room.

Very quietly, Joni-Pip went down the stairs and opened the door into the kitchen. As she walked over to the dresser to pick up a glass tumbler, she heard a rustling sound coming from behind her. She turned, expecting to see that Father had followed her down but the place was empty. Surprised, she turned back to the dresser. The rustling came again.

She spun round and nobody was there. She decided to stay looking behind her and sure enough the rustling came once more, only she realised it was coming from outside the kitchen window. The rustling sound got louder, so she decided to investigate.

"What on earth is that noise?" Joni-Pip said to herself as she walked through the porch towards the back door.

She opened the back door and was just about to step outside when a black hooded silhouette passed in front of the Moon and a shadowy figure ran speedily up the Log and Chain Path and disappeared under the cover of Windy Woods.

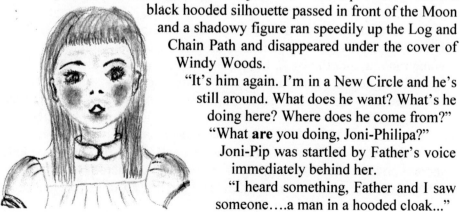

"It's him again. I'm in a New Circle and he's still around. What does he want? What's he doing here? Where does he come from?"

"What **are** you doing, Joni-Philipa?"

Joni-Pip was startled by Father's voice immediately behind her.

"I heard something, Father and I saw someone....a man in a hooded cloak..."

"Come on, Honey," said Father, ushering Joni-Pip back into the cottage and locking the door behind her. He straightened the Blackout Blind on the window of the door and then lifted it up, casting an odd look up the hill towards the trees of Windy Woods. "Anyway, Sweetheart, how do you know it was a man? If the figure was wearing a hood, it could have been a woman. Now to bed, Young Lady, or you'll be fit for nothing tomorrow!"

Joni-Pip couldn't sleep, so many wonderful and bewildering things were running around, inside her head. She couldn't wait to meet up with her friends in the morning to discuss all the astounding events of that day but she knew she had other things to do first. Firstly the Painting for the Family Party had to be finished. That sounded so nice! She kept thinking how her life had changed so dramatically since the After Pasture. It then occurred to her that the New Circle was still open because she remembered everything. She chuckled to herself because she knew why it hadn't closed.

She lay in her bed with the curtains open, looking up at Windy Woods, wondering about the mysterious hooded figure she kept seeing. The moon was still shining brightly through the trees. It was a strange but astonishing feeling, too, knowing that because of so many remarkable events, she was going to meet new people later on that day: people she had never actually met before in her First Circle but they would be friends and relations whom she would automatically bond with and memories would fill her mind about the times she had spent with them, in this new Orbit. She wasn't quite aware how many Circles it had been since her First but that didn't matter to her, she was so thrilled at the prospect of meeting them all.

One startling detail Joni-Pip had learnt in the Workhouse Barn, was that she had lost her Life again, as Father had warned. She could remember choking in the smoke, Ethelred-Ted abandoning them and Poppy being nowhere around. She also remembered banging on the windows with Hetty. The Wall of Time had gone. Everything had then gone black.

After she had accused 'Ethelred-Ted' of being a fraud, everything had then been explained to her; how her Life had been restored again. She remembered how confounded she was when a certain familiar figure had come running into the Barn. Laying on her bed, enjoying the beauty of the Moonlit night, she gazed at the stars. At first there only seemed a few but the more she looked, the more she saw; there were masses of them, millions of them, twinkling, flickering and some just shining brightly.

"What are you trying to tell me?" she whispered out loud. "I know there is something up there, some special secret in all those sparkly stars. I know there is an answer for that's going on down here, up there! Please tell?"

She fixed her eyes on those bright, night lights, awaiting a response and promptly fell into a peaceful, deep sleep.

Chapter 38

Reunion

"Joni-Philipa, Joni-Philipa, wake up quickly!"

Twelve-year-old eyelids stirred.

"Honey, please wake up!"

Her heavy eyes slowly opened and in the dim light they saw Father leaning over the bed holding a breakfast tray in his hands. Joni-Pip slowly lifted her head and blearily, she could just see two little figures standing either side of him.

"Wake up, Phiapa, please? We have been waiting ages for you to get up but Father said you needed to sleep longer, this morning," said Becky-Paige.

Joni-Pip sat up and held out both of her arms. Becky-Paige leaned over and hugged her. The other little figure then started to climb up on to the bed but she wasn't quite big enough to do it on her own. Father put down the tray and lifted her up and placed her beside Joni-Pip. Becky-Paige promptly climbed up on to the bed and sat herself down on the other side of her. Joni-Pip lovingly put her arms around both of her little sisters and kissed them both on the tops of their heads.

"My!" she said. "We make a special 'Sister Sandwich', don't we? We are a Becky-Paige, Elle-Sahara and Joni-Philipa sandwich!"

"I not a sandwich, Doni, I just a lickle girl," Elle-Sahara said huskily.

Joni-Pip looked at her and hugged her. Her heart was bursting with love.

"You are not just a little girl, Elle-Sahara; you my wonderful little sister and I love you so much," she said holding her closely. "I love you so much too, Becky-Paige!"

"Phiapa, why do you call me 'Becky-Paige'?"

"I like it! I like to be called Joni-Pip, too, so please call me it....all of you?"

"Joni-Pip, eh?" laughed Father. "I don't know if I can get used to that! Now get on with your breakfast, Young Lady, there's so much to be done!"

"What's going on in here?" came a familiar voice from the doorway. "Why all the laughing? Is everything all right?" Joni-Pip looked over to the door and saw her beautiful, sleek haired mother standing there.

"Mother, everything is just wonderful! You have no idea!"

Everybody looked at her and smiled. Joni-Pip unwrapped her arms gently from around her two little sisters, got out of bed and ran over and gave Mother the longest, tightest huggerly she could remember. Mother kissed her oldest daughter warmly.

"Mother, why did you give all your daughters two names, as their first name?"

"Simple. My name is Sarah Joan but I never ever get to be called Joan. I just write it when I fill out forms and it was read out when I got married. What's the point of that? It doesn't make sense having an unspoken name. I made sure all my girls used both the names they were given by simply putting a hyphen between them. Simple, as I said but very, very effective! We only gave Alexander one and we shorten that!"

"Hey, what's going on in here? Am I missing something?"

Alex appeared in the doorway. Joni-Pip walked to him and gave him a huge hug.

"J.P., are you all right?" he asked, returning the hug, equally strongly.

"Oh, Alex, it's so lovely to see you again, it seems ages...."

"I think you should come and eat your breakfast, right now, Honey," said Father.

"Yeah, p'raps you should, J.P.," said Alex gently. "Put your dressing gown on so you won't get cold," he unhooked it from off the door, with his arm still round her.

Alex then helped her put on his old, tatty but well-loved dressing gown. Joni-Pip pulled herself slightly away from her big brother and looked into his eyes.

'Does he know anything?' she thought to herself.

He smiled down at her and then tousled her hair.

"Go and eat your breakfast, like a good girl," he said softly.

"It's so dark in here. I must open the curtains," said Mother, walking over to the window and pulling back Joni-Pip's familiar, red check curtains.

"I did that," said Father. "I crept in earlier and the sun was streaming in. It was so bright. I thought....Joni-Pip....could do with a bit more sleep, so I closed them."

"We must get on," said Mother looking up the hill, "We're expected at the Crooked Cottage for the party at three o'clock and it's ten o' clock already! Mrs Broft has been complaining that somebody has helped themselves to lots of the party food. A whole American Cream Pie has gone wandering as well as other deserts! I knew it couldn't be any of you, Darlings because you are so looking forward to the party and you wouldn't want to spoil it. I said it was possibly a passing Tramp who was a bit hungry. Mrs Broft was not amused and not impressed. Poor Darling....oh well, whoever it was, I hope they enjoyed it!" ((Believe me, he did!))

It was such a lovely feeling for Joni-Pip being with them all. It didn't seem strange at all that she had only known Elle-Sahara for but a moment. She looked at each in turn and thought how wonderful they were. Everything was just spiffing! The whole of that morning would prove to be excellent too and the rest of the day.

Joni-Pip finished painting the picture with her two little sisters. It was a real team effort and despite Alex constantly interfering, by throwing thick brightly coloured paint balls all over them and the paper, they finally completed it. He felt that the occasional red, yellow, blue, pink or green splodge, added to the brilliance of the work.

As the Painting was a combination of Becky-Paige's, Elle-Sahara's and Joni-Pip's artistic talents, coupled with their big brother's pretty missiles, it turned out to be a rather unusual nightscape-cum-abstract. It had started out to be 'The Clappers', 'a very green and visual representation of the Nottinghamshire Countryside'. However, the end result was more like 'Clapham Common on Firework Night'. Oh, well.

"What shall we call it?" asked Joni-Pip.

"Do pictures have names, then?" asked Becky-Paige.

"Do pictures have names?" repeated Alex. "Do trains run on rails? Of course they do! How would you like it if we just called you 'Girl', R.P.?"

"Hmmm, I suppose so," replied Becky-Paige.

"Alex, how about you calling Rebekah-Paige, B.P. now? I call her Becky-Paige, it really suits her!" laughed Joni-Pip.

"B.P.? That sounds like a British Petroleum Company or a Boy Scout!" Alex laughed.

"Twinkle, twinkle, little star!" said Elle-Sahara, looking at the painting.

Alex and Joni-Pip looked at her and then at the Painting.

"Stars!" they repeated and then said together, "Perfect!" and both burst out laughing. Alex shook his head and wrote the title of the Painting in the right hand corner, then looked at Joni-Pip for her approval.

"Isn't this even better than just 'Stars'?"

"Spiffing!" said Joni-Pip, after reading the new Title.

The finished Masterpiece was hung up to dry by being pegged to Mrs Broft's clothes horse and placed very close to the open range in the kitchen. Joni-Pip did worry slightly that it might catch fire, so Mrs Broft and Alex moved it back away a bit. As they were doing so, Alex playfully pushed the clothes horse over, so that the picture nearly landed in the fire, itself. Joni-Pip and the girls looked on in horror. He then quickly pulled it upright, grinning cheekily at all of them.

Father and Mother were then summoned to inspect the morning's work.

They looked at the Painting closely, very closely.

"It's very, very...." Mother started.

"Different!" finished Father. The Girls looked disappointed in their parents' response to their amazing artistic strokes.

"Wonderfully different!" exclaimed Mother. "It's so....so...."

"Colourful!" finished Father. "I think we most definitely have three budding young Picasso's in our midst."

"Picasso?" questioned Becky-Paige.

"An artist of exceptional talents," replied Father.

"So, is it good? Do you like it?" asked Joni-Pip.

"Yes, very much," answered Mother.

"I hope you like my contrived contributions," quipped Alex, "I think they have somewhat added to the vibrance, giving it a Festive Feel, don't you?"

"So you had a hand in this then, Alex?" questioned Father.

"Yes, he chucked in the splodges and the splatterings," Joni-Pip replied.

"I think they've added to the sense of occasion, they have given it a sense of....'Carnivality'...." Alex said, rather seriously.

Mother and Father both looked at him and shook their heads.

"Alex!" they said together.

"What?

"You are a naughty boy and you know it!" they both said together.

"Oh well," said Joni-Pip, "at least Grandfather will know that it is from all of us!" then she added, "No matter how bad it looks!"

Everybody looked puzzled.

As they were making their way across Windy Woods to Grandfather's Crooked Cottage, Joni-Pip kept feeling this amazing sense of elation. Walking along, they all clutched something to take for the party. Before they had left, Father and Alex had gone into the shed and made a very nice but rather plain frame for the Painting. Father then wrapped it up in brown paper and string, so that Alex could carry it easily up and over the hill. Mother was carrying a tin of sausage rolls and a tin of cheese straws in a deep shopping bag. Mrs Broft had freshly baked these that morning. Joni-Pip was carrying a bowl of red jelly in a canvas bag. The girls had had great pleasure helping Mrs Broft make that. They used bottled strawberries and gelatine powder. Father carried a couple of collapsible wooden chairs. Becky-Paige carried a wrapped up bundle for Pass the Parcel and Elle-Sahara carried a bag of paper hats, which they had all made together out of old newspapers a few days before.

When they got to the top of the hill, Joni-Pip saw Poppy sitting on the bridge over the stream. Her thoughts had been far from her friends, since last night and she felt guilty. She let everybody walk on in front of her and then she turned to Poppy.

"I have no idea where he is, have you?" asked Poppy concerned.

"Who?"

"Ethelred-Ted, Silly, have you seen him this morning?"

'I've hardly given him a thought!' she mused but she daren't tell Poppy. Since she had been with Father in the OOMU, she had spared but a few seconds for him.

"Where do you think he might be, then?" asked Joni-Pip.

"Well, how should I know? I haven't seen him since I left you Lot at the Workhouse Fire, when I went to get Fred Finn and Grandfather in 1892!"

"You haven't?" asked Joni-Pip alarmed.

"When did **you** see him last, then?"

"When he JITTED and left Hetty and me with the children in the fire....look Poppy, I would love to stop and talk but I have to go to a party at Grandfather's. He has invited all of our friends and family round for tea this afternoon. There are going to be lots of new friends....and family....some I have never met before but thanks to us changing the Past, I now have a different Future," said Joni-Pip excitedly.

"I see, so you don't want to be with Hetty and me any more, now that you have new friends and family....and what's more, you don't want to help us search for Ethelred-Ted," said Poppy-Plump-Pij seriously, sadly and especially, sulkily.

"Sure, I want to be with you, Pops," said Joni-Pip softly, gently stroking Poppy's back. "I want to be with Hetty the Wee, as well and I want to look for Eth with you but I just can't right now," she continued, feeling very torn between her old life and her new. "Look, how about we meet up, say, at ten o'clock tomorrow morning? I will be at Grandfather's Cottage all day today....and this evening, so I just can't meet up at any time, at all, today. Tomorrow I am free, so we could meet up at the Ruin. I will meet both you and Het, O.K.?" Joni-Pip hoped that this would placate her friend: then a thought struck her. "Why don't you bring Macca?"

Poppy-Plump-Pij smiled.

"That would be so nice. I'll tell Hetty and go and ask Macca. See you at ten?" with that she took off flying high into the sky, disappearing over the tops of the trees.

Joni-Pip ran to catch her family up. She didn't want to think about Ethelred-Ted right now. She had been more than a little hurt, when he had abandoned her and Hetty in the Children's Dormitory, leaving them to face the fear of the flames without him. He also left without explaining where he was going and what he was going to do.

When she realised that the 'Ethelred-Ted' who was acting as 'The Ring Master' in the Barn after the Workhouse Fire, was in fact not Ethelred-Ted at all: she was a little cross, to say the least. She had no idea where he was or what he was doing and she didn't much care, either: not at that particular moment, that was. Besides that, until he was found, the Premium Pasture would not be over and this Circle would not be closed and she was really enjoying remembering everything.

"Come on, J.P.!" yelled Alex. "What's keeping you?"

In no time at all, she had caught them up.

Half-way across the Woods, a squadron of RAF planes flew over. All her family stopped and looked up into the sky and watched them.

"Did you hear the News, last night?" Father asked Alex in a low tone, as they started to walk together down the hill.

"What? Is anything going on, Father?" asked Joni-Pip, walking between them.

"Honey, it's fine. I don't want you worrying about this Pesky War," he replied.

Father and Son then walked on in silence. Joni-Pip continually got the sense that her parents and brother did everything they could to protect her from the horrors of what was really going on in those awful times.

As they passed the Ruin, she thought she heard somebody singing.

Grandfather was standing waiting for them at the door with somebody else when they arrived. Joni-Pip was staggered when this other person seemed so familiar to her. She knew, absolutely knew that she had seen her before: where though, she had no idea. It then dawned on her that this person must have been the older lady whom she had seen down at the Crooked Cottage and who had waved at them when they were up at the Ruin, the day before. The woman hugged her. It was probably one of the most amazing hugs Joni-Pip had ever had in her entire life. It seemed to go on forever!

"Darling, Darling," whispered this older lady, with huge tears rolling down her cheeks, "thank you, so much!"

Joni-Pip looked puzzled and studied her face. Yes, she did look so, so familiar to her but she wondered who on earth she was. Then she remembered she had seen this face through the windows in the OOMU and she had seen her photograph on Grandfather's parlour wall many times.

"I wished I had known you were my granddaughter, nobody explained," her Hugger continued, whispering into Joni-Pip's ear.

At first Joni-Pip had no idea what she was talking about: then it suddenly dawned on her who she was!

"Grandmother! Grandmother! Grandmother!" Joni-Pip shouted, giving her the biggest hug of her life. She cried and cried tears of joy. "How silly I am for not realising who you were when you waved at us, yesterday!"

"Come on, Cherry-Plum. How about a hug for your old Grandfather?"

Poppy's flight through the storm by Joni-Pip. 10/8/06

came the familiar voice of her beloved grandfather from inside the kitchen.

Joni-Pip was slightly apprehensive. She knew the kitchen was going to be different but as she entered, she was pleasantly surprised. Yes, there were a few differences but only minor ones. In Joni-Pip's First Circle, Grandfather had kept the kitchen almost exactly as Grandmother had left it, when she had died during the Spanish 'Flu Pandemic of 1918/1919 ((a horrible Influenza that killed more people in a year than the Black Death of the Middle Ages, killed in a century. A common estimate of the number who died, was 21 million but now some experts judge that figure to be more like 50 or even 100 million))! Anyway, the kitchen was still very familiar, with the fully gathered, green check curtains both around the sink and at the window. The kitchen table and chairs were just the same.

Grandfather looked at her lovingly and gave her a wonderful hug.

"Thank you so much, My Darling Girl!" he whispered.

Joni-Pip didn't say anything, she just stored the words of both of her grandparents in safekeeping, tucked up in her heart.

What an amazing day it was proving to be!

Grandmother suggested they join the rest of the family in the Parlour.

There was one thing, though, that struck Joni-Pip as odd. As she walked down the hallway, which led to the Parlour, instead of Grandfather's familiar Landscape, on one wall hung a collection of drawings. They were obviously all done by children. There were four of them. The first one was of a pigeon flying through a storm. Joni-Pip examined it. The picture was entitled, **'Poppy's flight through the storm, by Joni-Pip'**. She had no recollection of drawing it.

'How can it be?' she thought to herself. 'This is entirely impossible!'

The second was of a hedgehog, a bird and a familiar looking Teddy Bear, all jumping over a wall and was entitled:-

'Ethelred-Ted, Hetty the Wee and Poppy-Plump-Pij, by Becky-Paige'.

'This has to be the Wall of Time!' Joni-Pip thought. 'But how can it be? Becky-Paige doesn't know anything about it. What's going on?'

Suddenly Joni-Pip was uneasy. She turned to Grandfather who was following her closely down the hallway, pointed to this picture and asked,

"Grandfather....how did this picture get here....when did it get here? Did Becky-Paige really draw it? How could she?"

Grandfather looked at her and put his arm around her shoulder.

"Cherry-Plum, what is the matter? You have gone quite pale....you all painted them last month....don't you remember? All of you came over for the afternoon, you couldn't play out as it was raining and you asked me to

384

tell you what to draw and I suggested the Nursery Rhyme, 'Three Toys in Time'," laughed her grandfather.

"What do you mean 'Three Toys in Time'?" she asked him in horror.

"You know that famous old rhyme, don't ask me to quote it all but it goes something like this....

'Three toys sat in the Parlour, watching days go by.
Waiting for Awakenings, then o'er the Wall they'd fly.
A workhouse stood in the Wood, hiding tears of shame.
The Three Toys JITTED in Time, to save the O'Hara name.
The Three Toys in Time then saved, countless hearts and life.
A hedgehog, Pigeon and Ted, over a Wall of Ice.
Three Toys in Time, Three Toys in Time.'

"Why am I singing this? You know it better than I do!" he laughed.

"I don't Grandfather, I have never heard it, ever!" she shouted.

"Cherry Plum, whatever has got into you? Are you feeling unwell?"

"Everything all right?" asked Father from behind them both.

Joni-Pip and Grandfather turned round and looked at him.

"Hurry along, you are blocking the way! Mind the Gap!" laughed Father.

"Oh, sorry!" laughed back Grandfather; both men then walked on.

Joni-Pip stared at the third picture on the wall. It was entitled, **'Ethelred-Ted, Hetty the Wee and Poppy-Plump-Pij, by Elle-Sahara'**.

Joni-Pip couldn't believe it. Surely it was a picture of her three special friends, jumping over the Wall of Time? But it couldn't be, Elle-Sahara didn't know Hetty and Poppy. How could she draw the Wall of Time? How did she know about it?

Joni-Pip then looked aghast at the last picture. It was a beautiful, vibrant painting of a red and yellow Teddy Bear, obviously done by a very small child. The writing on it sent a cold, cold shiver down her spine. It said, **'Red-Ted-Ted by Beth Garador'**.

'Beth Garador?' she thought to herself. 'Beth Garador. Who are you? Where are you? Or more importantly, when will you be?'

Joni-Pip looked carefully at the huge Hallstand standing in the hallway. Something so bugged her about it. Her eyes searched the oak panels either side of it, for a clue but nothing came. She looked again at the picture and drew back her breath, as there, in the reflection of the glass was Flip's face. They smiled at each other. Joni-Pip stared closely and then Flip vanished. Suddenly, she had this 'hard-to-believe' feeling that she had done all this

385

Three Toys in Time

(by Joni-Philipa)

Three toys sat in the Parlour,

Watching days go by.

Waiting for Awakenings,

Then o'er the Wall they'd fly.

A workhouse stood in the Wood,

Hiding tears of shame.

The Three Toys JITTED in Time,

To save the O'Hara name.

The Three Toys in Time then saved

Countless hearts and life.

A hedgehog, Pigeon and Ted,

O'er a Wall of Ice.

Three Toys in Time, Three Toys in Time....

Ethelred - Ted, Hetty the Wee
and Poppy - Plump - Pij
by Elle - Sahara

before. She knew that she was about to go into the Parlour: she knew where everyone would be sitting: she knew what they would say to her. She looked quickly back along the Hall wall and there was the familiar Landscape, which Grandfather had painted when he was at College. All of

Red-Ted-Ted by Beth Garador

the other four pictures had gone.

"Oh no," she said, "not again.... Déjà Vu!"

Soon everyone was snuggled cosily in the Parlour round the fire drinking freshly brewed tea. Grandmother said she had everything ready and just wanted to enjoy a few peaceful moments with her daughter, Sarah and her family, before the other guests arrived. She had invited the others to come for four o'clock, so they had enough time to enjoy a leisurely cup of tea and a natter. Becky-Paige and Elle-Sahara sat on the rug playing with the kittens. Joni-Pip had so many thoughts running around her head that she found it hard to concentrate.

"Everything O.K.?" asked Mother, "You seem a million miles away!"
"I think she's just tired, aren't you, Honey?" Father replied for her.
Joni-Pip wasn't even aware they were talking, she just ignored them.
"J.P., I think you are becoming Me the older you get," laughed Alex.
"Yes, Alex, she truly is absent-minded today!" chuckled Grandfather.
"Goodness Gracious, how will the World cope with two of them?"
"We'll manage, Sarah," laughed Grandmother, "just about...I think!"
They all laughed together.
"What's so funny, then?" asked Joni-Pip innocently. "What?"
With that all the adults in the Parlour went silent; looked at each, then at Joni-Pip and burst into uproarious laughter. Joni-Pip looked puzzled.
"What did I say?" she asked but they were all splitting their sides.
She never did find out what they were laughing about.
It wasn't long before the others began to arrive.

First, it was her Auntie Sylvia and Uncle Richard with her two cousins. It was a strange meeting because she hadn't actually seen them through one of the tiny windows in the OOMU. It was 'strangely normal', Joni-Pip decided as looking at Auntie Sylvia was just like looking at a slightly younger version of Mother. As her new aunt hugged her, Joni-Pip knew that they had a very close relationship in this new part of her POOL. She immediately realised that, as they only had two sons, Uncle Richard and Auntie Sylvia treated her as their own daughter.

Then came the astonishing meeting with her two cousins.

Steve, was fifteen and Craig was thirteen. Joni-Pip was astounded.

"We've met before, haven't we?" she said to the boys. "With the Two Men in Long, Black Coats, only you were older? That's amazing! Did you find everything? "

"You're obviously one of the BIGS then?" came Craig. "Full of British Instinctive Good Sense! What men in long, black coats, you Nolly?"

"What, on earth, are you on about?" Steve asked Joni-Pip, frowning.

"Yeah, sure we were older last time we met....two months ago!" laughed Craig. "What are you like?"

Both the boys hugged her and she knew them all right; even though they had no idea what she was talking about. She knew they would one day. She knew she would understand everything, too; she just had to wait.

"How's our Yankee Girl, anyway?" Steve grinned.

"Yankee Girl? Yes, of course! Not so much of your cheek!" replied Joni-Pip laughing. "Aren't I your Yankee Cuz, anyway? How's Flip?"

"Yankee Cuz? Hmmm....like that! I'll call you it from now!" said Steve.

"Flip?" said Craig. "Who's he? Great name, mind!"

"Flip, you know, the girl you were with in Archimedes' Quission Hut and other places recently, when you were looking for the Old Mine."

The two boys looked puzzled.

"The Girl? Which Girl? When have you seen us recently?" asked Steve.

"You won't remember, you can't remember, it hasn't happened yet!" she said seriously. Her cousins looked her and both shook their heads.

"What books have you been reading, or wireless stories have you been listening to? D'you realise how Crackers you sound, J.P.?" laughed Craig.

"Yeah, you sound as if you've flipped, Yankee Cuz!" grinned Steve.

"Flipped, she surely does! Hey, that's a great name, we should call **you** Flip: after all you are Joni-**Philipa**! Flip sounds good!" laughed Craig.

"Yeah, I'll second that!" said Steve. "It suits you....forget about this make- believe Flip. It's a spiffing name, isn't it Flip, my Yankee Cuz?"

Joni-Pip was astounded. Lots of memories began flooding her mind. She remembered her cousins' beautiful house by the sea. She remembered one particular time when she was sitting on the veranda with Eth, looking out, across Auntie Sylvia's and Uncle Richard's garden, to the sea. It was a great garden. She remembered Becky-Paige walking up and down the garden path pushing her doll's pram. Cinders, their grey cat, was patiently studying a Mouse's nest, while Candy, their white cat, lay sleeping on the veranda wall, snoring. The memory was so vivid and made her feel warm.

Amelia Plate, her husband, Colin Finn and their daughters, Jean and Kathleen arrived. Colin was now Farmer Finn, himself! As Fred Finn had become a doctor, Colin, who was his younger brother now ran the farm with his nephew, James Finn (Father's best friend, whom he called Taff). Colin looked after the running of the financial side of Finn's Farm, while James took care of all the 'hands on' work: the actual farming of the land.

Joni-Pip's meeting with Amelia Plate was very emotional. Why, it had only been a few hours before, that a little eight-year-old Victorian girl had fallen asleep on her shoulder in the Workhouse Barn after they had been saved from the scorching flames of the Workhouse Fire. Joni-Pip was so pleased the Circle was still open and the Premium Pasture had still not been completed. She could remember all the events of the last few weeks so vividly. She couldn't help but remember that everything that had happened was in order to change the life of this person, this special person, who stood before her, open-armed, right now.

They ran to each other, hugged and cried tears of joy.

"Joni-Pip!" exclaimed Amelia Plate, joyfully. "Joni-Pip, Joni-Pip, Joni-Pip, how incredible it is to see you again!"

Joni-Pip and Ethelred-Ted sat on Auntie Sylvia's & Uncle Richard's porch looking across at the sea, while Cinders patiently studied the mouse nest and Candy snored.

Chapter 39

The Rescue

"So how was the party then, Ma Pet?"

Hetty was sat on one of the few remaining walls of the Workhouse Ruin.

"Swell!" enthused Joni-Pip. "Actually it isn't over yet. I don't suppose it will end until this evening. Mother is so pleased to be able to spend time with her family: especially Auntie Sylvia. They set off from Barmouth yesterday morning. It's a long way and they are not leaving until later this afternoon. They like to spend as much time as they can together, which is quite rare, what with petrol rationing and all that."

"I hope they don't miss you today and come running out to find you, Pudding. We need you here with us at the moment," said Poppy seriously.

It was a beautiful, peaceful May morning. The sun was shining, the sky was blue and the birds were twittering happily, buzzing around in their busy lives.

"Poppya 'assa explaina to me thata you hava losta Ethelreda-Tedda: thees eeza a pity. Whera yoowa thinka 'ee mighta be?" asked Macca, while balancing precariously on one of the flimsier branches of The Major Oak.

"Life in the Wood," came a muffled singing voice.

Everybody stopped dead in their tracks and stood completely still.

"....is so good! Life in the Wood is fun!" the singing continued.

"Can you hear that, Ma Pets?"

"Where on earth is it coming from?" questioned Joni-Pip.

"Who, on earth, is it coming from?" asked Poppy-Plump-Pij.

"I donta knowa abouta youa, mya friendsa but eeta eesn't so gooda....zis singing!" said Macca seriously.

"I expect you think not, what with you being an opera singer and all that, Macca!" laughed Joni-Pip. She then walked towards the stifled singing but it seemed to trail away. Hetty climbed down the wall and followed her. Joni-Pip kept walking in one direction and then another, turning around and going in a different direction. Each time she thought that she had found the source of the singing, it seemed to move.

"This is a wee mystery, Ma Pets."

"I'll fly round....hang on a minute, I've just thought of something...."

The others stopped and turned and looked at her.

"What's the song that's being sung?"

"Life in the Wood," replied Hetty the Wee and Joni-Pip together.

"Eeza it? I 'aven'ta 'erada ofa thisa songa befora. Oooa wrota eet?"

"Grandfather and Ethelred-Ted!" said Poppy, Hetty and Joni-Pip.

Then they all looked at each other and chorused, "Ethelred-Ted!"

"My point exactly!" said Poppy-Plump-Pij. "Besides we three, the only other people who know that song, are Grandfather and Ethelred-Ted."

"Of course!" said Joni-Pip. "Why didn't we think of that before?"

"Good thinking Poppy, Pet!"

"The singing is coming from Ethelred-Ted then but where is he?"

"Let's make a really thorough search, Joni-Pip" Hetty replied, scurrying off and weaving her little body in and out of the bricks and stones.

"Trees grow so high," continued the singing.

"Er....whya youa notta calla 'ima?"

"And we're not stupid, then?" laughed Joni-Pip.

"Ethelred-Ted! Ethelred-Ted! Where are y', Laddie?"

"Ethelred-Ted! Ethelred-Ted! Where are you?" called Joni-Pip.

The singing continued. Poppy took off and circled around the Ruin.

"I don't know about You Lot but isn't the singing, kind of....in the air..?"

"It sounds like he is in a tunnel, to me," said Hetty, pushing over stone after stone, trying to find a secret tunnel, which went deep into the ground.

Although she couldn't remember it, her experience in Tunnel 6 had really got to her and she had this desire to find the secret passages again.

"He must be somewhere," said Joni-Pip puzzled, "but where?"

They all continued calling out his name.

"D' y' think he can hear us, Lambs?"

Macca, joining them in their search, took off and flew very low to the ground, circling around the broken walls of the Ruin. He put his head on one side, straining to locate the far-from-pleasing voice. He flew towards the old propped up chimney, where Grandfather found Amelia Plate's note. He landed right on top of the chimney and thrust his head down, as far as it could go.

"Lean by the stream, Lean dream and dream," came the quite distinctive voice below him.

"I founda 'eem!" he shouted to the others. "'Eez 'eyah!"

"Where? Where is he then?" Poppy flew and joined him on the chimney.

"Are you sure?" asked Joni-Pip, looking round and up at the two birds.

"That's wonderful, Hen!"

Macca looked disdainfully at the hedgehog.

"Ooo, no offence meant, Laddie. It's just a Scottish term of affection."

"I foragiva youa buta 'ha hen'? Eez thisa nota ha lady terma?"

"No, definitely not, I call everyone, Laddie or Lassie: 'Hen'," said Hetty walking over with Joni-Pip; they stood by the old fire place and looked inside.

"Life in the Wood is so good," went the voice of their friend.

"Where exactly is he, then?" asked Joni-Pip, peering up into the old chimney. "I can hear him but I can't see anything. Can anyone else?"

"No, nothing from up here." Poppy's voice echoed down the chimney.

"Shall we do a bit of tunnelling then, Ma Pets?"

"Tunnelling?" her three friends repeated.

"Y' ken, let's pull a few bricks away, I'm quite sure that he's in here somewhere. I love tunnelling!" She started pulling bricks out of the fireplace.

Macca and Poppy flew down to the ground. Soon all of her friends were helping her. They removed bricks and sticks and stones and bits until the fireplace was free of rubbish.

"This is ridiculous!" said Joni-Pip, wiping her brow and leaving a wiggly trail of black soot across her forehead. "He just has to be here but where?"

"Whena youa lasta see 'eem?"

"When Het and I were in the Children's Dormitory in 1892. We watched him jump over the Wall of Time and that was it," answered Joni-Pip.

"He's not been seen since, Ma Lambs, so he could 'a come back and landed in the middle of the fire or he could 'a come back after the fire...."

"Ora 'ee coulda landida soma whera elsa in ze 'ousa....and gotta 'imself trappeda!"

He peered this time **up** the chimney, from down in the fireplace.

"Good point!" said the others, looking at each other.

"If that was true, why didn't he just JIT and come home?" said Joni-Pip.

"Hmmmm....good question...." said Hetty thoughtfully. "I think that Eth got stuck in Time somehoo and he's waitin' for us t' rescue him."

"Poppy, what would you do?" asked Joni-Pip.

Poppy flew up on to the branch of a tree and put her head on one side.

"I would fly back over the Wall of Time and come home to 1942."

"Yes, Pops of course you would but supposing you were trapped somehow....the flames were getting closer and for some reason you just couldn't get to the Wall of Time....or it had disappeared somehow...."

"I woulda 'ide," answered Macca, once more poking his head up the chimney only this time he called out, "Ethelreda-Teda, whera ara you?" He loved the sound of his own voice, echoing up the chimney. The acoustics were perfect. In fact, they sounded so good that he started to practice a few scales and arpeggios.

The others ignored him.

"Exactly!" exclaimed Joni-Pip.

"And wait for Y' Lot to find me!" finished Hetty the Wee.

"Exactly!" said Joni-Pip again.

"Where would be a good place to hide for fifty yearsful?" asked Poppy.

They all looked at her and laughed.

"I don't think there could ever be a 'good' place to hide f' so long, Ma Lamb!"

"Well, he didn't have a lot of choice in the Workhouse did he?"

"Personally, I would try and find a safe place....away....well, as far as possible, away from the flames...." said Joni-Pip thoughtfully, "as we did when my beautiful city of Bath was bombed earlier this year!"

They all remained silent for a moment, then they looked at each other.

"The Cellar!" they shouted together.

"The Cellar? Well, if he is in the Cellar, then we have come full circle since leaving Bath to come and live in the wood!" said Joni-Pip.

"So, what are we waiting for? Let's hunt the Cellar!" cried Poppy, as if they were just beginning a party game at the Crooked Cottage.

"Where d' we start, Ma Pets? Where shall we start tunnelling?"

The others looked at her and giggled.

"You have your wish at last, Het! Let's tunnel!" enthused Joni-Pip.

All of them hurried around overturning stones, bricks, twigs and rubble. Macca flew across the ground and landed on a pile of bricks, just to the right of the chimney. He pushed a few bricks to one side and the singing, definitely, got slightly louder.

"'Elpa me, I thinka I finda 'eema!" he shouted to the others.

They ran and helped him push the remaining bricks out of the way. They pulled at the tufts of long grass and there on the ground was a metal grille.

"By the reeds of the river," came a familiar voice below them.

"Ethelred-Ted! Ethelred-Ted! We have found you!" Joni-Pip shouted down through the metal bars of the grille. She could see nothing.

"About time too!" replied the voice from the darkness. "Do you know how long I have been down here?"

"Fifty years!" they all shouted down to him.

"Fifty years?" questioned the voice. "Of course not, it can't be....is it really? No? M, M 'n M, have I been busy! It only seems like a few hours!"

"How are we going to get you out?" asked Poppy, peering into the pit.

"If I knew that, I would have got out long ago!" came a frosty reply.

Operation Grille commenced! They pulled and they pushed; they tugged and they dug; they scraped and they scratched: they ripped and they picked: they plucked and they pressed; they tore and they dragged; they split and they shook; they jostled and they shoved....but of course the grille didn't move: not a hundredth of an inch!

Strained and grazed, Joni-Pip stopped.

393

"People, I don't think this is going to work," she said, once more wiping the sweat off her brow. This time it left a trail of tiny pieces of grass, twigs and mud, mixed in with the soot.

"A bit more of that on ye forehead, Ma Pet and we might mistake ye for a wattle and daub hut!" laughed Hetty the Wee.

They stopped working and examined Joni-Pip's decorated face and hair.

"She looks more like a warrior to me!" laughed Poppy-Plump-Pij.

"What's wrong with my face?" asked Joni-Pip, wiping it again, which of course smeared the mud even more widely....over her cheeks this time.

"I think ye might just look like an ancient Anglo-Saxon," Hetty laughed. "If not that old, y'd be right at home in the Camp of King Ethelred, himsel'!"

"To fight the dangerousful Danes?" asked Poppy-Plump-Pij.

"What? What are You Two going on about, now?" Joni-Pip moaned.

"Hurry up, You Lot! You've made plenty of mess down here!"

Nobody took any notice of the voice below them.

"Eeta eeza youra face, youra haira....eeta eeza nota so preeetty!"

"What d'you expect," Joni-Pip asked the Macaw sarcastically, "a top Paris Fashion model? I have been working, you know and jolly hard, too!"

"What's going on up there?"

"I notta meana upseta you: Macca saya sorreeyah!" he said sheepishly.

"It's all right, Macca, I think I'm just a bit overwhelmed by everything that has happened in my life recently. I feel a bit tired and edgy. Sorry!"

"Are you anywhere near getting me out of here, yet? Please?"

Macca, Poppy, Joni-Pip and Hetty all stopped and looked at each other.

"No!" They shouted down into the darkness of the grille.

"I only asked!" replied the lonely voice beneath them.

"I think we must go and get Father and Grandfather and they can lift the grille up and we can lower a rope down to hoist you up!"

"I'll go and get them!" said Poppy, immediately taking off, swooping around her friends then flying into the air and disappearing down the hill.

"What's going on here?" came a gruff voice from behind them.

They turned their heads and looked into the face of Nuttingham Squirrel.

"What's happened? What are you doing? Who are you talking to? Who is down there? Why is he down there?" he interrogated.

"Er....it's Ethelred-Ted," replied Joni-Pip.

"He's kind of stuck," replied Hetty the Wee.

"We trya 'elpa 'eem," replied Macca.

"How did he get down there, then?" asked Nuttingham Squirrel, walking over to the grille and looking down into the murky depths below.

"He's been down there a long time." Joni-Pip shook her head.

"What do you mean, 'a long time'?" shot the squirrel.

"Ah, a long time indeed," added Hetty, also shaking her little head.

"What do you mean, 'a long time indeed'?" snapped the squirrel. "He couldn't have been down there a long time!"

"Oh, 'ee 'as....sucha longa tima!" said Macca nodding his head.

"What are you all talking about? What nonsense is this?" Nuttingham Squirrel shook his head and looked closely down into the cellar.

"You wouldn't understand but believe us, he has been down there for what seems like, years," said Joni-Pip seriously.

"Nuts and Nonsense! Why, he was only in my house drinking and eating with me less than two days ago!" grumbled the squirrel, then scuttling off.

"What?" exclaimed Joni-Pip, Macca and Hetty the Wee together.

"He must be mistaken....no, of course, The Great Store and all that....it was shown to Ethelred-Ted in 1942, although we learnt about it in 1892!" laughed Joni-Pip.

They all remained silent for a little while.

"Let's have another go, Ma Pets!" encouraged Hetty the Wee.

"I zinka zees eeza good idee!" added the Macaw.

"If we can lift this grille up then we can winch him up somehow," said Joni-Pip.

They all began to claw and paw again.

In no time at all, Poppy circled back round them, landing on the top of the chimney.

"They'll be coming!" she said. "I'll join you in a mo, I just need a rest!"

"Well done, Pops, it's so lovely that you can fly. It would have taken me ages to go and get them," said Joni-Pip appreciatively. "I did love the feeling that I was flying in the KOL, though....it was marvellous!"

"T'was indeed, Hen! Hmmm....a flying hedgehog! It was breathtaking!"

"Iya ama so 'appy, Iya toowah 'ava privilega toa dowah eet!"

A splashing sound was heard coming from behind them.

"What was that?" asked Joni-Pip, turning and looking up towards the bridge. "It sounds as if someone is crossing the stream."

"I didn't hear anythin', Pet." Hetty looked behind her towards the bridge.

The splashing continued. Joni-Pip headed up the hill following the noise.

"There's somebody up there, there must be," she shouted down to them.

"It's probably Alex, Lambie," said Hetty, "or Farmer Finn or someone!"

"What are they doing in the stream, then? Daft if you ask me!" she said.

By the time Joni-Pip reached the bridge, the splashing had stopped. She heaved herself up on the wall and looked down into the disturbed waters.

"Somebody has been walking across the stream, there's no mistake," she said to herself, "I wonder who...or what, even? Silly me, perhaps it was one of the Farm dogs. I expect Farmer Finn will turn up in a minute!"

As she sat there, dangling her legs over the edge of the beautiful bridge, she heard a cough coming from up in the thick of the trees.

"Who's there?" she asked the empty space. "Hey, I heard you cough, so I know you are around. Who are you? Come and speak to me!"

Twigs and leaves crunched and splintered as footsteps raced away from her.

"Come back, I want to talk to you!" Joni-Pip cried out but as she did so she suddenly thought, 'What am I doing? He might be dangerous. He might be a Spy or a villain of some sort. He might be an escaped prisoner!'

She continued to look up into the trees and just caught the back of a figure as it came out from behind one tree and crossed a small gap until it disappeared behind another tree.

"I must follow him," she whispered to herself as she slipped off the wall, crossed the woodland path and clambered up through the trees. It wasn't long before she reached the other side of the wood and when she finally got to the brow of the hill, she looked down over towards the train track, just in time to see the mysterious hooded figure enter into the black mouth of the railway tunnel and disappear into the darkness.

"Drat!" she said, "I wonder where he's off to? I'd better go back now!"

When she arrived at The Ruin, she heard voices coming up the hill.

"Welcome One and All!" said Joni-Pip walking down to greet them. "I'm so glad you have come!"

"Who is this Creature?" asked Father, pulling at some of the dead leaves that had got caught in her hair.

"New hat have we?" laughed Taff.

"What have you been doing, Cherry Plum?" Grandfather grinned.

"My, with a bit more carefully arranged dishevelling, you will look decidedly like me!" laughed Archimedes Spindlethrop.

"What?" asked Joni-Pip, not quite understanding what all the fuss was about. She didn't care, anyway, she just hugged them all and walked back up with them to show them the grille.

"It's impossible I'm sure!" she said.

"What do you mean?" laughed Father. "We can move anything!"

"The Fit Force! That's us!" laughed James Finn.

"The Fit Force? More like the Feeble Force!" laughed Archie Spindlethrop.

"The Frail Force, more like!" added Grandfather.

"Oh, Uncle Archie! It's so lovely to see you, again!" said Joni-Pip and frowned.

"Well, let's see what we can do to rescue our young friend!" said Father.

All of them examined the grille and looked down into it.

"I think it's cemented in," said James Finn, "no wonder you couldn't move it!"

"No wonder!" said Joni-Pip rubbing her sore scratched hands and arms.

"The cement might crack, it's so old," said Grandfather.

"Hmmm! Like somebody else I know!" laughed Archie, looking at him.

"That's enough of your cheek, Young Man!" Grandfather chuckled.

Father had brought a rope and tried pushing one end through one of the narrow spaces between the metal bars. The rope was thick and heavy and James got down on his knees to help him but they couldn't do it. Grandfather had brought a garden fork with him so he used the prongs to push the rope firmly through one of the spaces.

"By the way, have any of You Lot been in my shed? When I went to get this fork, somebody had left a pile of stuff on my workbench. I usually keep it in my old Victorian Coronation Tin, which has gone missing. All the stuff is there. My best hammer has disappeared, too. It's a mystery!"

Everybody shook their heads: that was except Joni-Pip, Hetty and Poppy. They just looked at each other.

"What would anybody want with that rusty old tin?" laughed Archie.

"Well, I liked it, actually! Let's try and get this thing moving, shall we?"

With a great deal of effort, the rope finally went through the gap. They then tried to hook the rope back up between the bars, through another space.

"Will we ever hook this?" asked Archimedes.

"Not if we trust in somebody's hooking skills, the last time we went fishing!"

"What? I am an expert Angler!"

"It depends what kind of angling we are referring to here, doesn't it?" said Grandfather. "After all, if we are talking about angling for the branches of the trees, then I admit you are indeed an expert."

"What?" laughed Archimedes. "I only caught the trees once when I cast."

"What was that?" asked James Finn, laughing. "You hooked the trees?"

"He is also an Expert Angler of another kind!" said Grandfather seriously.

Everybody stopped at this comment.

"I don't think we need to go into this, now, do we?" pleaded Archimedes.

"Want to know what else he hooked, once? It wouldn't have been so bad if he hadn't got so excited. Everybody ran over to watch him land such a huge catch! One of the nearby anglers had his Box Brownie ready to snap the picture of the year for the Angling Times. The lake was lined with spectators, eager to catch a glimpse of the biggest and heaviest fish ever to come out of Loxley Lake. They all watched with baited breath, as Archie wrestled to reel in the Catch of the Century. They gasped as it nearly got away and then finally he reeled in enough line to hoist the fish out of the water and into the net; they looked saw the hugest, the most enormous, the biggest ....BOOT....they had ever seen, covered in reeds and weeds! It was at least a size 14!"

Everyone burst into uproarious laughter.

"Don't be so mean!" laughed Joni-Pip.

The May morning air was filled with the sound of uncontrollable laughter. Joni-Pip couldn't help but feel incredibly happy. How wonderful it was to see her Grandfather laughing with his old arch enemy of a former Circle. Still giggling, they finally hooked the rope back up between the bars and then tied it in a firm knot. They then all formed a line and resembling a team of Tug-of-war contestants, pulled at the rope, trying to shift the only known way into the cellar of the Workhouse.

"Heave-ho, M' Hearties!" cried Grandfather: they all pulled.

"Yo-heave-ho!" chanted Father and Archimedes: they all tugged.

"Yo-heave-ho!" repeated James Finn: they all hauled.

Just then, emerging from behind a tree, unseen to them all, a figure appeared. He stood behind them looking closely at what they were doing and then joined them, by pulling on the very end of the rope.

"Once more, Heave-ho M' Hearties!" encouraged Grandfather: they all yanked.

Once again, the grille didn't move....not an inch....not a tiny millimetre.

"What are we actually doing?" asked the latest Team member.

"Getting the grille off," replied James Finn, turning and looking at him.

"I see! What for?"

"So we can rescue Ethelred-Ted," replied James looking back and then looking back again and promptly letting go of the rope: the other men then fell in a heap.

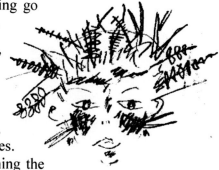

"Why did you let go, you Ninny?" asked Father.

"That was a daft thing to do, by Basil!" laughed Grandfather.

"Jim, you could have warned us first, before you let go!" chuckled Archimedes.

"Farmer Finn, why do that; is anything the matter?" asked Joni-Pip concerned.

James didn't reply, he just smothered the smirk on his face and waited.

They then all disentangled themselves from each other, got back on their feet again and began to brush themselves down.

"That looked so funny!" came a familiar voice.

Everybody stopped what they were doing and looked round. They all looked at the owner of that voice and looked again.

"Ethelred-Ted!" they all said, looking at him in amazement.

"How on earth?" asked Joni-Pip, now resembling a well camouflaged commando.

"What?" asked Ethelred-Ted innocently. "And what do you look like?" he said screwing up his face.

"What?" replied Joni-Pip, picking some of the twigs and grass out of her hair and trying to smooth the matted mess down.

"How come you are out?" asked Father. "We have been commandeered to rescue you from the confines of the Workhouse Cellar."

"It was Jack who took my tin!" exclaimed Grandfather, suddenly remembering all the dialogue in the Barn after the Workhouse fire.

"Of course!" said Archimedes Spindlethrop and then he added, "Yes, Ethelred-Ted, how come we were wrenched away from our important work, in order to get you out of the cellar when you are already out of the cellar?"

"Sorry, Old Chap, nice to see you. What important work were you engaged in....some difficult experiment?" asked Ethelred-Ted eagerly.

"Very difficult!" replied Father.

"Very difficult, indeed!" added Grandfather.

"Very, very, difficult!" said James Finn emphatically.

"What were you doing?" asked Joni-Pip, wiping her face with her arm.

"Drinking tea!" chorused the four men together.

Chapter 40

Minds and Mines

"It was such a surprise to me, when I realised that you were missing on the night of the Workhouse Fire, Eth."

"It was a surprise to me when I couldn't get out of the Workhouse, at all!"

"It must have been a mite scary fer y', Laddie."

"Yes, Hetty, it was. I'd been looking for You Lot, the night of the fire but then I tripped and the next thing I knew, I was in the cellar. I tried to get out. I climbed the stairs up to the door, which I presumed led into the Workhouse but it was locked. I just couldn't budge it. I crawled up the chute I had slid down but there was a little door at the top and some Nolly had locked it from the outside. I called for ages but nobody heard me. I went to use my F.B. and to my horror, I couldn't find it. It was almost pitch black: I just sat. You should hear the poems and songs I've composed and written! My favourite, you'll love, is called 'Three Toys in Time'!"

"P'raps we will later!" Joni-Pip said, feeling very peculiar.

After the 'rescue', Eth explained that Nuttingham Squirrel had appeared down in the cellar; he had got in by unbolting the hatch from the outside and then had helped him to clamber through the opening and up the chute. The bear had no idea about the metal grille and what exactly his friends had been doing to try and move it. Every time he had asked them anything, they had either ignored him or spoken to him as if it didn't concern him. Eth had thanked his new found friend before he scurried off and then he had walked round from behind his favourite tree to find his friends.

Ethelred-Ted was surprised to see them having fun in a Tug-of-war and wanted to join in. It was a very normal sort of thing to want to do and he couldn't quite understand how the others could feel peeved about that.

The men had had a good laugh together and then left. Joni-Pip, Hetty and Poppy said they were very cross for not remembering about the hatch and the coal chute and that if they had, they would have rescued Ethelred-Ted sooner and with much less effort: although they all agreed that having the men with them had been so funny. As Joni-Pip and her friends had much to discuss and Ethelred-Ted was in a desperate need of some exercise and a very overdue Munch Break, they decided to go for a walk into Edwinstowe. The four of them walked across the woods and down the hill. When they got to the Crooked Cottage, Joni-Pip popped in and came out with some sandwiches and a bottle of Grandfather's blackcurrant cordial. Eth, Hetty and Poppy decided not to go in, as there were too many things to talk about. They then made their way down Lily Lane towards Edwinstowe. Eth was busily munching and drinking.

"I was staggered when he ran into the barn," said Joni-Pip.

"Who?" asked Eth, wiping some dark red blobs of drink from around his mouth.

"Yes, how surprised we all were? Why was he there?" asked Poppy.

"Who?"

"Yes, Poppy, Ma Lamb, that's exactly what I wanted t' know!" laughed Hetty. "There we were in 1892, the children had been saved from the Workhouse Fire...."

"Who are you on about?" asked Ethelred-Ted, tucking into his next sandwich, slightly annoyed that no one was paying any attention to him.

"Grandfather, Fred Finn and Archimedes Spindlethrop were all youngful men...." continued Poppy-Plump-Pij, "....it was so weirdful!"

"Who ran into the barn? Who was it that you were so surprised to see?" Ethelred-Ted was exasperated but he still munched away at his fresh egg sandwich.

"Father was older than Grandfather," mused Joni-Pip. "It all seemed so odd. James Finn was older than his father, Fred: most peculiar."

"Hmmm! Who exactly was it that ran into the barn?" Ethelred-Ted said very deliberately and very slowly and then he took another gulp of blackcurrant cordial. "Nobody makes blackcurrant cordial like Grandfather!"

"We thought that it was **you** getting us all to tell our stories," said Poppy.

"Me?" Eth paused before he took another swig from the bottle.

"Yes, Ye, Ma Pet, ye stood in the middle and we sat round yer in a circle."

"I did?" he asked, examining the deeply piled, mashed egg between the two slices of freshly baked bread. "Crumbs, I've missed eating; you've no idea!"

"You were marvellousful. We all thought it was you, of course," said Pops.

"I was marvellous?" Ethelred-Ted beamed and slightly choked on his sandwich. He then spat gently into his paw and brushed it away. "The only thing I don't like about egg sandwiches, is the occasional bit of...."

"Egg shell!" finished all three of his friends together.

"Oh, so you are aware that I am here, then. Hmmm, I seem to remember you were saying that I was marvellous, Poppy, weren't you?"

"Yes but we only **thought** that you were but we were wrongful."

"That was until I saw you hadn't got a poorly arm!" laughed Joni-Pip.

Eth quickly put his paw over the wound on his arm, leaving an eggy trail on it.

"Right....when he, whoever he might be, came running in, you all knew who the bear was, then?" he asked, trying to brush the egg off his arm.

"Yes we did!" they all said together.

"Who was it? What? How? Why? Come on, People-Folk, tell me....I need some answers. Who was this mystery figure that ran into the barn, then? What had happened....tell me?" he asked, taking another bite of his delicious sandwich.

So, Dear Reader, let us go back and listen to the conversation in the Workhouse barn on the night of May 4$^{th/}$5th 1892, shall we?

Everybody turned as a strange figure ran into the barn.

"Jack!" exclaimed Joni-Pip, Hetty the Wee and Poppy-Plump-Pij together.

Of course only they recognised him from their meeting in Marley's Barn in 1942. Only they had been in contact with him through his mobile 'phone, when he had JITTED back to 2007. All three of them looked at the Bear in the middle of the Circle in the Workhouse Barn. He hadn't stood out from the others as being particularly tatty: everybody did! After all, fighting a fire and rescuing lots of children meant they could hardly keep themselves clean!

"Red-Ted!" Hetty, Poppy and Joni-Pip cried.

Red-Ted looked sheepish and nodded but he was only interested in Jack.

"I've done it!" Jack said triumphantly.

"Great stuff! If not, I thought we might have to tell those OGOFS to Bog Off!" said Red-Ted making Jack laugh. "I knew it would work! I knew it! I knew it!" Red-Ted continued, feeling slightly guilty at what he had just said.

"I couldn't see how....but you are all here, so it must have! Hey, You Guys!" Jack greeted Joni-Pip, Poppy and Hetty and then he turned back to Red-Ted. "So, I've done it! They are there! The Circle Continuum is staggering!"

"Sure is and they sure are! How d'you think we managed to save the children?"

"Shucks, yeah! That's so neat!"

"Excuse us but what are you talking about, by Basil?" asked a young Grandfather. "And what's more, who on earth are you?" he pointed at Jack.

"Phew!" said Jack, looking around. "Who are all these people?"

"Spiffing to see you again!" Joni-Pip gave him a hug. "Come, sit down and explain!"

Jack started to follow Joni-Pip but Red-Ted pulled him back gently.

"Everybody, this is Jack, he lives in the United States, in 2007 with me and his parents of course. As you can hear he is American. Grandfather, er Sam, Jack is your Great, Great Grandson. He is Phil's son, Alex...." he said gesturing towards Father, "he is Alex's Grandson!"

Father and Grandfather both got up from where they were sitting and walked over to Jack. First of all Father hugged him.

"Great to meet you! So you're my Great, Grandson, Jack. I'm real glad that we still have American blood in the family! I thought they'd all end up as True Brits!"

"It sure is great to meet you, too, Great Grandfather!" Jack beamed.

Grandfather, a young Sam Regan, aged twenty six, then hugged Jack.

"I'm delighted to meet you, Jack. Apparently, Phil here, Joni-Pip's father, is my son-in-law, married to my daughter, Sarah and you are their son, Alex's, grandson....so that makes you my Great, Great, Grandson. Right?"

"Spot on!" said Red-Ted.

"All right then, now we know **who** Jack is," said Fred Finn, "**why** is Jack here?"

"Yes!" chorused everybody.

"Jack said, 'I've done it! They are there!'" said James. "Why was that?"

"Good questions, good questions!" said Red-Ted. "Let me explain."

Father, Grandfather and Jack went to go and sit down on the bales of hay but before Red-Ted had chance to begin, Grandfather turned round.

"If you are not Ethelred-Ted, then, who are you, by Basil?"

"This is Red-Ted, Grandfather," replied Joni-Pip, "he is Ethelred-Ted, only he lives in the next century....no, in the one after that....this is the Nineteenth Century, isn't it? I live in the Twentieth Century and Red-Ted and Jack come from the Twenty First Century and they live in the United States."

"Yes, I am Red-Ted from 2007," laughed Red-Ted, "just a very old Ethelred-Ted, really. I'm a bit tatty **and** I have a new wound, here on my side." He rubbed his scorch mark. "I did it in 1892: wow that's now! Do you all realise that's over a hundred years before the time I'm living in, in 2007? By the way, I had my arm replaced when I had an accident....but that's another story....this latest story all started after Jack had received his cell 'phone in the post. You see, we had left it in 1942...."

"Cell 'phone?" asked all the men together.

"Of course, none of you would know what a cell 'phone is."

"It's this! Brits call it a mobile!" said Jack, holding up his little 'phone. Everybody strained to look at it; having no idea what it was or could do.

"That pathetic little thing? What can that do?" laughed Archimedes.

"Perhaps you should demonstrate, Jack?" suggested Red-Ted. "Let's see, it's just after two in the morning in England, so where we live in the States, is seven o'clock in the evening. Telephone....I know, Jack, call your grandfather."

Jack immediately tapped out some numbers on the keypad of his 'phone.

"I'll put it on loud speaker and then you can all hear our conversation."

Everybody in the barn remained silent. Archimedes and Grandfather were incredulous when they heard a very clear voice answer: bear in mind this was 1892 and only two of them had ever seen an ordinary telephone before.

"Hello," came the voice from the little 'phone.

"Hello," said Jack, "is that you, Grandpa?"

"Hello, Jack, where are you? What are you doing?" came the voice again and Father felt a strange thrill come over him.

"Grandpa, I am with an old friend of yours....well he....he knew your Dad, anyway," said Jack. "He would love to say, 'Hello' to you."

Jack walked over to where Father was sitting on a bale of hay.

"Who is he? What's his name?" asked the voice from the 'phone.

"His name is Philip, Phil, just say hello, please Grandpa?" asked Jack.

"Sure, Jack!" came the Speaker from the Future.

"Say 'hello'," Jack whispered to Father, handing him the 'phone.

Clumsily, Father took the 'phone, looked at it and then very awkwardly held it up to his cheek. Jack moved it over to his ear.

"Hello," Father said into the 'phone, "who is this?"

"Hello, it's me, Alex Garador....so you knew my Father, did you?"

"Yes," replied Father, stunned and shaking because Alex still sounded like Alex, only of course he was now an elderly man of eighty one and his years of living in America had left him with a definite Anglo-American accent.

"Are you there?" came Alex's voice again. "You knew Philip Garador then? You sound rather young to have known my Father," said Alex.

"Er....I did when I was a lad," answered Father, he couldn't believe what he was hearing and he certainly couldn't believe what he was saying.

"You sound very familiar to me," said Alex, "have we met before?"

"I think so," faltered Father.

"When? My Father died in 1992, that was fifteen years ago," said Alex.

The Listeners in the Barn gasped.

404

"How old was he when he....er...." started Father. "Er....how did he....?"

"He was ninety and he died peacefully in his sleep."

"Oh, I see, that's good then." Father smiled to himself and nodded.

"I think you had better say, 'Goodbye' now. I don't want my battery dying!" Jack whispered to Father.

"Goodbye!" said Father to Alex. "I'm sure we'll meet soon, very soon."

"Goodbye," said Alex to Father, "it was so good to speak to you, too and I hope we do meet. I enjoy talking about the old days!"

Jack took the 'phone back and spoke to his Grandpa.

"I'll catch you later, Grandpa, 'bye!"

"Good bye, Jack, I hope you won't be out too late, you know how your Mom worries," said Alex.

"I won't, Grandpa. See ya!" Jack replied, switching off the 'phone.

"Whew!" said everyone in the Barn.

Father sat totally overwhelmed. Joni-Pip walked over and hugged him.

"I remember when I first did that, it wasn't quite the same; I spoke to myself and I was an old lady of seventy seven! I couldn't stop thinking about it. It's obvious why when we are given the gift of Déjà Vu we have to forget everything so soon after; it would be just too much to keep in our hearts and minds....just too, too much!"

Everybody smiled at her.

"Let me get this straight," said Archimedes Spindlethrop to Jack, "was Phil actually talking to his son....Alex....your Grandpa?"

"He sure was!"

"Using that tiny contraption?"

"He sure was!"

"He was speaking from the year 2007....two centuries in front of us?"

"He sure was!" chorused Joni-Pip, Hetty, Poppy, Red-Ted and Jack.

"Staggering!" said Archimedes. "So, it's not pathetic, at all! I must become an Inventor and invent a portable speaking machine! Please may I examine it carefully?"

"Right, You Guys," said Red-Ted, "I must resume our story: there's a great deal to explain and Time is running out. I started to tell you that when we received Jack's cell 'phone, Jack's mobile back...."

"That was probably **the** most wondrous thing in all of this," interrupted Jack. "I left my cell 'phone in 1942 and that kept the Circle from closing up, ending the Orbit. We had to work out how to get it back to 2007."

"That astounded me, Ma Pets!"

"I still haven't a clueful how that worked." Poppy shook her head.

"It was Red-Ted's brilliant idea," said Jack.

"It was but there was a massive problem," said Joni-Pip. "Jack's phone

405

battery had died. You now come in, Grandfather." She looked at Sam.

"Me?"

"Yes, you made us this thingy to make Jack's hattery come alive again."

"I think you mean battery, Pops," said Red-Ted kindly.

"Yes, Grandfather, you charged the battery in Jack's little telephone by joining up all these torch batteries with two torch bulbs. It was so clever, it made the amount of volts it needed," she beamed at her young grandfather.

"Did I, by Basil?"

"So you learn to do something useful, eventually, then?" laughed Archie.

"Enough of your cheek, Archie Spindlethrop!" laughed Grandfather.

Joni-Pip then explained to them all, the wonder of getting Jack's cell phone back to the Future, by using the Captain's Chest.

"Whew!" said everyone again when she had finished.

"Yet it all happened within a few hours: instantly really!" laughed Jack. "It sure astonished me....that was Red-Ted's idea!"

Red-Ted grinned and continued,

"Once the cell 'phone arrived back at Jack's house, we expected everything to finally wind up. With the Circle being complete, we presumed the next Orbit would start. We began to think that any minute we would forget all the amazingly wonderful things that had happened but we didn't."

"I went round to Grandpa's house and asked where Auntie Joni-Pip was," said Jack seriously. "My Grandpa; you know Joni-Pip, your brother Alex, he looked at me and frowned. It was a perfectly normal question to ask him, as she was visiting him from England. I couldn't believe it when he said, 'That's not very funny, Jack, why the Dickens did you ask me that?' I replied that I would like to talk to her again, as I so enjoyed hearing all her stories about the life in the wood and Knotty Knook, during the War, especially with Poppy and Hetty the Wee. Grandpa just went white and asked, 'Jack are you ill? Have you been seeing and hearing things?' I told him that I sure wasn't ill. Then he shook me, by saying, 'Jack, my little sister, Joni-Philipa, my little J.P., she died in 1942.' I was horrified. I raced home and told...."

"Me," continued Red-Ted. "We just couldn't believe it. We knew something had gone horribly wrong. We had no idea what. All traces of Joni-Pip had disappeared from 1942....we were back to square one."

"I tried to 'phone my Auntie Amanda in England but she didn't exist! Of course she didn't exist because her mother, Joni-Pip had died, aged twelve, in 1942," continued Jack. "I raced back to Grandpa's and asked him how Joni-Pip had died; did she fall off a ladder in Marley's Barn? When Grandpa started to cry, I felt so terrible. He told me that his little sister, Joni-Philipa, had gone missing one night and she had never been seen since. At first they thought that she had been taken from her bed while she was sleeping but they discovered that her Wellington boots and outdoor coat were missing, which made them change their minds. They decided that she had gone out one night willingly and she had simply vanished. He told me it was all in the newspapers and detectives from Scotland Yard came up to Nottinghamshire from London. What a mystery! They searched the Mine Areas, they dredged the lakes, they scoured every inch of Sherwood Forest. It was the biggest search England had known. She was never found. How terrible that was for all her family," Jack said solemnly.

Just then, Joni-Pip felt a tap on her shoulder. She turned round.

"Flip, what, on earth, are you doing here?" she gasped in utter disbelief.

"I just wondered if you want to come with us? It's all right, this Lot can't see us, we're in a SOT, they'll know and see nothing. It's a Stop In Time, a SIT for them," said Flip. "A SIT is when Time stands still it simply stops."

"A slot, which slot? What's that?" asked Joni-Pip.

"Not a slot, a SOT," chuckled Steve, "a Seam Of Time. It's like a seam in your clothes: it joins two pieces of Time together, at the same location.

"Where are we going, then?" asked Joni-Pip. "Who are those two men?"

"This is James Finn and Father and they know who you are, although you will all forget. We had a bit of a job getting them here," chortled Flip.

Joni-Pip smiled at the two men; she felt very odd. They smiled back.

"We were galloping along, behind Knotty Knook, trying to get Colonel Durnford to follow us, when the Wall of Time appeared, frightening the horses," started James.

"So, Daughter, are you coming with us?" laughed a young Father.

Immediately in front of Joni-Pip stood a smooth sheet of water, similar to the Wall of Time, only with no ice bricks. She remembered seeing one briefly before, in Tunnel 6, with Freddie, Jem and the wounded soldier but no-one had explained what it was. Flip took her by the hand and they just walked straight through it! They emerged the other side and walked down the hill, past a different-looking, much newer, not so crooked, Crooked Cottage and then up towards the Clappers. It was wonderful for Joni-Pip, she knew she was in a different, much earlier Time but everything was still so familiar. She kept looking sideways, very shyly at Father and he kept smiling back at her; only his was a massive, massive grin!

"Right, James, lead on!" said Flip. "It's a good job the moon is full."

Joni-Pip looked into the sky; the light, bright stars seemed to beckon her.

They circled the Clappers until they came to a huge rock: behind it were some dense bushes. The men pulled at some branches and revealed a cave mouth. It was so well concealed, nobody would have guessed it was there.

"Father showed me this hidden entrance, when I was a lad," said James. "My grandfather had wanted it blocked off but my father left it to get in here, in case there was an emergency. There are some really old-fashioned type lamps we can use, don't worry, well there were last time I was here!"

James waited for them to stand in the dark access, then he pulled the bushes back over so that nobody passing might see anything. He then took a fairly new looking lantern, not old at all, from a shelf and some kind of flint and lit the wick.

"This would be a spiffing place to hide Colonel Durnford and his Regiment, Farmer Finn," said Joni-Pip to James, who laughed.

"Now, that's a thought! This will become the reception area for the Miners in a few hundred years! From here we have to use the hand-pulled Lift. We have four men with us, so it won't be a problem for you girls!" he looked at Steve and Craig.

They followed him to a heavy iron gate, which filled up a huge archway. James pulled a few levers and the iron gate cranked noisily to one side. Once opened, James stepped on to a square, wooden platform. The others followed. Joni-Pip was a bit hesitant but Father, still holding her hand, helped her over. As soon as everyone was safely stationed on the stand, James closed the iron gate. He then instructed Steve to join Father and Craig to join him. They unwound two very thick ropes that were wound round gigantic metal cleats.

"It's a bit antiquated. This place was used hundreds of years ago. Stay in the middle, Girls. Ready Men? We must do this as slowly as we can!"

Bit by bit, the Boys let out the rope and the Lift descended into the ground. The air became decidedly colder, the lower they dropped and the walls surrounding them seemed to get closer and closer, the further they sank. Joni-Pip and Flip stood in the very middle of the platform, hugging each other. Occasionally the Lift would scrape against the wall and judder, almost to a standstill. The men would then push the platform away from the walls, while still gripping the sturdy ropes.

'Why did I come?' Joni-Pip thought to herself. 'I could be safe in the Workhouse Barn now, if I hadn't.'

"You Girls, all right?" asked a concerned Father, which made Joni-Pip smile and think how beautiful he was when he was only twenty.

Suddenly the Lift smacked against one of the walls of the deep, vertical tunnel. The lantern that James had put in the middle of the platform fell on to its side. Immediately James stretched to steady it and lost his grip on the rope. Craig tried desperately to keep hold of the rope, at the same time as Steve, not aware of what had happened, pushed the Lift free of the wall. The Lift swayed and jerked uncontrollably and rapidly they began to gain speed. Flip grabbed the lamp but it slipped out of her hands and the oil spilled out on to the wooden platform and burst into flames. She quickly took off her jacket and started to beat at the blaze.

"James, the rope!" she screamed.

"Woooow!" shouted James, trying to grab the rope; in the process, the coarse, thick twine, burnt into his hands. Both girls ran to help but the Lift was going faster and faster; the walls seemed to fly past them!

"Oh, dear me!" said Craig and they all burst out laughing.

Smoke began to fill the shaft and they all started to cough and choke as the flames took hold. It got hotter and hotter.

'Not again!' thought Joni-Pip.

"I just hope we reach the bottom before the platform burns in half!" shouted Father, struggling to take off his jacket while still holding his rope.

"What shall we do at the bottom?" asked Steve, still pulling frantically at the same rope. "How deep is it? It will be a bit of a bump!"

"We have to stop this!" shouted back James. "Let's just try and concentrate on slowing the Lift down, shall we?"

'This is hopeless,' thought Joni-Pip, beating at the flames with Father's jacket. 'I don't want to have anything more to do with fires....ever!'

Suddenly the Lift thumped against one of the walls, jolting violently and shaking its hapless occupants but the good thing was....it slowed it down.

"We must be nearly there!" shouted James. "It's not travelling very fast now, so when I say 'Jump', then jump sideways and off the platform!"

The Lift slowly cranked its way lower and lower, scraping the wet walls as it went. James then grabbed Joni-Pip's hand and shouted,

"Jump!"

All six of them leapt sidelong into the air and tumbled on to the uneven ground. The Lift continued on its journey downwards. They scrambled up quickly and leaned over into the abyss they had escaped from, watching the last moments of the unfortunate Lift, as it crashed into a murky pool below. The flames flared for a bit then went out, engulfed by the water.

James had had the presence of mind to quickly light a lantern, which was hanging on a side wall. All six of them gathered around this beacon.

"Welcome to the Ancient Old Mine!" he announced seriously.

"How do we get out then? The same way as we came in?" asked Craig.

Everyone laughed and James led the way through, into a large cavern.

"Take this, Phil," he said to Father, handing him the lamp and then lighting two more and giving them to the boys: he then lit one for himself. The girls held hands and then they all followed James. "We'll need all these lamps. It's a good job I've JITTED here before. My father took me down here when I was a lad. He said things couldn't have changed for hundreds of years: he was right! I know all of the passages," James continued as he started to lead them down a path that ended in a solid wall. "Well, almost all of them!" he laughed.

"Is it far, Jim?" asked Father, which Joni-Pip noticed was in a much stronger American accent than she was accustomed to hearing.

"Yes, a bit of a walk. Do you know Clipstone, Flip? Joni-Pip?"

"Yes, I do, it's not too far from Edwinstowe....or is it?" replied Flip.

They ventured on for what seemed like miles, through passages and into little grottos; under archways and over natural bridges, even crossing underground lakes. Joni-Pip was still not too good with tunnels. It wasn't the low ceilings or the dripping wet walls, which disturbed her and the ground beneath their feet was uneven but pretty flat, so it wasn't even particularly tiring: what made her shudder, were the scary shadows around her; monstrous images on the walls and ceilings, cast by the lights from the lanterns the boys carried.

They continued on their way, the men quipping jokes and the lads making witty comments until they arrived at a huge wooden door. James put his lantern on the ground and unlocked it using a massive metal key.

"Nearly there....if my memory serves me rightly!"

Father helped James push open the immense door, which creaked loudly. They heard movement, a muted, rustling sound as they entered and crossed into yet another empty cavern. James took them to one of the archways and instead of going through it, he found a lever, high up on the wall beside it. He pulled on it. Nothing happened. He tried again. Nothing happened. He tried once more with the same result. He sighed and said,

"This can't be happening! This can't be right!"

Father held his lamp up and examined the wall; he walked to another archway and high above his head was a rock jutting out, he put his hand behind the rock and pulled at something.

Slowly a small section of the wall lumbered to one side, noisily scraping little rocks and stones under it. The four boys held up their lanterns and all six of them stood open-mouthed as a Medieval Hooded Figure, dressed in Lincoln Green, walked towards them with a bow strapped across his back.

"Robin Hood?" questioned James, Father and Joni-Pip, incredulously.

"The very same! Where did you come from, My Good Fellows?" he laughed, extending his arm and shaking hands with all the men. "I thought my Men and I were done for along with these good folk," he gestured to the others huddled in the dank room.

He looked at Flip and a huge beam spread across his handsome face.

"Maid Flip, my Hughog!" Robin exclaimed, hugging Flip and lifting her up. "Steve, Craig, Greetings!" he said shaking the boys hands strongly. "We meet again! Have you shot any more unfortunate squirrels out of the Sherwood Trees, Maid Flip? Forsooth, I'm content we managed to save the poor creature!" he laughed heartily and was joined by His Men.

"It took some nursing, Maid Flip, we only wish you had tarried a little longer then you would have known how difficult a task it was to keep the hapless squirrel alive but as Robin said, we accomplished it so you didn't have the blood of the ill-fated rodent on your badly aimed arrow!" laughed a huge archer, making a stunned Flip shake her head and loudly draw in her breath.

Then in turn, Robin Hood's companions picked her up and hugged her!

"How true that was, Little John!" Robin Hood laughed loudly.

"Thank you for letting me come," Joni-Pip whispered, "it's so exciting!"

"What is exactly going on?" Father asked The Bowman.

"Sadly, my Good Man and True, I thought that Prince John had finally got the better of us. The Brutish Brigand captured these poor peasant families as Hostages, luring us to try and release them. He imprisoned them in these damp dungeons, underneath his Palace of Clipstone."

"Woe for us, we were betrayed and Prince John threw us down here to 'starve and rot', I think he said, didn't he Robin?" laughed another bowman, dressed all in red.

"'Tis true what Will says," the Hooded Leader replied.

"Well, we have come to change all that," said Steve, "you will not actually end your days down here! History will be re-written!"

"History will now say 'Prince John was outwitted by a Band of Outlaws when Robin Hood and his Merry Men released the Hostages'," began Craig.

"....'Who were held in the Dungeons, beneath the King's Palace, at Clipstone'...." finished a still very bemused and astonished Flip.

"I'm confused! Nevertheless, we must away!" said Robin Hood. "Make haste! There is no time to lose! We must escape before we are discovered!"

"Er...." said James, turning and peering outside, "how are we going to get back up, we don't have a Lift, well, not a proper one, anymore!"

"It's a Lift then, Jim but not a Lift as we know it!" laughed Father.

"Does any one of you Good People have any vittles? I would indeed so enjoy a morsel of a Munch Break!" said a jovial, plump monk: much to

Joni-Pip's amazement!

Joni-Pip picked up one of the lanterns on the floor, left the Dungeon and walked to examine all of the archways surrounding the large room outside. She had gone round four of them and went to the next and called out,

"Over here, You Lot! I've found something! Look!"

The Captives filed out of the Dungeon; the Peasants, Will Scarllet, Little John, Friar Tuck, the rest of the Merry Men and the Master Bowman, himself, Robin Hood.

Father, James, Craig, Steve and Flip followed. They all looked up.

"See, Flip! Tunnel 5!" said an elated Joni-Pip, holding up her lamp and pointing to the carved number '5' on the wall. "It has to lead somewhere near Tunnel 6, surely?"

"Of course, it does! You clever girl! Let's go," said Flip, then she looked back, "but not before we have closed the door. I hate leaving them open!"

"Good thinking!" said Father. "We don't want King John pursuing us into the Future!" With that he walked back over to the secret doorway, pulled the lever and the wall slowly ground and rumbled back into place.

"Wonderful!" said Robin Hood. "Prince John will be incensed on discovering our disappearance! He will wonder how we escaped! How jolly is that? I would love to be there to see his face! What rapture!"

"No, Robin, we will not return to view such a thing, however gratifying and tempting that vision might prove to be!" laughed Will Scarllet.

"Owh!" said the disappointed Medieval Hero. "Think how agreeable that would be!"

"Is this the reason you needed to know the whereabouts of the Old Mine?" Joni-Pip asked Steve. "So it was nothing to do with the Two Men in Long, Black Coats, then? We got it all wrong?"

"We still don't know what that's all about and yes, it was me actually. In the History Books it said that Robin Hood and some of his Merry Men, died in the Dungeons of The King's Palace, at Clipstone. I was sad and mad and wanted to change that. So we did some research and discovered that there was a secret tunnel from the Old Mine to Clipstone," Steve replied.

"But I couldn't remember where the Old Mine was!" laughed Flip.

"But now it is accomplished. We have changed the Past!" grinned Craig.

"But I am here." Joni-Pip stood up; she was back in the barn, unaware of her amazing encounter and adventure with the Famous Legendary Outlaw. "How did that happen? When did I disappear? It doesn't make any sense."

"It does, it sure does," said Father, also standing up. "I remember carrying your lifeless body out of the Workhouse Fire. It was the worst moment of my life. Don't you remember me warning you not to go over the Wall of Time, Honey? Don't you remember me telling you that you had died in the Fire?"

"Yes, Hen, it was after Father had told us that he had been petrified in the Keep of Bad Memories, don't y' remember?"

Joni-Pip walked over to Father and hugged him.

"Yes, Father, I do remember you warning me but I am still here. I came out of the Fire safely. It was very, very scary but we made it."

"What did you do, then, Jack?" asked Grandfather. "You must have done something because Joni-Pip is still with us."

"We made lots of enquiries about Great Auntie Joni-Pip and there was nothing, absolutely nothing."

"It was all such a mystery to us," continued Red-Ted, "but....we still had memories of everything that had happened...."

"So we knew the Circle was not closed and we were still in the Pasture."

"That's right, Jack. In the end, after much discussion, we decided that the only thing we could do, was to jump back over the Wall of Time and make some investigations. Which we did, didn't we?" continued Red-Ted.

"Yeah, we both came back to 1942, with Macca and paid a visit to Edwinstowe Library...." answered Jack.

"Seamus!" said Joni-Pip and Hetty the Wee, looking at each other.

"Yes," said Red-Ted, "Seamus helped us to find the Newspaper Report on the Workhouse Fire and after what we saw, we knew we had to get back to 1892. So we jumped back over the Wall of Time again and landed....too late!"

"What did you see in the Newspaper Report, then?" asked Archimedes. "It must have been very dramatic for you to feel that you had to come back here."

"We saw a picture of Father and James and they were part of the Rescue Team. We then read another article about a mysterious little girl, who had died. Nobody knew where she came from, she didn't belong in the Workhouse," answered Jack.

"Because Joni-Pip had disappeared, along with her Wellington boots and outdoor coat, we guessed that she was that 'little girl' and that she had JITTED and died in the Workhouse Fire. We thought that Father and James had JITTED, too, to try and save her but had failed," said Red-Ted.

"We came back here but it was all too late. All the children and Joni-Pip had died. What puzzled us was where was Ethelred-Ted?" Jack shrugged.

"Hmmm!" mused Red-Ted. "I knew the only way to find out was to go into the Observatory of Memories Unknown, then I would know where Ethelred-Ted, was, while all this was going on."

"Observatory of Memories Unknown? That sounds some great place!" said Fred Finn. "Or is it?"

"Yes, it is a great place; it's the place you go to after you have started a new Circle. It fills in the new memories that you have, after the Past has been changed. It's amazing!" replied Red-Ted. "It's called the OOMU."

"That sounds exceedingly complicated," said Grandfather.

"Look, it isn't, it's wonderful and you would all love it but I really haven't got time to explain it right now," replied Red-Ted. "We're rapidly running out of time. All I will say is that I JITTED, went into the KOL and entered into the OOMU and there, through one of the windows, I saw myself, well, Ethelred-Ted, actually, sipping tea and eating buns with Nuttingham Squirrel in his Underground Apartment and it was on the night of the Workhouse Fire!"

"How d'you know when it was, it could've been any time?" asked Fred.

"You take it as read!" said Red-Ted to Fred.

"Red-Ted was most upset when he saw himself and realised that he had left Joni-Pip and Hetty the Wee to face the flames, while he was drinking tea, eating buns and making peace with an obnoxious squirrel," said Jack.

"Once more, I felt it was my fault that Joni-Pip had lost her life: so right then and there I knew something had to be done. I had to find a way of saving her and all the children....and Hetty, of course!" said Red-Ted sadly.

"We knew they had been trapped. In the newspaper, Gavin Fielding, the local Reporter, had written that all the doors and windows were locked in the Workhouse, so none of the children could escape. Nobody could get into them and nobody could get out," said Jack, equally sadly.

"In the OOMU, I saw the OGOFS' Great Store and in there, I told you that there were loads of various sized...." started Red-Ted.

"Keys!" said everyone.

"Right! I went back to 1942 and asked Nuttingham Squirrel if I could borrow the keys to the Workhouse. He said I couldn't," started Red-Ted.

"How mean!" said Archimedes Spindlethrop.

"Yes!" echoed everybody else. "How mean!"

"No!" said Red-Ted. "You don't understand, he just **couldn't** help; the keys to the Workhouse weren't in the Great Store. There were loads of other keys found but not them. He said he would have known if they were there because everything is labelled: day and date. As well as that, there were bunches of keys but only little ones. The Workhouse keys had never been found. So, I reasoned that the only way to do it, was to come back here, in 1892 and make sure the keys were put somewhere where I could find them and use them. So earlier....tomorrow morning....sadly....after it was too late...."

Everybody looked totally confused.

"We JITTED," continued Red-Ted, "to try and find the keys. We searched everywhere. Some Firemen were still around, checking everything was safe."

"Yeah, twice I was told to go away....which of course I didn't: well I couldn't could I? We had a very important Quission," said Jack seriously.

The door of the Workhouse Barn opened and in walked some women carrying baskets ladened with flasks of fresh cocoa and platters of cheese and pickle, as well as egg, sandwiches. A Munch Break? Red-Ted was delighted!

"Thank you, Rosemary," said Fred to one of the women.

"Hello, Fred," she replied, "what a terrible night! I'm so glad that everybody has got out safely. Your mother kindly sent all this!"

"Good show!" he laughed.

Rosemary walked into the corner to some of the others in the Barn.

"Who is that?" asked Joni-Pip. "She looks so familiar."

"That's pretty Rosemary Brown, well, she used to be called that. Her name is now Rosemary Duke," laughed Archimedes. "Fred quite liked her once but Dennis Duke beat him to it. She is married to him now."

"I know who she is!" said Joni-Pip, to her friends. "That's Mrs Broft's mother. She told me her mother's name. She looks like her!"

"Yes, she does!"

415

"These egg sandwiches are so delicious!" said Red-Ted munching his way through an enormous, deeply filled sandwich. "Did the eggs come from your chickens then, Farmer Finn....er Fred?"

"Yes, they did and you know what my Father always says?" said Fred. "'If you feed the chickens well, then the chickens feed you well'!"

"How horrible!" said Joni-Pip.

"But they give us lovely eggs!" said Fred innocently.

"Yeah right and the rest!" laughed Jack.

Another pretty young woman came up to James Finn and offered him some more hot cocoa and another sandwich.

"Thanks," said James, taking a sandwich carefully from the plate and taking a hearty bite. He then turned and smiled at her. Then he looked at her again. He turned deathly pale: drew in his breath, in shock, which made him choke and then he promptly sprayed her with a spluttered, eggy, shower. A shiver came over him.

"M....Er....M....er....what's your name then....er....Mary? I'm so sorry," he stumbled and in trying to wipe the egg from her unfortunate coat, he smeared the yellow and white lumpy mixture, spreading it so that it covered a wider area.

For some reason Mary didn't object, she just laughed.

"Sir, you know my name, you just called me Mary, so why did you ask me what it was? I do not know you, do I?"

James went whiter still and spluttered again.

"Er....no I don't suppose you do....have you met, my Fa....my....my.... have you met Fred Finn, yet?"

"No, I don't care much for him. I have heard a great deal about him from my friend, Rosemary and I don't think I would ever like him!" said Mary turning to walk away from him. "He seems to like the ladies a bit too much!"

James ran over to Fred, his father and dragged him towards Mary.

"Fred, I want you to meet Mary....Mary I want you to meet Fred...."

Fred turned and looked at Mary, a huge smile spread across his face.

"How do you do?" he asked, holding out his hand.

Mary did not extend her hand and said very abruptly,

"Sir, as you can see, I am carrying a very large platter in one hand and a flask of hot cocoa in the other, it is impossible for me to shake your hand."

Fred just smiled at her, completely unaware of what she had said.

James looked at his younger father and then nudged him.

"Can't you see, Fath....Fred....Mary can't shake your hand."

Fred continued grinning like a greedy boy, let loose in a Bakery.

"Fa....Fred....help Mary with her plate!" urged James.

Fred still stood there, beaming at the lovely Mary.

"Look," said James very seriously, "I would very much like to exist when I return shortly to 1942....and as painful as it might seem....this young lady is not very impressed with you....not at all....so stop grinning at her; take the plate from her and help her with the sandwiches! Please? For my sake? Pleeeeeeze?"

Fred looked at Mary, looked back at James again and then, looking back again, saw her ladened with flask and platter. It suddenly dawned on him that he should be helping this beautiful young lady, not just ogling at her! He quickly relieved her of the platter of sandwiches and then attempted to take the flask out of her hand.

"That's fine," she said, "I can manage the flask. Do you want to take the plate round for everybody, then?"

"Er....no," replied Fred.

James looked aghast.

"I will take the plate round for you!" said Fred, smiling at pretty Mary.

Mary smiled at Fred. Fred beamed. James sighed with relief.

Soon the women left but not before everyone had been fed and watered and not before everybody had thanked them for their extreme kindness and not before Fred had expressed his desire to call on Mary later that week.

James was so happy: so exceedingly happy.

"Right, Red-Ted, where were you in your story?" asked Archie Spindlethrop. "I am intrigued!"

"We all are!" added Grandfather.

Everybody sat back on the bales of hay, with Red-Ted in the middle.

"Jack and I were searching for the keys to the Workhouse, remember? We looked everywhere and found nothing. We decided that the only other place that we hadn't searched was down in the cellar. We knew that was where the fire had broken out but how could we get down into the cellar? The fire had destroyed most of the downstairs of the building and smouldering beams were everywhere, blocking all the doors. We walked round the blackened building but we couldn't find the door to the cellar."

"After a lot of poking around, we managed to locate this metal hatch. It was still warm but we lifted it up: it was right to one side of the burnt out building. When we opened it there was a kind of chute, so we had a warm slide down into the cellar. It sure was fun!" laughed Jack.

"Yes it was, although I kinda worried that I might singe my fur....how mean, You Lot all are!" he said when everyone laughed.

"Wasn't it dark, down there?" asked James Finn.

"How did you manage to see anything?" asked Father.

"Yes, it was dark, very dark," replied Red-Ted.

"I always carry my pencil torch with me so we managed to look round."

"Pencil torch?" questioned the men from 1892.

Jack took his pencil torch out of his jacket pocket and held it up for everyone to see. He switched it on and they all gasped.

"It was still quite difficult but we managed to search through the rubble and lo and behold there it was on the floor, lying abandoned and forgotten; one large and very heavy bunch of Workhouse Keys," said Red-Ted. "Don't forget the fire broke out down there, so we presume the man who accidentally started the fire dropped them in panic, or drunkenness. We then had to quickly decide how best it was to make sure that the keys were kept safe, so that we could easily get our hands on them, in order to unlock the doors and windows and get the children out safely, in 1892."

"We decided that I should JIT and hide the keys: guess where?"

Everybody shrugged their shoulders and shook their heads.

"Down the hatch!" said Red-Ted and Jack together.

"I hid them in the cellar: the safest place, only in 1942. I have just got back!" said Jack enthusiastically. "They weren't there long....only a few minutes, really!"

"I picked them up almost immediately they were put there! Actually I picked them up before they were put there, in my Circle Continuum, but in 1942 I picked them up after they were put there, " laughed Red-Ted. "Pretty, pretty amazing eh?"

"Confounding! No wonder they were never found in 1892!" laughed Joni-Pip.

"What?" asked Jack and Red-Ted together: then they thought about it, looked at each other and said, "Of course!"

"How canny is that? Y' Two hiding them, Ma Pets!" giggled Hetty.

"Of course!" said everyone else.

"I'm still puzzled, though. How did it actually work?" asked Joni-Pip. "How did you get them Red-Ted, before Jack had actually put them there? That's got to be impossible! How did you both manage to make separate jumps back over the Wall of Time? You only have one F.B.. Why did you hide them in 1942 and not in 1892?"

"I beg your pardon? I have the F.B. that Jemmy gave me in 2007," replied Jack.

"And I have the F.B. that Jack gave me in 1942,"said Red-Ted.

"In saying that, though, we do actually have three F.B.'s in our possession," laughed Jack, "very soon, Eth from 1942, will JIT back."

"Only after he's polished off a large plate of biscuits and buns," laughed Red-Ted. "Right now, in 1942, he's still with Nuttingham and when he comes, for some reason, he'll bring some ice cubes for the Wall of Time!"

"I think we can safely say that when he discovers that it's too late to save the children, Joni-Pip and Hetty, he'll be so upset, he'll panic and run about trying to find out what's gone on and what's happened to them," explained Jack, "not knowing that by then, you'll all be back in 1942."

"In that panic, he'll drop his F.B. he should be guarding. It doesn't seem to like being dropped, nor does anyone, I suppose," said Red-Ted.

"And....we happened to see it lying on the ground when we came back too late, in an hour or so's time!" laughed Jack.

Everybody looked totally and utterly confused, yet again.

"I see, Ma Lambs, where Y' Two are coming from now."

"Me, too!" agreed Joni-Pip.

"I haven't got a clueful!" added Poppy; another oxymoron phrase.

"It means that as we have his F.B., he'll be stuck in Time!" said Jack.

"Let me go over this spectacular part of the story again. I can't really believe the gamble worked. I told Jack to go back to 1942 with the Workhouse Keys and said to hide them in the cellar. Be both jumped at the same time, only I JITTED back to 1942 and **picked up those very keys**....I'd set my F.B. to two hours **after** Jack's, hoping that gave him enough time to do everything we had discussed. We knew he couldn't take anything permanently from 1892 or 2007, or the Circle would never close up. He obviously managed it and when I went back and landed....amazingly, I saw Father and James Finn and 'myself' jump over the Wall of Time and disappear then I went and took the keys out of the cellar and immediately jumped back, here."

"I remember," said James and Father together.

"Time was running out! We knew Jack would take much longer because he had to find a safe way of hiding the keys. What we'd done was use the same idea as we used with the cell 'phone; only in reverse. I went back and picked up the keys at eleven thirty May 4th 1942. Jack knew he had to get them there before then!"

"Eleven thirty?" Jack said alarmed. "I looked at my 1942 watch and the hands said 'eleven twenty seven'! Whew! That was close but we made it! Just! It took a bit of doing but so much was at stake. I borrowed some wood from Grandfather's shed at the Crooked Cottage. I don't think you'll mind, will you, Grandfather?" laughed Jack.

"I'm sure I won't!" Grandfather looked confused: everyone laughed.

"I made a wooden box," started Jack, "it's so easy to locate stuff in your shed, Grandfather, it's all labelled and stacked so tidily, you're so organised!"

"Sam? Organised? Sir, you are mistaken!" laughed Archimedes.

"Surprisingly he can in 1942, believe me!" said Jack. "I emptied a tin and put the keys in it. Hmmm, a tin is going to go missing from your shed, too, sorry, Grandfather....don't moan when you find the contents of one of your tins, emptied all over the work bench in 1942, will you? After all it was to save your granddaughter! Quite a nice tin actually....it had a king on it! There's a Queen of England now! Oh silly me, so there is here, in 1892! Anyway, when I had finished the box with your 'borrowed' wood and hinges, Grandfather, I put the tin that held the keys into the wooden box and then I had to go and search for the old hatch that lead down to the cellar of the Workhouse...."

"You hammered nails without attracting any attention?" asked Fred.

"Good question. That's exactly what I was thinking....er Father," said James Finn, laughing once more at the preposterousness of calling a much younger man, 'Father'. Fred looked at his son and smiled.

"Great minds and all that!"

James smiled back and nodded: then he thought to himself,

'I would wager a bet that there aren't that many men who have introduced their Father to their Mother, as I have just done!'

"I carried everything up into the woods, hoping that the hammering wouldn't be heard. Trouble is, I was disturbed by this pesky squirrel! He was such a pain, moaning at me for being a 'noisy boy'! 'Didn't I know there was a War on?' I told him to go away and just ignored him," said Jack seriously. "I had to find the hatch that led down into the cellar. I searched and searched and I finally found it, behind a large tree with a low branch across the path."

"The Major Oak!" said Hetty, Joni-Pip and Poppy-Plump-Pij together.

"I cleared away the overgrown grass and the stones, which were on the hatch, so that Red-Ted could pull it up easily," explained Jack.

"That was no problem. I found the hatch immediately, just behind my tree, I didn't even have to scrape around the edges: it came straight up!"

"Of course it did, Red-Ted, I had only just done it!"

"Oh yeah, of course; Nolly Me!"

"I still don't understand why you felt you had to hide the keys, back in 1942. Why couldn't you have hidden them in this Time?" asked Joni-Pip.

"We thought it was best to take them back into the Future, we didn't have a lot of time to make a decision," continued Red-Ted. "As well as that, we knew the OGOFS hadn't found the keys...."

"We also knew the keys had never been found in 1892, so to make sure that we had them, we felt it was necessary to take them completely away, out of this Time and bring them back ourselves....making sure they weren't ever lost," added Jack.

"The simplest way to solve everything," said Red-Ted. "Did I say

SIMPLE?"

"Well it worked! Look you're all here! You're all safe!" Jack was happy.

"It nearly didn't work though, Jack," said Red-Ted seriously. "When I JITTED back to the Workhouse with the keys, because the Wall of Time Eth was using was still in the Children's Dormitory, my Wall of Time took me outside the dormitory door. There obviously wasn't enough room for both of them in the same area....I nearly caught fire the flames were so ferocious," said Red-Ted gently rubbing the scorch marks on his side.

"You Poor Thing!" said Jack. "I had no idea. I thought that you'd JIT and unlock all the doors and windows and everyone would get out safely."

"Er....not quite!" replied Red-Ted, remembering the fury of the flames.

"That was so very odd," said Hetty, "we saw Ethelred-Ted leaving the room, disappearing over the Wall of Time, at the same time as we saw him coming in through the door, after he had finally managed to unlock it."

"But that wasn't him, it was you, Red-Ted! Were we glad to see you! It was then that I had such a strong feeling of Déjà Vu again: of course it was another Circle! Thank you! Hey, no wonder the keys were never found: you took them! Come and get a hug from this Hug-hog!" said Joni-Pip, hugging them both and then looking extremely puzzled at what she had called herself.

"Can we go back to your house, soon, Uncle Archie?" came a tiny voice.

Amelia Plate had left sitting on the bale of hay, in between her uncle and Joni-Pip and had fallen asleep, curled up in a corner on a deep pile of hay.

Archimedes Spindlethrop walked over and lifted her up from the floor.

"Sorry, Sweetness," he said gently, "I have been so interested in all these amazing goings on that I had completely forgotten about my little niece!"

"There is one thing I want to do first, Uncle Archie, before we go, if you don't mind. Have you got a piece of paper, please?" asked little Amelia.

"Er....No! Has anyone got a piece of paper handy?" asked Archimedes.

Everybody laughed and looked heavenward.

"I have!" said Joni-Pip, taking out an envelope from her pocket: inside the envelope was a folded piece of white paper; she looked at Grandfather. "You never know when you might need it!" she laughed.

"That's a good idea, I will remember that!" said Grandfather seriously.

Joni-Pip then took out the fountain pen that he had given her in 1942.

"Here you are, Amelia," she said, offering her both the pen and paper, "I always carry a pen, too, you never know when you might need that, either!"

"Thank you, Joni-Pip, I so need to do this!" smiled Amelia.

Joni-Pip smiled back, exhausted but happy.

Amelia took the paper and started to write on it.

Chapter 41

The Keep of Bad Memories

Suddenly through the darkness streaked a huge hand of forked lightning, digging its fingers into the large oak that stood by the Workhouse Barn and splitting it in two. Immediately there began a creaking and a cracking. The still night air was filled with an almighty clap of thunder followed by a loud groaning and a thousand rips and splits, which eventually grew into a thunderous crash as the large oak, which once stood proudly guarding the Workhouse, keeled over and landed right on top of the barn roof. The barn juddered and quaked. The sleeping children woke up and started crying. All the men jumped to their feet. The barn, which had at first become a harbour of peace and safety, now became an open sea of turmoil and panic.

"What on earth?" asked Father, running to open the Barn door. "I can't open the door, its somehow got wedged!" He shouted to the men behind him. They joined him in trying to shove the door open. Five strong backs pushed and thrust at the double, wooden doors of the barn to no avail.

"It's got to be the Old Oak Tree," said Fred, nodding hopelessly.

"How can we get out? Is there another way?" asked Joni-Pip.

"A barn with two ways out? Hmmm, I don't think so!" said Sam Regan.

One of the children came running up to Father and tugged at his sleeve. Father turned and looked at him....the boy pointed. The vibrations on the barn roof had caused a lighted lantern to fall off its hook on to a bale of hay. It was blazing fiercely.

"Where's some water?" yelled James across the barn. He took off his jacket and started beating at the flames. Nobody answered.

"There are some barrels of paraffin, or something, in the corner; we must get them away from the flames!" yelled Sam, running to the barrels and trying to roll them on to their sides even though they were very heavy and very difficult to shift.

"You all right in there? Everybody all right?" a voice came from outside.

"So far but we have a fire to fight in here!" Father shouted back to him.

"We're The Firemen. Some branches are blocking the door. The main trunk is leaning on the roof. We've saws and choppers but the tree is huge. Can you hold out?"

"We haven't much choice," replied Grandfather solemnly.

The roof moaned. The flames were ferocious. Some were choking in the smoke.

"Red-Ted, we must do something!" said Jack. They looked at each other in silence, then they both grinned. "D'you think it will work?" asked Jack.

"We try or we die!" laughed Red-Ted. "Right everyone!" he shouted but at first, nobody could hear him, so he went to Father and yanked at his sleeve. "Jack and I have an idea!"

"It's hopeless. We can't change the Past, however hard we try," mumbled Father.

"You did! You saved Colonel Durnford's entire Regiment in Isandlwana!"

"O.K. perhaps we can only do it once, then," Father replied gloomily.

"Please, Father, can you call everyone to attention?" Red-Ted begged.

"O.K. but it won't work," surrendered Father, walking away from the door and then shouting very loudly, "Jack and Red-Ted have an idea, so please listen to them!"

Everyone stood still, waiting to hear what to do, surrounded by the angry flames.

"Please all stand as close as you can to the door!" Red-Ted commanded.

Everyone obeyed. Joni-Pip and Poppy herded the children together.

"Are y' thinking what I'm thinking, Ma Pets?"

"I can't see how!" replied Joni-Pip. "Where are they going to get ice from?"

"Keep clear!" ordered Red-Ted.

Jack unfolded the F.B. and true to form, the little green silk handkerchief was transformed into a large, firm board. The flames around them got closer and closer. The Wall of Time grew taller and wider. Everyone gasped as they watched each amazing brick of water form like ice blocks, one out of another.

When the Wall was finally, fully formed, Jack gave the instructions.

"Right, Guys, we are not quite sure what's going to happen but at least we will be away from the flames. As you approach the Wall of Time just simply jump, O.K.?"

"Where did you get the ice from?" asked Joni-Pip.

"Ice? What on earth did we need ice for?" Jack asked puzzled.

"To put on the F.B. to make the Wall of Time."

"What?"

"Ice: an ice cube for each of the four star symbols."

"What are you going on about? You just touch the stars!" Jack laughed.

"Joni-Pip, you Hetty and Poppy take the children. Jack, the men and I, will follow behind you!" ordered Red-Ted calmly.

"Children," Joni-Pip said, "get into pairs, walk up to the Wall and jump over it!"

"But I can't jump," said a little black boy.

Joni-Pip knelt down in front of him as he seemed so sad. She clasped his hands.

"Hurry, Joni-Pip!" urged Red-Ted. "There's just no time to spare, for this!"

"What's your name, Honey?" Joni-Pip asked the little boy.

"It's Sunshine Kwame but most people just call me Sunshine."

"Why can't you jump, Sunshine Kwame?"

The little boy pulled up his nightshirt and exposed a badly twisted leg.

"Sunshine, hold my hand and you can jump with me," she said taking the hand of Amelia Plate and saying to the other children, "Everyone, go to the Wall and jump!"

They approached the Wall, smiled and then all jumped together. Poppy led a small group of children and jumped with them. Hetty did the same. Up they all went.

Soon everybody had left the burning barn.

Joni-Pip and Hetty were expecting to go over the Wall of Time and enter into the KOL with the patterns swirling around them. That, however, did not happen.

As they took off, they were indeed taken into the air but as they began to be whisked over the Wall of Time, they met some others coming over the Wall in the opposite direction and they all tumbled down a long spiral chute. Children, animals and toys seemed to be everywhere! It was chaotic. They seemed to be falling and plunging and twirling and swirling and rolling and turning, on and on for miles.

Finally they all came to a halt, toppling into a huge circular observatory!

"What on earth was that?" said Joni-Pip, looking round the vast, packed room. "Where did all these people come from?" she asked Poppy and Hetty as they lay with the children, dishevelled and untidily on the floor.

"That was the best thing ever!" laughed Sunshine. "Can we do it again? Please?"

"Everyone O.K?" Joni-Pip stood up and brushed herself down.

"Yes!" came a loud reply from all the smiling children.

"Hi, J.P., that was fun!" came Craig's familiar voice.

"Hey, Yankee Cuz, how's you?" Steve called across the massive round room.

"Joni-Pip, what happened? We'd come to save you from the Workhouse

424

Barn!"

"Flip!" Joni-Pip called and weaved her way through the crowd to them.

On her way over, a young girl stopped her and hugged her. She had her hair tied up in a pony tail and wore a tee-shirt with the words 'Milton Keynes' written across it.

"Be of good cheer, you must be Joni-Pip? So sorry, we caused the accident I am afraid: the MTC, The Mid-Time Collision over the WOT. We had JITTED to save you from the explosion in the Workhouse Barn. In the first Circle that didn't happen. The Barn wasn't used. The Past was changed when the Children were saved so every-thing was different. My name's Jemmy, you don't know me but I know about you. Where's Jack? I'm his Great Niece, we met when we JITTED to save his brother...."

"Grant! I remember, I do know about you, too! They told us. Pleased to meet you, Jemmy. Are Acker and Reddy with you?" Joni-Pip looked around the room.

"Yes, of course. They are getting acquainted with Hetty the Wee and Poppy-Plump-Pij and Macca, naturally. Where is Jack? Do you know?"

"I have no idea. He must be here somewhere with Red-Ted, my father and all the other men. They were supposed to jump after us. Where are we, exactly?" she said, scouring the area for familiar faces.

"Joni-Philipa!" Father's voice came across the air and Joni-Pip scanned the room but she couldn't see him.

Finally she met up with Flip, Steve and Craig. They had a Circle Hug.

"You Lot, I just have to know something. When you open the F.B. how do you make the Wall of Time grow?" asked Joni-Pip.

"Touch the Stars!" all three of them said together, puzzled.

"That's exactly what Jack said. What does that mean? How?"

"Exactly what it says: think about it and it will come to you!" Flip laughed.

"Look who's over there!" Steve pointed. "Robin Hood and his Merry Men!"

"How spiffing! There are some fun times to come with them, methinks! I can see Colonel Durnford and his Regiment, over there, too! I hope he hasn't got the 20,000 Zulus with him. Where will they all fit?" asked Joni-Pip, anxiously.

"Mmmmm....interesting thought!" said Craig, "I can't see any sign of the Warriors but I can see two men we know, look!"

Joni-Pip went up to the men Craig pointed out and hugged them.

"Hello again, Father," she said to a twenty-year-old, Philip Garador.

"I didn't think we would meet again until you were born, Joni-Pip," he said. "D'you mind if we call you Joni-Philipa, after me, instead of Joni-

425

Pip?"

"Cripes!" said Joni-Pip, shaking her head. "That takes a lot of working out!....Did you get back through the SOT, O.K., Farmer Finn?"

"No problems. That was a marvellous meeting with Robin Hood, eh....?"

"Attention everybody!"

1942 Father's voice was heard, shouting above the chattering and hubbub.

"Attention everybody!" the nattering and buzzing stopped. "As you can see we have a situation here. We, us guys, have had a discussion and come to the conclusion that the MTC broke an Orbit. Consequently, we have all of us here together, enmasse. Some of you will no doubt meet yourselves; yes they are really you, only from another Time, another Circle. I'm here twice....from 1922 and 1942....weird....very odd....but nevertheless amazing! Everyone of us is a JIT...." Father continued. "Get yourselves acquainted because we haven't got long! We're just discussing the best way to get us all home and back to our loved ones! Accidentally, Jack used a 'borrowed'....well, Eth's, F.B., instead of his own....he did have three to chose from, an easy mistake but sadly it means if you look around there is only one way out of this room! There is no Arch, no Pool of Colours, no Keep of Good Memories and no OOMU! We'll keep you posted as to what to do....when we know." Father's voice trailed away.

Joni-Pip quickly made her way over to find Hetty and Poppy.

"You know what that means? Something we've always dreaded."

"The Keep of Bad Memories!" said Hetty and Poppy together.

"The Children? How can we take them through that terrible place?"

"What I don't understand is, why isn't Ethelred-Ted here?" asked Poppy.

"He's probably eating buns and things...." started Hetty.

"I heard that! No, I am not! It's weird, Joni-Pip, everyone who has JITTED in your Orbits, is here and loads more. I don't quite understand. P'raps you'll meet them in the Future. There are three of me: me, Red-Ted and Reddy!"

Before she had time to reply, there came a loud battering sound from outside the walls of the round chamber. It was thunderous and terrifying!

"What's that?" shouted Joni-Pip. In seconds Steve had found them.

"Look out of one of the windows!" he pointed.

In the confusion, Joni-Pip hadn't thought to see what was outside the room. They threaded their way in and out of the people and over to the wall.

As she looked through the glass she shrunk back in fright, for there she came face to face with a War–painted Zulu! She re-coiled in terror!

"There are those soldiers in strange uniforms out here!" said Ethelred-

Ted, looking outside. "Can't see the Two Men in Long Black Coats, though!"

"Of course you can't," said Poppy, "I flew up to take a look a minute ago and saw them talking to a wounded soldier. They are on the other side of the room!"

"I'll go and have a look!" said Steve intrigued and he hurriedly left them.

The clapping sound of the Warriors outside sent shivers down Joni-Pip's spine. She felt a tap on her shoulder. She turned round and there, to her astonishment, was a smiling Zulu!

"Hello!" she said, immediately recognising him as the Zulu who touched her gently on the head with his spear. She took his hand and shook it, much to his surprise and amusement: he then bowed slightly and walked off.

"Right, Everybody, it seems we have no choice!" Father's voice could hardly be heard above the racket coming from outside the room. "We all have to go into the Keep of Bad Memories. We can only go out through one person's memories and I have volunteered. Stick together and remember all the things you might see and hear are just my memories, my bad memories, they can't hurt you! Please don't rush or somebody might get hurt! I will go first!"

"No, you won't! I'll lead the way. It will be my memories!" Joni-Pip shouted across to him. Everyone turned and looked at her. She marched into the middle of the room where Father stood. "You are all here because of my accident in Marley's Barn, aren't you?"

Colonel Durnford and his Regiment, Robin Hood and his Merry Men, the wounded soldier and the Two Men in Long Black Coats looked at each and shrugged.

"What is she on about?" Craig asked, leaning over to Flip.

"Leave her! She'll learn soon enough, how insignificant she is in all this!"

"Well, even if you're not," Joni-Pip faltered, "it's about time I did something for others. I've been a spoilt and selfish brat all my life, so it's my chance to show everyone I have changed, I have so changed! I'll go first! I won't let you down!"

Without giving anyone the opportunity to stop her, Joni-Pip unbolted the trap door in the middle of the room, opened it up and started to go down the stairs. Father tried to pull her back but she had walked into The Keep of Bad Memories first. There was nothing that he could do. She would now have to face her bad memories, all alone!

Immediately Joni-Pip had descended three or four of the cold, uneven steps, she heard the soft, rushing, humming sound she had heard in the OOMU.

When she reached the bottom step, the Air Raid sirens started. The sound of the wailing made her shiver but she was determined to stay calm. The memory of that night in the cellar came flooding back. Soon she had reached a dark, long and damp passage. She was petrified. It took her back to a visit she and her family once made to Dover Castle before the War. They had been guided through the secret tunnels under the Castle as part of their tour. The place had fascinated but terrified her. She could hear the water as it dripped down the wet walls. It was so cold! There was an eerie, dim glow coming from a few small oil lamps hung, now and again, along the way. She had to keep looking straight ahead of her, as the light from the lanterns transformed her shadows into ugly monsters on the wall. The siren suddenly stopped. Soon the bombing started. Each explosion made her jump but on she walked. Then came the acrid smell of the burning and the smoke. The noise above her and around her made her heart beat faster and faster, she shuddered and shook but battled on boldly. Suddenly everything went pitch black. She so wanted to curl up on the floor and hide from her mind but she knew everyone's future lay solely in her hands!

The squeaking then began. The scuffling of tiny claws. Straight away she knew what they were. Rats! She could feel them crawling over her feet. Scratching at her legs. Hundreds and hundreds of them; she needed to screech and shriek but she didn't!

'This isn't real! This isn't real! This is just one of my Nightmares!' she thought, even though her flesh was creeping with fear. 'They can't hurt me! They just can't!'

A gloomy light appeared and she thought it must all be over but then she heard a faint munching. The noise got steadily louder and louder, until it was deafening. Then she saw them, all marching straight towards her. It was an army of huge Soldier Ants! Their bodies were crisp and red and shiny like shells and their antennae stretched high into the air, quivering and searching for their next dinner. Joni-Pip's body shuddered in dread as the largest of the ants climbed up and over her body. She looked up and could see the sections of its huge under parts as it past over her, touching her skin.

She felt so sickened and just needed to run and scream and scream but she didn't, even though it made her quake in terror; bravely, she went on.

'This isn't real! This isn't real!' she thought again to herself, as one after the other of these huge insects crunched slowly over her. She could hardly breathe in horror. She closed her eyes and tried to think of something nice but on and on the giant ants scrunched; thousands and thousands and thousands of them!

Just as she thought it was finished, she heard a swishing sound and the ground beneath her feet shook. Something coarse and wet then licked her cheek. She turned and stared straight into the face of a small Iguana. She shrunk back in horror but felt relief, as it was only little....but then came the rest! Big, ugly, scaly reptiles, lolloping, Quasi-Modo-like towards her with their curly tongues coiling around her face and arms. Her skin quivered and crawled in revulsion but she knew she had to go on: so many and so much depended on her and her alone! She had no choice!

Suddenly she was in sunlight, lying in her bedroom at Knotty Knook, in Berry Bush. She was alone. She looked around the room. In her fireplace burned a log-fire. She looked up to the mantelpiece and there was her old, brass alarm clock, ticking away. Everything was normal again. What a relief! Her eyes then wandered over the wall paper. It was floral. All of a sudden, from out of one the flowers came an ugly, monstrous head. Its mouth opened and huge teeth came shooting straight towards her, followed by a long, pointed tongue. Joni-Pip hid her face under the bed clothes and closed her eyes but the monsters kept appearing and looming straight into her face, one after another; ugly, hideous creatures with gruesome faces.

She let out a silent scream but kept thinking of all those relying on her.

Next came the snakes! Millions of them wriggling and squirming in front of her. Thick and slimy: slithering along the road: a wall of them, six feet high! She shuddered and shook violently. Then she remembered and said out loud,

"I'm hallucinating. Doctor Evans told Mother it was my high temperature when I had Pneumonia. Now, it's simply a bad memory and it can't hurt me!"

The loud clapping of the Zulus then began! Thousands of them ran in front of her, chanting One came running up towards her, she could hear his breath and feel the skin of his shield, on her face! She so wanted to run but she didn't, she began to walk up some steps. At the top was a Pool. It wasn't the pretty Pool of Colours. It was a pool of thick, lumpy, orange gruel.

"Done it! Done it!" she shouted triumphantly. "I can't believe I've actually conquered The KOBM! I am Victor of the KOBM! Oh, well....great reward!"

She held her nose and jumped into the sticky Pool Of Orange Porridge!

Just then, the doors of the Workhouse Barn flew open and in ran a tatty red and yellow Teddy Bear with a big patch on his side, a young girl and a kind of Macaw-like pigeon.

"I know what's going to happen! Talk about Déjà Vu!" said Joni-Pip.

"Get out now, all of you! Run! Run! Out! Get out! Get out, now!"

shouted the girl.

"Don't ask questions, just run!" said the tatty Teddy Bear.

"Do as he says, Guys!" squawked the Macaw, in a clear American accent.

"Macca?" asked Poppy-Plump-Pij.

The bird turned and smiled at Poppy-Plump-Pij, the smile said it all.

"Grandma, it's me, Acker, your grandson. Please leave the Barn....now!"

Poppy looked confused.

The girl, the Teddy Bear and the half-Macaw ran round the Workhouse Barn, herding everyone outside into the cold night air. Nobody panicked but obediently they just did as they were told.

"You must get as far away from the Barn as you can!" said the Bear. "When is it that I actually learn to stop talking?" he mumbled to himself.

"What's going on?" asked Archimedes Spindlethrop.

"Oh, hello, Archimedes, how nice to see you again!" said the Bear, running off and helping Hetty the Wee to get out safely.

Soon everybody stood huddled in a small group, about fifty yards or so away from the Barn, all shivering because of the cold.

"What is this all about?" asked Father.

"Something is going on but I can't see anything!" replied Grandfather.

"Is everyone out, Reddy?" shouted the girl.

"Yep, it sure is!" shouted back the Bear. "I'll just check the barn again!"

"Hey, what's with all this evacuation?" Jack asked.

The girl turned and looked, giving him a huge smile.

"Hey, Great Uncle Jack, how are you?" she grinned. "So, so sorry about all this but you will see why we had to come back, in a minute!"

"Who are you?" asked Jack, peering at the girl through the darkness.

"It's me, Jemmy! Don't you remember? We came back to save Grant!" She ran off, back towards the Barn.

"Shucks!" exclaimed Jack. "How many Circles have we got here now?"

"Isn't it great? We can remember other Pastures?" said Red-Ted. "It's just like an atom with all the electrons orbiting around the nucleus!"

Hetty the Wee, Poppy-Plump-Pij, Joni-Pip and Jack all agreed.

The visiting Bear and the girl ran into the Barn.

"Are they all right?" asked James Finn.

"Why did they get us all out?" Fred Finn questioned, looking puzzled.

"I think we're about to find that out!" answered Red-Ted, half-smiling.

Suddenly, across the darkness, came a huge hand of forked lightning. It struck the large oak that stood by the Barn, splitting it in two. There followed a colossal clap of thunder, which boomed like all the bombs that dropped on Bath, put together.

"It's going! It's going!" shouted Jemmy, running out of the barn doors.

The night air was filled with a thousand cracks and splits, which grew into a thunderous crash as the large oak, which once stood proudly guarding the Workhouse, keeled over and landed right on top of the barn roof. For a second or two, the sturdy barn roof held its own: the solid, wooden beams creaked and groaned, giving their all but the sheer bulk of the oak was too enormous and the tremendous weight of the mighty tree was just too much. The massive oak sheered straight through the barn, crashing and thudding heavily onto the floor. Within seconds, a huge orange flame lit up the night sky and the barn exploded into a ferocious and merciless inferno.

Everybody looked on in horror, realising how close they had all come to being engulfed in the blaze.

"Our lives have just been saved, yet again, Hens," said Hetty the Wee.

The small crowd of onlookers stood in silence, watching the Workhouse Barn disappear in the flames. Then down came the torrents!

"Hey, that was close!" shouted Jemmy, her voice was practically swallowed up by the tumultuous noise of the rain, the lightning and the thunder. She looked around.

"Where's Reddy?" she said in panic.

"I don't know!" replied Red-Ted.

"The last time I saw him he was going into the Barn," said Jack.

"Oh....no....no!" shouted Jemmy. "He's got to be out! He must be out!"

Everyone silently looked at her in horror, knowing it was impossible for anyone to survive the burning heat of those hungry, angry flames.

431

Chapter 42

Questions and Answers at the Library

"Well, well, so I will be a hero in my old age?"

"It seems so!" said Joni-Pip; she hadn't told him all that had happened.

"It was unbelievable, thinking that only a few moments before the oak tree fell, we were all happily talking in the Workhouse Barn," said Poppy.

"So what happened next?" asked Eth, watching some warplanes fly over.

Just then the Warden of the Home Guard came tearing up on his bike.

"Out of my way! I am on important War Business!" he shouted, making them jump into the ditch beside the grass verge; they all looked over the top of the bank and watched him haring down the road. "I have important questions to ask the Vicar!"

"Most important," said Ethelred-Ted poshly, " 'Will there be cucumber or tomato sandwiches?' "

They all roared with laughter.

"Where were we before that rude, funny man interrupted us?" asked Het.

"Right...Red-Ted thought the Premium Pasture was almost up; he wasn't right though because we're obviously still in it....or are we?" broke out Joni-Pip.

"It seems like it, Hen, we're still remembering everything, aren't we?"

"Anyhow, we all had to say our 'goodbyes'. It was very sadful and it was so strange seeing Acker, my grandson; very, very beautifulful, though."

"Crumbs, yes, Pops. Where is Macca, we haven't seen him since the Tug-of-war, didn't he want to come to Edwinstowe with us?" asked Eth.

"He went back to see Franco. They're practising a new song to sing at the Village Fete next month," said Poppy rather dolefully.

"That should be nice, I look forward to that!" said Joni-Pip. "I'll never forget when I first heard them singing together, up at Marley's Barn. It was the most amazing duet I have ever heard: written by Bizet, from the Opera 'The Pearl Fishers'. It was spectacular. Just imagine an opera singing parrot! We are so blessed knowing him!"

"Macaw; Pudding," corrected Poppy, "and yes we are blessed indeed having him!"

"So, to get us back to 1892, what happened after the Workhouse Barn burned down?" asked Ethelred-Ted.

"Nothing much really," started Joni-Pip, "well, actually we had a very brief but interesting discussion with Jemmy and Acker."

"Er....yes we did, Ma Lamb, despite the....the...."

"We asked about life in 2042....we asked about work and schools...." Joni-Pip interrupted. "Isn't it amazing, in 2042 they don't have offices."

"They don't?" asked Ethelred-Ted.

"Jemmy said they have these old things, covered in Tumbleweed, which used to be known as 'offices'. She said something called 'The Net', will make everyone work from home. She said children won't even go to school any more; they will be educated by this Big Net," finished Joni-Pip.

"That sounds terrible: being caught in a Net. I don't think I'm going to like some of the things that will happen in the Future," mused Eth.

"I don't think you will, Pud. No, not at all," said Poppy quietly.

There was a silence.

"Then we simply said, 'goodbye' t' everyone and hugged everyone," said Hetty, breaking the solemnity, "that's about it."

"It was a very painful parting, though," said Joni-Pip, "we knew that once the Circle had closed, we would forget each other...."

"So the JITS all jumped back over their Walls of Time....Macca and I flew over....does that make us FITS?" asked Poppy-Plump-Pij.

Hetty the Wee, Ethelred-Ted and Joni-Pip looked at her, looked at each other and then burst out laughing.

"What?"

The others continued to laugh.

"Look, if everyone who 'Jumps in Time', is a JIT, then everyone who 'Flies in Time', must surely be a FIT!"

"True, true, Poppy, you are indeed....You, Macca and Acker, of course, are all FITS!" said Ethelred-Ted and then promptly exploded into more laughter.

"What? What's so funny about being a FIT?"

"Nothing!" laughed her friends.

"M, M 'n M, Pops," said Joni-Pip, "that sounds hilarious! You never know, though, one day, being Fit, might just be a complement!"

"I jolly well hope so!" said Poppy firmly. "It's just not funnyful!"

With that, once more, the other three shrieked with laughter

"What?" she laughed.

After they had restored their composure, Joni-Pip continued,

"Folks, I will finish this story: after the JITS and the...." Joni-Pip looked at Poppy respectfully, "FITS left Sam, Archie, Fred and Amelia in 1892....I went into the OOMU with Father, then we arrived back here!"

"So that's it?" asked Ethelred-Ted.

"Well, no; I have a new little sister, who is gorgeous and she is called Elle-Sahara and I have a new grandmother....which is totally, totally spiffing...."

"What?" exclaimed Eth. "A new grandmother? How wonderful!"

"Fred became a doctor and nursed Grandmother through the Spanish 'Flu Epidemic of 1918/19, so she didn't die. I have more new family; cousins and an aunt and uncle and there is someone else I want you to meet soon!"

The Four of them walked down Edwinstowe High Street together. Everything was much the same. The village was still very pretty with thatched cottages, a few little shops, Goff's the Butchers, the Bakers, a little grocery store, the Post Office, the Old Stopping Cells and the Old Blacksmith's Forge.

As they walked past Edwinstowe Library, Seamus came out and called them over, he then walked back inside. There was nobody else in the Library.

"Top of the mornin' to ye!" Seamus greeted them loudly.

"Good morning to you, Seamus," said Poppy-Plump-Pij, "I have heard a lot about you. This is my first visit to the Library."

Seamus beamed from ear to ear and shook her wing gently.

"Are you by any chance Poppy, Miss Poppy-Plump-Pij, **the** Poppy-Plump-Pij?"

"Yes," replied Poppy, slightly embarrassed by Seamus' enthusiasm.

"We meet at last!" said Seamus, still shaking Poppy-Plump-Pij's wing. "I've waited so long but I knew you would come!"

Joni-Pip and her friends were quite taken aback by the Librarian's obvious interest in Poppy. The wing shake was incredibly, incredibly long.

"Good morning, Seamus and how are you today?" asked Joni-Pip.

"I am well, t'ank you and all the better for seeing ya and yer friends."

"Good morning, Seamus, does anyone ever read these books, Ma Pet?"

"Oh, they do indeed!" replied Seamus surveying the empty library.

"Good morning, Seamus, how's life treating you?" asked Ethelred-Ted.

"Well now, the reason I called ya to come in, was because I have a mystery on ma hands and I have a question for y'all. It's most peculiar."

The Librarian then walked off and disappeared behind one of the huge book cases.

His visitors looked at each other and shrugged their shoulders.

"Come on then!" Seamus called, poking his head back round a corner.

The four of them stood still.

"Well, aren't ya comin'?" He leant his head forward, beckoning them. They followed him. He walked along a couple of aisles and then entered the Reference Section of the Library. He ran his fingers along a row of volumes, pulled out the File marked '1892', carried it to the stand and then opened it.

"What d'ye make of this?" he asked, looking at each of them in turn.

Poppy flew up on to the stand and peered at the newspaper it displayed. Hetty the Wee climbed up on to the table by the stand, using a chair and Joni-Pip and Ethelred-Ted stood in front, examining the News Report.

"It's the Workhouse Fire!" said Joni-Pip.

"It is but do you notice somet'ing strange about it?" Seamus frowned.

"What the write up, Ma Lamb?"

"No, the photograph....I can't understand it!" he said scratching his head. "You Lot have been in and out of my Library so much, recently that I t'ought I'd have a look and investigate what was intriguin' y'all. You could have blown me down with a chicken when I saw it!"

Joni-Pip and Hetty the Wee and Ethelred-Ted stifled a laugh.

"What are we looking for?" Poppy strained her neck to get a good look.

"Just keep on lookin' and y'll surely notice it!"

Everybody examined the photograph thoroughly.

"Now, let's see," said Joni-Pip, "this is a picture of those who took part in the Rescue....yes?"

"Right!"

"It must have been taken the morning after the Fire?" asked Poppy.

"Right again."

"There are the men. We know some of them. Right?" asked Eth.

"Right!"

"There is young Archimedes Spindlethrop," said Hetty the Wee.

"Right!"

"And there is young Grandfather," said Poppy-Plump-Pij.

"Right!"

"There is young Fred Finn," said Joni-Pip.

"And there is Ethelred-Ted," said Hetty the Wee.

"Right!" he looked at them strangely, "and what would he be doin' there, I ask myself?" he turned and looked directly into Ethelred-Ted's face.

"And there is Ethelred-Ted," said Poppy-Plump-Pij.

"And there is Ethelred-Ted, again!" said Joni-Pip.

"Hmmmm! Now that's a mite interestin'! T'ree Et'elred-Ted's!"

Everyone strained to examine the photograph again and sure enough, there was Ethelred-Ted standing next to Grandfather on one side of the group, then there was Ethelred-Ted standing next to Archie on the other side of the picture and finally there was Ethelred-Ted kneeling down in front of them all!

"At first I t'ought there must be lots of Bears like you, Et'elred-Ted."

"Why not? Three Bears, eh? Sounds like a good fairy story to me!"

laughed Ethelred-Ted, nervously rubbing his chin.

"But just ya be takin' a closer look."

They all leaned forward and really scrutinised the photograph.

"The one next to Grandfather is holding his arm and look no scar, no stitches! I remember Joni-Pip tellin' me about your nasty tear and how she sewed y' up! So that can't be ya!" said Seamus almost accusingly.

All four of them smiled sheepishly.

"Now look at ya on yer knees, yer wearin' my woolly hat wit' t'e red bobble on t'e top! There's no denyin' it's you! But I gave it to ya only a few days ago and this photograph was taken in 1892. Explain t'at? And who t'e Derry is this one?" he asked, pointing to the third Ethelred-Ted in the picture.

"Red-Ted!" all four of them replied.

"He said he came back twice, at least. No wonder there are two Red-Teds!" said Joni-Pip, looking really, really, really closely at the photograph.

"Red-Ted? And who t'e Derry is Red-Ted? Who are t'e two Red-Teds?"

"He was the bear who came with the young American boy, remember?"

"Wasn't t'at you then?" he asked Ethelred-Ted, scratching his head.

"Yes!" replied Hetty the Wee and Poppy-Plump-Pij together.

"No!" replied Ethelred-Ted and Joni-Pip together; at the same time.

"I see....well, either it was or it wasn't. Which one is it going t' be? Is it you or is it not, Et'elred-Ted?" Seamus asked very seriously.

"Well, it is and it isn't!" replied Ethelred-Ted, nodding his head many times.

"I see and t'at makes sense then!" said the Irishman dryly.

"It's a long, story, Seamus and I doubt if you would believe it, even if we told you," started Joni-Pip.

"And why not? Why wouldn't I believe y'? I t'ought y' were m' friends?"

"O.K., Seamus, it sounds preposterous and until I saw this photograph, I wouldn't have believed it was possible myself. All of those bears in the photograph are me....only each one of them is from the future...."

"Now we're really making sense, I show y' a photo that was taken in 1892, which was 50 years ago and y' tell me that the bears in the picture are from t'e future. Hmmm....that's about as clear t' me as a sixpence. Explain?" said Seamus, ignoring the giggles from Joni-Pip and Hetty the Wee.

"I think Ethelred-Ted means that in 1892, he had come from the future, from now, 1942," said Joni-Pip, stifling her amusement.

"Yes, that's what I meant," started Ethelred-Ted. "You see, Seamus, the other day, when the Bear who looked like me came into the Library with that young lad, they had come...."

"All t'e way from t'e Future?" asked Seamus.

"Er....Yes!" everyone replied.

"Y' expect me to believe t'at?" he asked, looking at each visitor in turn.

"Er....Yes!" everyone replied again.

"Well...." began the Librarian, "tell me who this is?" he asked, pointing to a figure in the photograph who stood just behind one of the Red-Ted's.

They all stretched their heads forward, examined the picture, looked at each other and said together,

"Jack!"

"T'at's the boy, isn't it? The boy who came in here with his loud music coming from a small wireless with no wires and no valves. I recognised his hat. T'was the most amazing t'ing I'd seen; not t'e hat, of course, t'e musical contraption. I asked if I could look at it. I even turned it up loud, despite my strict rule on silence in the Library. The words on the side of the little magic music box were a big clue as to where he came from, 'Sony 2007'. They'd come from all t'at Time ago....will be .... is .... whatever?"

"Yes, it was actually 2007....so you knew!" said Ethelred-Ted.

"Why have you been asking us, when you knew?" asked Joni-Pip.

"You are mean, Seamus," laughed Poppy-Plump-Pij.

"And here we are trying to explain what seems impossible and y' knew all the time!" said Hetty the Wee, sounding slightly cross.

"I didn't **know**," said Seamus slowly, "I kind of **guessed**. I had t'is feelin', y' see. I've been waitin' so long: so, so long but I knew you would turn up one day. Come into my office and have a cup of tea and I will explain everyt'ing!"

They all looked at each other puzzled. Joni-Pip turned to Ethelred-Ted and mouthed the word 'waiting'. Ethelred-Ted frowned and shrugged.

None of them had ever been into the Library Office. It was more like a conservatory than an office. Everywhere they looked, on every window sill and every available floor space, there stood beautiful, flourishing pot plants. The room smelt fresh and the air felt invigorating. It had that lovely warm, damp, soily smell about it: that smell only found in greenhouses.

"What a bonny place is this!" exclaimed Hetty the Wee. She used a stool and climbed up on to one of the many windowsills. She sniffed at the lush, green plant in front of her. "Oooh, that's a delight f' sure!" she enthused.

Poppy-Plump-Pij took off and gently hovered over some of the numerous huge, thick, fleshy, green leaves of the plants.

"I have never seen these types of plants before and I have flown over so many, Pudding," she said, "where have they come from?"

Joni-Pip walked about the large, airy room, examining everything.

"These plants are so unusual, Seamus. Your Office reminds me of somewhere my parents took me before the War. It's a special place in London."

"Kew Gardens?" asked Ethelred-Ted. "I remember us going. It was one of the most amazing places Father had ever taken us to. How I longed to be able to get up and walk about! If I'd known it was like that here, I'd have asked to visit sooner. It's charming, Seamus. Edwinstowe's very own, Kew Gardens!"

"Well, I'm glad it meets with yer approval," he laughed, delighted that they were enchanted with his Office. "Let's be puttin' t'e kettle on!"

Soon they were all drinking tea amid exotic and luxuriant plants.

"I shouldn't think these would normally grow in England, would they, Seamus?" asked Ethelred-Ted. "They've got to be tropical."

"Indeed. T'is room is Sout' facin', plenty of windows, plenty of sunlight: it's a conservatory, really. I always keep it warm t'rough t'e Winter, by keepin' t'e boiler stoked up. Sherwood Forest has plenty of trees t' keep t'e fires goin'!"

"Seamus, where did you get these tropical plants from?" asked Joni-Pip, running her hand over one of the deep, green, shiny, succulent leaves.

"It's a long story but in actual fact, it's somet'ing t'at will interest y'a great deal," said Seamus sipping his tea and then leaning back in his chair.

All of his visitors looked at him, giving him their very closest attention.

"I have been waitin', ye see," he said seriously.

"Waiting?" questioned four voices together.

"Waitin'....for an opportunity to tell y' who I really am."

Joni-Pip, Ethelred-Ted, Hetty and Poppy looked aghast and said,

"Who are you, Seamus?"

"I was born in Ballymahon, Southern Ireland, in 1904, that makes me 38 years old, this year. My mot'er was Bridie O'Hara, a beautiful Irish Colleen and my father was an Englishman. I was ten years old when the Great War broke out in 1914 and my father went to fight for England. He didn't have to because he lived in Ireland but he wanted to serve his King and Country. After the War, he returned home to my mot'er and me but he was a very sick man. He had spent a long time, knee deep in freezin', muddy water in the Trenches and his kidneys never recovered. My mot'er and I nursed him but he finally died of acute nephritis, kidney failure, in 1920. I was sixteen years old."

"How awful, Seamus," said Joni-Pip gently, "you were only Alex's age."

"While he was dyin', he told me about his life before he met my mot'er. He said t'at he had married a beautiful English girl but then he went away

438

in his work to Africa and while he was there, he caught Malaria and continually suffered from very high fevers. He obviously didn't die but he was very seriously ill for several years. While he was ill, he had asked his English nurse to write to his wife and tell her where he was and what had happened to him. The letters, although written, were never sent. The nurse had fallen in love with my father and hoped that he would stay in Africa, never returning to England. In fact, my father discovered t'at the nurse had kept givin' him herbal sleepin' drafts, to make him feel drowsy so t'at he believed he was still ill. When everyt'ing finally came out, you can imagine how furious my father was! He immediately returned to England from the Gold Coast and made enquiries about his wife."

"You are going to tell me they lived happily ever after?" said Poppy.

"Was she all right, Hen?"

"It had been a long time since he'd been away, over eight years and he daren't just arrive at t'e house he'd shared with his beautiful young wife. He wanted to let her know gently t'at he was alive. He worried the shock of him just walkin' in might be too much for her. He'd never stopped lovin' her; in fact t'e t'ought of her beautiful smile kept him alive, givin' him a reason to want to get better. So, in disguise he stayed at a local Inn."

"Was she still alive?" Ethelred-Ted asked earnestly.

"Yes, she was but somet'ing terrible had happened," he said poignantly.

"Oh no!" his Listeners all said.

"When he had gone off on his travels, he had not only left a wife behind but he had left a child as well and he found out t'at his child had died."

"Oh, Seamus, your poor father!" said Poppy-Plump-Pij.

"He was told t'at his wife had married again and t'at the man she married adored her. He was so devastated about his child and so angry with himself for leavin' 'em both in the first place. He just couldn't forgive himself, although he had done it all for them, to give them a good life in England. So, he made the biggest sacrifice of his life," he said, tears filling his eyes.

Hetty the Wee, Poppy, Ethelred-Ted and Joni-Pip held their breath.

"My father left....he left wit'out seeing his wife, wit'out even havin' a glimpse of the woman he loved!" finished the Librarian.

All of his visitors had tears in their eyes and remained silent for a while.

"That's such a sad story, Seamus," Joni-Pip began softly.

"My father asked me, if ever I came to England, to keep an eye on his first wife. I came to England but sadly, she had died at about the same time as my father: she was frail, y' see. It had been just too hard on her. T'e t'ing I was really sad about, too, was the child....I was an only child, myself and how I wished I had a brother or a sister!"

"Seamus, when we first came in here, you said that your story would interest us....that you had been waiting...." started Ethelred-Ted.

"I am comin' to t'at, right now. When ya first started comin' in here and askin' to read the papers of 1892, I got an inklin' that you were The Ones."

"The Ones?" they all repeated.

"Yes, The Ones," he repeated again, "the Ones my father told me about."

"Your father told you about us? That's impossible!" said Ethelred-Ted.

"Before I explain, there is one more detail I must relate to ya," said the Librarian. "It was the cruellest twist of all for my dear mot'er."

"Oh, Seamus, what more painful things have you to tell?" asked Joni-Pip. "Can we bear to hear them?"

"You must, you must, it is so, so important," said the Irishman, putting his head in his hands.

Ethelred-Ted stood up from his chair and put a paw consolingly on Seamus' shoulder and asked gently,

"Is this too much for you, Seamus, do you want to leave it for now?"

"No, t'ank ya.....it was such a coincidence, an unbelievable coincidence, y' see, ma mot'er wasn't born in Ireland but here in Edwinstowe."

Everyone looked shocked. Joni-Pip went to say something but Ethelred-Ted looked at her and shook his head slowly: she remained silent.

"My mot'er's father, my grandfather had a good, responsible job here. My mot'er lived here with her parents, enjoying a happy life until she was twelve. Unfortunately, my grandfather ended up in disgrace, in prison, so my grandmother took my mot'er and returned to Ballymahon, the small town where her mot'er came from. It was there that my mot'er met my father and eventually I was born. Neither of us knew anything about my father's sad life, until he was dyin'. Then, to my mot'er's horror, my father told her that his little child had died in a terrible tragedy, right here near Edwinstowe, that her father, my grandfather, Paddy O'Hara had caused!"

"Baddie A Jara? A jar of what, Pudding?" asked Poppy-Plump-Pij.

Everybody looked at her and smiled; even Seamus, which was a good thing as the conversation had become very heavy, very intense.

"Paddy O'Hara? Where have I heard that name before?" asked Eth.

"I remember where, Laddie. Why didn't we link the two names before? Y' are Seamus O'Hara, aren't ye?"

"I am indeed," he nodded.

"I remember, too," said Joni-Pip, "it was your grandfather who caused the Workhouse Fire!"

"I'm afraid it was."

"Whew!" said his visitors: they remained speechless for a little while.

"Did your father ever find out?" asked Ethelred-Ted.

"No, my mot'er never told him. How could she? My grandfather was sent to prison because he was responsible for all t'e little children dying in t'e fire. My mother never told him a t'ing. It was hard enough knowin' t'at her father had caused t'is dreadful tragedy but to find out t'at it was her father's fault t'at the man she married had lost his own child, t'at was almost unbearable for her."

"So...." started Hetty the Wee.

"On his death bed, my father told me t'at he knew t'at everythin' was going to be put right...."

"He did? But how?" asked Ethelred-Ted.

"He told me t'at on the very first day he saw his pretty new 'wife to be', he had the most amazin' encounter. At first he t'ought he must be dreamin' but then, exactly a year later, he had another very brief encounter, which verified in his mind t'at it was true. I have been waitin' for y' to turn up and here y'all are!" He beamed from ear to ear. "Especially you, Poppy!"

Poppy flew down to perch on the rounded, wooden arm of his chair.

"Especially me?" she asked, looking up at him sweetly.

"Yes, my father said t'at t'e first time he came walkin' t'rough t'e woods round here, he met a young man who was nursing an injured pigeon...."

"When was this, then?" asked Hetty the Wee.

"Now let's see....it was the year before he got married...."

"It was in 1882!" nodded Poppy and then she carried on, "I had just flown back over the Wall of Time and picked up my tin of Oat Scones for Bullet. I was exhausted and Fred Finn and your father helped me."

Hetty, Eth and Joni-Pip all looked at Poppy. With everything that had gone on recently, Poppy had just not got round to telling them about this.

"So, you know Seamus' father, Poppy?" asked Ethelred-Ted.

"Yes, I do!"

"How come we don't, then?" asked Joni-Pip.

"Because You Lot stayed down in the Stable Courtyard, didn't you? I was up on the Clappers, remember?" she smiled.

"My father told me t'at this wood pigeon, called Poppy, had explained t'at she and her friends had come from t'e Future and t'at they had come to make a Bad Past into a Better Future," explained Seamus. "She also told him that in a year from then, in 1883, he would be in this same place. He would be up on the Clappers having an argument with t'ree friends about his fort'coming marriage. One of them t'ought it unfair of him to keep travellin' and leavin' her. This Poppy also told my father t'at she would land on t'e branch of a tree at t'is time and my father and Fred Finn would say 'hello' to her and she would say, 'I don't know you!' and fly off."

"Now, I remember. Poppy, you told us about this conversation the first time we tried to JIT, didn't you?" said Ethelred-Ted.

441

"JIT?" asked Seamus.

"Jump in Time, Hen."

"Ah!" said Seamus. "So, when it all happened, my father knew it wasn't a dream. He had spoken to a real, live wood pigeon and he told me t'at he believed t'at one day, she and her friends would turn up and make...." Seamus began and the others finished,

"A BP into a BF!"

"Exactly and you have!" cried Seamus. "You changed t'e Past....you saved all the children! It's in the newspaper. T'ank ya, t'ank ya, so much!"

"Seamus, this is all so puzzling. It struck me as peculiar that you were able to speak to Ethelred-Ted right from the start. Alex, my brother, still can't speak to him. So, how come you can?"

"Also, Seamus, how come your father remembered all about our visit from the Future? Once everything is accomplished and the Circle is closed, you should forget everything?" Ethelred-Ted said and then added, "Not that he met us but he must have known about us, from Poppy!"

"It doesn't make sense, none at all, Ma Pet."

"Ah.... but it does!" replied Seamus. "I have one t'ing left...."

"Seamus....who is your father then?" asked Hetty the Wee. "You haven't told us. Should I know him?"

"No, Het, I don't think you know him. I don't think you ever met him but you do know of him. You do know all about him!" answered Poppy.

"I do?" asked Hetty the Wee.

"Yes, Silly...." Poppy-Plump-Pij laughed again.

"My father was Edmund Plate," said Seamus, "didn't you guess?"

"No, we didn't! Of course, of course!" cried Joni-Pip and Ethelred-Ted.

"This is all so unbelievable! I love it!" laughed Poppy-Plump-Pij.

They had a Circle Hug and then Joni-Pip pulled away and said seriously,

"Seamus, as you're the son of Edmund Plate, there's someone I want you to meet. I was just on my way to take my friends: you must come, too!"

"Now, t'at sounds intriguing, I can't wait! But before we go, there is one t'ing I have to do....I hope t'is will explain everythin'," he said, grinning.

They all looked intrigued as he walked over to a cupboard, opened the door and took something out. He kept his back towards them so that they couldn't see what it was. He put it on the desk. Poppy shouted with joy.

"My tin, my Coronation tin....Grandfather wasn't the only one who lost his....this was the tin I flew over the Wall of Time with, to take Bullet his Oat Scones in! I left it up on the Clappers in 1882!"

Chapter 43

The Granting

They all felt invigorated as they left and came out into the sunny air of that May day in 1942. Seamus decided that he would come along a little later, after he had turfed out the 'Reader' and the Library closed for lunch.

Edwinstowe didn't seem any different from before to them but there was one wonderful change. No longer did a little, empty shop stand forlorn, forgotten and derelict along Edwinstowe High Street. No longer did children have to peer between the rough, gnarled, nailed planks in order to get a glimpse of the, once-enticing, wonders within and no longer was anyone barred or prevented from either coming or going inside. The Pretty Posy was once again a bustling little shop. Although it still bore the name, it no longer sold pretty posies or pretty plants. This was 1942 and there was a War on, a devastating war that changed everything in England. Now, there wasn't much of a demand for cut flowers or plants in this historic Nottinghamshire village. The Pretty Posy had become a little Haber- dashery, which sold almost anything and everything: from buttons, elastic, silk skeins, string, cotton, wool, pegs, press studs, sewing needles, darning needles, knitting needles, brown paper, crepe paper, crepe bandages and cord; to dish clothes, table cloths, floor cloths, tea towels, terry towels, terry nappies, sheets, pillow cases and eiderdowns. It also stocked disinfectant, soap, washing powder, plasters, gauzes, liniment, slings, antiseptic lotions and potions and of course most essential; safety pins.

Ethelred-Ted, Hetty, Joni-Pip and Poppy stood in front of the shop, peering through the gleaming, clear glass of the little square windows.

"Cripes, this is different! Really different!" laughed Ethelred-Ted.

"It sure is, Eth!" agreed Joni-Pip.

"How bonny it looks inside," said Hetty, standing on the window sill.

"This is a good thing we have done!" said Poppy, taking off and circling round her friends and then flying up and landing on top of the green and white striped canopy that curved and hugged the front of the shop.

A regiment of soldiers marched past them, compelling them to climb several stone steps and stand in the shelter of the shop porch.

"Yes, saving Jemimah Plate brought about so many good changes and this must be one of my favourites. I hated this shop looking so lonely and lost. I wish we could have stopped this stupid War, though!" said Joni-Pip.

"Well, well, well," came a familiar, booming voice behind them.

"Constable Cruckleton!" they all said.

"Good day to you all and how are you today?"

"Fine, thanks," said Joni-Pip. "How are you, Constable Cruckleton?"

"I am fine, too, thank you."

"Where is your little feathered friend, then?" he looked up.

"I'm here, Pudding," said Poppy, peering over the edge of the canopy.

"I see you!" said the jovial policeman; then he turned to Joni-Pip, "You've come to see your Auntie then?"

Joni-Pip and all of her friends looked puzzled.

"Er....have I?" she replied, thinking how stupid she sounded.

"I'll be off, a Report came up to the Police House from the Home Guard, this morning. Somebody said they heard a loud hammering and banging as they were walking through Windy Woods on their way home from their Late Shift, on Guard Duty, last night. It was coming from the Ruin. It's probably nothing but I have to investigate. It might be somebody up to no good. I don't think it's an Invasion or anything. Good day to you!"

"Good bye, Constable Cruckleton," all of them said together. When he had walked a little way up the High Street, the others looked at each other.

"Jack and the box!" they all said and laughed.

"Hello, Darlings, what's so funny?" came a voice from inside the shop.

All four of them turned round and Hetty, Poppy and Joni-Pip recognised the face of another old friend, even though she was much, much older now.

"Amelia Plate!" they all said: Eth stepped forward and held out his paw.

"We meet at last!" he said. "How do you do, Amelia? You have no idea what adventures we have been through in order to save you."

Amelia Plate looked puzzled and Ethelred-Ted reasoned that was because she couldn't still be in the Pasture.

"I am very pleased to meet you but I thought we had already met, on the night of the Workhouse Fire," she said softly.

"That was Red-Ted from 2007, remember?" explained Hetty the Wee.

"But there was another one."

"That was Reddy, he was from 2042," said Poppy, flying down to them.

"How many of you are there, then?" Amelia frowned, smiled and then her face changed as she said sadly, "Was that the one who was...."

"So brave!" interrupted Joni-Pip. "This is Ethelred-Ted....the original one ....the one Father bought me from Germany when I was a baby."

"I see. I'm very pleased to meet you," Amelia Plate said to Ethelred-Ted. "Where were you, when these brave friends were saving us from the fire?"

"Er....busy...." replied Ethelred-Ted.

Just then Seamus arrived. Grinning, Joni-Pip grabbed him by the arm.

"Seamus, I have somebody I want you to meet," she said, leading him to

444

the owner of the shop. "Amelia, I have somebody I want you to meet."

Amelia and Seamus looked at each other, looked at Joni-Pip and shrugged their shoulders. They shook hand politely.

"Enchanted to meet you....er....was it Amelia?" asked Seamus.

"Pleased to meet you, whoever you are!" laughed Amelia.

"This is Seamus, the Librarian, actually he is more than a Librarian."

"He is?" asked Hetty the Wee, Ethelred-Ted and Poppy-Plump-Pij.

"Seamus is the son of Edmund Plate," explained Joni-Pip.

"Sorry....he is the son of whom?" Amelia asked, shaking her head.

"Edmund Plate was my father," answered Seamus.

"I thought you were Seamus O' Hara, the Librarian. I've heard of you."

"That's my mot'er's name, O' Hara....I took my mot'er's name....my father was Edmund Plate, the Explorer," said Seamus.

Large tears began to roll down Amelia's face.

"But Edmund Plate was my father, too and he was lost at sea when I was a little girl...." Amelia began to sob.

Seamus pulled Amelia in to him and hugged her. He started to cry.

"Then you are....my....sister!" he whispered. "I saw a Shooting Star once, when I was waterin' me plants in me conservatory. I wished so hard for a sister but I never dreamt I would get t'e little one I lost, back! The little one who died in the Workhouse Fire. It's just amazin'. It's phenomenal!"

"You really....you really, truly....are my brother?" Amelia whispered.

The two of them hugged and cried and cried and hugged.

"T'is is the best present I could ever have had in ma whole life, Joni-Philipa," said Seamus, ruffling Joni-Pip's hair. "T'ank you so, so kindly!"

"Joni-Pip, how can this be? Is it all your doing, then?" asked Amelia.

"Er, you could say I've had a little hand in it, that's all; a tiny, tiny hand but Eth, Poppy and Hetty have all had just as much to do with it as me!"

Amelia suddenly pulled away from Seamus.

"Don't go away, my new Brother, we've loads to talk about but I've something very important to do, myself. Come in all of you, I have some visitors who want to talk to Joni-Pip!" she beckoned them into the shop.

They followed Amelia Plate as she walked straight through the beautifully laid out shop. Everything was in its place and neatly displayed. She led them into a spacious, light, back room. Seamus, Ethelred-Ted, Poppy-Plump-Pij and Hetty the Wee held back and stood in the doorway.

"Hello Darling!" came a voice that was so similar to Amelia's.

Joni-Pip was astonished to see that sitting around the room were three special women from her own family.

"Mother! Auntie Sylvia! Grandmother!" said Joni-Pip, running and hugging them one by one. "What are you all doing here?"

445

Mother was sitting in an armchair and looked at her puzzled and said,

"Darling, what do you mean, what are we all 'doing here'? Auntie Sylvia and Grandmother came up with me, so that Amelia could say 'good bye' to Sylvia before she leaves this afternoon."

"I see," said Joni-Pip, "and that's as clear as clay!"

Amelia stepped forward, smiled knowingly at Joni-Pip and said,

"I don't know when it will be that I will see my little **sister** again!"

"Sister?" she whispered, her heart leaping.

Amelia Plate walked over to Joni-Pip and put her arms around her.

"Joni-Philipa," she whispered back, "yes, your Auntie Sylvia is my youngest sister, my baby sister....how silly we didn't say yesterday!"

"So Mother, my mother is your sister, too!" Joni-Pip whispered to Amelia Plate. "That means you are my Auntie Amelia and Archimedes is....my Great Uncle....Crumbs and when he was young and talking in the Workhouse Barn, he looked just like Alex does now! I knew I knew him!"

"I was there remember? He does look so like him!" whispered Amelia.

"So, my Grandmother is...." Joni-Pip started but she couldn't continue, her mind was racing, "she can't be.....that's impossible! No! No!"

"Yes, Darling....yes she is...." Amelia still whispered.

"My Grandmother is...." started Joni-Pip.

"Jemimah Plate!" whispered Eth, Hetty and Poppy and they all clapped their paws, claws and hands.

"How? Why? When?" whispered Joni-Pip to Amelia.

"Your Grandfather, Sam Regan, married, my mother, Jemimah Plate, seven years after my Father," Amelia stopped and looked over at Seamus, "our father, Edmund Plate disappeared and then they had two more daughters, your mother, Sarah and Sylvia. So, I'm their half sister, we all have the same mother, Jemimah Plate, now Jemimah Regan!"

"Grandmother, when I was five, I saw a Shooting Star in Wales and I made a wish for you!" Joni-Pip shouted, running across the room to Jemimah, her grandmother and giving her the biggest, the longest huggerly she could ever remember!

Joni-Pip was ecstatic. All the time she had been JITTING, it had never occurred to her that she was related to Amelia Plate. It had never occurred to her that she was related to Jemimah Plate, either and it had most certainly, never, ever occurred to her that she was related to Archimedes Spindlethrop. Why hadn't anybody told her? She then pulled away from Grandmother and ran and hugged, first of all her Auntie Sylvia, then

446

Mother, then all her friends, whispering,

"I am truly a Hughog! Robin Hood told me! It's a real Fairy Story!"

"You said, 'our father, Edmund Plate', Amelia?" asked Grandmother.

A huge beam spread across Amelia's face. She walked over to Seamus and gently pulled him into the room.

"Yes, I did. Let me introduce You Two. Seamus is the son of Edmund Plate, Mother. He is my younger, half-brother. Isn't it incredible? I have a brother! Seamus, this is my mother, Jemimah, your father's first wife!"

Jemimah Plate just stared for a moment in disbelief. Then her face changed from astonishment into delight! She swept Seamus into her arms.

"I can't believe it!" wept Grandmother. She pulled away from him and examined his face. She gently ran her long fingers over the tears rolling down his cheeks.

"My, my, you are your father's son....you have his beautiful, big, brown eyes and his incredible smile. It is unbelievable!
It is as if he has been returned to us....after all these  years! My Edmund, my beautiful Edmund. My Edmund's son! What an amazing gift!"

There was one thing left for Amelia Plate to do.

"I think I have something of yours, Joni-Pip."

"What's that, Auntie Amelia?"

"I've something that sadly, I must give back!"

"You do?"

"It's in my pocket, are you ready?"

Amelia Plate reached in her pocket and took out an old, yellowish, creased envelope. She looked at it, smiled, sighed and then gave it to her niece.

"Thank you, Auntie Amelia but why did you say it was mine? How?"

Joni-Pip opened it very carefully and then slipped the folded piece of paper out. Very slowly, so as not to tear the old, fragile paper, which was now brown from age, Joni-Pip unfolded the single piece of paper. She held it out in front of her and read the words written on it out loud. Her eyes lit up and a huge, wide smile beamed across the breadth of her face. She read them again and again then she handed the paper back to Amelia. Her Aunt smiled and nodded, looking over the words she had written so long ago, not realising what an extraordinary adventure they would cause.

"Well, I never!" said Joni-Pip. "So this is what all this has been all about? It's so amazing, so unbelievable and it was all for you, Amelia!"

"For me? What are you talking about, Silly Girl! It wasn't for me! Nothing was! Don't you see? It was just for Joni-Philipa Garador, YOU!"

"For me? For me? It was all for me? It can't have been! No! It can't be! Not for me it was for you!"

"Silly, it was for **you**. To grant **your** wish. A full Circle, Joni-Pip, can't you see? An Orbit! Just to complete your POOL. Work it out quickly. We haven't got long! This Pasture will soon be over and we will all forget!"

Joni-Pip and her three friends all looked at each other. Everything then began to fall into place. Everything now made sense. All the things that had happened, hadn't been for Amelia Plate, it hadn't been for her, at all! So many Circles had been opened. So many Circles needed closing. It **had** been for a little girl but all along they had got the wrong little girl!

Joni-Pip just stood there, trying to take in the enormity of it all. There were so many things that had happened over the last few weeks. She and her friends had enjoyed so many spectacular and fantastic adventures and every one had been needed, in order to grant Joni-Philipa Garador her wish. Everything they had experienced seemed to flash through her mind. It was astounding. She seemed to re-live each event in those few moments.

"Seamus, there is one thing I am not too sure about. Didn't you see a Shooting Star, too and hasn't your wish been granted?" asked Joni-Pip.

"I did indeed! It has indeed! I have, not only **a** sister but I have my own sister back, the very one I lost. How about t'at for a wish come true! It's purely amazin'! Can't believe it. I wish ma dad was here to be with us all!"

"Yes, of course but you saw a Shooting Star, so you must have been in the OOMU and looked straight into your own eyes in the Past! When?"

"I don't remember!" Seamus shook his head.

"It might not have happened to him yet, Joni-Pip," said Ethelred-Ted.

"Something to look forward to, then brother! An Adventure!" laughed Amelia walking over to him and linking her arm in his.

"What are y' sayin' to me, sister? Me? Seamus O'Hara have an adventure like t'is. I hardly t'ink so! I'm just a humble Librarian doin' me job!"

"I think our wishes were linked, Seamus," said Joni-Pip, walking over to him and hugging him: she was indeed now, The Little Hughog!

Joni-Pip paused for a moment, then turned and looked at the paper

Amelia was holding in her hand. Joni-Pip frowned at it and grinned.

Her face then suddenly changed and she looked very, very puzzled.

"That's a really strange note, Auntie Amelia. Did you write it in 1892 Have you kept it since 1892? It's very old. Why did you write it? What does it mean? What's it got to do with me? Has it got anything to do with me?" the twelve-year-old laughed, screwing up her pretty face, "Why did you say it was mine? 1892....are you joking? How could it be?"

A vision of a smiling pilot flashed into her mind. Joni-Pip scratched her head and the face disappeared. She picked up her red and yellow Teddy Bear, who was now lying, flopped on the floor and hugged him. A little brown hedgehog went scurrying through the shop, along Edwinstowe High Street and disappeared, heading towards Marion's Meadow and a plumpish wood pigeon walked out of the Pretty Posy and then took off and went flying up towards Windy Woods.

Suddenly, the door burst open and Flip ran in.

"Mother please come quickly," she tore across to her, "hurry, Mother, we need you so urgently to help."

Flip pulled Mother, dragging her over to the door.

Amelia Plate
May 5th
1892
Age 8 years
Yesterday I worked
all day
Today I worked
all day
But Tomorrow
Who knows?

"Do I know you? Yes, I do, don't I? Why are you calling me Mother?"

"We will explain later but you must come and help, please, Mother?"

"What's going on?" asked Seamus. "Who are you?"

"Oh, hello, Seamus!" Flip said turning, looking at him and smiling.

"I don't know ya, do I? How in Chicken's name d'ya know me?"

"Sorry, no time to explain, we need Mother's help right now!" Flip said, pulling Mother out through the door of the back room and into the shop.

The rest of them followed and looked from the doorway. Ethelred-Ted jumped out of Joni-Pip's arms and stood upright, peering into the shop.

"I hope you can do something, before it's too late!" begged Flip. "He's half-dead! You're such a wonderful nurse, Mother! Oh, hi, Eth, Joni-Pip!".

Joni-Pip and Eth poked their heads round and peered into the shop. There were Steve and Craig propping up a man between them. Blood was seeping out through rough bandages, which were untidily wrapped around his arms, chest, legs and head. Mother immediately ran to him and helped him down on a chair. He groaned as she gently examined his terrible wounds.

"Right, Amelia, Sylvia, Joni-Philipa, I need hot water, soap, bowls, clean bandages and antiseptic lotion. Now!" she commanded magnificently.

The girls jumped and rushed around the shop, searching for her demands.

"Don't I know you boys?" asked Sylvia picking up armfuls of bandages.

"Oh, hello Mum," said Craig: Auntie Sylvia went quite pale.

449

"Sorry, Mum, this must be so confusing, we'll explain later," said Steve.

"Who is this man?" asked Grandmother, frowning. "Don't I know him?"

"I don't quite think so Grandma!" Laughed Steve.

"I'm quite sure I do! Who are **you**, anyway? You look so familiar? Do you work on Finn's Farm with Colin?" asked a perplexed Grandmother.

"I should hardly think so, Grandma, it's me, Steve, only I am not this old yet! This poor man, he's an airman, a badly wounded airman. We have to help him, we've been asked to help him, by Freddie and Jem."

"And Col, don't forget, Steve. We need to hurry and get back, really. Our Own Mission with Robin Hood is accomplished!" laughed Craig.

"At last! Please help him before he dies?" Flip asked Mother solemnly.

"He's from the Great War!" added Craig.

"The Great War?" said Jemimah, Amelia, Sylvia, Mother and Seamus.

"Why, that ended twenty four years ago!" said Sylvia opening a packet of fresh, white cloths ready to bathe the Casualty.

Grandmother went over to the soldier, crouched down and lifted up his bleeding face, cupping it in her hands. The others flew around, preparing to soothe his wounds, dress his burns and bind up his bleeding gashes.

Joni-Pip suddenly remembered seeing the Piano Player and the soldier in the Pretty Posy, she could even hear the beautiful music in her head.

"What exactly is going on here? This is so peculiar, so very odd. I need to know! I need answers! Who is this soldier?" Joni-Pip turned to Eth.

"Search me!" laughed Eth. "We'll understand if we're just patient but right now, the 'patient' we should be concerned about is this poor man!"

"Timothy!" Jemimah gasped. "Timothy Scott Gore! What are you doing here? How did you get here? It's impossible. You can't be much more than twenty now, yet you were that old in 1912! Where have you come from?"

The poor man groaned and closed his eyes in pain. He looked up at Grandmother and faintly smiled and as he did so, for the first time Joni-Pip saw his face clearly and gasped, too.

"You! I saw you in the garden in Bath on the night of the raid! You keep coming into my mind! Why? I don't know you but you seem familiar. Do I know you? You were flying a strange plane, behind a Messerschmitt! Where do you come from? Who are you?" cried Joni-Pip.

"Who are **you**? Who are all these people? Where are the other three? I want Jem! Where am I? I thought I was going to be hidden, going to be safe," the pilot whispered feebly gesturing towards the shop door.

Everyone turned and saw a small regiment of strangely dressed soldiers, standing outside the shop and peering through the window.

"I am done for," the wounded pilot grimaced in pain, "it's too late!"

Joni-Pip looked at the soldiers and saw the distinctive sparkly glitter....

Chapter 44

The Keeper of Stars

The little twigs snapped under her feet, as Joni-Pip walked over the hill and across Windy Woods towards The Crooked Cottage. It was nearly the end of May, 1942 but sadly, not nearly the end of the War. She was on her way to have lunch with her grandparents. Her life had really changed of late but she was totally unaware of it. All of the Circles had closed and her life was back to normal again, although, for some reason she felt more grown up. Her new adult view of life had its toll on one person, however.

"J.P., hang on!"

Joni-Pip turned round and waited for her brother. They seemed to get on much better nowadays; engaging often in lively discussions about anything and everything. Their parents were so pleased with this turn of events.

"What have you brought him for?" laughed Joni-Pip derisively when she saw Alex was carrying Ethelred-Ted under his arm.

"Sorry! I saw him lying on the Conservatory floor by your slippers and I presumed you had forgotten him in your eagerness to eat your lunch! What are we having, by the way?"

"Alex, have you invited yourself, you Greedy Boy?"

"Grandmother won't mind!" grinned Alex, handing over her bear.

"Thank you, Alex but I feel I have, kind of, grown out of him recently."

"Nonsense, J.P., nobody ever 'grows out' of their teddy bears!"

They arrived at the Crooked Cottage and were greeted by the wonderful smell of freshly baked bread. As usual, Grandmother had prepared them both a delicious Lunch. She guessed Alex might decide to come along.

After they had all been fed and watered satisfactorily, in true English style everyone went into the Parlour to enjoy a pot of freshly brewed tea. Grandmother realised she had forgotten to bring in the milk jug, so Joni-Pip was sent back to the kitchen to fetch it. As she walked along the hallway, she stopped and looked at the Painting Masterpiece, which had been duly hung in pride of place next to Grandfather's Landscape. The more she looked at it, the more it looked like a firework display or a starry night sky. Something about it mesmerised her, she couldn't stop staring.

"I'm starving, Joni-Pip. I'm going back to the kitchen to have lunch, as you're all in the Parlour. If not, I'll just squeeze in a Munch Break!"

Joni-Pip was startled by Ethelred-Ted, standing beside her.

"Not now, you are not!" came a strange voice from behind them. "It is

The Time. You must both follow me! Please don't turn round until I say."

Ethelred-Ted and Joni-Pip both wanted to but they obeyed and although she didn't exactly look, she glanced in the Hallstand mirror and saw a tall, figure. She drew in her breath as she was sure he was the familiar figure she had caught glimpses of recently, dressed in a long, grey, hooded cloak. The hood cast a deep shadow over the wearer's face.

"I am a Keeper of Stars, a KOS," he said, pulling the brush on the Hallstand and opening the way into Tunnel 6. Obediently they followed, Joni-Pip closing the doors firmly behind them. The hooded KOS lit a lantern and then they walked through the many dark, damp, low passages and tunnels, until finally they emerged in the woods, up on the Clappers. The KOS then lead them into a clearing and to Ethelred-Ted's and Joni-Pip's astonishment, there, in front of them, was a huge, spinning Orbit. The strange KOS stepped right into it, as if it was a capsule on the London Eye. He beckoned to them. Terrified, Ethelred-Ted went to run back but Joni-Pip dragged him by the arm and pulled him into the Orbit. It was incredible inside! They stood in a roomy observatory, similar to the OOMU, with windows all around! They could walk about quite freely. The noise it made reminded Joni-Pip of the times she used to have her bicycle upside down, resting on its saddle and handle bars and she would turn the pedals round and round very fast. The wheels would make a high pitched whizzing sound as they spun. The Orbit sounded the same; somehow it was a comforting and calming hum.

The KOS then raised his arm and the Orbit began to rise up, through and above the trees. Both of them looked out and down. Below them was Finn's Farm. As they climbed higher, they saw The Crooked Cottage, Knotty Knook, Edwinstowe, Hideaway Cottage and the Prisoner of War Camp in Norton Cuckney. Soon they went through the clouds and above them. It was beautiful; the Orbit was spinning round all the time. The sky then got darker and darker and they caught sight of the stars above them: thousands of them. They sped right up to the stars. Next the Orbit gently turned upside down and they slowly began to descend. They now viewed the stars below them; a bird's eye view, in fact. Before long, it became obvious that these weren't stars, at all. They were clearly the tops of colossal, strange structures, which formed an enormous Metropolis. The Visitors were then moved away and down slightly and they experienced the same incredible feeling they had, every time they jumped over the WOT and flew through the KOL. The Two Travellers then had a side view of the City, as they gently soared around these odd Keeps. It was as if they were flying in a light aircraft, around the tall buildings of Manhattan, New York, at night time. It was breathtaking! Instead of white light, though, coming from the windows of this City of Towers, there were beautiful, multi-coloured beams of light. As they glided, they felt as if they were riding high on a huge Ferris Wheel that very slowly and extremely gently, took them on a horizontal, vertical and diagonal ride. They smoothly circled round and round for a while; up and down and sideways, twisting and turning, like electrons in their orbits. It was unbelievably exhilarating and so exciting. They kept gasping at the sheer wonder and beauty of it all.

As they travelled, they glanced through some of the innumerable windows and briefly caught glimpses of people they knew and loved, doing both ordinary everyday things, as well as extraordinary things. They saw people they didn't know, doing the same. The City truly buzzed with action: humming with excitement, movement and fun: most extraordinary!

Eventually, they came to a halt, landing on a huge, round platform. It was purely an Observation Table, having no bars or railings, nothing to hold on to, nothing to keep them secure. The KOS walked out of the Orbit and then beckoned them to follow. Joni-Pip worried that if she went too close to the edge, she would fall over. Ethelred-Ted just stepped out and strode around, looking out; Joni-Pip then followed. As far as they could see, there were thousands and thousands of these buildings, all coming up, towering above white woolly clouds. It was total magnificence!

"Welcome to COS, the City of Stars!" said the KOS. "Its full title is the 'City of Stars - Meaning of Stars' but you know how things get abbreviated. The same goes with my title. I am known as a KOS in the COS in the KOL! I am so thrilled it is The Time I have waited so long!"

As they were no longer flying around, it gave them the opportunity to really examine everything they could see. Each tower had a circular section, which was much larger than the main stem of the building. These parts of the structures were the ones emitting the beautiful coloured light from their windows. They realised these must be the Observatories. The straight, unmoving part of the strange towers had little windows, too but only bright, white, light, shone out of these. Looking closer, they saw that the Observatories were situated on different levels of these tall, round, huge towers. As they watched, they realised nothing ever stood still. The Observatories were the only part of the cylinders that were changing their positions every now and then: moving like rings, up and down on a finger. It was a scene of motion, power and energy. They were entranced by this immense Secret City above the clouds; it filled them with awe and wonder. They walked around the Observation Table, pointing, chatting and gasping over this weird and wonderful spectacle. The KOS looked on silently.

"Wow! Are these **all** Kaleidoscopes of Life?" Joni-Pip asked the KOS.

"Of course. You thought there was only one, didn't you, Joni-Philipa? When you entered into the different Keeps and Observatories, you were always in the same Room; only it moved up and down, around the Kaleidoscope of Life, depending where you were heading, of course. As you walked up and down any of the steps, the Observatory would move into place. Do you remember hearing a high-pitched humming sound?"

"I do! So that's what the noise was! This is all so 'out of this world'!"

"It is The Time, Joni-Philipa, your time, The Time here in the COS when you are given the answers you've been seeking: the Secret of the Stars: the reason for all you have witnessed recently! Do you realise, Ethelred-Ted, all the time you struggled with the Formula, you just needed to touch the four star symbols on the F.B. at the same time; you didn't need ice! All those trials and it was there in front of you! The Wall of Time, the WOT, grows if you touch the stars. It works on the same principle as the F.B., it starts as liquid and then grows into a solid. The molecular structure of the F.B. is very similar to water, that's why it feels so strange when it is small."

"What, the four little star symbols were exactly that, Stars? The stars were the answers! How wrong we've been about so many things! Whew! Hasn't it been worth the wait, though, to witness all these incredibly, amazing things and find the answers," said Eth in awe. "Thank you so!"

"Don't thank me, I'm just a JIT, like you. The only difference is that I have JITTED a hundred times. I then became a Keeper of Stars and so will you, one day. The moment you become a Centurion JIT, then Keeper Status is Invested on you. It's a great moment, your Investiture, a grand celebration! You'll love it! It's fun and exciting but sometimes a bit sad."

"What does it mean then, Keeper of Stars?" asked Joni-Pip.

"The job of a KOS is to nurture Fledgling JITS. They are known as Little Stars. When a new candidate qualifies, obviously he or she needs guidance and protection. That's what has been happening with you, Joni-Philipa."

"Me? Have you been guiding me and protecting me?"

"Yes."

"How? I have only seen little glimpses of you and you always ran away."

"I've been there for a few years now, keeping a careful watch over you."

"A few years? That can't be, we have only just become JITS recently!"

"Everything done from COS is unseen for you, Joni-Pip, until now. To break you in gently, so as not to alarm you, too much, you were allowed to see little hints of my presence. You never would have caught me, how ever hard you had tried, sorry! Things are different now that you have finally completed a Circle successfully, after many trials and bumps on the way, I might add. You are now in The Time, that's why you are here, to learn what it's all about! It is known as 'The Time' because it is the time for you to learn the Secret of the Stars. The City of Stars, COS, is the exact Centre, the place where changes in the Past can be made and maintained. Isn't it incredible? I remember how I felt when I was first given the Secret of the Stars, I could hardly contain myself I was so thrilled and now you, you, Joni-Philipa Garador, you are officially entrusted with this secret! Please tell it to no-one. I have to ask you both to sign this Declaration, please?"

The KOS then took out a small box which was tucked beneath his long cloak. When he opened it, it grew and grew until it became a very large tome, which he could hardly carry. Balancing the book on his left forearm, he reached underneath the thick, leather, back cover and pulled out a lever, which he straightened, forming a leg. He then pulled out another lever, straightened it and formed it into a second leg. The KOS then firmly slotted each leg into two small holes on the Observation Table. He opened up the huge volume, turning over pages and pages of signatures.

"This is The Tome of Time, it is an extremely ancient record of many Declarations and there are some very, very famous signatures in here."

"M, M 'n M," exclaimed Ethelred-Ted, "can I read some of those?"

"Sorry, only when you are a KOS. Right, Entry No. 111,332,445,567 is yours," said the KOS, taking a small pencil from his pocket: he opened it like a pen knife so that it became much longer and when he gave it to Joni-Pip, it became a sparkler, emitting little stars from the top. Joni-Pip jumped in surprise, "It's fine, you can write with it, it's a star pen!" he laughed.

Joni-Pip wrote her name on the Declaration, followed by Ethelred-Ted.

"Wow, that is really spiffing! I feel so honoured that I have been told the Secret of The Stars. Honestly, I don't really know what to say. I still don't understand how you have protected me, though," she handed back the pen.

"I've been invisibly with you, through everything! I was there when Flip first turned up at the Bentley and when you were being a bit naughty and experimenting in Archimedes' Quission Hut. I was there in the Stable Courtyard at the time of the Accident and at the Work House Fire. I've been guiding you and protecting you throughout all your JITTING!"

455

"Invisibly? How have you guided me?"

"A KOS has to give their Fledgling JIT something of their's somehow and that object is the link between JIT and KOS. You'll do the same when you become a KOS and are given the charge of your first Fledgling JIT."

"I still don't understand," said Joni-Pip seriously, shaking her head.

"You will! Anyway, it's time to go but before then, I've one more thing to do. I love this," the KOS chuckled and lifted up his arm, gently sprinkling lots of tiny little stars all over their heads. "From now on, any JITTING you do, or any JIT who visits you in your POOL, will come with stars. You only get these in your POOL after your first successful Circle!"

They were invited by the KOS to step back into the Orbit and once again were lifted up, over the tops of the Kaleidoscopes. Now they could quite clearly see that they were viewing them from above: as they were taken higher and higher, they could only see the star-shapes of their roofs.

"Before we go back," said the KOS, "I have a final wonder to show you. The City Centre of COS. I think you'll both find this totally fascinating!"

They hovered for a while above the top of the Central Part of the City. It was in a perfect rectangle, the buildings forming a huge strange pattern from above. Then it suddenly dawned on them both and they shouted out,

"The City Centre, it makes the Formula Board, it's the F.B.!"

"Yes, all the buildings are designed in the shape of the Formula, as seen from above. Clever stuff, isn't it? Right we must leave I'm afraid."

Soon there was simply a star-filled, night sky again. Then the sky turned into countless stars in a picture frame. Joni-Pip's eyes then focused on the right hand corner of the vibrant painting she was staring at in Grandfather's hallway. The bold black letters that Alex had written, spelled out:

COSMOS by The Garadors May 1942.

Joni-Pip turned, looked at Ethelred-Ted and beamed knowingly.

"C'mon J.P., have you got that milk yet? I'm simply dying for a cup of tea!" said Alex joining her in the hallway. He then looked at her and then at the picture. "Didn't we do well?" he grinned. "Specially my paint balls!"

Joni-Pip was very quiet as she and Alex walked back to Knotty Knook, past the Ruin, through Windy Woods and down the Log and Chain Path.

"I'm sorry I said that I feel I have, kind of, grown out of Ethelred-Ted, Alex," she said, as they took their boots off and put on their slippers.

"That's all right, J.P. I knew you hadn't really, you can't fool me!"

Later that night, Joni-Pip lay on her bed, looking up into the beautiful night sky, which teemed with countless twinkling stars.

A squadron of Lancasters rumbled over, reminding her of the times.

"This ridiculous War! Why doesn't it end?" she said out loud, then she turned her attention to the amazing array of stars in the velvety heavens.

"Nobody would ever believe what happened to us earlier today, or what we have seen, Eth, would they?" she whispered to her Teddy Bear, who sat on the windowsill also looking up at the stars. "Or where we have been?"

"Never....but do you think we will always remember things now?"

"I hope so, Eth, I really hope so! What an amazing time we have had. I keep pinching myself and thinking, 'No it didn't really happen', do you?"

"Yes but as I passed the Hall mirror earlier, guess what I saw in my fur?"

"Of course, what a Nolly I am! I saw them in my hair, too, when I was brushing my teeth! They are so beautiful!"

"Stars!" they both said together.

"So it is all real. It is all true!" said Joni-Pip, wistfully. "I can't believe that I didn't want to come and live here a few weeks ago! Was I mad?"

"So you think that the life in the wood isn't that bad, now?" laughed Eth.

"No, not bad at all. In fact, I can truthfully say that the life in the wood is spiffing, super spiffing!" She laughed heartily.

"Aren't you asleep, J.P.?" Alex called from her doorway.

"I'm not sleepy, Alex," she replied, lifting her head and smiling at him.

"O.K., I'll just pull up your door then everyone will think you're asleep."

"Thank you, Alex, Goodnight!" said Joni-Pip, watching her door as he slowly closed it.

"Goodness!" she said. "It's been there all along, the link with my KOS!"

She lay there, just staring at Alex's old, worn out dressing gown.

"Goodnight, Flip, my Little Star," Alex called softly from outside her door.

THE END

The
CIRCLES
Trilogy

BOOK TWO

The Life by the Sea with
JONI-PIP

CARRIE KING

BOTHY BOOKS

458

Chapter 1

Changes from the Skies

It was a beautiful sunny August afternoon and Flip was walking back across the Field of Smells from the beach. She had climbed up the cliffs with her cousins, Steve and Craig, whom she was staying with for the Summer Holidays.

Much to his annoyance, she had left Ethelred-Ted back at Aunty Sylvia's and Uncle Richard's house with Becky-Paige and Elle-Sahara, her two younger sisters. The house, which was called 'Two Beach View', was a beautiful Edwardian Villa and lay on the outskirts of the village of Merricliff, a few miles outside of Barmouth, West Wales. Ethelred-Ted objected most strongly to this action, on the basis that he hated being dressed in a pink, woolly jumper and being pushed around in Becky-Paige's doll's pram by Elle-Sahara. The indignity of it! Why after all he was a hero! Well, he thought he was. He didn't know why or where, of course but he knew it, he just knew it. At some time or other or more accurately in some Time or other, he had a vague, niggly feeling that he had been a Super Hero, no less.

It was now 1944 and the War was still raging across Europe. Almost the entire coastline of Britain was sown along the shore with huge rolls of barbed wire, like massive coils of embroidered chain stitch. Although this marred the spectacular views across the beaches, it didn't stop the children of this beautiful Island from enjoying the normal things that delight at the seaside.

As they wandered back towards the house across the Field of Smells, a name given to this particular patch of land by these three young people, the peace of the still afternoon was interrupted by the staccato sound of a spluttering engine in the skies above them. They all looked up into the clear blue sky, shielding their eyes from the blinding sun, trying to locate the whereabouts of the obvious ailing aircraft that rapidly seemed to be getting closer and closer, until it seemed to be just over their heads.

"There it is!" shouted Craig, pointing immediately above them. "Get out of the way....run for it....Flip, take cover!"

Flip looked up and as the aeroplane approached, it banked slightly and she saw the head of a pilot, wearing a balaclava and goggles. For a split second the pilot turned, looked straight at her....a fleeting feeling of recognition flooded over her. She took off her baseball cap and used it to wave at him!

"What are you doing, Flip? Take cover!" Craig repeated his command.

All three of them immediately looked around the flat empty field. There wasn't a rock or stone even, behind which they **could** take cover. They all shrugged and immediately lay flat on the ground and protected their heads with their arms.

They lay as still as stones. The engine noise above them got increasingly louder and louder as it coughed and choked, seemingly inches above their sprawling bodies. They could feel the cold air from the propellers as it passed over their

459

arms and continued on its way across the Field of Smells and then disappeared over the top of the cliffs, which dropped down onto the beach.

The malaise noise of the plane then suddenly changed. Instead of the splutterings, it gave out the loud screaming, almost wailing sound that all aircraft make, when they are rapidly losing altitude and are heading, uncontrollably, to earth. There was an eerie silence, followed by an almighty explosion and huge red and yellow flames appeared above the top of the cliffs. Thick brown smoke then billowed its way towards them, like the enormous, curling, menacing tentacles of a gigantic sea monster.

Craig, Steve and Flip all began to choke in the smoke. Flip suddenly had a feeling that she had experienced this before but she couldn't recollect where on earth it was. She remembered being engulfed in thick, coily smoke; choking and coughing and then everything going black.

It had been two years since Joni-Pip, Hetty the Wee, Poppy-Plump-Pij and of course Ethelred-Ted, himself, had saved the children from the Workhouse Fire in Berry Bush, Nottinghamshire, England.

Life had changed so much but they, of course, didn't realise it. Saving Jemimah Spindlethrop and then Amelia Plate had brought about so many extraordinary differences to them all but it had solely been to grant the wishes of two people.

"Come on, You Two, somebody down on the beach needs our help!" Steve shouted to the others as he headed back towards the 39 Steps.

There used to be 40 but one of them, the very last one that stretched down on to the beach, was missing, so they felt it appropriate and complimentary, to name them after John Buchan's amazing, suspense-filled, intriguing 1915 novel, **The Thirty-Nine Steps.** The steps were made up of thick railway sleepers (ties), which had been leftover when the railway track had first been laid through Merricliff, fifty years previously.

"I think it's a bit too late for that!" replied Craig but he still joined his brother and they both ran through the brown murkiness and into the cloud of smoke.

Flip hesitated. The faint feelings she had, were enough to make her think twice about running straight into the arms and acrid smell of this huge brown Octopus but run she did.

For a moment they could see nothing and then the darkness cleared and to their astonishment, loud explosions and missiles shot in all directions, over their heads.

"What the?" shouted Craig, as he ducked and dodged the deadly bullets that whistled in a steady array over his body.

"It appears...." started Steve, "that we have run straight into a Battle Ground....that's impossible....why less than ten minutes ago we were walking along the beach in brilliant sunshine...." before he had time to finish, a man in strange battle dress appeared.

"What on earth are you kids doing here? How did you get here?" he yelled. "Get down as low as you can and follow me! Now!" he ordered.

Without hesitation, The Three Intruders crouched down and followed him.

Flip looked around her. Nothing looked familiar. Instead of the 'brilliant

460

sunshine', the sky was grey and cloudy. Whether that was from the smoke from the gunfire, she didn't know. There was no beautiful blue sea: no white crested waves: no soft, fine, golden sand: no sea gulls twisting and calling in the clear blue sky.

It was pretty obvious they were 'somewhere else', wherever that might be.

The soldier in front of them was tall and lithe and quickly led them to the entrance of a dug out shelter, which was heavily protected by large rocks. He had to duck down to get into the shelter and the other three followed him. Inside, the air smelt damp and soily. It reminded Flip of Seamus O'Hara's conservatory, behind the Library in Edwinstowe, Nottinghamshire.

"You'll be safe in here," said the soldier, gesturing towards some wooden chairs that were pushed up under a large, wooden table. "Sit down and wait, I must get back to my Men." With that he started to leave. He then turned round and for the first time, he smiled at them, "What the Blazes are you kids doing here in the middle of a battle?" With that, he disappeared.

Once again, Flip had the same fleeting feeling of recognition. What was it about this soldier's smile that was so familiar to her?

"Well, not meaning to pinch Ollie Hardy's catch phrase or anything, all I can say is 'That's another fine mess you've got us into'!" laughed Craig. "Where the Dumplings are we?"

Steve shook his head, then scratched it and replied,

"I have absolutely no idea. It's all so impossible. One minute we are walking across the Field of Smells and the next minute we appear to be in the middle of a battle. What's going on?"

"But we weren't, were we?" Flip questioned her cousins.

Both the boys looked at her and raised their eyebrows.

"We weren't in the Field of Smells when everything changed," she continued.

"But we were, Flip," answered Steve.

"Ye-ah!" agreed Craig.

"We weren't....it was the brown smoke....everything changed when we went through the brown smoke!" she finished.

Her two cousins remained silent and thought about what she had said.

"You're right, Yankee Cuz," laughed Steve, running his hand through his thick, black mop of wavy hair, "brown smoke, eh? That's kind of a weird colour for smoke, isn't it?"

"Yes, I suppose it is. Smoke's usually grey or black. Flip's right though, it was when we came through the brown smoke that things had changed," said Craig thoughtfully. "Before we ran into the smoke it was 1944 and when we came out of it, it was in....well, I have absolutely no idea....but I think it is definitely in....a few years ago!"

"And that makes good English!" laughed his brother.

"I think we ought to do a bit of investigating, don't you?" Flip said looking further into the Dugout. "Perhaps then we'll get some idea where we are."

TO BE CONTINUED

461

Who is Timothy Scott Gore? Who is Herr Geronnenblut? Why is his capture so important to 'National Security'? Who are the Men in Long Black Coats and the small Regiment of Strange Soldiers? What is the secret in the smoke? Who is Beth Garador? Who is besieging The Planet of the Blue Rings and why? What is the importance of The Sky Sweepers? Find the answers to these questions and much, much more, in Carrie King's forthcoming, BOOK TWO of The CIRCLES Trilogy 'THE LIFE BY THE SEA WITH JONI-PIP'.

The
CIRCLES
Trilogy

BOOK TWO

The Life by the Sea with

JONI-PIP

A Special Request from the Author

Dear Reader, if it is at all possible, please keep The KOS in the COS in the KOL's identity a secret by signing this Declaration?

I am depending on you!

Thank you so much,
Carrie King

10:01:10

Carrie King

I, the undersigned, as a Reader of The CIRCLES Trilogy BOOK ONE, The Life in the Wood with Joni-Pip, do promise, as far as it is in my power to do so, not to divulge the identity of the KOS in the COS in the KOL

Name... Date......................................

Witnessed by.. Date......................................

If you would like to join the Worldwide Circleites Club, entirely run by Joni-Pip, herself, please e-mail the website.

www.joni-pip.com

Words of Appreciation for Joni-Pip

This book is incredible and I don't know the meaning of the word 'bias'! You've never read anything like this before!   Joni (14)

A truly amazing story: not a dull moment. It grabs you from the first page and keeps you hooked 'til the last. You will just have to read it again!   Liam (14)

Thank you for a brilliant read. I look forward to the next two.   Caroline (13)

I completely adored Joni-Pip!   Subul (11)

I've read Joni-Pip, it's totally cool!   Samuel (11)

Joni-Pip is FANTASTIC! I just couldn't put it down!   Olivia (13)

I've finished Joni-Pip. Its really great, it has a lot of adventures in one book. If you could make the book into a film, it would be really good.   Sarah (14)

Joni-Pip is SO good, it is the best book I've ever read!   Eryn (8)

Joni-Pip is the best book I have ever read. I have read it six times now and I will never get bored with it!   Albrecht (11)

Brilliant read, on the edge of your seat stuff. Kept me guessing right to the end!
                                                                Michelle Taylor (37)

I loved the book, I just cant wait for the next.   Karoline Jeffery (26)

I loved Joni-Pip, I never dreamt the ending, what a great surprise!   Wesley (19)

I absolutely loved the first Joni-Pip and I look forward to reading the next two.
                                                                         Ash (38)

I love Joni-Pip. I have many books and this is my favourite. I have signed the declaration at the end.   Amy (13)

Joni-Pip is a brilliant book! I really enjoyed it.   Arantxa (13)

I've just finished reading Joni-Pip, it was awesome. I loved it, it was fantastic!
                                                                         Amalie (11)

Brilliant Read! I can't wait for Book Two!   Andy (52)

Words of Appreciation for Joni-Pip continued:

I was hooked from the first chapter; it was so exciting, surprising and unexpected!
Matt (15)

Need a Holiday? Joni-Pip is the best 'get away' ever! Couldn't put it down.
Josephine (41)

Truly a fantastic read: the most wonderful book I've ever read: read it and see!
Mandy (40)

I so really enjoyed reading Joni-Pip. When is Book Two?   Martin (42)

Joni-Pip is so exciting, they keep going back in time. I can't wait for Book Two!
Muhtasim (12)

Truly inspiring, positive and mind-stretching!   Danielle Lloyd (28)

Totally Spiffing! The last but one chapter was fantastic, my fave!   Paige (12)

Joni-Pip is like nothing I've ever read before. I loved every minute of it.
Marley (15)

Joni-Pip is sheer magic, a really enchanting story!   Jose McKinnon (88)

I just wanted you to know what my friends at school have said about Joni-Pip.
Totally Spiffing! Fantastic! Fabulous! Couldn't put it down. Totally loved it!
Took it everywhere!   Jessica (14)

We have lots of the children reading their **Joni-Pip** books on the playground -
even during the cold blast!   Mark Welch (Headmaster)

What a great story! I love the way the strands are weaved through the book &
different characters recall their stories.   Jane (Learning Resource Manager)

A rare feast.....a fabulous journey!   R.J.Ellory (A Quiet Belief in Angels)

I finished Joni-Pip within a few days; I was absolutely enchanted from the very
first chapter. I loved every page and I'm now reading it for the second time
Rhiannon (17)

Joni-Pip never goes the way you think it's going to go right to the end. All the
characters are funny and are lovely. It was hard to put the book down!
Eliza (13)